mjf

BERNARD MALAMUD

THE FIXER

THE NATURAL

THE ASSISTANT

MJF BOOKS
NEW YORK

Published by MJF Books
Fine Communications
POB 0930
Planetarium Station
New York, NY 10024-0540

Library of Congress Catalog Card Number 92-60777
ISBN 1-56731-001-X

This edition published by arrangement with Farrar, Straus & Giroux, Inc.

Manufactured in the United States of America

MJF Books and the MJF colophon are trademarks of Fine Creative Media, Inc.

10 9 8 7 6 5 4 3 2 1

CONTENTS

THE FIXER

For Paul

I

From the small crossed window of his room above the stable in the brickyard, Yakov Bok saw people in their long overcoats running somewhere early that morning, everybody in the same direction. Vey iz mir, he thought uneasily, something bad has happened. The Russians, coming from streets around the cemetery, were hurrying, singly or in groups, in the spring snow in the direction of the caves in the ravine, some running in the middle of the slushy cobblestone streets. Yakov hastily hid the small tin can in which he saved silver rubles, then rushed down to the yard to find out what the excitement was about. He asked Proshko, the foreman, loitering near the smoky brickkilns, but Proshko spat and said nothing. Outside the yard a black-shawled, bony-faced peasant, thickly dressed, told him the dead body of a child had been found nearby. "Where?" Yakov asked. "How old a child?" but she said she didn't know and hurried away. The next day the *Kievlyanin* reported that in a damp cave in a ravine not more than a verst and a half from the brickworks, the body of a murdered Russian boy, Zhenia Golov, twelve years old, had been found by two older boys, both fifteen, Kazimir Selivanov and Ivan Shestinsky. Zhenia, dead more than a week, was covered with stab wounds, his body bled white. After the funeral in the cemetery close by the brick factory, Richter, one of the drivers, brought in a handful of leaflets accusing the Jews of the murder. They had been printed, Yakov saw when he examined one, by the Black Hundreds organizations. Their emblem, the Imperial double-headed eagle, was imprinted on the cover, and under it: SAVE

RUSSIA FROM THE JEWS. In his room that night, Yakov, in fascination, read that the boy had been bled to death for religious purposes so that the Jews could collect his blood and deliver it to the synagogue for the making of Passover matzos. Though this was ridiculous he was frightened. He got up, sat down, and got up again. He went to the window, then returned hastily and continued to read the newspaper. He was worried because the brick factory where he worked was in the Lukianovsky District, one in which Jews were forbidden to live. He had been living there for months under an assumed name and without a residence certificate. And he was frightened of the pogrom threatened in the newspaper. His own father had been killed in an incident not more than a year after Yakov's birth—something less than a pogrom, and less than useless: two drunken soldiers shot the first three Jews in their path, his father had been the second. But the son had lived through a pogrom when he was a schoolboy, a three-day Cossack raid. On the third morning when the houses were still smoldering and he was led, with a half dozen other children, out of a cellar where they had been hiding he saw a black-bearded Jew with a white sausage stuffed into his mouth, lying in the road on a pile of bloody feathers, a peasant's pig devouring his arm.

2

Five months ago, on a mild Friday in early November, before the first snow had snowed on the shtetl, Yakov's father-in-law, a skinny worried man in clothes about to fall apart, who looked as though he had been assembled out of sticks and whipped air, drove up with his skeletal horse and rickety wagon. They sat in the thin cold house—gone to seed two months after Raisl, the faithless wife, had fled—and drank a last glass of tea together. Shmuel, long since sixty, with tousled gray beard, rheumy eyes, and deeply creased forehead—dug into his caftan pocket for half a yellow sugar lump and offered it to Yakov who shook his head. The peddler—he was his daughter's dowry, had had nothing to give so he gave favors, service if possible—sucked tea through sugar but his son-in-law drank his unsweetened. It tasted bitter and he blamed existence. The old man from time to time commented on life without accusing anyone, or asked harmless questions, but Yakov was silent or short with answers.

After he had sipped through half his glass of tea, Shmuel, sighing, said, "Nobody has to be a prophet to know you're blaming me for my daughter Raisl." He spoke in sadness, wearing a hard hat he had found in a barrel in a neighboring town. When he sweated it stuck to his head, but being a religious man he didn't mind. Otherwise he had on a patched and padded caftan from which his skinny hands hung out. And very roomy shoes, not boots, which he ran in, and around in.

"Who said anything? You're blaming yourself for having brought up a whore."

Shmuel, without a word, pulled out a soiled blue handkerchief and wept.

"So why, if you'll excuse me, did you stop sleeping with her for months? Is that a way to treat a wife?"

"It was more like weeks but how long can a man sleep with a barren woman? I got tired of trying."

"Why didn't you go to the rabbi when I begged you?"

"Let him stay out of my business and I'll stay out of his. All in all he's an ignorant man."

"Charity you were always short of," the peddler said.

Yakov rose, enraged. "Don't talk to me about charity. What have I had all my life? What have I got to give away? I was practically born an orphan—my mother dead ten minutes later, and you know what happened to my poor father. If somebody said Kaddish for them it wasn't me till years later. If they were waiting outside the gates of heaven it was a long cold wait, if they're not still waiting. Throughout my miserable childhood I lived in a stinking orphans' home, barely existing. In my dreams I ate and I ate my dreams. Torah I had little of and Talmud less, though I learned Hebrew because I've got an ear for language. Anyway, I knew the Psalms. They taught me a trade and apprenticed me five minutes after age ten—not that I regret it. So I work—let's call it work—with my hands, and some call me 'common' but the truth of it is few people know who is really common. As for those that look like they got class, take another look. Viskover, the Nogid, is in my eyes a common man. All he's got is rubles and when he opens his mouth you can hear them clink. On my own I studied different subjects, and even before I was taken into the army I taught myself a decent Russian, much better than we pick up from the peasants. What little I know I learned on my own—some history and geography, a little science, arithmetic, and a book or two of Spinoza's. Not much but better than nothing."

"Though most is treyf I give you credit—" said Shmuel.

"Let me finish. I've had to dig with my fingernails for a living. What can anybody do without capital? What they can do I can do but it's not much. I fix what's broken—except in the heart. In this shtetl everything is falling apart—who bothers with leaks in his roof if he's peeking through the cracks to spy on God? And who can pay to have it fixed let's say he wants it, which he doesn't. If he does, half the time I work for nothing. If I'm lucky, a dish of noodles. Opportunity here is born dead. I'm frankly in a foul mood."

"Opportunity you don't have to tell me about—"

"They conscripted me for the Russo-Japanese War but it was over before I got in. Thank God. When I got sick they booted me out. An asthmatic Jew wasn't worth the trouble. Thank God. When I got back I scraped again with my broken nails. After a long runaround which started when I met her, I married your daughter, who couldn't get pregnant in five and a half years. She bore me no children, so who could I look in the eye? And now she runs off with some stranger she met at the inn—a goy I'm positive. So that's enough—who needs more? I don't want people pitying me or wondering what I did to be so cursed. I did nothing. It was a gift. I'm innocent. I've been an orphan too long. All I have to my name after thirty years in this graveyard is sixteen rubles that I got from selling everything I own. So please don't mention charity because I have no charity to give."

"Charity you can give even when you haven't got. I don't mean money. I meant for my daughter."

"Your daughter deserves nothing."

"She ran from one rabbi to another in every town I took her, but nobody could promise her a child. She ran to the doctors too when she had a ruble, but they told her the same thing. It was cheaper with the rabbis. So she ran away—may God protect her. Even a sinner belongs to Him. She sinned but she was desperate."

"May she run forever."

"She was a true wife to you for years. She shared your every misfortune."

"What she caused she shared. She was a true wife to the last minute, or the last month, or the month before that, and that makes her untrue, a black cholera on her!"

"God forbid," cried Shmuel, rising. "On you!"

Eyes agitated, he thickly cursed the fixer and fled from the house.

Yakov had sold everything but the clothes on his back, which he wore as peasants do—embroidered shirt belted outside his trousers, whose legs were stuffed into wrinkled high boots. And a peasant's worn and patched, brown sheepskin coat, which could, on occasion, smell of sheep. He had kept his tools and a few books: Smirnovsky's *Russian Grammar,* an elementary biology book, *Selections from Spinoza,* and a battered atlas at least twenty-five years old. He had made a small bundle of the books with a piece of knotted twine. The tools were in a flour sack tied at the neck, the crosscut blade protruding. There was also some food in a cone of newspaper. He was leaving behind his few ruined sticks of furniture—a junkman had wanted to be paid to take them—and two sets of cracked dishes, also unsaleable, that Shmuel could do with whatever he wanted—use, ax, or fire—they were worth nothing. Raisl had had two sets for her father's sake, for herself it made not much difference. But in exchange for the horse and wagon the peddler would get a fairly good cow. He could take over his daughter's little dairy business. It could hardly pay less than peddling. He was the only person Yakov knew who peddled nothing and sold it, in bits and slices, for real kopeks. Sometimes he traded nothing for pig bristles, wool, grain, sugar beets, and then sold the peasants dried fish, soap, kerchiefs, candy, in minute quantities. That was his talent and on it he miraculously lived. "He who gave us teeth will give us bread." Yet his breath smelled of nothing—not bread, not anything.

Yakov, in loose clothes and peaked cap, was an elongated nervous man with large ears, stained hard hands, a broad back and tormented face, lightened a bit by gray eyes and brownish hair. His nose was sometimes Jewish, sometimes not. He had to no one's surprise—after Raisl ran away—shaved off his short beard of reddish cast. "Cut off your beard and you no longer resemble your creator," Shmuel had warned. Since then he had been admonished by more than one Jew that he looked like a goy but it had caused him neither to mourn nor rejoice. He looked young but felt old and for that he blamed nobody, not even his wife; he blamed fate and spared himself. His nervousness showed in his movements. Generally he moved faster than he had to, considering how little there was to do, but he was always doing something. After all, he was a fixer and had to keep his hands busy.

Dumping his things into the open wagon, a rusty water bucket hanging under it between the back wheels, he was displeased with the appearance of the nag, a naked-looking animal with spindly legs, a brown bony body and large stupid eyes, who got along very well with Shmuel. They asked little from each other and lived in peace. The horse did mostly as he pleased and Shmuel indulged him. After all, what difference did a short delay make in a mad world? Tomorrow he would be no richer. The fixer was irritated with himself for acquiring this decrepit beast, but had thought better a lopsided exchange with Shmuel than getting nothing for the cow from a peasant who coveted her. A father-in-law's blood was thicker than water. Although there was no railroad station anywhere around, and the coachman came for travelers only every second week, Yakov could have got to Kiev without taking over the horse and wagon. Shmuel had offered to drive him the thirty or so versts but the fixer preferred to be rid of him and travel alone. He figured that once he got into the city he could sell the beast and apology-for-dray, if not to a butcher, then at least to a junk dealer for a few rubles.

Dvoira, the dark-uddered cow, was out in the field behind the hut, browsing under a leafless poplar tree, and Yakov went out to her. The white cow raised her head and watched him approach. The fixer patted her lean flank. "Goodbye, Dvoira," he said, "and lots of luck. Give what you got left to Shmuel, also a poor man." He wanted to say more but couldn't. Tearing up some limp yellowing grass, he fed it to the cow, then returned to the horse and wagon. Shmuel had reappeared.

Why does he act as though he were the one who had deserted me?

"I didn't come back to fight with anybody," Shmuel said. "What she did I won't defend—she hurt me as much as she did you. Even more, though when the rabbi says she's now dead my voice agrees but not my heart. First of all she's my only child, and since when do we need more dead? I've cursed her more than once but I ask God not to listen."

"Well, I'm leaving," Yakov said, "take care of the cow."

"Don't leave yet," Shmuel said, his eyes miserable. "If you stay Raisl might come back."

"If she does who's interested?"

"If you had been more patient she wouldn't have left you."

"Five years going on six is enough of patience. I've had enough. I might have waited the legal ten, but she danced off with some dirty stranger, so I've had my fill, thanks."

"Who can blame you?' Shmuel sighed sadly. He asked after a while, "Have you got tobacco for a little cigarette, Yakov?"

"My bag is empty."

The peddler briskly rubbed his dry palms.

"So you haven't, you haven't, but what I don't understand is why you want to bother with Kiev. It's a dangerous city full of churches and anti-Semites."

"I've been cheated from the start," Yakov said bitterly. "What I've been through personally you know already, not to mention living here all my life except for a few months in the army. The shtetl is a prison, no change from the days of Khmelnitsky. It moulders and the Jews moulder in it. Here we're all prisoners, I don't have to tell you, so it's time to try elsewhere I've finally decided. I want to make a living, I want to get acquainted with a bit of the world. I've read a few books in recent years and it's surprising what goes on that none of us knows about. I'm not asking for Tibet but what I saw in St. Petersburg interested me. Whoever thought of white nights before, but it's a scientific fact; they have them there. When I left the army I thought I would get out of here as soon as possible, but things caught up with me, including your daughter."

"My daughter wanted to run away from here the minute you got married but you wouldn't go."

"It's true," said Yakov, "it was my fault. I thought it couldn't get worse so it must get better. I was wrong both ways so now enough is enough. I'm on my way at last."

"Outside the Pale only wealthy Jews and the professional classes can get residence certificates. The Tsar doesn't want poor Jews all over his land, and Stolypin, may his lungs collapse, urges him on. Ptu!" Shmuel spat through two fingers.

"Since I can't be a professional on account of lack of education I wouldn't mind being wealthy. As the saying goes, I'd sell my last shirt to be a millionaire. Maybe, by luck, I'll make my fortune in the outside world."

"What's in the world," Shmuel said, "is in the shtetl—people, their trials, worries, circumstances. But here at least God is with us."

"He's with us till the Cossacks come galloping, then he's elsewhere. He's in the outhouse, that's where he is."

The peddler grimaced but let the remark pass. "Almost fifty thousand Jews live in Kiev," he said, "restricted to a few districts, and all in the way of the first blow that falls if a new pogrom should come. And it will fall faster in the larger places than it falls here. When we hear their cries we will rush into the woods. Why should you walk straight into the hands of the Black Hundreds, may they hang by their tongues?"

"The truth of it is I'm a man full of wants I'll never satisfy, at least not here. It's time to get out and take a chance. Change your place change your luck, people say."

"Since the last year or so, Yakov, you're a different man. What wants are so important?"

"Those that can't sleep and keep me awake for company. I've told you what wants: a full stomach now and then. A job that pays rubles, not noodles. Even some education if I can get it, and I don't mean workmen studying Torah after hours.

I've had my share of that. What I want to know is what's going on in the world."

"That's all in the Torah, there's no end to it. Stay away from the wrong books, Yakov, the impure."

"There are no wrong books. What's wrong is the fear of them."

Shmuel unstuck his hat and wiped his brow with his handkerchief.

"Yakov, if you want to go to foreign parts, Turks or no Turks, why not to Palestine where a Jew can see Jewish trees and mountains, and breathe the Jewish air? If I had half a chance there's where I'd go."

"All I've had in this miserable town is a beggarly existence. Now I'll try Kiev. If I can live there decently that's what I'll do. If not, I'll make sacrifices, save up, and head for Amsterdam for a boat to America. To sum it up, I have little but I have plans."

"Plans or none you're looking for trouble."

"I've never had to look," said the fixer. "Well, Shmuel, good luck to you. The morning's gone so I'd better go."

He climbed up onto the wagon and reached for the reins.

"I'll ride with you as far as the windmills." Shmuel got up on the seat on the other side.

Yakov touched the nag with a birch switch the old man kept in the holder, a hole bored into the edge of the seat, but the horse, after an initial startled gallop, stopped short and stood motionless in the road.

"Personally I never use it," the peddler remarked. "It's there as a warning. If he dawdles I remind him it's there. He seems to like to hear me talk about it."

"If that's the case I'm better off walking."

"Patience." Shmuel smacked his lips. "Gidap, beauty—he's very vain. Whenever you can afford it, Yakov, feed him oats. Too much grass and he's prone to gas."

"If he's prone to gas let him fart." He flicked the reins.

Yakov didn't look back. The nag moved along a crooked road between black plowed fields with dark round haystacks piled up here and there, the peasant's church visible on the left in the distance; then slowly up the narrow stony cemetery road, a few thin yellow willows amidst the graves, and around a low tombstone-covered hill where Yakov's parents, a man and woman in their early twenties, lay buried. He had considered a visit to their weed-strewn graves but hadn't the heart at the last minute. The past was a wound in the head. He thought of Raisl and felt depressed.

The fixer snapped the rod against the nag's ribs but got no increase of motion.

"I'll get to Kiev by Hanukkah."

"If you don't get there it's because God wills it. You won't miss a thing."

A shnorrer in rags called to the fixer from beside a tilted tombstone. "Hey, there, Yakov, it's Friday. How about a two-kopek piece for a Sabbath blessing? Charity saves from death."

"Death is the last of my worries."

"Lend me a kopek or two, Yakov," said Shmuel.

"A kopek I haven't earned today."

The shnorrer, a man with ugly feet, called him goy, his mouth twisted, eyes lit in anger.

Yakov spat in the road.

Shmuel said a prayer to ward off evil.

The nag began to trot, drawing the rickety wagon with its swinging bucket banging the axle past the cemetery hill, down the winding road. They drove by the poorhouse, a shabby structure with an addition for orphans, which Yakov averted his eyes from, then clop-clopped across a wooden bridge into the populous section of the town. They passed Shmuel's hut, neither of them looking. A blackened bathhouse with boarded windows stood near a narrow stream and the fixer felt suddenly itchy for a bath, thinking of himself in the thick steam, slapping his soapened sides with a twig brush as the attendant poured water on his head. God bless soap and water, Raisl used to say. In a few hours the bathhouse, steaming from its cracks, would be bulging with Jews washing up for Friday night.

They rattled along a rutted dusty street with thatched cottages on one side, open weedy fields on the other. A bigwigged Jewess, sitting on her doorstep, plucked a bloodynecked hen between her knees, as she cursed out a peasant's sow rooting in the remnants of her potato garden. A pool of blood in the ditch marked the passage of the ritual slaughterer. Farther on, a bearded black goat with a twisted horn, tethered to a post, baaed at the horse and charged, but the rope around his neck held and though the post toppled, the goat was thrown on its back. The doors of some of the cottages hung loose, and where there were steps they sagged. Fences buckled and were about to collapse, without apparent notice or response, irritating the fixer, who liked things in place and functioning.

Tonight the white candles would gleam from the lit windows. For everybody else.

The horse zigzagged towards the marketplace, and now the quality of the houses improved, some large and attractive, with gardens full of flowers in the summertime.

"Leave it to the lousy rich," the fixer muttered.

Shmuel had nothing to say. His mind, he had often said, had exhausted the subject. He did not envy the rich, all he wanted was to share a little of their wealth—enough to live on while he was working hard to earn a living.

The market, a large open square with wooden houses on two sides, some containing first-floor shops, was crowded with peasant carts laden with grains, vegetables, wood, hides and whatnot. Around the stalls and bins mostly women clustered, shopping for the Sabbath. Though the market was his usual hangout, the fixer waved to no one and no one waved to him.

I leave with no regret, he thought. I should have gone years ago.

"Who have you told?" Shmuel asked.

"Who's there to tell?" Practically nobody. It's none of their business anyway. Frankly, my heart is heavy—I'll tell the truth—but I'm sick of this place."

He had said goodbye to his two cronies, Liebish Polikov and Haskel Dembo. The first had shrugged, the other wordlessly embraced him, and that was that. A butcher holding up by its thick yellow feet a squawking hen beating its wings saw the wagon go by and said something witty to his customers. One of these, a young woman who turned to look, called to Yakov, but by then the wagon was out of the marketplace, scattering some chickens nesting in the ruts of the road and a flock of jabbering ducks, as it clattered on.

They approached the domed synagogue with its iron weathercock, a pock-marked yellow-walled building with an oak door, for the time being resting in peace. It had been sacked more than once. The courtyard was empty except for a black-hatted Jew sitting on a bench reading a folded newspaper in the sunlight. Yakov had rarely been inside the synagogue in recent years yet he easily remembered the long high-ceilinged room with its brass chandeliers, oval stained windows, and the prayer stands with stools and wooden candleholders, where he had spent, for the most part wasted, so many hours.

"Gidap," he said.

At the other side of the town—a shtetl was an island surrounded by Russia—as they came abreast a windmill, its patched fans turning in slow massive motion, the fixer jerked on the reins and the horse clopped to a stop.

"Here's where we part," he said to the peddler.

Shmuel drew out of his pocket an embroidered cloth bag.

"Don't forget these," he said embarrassed. "I found them in your drawer before we left."

In the bag was another containing phylacteries. There was also a prayer shawl and a prayer book. Raisl, before they were married, had made the bag out of a piece of her dress and embroidered it with the tablets of the Ten Commandments.

"Thanks." Yakov tossed the bag among his other things in the wagon.

"Yakov," said Shmuel passionately, "don't forget your God!"

"Who forgets who?" the fixer said angrily. "What do I get from him but a bang on the head and a stream of piss in my face. So what's there to be worshipful about?"

"Don't talk like a meshummed. Stay a Jew, Yakov, don't give up our God."

"A meshummed gives up one God for another. I don't want either. We live in a world where the clock ticks fast while he's on his timeless mountain staring in space. He doesn't see us and he doesn't care. Today I want my piece of bread, not in Paradise."

"Listen to me, Yakov, take my advice. I've lived longer than you. There's a shul in the Podol in Kiev. Go on Shabbos, you'll feel better. 'Blessed are they who put their trust in God.' "

"Where I ought to go is to the Socialist Bund meetings, that's where I should go, not in shul. But the truth of it is I dislike politics, though don't ask me why. What good is it if you're not an activist? I guess it's my nature. I incline toward the philosophical although I don't know much about anything."

"Be careful," Shmuel said, agitated, "we live in the middle of our enemies. The best way to take care is to stay under God's protection. Remember, if He's not perfect, neither are we."

They embraced quickly and Shmuel got down from the wagon.

"Goodbye, sweetheart," he called to the horse. "Goodbye, Yakov. I'll think of you when I say the Eighteen Blessings. If you ever see Raisl, tell her her father is waiting."

Shmuel trudged back towards the synagogue. When he was quite far away Yakov felt a pang for having forgotten to slip him a ruble or two.

"Get on now." The nag flicked an ear, roused itself for a short trot, then slowed to a tired walk.

"It'll be some trip," the fixer thought.

The horse stopped abruptly as a field mouse skittered across the road.

"Gidap, goddamit"—but the nag wouldn't move.

A peasant passed by with a long-horned bullock, prodding the animal with a stick.

"A horse understands a whip," he said across the road in Russian.

Yakov belabored the beast with the birch rod until he drew blood. The nag whinnied but remained tightly immobile on the road. The peasant, after watching awhile, moved on.

"You son-of-a-bitch," said the fixer to the horse, "we'll never get to Kiev."

He was on the point of despair when a brown dog rustling through a blanket of dead leaves under some trees came onto the road, yelping at the horse. The nag hurried forward, Yakov barely grabbing the reins. The dog chased them, barking sharply at the horse's hooves, then at a turn in the road, disappeared. But the wagon rolled on, bucket rattling, its wheels wobbling, the nag trotting as fast as it could.

It clip-clopped along the hard dirt road, on one side of which flowed a mild stream below a sloping embankment; and on the other were the scattered log huts of a peasant village, their roofs covered with rotting straw. Despite poverty and the antics of too many pigs the huts looked better than the shtetl cottages. A bearded peasant chopped wood, a woman pumped water from the village well. They both stopped to stare at him. A verst from his own town and he was a stranger in the world.

The horse trotted on, Yakov gazing at the fields, some plowed under, where oats, hay, sugar beets had grown, the haystacks standing dark against the woods. A crow flew slowly over the stubble of a wheatfield. The fixer found himself counting sheep and goats grazing in the communal meadows under lazy thick clouds. It had been a dank and dreary autumn, the dead leaves still hanging on half the trees in the woods around the fields. Last year at this time it had already snowed. Though as a rule he enjoyed the landscape, Yakov felt a weight on him. The buzz and sparkle of summer were gone. In the violet distance the steppe seemed melancholy, endless.

The cut on the horse's flank, though encrusted, still oozed red droplets and drew fleas he switched away without touching the animal. He thought his spirits would rise once he was out of the shtetl but felt no relief. The fixer was troubled by discontent, a deeper sense that he had had no choice about going than he wanted to admit. His few friends were left behind. His habits, his best memories such as they were, were there. But so was his shame. He was leaving because he had earned a worse living—although he hadn't become a gravedigger—than many he knew with fewer brains and less skill. He was leaving because he was childless husband—"alive but dead" the Talmud described such a man—as well as embittered, deserted one. Yet if she had been faithful he would have stayed. Then better she hadn't been. He should be grateful to be escaping from a fruitless life. Still, he was apprehensive of going to a city of strangers—Jews as well as Gentiles, strangers were strangers—in a sense a forbidden place. Holy Kiev, mother of Russian cities! He knew the towns for a dozen versts around but had only once, for a week in summer, been in Kiev. He felt the discontent of strangeness, of not knowing what was where, unable to predict or clearly visualize. All he could think of were the rows of shabby crowded tenements in the Podol. Would he go on in the same useless poverty and drab experience amid masses of Jews as poor as he, or somehow come to a better way of life? How at his age?—already thirty. Jobs for him were always scarce. With just the few rubles in his pocket how long would he last before starving? Why should tomorrow be better than today? Had he earned the privilege?

He had many fears, and since he rarely traveled long distances, had fears of traveling. The soles of his feet itched, which meant, the old wives said: "You will journey to a far-off place." So, good, but would he ever get there? The horse had slowed down again, a black year on its stupid head. Suppose those clouds, grown dark and heavy, cracked open on their undersides and poured snow upon the world. Would the horse make it? He pictured the snow falling thickly, in a few minutes turning the road and fields white so you couldn't see where one ended and the other began, the wagon filling up with snow. The nag would stop. Yakov might switch him till his bones gleamed through the blood but the animal was the type that would quietly lie down in the snow to spite him. "Brother, I'm tired. If you want to go on in this storm, go in good health. But not me. I'll take sleep and if it's sleep forever, so much the better. At least the snow is warm." The fixer saw himself wandering in drifts until he perished.

But the horse said nothing, and it didn't look like snow—or rain either. It was a brisk day beginning to be windy—it raised the nag's mane—and though the horse moved leisurely it moved steadily. Yet as they went through a grove of black-branched trees, the leafless twigs darkly intertwined high above Yakov's head, the small wood grew gloomy, and the fixer still searching for a change in the weather became actively nervous again. Shading his eyes in the queer light, he peered ahead—a winding road, absolutely snowless. Enough of this, he thought, I'd better eat. As though it had read his mind the nag came to a stop before he pulled the reins. Yakov got down off the seat, and taking hold of the bridle, drew the horse to the side of the road. The horse spread its hind legs and spattered a yellow stream on the road. Yakov urinated on some brown ferns. Feeling better, he tore up several handfuls of dry tussocky grass, and since he could locate no feedbag in the wagon, fed it in fistfuls to the nag. The horse, its sides heaving, chewed with its eroded yellow teeth until the grass foamed. The fixer's stomach rumbled. He sat under a sunlit tree, raised his sheepskin collar, and opened the food parcel. He ate part of a cold boiled potato, chewing slowly, then half a cucumber sprinkled with coarse salt, with a piece of sour black bread. Ah, for some tea, he thought, or if not that, some sweetened hot water. Yakov fell asleep with his back to the tree, awoke in a hurry, and climbed up on the wagon.

"It's late, goddamit, come on, move."

The nag wouldn't budge. The fixer reached for the switch. On second thought he climbed down, unhitched the rusty bucket and went looking for water. When he found a little stream the pail leaked, but he offered it, half full, to the horse, who wouldn't drink.

"Games I don't play." Yakov poured out the water, hitched the bucket on the hook under the wagon, and stepped up to the seat. He waved the switch till it whistled. The nag, lowering his ears, moved forward, if one could call it movement. At least it wasn't where it had been before. The fixer again whistled the air with the switch, and the horse, after an indecisive minute, began to trot. The wagon rattled on.

They had gone on a while when the wagon caught up with an old woman, a pilgrim walking slowly in the road, leaning on her long staff, a heavy peasant in black, wearing men's shoes and carrying a knapsack, a thick shawl wrapped around her head.

He drew over to the side to pass her but as he did Yakov called out, "A ride, granny?"

"May Jesus bless you." She had three gray teeth.

Jesus he didn't need. Bad luck, he thought. Yakov helped pull her up to the wagon seat and touched the nag with the birch whip. To his surprise the horse took up his trot. Then as the road turned, the right wheel struck a rock and broke with a crunch. The wagon teetered and sagged at the rear, the left wheel tilted inward.

The old woman crossed herself, slowly climbed down to the road, and walked on with her heavy stick. She did not look back.

Yakov cursed Shmuel for wishing the wagon on him. Jumping to the ground he examined the broken wheel. Its worn metal ring had come off. The wooden rim had caved in, splintering two spokes. The split hub leaked axle grease. He groaned.

After five minutes of stunned emptiness he got his tool sack out of the wagon, untied it and spread out the tools on the road. But with hatchet, saw, plane, tinsmith's shears, trisquare, putty, wire, pointed knife and two awls, the fixer couldn't fix what was broken. Under the best conditions it would take him a day to repair the wheel. He thought of buying one from a peasant if he could get one that fitted, or nearly fitted, but if so where was the peasant? When you didn't need them they were in your beard. Yakov tossed the pieces of broken wheel into the wagon. He tied up his tools and drearily waited for someone to come. Nobody came. He considered returning to the shtetl but remembered he had had enough. The wind was colder, sharper, got under his coat and between the shoulder blades. The sun was setting, the sky turning dark.

If I go slow maybe I can make it on three wheels to the next village.

He tried it, sitting lightly as far to the left on the seat as he could, and begged the nag to take it easy. To his relief they went forward, the back wheel squeaking, for half a verst. He had caught up with the pilgrim and was about to say she couldn't ride when the other rear wheel, grinding thickly against the axle, collapsed, the back of the wagon hitting the road with a crashing thud, the bucket crushed. The horse lurched forward, snorted and reared. The fixer, his body tipped at a perilous angle, was paralyzed.

Eventually he got down off the seat. "Who invented my life?" Behind him was the empty treeless steppe, ahead the old woman. She had stopped before a huge wooden crucifix at the side of the road, crossed herself, and then slowly sinking to her knees, began to hit her head against the hard ground. She banged it until Yakov had a headache. The darkening steppe was here uninhabited. He feared fog and a raging wind. Unhitching the horse and drawing him out from under the wooden yoke, Yakov gathered together the reins. He backed the nag to the wagon seat, and climbing up on it, mounted the animal. No sooner up than down. The fixer placed his tool bag, book bundle, and parcels on the tilted seat, wound the reins around him, and remounted the horse. He slung the tools over his shoulder, and with his left hand held the other things as they rested on the horse's back, his right hand grasping the reins. The horse galloped forward. To Yakov's surprise, he did not fall off.

They skirted the old woman, prostrate at the cross. He felt foolish and uncertain on the horse but hung on. The nag had slowed to a trot, then to a dejected walk. It stood stock still. Yakov cursed it into eternity and eventually it came to life, once more inching forward. When they were on the move, the fixer, who had never sat on a horse before—he couldn't think why except that he had never had a horse—dreamed of good fortune, accomplishment, affluence. He had a comfortable home, good business—maybe a small factory of some kind—a faithful wife, dark-haired, pretty, and three healthy children, God bless them. But when he was becalmed on the nag he thought blackly of his father-in-law, beat the beast with his fist, and foresaw for himself a useless future. Yakov pleaded with the animal to make haste—it was dark and the steppe wind cut keenly, but freed of the wagon the horse examined the world. He also stopped to crop grass, tearing it audibly with his eroded teeth, and wandering from one side of the road to the other. Once in a while he turned and trotted back a few steps. Yakov, frantic, threatened the switch, but they both knew he had none. In desperation he kicked the beast with his heels. The nag bucked and for a perilous few minutes it was like being in a rowboat on a stormy sea. Having barely survived, Yakov stopped kicking. He considered ditching his goods, hoping the lightened load might speed things up, but didn't dare.

"I'm a bitter man, you bastard horse. Come to your senses or you'll suffer."

It availed him nothing.

By then it was pitch dark. The wind boomed. The steppe was a black sea full of strange voices. Here nobody spoke Yiddish, and the nag, maybe feeling the strangeness of it, began to trot and soon came close to flight. Though the fixer was not a superstitious man he had been a superstitious boy, and he recalled Lilith, Queen of Evil Spirits, and the Fish-witch who tickled travelers to death or otherwise made herself helpful. Ghosts rose like smoke in the Ukraine. From time to time he felt a presence at his back but would not turn. Then a yellow moon rose like a flower growing and lit the empty steppe deep into the shadowy distance. The distance glowed. It'll be a long night, the fixer thought. They galloped through a peasant village, its long-steepled church yellow in moonlight, the squat thatched huts dark, no lights anywhere. Though he smelled woodsmoke he saw none. Yakov considered dismounting, knocking on a strange door and begging for a night's lodging. But he felt that if he got off the horse he would never get back on. He was afraid he might be robbed of his few rubles, so he stayed put and made uncertain progress. The sky was thick with stars, the wind blowing cold in his face. Once he slept momentarily and woke in shivering sweat from a nightmare. He thought he was irretrievably lost, but to his amazement, before him in the distance rose a vast height glowing in dim moonlight and sprinkled sparsely with lights, at the foot of which ran a broad dark river reflecting the half-hidden moon. The nag stopped jogging and it took them an almost endless hour to make the last half verst to the water.

3

It was freezing cold but the wind was down on the Dnieper. There was no ferry, the boatman said. "Closed down. Closed. Shut." He waved his arms as though talking to a foreigner although Yakov had spoken to him in Russian. That the ferry had stopped running sharpened the fixer's desire to get across the river. He hoped to rent a bed at an inn and wake early to look for work.

"I'll row you across for a ruble," the boatman said.

"Too much," Yakov answered, though deadly tired. "Which way to the bridge?"

"Six or eight versts. A long way for the same thing."

"A ruble," the fixer groaned. "Who's got that much money?"

"You can take it or leave it. It's no easy thing rowing across a dangerous river on a pitch-black night. We might both drown."

"What would I do with my horse?" The fixer spoke more to himself.

"That's none of my business." The boatman, his shoulders like a tree trunk, and wearing a shaggy grizzled beard, blew out one full nostril on a rock, then the other. The white of his right eye was streaked with blood.

"Look, mate, why do you make more trouble than it's worth? Even if I could haul it across, which I can't, the beast will die on you. It doesn't take a long look to see he's on his last leg. Look at him trembling. Listen to him breathing like a gored bull."

"I was hoping to sell him in Kiev."

"What fool would buy a bag of old bones?"

"I thought maybe a horse butcher or someone—at least the skin."

"I say the horse is dead," said the boatman, "but you can save a ruble if you're smart. I'll take him for the cost of the trip. It's a bother to me and I'll be lucky to get fifty kopeks for the carcass, but I'll do you the favor, seeing you're a stranger."

He's only given me trouble, the fixer thought.

He stepped into the rowboat with his bag of tools, books, and other parcels. The boatman untied the boat, dipped both oars into the water and they were off.

The nag, tethered to a paling, watched from the moonlit shore.

Like an old Jew he looks, thought the fixer.

The horse whinnied, and when that proved useless, farted loudly.

"I don't recognize the accent you speak," said the boatman, pulling the oars. "It's Russian but from what province?"

"I've lived in Latvia as well as other places," the fixer muttered.

"At first I thought you were a goddam Pole. Pan whosis, Pani whatsis." The boatman laughed, then snickered. "Or maybe a motherfucking Jew. But though you're dressed like a Russian you look more like a German, may the devil destroy them all, excepting yourself and yours of course."

"Latvian," said Yakov.

"Anyway, God save us all from the bloody Jews," the boatman said as he rowed, "those long-nosed, pock-marked, cheating, bloodsucking parasites. They'd rob us of daylight if they could. They foul up earth and air with their body stink and garlic breaths, and Russia will be done to death by the diseases they spread unless we make an end to it. A Jew's a devil—it's a known fact—and if you ever watch one peel off his stinking boot you'll see a split hoof, it's true. I know, for as the Lord is my witness, I saw one with my own eyes. He thought nobody was looking, but I saw his hoof as plain as day."

He stared at Yakov with the bloody eye. The fixer's foot itched but he didn't touch it.

Let him talk, he thought, yet he shivered.

"Day after day they crap up the Motherland," the boatman went on monotonously, "and the only way to save ourselves is to wipe them out. I don't mean kill a Zhid now and then with a blow of the fist or kick in the head, but wipe them all out, which we've sometimes tried but never done as it should be done. I say we ought to call our menfolk together, armed with guns, knives, pitchforks, clubs—anything that will kill a Jew—and when the church bells begin to ring we move on the Zhidy quarter, which you can tell by the stink, routing them out of wherever they're hiding—in attics, cellars, or ratholes—bashing in their brains, stabbing their herring-filled guts, shooting off their snotty noses, no exception made for young or old, because if you spare any they breed like rats and then the job's to do all over again.

"And then when we've slaughtered the whole cursed tribe of them—and the same is done in every province throughout

Russia, wherever we can smoke them out—though we've got most of them nice and bunched up in the Pale—we'll pile up the corpses and soak them in benzine and light fires that people will enjoy all over the world. Then when that's done we hose the stinking ashes away and divide the rubles and jewels and silver and furs and all the other loot they stole, or give it back to the poor who it rightfully belongs to anyway. You can take my word—the time's not far off when everything I say, we will do, because our Lord, who they crucified, wants his rightful revenge."

He dropped an oar and crossed himself.

Yakov fought an impulse to do the same. His bag of prayer things fell with a plop into the Dnieper and sank like lead.

II

Where do you go if you had been nowhere? He hid at first in the Jewish quarter, emerging stealthily from time to time to see what there was to see in the world, exploring, trying the firmness of the earth. Kiev, "the Jerusalem of Russia," still awed and disquieted him. He had been there for a few hot summer days after being conscripted into the army, and now, again, he saw it with half the self—the other half worried about his worries. Still, as he wandered from street to street, the colors were light and pretty. A golden haze hung in the air in the late afternoons. The busy avenues were full of people, among them Ukrainian peasants in their native dress, gypsies, soldiers, priests. At night the white gas globes glowed in the streets and there were thick mists on the river. Kiev stood on three hills, and he remembered his first trembling sight of the city from the Nicholas Bridge—dotted with white houses with green roofs, churches and monasteries, their gold and silver domes floating above the green foliage. He wasn't without an eye for a pretty scene, though that added nothing to his living. Still, a man was more than a workhorse, or so they said.

The other way, across the glassy brown river—the way he had come on a dying horse—the steppe stretched out into the vast green distance. Only thirty versts and the shtetl was invisible, gone—poof!—lost, maybe expired. Though he felt homesick he knew he would never return, yet what would it come to? More than once Raisl had accused him of being afraid to leave and maybe it was true but at last it wasn't. So

I left, he thought, what good will it do me? Was she back? he wondered. He cursed her when he thought of her.

He went where he had not been before, speaking in Russian to anyone who spoke to him—testing himself, he explained it to himself. Why should a man be afraid of the world? Because he was, if for no other reason. Numb with fear that he would be recognized as a Jew and ordered out, he stealthily watched from the gallery of a church as the peasants, some with knapsacks on their backs, knelt and prayed at the altar before a tall gold crucifix and a jeweled ikon of the Madonna, as the priest, a huge man in rich thick vestments, chanted the Orthodox service. The fixer had the shivers as he looked, and the strange odor of incense increased his nervousness. He almost rose out of his boots as he was touched on the arm and saw at his side a black-bearded hunchback who pointed to the peasants below smacking their heads against the flagstone floor and kissing it passionately. "Go thou and do likewise! Eat salted bread and listen to the truth!" The fixer quickly left.

Stupefied that he dared the adventure, he afterwards descended to the Lavra catacombs—under the old monastery on the Pechersky hill overlooking the Dnieper—amid a group of frightened pasty-faced peasants holding lit candles. They moved in a loose line along low, damp-smelling passages, where through barred windows he caught glimpses of the saints of the Orthodox Church lying in open coffins, covered with shabby cloths of red and gold. Small red lamps glowed in the walls under their ikons. In a candle-lit cell, as the line moved on, a monk with rattail hair to his shoulders held out a relic of "the hand of St. Andrew" for the faithful to kiss, and each knelt to touch the parchmented hand to his lips. But though Yakov had considered a quick kiss of the bony fingers, when his time came to kneel, he blew out his candle and groped his way on in the dark.

Outside there was a crowd of beggars, some of them armless and legless cripples from the late war. Three were blind. One rolled his eyes inward. One bulged his so that they looked like fish eyes. And one read sonorously "by divine inspiration" from a book of gospels which he held in his hands. He stared at Yakov and Yakov stared at him.

2

He lived in the heart of the Jewish quarter in the Podol District in a teeming tenement hung with mattresses airing and rags of clothing drying, above a courtyard crowded with wooden workshops where everyone was busy but no one earned much of anything. They stayed alive. The fixer wanted better, at least better than he had had, too much of nothing. For a while, during the cold rains of late autumn, he confined himself to the Jewish section, but after the first snowfall in the city—about a month after he had arrived—he began to edge out again, looking for work. With his tool sack slung over his shoulder he trudged from street to street through the Podol and Plossky, the flat commercial districts reaching to the river, and went up the hills into neighborhoods forbidden to Jews to work in. He sought, he continued to say to himself, opportunities, though in seeking them he sometimes felt like a spy behind enemy lines. The Jewish quarter, unchanged in ages, swarmed and smelled. Its worldly goods were spiritual goods; all that was lacking was prosperity. The fixer, having left the shtetl, resented the lack. He had tried working for a brushmaker, a man with a foaming beard who had promised to teach him the business. The wages were soup. So he had gone back to being a fixer and it came also to nothing, sometimes soup. If a window was broken they stuffed it with rags and said a blessing. He offered to replace it for a pittance, and when he had done the work they gave him thanks, blessings, a plate of noodle soup. He lived frugally in a low-ceilinged cubicle, in a printer's assistant's flat—Aaron Latke's, sleeping on a bench covered with burlap sack; the flat was crowded with children and smelly feather beds, and the fixer, as he parted with kopeks and earned none, grew increasingly anxious. He must go where he could make a living or change his craft, maybe both. Among the goyim his luck might be better, it couldn't be worse. Besides, what choice has a man who doesn't know what his choices are? He meant in the world. So he walked out of the ghetto when no one was looking. In the snow he felt anonymous, in a sense unseen in his Russian cap and coat—any unemployed worker.

Russians passed him without looking at him and he passed them. Having been told he did not look Jewish he now believed it. Yakov trudged in the snow up the hill to the Kreshchatik, the broad main street, trying kiosks, shops, public buildings, but finding little to do, a few odd jobs, payment in greenish coppers. At night in his cubicle, a glass of hot tea cupped in his reddened hands, when he thought of returning to the shtetl he thought of death.

Latke, when the fixer said this aloud, looked at him in popeyed horror. He was a man with arthritic hands and eight half-starving children. The pain hindered his work but not his labor.

"For God's sake, patience," he said. "You're not without brains and that's the beginning of luck. Afterwards, as they say, your ox will calve."

"To have luck you need it. I've had little luck."

"You've just come green from the country, so at least be patient till you know where you are."

So the fixer went looking for luck.

One desperate evening, the gas lamps casting a greenish glow on the snow, Yakov, trudging at twilight in the Plossky District, came upon a man lying with his face in the trodden snow. He hesitated a minute before turning him over, afraid to be involved in trouble. The man was a fattish, bald-headed Russian of about sixty-five, his fur cap in the snow, his heavy face splotched a whitish red and blue, snow on his mustache. He was breathing and reeked of drink. The fixer at once noticed the black and white button pinned to his coat, the two-headed eagle of the Black Hundreds. Let him shift for himself, he thought. Frightened, he ran to the corner, then ran back. Grabbing the anti-Semite under the arms he began to drag him to the doorway of the house in front of which he had fallen, when he heard a cry down the street. A girl wearing a green shawl over a green dress was running crookedly towards them. At first he thought she was a crippled child but then saw she was a young woman with a crippled leg.

She knelt, brushed the snow from the fat man's face, shook him and said breathlessly, "Papa, get up! Papa, this can't go on."

"I ought to have gone for him," she said to Yakov, cracking her knuckles against her breast. "This is the second time this month he's fallen in the street. When he drinks in the tavern it becomes an impossible situation. Kindly help me get him home, sir. We live only a few doors from here."

"Take his legs," said Yakov.

With the girl's help he half carried, half dragged the fat Russian up the street to the three-story yellow brick house with a wrought-iron awning above the door. The girl called the porter, and he and the fixer, she hobbling up after them, carried her father up the stairs into a large-roomed, well-furnished flat on the first floor. They laid him on a leather couch near the tile stove in the bedroom. A Pekinese began to yelp, then growled at the fixer. The girl picked the dog up, deposited it in another room, and at once returned. The dog barked shrilly through the door.

As the porter removed the man's wet shoes he stirred and groaned.

"With God's help," he muttered.

"Papa," said his daughter, "we owe thanks to this good man for assisting you after your accident. He found you face down in the snow. If not for him you would have smothered."

Her father opened his humid eyes. "Glory be to God." He crossed himself and began quietly to cry. She crossed herself and dabbed at her eyes with a handkerchief.

As she was unbuttoning her father's overcoat, Yakov, after staying for a last deep breath of the warmth, left the flat and went down the stairs, relieved to be out.

The girl called to him in a tight high voice from the top of the stairs and quickly hobbled down after him, holding to the banister. Her face was sharp, her green eyes searching, hungry. She seemed about twenty-five, slightly built, her torso long, with thick honey-colored hair that she wore loose around the shoulders. She wasn't pretty but she wasn't plain, and although he was sorry for her crippled leg he felt for her a strange momentary revulsion.

She asked him who he was, not quite looking at him, her eyes lowered, then shifting to a direct glance. She stared at the sack of tools on his shoulder.

He told her little: he was a stranger, recently from the provinces. It occurred to him then to remove his cap.

"Please come back tomorrow," she said. "Papa says he would like to thank you when he is in a better frame of mind, but I will tell you frankly you may expect something more than mere thanks. My father is Nikolai Maximovitch Lebedev—semi-retired—he was already retired but he had to take over his brother's business affairs at his death—and I am Zinaida Nikolaevna. Please call on us in the morning when Papa is himself. He's usually at his best then, though never at his very best since my poor mother's death."

Yakov, without giving his name, said he would return in the morning and left.

Back in his cubicle in Aaron Latke's flat, he wondered what was "more than mere thanks." Obviously the girl meant some sort of reward, possibly a ruble or two, and with luck, five. But he had doubts whether to go back there. Should he take a reward from a self-advertised Jew hater? He hadn't for a minute been comfortable in his presence, or the girl's. Then either better not go, or tell the old man who he was indebted to and leave. But that wasn't what he wanted to do. Yakov sweated in his thoughts, the drunkard's two-headed eagle staring him in both eyes. He slept badly and woke with a new thought. Why not a ruble or two if it kept a Jew alive? What better service from an anti-Semite? He recalled a Russian saying: "A fearful wolf should stay out of the forest," but decided to go anyway, take a chance, or how would he know what went on in the world?

So he returned to the house in the Plossky without his bag of tools, though he could not dress up, nor did he want to. Zinaida Nikolaevna, wearing an embroidered peasant blouse and skirt, with two green ribbons plaited into her hair and some strings of yellow glass beads at her throat, led him to her father's bedroom. Nikolai Maximovitch, in a loose wadded robe with a fur collar, sat at a table by a curtained window, a huge book open before him. On the wall behind hung a large chart in the form of a tree showing by way of white printed slots on its thickest black branches the descent of Nicholas II from Adam. A framed portrait of the Tsar sitting with the pale-faced Tsarevitch hung above that. The house was overheated. The little dog snarled at the fixer and had to be carried out of the room by the cook.

Nikolai Maximovitch rose slowly, an old man with wrinkled, red-rimmed, wet melancholy eyes, and welcomed Yakov without embarrassment. The fixer, thinking of his Black Hundreds button felt for him contempt, and a portion of the same for himself. His throat tightened. Though he wasn't trembling, he felt he might be.

"Nikolai Maximovitch Lebedev," the fat Russian said, offering his soft pudgy hand. A thick gold watchchain hung on his paunch, and his vest was dusty with snuff grains.

Yakov, after a slight hesitation, shook hands, answering as he had planned, "Yakov Ivanovitch Dologushev." To have given his name might have finished off the reward. Yet he felt ashamed and sweaty.

Zinaida Nikolaevna busied herself with the samovar.

Her father indicated a chair for the fixer.

"I have a good deal to thank you for, Yakov Ivanovitch," he said, resuming his seat. "I lost my footing in the snow, no doubt there was ice under it. You were very kind to assist me—not everyone would have. Once, under quite different circumstances—I began to drink only after the death of my beloved wife, a woman of exceptional qualities—Zina will affirm the truth of what I am saying—I fainted from illness on Fundukleyevsky Street, in front of a coffee shop, and lay on the pavement with a gash in my head for an unconscionable time before anyone—in this case a woman who had lost a son at Port Arthur—bothered to come to my assistance. Nowadays people are far less concerned about their fellow humans than in times past. Religious feeling has shrunk in the world and kindness is rare. Very rare indeed."

Yakov, waiting for him to come to the reward, sat tightly in the chair.

Nikolai Maximovitch regarded the fixer's worn sheepskin coat. He took out his snuffbox, inserted a pinch in both nostrils, blew his nose vigorously in a large white handkerchief, sneezed twice, then after a few futile attempts, succeeded in thrusting the box back into his robe pocket.

"My daughter informs me you were carrying a bag of tools yesterday. What is your trade, if I may ask?"

"Repairs, et cetera, of all kinds," Yakov answered. "I do carpentering, also painting, and roofing."

"Is that so? Are you presently employed?"

The fixer, without thought, said he wasn't.

"Where are you from if you don't mind saying?" said Nikolai Maximovitch. "I ask because I have a curious nature."

"From the provinces," Yakov answered, after a moment's hesitation.

"Ach—really?—a country boy?—and a good thing, may I say. The country virtues are not to be denied. I'm from the region of Kursk myself. I've pitched hay in my time. Do you come to Kiev as a pilgrim?"

"No, I came for work." He paused. "Also, if possible, for a little education."

"Excellent. You speak well although with a provincial accent. But grammatically. Have you had some schooling?"

Blast his questions, the fixer thought.

"I've read a little on my own."

The girl was watching him through lowered eyelids.

"Do you also read in the Holy Scriptures?" asked Nikolai Maximovitch. "I presume you do?"

"I know the Psalms."

"Wonderful. Did you hear, Zina?—the Psalms, wonderful. The Old Testament is admirable, the true prophecy of Christ's coming and his redemption of us through death. However, it is in no way equal to the preachings and parables of Our Lord, in the New Testament. I have just been rereading this." Nikolai Maximovitch glanced down at the open book and read aloud:

" 'Blessed are the poor in spirit; for theirs is the kingdom of heaven.' "

Yakov, grown pale, nodded.

Nikolai Maximovitch's eyes were humid. He had again to blow his nose.

"He always cries when he reads the Sermon on the Mount," said Zinaida Nikolaevna.

"I always cry." Clearing his throat, Nikolai Maximovitch read on: " 'Blessed are the merciful; for they shall obtain mercy.' "

Mercy, the fixer thought, it makes him cry.

" 'Blessed are they which are persecuted for righteousness sake; for theirs is the kingdom of heaven.' "

Come already to the reward, thought Yakov.

"Ah, this is most moving," Nikolai Maximovitch said, having to wipe his eyes again. "You know, Yakov Ivanovitch, I am in some ways a miserable man, melancholic, a heavy drinker, yet something more than that although I recently set my clothes on fire while smoking a cigarette when a piece of hot ash fell on my trousers, and if Zina had not alertly poured a pitcher of water over me, I would now be a burnt corpse. I drink because I happen to be more sensitive than most—I feel much too keenly the sorrows of life. My daughter will attest to that."

"It's true," she said. "He is a man of more than ordinary feeling. When our former little dog Pasha died of a distemper, Papa couldn't eat for weeks."

"When Zina was a child, after her severe illness I wept every night over her poor crippled leg."

"It's true," she said, her eyes moist.

"I tell you this so that you may know the kind of person I am," Nikolai Maximovitch said to Yakov. "Zina, please serve the tea."

She brought the tea to the marble-top table on a thick silver tray, with two clay pots of whole-fruit jam, raspberry and peach; and Viennese rolls, and butter.

It's mad, I know, Yakov thought. Tea with rich goyim. Yet he ate hungrily.

Nikolai Maximovitch poured a little milk into his tea and ate a buttered roll. He ate with gulping noises, as though drinking what he ate. Then he sipped again from the hot glass and set it down, patting his snuff-swollen lips with a linen napkin.

"I would like to offer you a modest reward for your timely assistance."

Yakov hastily put down his glass and rose.

"I ask for nothing. Thanks for the tea and I'd better be off."

"Spoken like a Christian, but please sit down and listen to what I have to say. Zina, fill Yakov Ivanovitch's glass and put plenty of butter and conserves on his roll. Yakov Ivanovitch, what I have to say is this. I have an empty flat on the next story, recently vacated—the tenants proved entirely unsuitable—four fine rooms that need painting and repapering. If you care to undertake the task I offer forty rubles, which is more than I would ordinarily pay, considering the fact that I furnish the paint and other materials; but the circumstances in this case are different. It is, of course, a matter of gratitude, but wouldn't you rather work than peremptorily receive from me some silver coins? Is money ever valuable if it is come by without labor? An offer of work is an appreciation of merit. Notwithstanding you did me the greatest of favors—I might have suffocated in the snow, as Zina points out—isn't my offer of work a more estimable reward than a mere payment of money?" He looked eagerly at Yakov. "Therefore will you accept?"

"In the way you put it, yes," said Yakov. He got up quickly, said he had to be going, and after stumbling into a closet on his way out, hurriedly left the apartment.

Though he worried what he was getting into and changed his mind every half hour as he lay restlessly on his bed-bench that night, the next morning he went back. He returned for the same reason he had gone the first time—to collect his reward. What he earned for his work in this case was the reward. Who could afford to say no to forty rubles—a tremendous sum? Therefore why worry about returning? Go, do the job quickly, collect the money, and when you have it in your pocket, leave the place once and for all and forget it. After all it's only a job, I'm not selling my soul. When I'm finished I'll wash up and go. They're not bad people. The girl's direct and honest in her way, though she makes me uneasy, and as for the old man, maybe I misjudged him. How many goyim have I known in my life? Maybe someone stuck that Black Hundreds pin on his coat when he was drunk in the tavern. Still, if it's really his own I'd like to ask him straight out, "Nikolai Maximovitch, will you please explain how you can cry for a dead dog yet belong to a society of fanatics that urges death on human beings who happen to be Jews? Explain to me the logic of it." Then let him answer that.

What also troubled the fixer was that once he went to work, even though the "reward" made it different from work though not less than work, he might be asked to produce his passport, a document stamped "Religious Denomination: Judaic," which would at once tell Nikolai Maximovitch what he was hiding from him. He chewed his lips over that but decided that if the passport was asked for he would say the police in the Podol had it; and if Nikolai Maximovitch insisted he must produce it, that was the time to quit or there would be serious trouble. It was therefore a gamble, but if you were against gambling, stop playing cards. He guessed the Russian was probably too muddled to ask for the passport although he was required to by law. Still, after all, it was a reward, maybe he wouldn't. Yakov was now somewhat sorry he hadn't at once identified himself as a Jew by birth. If that had killed off the reward, at least there would be no self-contempt. The more one hides the more he has to.

He did an expert job on the flat—scraped the walls clean of paper, and the ceilings of flakes and loose patches. He plastered where he had to, then thickly calcimined the ceilings—nothing but the best for Nikolai Maximovitch. And he pasted the wallpaper neatly though his experience with papering was limited—in the shtetl only Viskover, the Nogid, was that fancy. Yakov worked all day and into the night by yellow gaslight to get the job done, collect his rubles, and disappear. The landlord, stopping now and then to catch his breath, labored up the stairs each morning to see how the work was progressing, and expressed himself as most pleased. In the afternoon he got out his vodka bottle, into which he had cut strips of orange peel, and by sunset was drunk. Zina, unseen during the day, sent up the cook, Lidya, with a snack at lunchtime—a fish pie, bowl of borscht, or some meat dumplings so delicious it seemed to the fixer he would have done the job for the food alone.

One night Zina limped up the stairs, expressing surprise he was working so late. She asked Yakov if he had eaten since lunch, and when he said he was not hungry she suggested, nervously laughing, that he eat supper with her, Papa having already retired and she liking company. The fixer, greatly surprised by the invitation, begged off. He had, he explained, too much to do, and apologized for his clothes. Zina said not to mind that. "Clothes can be shed in a minute, Yakov Ivanovitch, but whether they are or not cannot change a man's nature. He's either kind or he's isn't, with or without clothes. Besides I don't care for excessive formality." He thanked her but said he couldn't take the time off from work. There were two more rooms to do. The next evening she came up again and somewhat agitatedly confessed she was lonely; so they ate together in the kitchen downstairs. She had dismissed Lidya and throughout the meal talked constantly, mostly of her childhood, the young ladies' school she had attended, and the pleasures of Kiev in the summertime.

"Days are long and hot, but nights are languorous and starlit. People refresh themselves in their flower gardens and some walk in the parks, drink kvass and lemonade, and listen to the symphonies. Have you ever heard *Pagliacci,* Yakov Ivanovitch? I think you would love Marinsky Park."

He said he did not mind parks.

"The Contract Fair opens in the spring, it's most entertaining. Or if you like there's a cinematograph to go to on the Kreshchatik."

Her eyes darted glances as she spoke and when he looked at her she glanced away. Afterwards the fixer, made nervous by her chatter, excused himself to go back to work, but Zina followed him up the stairs to watch him paste on the wallpaper she had selected, bunches of blue roses. She sat on a kitchen chair with her legs crossed, the good one over the crippled, and cracked and ate dried sunflower seeds, rhythmically swinging her leg as she watched him work.

Then she lit and awkwardly smoked a cigarette.

"You know, Yakov Ivanovitch, I couldn't possibly treat you as an ordinary common laborer for the simple reason that you aren't one. Certainly not in my eyes. Really you are a guest who happens to be working here because of Papa's idiosyncratic ways. I hope you realize that?"

"If you don't work you don't eat."

"Quite true, but you are more intelligent and even genteel—at any rate, sensitive—please don't shake your head over that—than the average Russian laborer. I can't tell you how exasperating they can be, particularly Ukrainians, and really we dread having repairs or improvements made. No, please don't deny it, anyone can sense you are different. And you told Papa you believe in the necessity of an education and would like to further your own. I heard you say that and approve very much. I too love to read, and not only romances. I'm sure you'll find excellent opportunities for yourself in the future, and if you are alert may some day be as comfortably off as Papa."

Yakov went on papering.

"Poor Papa suffers dreadfully from melancholia. He gets quite drunk by nightfall and has no appetite, to speak of, for supper. He usually falls asleep in his chair, Lidya removes his shoes, and with Alexei's help we get him to bed. At night he awakes and says his prayers. Sometimes he undresses himself, and it's almost impossible to find his clothes in the morning. Once he put his socks under the rug, and I found his drawers, all wet, in the water closet. Usually he isn't awake till midmorning. It's hard on me, of course, but I can't complain because Papa's had a difficult life. And there's no one to keep me company in the evening but Lidya and at times Alexei when he happens to be fixing something, but quite frankly, Yakov Ivanovitch, neither of them has an idea in his head. Alexei sleeps in the basement, and Lidya's small room is at the back of the flat off the terrace beyond Papa's bedroom; and since I would rather read at night than listen to her go on and on, I dismiss her early. Sometimes it gives me pleasure to be the only one up in the house at night. It's very cozy. I light the samovar, read, write letters to old friends and crochet. Papa says I make the most remarkable lace doilies. He marvels at the intricacy of the patterns. But most of the time," she sighed, "to tell the truth, it can be dreadfully lonely."

She chewed a sunflower seed disconsolately, then remarked that although she had been crippled through illness as a child, she had always been considered attractive by the opposite sex and had had more than one admirer.

"I don't say this to flaunt myself or be brazen but because I don't want you to think of me as being at a disadvantage with regard to the normal experiences of life. I am nothing of the sort. I have a quite attractive figure and many men notice me, especially when I'm dressed up. Once in a restaurant a man ogled me so insistently Papa went over to him and demanded an explanation. The man humbly apologized and do you know, Yakov Ivanovitch, when I got back home I broke into sobs."

Gentlemen called on her of course, Zina went on, but unfortunately not always the most sensitive or worthy, a situation more than one of her friends had to put up with. Sensitive, dependable men were rare, although such persons could be found in all classes, not necessarily gentry.

He listened with one ear, aware that her glance traced his every move. Why does she bother? he asked himself. What can she see in a man like me whose advantages are all disadvantages if I have it right? I have little wit in Russian, it's a heavy language for me. And if I said "Jew" aloud she'd run in six directions. Yet she often entered his thoughts. He had been a long time without a woman and he wondered what it would be like to be in bed with her. He had never had a Russian woman, though Haskel Dembo had slept with a peasant girl and said it was the same as with any Jewess. The crippled leg, Yakov thought, would not bother him.

He finished papering the fourth room that night and except for the woodwork the job was done. Two days later when it was all but finished, Nikolai Maximovitch unsteadily ascended the stairs to inspect the flat. He went from room to room, running his fingers over the wallpaper, looking up at the ceilings.

"Outstanding," he said. "Quite outstanding. An honest and attractive piece of work, Yakov Ivanovitch. I congratulate you."

Later he said as though in afterthought, "You must excuse me for asking, but what are your political predilections? Surely you're not a Socialist? I ask in the strictest confidence without attempting to pry, and not in the least accusatorily. I ask, in a word, because I am interested in your future."

"I am not a political person," Yakov answered. "The world's full of it but it's not for me. Politics is not in my nature."

"Very good, indeed. Neither am I, and much better off in the bargain if anyone should ask. Yakov Ivanovitch, don't think I will soon forget the quality of your craftsmanship. If you should care to go on working for me, though in another, and may I say, advanced capacity, I would be more than happy to employ you. The truth of the matter is that I am the owner of a small brickworks nearby, although in a contiguous district. I inherited it from my elder brother, a lifelong bachelor who went to his final reward half a year ago after suffering from an incurable disease. I tried to sell the factory but the offers were so disgraceful that, although I have little heart or, at this time of my life, head for business, I have kept it going, although, I confess, barely profitably. My foreman Proshko is in charge, an excellent technical person who is otherwise an ignorant man, and confidentially, the drivers who work under him have not been accounting for every brick that leaves the yard. I would like you to go in as a sort of overseer to handle accounts and, on the whole, look after my interests. My brother was involved in every phase of the operations, but I have little patience with bricks."

Yakov, though he had listened with excitement to the proposition, confessed he was without experience in business. "I know nothing about bookkeeping."

"Common sense is what's needed in business once honesty is assured," said Nikolai Maximovitch. "What there is to learn you will learn as you go along. I usually visit for an hour one or two mornings a week, and what you don't know I'll try to help you with, though I frankly confess my knowledge is limited. There's no need to protest, Yakov Ivanovitch. My daughter, whose judgment in these matters I respect, has the highest opinion of your merit, and you may believe me, I thoroughly share it. She considers you a man of sobriety and sound sense, and I am confident that after you have mastered the fundamentals you will do a responsible and effective job. During the period of your—ah—apprenticeship I will pay you forty-five rubles monthly. I hope that's satisfactory. But there is another advantage for you that I should mention, frankly one that will work to our mutual benefit. My brother converted part of a loft over the brickyard stable into a warm and comfortable room, and you may live there without payment of rent if you accept my offer."

The forty-five rubles astounded and tempted the fixer.

"What is it an overseer does? Excuse the question, but I'm not a man of the world."

"Worldliness is vanity, it doesn't appeal to me. The overseer manages the business end of the enterprise. We manufacture about two thousand bricks daily—many fewer than we used to—a thousand or so more during the building season, not quite so many this time of the year; and it has been fewer lately although we have a contract with the Kiev Municipal Council for several thousands of bricks. The Tsar himself has given orders for civic improvements to be made before the Romanov Jubilee, and the Municipality is tearing up wooden walks and laying down entire streets of brick sidewalk, though this is done of course when the weather permits, not in the winter snow. And we also hold a small contract for bricks for the restoration of certain fortifications above the Dnieper. Yes, I would expect you to keep track of orders received and, to be sure, of the exact number of bricks manufactured as well as those carted out. These figures you will get from Proshko, but there are ways of checking. You will also send out statements requesting payment and enter payments received in the ledger. Once or twice weekly you will turn over bank drafts and other monies to me, and in the meantime keep them safe in the strongbox. Proshko will of course retain the responsibilities of the technical foreman, and I will tell him I expect him to place all orders for supplies through you. You will also make out the wages inventory and pay the workers at the end of the month."

Though beset by self-doubt and every kind of fear, Yakov was thinking this might be his important chance. A few months' experience at this kind of work and other opportunities might open up for him. "I'll think it over carefully," he said, but before Nikolai Maximovitch had descended the stairs, he had accepted.

The landlord returned with a vodka bottle to wet the bargain. Yakov had two drinks and his uneasiness wore off. He was preparing himself for a better future, he told himself. He slept for a while on the floor and later finished the last of the woodwork, once more uneasy.

It was nightfall. After he had swept and cleaned up, soaked the paintbrushes in turpentine, and washed, he heard Zina limping up the stairs. She was wearing a dress of blue silk, her hair up and encircled with a white ribbon, her cheeks and lips delicately rouged. She invited Yakov to eat with her again. "In celebration of the completion of your fine work, and most of all, to your future relationship with Papa, though he has already retired and we shall be alone."

He had the old excuses, was even a little irritated by the invitation and wanted to escape, but she would not hear of it. "Come, Yakov Ivanovitch, there's more to life than work."

It was news to him. Still, he thought, the job's done here and this is the last I'll see of her. So what's wrong with farewell?

On the kitchen table Zina had laid out a feast, even some food he had never seen before. There were stuffed cucumbers, raw Danube herring, fat sausages, pickled sturgeon with mushrooms, assorted meats, wine, cakes and cherry brandy. The fixer, overwhelmed by the spread, felt at first self-conscious. If you've had nothing you're afraid of too much. But he swept that aside and ate hungrily those things he had eaten before. He sucked the red wine through delicious chunks of white bread.

Zina, open and happy, and looking more attractive than he had ever seen, picked here and there at sweet and spicy things and filled her wineglass often. Her sharp face was flushed, she talked about herself and laughed at nothing at all. Although he tried to think of her as possibly a friend she remained strange to him. He was strange to himself. Once, staring at the white tablecloth, he thought of Raisl but put her out of his mind. He finished the meal—he had never in his life eaten so much—with two glasses of brandy, and only then began to enjoy the "party."

When she cleared the table Zina's breath was heavy. She brought out a guitar, plucked it, and in a high thin voice sang, "Ech, my pack is heavy." It was a sad song and filled him with mild melancholy. He had thought of getting up to leave, but the kitchen was warm and it was pleasant to sit there listening to the guitar. Then she sang, "Come on, come on, my darling angel, come and dance with me." When she put down her guitar, Zina looked at him in a way she never had before. Yakov understood at once where they were. Excitement and foreboding flowed into one feeling. No, he thought, it's a Russian woman. If she slept with me and found out who I was she'd cut her throat. Then he thought, it's not always so, there are some who wouldn't mind. For himself he was willing to experience what there was to experience. But let her lead.

"Yakov Ivanovitch," Zina said, pouring herself another glassful of wine which she at once drank down, "do you believe in romantic love? I ask because I think you guard yourself against it."

"Whether I do or don't it doesn't come easily to me."

"I heartily agree that it oughtn't to come too easily," Zina said, "but it seems to me that those who are serious about life—perhaps too serious—are slow to respond to certain changes in the climate of feeling. What I mean to say, Yakov Ivanovitch, is that it's possible to let love fly by like a cloud in a windy sky if one is too timid, or perhaps unable to believe he is entitled to good fortune."

"It's possible," he said.

"Do you love me—just a little. Yakov Ivanovitch?" she asked quickly. "I've sometimes noticed you looking at me as though you might. For instance, you smiled at me quite delightfully a few minutes ago, and it warmed my heart. I dare ask because you yourself are very modest and tend to be conscious—overconscious, I would say—that we are from different classes, though I believe much alike as people."

"No," he said. "I can't say I love you."

Zina flushed. Her eyelids fluttered. After a long minute she sighed and said in a smaller voice, "Very well, then, do you like me at all?"

"Yes, you have been kind to me."

"And I like you too, indeed I do. I think you are serious and a well-informed person."

"No, I am half an ignoramus."

She poured herself some cherry brandy, sipped from the glass and put it down.

"Oh, Yakov Ivanovitch, please for a moment let up on your seriousness and kiss me, I dare you to kiss me."

They got up and kissed. She groped for him, her body clinging tightly to his. He felt for an instant an anguished pity for her.

"Shall we stay here longer?" she whispered, breathing

heavily, "or would you care to visit my room? You've seen Papa's but not mine."

She looked him full in the face, her green eyes lit dark, her body hot, still clinging. She seemed to him an older woman, possibly twenty-eight or nine, someone used to looking out for herself.

"Whatever you say."

"What do *you* say, Yakov Ivanovitch?"

"Zinaida Nikolaevna," he said, "excuse me for asking you this question but I don't want to make a serious mistake. I've made my share of them—every kind you can think of but there are some I don't want to make again. If you are innocent," he said awkwardly, "it would be better not to go any further. I say this out of respect for you."

Zina reddened, then shrugged and said frankly, "I'm as innocent as most, no more nor less. There's nothing to worry about in that regard." Then she laughed self-consciously and said, "I see you're an old-fashioned person and I like that, although your question to me was hardly discreet."

"If one why not another? What about your father? What I mean to ask is, is it likely he might find out if we go to your room?"

"He never has," she said. He was momentarily surprised at her answer and then accepted it without another question. Why wrestle with a fact?

They went silently along the corridor, Zina hobbling, Yakov tiptoeing behind her, to her perfumed bedroom. The Pekinese, lying on the bed, looked at the fixer and yawned. Zina picked it up and went again down the hall to lock it in the kitchen.

Her room was full of knickknacks on numerous small tables, and pictures of kerchiefed girls on the wall. Peacock feathers stuck out from behind the frame of a mirror. In the corner of the room hung an ikon of the Holy Mother with a small red oil lamp lighted before it.

Should I stay or should I go? Yakov thought. On the one hand it's been a long season without rain. A man is not a man for nothing. What do the Hasidim say? "Hide not from thine own flesh." On the other hand what does this mean to me? At my age it's nothing new. It means nothing.

When she returned he was sitting on the bed. He had taken off his shirt and undershirt.

Yakov watched uneasily as Zina, after removing her shoes, knelt at the ikon, crossed herself, and for a moment prayed.

"Are you a believer?" she asked.

"No."

"I wish you were, Yakov Ivanovitch," she sighed.

Then she rose and asked him to undress in the lavatory while she got ready in the bedroom.

It's her leg, he thought. She'll be under covers when I come in. Better that way.

He removed his clothes in the lavatory. His hands still stank of paint and turpentine, and he soaped them twice with her pink bar of perfumed soap. He smelled them again but now they stank of the perfume. If there's a mistake to make I'll make it, he thought.

Seeing himself naked in the mirror he was at first uneasy, then sickened by what he was about to do.

Things are bad enough, so why make them worse? This isn't for me, I'm not the type, and the sooner I tell her the better. He went into the bedroom, carrying his clothes.

Zina had braided her hair. She stood naked, her bosom full, sponging herself from a white bowl, in the gaslight. He saw a dribble of bright blood run down her crippled leg and said, stupefied, "But you are unclean!"

"Yakov!—You startled me." She covered herself with the wet cloth. "I thought you would wait till I called you."

"I didn't know your condition. Excuse me, I had no idea. You didn't mention it, though I realize it's personal."

"But surely you know this is the safest time?" Zina said. "And there's no inconvenience to speak of, the flow stops the minute we begin."

"Excuse me, some can but I can't."

He was thinking of his wife's modesty during her period and until she had been to the baths, but could not say that to Zina.

"Excuse me, I'd better be going."

"I'm a lonely woman, Yakov Ivanovitch," she cried, "have mercy a little!" but he was already dressing and soon left.

3

One night in the dead of winter, in the cold thick dark at 4 A.M., after the drivers Serdiuk and Richter had come for two teams of horses—leaving six horses in the stalls—and he had heard them clomp out of the stable and clack dully across the snow-covered cobblestones, Yakov, who had been two days in the brickyard, got quickly out of bed, lit a short candle and hurriedly dressed. He sneaked down the outer stairs from his room above the stable and went along the fence of palings, past the squat brick-kilns to the cooling shed. Motionless in the wet cold, he watched the drivers and their helpers, in steaming sheepskins, the horses' flanks steaming, loading the straw-covered long wagon-trucks with large heavy yellow bricks. The work progressed slowly, helper tossing a brick to helper, who tossed it to the driver on the wagon, who laid it in place. After what seemed to him an endless time standing in the dark, blowing on his hands and trying soundlessly to stamp the cold out of his boots, Yakov had counted three hundred and forty bricks loaded into one wagon, and four hundred and three into another. Three other wagons at the shed went unused. But in the morning when Proshko, the foreman, presented him with the voucher in the stuffy low-ceilinged shack where Yakov sat at a table stacked with ledgers and bundles of useless papers from the past, the badly written numbers scrawled on a torn piece of wrapping paper came to a total of six hundred ten bricks, instead of seven hundred forty-three, and the fixer ground his teeth in anger at the cold-blooded nerve of the thievery.

Though Yakov was desperately eager for work, he had reluctantly accepted Nikolai Maximovitch's offer, at the last minute almost in panic trying to back out when he learned that the Lukianovsky, where the brickyard was located—near a cemetery, with a few houses and trees scattered around and beyond it, more heavily on the far-off side about half a tombstoned verst away—and where he was expected to live, was a district forbidden to Jews to reside in. He had then told the owner of the brickworks that he would not take the job because he had many doubts he could do the work as it should be done. But Nikolai Maximovitch, advising him not to be hasty, had pooh-poohed his doubts.

"Nonsense, you will do better than you suppose. You must learn to have confidence in your natural abilities, Yakov Ivanovitch. Just follow my late brother's method with the ledger—old-fashioned but accurate—and you will master the system as you go along." Yet puzzled somewhat, he raised his offer by three rubles a month, and Yakov trying every way to convince himself to take the job, then suggested it would be more convenient for him if he could go on living in the Podol—he never said where in the district—and come to work very early each morning. It wasn't too far a walk from where he lived. The electric trolley, which stopped close by the brickyard, did not run after dark.

"Unfortunately you won't be of much use to me living in the Podol," said Nikolai Maximovitch. They were talking in the brickyard on a cloudy end-of-January day—a pall of black smoke hung over the kilns—and Nikolai Maximovitch still wore his Black Hundreds button on his coat, which Yakov, when speaking to him—he saw himself unable to detach his eye if once he stared at it—had to ignore or look around, for the button loomed large and unsettling.

"It is not what goes on here during the workday that worries me so much," the anti-Semite said, "although I assure you that worries me too; but I am deeply concerned with what happens in the early morning hours when the wagons are being loaded for the first deliveries. Daylight is too strong for a thief. It's in the dark when the ghosts are flying and good people are lying abed that he does his dirty work. My late-lamented brother, who had little respect for sleep—one must respect it or it will not respect him—was here at 3 A.M. in every weather to oversee each and every wagonload. I am not asking you to do the same, Yakov Ivanovitch. That sort of dedication to a business enterprise is fanatic and in his case led, I am convinced, to my brother's early death." Nikolai Maximovitch crossed himself with eyes shut. "But if you were to look in on them in the early morning hours, and also unexpectedly during other loadings, counting off aloud a close estimate of the number of bricks in the trucks, it might tempt them not to overdo it. I expect some thievery—humans are humans—but of necessity there has to be a limit. It would be impossible for me to get a reasonably just price for this factory if it should go bankrupt."

"How do they steal?" the fixer had asked.

"I suspect the drivers under Proshko's supervision or connivance. They take out more than they account for."

"Then why don't you give him the boot?"

"More easily said than done, my dear boy. If I did I would have to shut down the plant. He is an excellent technical man—one of the best, my brother used to say. I confess it is not my purpose to catch him thieving. As a religious person I want to keep him from it. And wouldn't you say it was the more sensible as well as charitable thing? No, let's arrange it as I say. Take the room above the stable, Yakov Ivanovitch. It's yours without a single kopek of rent."

Since he had not mentioned the fixer's papers—neither the passport necessary for new employment, nor the residence certificate he would need, Yakov uneasily took the chance and accepted the job. He had for a fleeting minute again considered saying he was a Jew—just quietly informing Nikolai Maximovitch: "Well, you ought to know what the situation is. You say you like me; you know I'm an honest worker and don't waste the boss's time, then maybe it won't surprise you to hear I was born Jewish and for that reason can't live in this district." But that was of course impossible. Even supposing—a fantastic suppose—that Nikolai Maximovitch, two-headed eagle button and all, overlooked the confession in his own interests, still the Lukianovsky was not for Jews, with certain unusual exceptions, and if a poor fixer were exposed as one living there he would be in serious trouble. It was all too complicated. For the first week Yakov was daily on the verge of leaving, escaping from the place, but he stayed on because he had heard from Aaron Latke that counterfeit papers of various kinds were available to prospective buyers at a certain printing establishment in the Podol, for not too large a sum, and though the thought of acquiring such papers gave him severe sweats, he decided he ought to keep it in mind.

When Proshko brought in the voucher the morning after Yakov had spied on the drivers loading the wagons, though the fixer's heart beat loudly when he saw the false figure on the paper, he informed the foreman that Nikolai Maximovitch had told him to be present at night when the wagons were loaded, and since it was his responsibility, he would be there from now on. Proshko, a burly, thick-eared man with a rough beard, who wore high rubber boots muddy with yellow clay and a long dirty leather apron, gazed at the fixer with intense small eyes.

"What do you think goes on in the wagons at night? Are the drivers on their knees fucking their mothers?"

"What goes on goes on," said Yakov nervously, "but the number of bricks you loaded last night and this figure on your paper don't agree, if you'll excuse me for saying so."

He then wished he had said it differently, though how was it possible to say it differently to a thief?

"How would you know how many bricks were loaded?"

"I stood near the shed last night, counting them, according to Nikolai Maximovitch's direction. In other words, I did as he told me." His voice was thick with emotion, as though the bricks belonged to him, although the strange thing was they belonged to an anti-Semitic Russian.

"Then you counted wrong," Proshko said, "this is the number we loaded." He tapped a thick finger on the paper on the table. "Listen, my friend, when a dog puts his nose into shit, he gets it dirty. You have a long nose, Dologushev. If you don't believe me look in a mirror. A man with a nose like that ought to be careful where he puts it."

He left the shack but returned in the afternoon. "What about your papers," he said, "have you registered them yet? If not, hand them over here and I'll have them stamped by the District Police."

"I'm obliged to you," Yakov said, "but that's already been seen to and done. Nikolai Maximovitch took care of it. You don't have to trouble yourself."

"Tell me, Dologushev," said Proshko, "why is it you talk Russian like a Turk?"

"And what if I am a Turk?" The fixer smiled crookedly.

"He who runs too fast raises the wind against him." Lifting his leg Proshko farted.

Afterwards Yakov felt too uneasy to eat supper. I'm the wrong man to be a policeman, he thought. It's a job for a goy.

Yet he did what he was asked to. He appeared in the shed every morning in the 4 A.M. cold and counted the bricks in the wagons. And when he looked out the shack window and saw them loading up during the daylight hours, he went outside to watch. He did it openly, preventing the thieves from their thievery. When Yakov appeared at the shed, no one spoke but the drivers sometimes stopped their work to stare at him.

Proshko no longer turned in vouchers each morning, so Yakov wrote his own. The bookkeeping was not so difficult as he had thought—he had caught on to the system, and besides there wasn't that much business. Once a week Nikolai Maximovitch, more drearily melancholic, arrived by sledge for receipts to be deposited in his bank, and after a month Yakov received a long congratulatory letter from him. "Your work is diligent and effective, as I foresaw, and I shall continue to vest in you my utmost confidence. Zinaida Nikolaevna sends her regards. She too applauds your efforts." But no one else did. Neither the drivers nor their helpers paid any attention to him, even when he tried to make conversation. Richter, the heavy-faced German, spat in the snow at his approach, and Serdiuk, a tall Ukrainian who smelled of horse sweat and hay, watched him, breathing heavily. Proshko, passing the fixer in the yard, muttered, "Bastard stool pigeon!" Yakov pretended not to hear. If he heard "Jew" he would dive into the sky.

Except for these he was on more or less decent terms with the other workers in the yard—he paid them on time, about fifty left from almost two hundred employed when the yard had turned out six or seven thousand bricks a day—and this was so despite the fact that Proshko was spreading nasty stories about him; one that Skobeliev, the yardkeeper, had told him was that the fixer had once done time as a convicted thief. But no one sought him out as a friend or kept him company when the brickyard was closed, so he was mostly alone. After work Yakov stayed in his room. He read by lamplight—though Nikolai Maximovitch had promised to install an electric bulb—for hours each night. His reading in the past was what he had accidentally come across; he now read what he wanted to know. He continued to study Russian, wrote out long grammatical exercises and read them aloud. And he devoured two newspapers every day, though they often gave him the shivers, both things reported as fact, and things hinted at; for instance, Rasputin and the Empress, new plots of terrorists, threats of pogroms, and the possibility of a Balkan war. So much was new to him, how is one to know all he ought to know? He began to haunt the bookshops in the Podol in his free time, searching for inexpensive books. He bought a *Life of Spinoza* to read during the lonely nights in his stable room. Was it possible to learn from another's life? And Russian history fascinated him. He went through stacks of pamphlets on the shelves in the rear of the shops. He read some on serfdom, the Siberian penal system—a terrifying account he had found in a bushel the bookseller had winked at. He read about the revolt and destruction of the Decembrists, and a fascinating account of the Narodniki, idealists of the 1870's who had devoted themselves to the peasants in an impulsive attempt to stir them to social revolution, were rebuffed by them, and turned from peasant-mysticism to terrorism. Yakov also read a short biography of Peter the Great, and after that a horrifying account of the bloody destruction of Novgorod by Ivan the Terrible. It had entered the madman's head that the city intended treason to him, so he had ordered a wooden wall built around it to prevent escape. Then he marched in with his army, and after putting his subjects through the cruelest tortures, daily slaughtered thousands of them. This went on in increasing savagery, the sound of horror rising to the sky as the wailing mothers watched their children being roasted alive and thrown to wild dogs. At the end of five weeks, sixty thousand people, maimed, torn, broken apart, lay dead in the foul-smelling streets as disease spread. Yakov was sickened. Like a pogrom—the very worst. The Russians make pogroms against the Russians—it went on throughout their history. What a sad country, he thought, amazed by what he had read, every possible combination of experiences, where black was white and black was black; and if the Russians, too, were massacred by their own rulers and died like flies, who were then the

Chosen People? Fatigued by history, he went back to Spinoza, reading chapters on biblical criticism, superstition, and miracles which he knew almost by heart. If there was a God, after reading Spinoza he had closed up his shop and become an idea.

When he wasn't reading, Yakov was composing little essays on a variety of subjects—"I am in history," he wrote, "yet not in it. In a way of speaking I'm far out, it passes me by. Is this good, or is something lacking in my character? What a question! Of course lacking but what can I do about it? And besides is this really such a great worry? Best to stay where one is, unless he has something to give to history, like for instance Spinoza, as I read in his life. He understood history, and also because he had ideas to give it. Nobody can burn an idea even if they burn the man. On the other hand there was the activist Jan De Witt, Spinoza's friend and benefactor, a good and great man who was torn to pieces by a Dutch mob when they got suspicious of him although he was innocent. Who needs such a fate?" Some of the little essays were criticisms of "Certain Conditions" as he had read about them in the newspapers. He read these over and burned them in the stove. He also burned the pamphlets he could not resell.

Something that unexpectedly bothered him was that he was no longer using his tools. He had built himself a bed, table, and chair, also some shelves on the wall, but this was done in the first few days after he had come to the brickyard. He was afraid that if he didn't go on carpentering he might forget how and thought he had better not. Then he got another letter, this from Zina, her handwriting full of surprising thick black strokes, inviting him—with her father's permission—to call on her. "You are a sensitive person, Yakov Ivanovitch," she wrote, "and I respect your ideals and mode of behavior; however, please don't worry about your clothes, although I am sure you can purchase new ones with the improved salary you are earning." He had sat down to reply but couldn't think what to say to her, so he didn't answer the letter.

In February he went through a period of severe nervousness. He blamed it on his worries. He had visited the place where he could get counterfeit papers, had found they were not impossibly expensive although they were not inexpensive, and he was thinking of having a passport and residence certificate made out under his assumed name. When he awoke, hours before he had to, to check the number of bricks in the trucks his muscles were tight, his chest constricted, breathing sometimes painful, and he was uneasy when he dealt with Proshko. Even to ask him the most routine questions troubled the fixer. He was irritable all day and cursed himself for trifling mistakes in his accounts, a matter of a kopek or two. Once, at nightfall, he drove two boys out of the brickyard. He knew them as troublemakers, one a pale-faced pimply boy of about twelve, the other like a peasant with a head of hair like hay, about the same age. They came into the yard after school, in the late afternoon, and pitched balls of clay at each other, broke good bricks, and hooted at the horses in the stable. Yakov had warned them to stay out of the yard. This time he caught sight of them through the shack window. They had sneaked into the yard with their book satchels and threw rocks at the smoke curling up from the kilns. Then they hit the chimneys with pieces of brick. Yakov had rushed out of the shack, warning them to leave, but they wouldn't move. He ran towards them to scare them. Seeing him coming, the boys hooted, touched their genitals, and clutching their satchels, sped past the supply sheds and scrambled up a pile of broken bricks at the fence. They tossed their book satchels over the fence and hopped over it.

"Little bastards!" Yakov shouted, shaking his fist.

Returning to the shack, he noticed Skobeliev watching him slyly. Then the yardkeeper hurried with his stick to light the gas lamps. After a while they glowed in the dusk like green candles.

Proshko, standing at the door of the cooling shed, had also been looking on. "You run like a ruptured pig, Dologushev."

The next morning a police inspector visited the fixer to ask if anyone in the brick factory was suspected of political unreliability. The fixer said no one was. The official asked him a few more questions and left. Yakov was not able to concentrate on his reading that night.

Since he was sleeping badly he tried going to bed just after he had eaten. He fell asleep quickly enough but awoke before midnight, totally alert, with a sense of being imperiled. In the dark he feared calamities he only occasionally thought of during the day—the stable in flames, burning down with him in it, bound hand and foot unable to move; and the maddened horses destroying themselves. Or dying of consumption, or syphilis, coughing up or pissing blood. And he dreaded what worried him most—to be unmasked as a hidden Jew. "Gevalt!" he shouted, then listened in fright for sounds in the stable to tell him whether the drivers were there and had heard him cry out. Once he dreamed that Richter, carrying a huge black bag on his back, was following him down the road by the graveyard. When the fixer turned to confront the German and asked him what he was carrying in the bag, the driver winked and said, "You." So Yakov ordered and paid for the counterfeit papers, though weeks went by and he did not claim them. Then for no reason he could think of he began to feel better.

He went through a more confident period, when for the first time in his life he spent money as though it was nothing more than money. He bought more books, paper to write on, tobacco, a pair of shoes to relieve him from boots, a luxurious jar of strawberry jam, and a kilo of flour to bake bread with. The bread did not rise but he baked it and ate it as biscuit. He also bought a pair of socks, a set of drawers and undershirt, and an inexpensive blouse, only what was necessary. One night, feeling an overwhelming hunger for sweets, he entered a candy store to sip cocoa and eat cakes. And he bought himself a thick bar of chocolate. When he counted his rubles later, he had spent more than he had bargained for and it worried him. So he returned to frugality. He lived on black bread, sour cream and boiled potatoes, an occasional egg, and when he was tempted, a small piece of halvah. He repaired his socks and patched his old shirts until there was nowhere he hadn't made a stitch. He saved every kopek. "Let the groats accumulate," he muttered. He had serious plans.

One night in April when the thick ice of the Dnieper was cracking, and Yakov—after selling the books he had recently bought and afterwards wandering in the Plossky District—was returning late to the brickyard, it began to snow unexpectedly. Coming up the hill approaching the cemetery, he saw some boys attacking an old man and scattered them with a shout. They ran like frightened rabbits through the graveyard. The old man was a Jew, a Hasid wearing a caftan to his ankles, a round rabbinic hat with a fur brim, and long white stockings. He slowly bent and retrieved from the snow a small black satchel tied with brown twine. He had been hurt on the temple and the blood dripped down his hairy cheek into his tousled two-forked gray beard. His eyes were dazed. "What happened to you, grandfather?" the fixer said in Russian. The Hasid, frightened, backed off, but Yakov waited and the old man replied in halting Russian that he had come from Minsk to see a sick brother in the Jewish quarter and had got lost. Then some boys had attacked him with snowballs embedded with sharp stones.

The streetcars were no longer running, and the snow was falling in thick wet flakes. Yakov was uneasily worried but thought he could take the old man into the brickyard, let him rest while he applied some cold water to his wound, then get him out before the drivers and their helpers came in.

"Come with me, grandfather."

"Where are you taking me?" said the Hasid.

"We'll wipe the blood off you, and when the snow stops I'll show you which way to the Jewish quarter in the Podol."

He led the Hasid into the brickyard and up the stairs to his room above the stable. After lighting the lamp, Yakov tore up his most tattered shirt, wet it, and wiped the blood off the old man's beard. The wound was still bleeding but it didn't bother the Hasid. He sat in Yakov's chair with his eyes shut, breathing as though he were whispering. Yakov offered him bread and a glass of sweetened tea but the Hasid would not accept food. He was a dignified man with long earlocks and asked the fixer for some water. Pouring a little over his fingers over a bowl, he then withdrew a small packet from his caftan pocket, some matzo pieces wrapped in a handkerchief. He said the blessing for matzos, and sighing, munched a piece. It came as a surprise to the fixer that it was Passover. He was moved by a strong emotion and had to turn away till it had gone.

When he looked out the window the snow was still falling but there were signs of a moon, a circle of dim light within the falling snow. It'll soon stop, he thought, but it didn't. The glow disappeared and once more it was dark and snowy. Yakov thought he would wait till the drivers arrived, quickly count the bricks, and when the snow stopped, sneak the old man out after the wagons had left and before Proshko came. If the snow didn't stop, the old man would have to leave anyway.

The Hasid slept in the chair, woke, stared at the lamp, then at the window and slept again. When the drivers opened the stable door he awoke and looked at Yakov, but the fixer made a sign for silence and left to go down to the shed. He had offered the Hasid his bed but when he returned the old man was sitting up awake. The drivers had loaded the wagons and were waiting in the shed for daylight. They had wrapped chains around the horses' hooves but Skobeliev had said if the snow got deeper they would not leave the yard. Now Yakov was worried.

In his room, huddled in his sheepskin coat, he stood watching the snow, then rolled and smoked a cigarette and made himself a glass of tepid tea. He drank a little, fell asleep on his bed, and dreamed he had encountered the Hasid in the graveyard. The Hasid had asked, "Why are you hiding here?" and the fixer had struck him a blow on the head with a hammer. It was a terrible dream and gave him a headache.

He awoke to find the old man staring at him, and his nervousness returned.

"What's wrong?" he asked.

"What's wrong is wrong," said the old man. "But now the snow has stopped."

"Did I say anything in my sleep?"

"I wasn't listening."

The sky had lightened and it was time to go, but the Hasid dipped the tips of his fingers into water, then unknotted the twine around his satchel, opened it, and removed a large striped prayer shawl. From the pocket of his caftan he took out a phylactery bag.

"Where is the east?" asked the old man.

Yakov impatiently indicated the wall with the window. Saying the blessing for phylacteries, the Hasid slowly wound one around his left arm, the other on his brow, binding the strap gently over the crusting wound.

He covered his head with the capacious prayer shawl, blessing it, then prayed at the wall, rocking back and forth. The fixer waited with his eyes shut. When the old man had said his morning prayers, he removed the shawl, folded it carefully and put it away. He unbound the phylacteries, kissed them, and packed them away.

"May God reward you," he said to Yakov.

"I'm much obliged but let's move on." The fixer was sweating in his cold clothes.

Asking the old man to wait a minute, he went down the snow-laden stairs and walked around the stable. The yard was white and still, the roofs of the kilns covered with snow. But the wagons, though loaded with bricks, had not yet left and the drivers were still in the shed. Yakov hurried up the stairs and got the Hasid and his satchel. They hastened through the spring snow to the gate. He led the old Hasid down the hill to the streetcar stop, but while they were waiting a sledge with tinkling bells drove by. Yakov hailed it and the sleepy driver promised he would take the Jew to his street in the Podol. When Yakov got back to the brickyard he felt he had been through a long night. He felt out of sorts and unreasonably depressed. On the way to the stable he met Proshko in high spirits.

When he entered his room Yakov had the sudden feeling that someone had been in it while he was out with the Hasid. He had the impression things had been moved, then set back not exactly in place. He suspected the foreman. The smell of horse manure and rotting hay seeped up from the stable. He hastily searched among his few possessions but could find nothing missing, neither household articles, his few books, nor rubles in the tin can. He was glad he had sold some of the books and burned the pamphlets; they were about history but some history was dangerous. The next day he heard that a body had been found in a cave nearby, then he read with fascinated horror a newspaper account of the terrible murder of a twelve-year-old boy who had lived in one of the wooden houses near the cemetery. The body was found in a sitting position, the boy's hands tied behind his back. He was clad in his underwear, without shoes, one black stocking hanging on his left foot; scattered nearby were a bloodstained blouse, a schoolboy's cap, a belt, and several pencil-smeared copy books. Both the *Kievlyanin* and *Kievskaya Mysl* carried a picture of him, Zhenia Golov, and Yakov recognized the pimply-faced boy he had chased out of the yard with his friend. One newspaper said the boy had been dead for a week, the other said two. When the Police Inspector had examined his swollen face and shrunken mutilated body, he had counted thirty-seven wounds made by a thin pointed instrument. The boy, according to Professor Y. A. Cherpunov of the Kiev Anatomical Institute, had been stabbed to death and bled white, "possibly for religious purposes." Marfa Vladimirovna Golov, the bereaved mother, a widow, had claimed the body of her son. There was a picture of her in both newspapers, pressing the boy's poor head to her grief-stricken bosom, crying desolately, "Tell me. Zheniushka, who did this to my baby?"

That night the river overflowed its banks, flooding the lower reaches of the city. Two days later the boy was buried in the cemetery, a few short steps from his home. Yakov could see from the window of his stable the trees still powdered with April snow, and wandering amid them and the thin tombstones, the black crowd, among them some pilgrims with staves. When the coffin was lowered into the grave, hundreds of leaflets exploded into the air: WE ACCUSE THE JEWS. A week later the Kiev Union of Russian People, together with members of the Society of the Double-headed Eagle, placed a huge wooden cross on the grave of the boy—Yakov watching from afar—at the same time calling on all good Christians, according to the newspapers that night, to preach a new crusade against the Israelitic enemies. "They want nothing less than our lives and country! People of Russia! Have pity on your children! Avenge the unfortunate martyrs!" This is terrible, Yakov thought, they want to start a pogrom. In the brickyard Proshko sported a Black Hundreds button on his leather apron. Very early the next morning the fixer hurried to the printer's for his counterfeit papers but when he arrived he found the place had burned down. He ran back to the stable and hastily counted his rubles to see if he had enough to get to Amsterdam and possibly New York. Wrapping up his few things, and slinging his bag of tools onto his shoulder, he was on his way down the stairs when a man who identified himself as Colonel I. P. Bodyansky, the red-mustached head of the Secret Police in Kiev, with several other officials, fifteen gendarmes wearing white looped cords across the breasts of their uniforms, a detachment of police, several plainclothes detectives, and two representatives of the Office of the Chief Prosecuting Attorney of the District Superior Court, about thirty in all, rushed up the stairs with drawn pistols and swords, confronting the fleeing Yakov.

"In the name of His Majesty Nicholas the Second," said the red-headed colonel, "I arrest you. Resist and you are dead."

The fixer readily confessed he was a Jew. Otherwise he was innocent.

III

In a long, high-ceilinged cell under the District Courthouse, a dismal faded stucco structure in the commercial section of the Plossky a few versts from the brickyard in the Lukianovsky, Yakov, in a state of unrelieved distress, could not blot out the sight of himself marching manacled between two tall columns of gendarmes on horses, their sabers drawn and spurs clinking as they hurried him along snowy streets tracked slushy by sledge runners.

He had begged the colonel to let him walk on the sidewalk to lessen his embarrassment, but was forced into the wet center of the street, and people on their way to work had stopped to watch. They gazed at first quietly, then in deep silence, broken by whispers, muttering and a few jeers. Most seemed to wonder what the parade was about, but then a uniformed schoolboy in a blue cap and silver-buttoned coat, poking his fingers up like horns over his head, danced in the snow behind the prisoner, chanting, "Zhid, Zhid," and that awoke murmurs, hoots, mockery. A small crowd, including some women, began to follow them, jeering at the fixer, calling him dirty names, "murdering Jew." He wanted to break and run but didn't dare. Someone flung a block of wood at him but it struck a horse that broke into a wild gallop, kicking up snow and running two squares before it was controlled. Then the colonel, a huge man in a fur cap, raised his saber and the crowd scattered.

He delivered the prisoner first to Secret Police Headquarters, a one-story brown building in a side street; then after a long annoyed telephone conversation, fragments of which the frightened prisoner sitting on a bench in the anteroom surrounded by gendarmes, overheard, the colonel escorted Yakov directly to an underground cell in the District Courthouse, leaving behind two gendarmes who patrolled the corridor with naked sabers. Yakov, alone in the cell, wringing his hands, cried out, "My God, what have I done to myself? I'm in the hands of enemies!" He hit his chest with his fist, bewailed his fate, envisioned terrible things happening to him, ending by being torn apart by a mob. Yet there were also moments of sudden hope when he felt that if he only *explained* why he had done what he had done, he would be at once released. He had stupidly pretended to be somebody he wasn't, hoping it would create "opportunities," had learned otherwise—the wrong opportunities—and was paying for learning. If they let him go now he had suffered enough. He blamed also egotism and foolish ambition, considering who he was, and promised himself it would be different in the future. He had learned his lesson—again. Then he jumped up and cried aloud, "What future?" but nobody answered. When an orderly brought in tea and black bread, he could not eat though he had eaten nothing that day. As the day wore on he groaned often, tore his hair with both fists, and knocked his head repeatedly against the wall. A gendarme saw him and strictly forbade it.

Towards evening, the prisoner, sitting immobile on a thin mattress on the floor, heard footsteps in the corridor other than the measured tread of the armed guard who had replaced the two gendarmes. Yakov scrambled to his feet. A man of medium height carrying a black hat and fur coat hurried along the dimly lit corridor to the dark cell. He ordered the guard to open the cell door, lock him in with the prisoner, and leave. The guard hesitated. The man waited patiently.

"I was ordered not to leave, if it's all the same to your honor," said the guard. "The Prosecuting Attorney said not to let the Jew out of my sight because it's a most important case. That's what I was told by his assistant."

"I am here on official business and will call you when I need you. Wait outside the corridor door."

The guard reluctantly opened the cell, locked the man in

with Yakov and left. The man watched till the guard had gone, then took a candle stub out of his coat pocket, lit it and set it in some drops of wet wax in a saucer. He held the saucer in his hand, studying Yakov for a long moment, then put it down on the table in the cell. Seeing his cold breath in the light he drew on his fur coat. "I am subject to lingering colds." He wore a darkish beard, pince-nez, and a thick scarf wrapped around his neck. Facing the fixer, he introduced himself in a quiet resonant voice.

"I am B. A. Bibikov, Investigating Magistrate for Cases of Extraordinary Importance. Please kindly identify yourself."

"Yakov Shepsovitch Bok, your honor, though there's nothing extraordinary about my foolish mistakes."

"You are not Yakov Ivanovitch Dologushev?"

"That was a stupid deception. I admit it at once."

Bibikov adjusted his glasses and looked at him in silence. He lifted the candle to light a cigarette, then changed his mind, set it down, and thrust the cigarette into his pocket.

"Tell me truly," said the Investigating Magistrate in a severe voice, "did you murder that unfortunate child?"

A fog of blackness rose before Yakov's eyes.

"Never! Never!" he cried hoarsely. "Why would I kill an innocent child? How could I have done it? For years I wanted a child but my luck was bad and my wife couldn't have one. If in no other way at least in my heart I'm a father. And if that's so how could I kill an innocent child? I couldn't think of such a thing, I'd rather be dead."

"How long have you been married?"

"Five years going on six, though I'm not really married now because my wife left me."

"Is that so? Why did she leave you?"

"To make it short and simple she was unfaithful. She ran off with an unknown party and that's why I'm in jail now. If she hadn't done that I would have stayed where I belonged, which means where I was born. This very minute I'd be sitting down to supper, such as it was, but it could have been worse. When the sun went down, whether I had earned a kopek or not, I headed straight for my hut. It wasn't such a bad place to be, now that I think of it."

"You're not from Kiev?"

"Not the city, the province. I left my village a few months after my wife left me and I've been here since November. I was ashamed to stay on there with things as they were. There were other reasons but that was what bothered me most."

"What other reasons?"

"I was fed up with my work—no work at all. And I hoped, with a bit of luck, to get myself a little education. They say in America there are schools where a grown man can study at night."

"You were thinking of emigrating to America?"

"It was one of my thoughts, your honor, though I've had many such and they've all come to nothing. Still in all, I'm a loyal subject of the Tsar."

The Investigating Magistrate found the cigarette in his pocket and lit it. He smoked silently, standing on the other side of the table, still studying Yakov's tormented face in the candlelight.

"I saw among your possessions when you were arrested a few books, among others a volume of selected chapters from the work of the philosopher Spinoza."

"That's right, your honor. Could I get them back? I'm also worried about my tools."

"In due course, if you are not indicted. Are you familiar with his writings?"

"Only in a way of speaking," said the fixer, worried by the question. "Although I've read the book I don't understand it all."

"What is its appeal to you? First let me ask you what brought you to Spinoza? Is it that he was a Jew?"

"No, your honor. I didn't know who or what he was when I first came across the book—they don't exactly love him in the synagogue, if you've read the story of his life. I found it in a junkyard in a nearby town, paid a kopek and left cursing myself for wasting money hard to come by. Later I read through a few pages and kept on going as though there were a whirlwind at my back. As I say, I didn't understand every word but when you're dealing with such ideas you feel as though you were taking a witch's ride. After that I wasn't the same man. That's in a manner of speaking of course, because I've changed little since my youth."

Though he had answered freely, talking about a book with a Russian official frightened the fixer. He's testing me, he thought. Still when all's said and done, better questions about a book than a murdered child. I'll tell the truth but speak slowly.

"Would you mind explaining what you think Spinoza's work means? In other words if it's a philosophy what does it state?"

"That's not so easy to say," Yakov answered apologetically. "The truth is I'm a half-ignorant man. The other half is half-educated. There's a lot I miss even when I pay the strictest attention."

"I will tell you why I ask. I ask because Spinoza is among my favorite philosophers and I am interested in his effect on others."

"In that case," said the fixer, partly relieved, "I'll tell you that the book means different things according to the subject of the chapters, though it's all united underneath. But what I think it means is that he was out to make a free man out of himself—as much as one can according to his philosophy, if you understand my meaning—by thinking things through and connecting everything up, if you'll go along with that, your honor."

"That isn't a bad approach," said Bibikov, "through the man rather than the work. But you ought to explain the philosophy a little."

"Who knows if I can," the fixer said. "Maybe it's that God and Nature are one and the same, and so is man, or some such thing, whether he's poor or rich. If you understand that a man's mind is part of God, then you understand it as well as I. In that way you're free, if you're in the mind of God. If you're there you know it. At the same time the trouble is that you are bound down by Nature, though that's not true for God who is Nature anyway. There's also something called Necessity, which is always there though nobody wants it, that one has to push against. In the shtetl God goes running around with the Law in both hands, but this other God, though he fills up more space, has less to do altogether. Whoever you end up believing in, nothing has changed much in the world if you're without work. So much for Necessity. I also figure it means that life is life and there's no sense kicking it into the grave. Either that or I don't understand it as well as it's said."

"If a man is bound to Necessity where does freedom come from?"

"That's in your thought, your honor, if your thought is in God. That's if you believe in this kind of God; that's if you reason it out. It's as though a man flies over his own head on the wings of reason, or some such thing. You join the universe and forget your worries."

"Do you believe that one can be free that way?"

"Up to a point," Yakov sighed. "It sounds fine but my experience is limited. I haven't lived much outside the small towns."

The magistrate smiled.

Yakov snickered but caught himself and stopped.

"Is such a thing as you describe it, true freedom, would you say, or cannot one be free without being politically free?"

Here's where I'd better watch my step, the fixer thought. Politics is politics. No use fanning up hot coals when you have to walk across them.

"I wouldn't know for sure, your honor. It's partly one and partly the other."

"True enough. One might say there is more than one conception of freedom in Spinoza's mind—in Necessity, philosophically speaking; and practically, in the state, that is to say within the realm of politics and political action. Spinoza conceded a certain freedom of political choice, similar to the freedom of electing to think, if it were possible to make these choices. At least it is possible to think them. He perhaps felt that the purpose of the state—the government—was the security and comprehensive freedom of rational man. This was to permit man to think as best he could. He also thought man was freer when he participated in the life of society than when he lived in solitude as he himself did. He thought that a free man in society had a positive interest in promoting the happiness and intellectual emancipation of his neighbors."

"I guess that's true, your honor, if you say so," said Yakov, "but as far as I myself am concerned what you said is something to think about, though if you're poor your time is taken up with other things that I don't have to mention. You let those who can, worry about the ins and outs of politics."

"Ah," Bibikov sighed. He puffed on his cigarette without speaking. For a moment there was no sound in the cell.

Did I say something wrong? Yakov thought wildly. There are times it doesn't pay to open your mouth.

When the magistrate spoke again he sounded once more like an investigating official, his tone dry, objective.

"Have you ever heard the expression 'historical necessity'?"

"Not that I remember. I don't think so though maybe I could guess what it means."

"Are you sure? You've not read Hegel?"

"I don't know his name."

"Or Karl Marx? He too was a Jew, though not exactly happy to be one."

"Not him either."

"Would you say you have a 'philosophy' of your own? If so what is it?"

"If I have it's all skin and bones. I've only just come to a little reading, your honor," he apologized. "If I have any philosophy, if you don't mind me saying so, it's that life could be better than it is."

"Yet how can it be made better if not in politics or through it?"

That's a sure trap, Yakov thought. "Maybe by more jobs and work," he faltered. "Not to forget good will among men. We all have to be reasonable or what's bad gets worse."

"Well, that's at least a beginning," the magistrate said quietly. "You must read and reflect further."

"I will just as soon as I get out of here."

Bibikov seemed embarrassed. The fixer felt as though he had disappointed him, although he was not sure why. Probably too much inexact talk. It's hard to make sense when you're in trouble, considering also your other natural disadvantages.

The magistrate after a while absently asked, "How did you bruise your head?"

"In the dark, in desperation."

Bibikov reached into his pocket and offered the fixer his cigarette box. "Have one, they're Turkish."

Yakov smoked in order not to affront the man, though he could not taste the cigarette.

Taking a folded paper and pencil stub out of his suit coat pocket the magistrate placed them on the table, saying, "I leave this questionnaire with you. We will have to know more biographical details since you have no police record. When you have answered each question and signed your name, call the guard and give him the paper. Be accurate in everything you say. I'll leave the candle with you."

Yakov stared at the paper.

"I have to hurry now. My boy has a fever. My wife gets frantic." The Investigating Magistrate buttoned his fur coat and put on a wide-brimmed black fedora that looked large for his head.

Nodding to the prisoner, he said quietly, "Whatever happens you must have fortitude."

"My God, what can happen? I'm an innocent man."

Bibikov shrugged. "It's a touchy thing."

"Have mercy, your honor; I've had little in my life."

"Mercy is for God, I depend on the law. The law will protect you."

He called the guard and left the cell. As the door was being locked he hurried away in the dimly lit corridor.

The fixer felt at once a sense of intense loss.

"When will you come back?" he shouted after him.

"Tomorrow." A distant door shut. The footsteps were gone.

"It's a long tomorrow," said the guard.

2

The next morning a new guard unlocked the cell, searched Yakov thoroughly for the third time since he had awakened, manacled him tightly with heavy handcuffs attached by a short thick chain, and in the presence of two other armed guards, one of whom cursed the prisoner and prodded him with his pistol, escorted Yakov, about as dead as he was alive, up two flights of narrow booming wooden stairs into the

Investigating Magistrate's office. In the large anteroom some clerks in uniform sat at long tables scratching on paper with wet pens. They gazed at him with intense interest, then looked at each other. Yakov was led into a brown-walled smaller office. Bibikov was standing at an open window, waving his hand back and forth to thin out the cigarette smoke. As Yakov entered he quickly shut the window and seated himself in a chair at the head of a long table. The room contained a bulky desk, several shelves of thick books, two large green shaded lamps, and a small ikon in the corner; on the wall hung a large sepia portrait of Tsar Nicholas II, bemedaled and immaculately barbered, staring critically at the fixer. The picture added to his discomfort.

The only other person in the room was Bibikov's assistant, a pimply-faced man in his thirties, with a thin beard through which his small chin was visible. He was sitting next to the magistrate at the short end of the table, and Yakov was told to take his seat at the other end. The three escorting guards at the magistrate's request waited in the antechamber. He, after barely glancing at the prisoner—almost distastefully the fixer thought—fished among some official documents in a pile before him and drew forth a thick one whose pages he thumbed through. He whispered something to the assistant, who filled a heavy fountain pen from a large bottle of black ink, wiped the nib with an ink-stained rag, and began to write quickly in a notebook.

Bibikov, looking ill-at-ease and tired, seemed changed from last night, and for a moment Yakov nervously wondered if it was the same man. His head was large, with a broad forehead and a pelt of dark graying hair. As he read he nibbled on his thin underlip; then he put down the paper, blew at his pince-nez, adjusted them with care and sipped from a glass of water. He spoke in a voice without warmth, addressing the fixer across the table: "I will now read you a portion of the deposition of Nikolai Maximovitch Lebedev, factory owner of the Lukianovsky District; that is, his factory is in the Lukianovsky—" Then his official voice changed and he said quietly, "Yakov Shepsovitch Bok, you are in a difficult situation and we must straighten things out. Listen first to a statement of the witness Lebedev. He says it was your intent from the outset to deceive him."

"It isn't true, your honor!"

"Just one minute. Please contain yourself."

Bibikov took up the document, turned to an inside page and read aloud:

" 'N. Lebedev: He whom I knew as Yakov Ivanovitch Dologushev, although he did me, by chance, a personal favor of some magnitude, for which I generously rewarded him, and my daughter treated him most considerately, was a less than honest man—more accurately, a deceitful one. He concealed from me, for reasons that are obvious—and well he might for I would never have employed him had I known what I do now—that he was in truth, although he attempted to hide it, a member of the Jewish Nation. I confess I felt a tremor of suspicion when I observed his discomfiture at a query I addressed him concerning the Holy Scriptures. In response to my question whether he had made it a habit to read the Holy Bible, he replied he was familiar only with the Old Testament, and blanched greatly when I proceeded to read him some telling verses from the New Testament, in particular from the Sermon on the Mount.'

" 'Investigating Magistrate: Anything else?'

" 'N. Lebedev: I also noticed an odd hesitancy, a sort of bumbling when he spoke his name for the first time, that is to say the assumed name, which he was as yet unfamiliar with. It did not, need I say, your honor, fit his Jewish tongue. Furthermore, for an ostensibly poor man he showed extreme reluctance—perhaps this is to his credit—to accept my generous offer of a position in my brickworks, and my suspicions were further aroused because he seemed uneasy when I had broached the matter of his living in the room above the stable on the factory grounds. He wanted to work for me and yet he was afraid to, naturally enough. He was troubled and nervous, constantly wetting his lips and averting his eyes. Since I am somewhat incapacitated in health—my liver gives me trouble and I suffer a marked shortness of breath—I had need of an overseer who would live on the premises and see that my affairs were kept in order. However, since the Jew had helped me when I became suddenly ill and collapsed in the snow, my suspicions were not long lasting, and I offered him the position. I believe he knew full well, when he accepted my unwitting offer, that the Lukianovsky District is sacred territory and forbidden to Jews for residence, except, as I understand it, for exceptional services to the Crown; and I take that to be the reason he made no attempt to turn over to me his papers so that I might deliver them to the District Police.'

" 'Investigating Magistrate: Did you ask for them?'

" 'N. Lebedev: Not directly. Yes, perhaps I did once and he made me some sort of fishy Jewish excuse or other, and then as I was having trouble with my health I neglected to remind him again. Had I done that and he refused my request, I would at once have ordered him off my property. I am a generous and lenient man, your honor, but I would never have tolerated a Jew in my employ. Please note, if you will, the sigillum on my coat lapel. I consider it a mark of this man's insolence that he was not quailed by it in my presence. For your information I am a former recording secretary of the Society of the Double-headed Eagle."

The magistrate laid down the paper, removed his glasses and rubbed his eyes.

"You have heard the deposition," he said to Yakov. "I have also read your questionnaire and am familiar with the responses, but I must now ask you to comment on the remarks of the witness Lebedev. Is the substance of them correct? Be careful in your reply. This, though not a trial, is a police investigation to see if an Act of Indictment is warranted."

Yakov rose in excitement. "Please, your honor, I don't know much about the law, and it isn't always simple to say yes and no in the right place. Would you let me speak to a lawyer for advice? I might even have a few rubles to pay if the police will return my money to me."

"Yes and no take care of themselves if a man tells the truth. As for consulting a lawyer, that is not possible at this stage. In our legal system the indictment comes first. After the preliminary examination the Investigating Magistrate and Prosecuting Attorney consult, and if both believe the suspect to be guilty, an Act of Indictment is drawn up and sent to the District Court, where it is either confirmed or disapproved by the judges. The defense may begin after the accused is informed that the indictment has been voted, and he is then given a copy of it. Within a week or so, possibly a bit more, the accused may select his counsel and inform the court."

"Your honor," Yakov said in alarm, "suppose a man is innocent of what they say he did? What's it all about is a confusion in my mind. One minute I think it's as clear as daylight and the crime we're talking about is a small one, no more than a mistake you might say, and the next minute you say things that make me shiver. For my little sin why should anybody accuse me of a big one? If I gave a false name to someone does that mean there's bound to be an indictment?"

"We will know in due course what is bound to be."

The fixer, sighing heavily, sat down, his manacled hands twitching in his lap.

"I have asked you to comment on the witness Lebedev's remarks," Bibikov said.

"Your honor, I give you my word I meant no harm. What I did wrong—even Nikolai Maximovitch admits it—I did with reluctance, against my will. The truth is I found him drunk in the snow. As a reward he offered me a job I didn't ask for. I could've refused it and I did once or twice, but my money was going fast, I had rent to pay and et cetera. I was getting desperate for work—my hands complain when they have nothing to do—so I finally took what he offered me. He was satisfied with the paint and papering job I first did, and he also told me I was a good overseer in the brickworks. I used to get up half past three every night to inspect the loading of the wagons. If he said it once he said it more than once. Ask him yourself, your honor."

"True, but didn't you give him a false name as your own? In effect, a gentile name? That was no accident I take it? That was your intent, wasn't it?"

The magistrate had forcefully thrust his face forward. Was this the man who said he admired Spinoza?

"It's my mistake, I admit it," said Yakov. "I gave him the first name that popped into my head. I wasn't thinking, your honor, and that's how a man comes to grief. When you're faced with a worrisome situation it's not so easy to keep your mind on what comes next. Dologushev is a one-eyed peasant near my village who slaughters pigs. But the truth of it is I really didn't want to live on the factory grounds. It got so I couldn't sleep from worrying so much. Nikolai Maximovitch mentions that I was afraid to take his offer to live in the stable. He says so himself in this paper you just read to me. I asked him if I could live in the Podol instead and walk to the job, but he said no, I had to live there. In other words it wasn't my idea in the first place. And he's mistaken if he thinks he asked for my passport. Maybe he thought he did but he didn't. He's a melancholy man and sometimes vague in his thoughts. I swear he never asked me. If he had, that would have ended it then and there. I would have thought the jig's up and gone home. It would have saved me a lot of misery."

"Still, you did live in the Lukianovsky, though fully aware it was illegal for you to do so?"

"That's as you say, your honor, but I didn't want to lose the job. I was hoping for a better life than I had." His voice had begun to plead, but noticing the magistrate's compressed lips and stern gaze, Yakov stopped speaking and inspected his hands.

"In the questionnaire," said Bibikov, snapping on his glasses and consulting another paper, "you state you are a Jew 'by birth and nationality.' Do I sense a reservation, and if so what is it?"

The fixer sat silent a minute, then looked up uncomfortably. "What I meant by that is I'm not a religious man. I was when I was young but lost my belief. I thought I mentioned that when we talked last night, but maybe I didn't. That's all I meant by that."

"How did it happen? I refer to your loss of religion."

"I guess there's more than one reason even though I don't recall them all. In my life, the way that it's turned out, I've had a lot to think about. One thought breeds another. Give me an idea and in two minutes there's a second pushing out the first. Also I've been reading a little here and there, as I mentioned to you, your honor, and have picked up a few things I never knew before. It all adds up."

The magistrate leaned back in his chair. "You haven't by some chance been baptized along the way? It might be convenient if you had."

"Oh, no, your honor, nothing at all like that. What I mean to say is I'm a freethinker."

"I understand that, though to be a freethinker assumes one would know how to think."

"I try my best," said Yakov.

"What do you think freethinker means?"

"A man who decides for himself if he wants to believe in religion. Maybe an agnostic also. Some do and some don't."

"Do you think it adds to your stature to be irreligious?"

My God, what have I said? the fixer thought. I'd better keep this simple and small or I'll dig my grave and they'll lay me in it.

He said hastily, "It's as you say, your honor, yes and no fall into place if you tell the truth. I'm telling the truth."

"Let's not complicate matters unnecessarily." Bibikov sipped from his water glass. "Legally you are a Jew. The Imperial Government considers you one even though you twist and squirm. You are so recorded on your passport. Our laws concerning Jews apply to you. However, if you are ashamed of your people, why don't you leave the faith officially?"

"I'm not ashamed, your honor. Maybe I don't always like what I see—there are Jews of all sorts, as the saying goes, but if I'm going to be ashamed of anyone, it might as well be myself." As he said this his color heightened.

Bibikov listened with interest. He glanced down at his notes, then looked up with eyes narrowed. Ivan Semyonovitch, the assistant, who reacted quickly to his remarks, often taking on the same facial expression as the magistrate, glancing at the notes from where he sat, leaned forward intently.

"The absolute truth, please," said the Investigating Magistrate sternly. "—Are you a revolutionary, either as a theorist or activist?"

Yakov felt the force of his pounding heart.

"Does it say that anywhere in your papers, your honor?"

"Please answer my question."

"No, I'm not. God forbid. That's beyond me, if you know what I mean. It's not my nature. If I'm anything I'm a peaceful man. 'Yakov,' I used to say to myself, 'there's too much violence in the world and if you're smart you'll stay out of it.' It isn't for me, your honor."

"A Socialist or member of any Socialist parties?"

The fixer hesitated. "No."

"Are you certain?"

"I give you my earnest word."

"Are you a Zionist?"

"No."

"Do you belong to any political party whatsoever? That would include Jewish parties."

"To none at all, your honor."

"Very well. Have you noted the response, Ivan Semyonovitch?"

"Every word, sir. I have it all," said the pimply assistant.

"Good," said Bibikov, absently scratching his beard. "Now there is another matter I wish to question you about. Wait till I find the paper."

"Excuse me, I don't meant to interrupt," Yakov said, "but I would like you to know that my passport was stamped 'Permission Granted' when I left my village. And when I got to Kiev, the very next day after my arrival which happened late at night—the next day I brought it to the passport section of the Police Station of the Podol District. It was also stamped there, your honor."

"That is already noted. I've examined the passport and your remarks are substantially correct. However, that isn't the matter I was about to bring up."

"It was only in the Lukianovsky, if you'll excuse me, your honor, that I didn't register. That was where I made a mistake."

"That is also noted."

"If you don't mind, I'd like to mention that I served for a short time in the Russian Army."

"Noted. A very short time, less than a year. You were discharged for illness, were you not?"

"Also because the war was over. There was no use for any more soldiers at that time."

"What was the illness?"

"Attacks of asthma, on and off. I would never know when they would hit me next."

"Are you still troubled with this ailment?" the magistrate said conversationally. "I ask because my son has asthma."

"Mostly it's cleared up though sometimes on a windy day I find it hard to draw a breath."

"I'm glad it's cleared up. Now permit me to go on to the next item. I will read from the deposition of Zinaida Nikolaevna Lebedev, spinster, age thirty."

This is terrible, the fixer thought, squeezing his hands. Where will it all end?

The door opened. The magistrate and his assistant looked up as two officials strode into the room. One, in a red and blue uniform with gold epaulets, was the officer who had arrested Yakov, Colonel Bodyansky, a heavy man with a cropped red mustache. The other was the Prosecuting Attorney Grubeshov, Procurator of thc Kiev Superior Court. He had that morning gone down to stare at the fixer in his cell without addressing a word to him. Yakov had stood frozen against the wall. Five minutes later the prosecutor had walked away, leaving him in a sweaty state of unrest.

Grubeshov placed on the table a worn portfolio with straps. He was a stoutish man with a fleshy face, sidewhiskers, thick eyebrows and hawklike eyes. A roll of flesh on the neck hung over his stiff collar, the tabs of which were bent over a black bow tie. He wore a dark suit with a soiled yellow vest and seemed to be repressing excitement. Yakov was again apprehensive.

Bibikov's assistant had at once arisen and bowed. At a warning glance from the magistrate, the fixer hastily got up and remained standing.

"Good morning, Vladislav Grigorievitch," said Bibikov, a little flustered. "Good morning, Colonel Bodyansky, I am examining the suspect. Kindly be seated. Ivan Semyonovitch, please shut the door."

The colonel brushed his fingers over his mustache, and the Prosecuting Attorney, smiling slightly at nothing in particular, nodded. Yakov, at the magistrate's signal, shakily resumed his seat. Both officials studied him, the Prosecuting Attorney, once more intently, almost as though appraising the fixer's health, weight, stamina, sending chills down his back; or as though he were a new animal in the zoo. But the colonel looked through him as though he did not exist.

He wearily wished he didn't.

Bibikov read part way down the typewritten first page of the paper in his hand, then flipped through several more pages before he glanced up.

"Ah, I have it here," he said, clearing his throat. "This is the key statement: 'Z. N. Lebedev: I felt from the first he was different or odd in some way but could not guess how basically so, or I would never have had anything to do with him, you may believe me. He seemed to me somewhat foreign, but I explained to myself that he was from the provinces and obviously lacking in education and cultivation. I can only say I was on the whole uncomfortable in his presence, although of course truly grateful that he had assisted Papa that time he slipped in the snow. Afterwards I detested him because he tried to assault me. I told him firmly I never wished to see him again—' "

"It's not true, I didn't assault her," Yakov said, half rising. "It's not true at all."

"Please," said Bibikov, staring at him in astonishment.

"Silence," said Colonel Bodyansky, pounding his fist on the table. "Sit down at once!"

Grubeshov drummed with his fingers.

Yakov quickly sat down. Bibikov glanced at the colonel in embarrassment. To the fixer he said firmly, "You will please control yourself, this is a legal investigation. I shall continue to read: 'Investigating Magistrate: Are you charging sexual assault?'

" 'Z. N. Lebedev: I'm sure he intended to assault me. By this time I had begun to suspect he might be a Jew but when I saw for certain I screamed loudly.'

" 'Investigating Magistrate: Explain what you mean that you saw "for certain." '

" 'Z. N. Lebedev: He—I saw he was cut in the manner of Jewish males. I could not help seeing.'

" 'Investigating Magistrate: Go on, Zinaida Nikolaevna, after you have calmed yourself. You may be embarrassed but it is best to speak the truth.'

" 'Z. N. Lebedev: He realized I would not tolerate his

advances and left the room. That was the last I saw of him, and I thank God.'

" 'Investigating Magistrate: Then there was no assault in the true sense of the word, if you will pardon me? He did not touch you or attempt to?'

" 'Z. N. Lebedev: You may say that but the fact remains he undressed himself and his intentions were to have relations with a Russian woman. That's what he hoped for, or he wouldn't have undressed and appeared naked. I'm sure you wouldn't approve of that, your honor.'

" 'Investigating Magistrate: There is no approval expressed or implied either of his conduct or yours, Zinaida Nikolaevna. Did you afterwards inform your father, Nikolai Maximovitch, of this incident?'

" 'Z. N. Lebedev: My father is not well and hasn't been in good health or spirits since the death of my poor mother. And his only brother died a year ago of a lingering illness, so I didn't wish to upset him further. He would have wanted to horsewhip the Jew.' "

"It is noted at this point the witness wept copiously."

Bibikov laid down the paper.

"Will you say now," he asked Yakov, "whether you attempted to force yourself upon Zinaida Nikolaevna?"

Ivan Semyonovitch filled the magistrate's water glass from a porcelain pitcher on the table.

"Absolutely not, your honor," Yakov said hastily. "We ate together twice on her invitation while I was working in the upstairs flat, and the last night—the night I finished painting—she afterwards invited me to her bedroom. Maybe I shouldn't have gone—that's obvious now—but it's not such a hard thing to do when you consider a man's nature. Anyway, I had doubts and the minute I saw she was unclean, if you'll excuse me for saying so, your honor, I left. That's the honest truth and I could try from now to the Day of Judgment and not make it truer."

"What do you mean 'unclean'?"

The fixer was distraught. "I'm sorry to mention such things but if a man is in trouble he has to explain himself. The truth of it is she was having her monthlies."

He lifted his manacled hands to wipe his face.

"Any Jew who approaches a Russian woman ought to be strung up," said Colonel Bodyansky.

"Did she state such was her condition?" Grubeshov spoke with a slight thickness of speech.

"I saw the blood, your honor, if you'll excuse me, while she was washing herself with a cloth."

"You saw the blood?" the Prosecuting Attorney said sarcastically. "Did that have some religious meaning to you as a Jew? Do you know that in the Middle Ages Jewish men were said to menstruate?"

Yakov looked at him in surprise and fright.

"I don't know anything about that, your honor, although I don't see how it could be. But getting back to Zinaida Nikolaevna Lebedev, what her condition meant to me was that it wouldn't do either of us any good, and I was a fool to agree to go to her room in the first place. I should have gone home the minute I finished my work and not be tempted by a table full of all kinds of food."

"Relate what happened in the bedroom," Bibikov said. "And please confine yourself to the question at hand."

"Nothing happened, your honor, I swear it with my whole heart. It's as I said before—and also the young lady in the paper you just read—I got dressed as quickly as I could and left. I assure you of that, and it was the last I saw of her. Believe me, I'm sorry it happened."

"I do believe you," said Bibikov.

Grubeshov, sharply startled, stared at the Investigating Magistrate. Colonel Bodyansky shifted uncomfortably in his chair.

Bibikov, as though justifying himself, said, "We found two letters, both identified by the witnesses as written in their hand. One was from Nikolai Maximovitch addressed to Yakov Ivanovitch Dologushev, praising his diligence as an overseer of the Lebedev Brickworks, and the other was from the daughter, Zinaida Nikolaevna, on a sheet of perfumed blue paper, inviting the suspect to call on her at her home and expressly stating in the letter that she was writing it with the permission of her father. I have both letters in my files. They were turned over to me by Captain Korimzin of the Kiev City Police, who found them in the office of the brickworks."

The colonel and Prosecuting Attorney sat like statues.

Again addressing Yakov, the magistrate said, "I gather from the date that the letter from the young lady was written after the incident already described?"

"That's right, your honor. I was working in the brickworks then."

"You did not write her as she requested?"

"I didn't answer the letter. I figured I was born with a lot more trouble than I needed and there was no sense searching for more. If you're afraid of a flood stay away from the water."

"Her later remarks to me though of informal nature," the magistrate said, "affirm your statement. Therefore, considering the circumstances—this does not mean that I admire your behavior, Yakov Bok—I will recommend to the Prosecuting Attorney that you not be charged with attempted sexual assault."

He turned to his assistant, who, nodding, wrote hastily.

The Prosecuting Attorney, flushing through his sidewhiskers, picked up his portfolio, pushed back his chair and got up noisily. Colonel Bodyansky also arose. Bibikov reaching for the water glass, knocked it over. Jumping up, he dabbed at the spilled water on the table with his handkerchief, assisted by Ivan Semyonovitch, who in dismay quickly gathered up the papers and began to dry those that had got wet.

Grubeshov and Colonel Bodyansky, neither speaking a word, strode sullenly out of the room.

When he had blotted up the water, the Investigating Magistrate sat down, waited till Ivan Semyonovitch had dried and sorted the papers, and though embarrassed at the incident, picked up his notes, and clearing his throat, once more addressed the fixer in his resonant voice.

"We have laws, Yakov Bok," he said grimly, "directed against any member of your faith, orthodox or heretic, who assumes or counterfeits a name other than that entered in his official birth records, which is to say for the purpose of one sort of deception or another; but since there are no forged or counterfeited documents involved in this case, and since there is at present no record of similar previous offenses by you, I shall be lenient this time and not press this charge, although I personally feel, as I have already informed you, that your deception was repugnant and it is only by the greatest good fortune that it did not become an even more reprehensible situation—"

"I thank you kindly, your honor—" The fixer wiped his eyes with his fingers.

The magistrate went on. "I shall, however, ask the court to charge you for taking up residence in a district forbidden to Jews, except under certain circumstances which do not in any way appertain in your case. In this regard you have disobeyed the law. It is not a capital crime but you will be charged and sentenced for a misdemeanor."

"Will I be sent to jail, your honor?"

"I am afraid so."

"Ach. But how long in jail?"

"Not very long—a month at least, possibly less, depending on the magistrate who sentences you. It will teach you a lesson you are apparently in need of."

"Will I have to wear prison clothes?"

"You will be treated the same as other prisoners."

There was a knock on the door and a uniformed messenger entered. He handed an envelope to Ivan Semyonovitch, who quickly passed it to Bibikov.

The Investigating Magistrate, his hand trembling a little, tore it open, read the handwritten note, slowly cleaned his glasses, and hastened out of the room.

Though he knew he could expect trouble—although he had half hoped he would be let off with a warning or even a severe dressing down and sent running back to the Jewish quarter—oh, with what pleasure he would run!—Yakov, after his first disappointment, felt relief that things weren't a lot worse. A month in jail is not a year, and three weeks are less; besides, if you wanted to look at it that way, rent was free. After his manacled march through the snowy streets, the mutterings of the crowd, and the terrible question the Investigating Magistrate had put to him last night in his cell, he had expected a calamity if not worse. Now things had calmed down. Practically, there was only this minor charge, and perhaps a lawyer could get the sentence reduced to maybe a week or nothing at all? It meant, of course, goodbye to some rubles from his savings—surely the police would return them to him—but a ruble he could earn, if not in a day, then in a week or month. Better a month spent grubbing for one than a month in prison. It didn't pay to worry over rubles. The main thing was to be free, and once they freed him, Yakov Bok would be less foolish in his dealings with the law.

The magistrate's assistant had hesitantly reached over to read the note that Bibikov had crumpled up and left on the table. After glancing at it he smiled vaguely; but when the fixer attempted a smile in return, the assistant vigorously blew his nose.

Then the Investigating Magistrate returned, breathing through his mouth, his face drawn and grim, followed into the room by Grubeshov and Colonel Bodyansky. Once more they seated themselves at the table, the Prosecuting Attorney again unstrapping his portfolio. Ivan Semyonovitch gazed at them with concern, but neither of the officials spoke. The assistant tested his pen, and held it ready to write. Grubeshov's smile was gone, his lips set. The colonel's expression was deadly serious. One look at them and vast fear again surged through Yakov. Cold sweat prickled his back. Once more he expected the worst. At least almost the worst.

"The Prosecuting Attorney will now ask you a few questions," Bibikov said quietly though hoarsely. He sat back and fiddled with his pince-nez string.

"If you please, first my question," said the colonel, nodding to Grubeshov, who was peering into the compartments of his portfolio. The Prosecuting Attorney, looking up, assented.

"Will the prisoner state," Colonel Bodyansky's voice boomed out in the room, "whether he is a member of certain political organizations I shall now name: Social Democrats, Socialist-Revolutionists, or any other groups including the Jewish Bund, Zionists of whatever ilk or stripe, Seymists, or Volkspartei?"

"I've already gone into that," Bibikov said with a touch of impatience.

The colonel turned on him. "Mr. Investigating Magistrate, the task of protecting the Crown from its enemies is under the jurisdiction of the Secret Political Police. Already there has been too much interference in our affairs."

"Not at all, colonel, we are investigating a civil offense—"

"Even a civil offense may be lèse majesté. I ask you not to intrude on my questions and I won't interfere with yours. Tell me," he said, turning to Yakov, "are you a member of any of those so-called political parties I have just named, or of any secret terrorist or nihilistic organizations? Answer truthfully or I will send you to the Petropavelsky Fortress."

"No, sir, none, not one," Yakov replied hastily. "I've never belonged to a political party or any secret organization such as you just mentioned. To tell the truth I don't know one from the other. If I were a better educated man I might, but as it is now whatever you ask me about them I can tell you very little."

"You will be severely punished if you are lying."

"Who's lying, your honor? As a former soldier, I swear I am not lying."

"Save your breath," said the colonel in disgust, "I've never met a Jew I could call a soldier."

Yakov's face turned a fiery red.

The colonel wrote furiously on a slip of paper, thrust it into his tunic pocket and nodded to the Prosecuting Attorney.

Grubeshov had drawn a black oilskin-covered notebook out of his portfolio and was, with arched brows, studying one of its closely handwritten pages. Then he put the notebook down, and though he stared at the fixer, seemed to be in a pleasant state of mind as he remarked in a dry but slightly thick voice, "Well, we have been amusing ourselves, Mr. Yakov Shepsovitch Bok, alias Dologushev, alias I know not what else, but I now have some serious questions to put to you and I request that you give them your most serious attention. By your own admission you are guilty of certain flagrant violations of Russian law. You have confessed to certain crimes and there is good reason—excellent reason—to suspect others, one of so serious a nature that I shall not name it until we have further sifted the evidence, which I propose to continue to do now, with the permission of my colleagues."

He bowed to Bibikov, who, smoking, gravely nodded in return.

"Oh, my God," groaned Yakov, "I swear to you I am innocent of any serious crime. No, sir, the worst I am guilty of is stupidity—of living in the Lukianovsky without permission, that the Investigating Magistrate says I can get a month in prison for—but certainly not of any serious crimes."

God forgive me, he thought in terror. I'm in a bad spot now, worse than quicksand. That's what one gets for not knowing which way he's running, to begin with.

"Answer this question precisely," said Grubeshov, referring to his notebook. "Are you a 'Hasid' or 'Misnogid'? Please take down his answers with extreme accuracy, Ivan Semyonovitch."

"Neither. I'm neither one nor the other," said Yakov. "As I told his other honor—if I'm anything at all it's a freethinker. I say this to let you know I'm not a religious man."

"That won't do you any good," said the prosecutor, suddenly irritable. "I was expecting just such a response, and of course it's nothing more than an attempt to divert the questioning. Now answer me directly, you are a circumcised Jew, aren't you?"

"I'm a Jew, your honor, I'll admit to that and the rest is personal."

"I've already gone through all this, Vladislav Grigorievitch," said Bibikov. "It's all in the notes of the testimony. Read it to him, Ivan Semyonovitch, it will save time."

"I must ask the Investigating Magistrate not to interrupt," Grubeshov said testily. "I have no interest in saving time. Time is immaterial to me. Please let me go on without useless interruption."

Bibikov lifted the pitcher to pour himself a glass of water but it was empty.

"Shall I refill it, your honor?" whispered Ivan Semyonovitch.

"No," said Bibikov, "I'm not thirsty."

"What's this freethinker business about?" said the colonel.

"Not now, Colonel Bodyansky, I beg you," said Grubeshov. "It is not a political party."

Colonel Bodyansky lit a cigarette.

Grubeshov addressed Yakov, reading aloud certain words from his notebook and pronouncing them slowly.

"There are those among you—are there not?—Jews who are called 'tzadikim'? When a Jew wishes to harm a Christian, or as you call him, 'goyim,' he goes to the 'tzadik' and gives him a 'pidion,' which is a fee of some sort, and the 'tzadik' uses the power of the word, in magical incantations, to bring misfortune on the Christian. Isn't that a true fact? Answer me."

"Please," said Yakov, "I don't understand what you want of me. What have I to do with such things?"

"You'll find out, if you don't already know, only too soon," said Grubeshov, flushing. "In the meantime answer me truthfully and directly without vomiting a mouthful of irrelevant questions in return. Tell me now, what do you Jews mean by 'afikomen'? I want the truth without varnish."

"But what has this got to do with me?" Yakov said. "What do I know about these things you're asking me? If they're strange to you they're strange to me."

"Once more I will direct you to limit yourself to my questions. I will tell you patiently for the last time that I am not interested in your personal comments. Keep in mind that you are already in very serious trouble and curb your tongue."

"I am not positive," said the fixer, disheartened, "but it's a matzo of some kind that's used in the Passover ceremony for protection against evil spirits and evil men."

"Write that all down, Ivan Semyonovitch. Is it magic?"

"To my way of thinking it's superstition, your honor."

"But you say it's the same as matzos?"

"Practically the same, I think. I'm not an expert in these things. If you want to know the truth I haven't much use for such matters. I have nothing against those who want to follow the customary ways, but for myself I'm interested in what's new in the world."

He glanced at the Investigating Magistrate, but Bibikov was looking out the window.

Grubeshov slid his fingers into the portfolio and withdrew something covered with a handkerchief. He slowly peeled the four corners of the handkerchief and triumphantly held up a triangle of broken matzo.

"This was found in your habitat in the stable at the brick factory. What have you to say now?"

"What can I say, your honor? Nothing. It's matzo. It's not mine."

"Is it 'matzo shmuro'?"

"I wouldn't know if it was or wasn't."

"I understand that 'matzo shmuro' is eaten by very religious Jews."

"I think so."

"How does it differ from ordinary matzo?"

"Don't ask me, your honor. I don't really know."

"I'll ask what I please. I'll ask until your eyes pop out. Do you understand that?"

"Yes, sir."

"Did you bake this matzo?"

"No."

"Then how did it get into your habitat? That's where the police found it."

"It was brought in by an old man, a stranger to me. I give you my earnest word. He was lost one night near the cemetery and I took him in till it stopped snowing. Some boys had hit him with rocks. He was frightened."

"Near the cemetery in the Lukianovsky this occurred?"

"Where the brickworks is."

"Was he a 'tzadik'?"

"Even suppose he was, what has that got to do with me?"

"Answer with respect!" The Prosecuting Attorney struck the table with his palm. The piece of matzo fell to the floor. Ivan Semyonovitch hastily retrieved it. He held it up for all to see, it had not broken. Bibikov wet his dry lips. "Answer courteously," he said.

Yakov, in a dull state, nodded.

Grubeshov again bowed to the magistrate. "My deepest thanks." He paused as though to say more, then changed his mind. "Did your friend the 'tzadik' come often to the stable?" he asked Yakov.

"He came that once. He was a stranger to me. I never saw him again."

"That was because you were arrested not long after his departure."

Yakov could not argue the point.

"Is it true that you hid other Jews in the stable and trafficked with them in stolen goods?"

"No."

"Did you steal systematically from your employer, Nikolai Maximovitch Lebedev?"

"As God is my judge, never a single kopek."

"Are you certain you did not yourself bake this matzo? A half bag of flour was found in your habitat."

"With respect, your honor, it's the wrong flour. Also I'm not a baker. I once tried to bake bread to save a kopek or two but it didn't rise and came out like a rock. The flour was wasted. Baking isn't one of my skills. I work as carpenter or painter most of the time—I hope nothing has happened to my tools, they're all I've got in the world—but generally I'm a fixer, never a matzo baker. What there is to fix I fix though it pays little and generally my luck in jobs has been bad. But I'm not a criminal, your honor."

Grubeshov listened impatiently. "Answer strictly to the point. Did the 'tzadik' bake the matzos?"

"If so not in my house. Who knows if elsewhere, he didn't tell me but I don't think so."

"Then some other Jew did?"

"It's probably true."

"It's more than probable," said the Prosecuting Attorney, glaring at him. "It's the truth of God."

When Yakov saw him peering again into his evil portfolio, he wrung his manacled hands under the table.

Grubeshov now slowly drew forth a long, stained rag.

"Have you seen this before?" He danced the stained rag over the table with his fingers.

Bibikov watched the dancing rag, absently polishing his glasses; Ivan Semyonovitch stared at it in fascination.

"I will describe it to you," said the Prosecuting Attorney. "It is part of a peasant's blouse similar to the one you are presently affecting. Was this rag, by some chance, formerly a possession of yours?"

"I don't know," said Yakov wearily.

"I advise you to think more carefully, Yakov Bok. If you've eaten no garlic your breath won't stink."

"Yes, your honor," Yakov said desperately, "it's mine more or less, although that's nothing to worry about. The old man I mentioned to you was hit on the head by a rock, and I used part of an old shirt I was no longer wearing—it fell apart on my back—to wipe the blood away. That's God's own truth and all there is to it, I swear."

"So you admit it's bloodstained," shouted the Prosecuting Attorney.

Yakov felt his tongue turn to dust.

"Did you ever chase any children in the brickworks yard in the vicinity of the kilns, in particular a twelve-year lad by the name of Zhenia Golov?"

The fixer was unable to reply.

Grubeshov, after glancing at Bibikov, smiled broadly as he mincingly asked the fixer, "Tell me, Yankel Jew, why are you trembling?"

3

Why does a man tremble?

When he was locked in the cell again there were three filthy straw pallets on the floor. One was his—what a misery that he could think of it as his; and two new prisoners were lying on the others. One was a hairy man in rags, the other a living skeleton. Both stank across the room, of dirt and poverty. Though neither paid any attention to him, the ragged one blinking at the wall, the other snoring, the fixer kept to the far corner of the cell. He felt abandoned, lost to the world.

"What will happen to me now?" he asked himself. And if it happens bad who will ever know? I might as well be dead. Recalling his father-in-law and wife, he could conjure neither of them close. Especially the wife. He thought of his father and mother, young people in their weedy graves, and their fate gave him no comfort. His frustrated innocence outraged him. He was unjustly accused, helpless, unable to offer proof or be believed. What horror would they accuse him of next? "If they knew me could they say such things?" He tried to comprehend what was happening and explain it to himself. After all, he was a rational being, and a man must try to reason. Yet the more he reasoned the less he understood. The familiar had become evil. What happened next was weighted with peril. That he was a Jew, willing or unwilling, was not enough to explain his fate. Remembering his life filled him with hatred for the way things went and were going. I'm a fixer but all my life I've broken more than I fix. What would they accuse him of next? How could a man defend himself against such terrible hints, insinuations, *accusations,* if no one was willing to believe him? Panic gnawed him. He was full of desperate thoughts of what to do next—somehow to sneak out of the cell and seek in the ghetto for the old man to tell the Russians that he had been hit on the head by a rock and Yakov had wiped away the blood?

The fixer goes from house to house, knocking on each thin door and asking for the tzadik but nobody knows him; then in the last house they know him, a saintly man, but he had long ago gone away. The fixer hurriedly travels on the train to Minsk and after months of desperate searching meets the old man, the moon on his rabbinic hat, coming home one evening from the synagogue.

"Please, you must go back to Kiev with me and prove my innocence. Tell the officials I didn't do what they say I did."

But the old tzadik does not recognize the fixer. He looks at him long but shakes his head. The wound on his temple has healed and he cannot now recall the night Yakov says he had spent with him in the room above the stable.

When the fixer remembered where he was he tore at his hands with his nails, and he tore at his face.

The snorer awoke with a gasp. "Akimytch," he cried out. "Formerly a tailor. I am innocent," he whimpered. "Don't beat me."

The other one snickered.

"Have you got a cigarette, Potseikin?" the former tailor asked the one on the other mattress. "A piece of butt?"

"Fuck yourself," said the blinker, a man with blood-shot eyes.

"Have you got a cigarette?" Akimytch asked Yakov.

"My bag is empty," said the fixer. He held it up.

"I'll bet you don't know why I'm here," Akimytch said.

"No."

"Neither do I. It's mistaken identity with me. I never did

what they say I did, may they choke to death on their mothers' milk. They mistook me for an anarchist."

He began to weep.

"I'm here because of a pack of pamphlets or whatever you call 'em," Potseikin said. "Some poor bastard, a man with wild eyes and a thick greatcoat says to me on Institutsky Street, 'Brother,' he says, 'I have to piss, so hold my bundle a minute, and when I come back here I'll slip you a five-kopek piece, on my honor.' What can you say to a man who has to piss? Could I say no to that? Then he might piss on me. So I held onto his bundle and in two minutes a pig-eyed detective comes running across the street and jabs a gun in my gut so hard it almost busts, and then he marches me off to the Secret Police without listening to a word I say. When we get there three big ones give me a going over with fat sticks till all my bones are cracked, and they show me where the pamphlets say to overthrow the Tsar. Who wants to overthrow the Tsar? Personally, I have only the highest regard for Nicholas the Second and the royal family, especially the young princesses and the poor sick boy, who I love as my own. But nobody believed me and that's why I'm here. It's all the fault of those bastard pamphlets."

"It's mistaken identity with me," said Akimytch. "What's it with you, pal?"

"The same," said Yakov.

"What did they say you did?"

He thought he oughtn't to tell them, but it came out quickly, in accusation of the accusers.

"They say I killed a boy—it's a dirty lie."

There was a deep silence in the cell. Now I've blundered, Yakov thought. He looked for the guard but he had gone for the soup pail.

The two on the straw pallets, their heads together, whispered in each other's ears, first Akimytch whispering, then Potseikin.

"Did you?" Akimytch asked Yakov.

"No, of course not. Why would I kill an innocent child?"

They whispered once more and Potseikin said in a thick voice, "Tell us the truth, are you a Jew?"

"What difference would it make?" Yakov said, but when they were whispering again he was afraid.

"Don't try anything or I'll call the guard."

The one in rags got up and approached the fixer, sneering. "So you're the bastard Jew who killed the Christian boy and sucked the blood out of his bones? I saw it in the papers."

"Leave me in peace," Yakov said. "I've done nothing like that to anybody, not to speak of a twelve-year-old child. It's not in my nature."

"You're a stinking Jew liar."

"Think as you like but let me alone."

"Who else would do anything like that but a mother-fucking Zhid?"

Potseikin pounced on the fixer and with his rotten teeth tried to bite his neck. Yakov shoved him off but Akimytch, foul-breathed, was on his back beating the fixer's head and face with his clammy bony hands.

"Christkiller!"

"Gevalt!" cried Yakov, flailing his arms. Though he whirled, ducked, and struck out with his fists, Potseikin hit him with a knee in the back as Akimytch struck him on the neck with both fists. The fixer went down, his mind darkened in pain. He lay motionless as they kicked him savagely, and felt as he passed out, a terrible rage.

Afterwards he woke on his mattress, and when he heard their snoring, retched. A rat scuttled across his genitals and he bolted up in horror. But there was a bit of horned moon at the small high barred window and he watched for a while in peace.

IV

The stable had burned to the ground in a matter of minutes, Proshko said, spitting at the fixer's feet, and it wouldn't surprise him if it were done with Jewish magic. He pointed to the blackened remains of the stalls where four maddened, rearing, trumpeting horses had died, and a crisscross pile of burnt and broken planks and timbers had fallen from the roof.

The mustached and bearded officials in the brickyard, some uniformed and booted, a few carrying umbrellas although it was no longer raining, and the Secret Police gendarmes, plainclothes detectives, and Kiev City Police—among them also an Imperial Army general with two rows of gold buttons and one of medals across his chest—looked on in silence as the foreman spoke. Grubeshov, in English bowler, mud-spattered gaiters, and rain cape, flushed at Proshko's testimony, whispered in Colonel Bodyansky's lowered ear, clutching his hand tightly, and the colonel earnestly whispered something in return as Yakov licked his dry lips. Bibikov, with small, yellow-muddy, ankle-length shoes, his winter scarf and large hat, standing behind two tight-faced Black Hundreds representatives wearing their accusatory buttons, chain-smoked cigarettes from a box he amiably offered around. Nearby, the pimply Ivan Semyonovitch accompanied an oldish priest of the Orthodox Church, Father Anastasy, a "specialist," Yakov had heard it whispered, "of the Jewish religion"; he was a round-shouldered man with a streaked beard, thin hands, and restless dark eyes, dressed in flowing vestments and round pot-hat which he pressed down with his palm when the wind blew. What he was expected to add to the miserable state of Yakov's affairs the fixer didn't know and was afraid to guess. Manacled, his legs chained, nervously exhausted, his body in flight though he tried with ten fingers to hold onto his mind, he stood with five armed guards at his back, apart from the rest. Though almost a month had gone by since his arrest he could still only half believe this had happened to him, someone who did not recognize himself in the dream he was dreaming; and listened stunned to Proshko, as though the accusation of the monstrous crime were both true and an irrelevancy, as though it had happened to someone he didn't know very well, in truth a stranger, although he clearly remembered fearing that something like this might happen to him.

Otherwise the brickyard was deserted on a gray and green overcast Sunday afternoon in what had been a cold May. None of the workers was around except for the drivers Richter and Serdiuk, who listened without speaking and occasionally spat, the Ukrainian holding his cap in his large red hand, ill at ease, the German staring darkly at the former overseer. Nikolai Maximovitch had been expected but Yakov knew it was too late in the day for him to leave the house sober. After a morning fog had thinned and lifted, it began to rain heavily; and it poured again in the afternoon. The horses drawing the half dozen carriages that had left at intervals from the District Courthouse in the Plossky, and met first in the brickyard, had splashed through puddles, and the motorcar carrying Yakov, Colonel Bodyansky and the gendarmes, had got stuck in the mud on a road in the Lukianovsky, drawing several people, and irritating the Prosecuting Attorney, who made it known to the chauffeur that he didn't want "the matter getting out." Not very much about the fixer had appeared in the newspapers. All they seemed to know was that a Jew from the Podol had been arrested "as a suspicious person," but not who or why. Grubeshov had promised more information at a later date in order not, presently, to impede the investigation. Bibikov, before they left the courthouse, had managed to convey this to Yakov, but not much else.

"Start from the beginning," Grubeshov said to Proshko,

dressed in his Sunday thick-trousered suit with short jacket. "—I want to hear your earliest suspicions."

The Prosecuting Attorney had planned this re-enactment, he had told the accused, "to let you know the inescapable logic of our case against you so that you may act accordingly and for your own benefit."

"But how for my benefit?"

"It will become clear to you."

The foreman blew his nose, wiped it in two strokes and thrust the handkerchief into his pants pocket.

"On one look I knew he was a Jew, even though he was faking that he was a Russian. It's easy enough to tell an onion from a radish if you're not color blind." Proshko laughed a little from the chest. "Yakov Ivanovitch Dologushev, he called himself, but I knew from the sound of it on his tongue that the name didn't fit him. A name belongs to you as your birthright, but it hung on him like a suit of stolen clothes. I felt in my blood he was a Jew the same way as you feel in the dark the presence of a ghost. Wait up, little brother, I thought to myself, something smells fishy here. Maybe it's his natural smell, or the way he talks Russian, or maybe it's the flatfooted way he runs when he chases young boys, but when I looked with both of my eyes open I saw what I already knew—he was a Zhid and no two ways about it. You can't make a gentleman out of a toad, as the saying goes, and a born Jew can't hide the Zhid in his face. This is a foxy bastard, I thought to myself, and he thinks he's got it hidden because he wears a belted sheepskin coat and has shaved off his Jewish whiskers and curls, and maybe it'll be a little slow smoking him out of his hole now that he's fooled Nikolai Maximovitch, but smoke him out I will, and with God's help it's what I did."

"Tell the details," said Grubeshov.

"It wasn't more than fifteen minutes after I first saw him that I went back to the office shack and asked him for his papers so as to hand them over to the District Police, and right off he showed me who he was. He lied that he had given them to the boss and he had registered them with the police. If a man talks crooked, I thought to myself, he's crooked elsewhere, and I'll watch out to see where else. I didn't have long to wait. Once when he was nosing around the kilns for purposes of his own, I sneaked into the shack and checked up on his figures in the books. He was crooked in his accounts and every day entered smaller amounts than he should so he could keep some rubles for himself—not so many, a Jew is cunning—maybe three or four or five a day that Nikolai Maximovitch had no suspicions of, and he saved himself a nice little pile in a tin can in his room."

"You're a liar," Yakov said, trembling, "you're the thief and you're putting it on me. You and your drivers stole thousands of bricks from Nikolai Maximovitch, and you hated me for watching you so you couldn't steal more."

Nobody was listening.

"What did he do with the rubles you say he stole?" Bibikov asked the foreman. "There were about ninety in the tin can, if I remember correctly. If he was stealing four rubles a day, let us say, he should have had many more."

"Who knows what a Jew does with money. I've heard it said they take it to bed with them and give it a fuck once in a while. I bet he gave most of it to the Zhidy synagogue in the Podol. They have plenty of uses for a Russian ruble."

"The Secret Police confiscated altogether one hundred and five rubles," Grubeshov announced after conferring with Colonel Bodyansky. "Keep your mouth shut," he said to Yakov. "Answer when you're spoken to."

"What's more," Proshko went on, "he sneaked other Jews into the brickyard, and one was one of those Hasids with a round hat, or whatever you call them, who prayed up there in the stable with this one here. The other one came when they thought nobody was around to watch them. They both tied horns on their heads and prayed to the Jewish God. I watched them through the window and saw them praying and eating matzos. I figured they baked some in the stove up there and I was right, there was half a sack of flour hidden under the bed that the police got. I kept track of them because I had my own suspicions, like I told you. I saw this one here sneaking around like a ghost at night, his face white and eyes strange, looking for something, and I also saw him chasing the boys that I told you about. I was worried he would do them some kind of harm, little knowing how right I was. One day two or three school kids came in the yard with their book satchels. I saw him chase them but they got away over the fence. Once I asked him, 'Yakov Ivanovitch, why did you chase those young school kids, they are good boys and all they wanted to do is to see how we make brick,' but he answered me, 'If they are so innocent Jesus Christ will protect them.' He thought Proshko wouldn't know what he meant by that but I did."

Yakov groaned.

"That's why I kept my eye on him and when I couldn't I told the drivers to watch him."

"That's so." Serdiuk, still smelling of horse, nodded, and Richter said yes.

"I saw them praying with their little black hats on, and I spied on them when they were baking those matzos. Then when the boy was murdered and they found him in the cave with all those wounds the morning it was snowing—when the snow came again in April—I saw this one take the other Jew with the round hat down the stairs and they left the brickyard in a hurry. I went up there, walking right in their footsteps in the snow so he wouldn't see I had been there, and that was the day I found pieces of matzos they had baked, half a bag of flour under the bed, his sack of tools, and that bloody rag I told you about. The devil scatters his dung wherever he goes.

"After that he wanted to set the stable on fire to burn the evidence but he saw I had my eye on him. When I met him in the brickyard the blood ran out of his face and he couldn't raise his eyes at me. That was after they had killed the kid. After the funeral I went to the police, and in a week they came and arrested him. They took the matzos away and the other things that I told you about, but I went up there with Serdiuk and Richter here, to tear up the floorboards—some had certain dark stains on them that we wanted to show the police. Just then we see an old graybeard Jew run out of the stable, and the next thing the place was up in roaring flames, and the whole stable burned down in less than five minutes, so it was just by luck we saved any of the horses. We saved six and lost four. If the fire had been an ordinary kind we would've saved the whole ten, but being as it was, there was something that made it burn as if the wind was caught in it, and it cried out like people were dying and ghosts were going to meet them. They had said some magic words from a Zhidy book, I'll swear to God, and upstairs where this one here had lived before they arrested him, the flames turned an oily green such as I never saw before, and then yellow, and then almost black, and they burned twice as fast as the fire in the stalls even though the loft was full of hay. In the stalls the fire burned orange and red, and it was slower, more like an ordinary fire, so we got six horses out of the burning stalls and lost the other four."

Richter swore every word was true and Serdiuk crossed himself twice.

2

Father Anastasy stiffly embraced Marfa Golov, the haggard mother of the martyred boy, a tallish, scrawny-necked woman with red-rimmed, wet, flecked gray eyes, and dark skin drawn tautly over her face, who tried to curtsy and collapsed in the priest's arms.

"Forgive us our transgressions, Father," she wept.

"You must forgive us, my child," said the priest, in a nasal voice. "The world has sinned against you. In particular, those who sin against our Lord."

He crossed himself, his hand like a bird, and so did some of the officials.

Marfa Golov, when Yakov first saw her waiting for the officials to arrive, was standing, with a thick-shawled neighbor who quickly ran off when the carriages appeared, on the sagging steps of a two-story wooden house with a peaked corrugated tin roof. The house overlooked a low-walled cemetery, and in the distance the brickyard, which Bibikov stopped to stare at, its chimneys smokeless on Sunday. It was a boxlike house that had once been painted white but was now weathered gray and peeling. The grassless front yard, muddy from the rain, was surrounded by a high unpainted fence, held together horizontally on the street side by long uneven darkly weathered boards. The road in front of the house where the carriages and motorcar waited was pitted and muddy, and the carriages looked like those of a funeral party except that there was no visible hearse. Marfa, thirty-nine, the newspaper had said, and vaguely pretty, with a tense distracted manner, eyes glancing in every direction, a drawn unhappy mouth and slight chin, wore for the occasion a dark-flowered blouse, long green skirt, and pointed two-tone button shoes. She had pinned a discolored cameo to her worn throat and thrown a light scarf over her shoulders. And she had on a new white hat topped with a bunch of bright cherries that caused some interested glances. When the fixer was led through the gate into the yard, Marfa burst into sobs. One of the officials in the Prosecuting Attorney's office and a gendarme nearby cursed the prisoner under their breaths yet loud enough for him to hear.

"It's surely the one," Marfa gasped.

"Which one is that?" Bibikov asked, snapping on his silver-rimmed pince-nez and staring at her.

"The Jew Zhenia told me about, who had chased him with a long knife."

"Note the identification," said Grubeshov to Ivan Semyonovitch. The assistant hadn't his notebook with him, but he mentioned it to one of the policemen, who wrote it down.

There was a green mildewed stone well in the yard and Bibikov peered down it but could see nothing.

He dropped a small stone down the well and after a while there was a splash. The officials looked at one another but the Investigating Magistrate walked away.

"The room's upstairs, your honor," Marfa said to the Prosecuting Attorney. "It's small as you'll see, but Zhenia was small himself for a lad his age. That's not from me, you'll notice, because I don't lack size but from his cowardly father who deserted us." She smiled nervously.

Marfa led them in and hurried upstairs to show the officials where the poor child had slept. They wiped their feet on a muddy rag at the door and went up in small hushed groups to stare into the dark tiny cubicle between a large untidy bedroom with a two-pillowed brass bed, and a room with a locked door Marfa said was a storeroom.

"What can a widow do with so many bedrooms? Generally I store things. When my aunt died she left me her furniture although I have enough of my own."

Yakov was ordered to go up after the others had seen the boy's room. He wanted not to go but knew that if he said so they would drag him up. He went slowly up the stairs in his clanking leg chains that rubbed his ankles sore, followed by three booted gendarmes who waited for him on the landing with drawn pistols. Marfa, Father Anastasy, Grubeshov, Ivan Semyonovitch and Colonel Bodyansky were in the corridor as the Jew glanced furtively into the boy's room. The fixer had wanted to look calmly and with dignity but had been unable to. It was as though he expected a wild animal in the room to spring out at him. He glanced fearfully into the tiny cubicle with torn wallpaper and unmade cot, the crumpled bedsheet gray, soiled, the faded blanket torn. Though the room and cot were strange to him, Yakov had a momentary hallucinatory thought he had seen them before. He then recalled his cubicle in the printer's flat in the Podol. This was what he remembered but he worried they thought he was thinking of something that would surely convict him were it known what.

"My darling Zhenechka hoped to be a priest," Marfa whispered loudly to Father Anastasy, dabbing at her reddened eyes with a scented handkerchief. "He was a religious child and worshipped God."

"It was reported to me that he was being prepared for the seminary," said the priest. "One of the monks told me he was a dear boy, in some respects a saintly boy. I understand he had already had a mystical experience. I was also told he loved our priestly vestments and hoped some day to wear them. His death is God's loss."

Marfa wept miserably. Ivan Semyonovitch's eyes clouded and he turned away and wiped them on his coat sleeve. Yakov felt like crying but couldn't.

Then Father Anastasy came down and Bibikov went up the stairs, squeezing past the gendarmes. He glanced casually into Zhenia's small room, looked around absently, then got down on his knees, and lifting the bedsheet, peeked under the bed. He touched the floor and examined his soiled fingertips.

"The floor may be dusty," Marfa said quickly, "but I always empty the chamber pot."

"Never mind that," said Grubeshov distastefully. "Well, what have you discovered?" he asked Bibikov.

"Nothing."

The Investigating Magistrate glanced quickly into Marfa's bedroom and stopped at the locked door of the other room as if he were listening, but did not try the knob. He then wandered downstairs. Marfa hurriedly attempted to make the boy's bed up but Grubeshov ordered her to leave it alone.

"It will take me only a minute."

"Leave it as it is. The police prefer it that way."

They went downstairs. Although it was drizzling outside, some of the officials were gathered in the yard. The others, including the prisoner and gendarmes who guarded him, met in Marfa's dusty disordered parlor that smelled of tobacco smoke, stale sweet beer, and cabbage. At Grubeshov's request, she pulled open the window vent, and with a dirty rag hastily wiped the seats of a half dozen chairs nobody sat down in. The prisoner was afraid to sit. Marfa tried to do something to the floor with a broom but the Prosecuting Attorney took it from her.

"This can wait, Marfa Vladimirovna. Please give us your fullest attention."

"I just thought I'd clean up a bit," she hurriedly explained. "To tell the truth, I wasn't expecting so many high officials. I thought the prisoner was coming to see what he had done and why should I clean up for a dirty Jew?"

"That'll do," Grubeshov said. "We're not interested in your household affairs. Go now into the story of what happened to your son."

"Ever since he was little he wanted to be a priest," Marfa wept, "but now he's a dead corpse in his grave."

"Yes, we all know that and it's a tragic story, but perhaps you ought to limit yourself to what you know about the details leading up to the crime."

"First shouldn't I serve tea, do you think, your honor?" she asked, distracted. "The samovar's boiling."

"No," he said. "We are very busy and have much to do before we can return to our homes. Please tell the story—

specifically of Zhenia's disappearance and death—how, for instance, you learned of it."

"You," he said to Yakov, who was gazing out the window at the rain in the chestnut trees, "you know well this concerns you so pay attention." In the time the fixer had been in prison the city had turned green and there were sweet-smelling lilacs everywhere but who could enjoy them? Through the open window he could smell the wet grass and new leaves, and where the cemetery ended there were birches with silver trunks. Somewhere nearby an organ grinder was playing a waltz that Zinaida Nikolaevna had played for him once on her guitar, "Summer Is Gone Forever."

"Go on, please," Grubeshov said to Marfa.

She lifted both hands to straighten her hat, then caught his eye and dropped them.

"He was an earnest boy," Marfa quickly began, "and never gave me much trouble as boys do. As for myself I'm a widow of stainless character, pure and simple. My husband, who was a telegrapher, deserted me, as I mentioned before, your honor, and a couple of years later died of galloping consumption, which served him right for the way he mistreated us. I support myself by hard work and that's why my house that you're in isn't the neatest, but my child has always had a roof over his head, and my life has been one of irreproachable toil. If you work like a horse you can't live like the gentry, if you'll pardon my frankness. We got along without the deserter. This house doesn't belong to me, I rent it and sometimes let out a room or two, though one has to be careful of riffraff, especially those not given to paying what they owe to others. I didn't want my child associating with such, so I rarely took boarders in—even though I had to work that much harder—and then only if they were genteel people. But even if he didn't have all the advantages, Zhenia had what he needed and wasn't above showing his appreciation by giving me help—not like some boys I could name you, for instance Vasya Shiskovsky in the next house from here. My own was an obedient lad, an angel. He once asked me if he should leave the ecclesiastical school and become a butcher's apprentice but I advised him, 'Zhenia, my good darling, it's best to go on with your lessons. Get an education and when you're rich some day, you can support your poor mother in her old age.' 'Mamenka,' he answered me, 'I will always take care of you even when you are old and sick.' He was a saintly child, and it didn't in the least surprise me when he came back from his Bible lesson one day and said he wanted to be a priest. My eyes were full of tears that day."

She glanced nervously at Grubeshov, who nodded slightly.

"Go on, Marfa Vladimirovna, tell now what happened towards the end of March, a few short weeks before the Jewish Passover this year. And speak more slowly so that we can comprehend everything you say. Don't slur your words."

"Are you paying attention?" he asked Yakov.

"The closest, your honor, though I honestly don't understand what this has to do with me. It's all so strange."

"Only be patient," Grubeshov said. "It will be as familiar and close as the nose on your face."

Several of the officials, including the army general, laughed.

"On the morning in the week you mention," said Marfa, darting a glance at the Jew, "it was a Tuesday I'll never forget in my life, Zhenia woke up and got dressed in his black stockings that I had bought him for his name day and left for school as usual at six in the morning. I had to work until long after dark that day, then attend to the marketing so I naturally didn't get home until late. Zhenia wasn't in the house and after I had rested a while—I've had painful varicose veins since giving birth to my child—I went to Sofya Shiskovsky, my neighbor in the next house down a ways, whose Vasya was in Zhenia's form in school, and asked him where my boy was. Vasya said he didn't know because though he had seen Zhenia after school, Zhenia hadn't come home with him as was usual. 'Where did he go?' I said. 'I don't know,' he answered. Ach, I thought, he is at his grandmother's, I won't worry. But on the same night I caught the flu. I had the shakes and shivers for three days and stayed in bed in a weak condition for three more, only getting up, if you'll excuse me, to go to the toilet, or boil up a little rice and water to sop diarrhea. Zhenia was missing for about a week—six or seven days to be exact, and when I made up my mind to get dressed and report it to the police he was found dead in a cave with forty-seven stab wounds on his body. The neighbors came into my house with slow steps and sad faces—they looked like dead folk and frightened me before they spoke—then when they told me what horror had happened to me, I cried out, 'My life is over because I've lost my reason to live!' "

Marfa put her hand to her eyes and tottered. Two of the officials stepped towards her but she held onto a chair and remained upright. The men withdrew.

"Excuse me," Bibikov said gently, "but how is it you waited six or seven whole days before thinking to report that your son was missing? If it were my son I would have reported it at once—at the very latest on the night he had not yet appeared in the house. It's true that you were sick but even sick people have been known to pull themselves out of bed and act in emergencies."

"It all depends on how sick they are, if you please, your honor. Whether it's your son or mine, when you're running a high fever and are nauseous besides, your thoughts aren't always at their best. I worried about Zhenia and had terrible nightmares besides. I was afraid he was in some kind of horrible trouble, but I thought I dreamed that because I was feverish. And while I was so sick with the flu, so was my neighbor Sofya, and also Vasya. No one came to knock on my door, as usually happens two or three times during the day. And Yuri Shiskovsky, Sofya's husband, is as likely to knock on a person's door when you need him as Father Christmas. We don't get along at all but that's a story for a winter night. Anyway, if someone had come into my house during those five or six days I would have split both his ears crying out my fears for my poor child, but nobody ever did."

"Let her go on with the story," Grubeshov said to Bibikov. "If necessary you can ask questions later."

The Investigating Magistrate nodded to his colleague. "I assure you it's necessary enough, Vladislav Grigorievitch, but as you please, I'll ask later. As for what else may be necessary, or even not so necessary, for instance this entire procedure during a time of investigation, I think we ought to discuss that too, at least in principle if for no other reason."

"Tomorrow," said Grubeshov. "We'll talk over everything tomorrow."

"Come now to the point of the matter, Marfa Vladimirovna," he said. "Tell us what Zhenia and Vasya Shiskovsky told you about the Jew before the fatal incident."

Marfa had listened intently to the exchange between the men, alternating uneasiness with apparent boredom. When Bibikov was speaking she cast nervous glances around her but lowered her eyes if anyone looked at her.

"Vasya also told me what I heard Zhenia say more than once—that they were afraid of the Jew in the brickyard."

"Go on, we're listening."

"Zhenia told me that one day when he and Vasya were playing in the factory yard they saw two Jews—it was toward nightfall—sneak through the gate and go up the stairs where this one lived."

She glanced at the fixer, then averted her eyes. He was standing with his head bowed.

"Excuse me for interrupting," Bibikov said to the Prosecuting Attorney, "but I would like to understand how the boys identified the two men as Jews?"

Colonel Bodyansky guffawed and Grubeshov smiled.

"Easily, your honor," Marfa said in excitement, "they were wearing Jewish clothes and had long rough beards, not nicely trimmed ones like some of the gentlemen here. Also the boys used to peek in the window and saw them praying. They wore black hats and robes. The boys were frightened and ran home here. I asked Vasya to stay for a cup of cocoa and slice of white bread with Zhenia, but he was scared sick and said he wanted to go home to his own house."

Grubeshov listened, standing with his thumbs locked behind him. "Please go on."

"I heard from the boys that this one here brought other Jews up in his stable. One was an old man with a black satchel that the Lord knows what they did with. Zhenia once told this one to his face that he would tell the foreman if he chased him again. 'And if you do that I'll kill you once and for all,' said the Jew. One day Zhenia saw him running after another boy in the brickyard, a lad not eight years old from the neighborhood around here, Andriushka Khototov, whose father is a street sweeper. The boy luckily got out through the open gate, thank the Lord. Then the Jew saw my Zhenia and chased him, but my Zhenia climbed the fence and escaped that time, though he told me his heart hurt because he did not think he would get over the fence before the Jew grabbed him. One day, hiding by the kiln, Zhenia saw two of the Jews try to catch a Russian child and drag him into the stable. But the boy was a smart one and bit, clawed, and screamed so loud they got frightened and let him go. I warned Zhenia more than once not to go back there or he might get kidnapped and killed, and he promised me he wouldn't. I think he didn't for a time, then one night he came home frightened and feverish, and when I cried out, 'Zhenia, what ails you, tell me quickly what happened?' he said that the Jew had chased him with a long knife in the dark among the gravestones in the cemetery. I got down on my knees to him. 'Zhenia Golov, in the name of the Holy Mother, promise me not to go near that evil Jew again. Don't go in that brickyard.' 'Yes, dear Mamenka,' he said, 'I will promise.' That's what he said, but he went back in there again, anyway. Boys are boys, your honor, as you already know. God knows what draws them to danger, but if I had kept him under lock and key in this house as I sometimes did when he was a little boy he'd be alive today and not a corpse in his coffin."

She fervently crossed herself.

"Marfa Vladimirovna, please tell us what else you were told by the two boys," Grubeshov said to her.

"I was told they had seen a bottle of blood on the Jew's table."

The army general gasped and the officials looked at each other in horror. Yakov stared whitely at Marfa, his lips working in agitation. "There was no bottle of blood on my table," he cried out. "If there was anything it was a jar of strawberry jam. Jam is not blood. Blood is not jam."

"Be quiet!" Grubeshov ordered. "We will inform you when it is your time to speak."

One of the gendarmes pointed his revolver at Yakov.

"Put that foolish gun away," Bibikov said. "The man is chained and manacled."

"Did you personally see 'the bottle of blood'?" he asked Marfa.

"No, but both of the boys did, and they told me about it. They could hardly talk. Their faces were green."

"Then why didn't you report that to the police? It was your duty to, as well as the other incidents you just enumerated, as for instance the suspect chasing your son with a knife. That is a criminal act. This is a civilized society. Such things must be reported to the police."

She answered at once: "Because I've had my fill of the police, if you don't mind me saying so, your honor, and with apologies to those of them present that never bothered me. I once complained to them that Yuri Shiskovsky, for reasons that will be kept to myself, struck me on the head with a block of wood, and all morning they kept me in the police station answering personal questions while they filled out long forms, as if I myself were the criminal and not that madman who they let go, although I had a bloody gash in my scalp, and even an idiot would know who had hit who. I can't afford to lose my time like that. I have to earn a living and that's why I didn't report what the boys told me."

"Which is understandable enough," said Grubeshov—turning to the general, who nodded—"although I agree with the Investigating Magistrate that such things should be reported at once. Now finish your story, Marfa Vladimirovna."

"I have finished, there's no more to tell."

"In that case," said the Prosecuting Attorney, addressing the officials, "it's best to move on."

He pulled a thin gold watch from his yellow waistcoat pocket and consulted it closely.

"Vladislav Grigorievitch," Bibikov said, "I must insist on my prerogative to question the witness."

Marfa's intent gaze at him changed from fear to anger.

"What have I done to you?" she cried out.

"Neither of us has done anything to the other, that's not the point. Marfa Golov, I would like to ask you a question or two. Please, Vladislav Grigorievitch, I insist. Unfortunately, I can't go into certain things just now, but one or two questions I insist on asking and I would like them answered honestly and directly. Is it true, for instance, Marfa Golov, that you receive stolen goods from a gang of thieves, one of whom is or was your lover who often visits this house?"

"You needn't bother to answer that," Grubeshov said, flushing. "It's irrelevant to the matter at issue."

"I insist it is not so irrelevant, Vladislav Grigorievitch."

"No, I don't receive such goods," said Marfa, white-lipped, her eyes darkening. "That's a filthy rumor spread by my enemies."

"Is that your response?"

"Of course it is."

"Very well, then. Is it true that a year ago last January you threw the contents of a phial of carbolic acid into the eyes of your lover and blinded him for life, a man whom you have since become reconciled with?"

"Is he the one who reported me?" she asked, enraged.

"Reported you?"

"Told you these filthy lies?"

"Boris Alexandrovitch, as your superior in rank, I forbid these questions," Grubeshov said, irritated. "If you have anything of that nature to ask, please do so in my office tomorrow morning, though I personally don't see how such irrelevancies can matter. They do not change the weight of the significant evidence. We must absolutely get on now. It's Sunday and we all have obligations to our families."

"What is the 'significant evidence' you refer to?"

"The evidence we have been engaged in collecting, including the evidence of history."

"History is not law."

"We will see about that."

"I must insist on a reply from Marfa Golov."

"I have no more to say than I've already said," Marfa answered haughtily. "He used to beat me up and I defended myself. My legs and back were black and blue for months where he beat me, and once he smashed me in the eye so hard it ran pus for three weeks."

"Is it true that he also beat your son, once so severely that the boy lost consciousness?"

"I forbid you to answer," Grubeshov shouted.

"Don't be a fool," Colonel Bodyansky said to Bibikov.

"The Jew killed my child," Marfa cried out. "Somebody ought to scratch his eyes." She ran to the window and called out of the open vent to the gravestones in the cemetery, "Zhenia, my baby, come home! Come home to your mother!"

She wept heartbrokenly.

She's insane, thought Yakov. So is her hat with the cherries.

"See how he glares at me like a starving wolf from the forest," Marfa, turning to the fixer, shouted. "Make him stop!"

There was a stir among the officials. Two of the gendarmes pinned the prisoner by his arms.

Marfa, glaring at him, attempted to remove her hat. Her eyelids fluttered, and moaning she sank to the floor. The hat rolled off her head, but before fainting she gazed loosely around to see where it was. Father Anastasy and Colonel Bodyansky bent to assist her.

When Marfa recovered only the police and gendarmes were in the room with her and the prisoner. Bibikov, to Yakov's misery, had left first, and he saw him, through the window, walk down the muddy road and get into a carriage alone. The dead boy's mother asked for her hat, blew on it, and put it carefully away in a sideboard drawer.

She covered her head with a coarse black shawl.

3

Grubeshov, in his bowler and wet rain cape, hovered over Father Anastasy with a large black umbrella as the wet-lipped priest, standing on a low flat rock, his voice rising and falling sometimes out of context with what he was saying, nasally recited the blood guilt of the Jewish Nation.

The group of officials and police had abandoned the carriages and motorcar at the bottom of an inclined street paved with rocks, lined on one side by a row of blackened shanties from which people stared at them out of windows and doorways, but no one came out to watch. A flock of pigeons rose in the street and two small white dogs, barking shrilly, darted into the houses as the crowd of officials approached. On foot they climbed first up the steps of a terraced hill from which the winding Dnieper was visible in the distance, then descended into a muddy ravine, and along it to the bottom of an almost perpendicular rocky hill with some caves in its face, in one of which the body of Zhenia Golov had been found. This cave, minutely described in the newspapers Yakov had read on the day of the discovery of the boy's body, one of those cut into the hill by religious hermits centuries ago, was about fifteen feet up its face. To get up into it one climbed the rough steps that had been hewn into the rocky hill. On top of it was a sparse birchwood grove with thin-trunked white trees full of chirping swallows, and beyond that lay a flat section of the outskirts of the city consisting of scattered houses and empty lots, about two versts from Nikolai Maximovitch's brick factory.

"There is from here an almost straight road from the brick factory where Zhenia was presumed to be killed," Grubeshov said.

"But, permit me, Vladislav Grigorievitch, to draw your attention to the fact that the road from Marfa Golov's house is just as straight and a little shorter," said Bibikov.

"In any case," the Prosecuting Attorney answered, "the most important evidence will be the testimony of the experts."

The priest, a long-haired, large-nosed man whose breath smelled of garlic, was standing under Grubeshov's umbrella before a loose semicircle of listeners but the Prosecuting Attorney had Yakov brought up close, the officials giving way as he was pushed forward, his chains rattling, by his guards. Bibikov, standing in the rear, looked on, impassively smoking. It was still drizzling and the fixer had lost his cap, unsettling him further, more than he thought possible in his present condition. It's only a cap, not my life; but the thought was a terrible one, because it was the first time he had admitted to himself he was afraid for his life. Fearing he was about to hear some secret fact that would absolutely condemn him once it was known, he stood inch-deep in the mud, breathing thickly, listening transfixed.

"My dear children," said the priest to the Russians, wringing his dry hands, "if the bowels of the earth were to open to reveal the population of human dead since the beginning of the world, you would be astonished to see how many innocent Christian children among them have been tortured to death by Christ-hating Jews. Throughout the ages, as described in their holy books and various commentaries, the voice of Semitic blood directs them to desecrations, unspeakable horrors—for example, the Talmud, which likens blood to water and milk, and preaches hatred of gentiles, who are characterized as being not human, no more than animals. 'Thou shalt not kill' does not apply to us, for do not they also write in their books: 'Murder the good among gentiles'? This, perfidy, too, is prescribed in their Kabbala, the book of Jewish magic and alchemy, wherein the name of Satan is invoked; hence there have been multitudes of slaughtered innocent children whose tears have not moved their murderers to mercy."

His eyes darted over the faces of the officials but no one moved.

"The ritual murder is meant to re-enact the crucifixion of our dear Lord. The murder of Christian children and the distribution of their blood among Jews are a token of their eternal enmity against Christendom, for in murdering the innocent Christian child, they repeat the martyrdom of Christ. Zhenia Golov, in the loss of his own warm blood, symbolizes to us our Lord's loss of his precious lifeblood, drop by cruel drop, as he hung in pain on the wooden cross to which the anti-Christ had nailed him. It is said that the murder of the gentile—any gentile—hastens the coming of their long-awaited Messiah, Elijah, for whom they eternally leave the door open but who has never, during all the ages since his first coming, bothered to accept the invitation to enter and sit in the empty chair. Since the destruction of their Temple in Jerusalem by the Legions of Titus there has been no sacrificial altar for animals in their synagogues, and it has come about, therefore, that the killing of gentiles, in particular innocent children, is accepted as a fitting substitute. Even their philosopher Maimonides, whose writings were suppressed in our country in 1844, orders Jews to murder Christian children. Did I not tell you they think of us as animals?

"In the recorded past," said Father Anastasy in his nasally musical voice, "the Jew has had many uses for Christian blood. He has used it for purposes of sorcery and witches' rituals, and for love potions and well poisoning, fabricating a deadly venon that spread the plague from one country to another, a mixture of Christian blood from a murdered victim, their own Jewish urine, the heads of poisonous snakes, and even the stolen mutilated host—the bleeding body of Christ himself. It is written that all Jews require some Christian blood for the prolongation of their lives else they die young. And in those days they considered our blood to be—this too is recorded—the most effective therapeutic for the cure of their diseases. They used it, according to their old medical books, to heal their women in childbirth, stop hemorrhages, cure the blindness of infants, and to alleviate the wounds of circumcision."

One of the Kiev police officials, Captain Korimzin, a man in a damp coat and muddy boots, secretly made the sign of the cross. Yakov felt faint. The priest, staring at him intently for a minute, went on, and although he spoke calmly his gestures were agitated. The Russians continued to listen with grave interest.

"There are those among us, my children, who will argue that these are superstitious tales of a past age, yet the truth of much I have revealed to you—I do not say it is all true—must be inferred from the very frequency of the accusations against the Jews. None can forever conceal the truth. If the bellman is dead the wind will toll the bell. Perhaps in this age of science we can no longer accept every statement of accusation made against this unfortunate people; however we must ask ourselves how much truth remains despite our reluctance to believe. I do not say that all Jews are guilty of these crimes and that pogroms should therefore be instituted against them, but that there are certain sects among them, in particular the Hasidim and their leaders, the tzadikim, who commit in secret crimes such as I have described to you, which the gentile world, despite its frequent experience with them, seems to forget until, lo! another poor child disappears and is found dead in this fashion: his hands tied behind his back, and his body punctured by a sharp weapon in several places, the number of wounds according to magic numbers: 3, 7, 9, 13, in the manner of such crimes of former times. We know that their Passover, though they ascribe it to other uses, is also a celebration of the crucifixion. We know that is the time they kidnap gentiles for their religious ceremonials. Here in our Holy City, during the Polovostian raids in the year 1100, the monk Eustratios was abducted from the Pechera Monastery and sold to the Jews of Kherson, who crucified him during Passover. Since they no longer dare such open crimes they celebrate the occasion by eating matzos and unleavened cakes at the Seder service. But even this act conceals a crime because the matzos and cakes contain the blood of our martyrs, though of course the tzadikim deny this. Thus through our blood in their Passover food they again consume the agonized body of the living Christ. I give you my word, my dear children, that this is the reason why Zhenia Golov, this innocent child who wished to enter the priesthood, was destroyed!"

The priest wiped one eye, then the other, with a white handkerchief. Two of the guards standing nearest the fixer edged away from him.

But then Yakov cried out, "It's all a fairy tale, every bit of it. Who could ever believe such a thing? Not me!" His voice quavered and his face was bloodless.

"Those who can understand will believe," said the priest.

"Be respectful if you know what's good for you," Grubeshov said heatedly in an undertone. "Listen and learn!"

"How can it be so if the opposite is true," the fixer shouted, his throat thick. "It's all right to theorize with a fact or two but I don't recognize the truth in what's been said. If you please, your reverence, everybody knows the Bible forbids us to eat blood. That's all over the book, in the laws and everything. I've forgotten most of what I knew about the sacred books, but I've lived among the people and know their customs. Many an egg my own wife would throw out to the goat if it had the smallest spot of blood on the yolk. 'Raisl,' I said, 'take it easy. We can't afford to live like kings,' but there was no getting the egg back on the table, either by hook or by crook, once she took it off, even admitting anyone wanted to, which I never did—you get used to the customs. What she did was final, your reverence. I never said, 'Bring back the bloody egg,' and she would have thrown it at me if I had. She also soaked for hours the little meat or chicken we ate, to wash out every fleck of blood, and then sprinkled it with salt so as to be sure she had drained out every last drop. The rinsings with water were endless. That's the truth of it, I swear. I swear I'm innocent of this crime you say I did, not you personally, your reverence, but some of the officials here. I'm not a Hasid and I'm not a tzadik. I'm a fixer by trade, it's a poorer trade than most, and formerly for a short time I was a soldier in the Imperial Army. In fact, to tell the whole truth, I'm not a religious man, I'm a freethinker. At first my wife and I quarreled about this but I said a man's religion is his own business, and that's all there is to it, if you'll pardon me for saying so, your reverence. Anyway, I never touched that boy or any boy in my life. I was a boy myself once and it's a time I find hard to forget. I'm affectionate to children and I would have been a happy man if my wife had given birth to a child. It's not in my nature to do anything such as has been described, and if anyone thinks so it's mistaken identity for sure."

He had turned to the officials. They had listened courteously, even the two Black Hundreds representatives, though the shorter of them could not hide the distaste he felt for the fixer. The other now walked away. One man in a round cloth cap smiled sweetly at Yakov, then gazed impassively into the far distance where the golden cupolas of a cathedral rose above the trees.

"You'd be better off confessing," Grubeshov said, "instead of raising this useless stink." He asked the priest's pardon for his language.

"Confessing what, your honor, if as I told you I didn't do it? I can confess to you some things but I can't confess this crime. You'll have to excuse me there—I didn't do it. Why would I do such a thing anyway? You're mistaken, your honor. Somebody has made a serious mistake."

But no one would admit it and a heavy sadness settled on him.

"Confessing how it was done," Grubeshov replied. "How you enticed the boy into the stable with sweets, and then two or three of you pounced on him, gagged his mouth, tied him hand and foot, and dragged him up the stairs to your habitat.

There you prayed over him with those black hats and robes on, undressed the frightened child, and began to stab him in certain places, twelve stabs first, then another making thirteen wounds—thirteen each in the region of the heart, on the neck, from which most of the blood is drawn, and on the face—according to your cabalistic books. You tormented and terrified him, enjoying the full shuddering terror of the child victim and his piteous pleas for mercy, in the meanwhile collecting his dripping lifeblood into bottles until you bled him white. The five or six litres of warm blood you put into a black satchel, and this, if I understand the custom, was delivered by a hunchback Jew to the synagogue in time for making the matzos and afikomen. And when poor Zhenia Golov's heart was drained of blood and he lay on the floor lifeless, you and the tzadik Jew with the white stockings picked him up and carried him here in the dead of night and left his corpse in the cave. Then you both ate bread and salt so that his ghost would not haunt you and hurried away before the sun rose. Fearing the discovery of the bloodstains on your floor, you later sent one of your Jews to burn down Nikolai Maximovitch's stable. That is what you ought to confess."

The fixer, moaning, wrung his hands and beat them against his chest. He looked for Bibikov but the Investigating Magistrate and his assistant had disappeared.

"Take him up to the cave," Grubeshov ordered the guards.

Shutting his umbrella, he quickly preceded them, scampering up the steps, and entered the cave.

The leg chains were too short for Yakov to climb the steep steps, so he was seized under the arms by two of the gendarmes and dragged and pushed up, the other guards following directly behind. Then one guard went into the cave and the others shoved the fixer in through the narrow stone opening.

Inside the dank cave, smelling of death, in the dim light of a semicircle of dripping candles fastened on the wall, Grubeshov produced Yakov's tool sack.

"Aren't these your tools, Yakov Bok? They were found in your habitat in the stable by the driver Richter."

Yakov identified them in the candlelight.

"Yes, your honor, I've had them for years."

"Look at this rusty knife and these awls cleansed of blood with this rag, and now deny these instruments were used by you and your gang of Jews to perforate and bleed the body of a sweet and innocent Christian child!"

The fixer forced himself to look. He gazed at the gleaming point of the awl, and beyond it, into the depths of the cave which he now saw clearly, everyone present, among them Marfa Golov, her head wrapped in a black shawl, her wet eyes reflecting the candle lights, wailing on her knees at the bier of her Zhenia, disinterred from his grave for the occasion, lying naked in death, the wounds of his gray shrunken pitiful body visible in the light of two long thickly dripping white candles burning at his large head and small feet.

Yakov hastily counted the wounds on the child's bloated face, and cried out. "Fourteen!"

But the Prosecuting Attorney replied these were two magic groups of seven, and Father Anastasy, the stink of garlic rising from his head, fell on his knees and with a quiet moan began to pray.

V

The days were passing and the Russian officials were waiting impatiently for his menstrual period to begin. Grubeshov and the army general often consulted the calendar. If it didn't start soon they threatened to pump blood out of his penis with a machine they had for that purpose. The machine was a pump made of iron with a red indicator to show how much blood was being drained out. The danger of it was that it didn't always work right and sometimes sucked every drop of blood out of the body. It was used exclusively on Jews; only their penises fitted it.

In the morning the guards came into the cell and awakened him roughly. He was searched carefully and ordered to dress. Yakov was manacled and chained, then marched up two flights of stairs—he had hoped to Bibikov's office but it was to the Prosecuting Attorney's across the hall. In the anteroom, on a bench against the wall in the rear two men in threadbare suits looked up furtively at the prisoner, then lowered their eyes. They are spies, he thought. Grubeshov's office was a large high-ceilinged room with a long ikon of a crucified blue-haloed Christ on the wall behind the prosecutor's desk, where he sat reading legal documents and referring to open law books. The fixer was ordered to sit in a chair facing Grubeshov, and the guards lined up behind him.

The day was uncomfortably warm, the windows shut against the heat. The prosecutor wore a light greenish suit with the same soiled yellow vest and black bow tie. His sidewhiskers were brushed, and he mopped his moist face and palms and wiped the back of his heavy neck with a large handkerchief. Yakov, disturbed by his bad dream of that morning, and almost unable to look at the Prosecuting Attorney since his performance at the cave, felt he was suffocating.

"I have decided to send you to the preliminary confinement cell in the Kiev Prison to await your trial," Grubeshov said, blowing his nose and cleaning it slowly. "It is, of course, not easy to predict when it will begin, so I thought I would inquire whether you had become more cooperative? Since you have had time to reflect on your situation, perhaps you are now willing to tell the truth. What do you say? Further resistance will gain you only headaches. Cooperation will perhaps ease your situation."

"What else is there to say, your honor?" the fixer sighed sadly. "I've looked in my small bag of words and I have nothing more to say except that I'm innocent. There's no evidence against me, because I didn't do what you say I did."

"That's too bad. Your role in this murder was known to us before you were arrested. You were the only Jew living in the district, with the exception of Mandelbaum and Litvinov, Merchants of the First Guild, who weren't in Russia during the time of the commission of the crime, perhaps on purpose. We suspected a Jew at once because a Russian couldn't possibly commit that kind of crime. He might cut a man's throat in a fight, or suddenly kill a person with two or three heavy blows, but no Russian would maliciously torture an innocent child by inflicting forty-seven deadly wounds on his body."

"Neither would I," said the fixer. "It's not in my nature, whatever else is."

"The weight of the evidence is against you."

"Then maybe the evidence is wrong, your honor?"

"Evidence is evidence, it can't be wrong."

Grubeshov's voice became persuasive. "Tell me the honest truth, Yakov Bok, didn't the Jewish Nation put you up to this crime? You seem like a serious person—perhaps you were unwilling to do it but they urged it on you, made threats or promises of certain sorts, and you reluctantly carried out the murder for them? To put it in other words, wasn't it their idea rather than yours? If you'll admit that, I'll tell you frankly—I'll put it this way—your life would be easier. We will not prosecute to the full extent of our powers. Perhaps after a short while you will be paroled and your sentence suspended. In other words, there are 'possibilities.' All we ask is your signature—that's not so much."

Grubeshov's face glistened, as though he were making a greater effort than was apparent.

"How could I do such a thing, your honor? I couldn't do such a thing. Why should I blame it on innocent people?"

"History has proved they are not so innocent. Besides I don't understand your false scruples. After all, you're an admitted freethinker, this admission occurred in my presence. The Jews mean very little to you. I size you up as a man who is out for himself, though I can't blame you. Come, here is an opportunity to free yourself from the confines of the net you have fallen into."

"If the Jews don't mean anything to me, then why am I here?"

"You are foolish to lend yourself to their evil aims. What have they done for you?"

"At the very least, your honor, they've let me alone. No, I couldn't sign such a thing."

"Then keep in mind that the consequences for you can be very grave. The sentence of the court will be the least of your worries."

"Please," said the fixer, breathing heavily, "do you really believe those stories about magicians stealing the blood out of a murdered Christian child to mix in with matzos? You are an educated man and would surely not believe such superstitions."

Grubeshov sat back, smiling slightly. "I believe you killed the boy Zhenia Golov for ritual purposes. When they know the true facts, all Russia will believe it. Do you believe it?" he asked the guards.

The guards swore they did.

"Of course we believe it," Grubeshov said. "A Jew is a Jew, and that's all there is to it. Their history and character are unchangeable. Their nature is constant. This has been proved in scientific studies by Gobineau, Chamberlain and others. We here in Russia are presently preparing one on Jewish facial characteristics. Our peasants have a saying that a man who steals wears a hat that burns. With a Jew it is the nose that burns and reveals the criminal he is."

He flipped open a notebook to a page of pen-and-ink sketches, turning the book so that Yakov could read the printing at the top of the page: "Jewish noses."

"Here, for instance, is yours." Grubeshov pointed to a thin high-bridged nose with slender nostrils.

"And this is yours," Yakov said hoarsely, pointing to a short, fleshy, broad-winged nose.

The Prosecuting Attorney, though his color had deepened, laughed thinly. "You are a witty man," he said, "but it won't do you any good. Your fate is foreseen. Ours is a humane society but there are ways of punishing hardened criminals. Perhaps I ought to remind you—to show you how well off you are—how your fellow Jews were executed in the not too distant past. They were hanged wearing caps full of hot pitch and with a dog hanging beside them to show the world how despised they were."

"A dog hangs a dog, your honor."

"If you can't bite don't show your teeth." Grubeshov, his neck inflamed, slashed the fixer across the jaw with a ruler. Yakov cried out as the wood snapped, one piece hitting the wall. The guards began to beat his head with their fists but the Prosecuting Attorney waved them away.

"You can cry to Bibikov from now to doomsday," he shouted at the fixer, "but I'll keep you in prison till the flesh rots off your bones piece by piece. You will beg me to let you confess who compelled you to murder that innocent boy!"

2

He feared the prison would go badly for him and it went badly at once. It's my luck, he thought bitterly. What do they say?—"If I dealt in candles the sun wouldn't set." Instead, I'm Yakov Fixer and it sets each hour on the stroke. I'm the kind of man who finds it perilous to be alive. One thing I must learn is to say less—much less, or I'll ruin myself. As it is I'm already ruined.

The Kiev Prison, also in the Lukianovsky, was a high-walled old gray fortress-like building with a large interior muddy yard, strewn on the iron gate side with junk piles—a broken wagon, rotting mattresses, blackened boards, barrels of rubbish, rock and sandpiles where prisoners sometimes worked with cement. A clear area between the administrative offices on the west and the main cell block was the promenade grounds. Yakov and his guards had got to the prison on a trolley, a ride of several versts from the District Courthouse where he had been in jail until then. At the prison the fixer was greeted by the cross-eyed warden, "Hello, blood-drinker, welcome to the Promised Land." The Deputy Warden, a lean, narrow-faced man with depthless eyes and a four-fingered right hand, said, "Here we'll feed you flour and blood till you shit matzos." The sub-officials and clerks rushed out of their offices to see the Jew, but Warden Gritzitskoy, a man of sixty-five, with a limp yellowish gray beard, a khaki uniform with gold epaulets, and a visored cap, shoved open a door and led the fixer into an inner office, where he sat down at his desk.

"I don't want your kind here," he said, "but I have no choice in the matter. I'm the Tsar's servant and follow his orders faithfully. You are the lowest of Jewish scum—I've read of your deeds—but nevertheless a charge of his Imperial Majesty Nicholas the Second. So here you'll stay till they tell me otherwise. You'd better behave yourself. Follow the rules and regulations and do as you're told. Quickly does it. Under no circumstances are you to attempt to communicate with any person outside this prison unless I authorize it. If you make trouble you will be shot in your tracks. Understood?"

"How long must I stay here?" Yakov managed to ask. "I mean considering I haven't yet been tried."

"As long as the proper authorities deem necessary. Now keep your questions to yourself and go along with the sergeant. He will tell you what to do."

The sergeant, a man with drooping mustaches, led the fixer down the corridor past some dingy offices from whose doorways the clerks were staring out, to a long room with a counter and several benches where he was ordered to undress.

Yakov changed into a sack-like white jacket, smelling of human sweat, and a pair of shapeless linen trousers. He was handed a shirt without buttons and a worn greatcoat that had once been brown and was now gray, to sleep in or under at night. As he was pulling off his boots to change into a pair of stiff prison shoes, a wave of oppressive darkness swept over him. Though he felt like fainting he wouldn't give them the satisfaction.

"Sit down in that chair for your haircut," the sergeant ordered.

Yakov sat down in a straightback chair, but as the prison barber was about to crop his hair with a pair of large clippers, the sergeant, checking his official paper, stopped him.

"Never mind that. The orders say let him keep his head of hair."

"It's always like that," said the barber, incensed. "These pricks are born with privileges."

"Cut it off!" shouted Yakov, "cut off my hair!"

"Silence!" ordered the sergeant. "Learn to follow orders. Move on!"

He unlocked a metal door with a large key and followed the fixer down a dimly lit dank corridor to a large crowded cell with a barred grating on one side, and a wall on the other containing two high small dirty windows through which little light penetrated. A smelly urinal, no more than an open drain, ran along the rear wall of the cell.

"It's the thirty-day cell," said the sergeant. "You stay here for a month and either you go on trial or they transfer you elsewhere."

"Where elsewhere?"

"You'll find out."

Wherever it is what difference does it make? the fixer thought blackly.

The noise in the cell quieted as the door clanked open, and the silence deepened as though a quilt had been thrown over the prisoners as they watched Yakov enter. After the door shut behind him they began talking and moving again. There were about twenty-five men in the room, their searing stench in the almost airless cell nauseating. Some sat on the floor playing cards, two men danced closely together, a few wrestled or sparred, fell over each other, got kicked and cursed at. An old fanatic jumped repeatedly from the seat of a broken stool. A man with a sick sunken face hammered his shoe with the heel of another. There were a few benches and tables in the cells but no cots or mattresses. The prisoners slept on a low wooden platform along the outer wall, raised a centimeter from the damp filthy floor. Yakov sat alone in the farthest corner, reflecting on his wretched fate. He would have torn out fistfuls of his hair but he was afraid to be noticed.

3

A guard with a gun outside the grating shouted "Supper!" and two other guards opened the cell door and delivered three steaming wooden pails of soup. The prisoners ran with a roar to the pails, crowding around each. Yakov, who had eaten nothing that day, got up slowly. A guard handed out a wooden spoon to one prisoner in each group around the three pails. Sitting on the floor before his pail, the prisoner was allowed to eat ten spoonfuls of the watery cabbage soup, thickened with a bit of barley, then had to pass the spoon to the next one in line. Those who tried to take extra spoonfuls were beaten by the others. After each prisoner had had his quota, the first began again.

Yakov edged close to the nearest pail but the one eating the soup, a clubfoot with a scarred head, stopped spooning, reached into the pail, and with a shout of triumph plucked out half a dead mouse, its entrails hanging. The prisoner held the mouse by the tail, hastily spooning down the soup with his other hand. Two of the prisoners violently twisted the spoon out of his hand and shoved him away from the pail. The clubfoot limped over to the men at the next pail and dangled the mouse in front of their faces, but though they cursed him into the ground no one left the pail. So he clumsily danced around with his dead mouse. Yakov glanced into the second pail, already empty except for a few dead cockroaches floating at the bottom. He did not look into the third pail. Nor did he care for the colorless tea that was served in tin mugs without sugar. He had hoped for a bit of bread but was given none because his name had not been entered on the bread list by the sergeant. That night when the other prisoners were snoring side by side on the platform, the fixer, wrapped in his greatcoat, though it was not a cold night, walked back and forth the length of the cell in the thick dark until the nails in his shoes bit into his feet. When he lay down exhausted, covering his face with half a sheet of newspaper he had found in the cell, to keep off the flies, he was at once awakened by the clanging bell.

At breakfast he gulped down the weak tea that smelled like wood rotting but could not touch the watery gray gruel in the pails. He had heard the wooden pails were in use in the bathhouse when they were not filled with soup or gruel. He asked for bread but the guard said he was still not on the list.

"When will I be?"

"Fuck you," said the guard. "Don't make trouble."

The fixer noticed that the mood of the prisoners to him, neutral to begin with, had altered. The men were quieter, subdued. During the morning they congregated in groups close to the urinal, whispering, casting glances at Yakov. The clubfoot from time to time appraised him with shrewd and cunning eyes.

Yakov felt icicles sprout in his blood. Something has happened, he thought. Maybe somebody told them who I am. If they think I killed a Christian boy they might want to kill me.

In that case should he cry out to the guard and ask to be transferred to another cell before they murdered him in this? And if he did would he live long enough to get there? Suppose the prisoners rushed him and the guards made no move to defend him?

During the morning "promenade," the ten-minute exercise break when the men marched in double lines of twelve around the yard, ten paces between each group, as armed guards, some with coiled bullwhips, stood at the foot of the high thick walls, the clubfoot, who had slipped into line next to Yakov, said in a whisper, "Why isn't your head shaved like the rest of us?"

"I don't know," Yakov whispered. "I told the barber to go ahead and do it."

"Are you a stool pigeon or a squealer? The men are suspicious of you."

"No, no, tell them I'm not."

"Then why do you sit apart from us? Who the hell do you think you are?"

"To tell the truth my feet hurt in these shoes. Also it's my first time in prison. I'm trying to get used to it but it's not so easy."

"Are you expecting any food packages?" asked the clubfoot.

"Who would send me packages? I have nobody to send me a package. My wife left me. Everyone I know is poor."

"Well, if you get one, share and share alike is my motto. That's the rule here."

"Yes, yes."

The clubfoot limped along in silence.

They don't know who I am, Yakov thought. From now on I'd better be sociable. Once they find out it will be blows, not questions.

But when the prisoners had marched back into the cell there were whispered arguments among them, and Yakov, remembering how he had been beaten in the District Courthouse cell, felt himself sweating hotly.

Afterwards, another prisoner, a tall man with humid eyes, detached himself from a group of others and approached Yakov. He was heavily built, with a pale hard intense face, an almost black neck, and thin bent legs. He walked forward slowly, oddly, as though afraid something might fall out of his clothes. The fixer, sitting on the floor with his back to the wall, scrambled up quickly.

"Listen, little brother," the other prisoner began, "I am Fetyukov. The prisoners have sent me to talk to you."

"If you're worried that I'm a stool pigeon," Yakov said hastily, "you've got the wrong worry. I'm here like everybody else, waiting for my trial. I haven't asked for any privileges, not that they would give me any. I'm not even getting a bread ration. As for my hair, I told the barber to go ahead and cut it off but the sergeant said not to, though don't ask me why."

"What are you accused of?"

The fixer touched his lips with a dry tongue. "Whatever they've accused me of I didn't do. I give you my word. It's too complicated to go into without turning it into a wearying tale, something I don't understand myself."

"I'm a murderer," said Fetyukov. "I stabbed a stranger at the inn in my village. He provoked me so I stabbed him twice, once in the chest, and when he was falling, once in the back. That was the end of him. I had had more than a drop or two, but when they told me what I had done I was greatly surprised. I'm a peaceful man, I never make trouble if you don't provoke me. Who would've thought I could murder anybody? If you had told me any such thing I would have laughed at you to your face."

The fixer, staring at the murderer, edged sideways along the wall. At the same time he saw two other prisoners sneaking up on him, one from either side. As he cried out, Fetyukov reached behind him whipping a short heavy stick out of his trousers. He struck Yakov a hard blow on the head. The fixer went down on one knee, holding both hands over his pain-wracked, bloody head, then fell over.

He awoke, lying on the clammy wooden platform. His head ached sickeningly and a searing pain throbbed on the left side of his skull. His fingers sought out the wet swollen cut on his scalp. Blood dripped from it. He was anguished. Would he be beaten every time he was moved to another cell and met other prisoners? The fixer dizzily sat up, blood trickling down his face.

"Wipe it off," advised an old man with cracked eyeglasses, peering down at him. It was the slop-pail man who took care of the excrement buckets, brought in drinking water, and occasionally swept the wet floor. "Use the water bucket by the door."

"Why do you hit a man who has done nothing to you? What have I done to you?"

"Listen, matey," the old man whispered, "wash the blood off before the guard comes or the men will kill you."

"Let them kill me," he shouted.

"I told you he's a shitnose squealer," the clubfoot said from the other side of the cell. "Finish him off, Fetyukov."

A nervous murmur rose among the prisoners.

Two guards came running in the corridor, one carrying a shotgun. They peered through the grating.

"What's going on here? Cut out the noise, you pigs, or you'll live on half rations for a week."

The other guard stared through the barred grating into the gloomy cell.

"Where's the Jew?" he called.

There was dead silence. The prisoners looked among themselves; some glanced furtively at Yakov.

After a while Yakov said he was there. A low murmur came from the prisoners. The guard pointed a shotgun at them and the murmur ceased.

"Where?" said the guard. "I can't see you."

"Here," said Yakov. "There's nothing to see."

"The sergeant wrote your name on the bread list. You'll get your six ounces tonight."

"In the meantime you can dream of matzos," said the guard with the gun. "Also the blood of Christian martyrs, if you know what I mean."

When the guards left the prisoners talked excitedly among themselves. Yakov felt renewed fright.

Fetyukov, the murderer, approached again. The fixer rose tensely, his hand clawing the wall.

"Are you the Jew they say has murdered a Russian lad?"

"They lie," Yakov said hoarsely, "I'm innocent."

The mutterings of the prisoners filled the cell. One of them shouted, "Jew bastard!"

"That's not why I hit you," said Fetyukov. "Your head wasn't shaved and we thought you were a spy. We did it to see if you would report us to the guard. If you had done that it would have finished you off. The clubfoot would have knifed you. We are going on trial and don't want anybody testifying what he has heard in this cell. I didn't know you were a Jew. But if I had I wouldn't have hit you. When I was a boy I was apprenticed to a Jew blacksmith. He wouldn't have done what they say you did. If he drank blood he would have vomited it up. And he wouldn't have harmed a Christian child. I'm sorry I hit you, it was a mistake."

"It was a mistake," said the clubfoot.

Yakov went unsteadily to the water bucket. The bucket

stank but he sank to his knees and poured some water over his head.

After that the prisoners lost interest in him and turned to other things. Some of them went to sleep on the platform and some played cards.

That night Fetyukov woke the fixer and gave him a piece of sausage he had saved from a package his sister had sent him. Yakov gobbled it up. The murderer also handed him a wet rag to press down the swollen cut on his head.

"Tell the truth," he whispered, "did you kill that lad? Maybe you did it for a different reason? You might have been drunk."

"For no other reason," Yakov said. "And I wasn't drunk. It never happened, I'm innocent."

"I wish I were innocent," sighed Fetyukov. "It was a terrible thing I did. The man was a stranger to me. One must protect strangers, it says so in the Book. I had had a drop, you understand, and the next thing I knew I grabbed up a knife and he was dead at my feet. God, who gives us life, lets it hang by a thread. One blow and it's torn away. Don't ask me why unless the devil is the stronger. If I could give that man his life again I would. I would say take your life and don't come near me again. I don't know why I did it but I don't want to be a murderer. Things are bad enough as they are, who needs worse? Now they'll pack me off to a prison camp in Siberia and if I live out my term I'll have to stay there the rest of my days."

Little brother," he said to Yakov, making the sign of the cross over him, "don't lose hope. The stones of the bridge may crumble but the truth will come out."

"And till then," sighed the fixer, "what of my wasted youth?"

4

His youth dribbled away.

He had been imprisoned almost three months, three times

longer than Bibikov had predicted and God only knew when it would end. Yakov nearly went mad trying to figure out what was happening to him. What was a poor harmless fixer doing in prison? What had he done to deserve this terrible incarceration, no end in sight? Hadn't he more than his share of misery in a less than just world? He tried desperately to put together a comprehensible sequence of events that had led inevitably from his departure from the shtetl to a prison cell in Kiev; but to think of all these strange and unexpected experiences as meaningfully caused by related events confused him. True, the world was the kind of world it was. The rain put out fires and created floods. Yet too much had happened that didn't make sense. He had committed a few errors and paid for them in more than kind. One dark night a thick black web had fallen on him because he was standing under it, and though he ran in every direction he could not extricate himself from its sticky coils. Who was the spider if it remained invisible? He sometimes though God was punishing him for his unbelief. He was, after all, the jealous God. "Thou shalt worship no other Gods before me," not even no Gods. He also blamed the goyim for their eternal hatred of Jews. Things go badly at a historical moment and go that way, God or no God, forever. Did it *have* to be so? And he continued to curse himself. It could have happened to a more dedicated Jew, but it had happened instead to a recent freethinker because he was Yakov Bok. He blamed his usual mistakes—he could not always tell those of the far-off past from those that had led directly to his arrest in the brickyard. Yet he knew there was something from the outside, a quality of fate that had stalked him all his life and threatened, if he wasn't careful, his early extinction.

He hungered to explain who he was, Yakov the fixer from a small town in the Pale, an orphan boy who had married Raisl Shmuel and had been deserted by her, a curse on her soul; who had been poor all his life, had grubbed for a living, and was poor in other ways too—if he was that one what was he doing in prison? Who were they punishing if his life was punishment? Why put a harmless man into a prison with thick stone walls? He thought of begging them to let him go simply because he was not a criminal—it was a known fact—

they could ask in the shtetl. If any of the officials—Grubeshov, Bodyansky, the warden—had known him before, they would never have believed he could commit such a monstrous crime. Not such as he. If only his innocence were written on a sheet of paper, he could pull it out and say, "Read, it's all here," but since it was hidden in himself they would know it only if they sought it, and they were not seeking. How could anyone look twice at Marfa Golov, note her suspicious ways and those crazy cherries on her hat, and not suspect she knew more about the murder than she was willing to admit? And what had happened to the Investigating Magistrate whom he hadn't seen now in more than a month? Was he still loyal to the law, or had he joined with the others in their vicious hunt for a guilty Jew? Or had he merely forgotten an expendable man?

During Yakov's first days in the courthouse jail the accusation had seemed to him almost an irrelevancy, nothing much to do with his life or deeds. But after the visit to the cave he had stopped thinking of relevancy, truth, or even proof. There was no "reason," there was only their plot against a Jew, any Jew; he was the accidental choice for the sacrifice. He would be tried because the accusation had been made, there didn't have to be another reason. Being born a Jew meant being vulnerable to history, including its worst errors. Accident and history had involved Yakov Bok as he had never dreamed he could be involved. The involvement was, in a way of speaking, impersonal, but the effect, his misery and suffering, was not. The suffering was personal, painful, and possibly endless.

He felt entrapped, abandoned, helpless. He had disappeared from the world and nobody he could call friend knew it. Nobody. The fixer berated himself for not having listened to Shmuel's advice and staying where he belonged. He had got himself in a terrible mess, for what? Opportunity? An opportunity to destroy himself. He had fished for a herring and had been snatched by a shark. It wasn't hard to guess which of them would eat meat. And though he had now, at last, a little understanding of what was going on, or thought he had, he could of course still not resign himself to what had happened. In a philosophical moment he cursed history, anti-Semitism, fate, and even, occasionally, the Jews. "Who will help me?" he cried out in his sleep, but the other prisoners had their own anguish, their own bad dreams.

One night a new guest was let into the cell, a fattish heavy-faced young man with a blondish beard and small hands and feet, who wore his own clothes. At first his manner was morose and he returned furtive glances to anyone who looked in his direction. Yakov observed him from the distance. The young man was the only fat one in a cellful of skinny prisoners. He had money, bribed the guards for favors, lived well on packages from the outside—two large ones in a week—and wasn't stingy with food or cigarettes. "Here, boys, eat hearty," and he would hand out whatever there was to spare, yet keep himself well supplied. He even passed around green bottles of mineral water. He seemed to know how to get along, and some of the prisoners played cards with him. The clubfoot offered to be his personal servant but he waved him away. At the same time he was a worried man, muttered to himself, shook his head in disagreement, and sometimes tore at his round wrists with dirty fingernails. One by one he pulled off the buttons of his shirt. Yakov, though wanting to talk to the man, skirted him in the beginning, possibly because he didn't know what to say to people with money, partly because the man obviously didn't want to be bothered, and partly for reasons he could not explain to himself. The new prisoner dispensed his favors with pretended cordiality, his eyes unable to conceal the fact that he was not a cordial man, and then withdrew. He sat alone often, muttering. Yakov sensed this one was aware of him. They both minded their business and looked each other over. One morning, after the promenade in the prison yard, they began to talk in a corner of the cell.

"You're a Jew?" said the fat young man, in Yiddish.

Yakov admitted it.

"I, too."

"I thought so," said the fixer.

"If you thought so why didn't you come over?"

"I thought I'd wait a little."

"What's your name?"

"Yakov Bok, the fixer."

"Gronfein, Gregor. Shalom. What are you in here for?"

"They say I killed a Christian child." He still couldn't say it keeping his voice steady.

Gronfein looked at him in astonishment.

"So you're the one? My God, why didn't you tell me right away? I'm happy to be in the same cell with you."

"Why should you be happy?"

"I heard they had accused somebody of killing the Russian boy they found in the cave. Of course the whole thing is a manufactured fake, but there's a rumor running around in the Podol that a Jew was arrested, though nobody has seen you or knows who. Whoever he is he's a martyr for us all. Is it really you?"

"It's me, I wish it wasn't."

"I had my doubts that such a person exists."

"Only that and no more," the fixer sighed. "My worst enemies should exist like this."

"Don't grieve," said Gronfein. "God will help."

"He will or he won't as it suits him, but if he doesn't I hope somebody else will soon, or they might as well put me in the ground and cover me up with earth and grass."

"Patience," Gronfein said absently. "Patience. If there's not one way, there's another."

"Another what?"

"As long as a man stays alive he can't tell what chances will pop up next. But a dead man signs no checks."

He began to talk about himself. "Of course I'm better off than some I can think of," Gronfein said, looking at Yakov to see if he agreed. "I have a first-class lawyer already working for me in what you could call unofficial ways, and I'm not afraid to part with a few hundred rubles if I have to, because there's more where they come from. What I do is I'm a counterfeiter. It's not honest but pays well, and so what if it takes away from Tsar Nicholas—he's got plenty he takes from the Jews. Still, if a bribe doesn't work this time I don't know what will. I've got a wife and five children and I'm getting a little worried. This is the longest I've spent in a cell. How long have you been here yourself?"

"Here about a month. Altogether three months since I was arrested."

"Whew." The counterfeiter gave Yakov two cigarettes and

a piece of apple strudel from his last package, and the fixer ate and smoked gratefully.

Next time they talked, Gronfein asked Yakov questions about his parents, family, and village. He wanted to know what he had been doing in Kiev. Yakov told him this and that but not too much. He did, however, mention Raisl, and Gronfein squirmed.

"Not so much of a Jewish daughter I'd say. My wife couldn't have such thoughts, not with a goy anyway, let alone do such a thing."

The fixer shrugged. "Some do, some don't. And some who do are Jewish."

Gronfein started to ask something, looked around cautiously, then whispered he would be interested in knowing what exactly had happened to the boy. "How did he die?"

"How did who die?" the fixer said, astonished.

"That Russian boy who was murdered."

"How would I know?" He drew away from the man. "What they say I did I didn't do. If I weren't a Jew there'd be no crime."

"Are you sure? Why don't you confide in me? We're both in the same pot."

"I have nothing to confide," said Yakov coldly. "If there was no fowl there are no feathers."

"It's tough luck," said the counterfeiter amiably, "but I'll do what I can to help you. Once they let me out of here I'll speak to my lawyer."

"For that I'll thank you."

But Gronfein had grown depressed, his eyes clouding, and said no more.

The next day he sidled up to Yakov and whispered, worried, "They say on the outside that if the government brings you up on trial they might start a pogrom at the same time. The Black Hundreds are making terrible threats. Hundreds of Jews are leaving the city as if fleeing the plague. My father-in-law is talking of selling his business and running to Warsaw."

The fixer listened in silence.

"Nobody's blaming you, you understand," Gronfein said.

"If your father-in-law wants to run away at least he can run away."

As they talked, the counterfeiter, from time to time, nervously glanced in the direction of the cell door, as if he were watching for the guard.

"Are you expecting a package?" Yakov asked.

"No, no. But if they don't let me out of here I'll soon go mad. It's a stinking place and I'm worried about my family."

He drifted away, but was back in twenty minutes with the remnants of a package.

"Guard what's left here," he said to Yakov, "maybe I'm getting some action after all."

A guard opened the door and Gronfein disappeared from the cell for half an hour. When he returned he told the fixer they were letting him out that evening. He seemed satisfied but his ears were flaming, and afterwards he muttered much to himself for more than an hour. Later he was calmer.

That's how it goes with money, Yakov thought. If you've got it you've got wings.

"Something I can do for you before I go?" Gronfein whispered, slipping the fixer a ten-ruble note. "Don't worry, it's guaranteed good."

"Thanks. With this I can get myself a few things. They won't give me my own money. Maybe I can buy a better pair of shoes from one of the prisoners. These hurt my feet. Also if your lawyer can help me I'll be much obliged."

"I was thinking maybe you want to leave me a letter to send to somebody?" said Gronfein. "Just write it out with this pencil and I'll mail it along. I have paper and an envelope or two in my pack. Stamps I'll paste on on the outside."

"With the greatest of thanks," Yakov said, "but who have I got to write to?"

"If you have nobody to write to," said Gronfein, "I can't manufacture you a correspondent, but what about your father-in-law that you told me about?"

"He's a poor man all his life. What can he do for me?"

"He's got a mouth, hasn't he? Let him start yelling."

"A mouth and a stomach but nothing goes in."

"They say when a Jewish rooster crows in Pinsk they hear him in Palestine."

"Maybe I'll write," said Yakov.

The more he thought about it, the more he wanted to write. He had a desperate desire to make known his fate. On the outside, as Gronfein had said, they knew somebody was in prison but not who. He wanted everyone to know it was Yakov Bok. He wanted them to know his innocence. Somebody had to know or he would never get out. Maybe a committee of some sort could be formed to help him? Maybe, if you knew the law, it was possible for a lawyer to see him before the indictment; if not that, he could at least urge them to produce the document so they could begin his defense. In another week it would be thirty days in this smelly detention cell and he had heard from no one. He considered writing to the Investigating Magistrate but didn't dare. If he should turn over the letter to the Prosecuting Attorney things might go worse. Or if he didn't maybe his assistant, Ivan Semyonovitch, might. In any case, it was too great a chance to take.

The fixer then slowly wrote two letters, one to Shmuel, and another to Aaron Latke, the printer who had rented him a room in his flat.

"Dear Shmuel," wrote Yakov. "As you predicted I got myself into serious trouble and am now in the Kiev Prison near Dorogozhitsky Street. I know it's impossible but try to help me as soon as you can. Who else can I appeal to? Your son-in-law, Yakov Bok. P.S. If she's back I'd rather not know."

To Aaron Latke he wrote, "Dear friend Aaron, your recent boarder Yakov Bok is now in the Kiev Prison, in the thirty-day cell. After thirty days God knows what will happen to me. What's happened already is bad enough. I am accused of killing a Russian child by the name of Zhenia Golov, who I swear I didn't touch. Do me a favor and take this letter to some Jewish journalist or maybe to a sincere philanthropist, if you happen to know of one. Tell them if they can get me out of here I'll work hard my whole life to pay them back. Only hurry because it's a desperate situation and getting worse. Yakov Bok."

"Good," said Gronfein, accepting the sealed letters, "that should do it. Well, the best of luck to you, and don't worry about the ten rubles. You can pay me when you get out. Where there's that there's more."

The guard opened the cell door and the counterfeiter hurriedly disappeared down the corridor, the prison guard trotting after him.

Fifteen minutes later Yakov was called to the warden's office. He handed the remnant of Gronfein's package to Fetyukov to watch, promising to divide it with him.

Yakov hurried through the hall with the guard's gun at his back. Maybe it's the indictment, he thought in excitement.

Warden Grizitskoy was in his office with the Deputy Warden and a stern-faced inspector in a uniform like a general's. In the corner sat Gronfein, his hat on and eyes shut.

The warden waved the two letters, out of their envelopes, that the fixer had just written.

"Are these yours? Answer truthfully, you son-of-a-bitch."

The fixer froze, his heart sinking. "Yes, your honor."

The warden pointed to the Yiddish script. "Translate these bird droppings," he said to Gronfein.

The counterfeiter opened his eyes long enough to read the letters aloud in Russian, in a quick monotone.

"You Zhid bloodsucker," said the warden, "how dare you break prison regulations? I personally warned you not to try to get in touch with anybody on the outside without my express permission."

Yakov said nothing, staring, sickened to the pit of his stomach, at Gronfein.

"He turned them over to us," the Deputy Warden said to the fixer. "A law-abiding citizen."

"Don't expect a moral man," Gronfein said to nobody in particular, his eyes still clamped shut. "I'm only a counterfeiter."

"You bastard stool pigeon," Yakov shouted at him, "why did you trick an innocent man?"

"Watch your language, you," warned the warden. "A foul heart, a foul tongue."

"It's every man for himself," Gronfein muttered. "I have five small children and a nervous wife."

"What's more," said the Deputy Warden, "we have it in writing that you also tried to bribe him to poison the yardkeeper who saw you attempting to kidnap the boy in the brickyard, and also to pay Marfa Golov not to testify against you. Isn't that the truth?" he asked Gronfein.

The counterfeiter, sweat trickling from under his hat down his dark lids, nodded once.

"Where would I get the money to pay for those bribes?" Yakov asked.

"The Jewish Nation would supply it," answered the inspector.

"Get him out of here," said the old warden. "The Prosecuting Attorney will call you when he needs you," he said to Gronfein.

"Stool pigeon!" Yakov shouted, "bastard traitor—it's a filthy lie!"

Gronfein, as though blind, was led out of the room by the Deputy Warden.

"This is the sort of assistance you can expect from your compatriots," the inspector said to Yakov. "It would be best for you to confess."

"We won't have our rules flouted by such as you," the warden said. "To strict confinement you go, and if you have any more letters to write you'll write them in your own blood."

5

He was being boiled alive in the smothering heat of the small solitary cell they had thrust him into, the sweat drenching his back and flowing from his armpits; but on the third night the bolt was shot back, a key grated in the lock, and the door opened.

A guard ordered him downstairs to the warden's office. "Get a move on, you fuck, you're more trouble than you're worth."

The Investigating Magistrate was there, sitting in a chair, fanning himself with a wilted yellow straw hat. He wore a crumpled linen suit and a white silk tie, his pallid face contrasting with his dark short beard as he talked earnestly with the Deputy Warden, an uneasy-eyed man with smelly polished boots, flushed, and self consciously irritated when Yakov entered. When the prisoner, ghastly gray and close to shock, limped into the room, the two officials momentarily stopped talking. The Deputy Warden, gnawing his lip, remarked, "It's an irregular procedure if you ask my opinion"; but Bibikov patiently differed. "I'm here in the pursuit of my official duties as Investigating Magistrate, Mr. Deputy Warden, so there is nothing to fear."

"So you say, but why close to midnight when the warden's away on vacation and the other officials are sleeping? It's a strange time to come here on business, if you ask me."

"It's a dreadful night after a dreadfully hot day," the magistrate said huskily, coughing into his fist, "but much cooler at this hour. In fact there's a veritable breeze off the Dnieper once you are in the street. To be frank, I was already in bed, but the heat in the house was unbearable and the bedsheets perspired more than I did. I tossed and turned, then I thought, it's useless, I'll get up. Once I had dressed it occurred to me it would be helpful if I got on with official matters rather than lay around drinking cold drinks that give me gas, and curse the heat. Fortunately, my wife and children are at our dacha on the Black Sea, where I will go to join them in August. Do you know the heat rose to 40.5 in the shade this afternoon, and must now be hovering around 33.8? I assure you it was all but impossible to work in my office today. My assistant complained of nausea and had to be sent home."

"Go on, then, if you want to," said the Deputy Warden, "but I have to insist that I stay here as a witness to your questions. The prisoner's under our jurisdiction, that's clear enough."

"May I remind you that your function is custodial and mine investigatory? The suspect has not yet been tried or sentenced. In fact there is no indictment up to now. Nor has he officially been remanded to prison by administrative decree. He is simply here as a material witness. If you will allow me, I am within my rights to question him alone. The time may be inconvenient, but it is so in a formal sense only; therefore I beg you to absent yourself for a brief period, say not more than a half hour."

"At least I ought to know what you're going to ask him

about in case the warden wants to know when he gets back. If it's about his treatment in this prison, I warn you flatly the warden will be annoyed if you ask about that. The Jew hasn't been made any exception of. If he follows the rules and regulations he gets the same treatment as everybody else. If he doesn't he's in for trouble."

"My questions will not refer to his prison treatment, although I hope it is always humane. You may tell Warden Grizitskoy that I was checking some testimony of the accused made before me at a previous date. If he would like more precise information, let him telephone me."

The Deputy Warden withdrew, casting a sullen glance at the prisoner.

Bibikov, after sitting a minute with two fingers pressed to his lips, moved quickly to the door, listened intently, then carried his chair and one for Yakov to the windowless far corner of the office, and motioned him to sit down.

"My friend," he said hurriedly in a low voice, "I can see from your appearance what you have been through, and I beg you not to think me remiss or without feeling if I do not comment on it. I have promised the Deputy Warden to confine myself to other matters, and besides our time is short and I have much to say."

"That's fine with me, your honor," muttered Yakov, struggling with his emotions, "but I would like to know if you could get me a different pair of shoes. The nails in these hurt my feet though nobody believes me. Either let them give me a different pair or lend me a hammer and pliers so I can fix them myself."

He sucked in his breath and wiped an eye with his sleeve. "Excuse me for being out of order, your honor."

"I see we're wearing similar linen garments," Bibikov joked, fanning himself slowly with his limp hat. He remarked in an undertone, "Tell me your size and I'll send you a pair of shoes."

"Maybe it's better not to," Yakov whispered, "or the Deputy Warden would know I complained to you."

"You understand it wasn't I but the Prosecuting Attorney who ordered your imprisonment?"

The fixer nodded.

"Would you care for a cigarette? You know my Turkish beauties?"

He lit one for him but after a few puffs Yakov had to put it out. "Excuse me for wasting it," he coughed, "but it's hard to breathe in this heat."

The magistrate put away his cigarette box. He reached into his breast pocket for his pince-nez, blew on them, and settled the glasses on his perspiring nose. "I would like you to know, Yakov Shepsovitch—if I may—that your case holds an extraordinary interest for me, and only last week I returned in a beastly stuffy, crowded train from St. Petersburg, where I had consulted the Minister of Justice, Count Odoevsky."

He leaned forward and said quietly, "I went there to submit the evidence I had already gathered, and to request that the charge against you be limited, as I had already suggested to the Prosecuting Attorney, strictly to the matter of your residing illegally in the Lukianovsky District, or perhaps even dropped altogether if you left Kiev and returned to your native village. Instead I was expressly directed to continue my investigation beyond the slightest shadow of a doubt. I will tell you in the strictest confidence what most troubled me is that although the Minister of Justice listened courteously and with obvious interest, I left with the unmistakable impression that he expects the evidence to confirm your guilt."

"Vey iz mir."

"This was not stated so specifically, you must understand—it was an impression and I may possibly be misinterpreting, although I don't think so. Frankly, the matter seemed to revolve around an imprecise use of language, further confused by hints, hesitations, odd questions I did not fully understand, shadowy remarks, and so forth. Nothing—even now—is said absolutely directly, yet I am under pressure, as it were, to uncover evidence close to the prevailing belief. The Minister of Interior also has been telephoning me regularly. I will admit these pressures have made me nervous. My wife tells me I am more difficult than usual to live with, and there are signs of gastric disturbances. In her letter today she urged me to see a doctor. And tonight," he went on, lowering his voice to the dimmest whisper, "I had the impression on my way here that my carriage was being followed by another, though no doubt I am suggestible in my present state of nerves."

He thrust his pallid face close to Yakov's, continuing to whisper: "But that's neither here nor there. To return then to the facts: Count Odoevsky at one point offered to relieve me of the 'burden' of this case if I felt 'pressed or unwell,' or the work had become 'distasteful' or seemed to go against what he referred to as 'your creed.' And I believe I caught a clear hint that the purposes of justice might better be served by an indictment of murder for ritual reasons, an accusation which is of course poppycock."

"As for the murder," said Yakov, "if I had a hand in it let me live forever a cripple in hell."

The Investigating Magistrate fanned himself slowly with his hat. After again glancing at the door he said, "When I told the Minister of Justice—quite directly told him, nothing minced or hedged, shadowy remarks do not explicate or uphold the law—that my evidence pointed in the opposite direction, towards acquittal of the major charge, he shrugged his shoulders—the count is an imposing man, handsome, well-spoken, discreetly perfumed—as though perhaps to indicate I had not yet achieved true wisdom. And that's apparently where we left it, with a shrug that may mean much or little, but in any case a doubt. I can say in his favor that he is a gentleman. But I will tell you frankly that with the Prosecuting Attorney, my colleague Grubeshov, there are not even the slightest doubts. He has, I would say, convinced himself, perhaps almost before the fact. I say this after careful consideration. Grubeshov has more than once emphatically requested from me—in fact he has insisted on it—a severe indictment of you, mincing no words—for Zhenia Golov's murder, and I have categorically refused. Of course that adds to my nervousness. Yet for all practical purposes you should know this matter can't go on in such a way much longer. If I don't draw up the indictment someone else will. They will get rid of me, if they possibly can, and then I'll be of no use to you whatever. Therefore I will pretend to cooperate with them while I continue my investigation, until I have a foolproof case. I will then once more submit the evidence to the Ministry of Justice, and if they insist on a prosecution, I may reveal my findings to the press, which could conceivably cause a scandal. I would hope so. In fact I am already planning anonymously to give out selected information to one or two highly placed journalists as to the true state of affairs regarding the nature of the evidence against you, which up to now consists in nothing more than anonymous accusations and provocative articles published by the reactionary press. I decided this as I lay awake tonight. My visit to you, which I decided on impulsively, is to inform you of my plans so that you will not think you are without a friend in the world. I know you are falsely accused. I am determined to continue this investigation to the best of my ability and powers in order to discover, and if necessary, publish the whole truth. I am doing this for Russia as well as for your sake and mine. I therefore request, Yakov Shepsovitch, though I understand how difficult your trials are, your confidence and patience."

"Thanks, your honor," said Yakov with a tremor in his voice. "If you're used to stepping out of the hut once in a while to take a breath of fresh air in your lungs while you look at the sky to see if it's going to rain tomorrow—not that it makes any difference—it's hard to go on living in a small dark solitary cell; still now I know there's somebody who knows what I did and what I didn't do, and who I trust, though I would like to hear what you mean about 'the true state of affairs' that you mentioned before when you were talking about the journalists."

Bibikov went again to the door, opened it softly, peered out, closed it carefully and returned to his chair, once more bringing his face close to Yakov's.

"My theory is that the murder was committed by Marfa Golov's gang of criminals and housebreakers, in particular her blinded lover, one Stepan Bulkin, who, thus, perhaps, revenged himself on her for the loss of his eyesight. The boy was grossly neglected by his mother. She is a wicked woman, stupid yet cunning, with the morals of a hardened prostitute. Zhenia had apparently threatened, possibly more than once, to expose their criminal activities to the District Police, and it is possible that the lover convinced her the child had to be done away with. Perhaps the incident occurred during a time of general drunkenness. The boy was killed, I am all but certain, in his mother's house, Bulkin taking the leading role in the beastly sacrifice. They obviously tortured the poor child, inflicting a large number of wounds on his body and soaking up the blood as it spurted forth, in order not to leave any telltale stains on the floor—I would imagine they burned the bloody rags—and finally plunging the knife deep into the child's heart. I have not been able to determine whether Marfa witnessed his death or had passed out drunk."

The fixer shuddered. "How did you find out about that, your honor?"

"I can't tell you except to say generally that thieves quarrel, and as I said before, Marfa is stupid, canny as she is. The true story will come out in time if we work patiently. We have reason to believe she kept her son's body in the bathtub for a week before it was removed to the cave. We are searching for one of the neighbors who is believed to have seen it there and soon thereafter moved out of the vicinity, frightened out of her wits I would guess, by Marfa's threats. To save their own necks, naturally the thieves are going along with the blood ritual accusation against you. How that originated we are not exactly sure. We suspect Marfa herself wrote an anonymous letter suggesting that Jews did the evil work. The original letter to the police was signed 'A Christian.' I know that, though I have not been able to put my hands on the document yet. At any rate the thieves will do whatever they can to uphold the charge, even if it means testifying against you as eyewitnesses to your 'crime.' They are frightened and dangerous men. And my assistant, Ivan Semyonovitch, has ascertained that Proshko and Richter burned down Nikolai Maximovitch's stable, though without the help of any Jewish demons."

"So that's how it is," sighed Yakov. "Behind the world lies another world. Excuse me, but does the Prosecuting Attorney also know what you just told me?"

Bibikov fanned himself leisurely with his hat.

"To be absolutely truthful I don't know what he knows or doesn't. I am not one of his confidants—but I suspect he knows more than he admits. I also know he is an ambitious and opportunistic man, a restless careerist. In his youthful days he was a strong Ukrainophil, but since attaining public office he has become more Russian than the Tsar. Someday, if God's mercy does not intervene, he will be a justice of our Supreme Court—it is without a doubt what he wants most. If that should happen there will be 'justice' without justice." The magistrate caught himself and paused. "I will be grateful to you if you do not repeat this, Yakov Shepsovitch, or my other remarks to you, to anyone. Like most Russians I talk too much; however I wanted in particular to ease your mind a bit. I ask this for our mutual protection."

"Who would I repeat it to even if there was somebody here who wasn't my enemy? But what I want to ask is, does the Prosecuting Attorney truly think I killed the boy, and does he really believe those things the priest said at the cave?"

"As to his true beliefs I must again confess my ignorance although I see him often in the course of official business. He tends to believe, in my opinion, what those around him believe. I don't pretend to know how much claptrap and superstition there is in his soul or what purpose it serves. But he is not a fool, I assure you. He knows our history and is quite familiar with the law though not greatly responsive to its spirit. He surely knows that Alexander I, in 1817, and Nicholas I, in 1835, by official ukase prohibited blood libels against Jews living on Russian soil, although it is quite true that these libels have been revived within the last generation to provoke pogroms for political purposes. I do not have to tell you there has been a disappointing retreat of progress in recent times, whatever it is we call progress, especially disappointing because of the little we have had since the Emancipation. There's something cursed, it seems to me, about a country where men have owned men as property. The stink of that corruption never escapes the soul, and it is the stink of future evil. Still, the original decrees have not been withdrawn and are therefore the law. If Grubeshov has at all looked into this subject, as I have recently, he will also know, for instance, that certain Roman Catholic Popes, including an Innocent, a Paul, a Gregory, and a Clement, whose numerical designations I have forgotten, issued certain interdictions against this accusation. I believe one of them called it 'a baseless and wicked invention.' Interestingly, I learned that this very same blood accusation made against the Jews was used by pagans of the first century to justify the oppression and slaughter of the early Christians. They too were called 'blood drinkers,' for reasons you would understand if you knew the Catholic mass. The blood mystique arose in a belief of primitive people that there is a miraculous power in blood. It is, of course, a most dramatic substance in color and composition."

"So if the Pope said no why does the priest say yes?"

"Father Anastasy is a charlatan. He has written a stupid anti-Semitic brochure in Latin which brought him to the attention of the United Nobility, who have urged him to testify against you. Around him much of the pogrom agitation is centered. It is interesting to me that quite shortly after the appearance of his brochure, Zhenia Golov was murdered. He is a defrocked Catholic priest, for some disgraceful act, we think an embezzlement of church funds, who only lately came from Poland and joined the Orthodox Church, whose Synod, incidentally, does not support the accusation against you, although it does not deny it. The Metropolitan of Kiev has informed me he will not issue a statement."

"That won't keep the water from boiling," the fixer muttered.

"I'm afraid not. Do you know any French, Yakov Shepsovitch?" Bibikov asked.

"Not that I can think of, your honor."

"The French have a saying, 'The more it changes, the more it remains the same.' You must admit there may be a certain truth to that, especially with reference to what we call 'society.' In effect it has not changed in its essentials from what it was in the dim past, even though we tend loosely to think of civilization as progress. I frankly no longer believe in that concept. I respect man for what he has to go through in life, and sometimes for how he does it, but he has changed little since we began to pretend he was civilized, and the same thing may be said about our society. That is how I feel, but having made that confession let me say, as you may have guessed, that I am somewhat of a meliorist. That is to say, I act as an optimist because I find I cannot act at all, as a pessimist. One often feels helpless in the face of the confusion of these times, such a mass of apparently uncontrollable events and experiences to live through, attempt to understand, and if at all possible, give order to; but one must not withdraw from the task if he has some small thing to offer—he does so at the risk of diminishing his humanity.

"Be that as it may," he went on, "if the Prosecuting Attorney had indulged in a bit of Old Testament research he would, I am sure, be familiar with the prohibitions in Leviticus that Jews may not eat any manner of blood. I can't quote it exactly—my notes are on my desk at home—but the Lord warned that whoever ate blood, Israelite or stranger, He would cut him off from his people. Nor would He afterwards allow King David to raise a temple to Him, because he had fought in many wars and spilled much blood. He is a consistent God, if not gentle. I have also learned from certain Russian authorities of the Old Testament and other Jewish sacred texts that there does not exist in those writings a record of any law or custom which permits a Jew to use blood, or specifically Christian blood, for religious purposes. According to those I have consulted—secretly, you understand—the prohibition against using any blood whatsoever for whatever purpose was never retracted or altered in later Jewish writings of law, literature, or medicine. There is not, for instance, any record of a prescription of blood for use in medicine, internal or external. Et cetera, et cetera. There are many such facts that Grubeshov ought to have familiarized himself with—and I assure you I am strongly contemplating submitting him a summary of my researches for his reflection. Frankly, Yakov Shepsovitch, I am embarrassed to belittle a colleague to you in this manner but I have come to the unhappy conclusion that whatever he knows, or may know through my intervention, that might be helpful to you in establishing your innocence is, if not actually useless, then at least antithetical to his aims and purposes. He also would like to have you convicted."

Yakov wrung his hands. "If so what am I to do, your honor? Will I be abandoned to die in this prison?"

"Who has abandoned you?" the Investigating Magistrate asked, looking at him gently.

"Not you, of course, and I thank what little luck I have for that. But if Mr. Grubeshov has no use for your evidence I might rot here for years. After all, how long are our lives? Couldn't you put out an indictment of some small sort against me so that I could at least see a lawyer?"

"No, that wouldn't work at all. Murder is what I would be compelled to charge you with. I'm afraid to start off that way. Your lawyer will appear in due course. But at present no lawyer can do as much for you as I, Yakov Shepsovitch. And when the time comes that he can, I'll see to it that you have a good one. I already have in mind someone who is a vigorous and courageous man of the most excellent reputation. I will sound him out in the near future, and I am sure he will agree to represent you."

The fixer thanked him.

Bibikov, after looking at his watch, suddenly rose. "Yakov Shepsovitch, what more can I tell you? Take heart in the truth and endure your trials. Sustain yourself in your innocence."

"It's not so easy, your honor. I'm not suited for this kind of life. I find it hard to imitate a dog. That's not exactly what I mean but turned around a bit it is. What I mean is that I'm sick of prison, also I'm not a brave man. To tell the truth I have terrible fears that never leave me, day or night."

"No one says it's easy. Still, you are not alone."

"In my cell I'm alone. In my thoughts I'm alone. I don't want to sound bitter to you because I'm thankful for your help—"

"My dear friend," said Bibikov gravely, "your bitterness doesn't offend me. My worry is not to fail you."

"Why should you fail me?" the fixer said, anxiously rising.

"Who can say?" Bibikov put on his limp hat. "Partly it is our situation in this unfortunate country that causes me doubt. Russia is such a complex, long-suffering, ignorant, torn and helpless nation. In one sense we are all prisoners here." He paused, combed his beard with his fingers, then said, "There is so much to be done that demands the full capacities of our hearts and souls, but, truly, where shall we begin? Perhaps I will begin with you? Keep in mind, Yakov Shepsovitch, that if your life is without value, so is mine. If the law does not protect you, it will not, in the end, protect me. Therefore I dare not fail you, and that is what causes me anxiety—that I must not fail you. Now permit me to say good night. Let us both somehow try to sleep and perhaps tomorrow will be better. Thank God for tomorrow."

Yakov seized his hand to press to his lips but Bibikov had gone.

6

A prisoner, an anguished and desperate man, was locked in the next cell. The minute in, he began to pound with his shoe, or both shoes, against the wall. The noise came through distantly and Yakov pounded back with his shoe. But when the man shouted he could somehow be heard, though not his words. They shouted to each other at various times of the day and night as loudly as they could—it sounded to the fixer as though someone was trying to tell him a heartbreaking tale, and he wanted with all his heart to hear and then tell his own; but the man's shouts, cries, questions, were muffled, indistinguishable. So were his, the fixer knew.

The isolation cells were rectangular cubicles, the walls of brick and cement, the outer wall containing a single three-barred window a half meter above the prisoner's head. The door was made of solid iron with a peephole at eye level, through which the guard, when he was there, peered; and though Yakov could understand what was yelled at him from the corridor, when either prisoner shouted at the other through the spy hole, neither could understand. The openings were small, and reverberations in the corridor muffled the words and turned them into noise.

Once a guard with a dark face and stupid eyes, appearing in the cell block, heard them shouting to each other and cursed them both. He ordered the other prisoner to shut up or he would beat his head to a pulp, and to Yakov he said, "No more noise out of you or I'll shoot your Jew cock off." When he was gone both men resumed beating on the wall. The guard came once a day with a bowl of watery, insect-ridden soup, and a slice of stale black bread; he also checked the cells at unpredictable intervals. Yakov would be sleeping on the floor, or pacing back and forth the meager distance of the cell; or sitting with his back to the wall, his knees drawn up, lost in despondent thought, when he became aware of a malevolent eye staring at him, which was at once withdrawn. From the number of doors opening in the morning when the guard and his assistant delivered the food, the fixer knew there were only two prisoners in that wing of cells. The other prisoner was on his left, and on the right the guards retreated fifty steps to another door which they opened with a key, then shut with a terrible thump and locked from the other side. Sometimes in the early morning hours, when the huge prison was steeped in darkness and silence although hundreds of men, more likely thousands, dreamed, moaned, snored and farted in their sleep, the prisoner in the next cell woke and began beating on the wall between them. He did this in quick bursts of sound, then slowly, as though he were trying to teach the fixer a code, and though Yakov counted the beats and tried to translate them into letters of the Russian alphabet, the words he put together made no sense and he cursed himself for his stupidity. He banged but what did it mean? Sometimes they uselessly banged on the wall at the same time.

To be imprisoned alone was the greatest desperation the fixer had known. He hadn't the wit, he told himself, to be this much alone. When the guards came with his bread and soup on his twelfth morning of solitary confinement, Yakov begged for relief. He had learned his lesson and would uphold every regulation if they kindly returned him to the common cell, where there were, at least, other faces and some human activity. "If you will tell this to the warden I'll thank you with my whole heart. It's hard to live without a little conversation once in a while." But neither of the guards answered a word. It wouldn't have cost them a kopek to give his message to the warden, but they never did. Yakov sank into silence, sometimes imagining himself in the Podol, talking casually to someone. He would stand under a tree in the tenement courtyard with Aaron Latke and say how badly things were going. (How bad was bad if you were free?) Just a homey few words, better in Yiddish, but good enough in Russian. Or since freedom, at the moment, was out of the question, if he had his tools he could, after a morning's work, break a small hole through the wall and talk with the other prisoner, maybe even see his face if he stepped back a little. They could tell each other the story of their lives and stretch it out for months, then start over again if necessary. But the other prisoner, either because he was disheartened or sick, had stopped beating on the wall, and neither of them shouted to the other.

If he had forgotten the man he suddenly remembered him. One night a distant moaning broke into his sleep. He awoke and heard nothing. The fixer beat on the wall with his heavy shoe but there was no response. He dreamed he heard footsteps in the corridor, then a smothered cry awakened him again, terrified. Something's wrong, he thought, I must hide. A cell door clanged and there were steps of more than one man in the corridor. Yakov waited tensely in the pitch gloom, about to cry out if his door moved, but the steps went past his cell. The heavy door at the end of the corridor thumped shut, a key turned in the lock, and that was the end of the noise. In the terrible silence that followed, he could not get back to sleep. He beat on the wall with both broken shoes, shouting until he was hoarse, but could rouse no response. The next morning he was not brought food. They are leaving me to die, he thought. But at noon, a drunken guard came in with his soup and bread, muttering to himself. He spilled half the soup over Yakov before the prisoner could grab the bowl.

"Here he kills a Russian child and lords it over us," the guard muttered, his breath thick with alcohol.

When he had gone it came to the fixer, as he was very slowly chewing his black bread, that the guard had not locked and bolted the door. The hair on the back of his neck prickled. He got up in excitement, thrust two fingers through the peephole and almost fainted as the door slowly opened inward.

Yakov was overwhelmed in confusion and fright. If I step out they'll kill me for sure. Someone must be waiting on the outside. He peered through the hole but could see no one. Then he shut the door softly and waited.

An hour, if not longer, went by. Again he opened the

creaking door and this time quickly looked into the hall. To the right, at the end of the cell block the concrete door stood ajar. Had the drunken guard forgotten to lock that too? Yakov slunk along the corridor, stopped a few feet from the door and at once hurried back. Yet he did not go into his cell. Once more he approached the heavy door and was about to pull it open when it came to him thunderously that he was acting faster than he could think. So he ran back to his cell, entered, and slammed the door shut. There he waited, his flesh freezing, his heart a growing pain. No one came. But the fixer had thought it out and was certain the guard had left the door open on purpose. If he went through it and sneaked down the stairs at the bottom another guard would confront him, the one with the stupid eyes. He would look at Yakov and slowly raise his pistol. In the prison log the warden would write: "The prisoner Yakov Bok shot in the stomach while attempting to escape."

But he slid out into the corridor again, his thoughts flooded with freedom, this time going the other way, astonished he hadn't thought of that before. He looked cautiously to the left and right, then peered through the peephole into the other prisoner's cell. A bearded man, swinging gently, hung from a leather belt tied to the middle bar of the open window, a fallen stool nearby. He was staring down where his pince-nez lay smashed on the floor under his small dangling feet.

It took the fixer an age to admit it was Bibikov.

VI

In the luminous dark the ghost of Bibikov appeared wearing a large white hat. He had no glasses pinched to his nose, they were gone, and he rubbed the bridge in embarrassment.

"A terrible thing has happened, Yakov Shepsovitch. These men are without morality. I fear they will kill you, too."

"No, no," cried Yakov. "I don't believe in superstition."

The Investigating Magistrate lit a rose-papered cigarette and sat silent; then tried to say something and began to fade. He slowly disappeared in the dark, his white self dimming, as though evening had come and then night; and the soft glow of the cigarette diminished until it was out. All that remained was the dark memory of him hanging from the window, his bulbous eyes staring at his smashed glasses on the floor.

All night the fixer sat huddled in the corner of the cell, filled with the dread of dying. If he slept a minute his sleep was steeped in the taste, smell, horror of dying. He lay motionless in a graveyard, rigid, terrified. In the black sky were black stars. If he stirred he would topple into an open grave, amid the rotting dead, their dead flesh and putrefying bones. But more than death he feared torture. He feared being torn and broken before he died. He saw them dragging into the cell terrible instruments, monstrous wooden machines that racked and crushed the body; they hung his remains from a window bar. At dawn, when the dirty eye staring through the hole in the door touched him, he woke from shadowy sleep begging for his life. As the door creaked open he cried out; but the guards did not strangle him. One of them, with his foot, shoved in a bowl of gruel without a cockroach in it.

All day the fixer walked in his cell, sometimes he ran, five steps, three, five, three, breaking the circuit to hurl himself against the wall, or smash his fists against the metal door with prolonged cries of grief. He mourned Bibikov with great sorrow, great bitterness. For weeks he had lived with this potential savior in his thoughts, this just and gentle man; depended on him somehow to free him from prison, the trap laid for him, from the crime itself, the horrifying accusation. His only peace had come from these thoughts, that a good man was assisting him, and because of him, when the trial came, he would be judged not guilty. He had pictured himself freed, hurrying back to the shtetl, or running off to America if he could raise the funds. But now these hopes and expectations, these reveries on which he had lived, were gone, snatched from him without warning. Who would help him now, what could he hope for? Where Bibikov had lived in his mind was a hopeless hole. Who would now expose the murderess, Marfa Golov, and her accomplices, and proclaim his innocence to the newspapers? Suppose she left Kiev, fled to another city—or country—would they ever lay eyes on her again? How would the world ever learn about the injustice that had been committed against an innocent man? Who could help him if no one but his jailers knew where he was? For aught he meant to anyone, Yakov Bok did not exist. If they had no plans to kill him outright, then they would kill him slowly by burying him alive in prison forever.

"Mama-Papa," he cried out, "save me! Shmuel, Raisl,—anybody—save me! Somebody save me!" He walked in circles, forgetting he was walking, inventing fantastic plans to escape, each making his heart ache because each was impossible. He walked all day and into the night, until his shoes fell apart, and then walked in his bare feet on the lacerating floor. He walked in almost liquid heat with nowhere to go but his circular entrapment, striking himself on his journey—his chest, face, head, tearing his flesh, lamenting his life.

His crooked feet hurt unbearably. Yakov lay down in exhaustion on the floor. Torture by his own instrument—pain of body on deep depression. His pulpy feet, the soles covered with live scabs and red pussing sores, were like bags blown up about to burst. Then the ankles disappeared as the swelling moved up his legs. The fixer lay on his back, breathing badly, noisily. At least if it were cooler. How long can I stand this? His feet felt as though they were bound in chains and laid on fire. Both legs bulged to the knees. He lay on his back wishing for death. A cold eye stared at him. Ultimately he placed it at the peephole, an eye gazing at his suppurating feet, but the one who looked had nothing to say; and said nothing. "Help my poor feet," Yakov cried out, "it's a terrible pain." Whoever he was, if he heard, said nothing. Then the eye in the hole was gone. The fixer, feverishly shivering, his clothes wet, moaned through another night of pain. In the morning a key turned in the door and Warden Grizitskoy entered. Thinking of Bibikov, Yakov shrank from him. But the cross-eyed warden looked real and even human, and what he had seen in the next cell, dreamlike, unreal; he was at times not sure he had seen it. He didn't dare ask about the Investigating Magistrate. If they knew he knew they might kill him at once.

"What tricks are you up to now?" the warden demanded.

"Please," Yakov said, "my feet are infected from the nails in my shoes. I need a doctor."

"There are no doctors for the likes of you."

The fixer wearily shut his eyes.

The warden left. In the afternoon he returned with an aid from the prison infirmary.

"He's poisoned his feet," said the aid.

"Is it serious?" said the warden, "or will it go away by itself?"

"Both feet are full of pus. It might become gangrene."

"It would serve the bastard right," said the warden.

"All right," he said to Yakov, "go down to the infirmary. I'd let you rot here but I don't want the cell to stink any more than it does, or it will get infected from your germs. Move quickly now."

"How can I walk?" said Yakov. "Could Fetyukov or somebody help me?"

"Perfect company for a fellow murderer," said the warden.

"Fetyukov is no longer present. He was shot for disobeying orders and resisting a guard."

"Shot?" said the stunned fixer.

"For insubordination. He insulted a guard. Let that be a lesson to you. Now move along quickly."

"I can't walk. How can I go if I can't walk?"

"If you can't walk, crawl. The devil take you."

Like a dog, thought Yakov. On his hands and knees he moved out into the corridor, then painfully toward the door leading to the stairs. Though he crawled slowly the pressure hurt his knees and he could not keep his battered feet from scraping the floor. But he forced himself not to cry out. The warden and infirmary aid had left, and a guard with a shotgun followed the fixer as he moved toward the concrete floor. Going down the steep wooden steps, he had the weight of his body on his trembling arms, his feet bumping each step, and he more than once almost fell headlong down the stairs. When he paused, the guard prodded him with the butt of his gun. By the time Yakov reached the bottom of the stairs both his hands were scraped raw, and both knees bled. His back was black with sweat and the veins bulged on his neck as he crawled forward along the corridor and out the prison door into the yard.

The infirmary was in the administration section, on the other side of the quadrangle from the prison cells. It was the time of the ten-minute afternoon promenade, and the prisoners opened their double files for the fixer as they watched him haltingly crawling across the dirt yard.

"Five kopeks on the Zhid mule," shouted the clubfoot. A prisoner in a torn greatcoat turned and struck him across the mouth. A guard beat the prisoner.

If I live will I make it? Yakov, nauseated, was close to fainting. Halfway across the yard his trembling arms gave out and he collapsed. Several prisoners broke from their lines, but the guard with the whip shouted it was forbidden. The sentries patrolling the yard pointed their rifles at the prisoners and they returned to the lines, but not the slop-pail man, the one with the cracked eyeglasses. He fished some burlap rags from a garbage pile in the corner of the yard and ran towards Yakov. Hurriedly he wound the rags around the fixer's hands and knees. The guard cursed but looked on When the rags were tied he prodded Yakov with his foot.

The fixer got up on his raw hands and bleeding knees and went on, blindly crawling across the yard. He climbed up the stone steps into the infirmary.

The surgeon, a bald-headed man in a soiled white linen coat that smelled of carbolic acid and tobacco, inspected Yakov's feet, smeared them with a thick yellow acrid salve out of a can, and after bandaging both feet with dirty bandages and swabbing his hands and knees with alcohol, ordered the fixer into bed. This was the first bed he had been in since his arrest. He slept for a day and a half. When he awoke, the surgeon, smoking a cigar, unwound the bandages and operated on his feet. He cut into the pussing sores with a scalpel, without anesthetic. The prisoner, biting his lips to be silent, cried out at each cut.

"This is good for you, Bok," said the surgeon. "Now you know how poor Zhenia felt when you were stabbing him and draining his blood, all for the sake of your Jewish religion."

That night as he lay in bed in the infirmary Yakov had trouble breathing. Though he took in great gulping hot breaths through his mouth, the air seemed thin and insufficient. He did not at first fear asthma because he had often had trouble breathing under stress yet had not been seriously sick for years. But then the air turned heavy and stale. It was like trying to breathe metal. His chest heaved. His lungs weighed like rock, his breathing turned heavily raspy and he felt sick. The fixer clawed the mattress. "Please, who needs more? I have enough." He sat up, gasping for help but none came. Yakov got out of bed, his bandaged feet oozing blood, and tottered to the barred window. He lay under it, wheezing as he fought to draw into his lungs a few drops of air. In the midst of his exertions, he fell into an exhausted and perilous half-sleep, dreaming he was expiring in a windowless cell, seeing in his drowning dreams the miserable orphans' home, a crumbling tilted shack he had spent his childhood in; Raisl running from him in terror as though he had threatened her with a meat cleaver; and his imprisonment for a lifetime in Siberia for the murder of a boy whose suffering dead face haunted him still. He dreamed he had come upon him in the woods, a child carrying his schoolbooks, and had grabbed and choked him unconscious on impulse; then with Proshko's help, as the boy lay on the ground still twitching, he stabbed him thirteen times in the chest and drained five litres of his bright blood, a magnificent liquid. All night Grubeshov, standing with both yellow gaitered feet on Yakov's chest, harangued the victim in a thick-voiced tirade, and though the fixer frantically implored Bibikov's help, the Investigating Magistrate, at his desk in another room, would or could not be disturbed.

2

The warden assigned him to a new cell, a large dampish one on the ground floor of the solitary block of the south building of the prison, to the right of the administrative section and infirmary.

"It's just to keep you closer to my eye," he said. "There's talk you might try to escape with the assistance of your Jewish cohorts, which I strongly warn you against, because if you attempt it you're sure to get shot."

He pointed to the notice on the wall:

Obey all rules and regulations without question. If the prisoner is insubordinate or insulting to a guard or prison official, or he attempts in any way to breach the security of this prison, he will be executed on the spot.

"Furthermore," said the old warden, "the guard receives a monetary commendation for defending the regulations, so watch yourself. A smart dog recognizes the whip and avoids the lash."

He helped himself to a pinch of snuff and sneezed twice.

Yakov asked if he could have another prisoner, some decent person, for company. "It's hard to live without another soul to talk to, your honor. How is one to ease his heart a little?"

"That's the least of my worries," said the warden.

"Then could I have some kind of an animal to keep, either a cat or maybe a bird?"

"A cat out of your rations?—you'd both starve. Either he'd eat you or you'd eat him. Anyway, this is a prison for criminals, not a tea parlor or clubhouse. You're not here for comforts or coddling but for strict punishment for the mean murder you committed against a harmless child. Only you Jew prisoners have the nerve to make such requests. I've had enough of it."

In the fall the weather was bad, rainy and cold, and Yakov could see his breath in the cell. The asthma was not bothersome until he caught a cold, then it came on again, usually badly. Some mornings the outer wall of the cell, fronting the prison yard, was covered with lacy areas of frost. The inside walls, a foot thick, of brick, broken stone and cement, were scabby and cracked. After a heavy rain the greater part of the stone-paved floor was moist with seepage from the earth. Part of the ceiling above the window dripped. On fair days the small barred window, about a meter above the fixer's head, though dirty, let in light. The light was dim and on rainy days disappeared in the dark. After supper Yakov was given a small smelly kerosene lamp without its glass chimney, that burned until morning and was then removed. But one night the lamp was not given to him because, the Deputy Warden said, kerosene cost money. The fixer asked for a candle instead, and the Deputy Warden said he would see about that, but the fixer never got the candle. The cell was pitch black all night. I'll get the candle when I get the indictment, Yakov thought.

When the wind was strong on the outside, cold air floated through the cracked window into the cell. Yakov offered to fix it if they would let him have a little putty and a ladder, but no one was interested. The cell was cold but at least he had a mattress, a thin lumpy straw pallet whose last occupant—Zhitnyak, the small-eyed, black-fingered day guard, told him—had died of jail fever. The fixer kept the mattress on the dry part of the floor. There were bedbugs in it but he managed to beat out and kill some. His back ached after he had slept on it, and the straw in the sacking stank of mold, but it was better than sleeping on the stone floor. In November they gave him a ragged blanket. He also had a three-legged stool in the cell and a greasy small wooden table, one leg shorter than the other three. He had a jug of water in one corner of the cell; and in the opposite corner he kept the smelly can he urinated and defecated in, when there was something to defecate. Once a day he was allowed to empty the slop can into one of the barrels that were trundled past the cells by another prisoner, who wasn't allowed to speak to the fixer and whom Yakov was forbidden to address. He could tell from where the trundle stopped in the corridor that the cells on both sides of him were empty. It was a solitary solitary.

The bolted cell door was made of three sheets of iron, once painted black but now largely rusted; it had a peephole at eye level covered by a metal disk that the guard slipped aside to look in. Once every hour or so during the day a single eye roamed the cell. Zhitnyak was usually there in the daytime and Kogin at night; some days their times overlapped, and occasionally they exchanged shifts. When Yakov secretly pushed aside the disk and looked through the peephole, he could see Zhitnyak sitting in a large chair against the wall, hacking with his pocket knife at a stick, looking at pictures in a magazine, or dozing. He was a heavy-shouldered man with hairy nostrils and blackened stubby fingers, as though he had once worked with grease or lampblack that he had never got off. When he stepped into the cell he smelled of sweat and cabbage. Zhitnyak had a pockmarked face and an impatient manner. He was surly and unpredictable and sometimes struck the fixer.

Kogin, the night guard, was a tall man with a gaunt face and watery eyes, worn with worry. He spoke in a deep voice that seemed to rise from the ground. Even his whisper was low and heavy. Often he paced the corridor as if he were the prisoner; Yakov could hear his boots going back and forth on the concrete floor. At night Kogin opened the spy hole and listened to the fixer's asthmatic breathing and when he talked or shouted in his sleep. Yakov knew he was there, because when his nightmares or sleep-shouting woke him, he saw the dim light from the hall through the hole, and he saw the disk slowly moved back into place. Sometimes he woke up as Kogin was shining a torch through the peephole. Sometimes he could hear the guard's heavy breathing at the cell door.

Zhitnyak was the more talkative of the two, though he said

little enough. Kogin at first did not speak to the fixer, but once after he had been drinking he complained that his son had come to nothing. "He does no steady work," the guard said in his deep voice. "When will he get himself a job? I've waited thirty years for him to become a man and I'm still waiting. 'Wait,' I tell myself, 'he will change. He will become a man,' but he never does. He even steals from me and I am his father. My wife says it's my fault for not hitting him when he was a child and up to bad tricks, but that's not my nature. I had enough of that from my own father, may he rot in his grave. What's more, the daughter doesn't behave well either, but I won't go into that. The son will one day end up in prison the same as you, and it will serve him right. That's all that comes from a father's love."

In October Yakov had begged the guards to light the brick stove in the cell, but the Deputy Warden at first refused to spare the wood. Then one day in November Zhitnyak opened the door and two close-cropped prisoners, who sneaked looks at Yakov, brought the fixer a small load of wood tied in bundles. He had had a cold and asthma, and maybe one of the guards had reported it to the warden, who perhaps felt he had to keep the prisoner alive. The warden, as Yakov saw him, was not a vicious man. He was at best a disciplinarian, at worst, stupid. The Deputy Warden was something else. The fixer shuddered at the man's depthless eyes, narrow face, and four-fingered hand. Whatever he looked at he seemed to gnaw a little. His small mouth was crafty and hiddenly hungry. His boots stank of dog turd or whatever he used to polish them with. The guards wore guns in their holsters, but the Deputy Warden had a large gun on each hip. He had taken his time giving his permission for Yakov to have wood. The fixer disliked and feared him more than anyone in the prison.

The tall upright yellow brick stove leaked smoke at the top through a cracked brick, but Yakov preferred the smoke to the cold. He asked for the stove to be lit in the early morning, to get the frost off the wall although a small puddle formed on the floor when the cell warmed up; and he asked for a lit stove before supper so that he could eat in comfort. If the cell was too cold he could not taste the few bits of cabbage in his soup. If the cell was warm he tasted each morsel. To save wood he let the stove go out in the late morning. Afterwards, with his fingers he scraped the cold ashes out of the pit under the grate, put in a little kindling and some pieces of wood, then before supper, Zhitnyak came in to relight it. He did not seem to mind doing that, though he would sometimes curse as he was doing it. Yakov's hair was still not cropped but once was clipped a little by the prison barber; he was not permitted to shave, and his beard was growing long.

"That's to keep you looking more like a Jew," Zhitnyak said through the peephole. "They say the warden is going to make you wear a Zhid caftan and a rabbi's round hat, and they're going to twist earlocks out of your hair over your ears so you'll look kosher. That's what the Deputy Warden said they'll do."

The prisoners in the other solitary cells down the hall were served their meager food by other prisoners who were not allowed to serve the Jew. In Yakov's case they had to give the food to Zhitnyak, or Kogin, and he handed it to the fixer. This annoyed Zhitnyak, and sometimes when he brought Yakov's gruel or cabbage soup and bread, he said, "Here's your bowl of Christ's blood, drink hearty, mate." To enter the cell, the guard on duty, sometimes backed up by another guard in the hall holding a shotgun, more often alone, unlocked the six three-ringed bolts that had been attached on the door the day Yakov had been put into his cell. Hearing the six bolts being snapped back one by one, four or five times a day, put the fixer on edge.

During the late autumn Yakov did not see the warden, then one day he appeared in the cell "for purposes of official business."

"They've found a fingerprint on Zheniushka's belt buckle so we'd better take yours."

A detective appeared with an ink pad and paper and took Yakov's fingerprints.

A week later the warden entered the cell with a large pair of scissors.

"They've found some hairs on the boy's body, and we want to compare them with yours."

Yakov uneasily gave him permission to cut his hair.

"You cut it," said Warden Grizitskoy. "Cut off six or eight

hairs and put them in this envelope." He handed Yakov the scissors and envelope.

The fixer snipped off several of his hairs. "How do I know you won't take these hairs and put them on the boy's corpse and then say you found them there in the first place?"

"You are a suspicious type," said the warden. "That's true of all your race."

"Excuse me, but why should the warden of a prison look for evidence of a crime? Is he a policeman?"

"That's none of your damn business," said the warden. "If you're so innocent let's have the proof of it."

A louse fell into the envelope with the hairs but Yakov let it stay.

One morning the warden entered the cell with a pen, bottle of black ink, and several sheets of foolscap paper for some samples of Yakov's handwriting. He ordered him to write in Russian, "My name is Yakov Shepsovitch Bok. It is true that I am a Jew."

Later the warden returned and asked the fixer to write the same words, lying on the floor. Then he had Zhitnyak hold the prisoner's legs as he stood on his head while writing his name.

"What's this for?" asked Yakov.

"To see if the change in position changes your writing any. We want all possible samples."

And twice a day since he had been in this cell there were inspections of the fixer's body; "searches" they were called. The bolts of the door were shot back, and Zhitnyak and the Deputy Warden, with his smelly boots, came into the cell and ordered the fixer to undress. Yakov had to remove his clothes—the greatcoat, prison jacket, buttonless shirt, which were never washed though he had asked that he be allowed to wash them; and then he dropped his trousers and long drawers. He was allowed to keep on his threadbare undershirt, possibly so he wouldn't freeze to death. They also made him remove the torn socks and wooden clogs he had worn since the time the surgeon had lanced the sores on his feet, and to spread his toes apart so that Zhitnyak could inspect between them.

"Why do you do this?" Yakov had asked at the time of the first search.

"Shut your trap," said Zhitnyak.

"It's to see you haven't hidden any kind of weapon up your ass or in your clothes," said the Deputy Warden. "We have to protect you."

"What weapons could I hide? Everything was taken from me."

"You're a foxy sort but we've dealt with your kind before. You could be hiding small files, nails, pins, matches or such; or maybe even poison pills the Jews gave you to commit suicide with."

"I have none of those things."

"Spread your ass," said the Deputy Warden.

Yakov had first to raise his arms and spread his legs. The Deputy Warden probed with his four fingers in Yakov's armpits and around his testicles. The fixer then had to open his mouth and raise his tongue; he stretched both cheeks with his fingers as Zhitnyak peered into his mouth. At the end he had to bend over and pull apart his buttocks.

"Use more newspapers on your ass," said Zhitnyak.

"To use you have to have."

After his clothes were searched he was permitted to dress. It was the worst thing that happened to him and it happened twice a day.

3

He sank into deep gloom. I'll be here forever. The indictment will never come. I can beg on both broken knees but they won't give it to me. They will never bring me to trial.

In December, frost appeared on the four walls in the morning. Once he awoke with his hand stuck to the wall. The air was dead icy air. The fixer walked all day to keep from freezing. His asthma was worse. At night he lay on the straw mattress in his greatcoat, covered with the blanket, gasping, snoring thickly, wheezing as he desperately fought to breathe.

The one listening at the peephole shut it and moved away. One morning Zhitnyak helped Yakov pile up a new load of bundles of wood almost chest high against the outer wall. And in the evening there were pieces of meat floating in the cabbage soup, and some round flecks of fat.

"What happened?" the fixer asked.

The guard shrugged. "The higher-ups don't want you dying on them. You can't try a corpse in court, as the saying goes." He winked and laughed a little.

Maybe this means the indictment is coming, Yakov thought in excitement. They don't want me looking like a skeleton in the court.

Not only was the food better, there was more of it. In the morning there were two extra ounces of bread and the gruel was thicker, barley with watery hot milk. And there was a half lump of sugar for the tea, which diluted the rotten taste a little. The fixer chewed slowly, savoring what he was eating. A cockroach in the bowl no longer bothered him. He plucked it out and ate, afterwards licking the bowl with his tongue. Zhitnyak brought the food into the cell and left at once. But he sometimes watched Yakov eat, through the spy hole, although the prisoner as he ate usually sat on the stool with his back to the iron door.

"How's the soup?" Zhitnyak asked through the hole.

"Fine."

"Eat hearty." When Yakov had finished the guard was gone.

Though there was more to eat, the fixer hungered for more. The minute after he had eaten he was hungry. He had visions of Zhitnyak appearing one day with a huge plate of well-seasoned chicken soup, thick with broad yellow noodles, a platter of meat kreplach, and half a haleh loaf from which he would tear hunks of sweet foamy bread that melted on the tongue. He dreamed of rice and noodle pudding with raisins and cinnamon, as Raisl had deliciously baked it; and of anything that went with sour cream—blintzes, cheese kreplach, boiled potatoes, radishes, scallions, sliced crisp cucumbers. Also of juicy tomatoes of tremendous size that he had seen in Viscover's kitchen. He sucked a ripe tomato till it dribbled from his mouth, then, to get to sleep, finally had to finish it off, thickly salted, with a piece of white bread. After such fantasies he could hardly wait for the guard to come with his breakfast; yet when it came at last he restrained himself, eating very slowly. First he chewed the bread until its hard texture and grain flavor were gone, then bit by bit swallowed it down. Usually he saved part of his ration for nighttime, in bed, when he got ravenously hungry thinking of food. After the bread he ate the gruel, sucking each barley grain as it melted in his mouth. At night he worked every spoonful of soup over his tongue, each pulpy cabbage bit and thread of meat, taking it in very small sips and swallows, at the end scraping the bowl with his blackened spoon. He was grateful for the somewhat more satisfying portions he was getting, and although he was never not hungry, after this somewhat better, more plentiful food, he was a little less hungry than he had been.

But in a week his hunger was gone. He awoke nauseated one morning and waited a long day for it to go away but only felt worse. He felt sick in his mouth, eyes and in the pit of his bowel. It's not asthma, he thought, then if so what's wrong with me? His armpits and crotch itched, he was cold inside himself and his feet were ice. He also had diarrhea.

"What's going on here?" said Zhitnyak when he entered the cell in the morning. "You didn't eat your last night's soup.

"I'm sick," said the fixer, lying in his greatcoat on the straw mattress.

"Well," said the guard as he scrutinized the prisoner's face, "maybe you might have jail fever."

"Couldn't I go to the infirmary?"

"No, you had your turn there already but maybe I'll tell the warden if I see him. In the meantime you better eat this barley gruel. It's got hot milk in with the barley, and that's good for sickness."

"Couldn't I get out in the yard for a breath of air? The cell stinks and I've had no exercise for a long time. Maybe I would feel better outside."

"The cell stinks because you do. You can't go out in the yard because that's against the regulations when you're in strict confinement."

"How long will I be kept that way?"

"You'd better shut up your questions. That's for the higher-ups to say."

Yakov ate the gruel and threw it up. He sweated violently, the mattress soaked. In the evening a doctor came into the cell, a young man with a sparse beard and brown fedora. He took the prisoner's temperature, examined his body, and felt his pulse.

"There is no fever," he said. "It's some kind of harmless stomach complaint. You also have a rash. Drink your tea and never mind the solid food for a day or two, then you can go back on regular fare."

He left quickly.

After fasting for two days the fixer felt better and went back to gruel and cabbage soup, though not to black bread. He hadn't the energy to chew it. When he touched his head hairs came off on his fingers. He felt listless, despondent. Zhitnyak watched him through the hole, peeking in from the side. The diarrhea occurred more frequently, and after it Yakov lay, enervated and panting, on the mattress. Though he was very weak he kept up the fire in the stove all day and Zhitnyak did not say no. The fixer still felt cold and nothing seemed to warm him. The one good thing was that there were now no searches.

He asked again to be sent to the infirmary but when the Deputy Warden came into the cell, he said, "Eat your food and cut out malingering. Starving is what makes you sick."

Yakov forced himself to eat and after a few spoonfuls it was not too bad. Later he vomited repeatedly although there was nothing left in his stomach. And at night he had terrible dreams, visions of mass slaughter that left him sleepless, moaning. When he dozed again people were being cut down by Cossacks with sabers. Yakov was shot running into the woods. Yakov, hiding under a table in his hut, was dragged forth and beheaded. Yakov, fleeing along a rutted road, had lost an arm, an eye, his bloody balls; Raisl, lying on the sanded floor, had been raped beyond caring, her fruitless guts were eviscerated. Shmuel's split and broken body hung from a window. The fixer awoke in nausea, afraid to sleep although when he was awake the thick foul-smelling sickness was worse to bear than his nightmares. He often wished for death.

One night he dreamed of Bibikov hanging over his head and awoke with a heavy taste in his mouth, as if his tongue had turned to brass.

He sat up in fright. "Poison! My God, they're poisoning me!"

He wept for a while.

In the morning he would not touch the food Zhitnyak had brought in, nor drink the tea.

"Eat," ordered the guard, "or you'll stay sick."

"Why don't you shoot me?" the fixer said bitterly. "It would be easier for both of us than this bastard poison.

Zhitnyak turned pale and hurriedly left the cell.

He returned with the Deputy Warden.

"Why do I have to spend so much time on one goddamned Jew?" said the Deputy Warden.

"You're poisoning me," Yakov said hoarsely. "You have no true evidence against me so you're poisoning my food to kill me off."

"It's a lie," said the Deputy Warden, "you're out of your head."

"I won't eat what you give me," Yakov cried. "I'll fast."

"Fast your ass off, it'll kill you just the same."

"Then it's your murder."

"Look who's accusing other people of murder," said the Deputy Warden, "the blood killer of a twelve-year-old Christian lad."

"You shithead," he said to Zhitnyak as they left the cell.

The warden soon hastily came in. "What are you complaining about now, Bok? It's against the prison regulations to refuse food. I warn you that any more unorthodox behavior will be severely punished."

"You're poisoning me here," Yakov shouted.

"I know of no poison," the warden said sternly. "You're inventing this tale to make us look ridiculous. The doctor reported you had a stomach cold."

"It's poison. I can feel it in me. My body is sick and shrunken and my hair is falling out. You're trying to kill me."

"To hell with you," said the cross-eyed warden as he left the cell.

In a half hour he was back. "It's not my doing," he said. "I never gave such orders. If there's any poisoning done it's on the part of your fellow Jews who are the most notorious well-poisoners of all time. And don't think I've forgotten your attempt, in this prison, to bribe Gronfein to poison or kill Marfa Golov so that she couldn't testify against you in court. Now your Jewish compatriots are trying to poison you out of fear you will confess your true guilt and implicate the whole nation. We just found out that one of the cook's assistants was a disguised Jew and packed hin off to the police. He's the one who was poisoning your food."

"I don't believe it," said Yakov.

"Why would we want you to die? We want you sentenced to a severe life imprisonment as a lesson for all to see of Jewish perfidy."

"I won't eat what you give me. You can shoot me but I won't eat."

"If you expect to eat, eat what you get. If not you'll starve."

For the next five days Yakov starved. He exchanged the sickness of poisoning for the sickness of starving. He lay on the mattress, sleeping fitfully. Zhitnyak threatened him with a whipping but nothing came of it. On the sixth day the warden returned to the cell, his cross-eye watering and face flushed. "I command you to eat."

"Only out of the common pot," Yakov said weakly. "What the other prisoners eat I will eat. Let me go to the kitchen and take my gruel and soup out of the common pot."

"It cannot be allowed," said the warden. "You mustn't leave your cell. You are under strict confinement. Other prisoners are not allowed to look at you. It's all in the regulations."

"They can turn their heads while I draw my rations."

"No," said the warden. But after Yakov had fasted another day he consented. Twice a day the fixer, accompanied by Zhitnyak holding his drawn pistol, went to the prison kitchen in the west wing. Yakov drew his bread rations in the morning and filled his bowl from the common pot as the prisoners working in the kitchen momentarily faced the wall. He did not fill the bowl too full because if he did Zhitnyak poured some of it back.

He returned to half starvation.

4

He begged for something to do. His hands ached of emptiness, but he got nothing. The fixer offered to repair furniture, build tables, chairs, other pieces they might need—all he asked for was a few boards and his sack of tools. He missed his crosscut saw with the tapered handle, his small German plane, the hammer and tri-square. He could still feel each tool with his fingers and remembered how each worked. The sharp saw could rip through a six-inch board in ten seconds. He liked the touch and smell of wood shavings. There were times he heard in his thoughts the two-toned buzz of the cross-cut and the responsible knock of the hammer. He remembered things he had built with his tools, and sometimes in his thoughts he built them again. If he had the tools—if not his own, any tools—and some pieces of wood, he might earn himself a few kopeks to buy underdrawers, a wool vest, a warm pair of socks—other things he needed. If he earned a little money he secretly hoped he might pay someone to smuggle out a letter; or if not a letter then a message to Aaron Latke. But the tools and wood were refused him, and he cracked his knuckles constantly to do something with his hands.

He asked for a newspaper, a book of some sort, anything he could read to forget the tedium. Zhitnyak said the Deputy Warden had told him reading matter was forbidden to prisoners who had violated the regulations. So were paper and pencil. "If you hadn't written those sneaky letters you wrote, you wouldn't be in strict confinement now." "Where would I be then?" Yakov asked. "Better off. You might still be in the common cell." "Do you know when my indictment is supposed to come?" "No, and neither does anybody else, so don't ask me." Once Yakov said, "Why did you try to poison me, Zhitnyak, what did I do to you?" "Nobody said there was poison in that food," the guard said uneasily. "All they told me was to give it to you." Later he said, "It wasn't my fault. Nobody wanted to hurt you. The Deputy Warden thought you might confess faster if you got sick. The warden gave him a tongue lashing." The next morning Zhitnyak brought the prisoner a birch twig broom. "If you want to have it here, then keep your mouth shut from now on. The Deputy Warden says he's fed up of you talking to me. I'm not supposed to listen any more."

The broom was a stick with a bunch of thin birch twigs tied to it with cord. Yakov used it to sweep the cell every morning, working not too hard at first because he still felt weak from his sickness; yet he needed exercise to keep his strength up. He had again asked to be let out in the yard once in a while but, as he expected, the request was denied. Every day he thoroughly swept the stone floor, the wet parts and the dry. He swept in the corners of the cell, lifted his mattress and swept under that. He swept in the crevices between stones and once uncovered a centipede. He saw it escape under the door and the thought of that gave him a headache. He also used the broom handle to beat the mattress, its covering threadbare and split on both sides, the discolored straw visible so that he stopped beating it lest it fall apart. And when he beat it the mattress gave off a stench. Yakov patted it with his hands each morning as though to freshen it.

As much as he could he tried to arrange things so as to break the monotony of long stretches of time. When the bell rang in the corridor at 5 A.M. he arose in the cold dark, quickly cleaned the ashes out of the stove with his hand, raising dust he could smell, sweeping the small pile of ashes into a box they had given him for the purpose. Then he filled the stove with kindling, dry twigs, and some larger pieces of wood and waited for Zhitnyak, sometimes Kogin, to come in and light it. Formerly, the guard lit the stove when he brought in the prisoner's breakfast, and now that Yakov went to the kitchen for it, he lit the fire after the fixer returned with his food. Twice a day Yakov was permitted to go to the kitchen, not willing, when the warden suggested it, to give up the privilege of leaving the cell for a few minutes, although the warden gave his personal assurance that the food would be "perfectly healthful" if it were once again brought from the kitchen by the prisoners who delivered it to the guards.

"You have nothing to fear from us, Bok," he said. "I can assure you that the Prosecuting Attorney is most eager, as are all the other officials, to bring you to trial. No one would want to kill you off. We have other plans."

"When will my trial be?"

"I can't say," said Warden Grizitskoy. "They're still collecting evidence. It takes time."

"Then if you don't mind I'd rather keep on going to the kitchen."

As long as I can, he thought. I've paid for the privilege. He thought they were letting him continue to go only because they knew he knew they had tried to poison him.

After that the number of searches of Yakov's person was increased to three a day. His heart raced after these experiences, hatred thickened in it, and it took him a while to calm down. Sometimes after a search, to get the vile taste of it out of him, he swept the cell a second and third time. Or he collected the ashes out of the pit and had the wood ready for lighting long before Zhitnyak came in to take him to the kitchen to draw his supper rations. Though the stove was smoky the fixer ate near it, and after he had drunk the last of his tea, he threw in another stick or two of wood and lay down on the mattress with a sigh, hoping he could fall asleep before the stove went out and the cell became freezing. Sometimes the drinking water was ice in the morning and he had to melt it.

Passing water was another way to pass time. He urinated often, listening to the noise as the water rose in the tin can. Sometimes he held his water until it came forth with such heat and force his teeth hurt. When the can was collected was another momentary diversion. And every second day one of the guards filled the jug of water from which he drank and washed. There were no towels and he dried his hands on his ragged coat, or at the stove, rubbing them till they were dry. Fetyukov had given him a broken comb with which the fixer combed his hair and beard. Twice, thus far, he had been allowed into the bathhouse in the presence of a guard, when none of the other prisoners was there, and was permitted to wash his naked body with tepid water from a wooden bucket. He was worried to see how thin he had become. They would not touch his hair but once when his head was very lousy, the prison barber doused it with kerosene and let him comb the dead lice out with a fine comb. His beard went uncut though nobody objected that he kept it combed. Occasionally when Yakov complained that his nails were too long, Zhitnyak cut them for him. Afterwards the guard collected the nail parings and put them into an oilskin pouch.

"What's that for?" asked Yakov.

"For an analysis they want to make," said the guard.

One morning something new appeared in Yakov's cell. An old prayer shawl and a pair of phylacteries had been left there after he had gone to the kitchen for his food. He examined the phylacteries, then put them aside, but he wore the prayer shawl under his greatcoat to help keep him warm. He was wearing a heavier prison suit than the one he had first got, though much used by other prisoners in the past and already falling apart. He also had a small cap with ear flaps that did not fit him, which he wore with the flaps down. The seams of his greatcoat had split in places. Zhitnyak loaned him a darning needle and some thread to sew them with; and Yakov received a blow in the face from the guard when he told him, afterwards, that he had lost the needle. He really hadn't; he had hidden it inside the stove. But the coat seams opened again and there was no thread. His wooden clogs had been taken from him and he now wore bast shoes without laces; he was not allowed to have a belt. When Yakov put the prayer shawl on, Zhitnyak watched through the spy hole, often looking in unexpectedly as though hoping to catch the fixer at prayer. He never did.

Yakov spent hours pacing in the cell. He walked to Siberia and back. Six or eight times a day he read the prison regulations. Sometimes he sat at the shaky table. He could eat at the table but there was nothing else to do at it that he could think of. If he only had some paper and pencil he might write something down. With a knife he could whittle a piece of firewood, but who would give him a knife? He blew on his hands constantly. He feared he might go crazy doing nothing. If only there were a book to read. He remembered how he had studied and written in his stable room in the brickyard, at the table he had built himself with his tools. Once, just after Zhitnyak had peeked in, the fixer quickly piled up the loose wood at the wall and climbed up on top of the pile to see if he could look out the window into the prison yard. He thought the prisoners might be there on their promenade. He wondered whether any of those he knew were still in prison, or had they got out. But he could not reach the window bars with his hands and all he saw out of it was a piece of leaden sky.

5

The newspaper strips he was given to clean himself with Zhitnyak forbade him to read though Yakov managed to read some of them anyway.

"It's because you're an enemy of the state," the guard said through the peephole. "They're not allowed to read anything."

During the endless empty days, to forget his misery a little, the fixer tried to remember things he had read. He remembered incidents from Spinoza's life: how the Jews had cursed him in the synagogue; how an assassin had tried to kill him in the street, for his ideas; how he lived and died in his tiny room, studying, writing, grinding lenses for a living until his lungs had turned to glass. He had died young, poor and persecuted, yet one of the freest of men. He was free in his thoughts, his understanding of Necessity, and in the construction of his philosophy. The fixer's thoughts added nothing to his freedom; it was nil. He was imprisoned in a cell, and even in memory because so much that had happened to him during a life that had perhaps, at times, seemed free, now seemed designed to lead to this imprisonment. Necessity freed Spinoza and imprisoned Yakov. Spinoza thought himself into the universe but Yakov's poor thoughts were enclosed in a cell.

Who am I to compare myself?

He tried to recall the biology he had studied, and reflected on as much of history as he could bring to mind. They say God appeared in history and used it for his purposes, but if that was so he had no pity for men. God cried mercy and smote his chest, but there was no mercy because there was no pity. Pity in lightning? You could not pity anything if you weren't a man; pity was a surprise to God. It was not his invention. And Yakov also recalled tales by Peretz, and some pieces he had read in the papers by Sholem Aleichem, and a few little stories he had read in Russian by Chekhov. He recalled things from the Scriptures, in particular, fragments of psalms he had read in Hebrew on old parchment. He could, in a sense, smell the Psalms as well as hear them. They were sung weekly in the synagogue to glorify God and protect the shtetl from harm, which they never did. Yakov had changed them, or heard them chanted, many times, and now in a period of remembrance he uttered verses, stanzas that he did not think he knew. He could not recall a whole psalm, but from fragments he put together one that he recited aloud in the cell in order not to forget it, so that he could have it to say. In the morning he said it in Hebrew, and in the dark as he lay on his mattress, he tried to translate the verses into Russian. He knew Kogin listened when he said them aloud at night.

"Behold, he travaileth with iniquity;
Yea, he conceiveth mischief, and bringeth forth falsehood.
He hath digged a pit, and hollowed it,
And is fallen into the ditch which he made."

"I am weary with my groaning;
Every night make I my bed to swim;
I melt away my couch with my tears."

"For my days are consumed like smoke,
And my bones are burned as a hearth.
My heart is smitten like grass, and withered;
For I forget to eat my bread."

"Unrighteous witnesses rise up;
They ask me things that I know not."

"For I have heard the whispering of many,
Terror on every side;
While they took counsel together against me,
They devise to take away my life."

"Arise, O Lord; O God, lift up Thy hand;
Forget not the humble."

"Break Thou the arm of the wicked."

"Thou shalt make them as a fiery furnace in the time of
Thine anger."

"He bowed the heavens also, and came down;
And thick darkness was under His feet."

"And He sent out His arrows, and scattered them;
And he shot forth lightnings, and discomfited them."

"I have pursued my enemies, and overtaken them;
Neither did I turn back till they were consumed."

He thought of himself pursuing his enemies with God at his side, but when he looked at God all he saw or heard was a loud Ha Ha. It was his own imprisoned laughter.

6

I scratch at memory. I think of Raisl. I'm in prison so what difference does it make? The first time I saw her she was riding in her father's rickety wagon, drawn by the bony nag of late memory. She sat with the sick mother amid their few shreds of household goods. Shmuel was on the seat talking to himself, or the horse's tail, or God; he went where the nag pulled, but wherever he went he was going backward. They were coming from some place, where I don't know. Where can you come from in the Pale that's so different from where you're going? Everywhere he tried to make a better living, and everywhere he couldn't so he tried some place else. He came to our town, and the mother, fed up with adventure, died on the spot. After that her grave kept him in one place. Also from such a hard-luck father what kind of daughter could you expect, so I stayed away from her. Naturally I stayed away for the months I was in the army, but I also stayed away from her when I got back, though not for long. (She would have done me a favor to have got married while I was gone.) Anyway, she was a pretty girl, intelligent and dissatisfied, with even then a sad face. At least the right eye was sad; the left was neutral, it reflected me. I saw her many times in the market before I got up the nerve to talk to her. She scared me, I wasn't sure I had what she wanted. I was afraid she would rub my nose in my future. Anyway I saw the other young men looking at her and I looked too. She was a thin lanky girl with small breasts. I remember her dark hair in braids, deep eyes, and a long neck. She wore in the morning what she had washed out at night; sometimes the clothes were damp. The father wanted her to work as a servant girl but she wouldn't. She bought a few eggs from a peasant woman and set up a little stall in the market. Whenever I could I bought an egg from her. She lived with Shmuel in a hut off the road near the bathhouse stream. When I came for a visit they seemed glad to see me, especially the father. He was looking for a husband for her and a dowry didn't exist. If it existed it was a cherry pit. But he knew my type, that I wouldn't ask questions and he wouldn't mention it.

We walked together in the woods by the water, she and I. I showed her my tools and once cut down a small tree with my saw. I fixed up their hut a little, made a bench, a cupboard, and a few shelves out of some boards I was saving. If there was a little chicken to eat I came also on Friday nights. Raisl blessed the candles and served the food, it was very nice. We liked each other but both had doubts. I think she thought, He won't move, he isn't ambitious, he'll stay here forever. What kind of future is that? I thought to myself, She's a complicated girl and won't be easy to satisfy. What she wants she'll drive me wild to get. Still, I liked to be with her. One day in the woods we became man and wife. She said no but took a chance. Later it bothered her. She was afraid for her child once she had one, that it would be born crippled or with seven fingers. "Don't be superstitious," I said. "If you want to be free, first be free in your mind." Instead she began to cry. After a while I said, "All right, you've cried enough, so before it happens again let's get married. I need a wife and you need a husband." At this her eyes got big and once again were full of tears. She didn't answer me. "Why don't you talk?" I said. "Say yes or no." "Why don't you say love?" she said. "Who talks about love in the shtetl?" I asked her. "What are we, millionaires?" I didn't say so but it's a word that makes me nervous. What does a man like me know about love? "If you don't love me I can't marry you," she answered me. But by then the father had his nose in my ear. "She's a doll, a marvelous girl, you can't go wrong. She'll work hard and both together you'll make a living." So I said love and she said yes. Maybe my poor future looked better than her own.

After we were married, all she talked about was we must get out of Russia, including the father, because things were getting worse, not better. Worse for us and worse for the Russians. "Let's sell everything and leave while we can." I answered her, "Even if we sell everything we'll have nothing. Believe me, there's no shortage of places to go to in this wide world, but first I'll work hard and we'll save a few rubles, and in that case who knows where we'll get to. Maybe it'll take a year or two and then we'll leave." She looked at me with a tight face. "After another year you'll never go; you're afraid to leave." Maybe she was right but I said, "Your father changed places every time he breathed and all he's collected is air. I'll stay in one place and build up a little capital, and then I'll think of leaving." That wasn't strictly the truth. I was in no hurry to run to another country. Some men are by nature explorers; my nature is to stay under the same moon and stars, and if the weather is wet, under the same roof. It's a strange world, why make it stranger? When I was in the Tsar's army I was less afraid of the world but once I got home again enough was enough. In other words, in those days to make me move, somebody had to push. So she pushed. But we didn't get along so badly until another year or two went by and we still had no capital, and we had no children. Raisl was depressed and either said nothing, or wept, and never left off complaining. Our hut was divided into two small rooms. At night she stayed in bed while I sat in the kitchen. It was at this time that I began to read more. I picked up books here and there, a few I stole, and read by the lamp. Many times after I read I slept on the kitchen bench. When I was reading Spinoza I stayed up night after night. I was by now excited by ideas and I tried to collect a few of my own. It was the beginning of a different Yakov. I thought of things I had never thought of before, and then when I began to read a little history and also a pamphlet about Nicholas I, the Tsar's father, I said to myself, "She's right, we ought to get out of here and the sooner the better."

But without a living where can you go? We went nowhere. By now it was coming to six years that we were married and still had no children. I said nothing but I was, in my heart, a disappointed man. Who could I look in the face? In her heart Raisl was frantic. She blamed it on her sins. Maybe on my sins. She was running again, in her big wig, to the rabbis, who had never helped her, if not in our town, then in the others. She tried magic and she tried spells. She recited verses from the Scriptures and drank potions squeezed out of parts of fish and hares. I don't believe in this kind of business. Anyway, as one might expect, nothing happened. "Why has God cursed me?" she cried. "What God?" I said. She was a desperate woman. "Will I be just like my father, will I always have *nothing?* Will I have less than my father?" By this time I was worn out living in a storm. She ran this way and that, she wept, she cursed her life. I said less and read more though the books didn't bring me a kopek unless I sold them. I thought I would take her to a big doctor in Kiev, but who would pay for it? So nothing happened. She stayed barren and I stayed poor. Every day she begged me to leave so our luck would change. "Leave," I said, "on whose wings?" Then I said, "Like your father's luck changed." So she looked at me with hatred. I began to stay away from the house. When I came in at night I slept in the kitchen. The next thing I knew they were talking about her in the taverns. Then one day she was gone. I opened the door and the house was empty. At first I cursed her like somebody in the Bible curses his whorish wife. "May she keep her miscarrying womb and dry breasts." But now I look at it like this. She had tied herself to the wrong future.

7

You wait. You wait in minutes of hope and days of hopelessness. Sometimes you just wait, there's no greater insult. You sink into your thoughts and try to blot out the prison cell. If you're lucky it dissolves and you spend a half hour out in the open, beyond the doors and walls and the hatred of yourself. If you're not lucky your thoughts can poison you. If you're lucky and get out to the shtetl you might call on a friend, or if he's out, sit alone on a bench in front of his hut. You can smell the grass and the flowers and look at the girls, if one or two happen to be passing by along the road. You can also do a day's work if there's work to do. Today there's a little carpentering job. You work up a sweat sawing wood apart and hammering it together. When it's time to eat you open your food parcel—not bad. The thing about food is to have a little when you want it. A hard-boiled egg with a pinch of salt is delicious. Also some sour cream with a cut-up potato. If you dip bread into fresh milk and suck before swallowing, it tastes like a feast.

And hot tea with lemon and a lump of sugar. In the evening you go across the wet grass to the edge of the wood. You stare at the moon in the milky sky. You breathe in the fresh air. An ambition teases you, there's still the future. After all, you're alive and free. Even if you're not so free, you think you are. The worst thing about such thoughts is when they leave you and you're back in the cell. The cell is your woods and sky.

Yakov counted. He counted time though he tried not to. Counting presupposed an end to counting, at least for a man who used only small numbers. How many times had he counted up to a hundred in his life? Who could count forever?—it piled time on. The fixer had torn some splinters off sticks of firewood. The long splinters were months, the short, days. A day was a bad enough burden of time but within the day even minutes could do damage as they piled up. When one had nothing to do the worst thing to have was an endless supply of minutes. It was like pouring nothing into a million little bottles.

At five in the morning the day began and never ended. In

the early evening dark he was already lying on his mattress trying to sleep. Sometimes he tried all night. During the day there were the regular checks through the spy hole, and three depressing searches of his body. There was cleaning out ashes, and making and lighting the stove. There was the sweeping of the cell to do, urinating in the can, walking back and forth until one began to count; or sitting at the table with nothing to do. There was the going for, and eating of, his meager meals. There was trying to remember and trying to forget. There was the counting of each day; there was reciting the psalm he had put together. He also watched the light and dark change. The morning dark was different from the night dark. The morning dark had a little freshness, a little anticipation in it, though what he anticipated he could not say. The night dark was heavy with thickened and compounded shadows. In the morning the shadows unfurled until only one was left, that which lingered in the cell all day. It was gone for a minute near eleven he guessed, when a beam of sunlight, on days the sun appeared, touched the corroded inner wall a foot above his mattress, a beam of golden light gone in a few minutes. Once he kissed it on the wall. Once he licked it with his tongue. After the sun had gone, light from the window descended more darkly. When he stole a newspaper strip to read, the darkness was on the paper. It was night at half past three in the afternoon in December. Yakov put wood in the stove and Zhitnyak, after they had gone for the night rations, lit it. He ate in the dark or by the light through the stove door left ajar. There was still no lamp, no candle. The fixer set a small splinter aside to mark the lost day and crawled onto his mattress.

The long splinters were months. He figured it was January. Zhitnyak wouldn't tell him, nor would Kogin. They said they were forbidden to answer such questions. He had been arrested in the brickyard in mid-April and had served in the District Courthouse jail for two months. He figured he had been in this prison another seven months, a total of nine, if not more. It would soon—soon?—be a full year of prison. He did not, could not, think past a year. He could not foresee any future in the future. When he thought about the future all he thought about was the indictment. He imagined the warden snapping back the six bolts and bringing in the indictment in a thick brown envelope. But in this thought, after the warden had left, the indictment had still not come and he was still counting time. How long would he wait? He waited with months, days, minutes on his heavy head, and with the repetitive cycles of light and dark piled on top of the long and short pieces of time. He waited with boredom sticking its fingers down his throat. He waited for an unknown time, a time different from all the time on his head. It was unending waiting for something that might never happen. In the winter, time fell like hissing snow through the crack in the barred window, and never stopped snowing. He stood in it as it piled up around him and there was no end to drowning.

One wintry day, sickened of time, he tore off his clothes. The rags fell apart in his hands.

"Bastards!" he shouted through the peephole at the guards, prison officials, Grubeshov, and the Black Hundreds. "Anti-Semites! murderers!"

They let him stay naked. Zhitnyak would not light the stove. The fixer's body turned blue as he walked frantically in the freezing cell. He shivered on the mattress, shook, with the prayer shawl and ragged blanket wrapped around him.

"By morning," the Deputy Warden said when he came in with the guard for the last search of the day, "you won't need clothes. You'll be frozen stiff. Spread your filthy ass."

But the warden entered before nightfall and said it was indecent to have a naked Jew parading around in the cell. "You could have been shot for less than this."

He flung at Yakov another threadbare suit of prison clothes, and another ragged greatcoat. Zhitnyak then lit the stove, but it took the fixer a week to get the ice out of his spine, and the cold hurt worse than before.

Then he began to wait again.

He waits.

8

The warden, in full uniform, delivered a message from Prosecuting Attorney Grubeshov to Yakov in his solitary cell.

"You're to get dressed in your street clothes and go to the Plossky Courthouse. Your indictment is ready."

The fixer, stunned, shut his eyes. When he opened them the warden was still there.

"How shall I go, your honor?" His voice broke.

"A detective will accompany you. Since it's a short distance you can go by streetcar. You will be allowed out for no more than an hour and a half. That is the time the Prosecuting Attorney requisitioned for you."

"Must my legs be chained again?"

The warden scratched his beard. "No, but you'll be handcuffed and there'll be strict orders to shoot you dead if you try anything in the least irregular. Furthermore, two Secret Police officers will be following you and the detective in case any of your cohorts attempt to communicate with you."

In half an hour Yakov was outside the prison, waiting with the detective for a trolley. Though the day was dreary and cold, the streets white in every direction, the leafless trees black against the frozen sky, everywhere he looked brought tears to the fixer's eyes. It seemed to him he was seeing for the first time how the world was knit together.

On the trolley he watched the shops and passers-by in the street as though he were in a foreign country. How moving it was that a peasant entered a store. The detective sat next to him, one hand in his overcoat pocket. He was a heavy-bellied man with eyeglasses and a gray fur cap, who sat silent. All the way to the courthouse the fixer worried what the indictment would say. Would it accuse him simply of murder, or of murder "for ritual purposes"? The evidence was non-existent, "circumstantial" at best, but he feared their ingenuity. When the purpose was frame-up, the evidence could be arranged. Yet whatever the indictment said, the important thing to him now was getting it so that he could talk to a lawyer. Once he had done that maybe they would not keep him in solitary confinement. Even if they put him in with a murderer it would be better than being so desperately alone. The lawyer would tell everyone who he was. He would say, "This is a decent man, he could never have killed a child." The fixer worried about getting the proper lawyer, wondering who Bibikov had had in mind, "a vigorous and courageous man of excellent reputation." Would Ivan Semyonovitch know, if he were permitted to ask him? Was the lawyer a Russian or a Jew? Which was best? And how would he pay him? Could a lawyer advise him if he had no money to give him? And even if he had a good lawyer, would he be able to defend him if Bibikov's files had fallen into the hands of the Black Hundreds?

Despite these worries, and though he was tightly handcuffed, a prisoner out of jail for a few minutes, Yakov enjoyed the trolley ride. The people around him and the movement of the car created an illusion of freedom.

At the next stop two men boarded the streetcar, and passing the fixer, saw his manacled hands. They whispered to each other, and when they sat down, whispered to others. Some of the passengers turned their heads to stare at him. Noticing this he shut his eyes.

"It's that bastard killer of a Christian child," a man in a knitted wool hat said. "I saw him once in a motorcar in front of Marfa Golov's house after they arrested him."

Some of the men in the car began to mutter among themselves.

Then the detective spoke calmly. "Everything is in good order, my friends. Don't excite yourselves for nothing. I am accompanying the prisoner to the courthouse, where he will be indicted for his crime."

Two bearded Jews wearing large hats hastily got off the trolley at the next stop. A third tried to speak to the prisoner but the detective waved him away.

"If they convict you," the Jew shouted at Yakov, "cry 'Sh'ma, Yisroël, the Lord our God, the Lord is one!' " He jumped off the moving trolley, and the two secret police, who had risen, sat down.

A woman in a hat with velvet flowers, when she went by, spat at the fixer. Her spittle dribbled from his beard. Soon the detective nudged him and they left the trolley at the next stop. They were trudging along on the snowy sidewalk when the detective stopped to buy an apple from a street vendor. He handed it to the fixer, who gobbled it down in three bites.

In the courthouse building Grubeshov had moved into a larger office with six desks in the anteroom. Yakov waited with the detective, nervously impatient to see the indictment. It's strange, he thought, that an indictment of murder should be so precious, yet without it he could not make the first move to defend himself.

He was summoned into the inner office. The detective, hat in his hand, followed him in and stationed himself at attention behind the prisoner but Grubeshov dismissed him with a nod. The Prosecuting Attorney sat stolidly at a new desk regarding the prisoner with squinting eyes. Little had changed but his appearance. He looked older and if that was so, how much older did Yakov look? He saw himself as bushy-haired, bearded, swimming in his clothes, and frightened to death.

Grubeshov coughed seriously and glanced away. Yakov saw no papers on his desk. Though he had made up his mind to be controlled before this archanti-Semite, he could not help himself and began to shiver. He had been trembling within and had suppressed it, but when he thought of what had happened to Bibikov, and how he himself had been treated and what he had endured because of Grubeshov, a bone of hatred thickened in his throat and his body shook. It trembled violently as though it were trying to expel a poisonous substance. And though he was ashamed to be shivering as though feverish or freezing in front of this man, he could not stop it.

The Prosecuting Attorney looked on in puzzlement for a minute. "Are you suffering a chill, Bok?" The slightly thick voice attempted sympathy.

The fixer, still uncontrollably shaking, said he was.

"Have you been ill?"

Yakov nodded, trying to mask his contempt for the man.

"A pity," said the prosecutor. "Well, sit down and try to control yourself. Let's get on with other matters."

Unlocking his desk drawer, he took out a pack of closely typewritten long sheets of blue paper. There were about twenty pages.

My God, so many? Yakov thought. His trembling subsided and he sat forward anxiously.

"So," said Grubeshov, smiling as though he understood the matter for the first time, "you have come for the indictment?" He fingered the papers.

The fixer, staring at them, wet his lips.

"I suppose you find incarceration a not very pleasant experience?"

Though moved to shriek, Yakov nodded.

"Has it altered your thinking, yet?"

"Not of my innocence."

Grubeshov laughed a little, pushing his chair away from the desk. "A stubborn man walks with both feet tied. I am surprised at you, Bok. I wouldn't exactly have called you stupid. I think you know your future is nil if you continue to be stubborn."

"Please, when can I see a lawyer?"

"A lawyer won't do you the least good. You may take my word for it."

The fixer sat tensely, silent but wary.

Grubeshov began to walk on his oriental rug. "Even with six or seven lawyers you will be convicted and sentenced to total solitary confinement for the rest of your life. Do you think a jury of patriotic Russians will believe what some shyster concocts for you to say?"

"I will tell them the truth."

"If the 'truth' is what you have told us, no sane Russian will believe you."

"I thought you might, your honor, since you know the evidence."

Grubeshov paused in his pacing to clear his throat. "I least of all, though I have given thought to the possibility that you were once a virtuous man who became the expiatory victim of his co-religionists. Would it interest you to know that the Tsar himself is convinced you committed the crime?"

"The Tsar?" said Yakov in astonishment. "Does he know about me? How could he think such a thing?" His heart sank heavily.

"His Majesty has taken an active interest in this case since he read of Zhenia's murder in the newspapers. He at once sat down at his desk and wrote me in his own hand the following: 'I hope you will spare no pains to unearth and bring to justice the despicable Jewish murderer of that lad.' I quote from memory. His Majesty is a most sensitive person and some of his intuitions are extraordinary. Since then I've kept him informed of the progress of the investigation. It is conducted with his full knowledge and approval."

Ah, it's bad luck, the fixer thought. After a while he said, "But why should the Tsar believe what isn't true?"

Grubeshov quickly returned to his desk and sat down. "He is convinced, as we all are, by the accumulative evidence conveyed in the testimony of the witnesses."

"What witnesses?"

"You know very well which witnesses," Grubeshov said impatiently. "By Nikolai Maximovitch Lebedev, for instance, and his daughter, refined and genteel people. By Marfa Golov, the long-suffering mother of an unfortunate son, a tragic but pure woman. By the foreman Proshko and the two drivers. By the janitor Skobeliev, who saw you offering sweets to Zhenia, and will testify in court that you chased the boy several times in the brickyard. It was through your intervention, Nikolai Maximovitch tells us, that the man was discharged from his job."

"I never knew he was discharged."

"There's a lot you don't know that you will find out."

Grubeshov went on naming witnesses. "I shall also cite testimony by your Jewish cellmate, Gronfein, whom you urged, as a favor to the Jewish community, to bribe Marfa Vladimirovna so she wouldn't testify against you. By a beggar woman who once asked you for alms, which you refused her, and who saw you enter a shop where knives are sharpened. By the proprietor of that establishment and his assistant, who will say two of your knives were sharpened to the highest pitch and then returned to you. By certain religious figures, scientists of Jewish history and theology, and alienists who are authorities on the Jewish mind. We have already gathered more than thirty reliable witnesses. His Majesty has read all the relevant testimony. When he last visited Kiev shortly after your arrest, I had the honor to inform him, 'Sire, I am happy to report that the guilty culprit in Zhenia Golov's murder has been apprehended and is now in prison. He is Yakov Bok, a member of one of the Jewish fanatic groups, the Hasidim.' I assure you His Majesty bared his head in the rain and made the sign of the cross to express his thanks to the Lord for your apprehension."

The fixer could see the Tsar crossing himself, bareheaded in the rain. For the first time he wondered if it were a matter of mistaken identity. Could they have confused him with someone else?

The prosecutor opened a side drawer of his desk and took out a folder of newspaper clippings. He read from one: " 'His Majesty expressed himself as justified in his belief that the crime was the dastardly work of a Jewish criminal who must be properly punished for his barbaric deed. "We shall do whatever is necessary to protect our innocent Russian children and their anxious mothers. When I think of my own wife and children I think of them.' " If the ruler of the Russian State and its people is wholeheartedly convinced of your guilt, what chance do you think you will have for a verdict of not guilty? None, I assure you. No Russian jury will free you."

"Still," said the fixer, sighing brokenly, "the question is of the worth of the evidence."

"I have no doubts of its worth. Do you have any better evidence?"

"What if certain anti-Semitic groups committed the murder to cast suspicion on the Jews?"

Grubeshov banged his fist on the desk. "What a monstrous canard! It takes a Jew to shift the blame of his crime onto his accusers. You are apparently unaware of your own admissions, yes, confessions of guilt." He had begun to sweat and his breath whistled in his nose.

"Mine?" said Yakov, on the verge of panic. "What admissions? I have made none."

"You may think not but there is already a record of more than one confession you have made in your sleep. The guard Kogin has compiled it in his notebooks, and the Deputy Warden also heard you when he listened at the cell door at night. It's obvious that your conscience is heavily burdened, Yakov Bok, and for good and sufficient reason. There is much crying out against the abhorrent nature of your crime, sighs, ejaculations, grunts, even sobs of remorse. It is because you obviously feel some sorrow for what you have done that I am willing to talk to you in this kindly way."

Yakov's eyes again crept to the papers on the desk.

"Could I see the indictment, your honor?"

"My advice to you," Grubeshov said, wiping his neck with a handkerchief, "is to sign a confession saying you committed the murder unwillingly, under the influence of your religious cohorts. Once that's done, as I informed you the last time I talked to you, something to your advantage can be arranged."

"I have nothing to confess. What can I confess to you? I can only confess my miseries. I can't confess the murder of Zhenia Golov."

"Listen, Bok, I speak to you for your own good. Your position otherwise is hopeless. A confession by you will have more than one beneficial effect. For your fellow Jews it may prevent reprisals. Do you know that at the time of your arrest Kiev was on the verge of a massive pogrom? It was only the fortuitous appearance of the Tsar to dedicate a statue to one of his ancestors that prevented it. That won't happen a second time, I assure you. Think it over, there are strong advantages for you. I am willing to see to it that you are secreted out of prison and taken to Podovoloshchisk on the Austrian border. You will have a Russian passport in your pocket and the means of transportation to some country outside of Europe. This includes Palestine, America, or even Australia, if you choose to go there. I advise you to consider this most carefully. The alternative is to spend your lifetime in prison under circumstances much less favorable than those you are presently enjoying."

"Excuse me, but how will you then explain to the Tsar that you let a confessed murderer of a Christian child go?"

"That part doesn't concern you," said Grubeshov.

The fixer didn't believe him. A confession, he knew, would doom him forever. He was already doomed.

"The warden said you would give me the indictment."

Grubeshov uneasily studied the top sheet of the paper, then put it down. "The indictment requires the signature of the Investigating Magistrate. He is away on official business and has not yet returned to his office. In the meantime I want to know what your response is to my more than reasonable proposal?"

"I have enough to confess but not that crime."

"Ach, you are a stupid Jew."

Yakov readily agreed.

"If you have hopes of the sympathy and perhaps assistance of Magistrate Bibikov, you had better give them up. He has been replaced by another."

The fixer clamped his teeth tight to keep from going into shudders again.

"Where is Mr. Bibikov?"

Grubeshov spoke restlessly. "He was arrested for peculating from official funds. While awaiting trial, overwhelmed by his disgrace, he committed suicide."

The fixer shut his eyes.

When he opened them he said, "Could I speak to his assistant, Mr. Ivan Semyonovitch?"

"Ivan Semyonovitch Kuzminsky," said the Prosecuting Attorney coldly, "was taken into custody at the Agricultural Fair last September. He did not remove his hat when the band played 'God Save the Tsar.' If my memory is correct he was sentenced to a year in the Petropavelsky Fortress."

The fixer gasped silently.

"Do you get the point?" Grubeshov's face was taut, sweaty.

"I am innocent," the fixer shouted hoarsely.

"No Jew is innocent, least of all a ritual assassin. Furthermore, it is known you are an agent of the Jewish Kahal, the secret Jewish international government which is engaged in a subterranean conspiracy with the World Zionist Organization, the Alliance of Herzl, and the Russian Freemasons. We also have reason to believe that your masters are dickering with the British to help you overthrow the legitimate Russian government and make yourselves rulers of our land and people. We are not exactly naïve. We know your purposes. We have read the 'Protocols of the Elders of Zion,' and the 'Communist Manifesto,' and fully understand your revolutionary intentions!"

"I am not a revolutionist. I am an inexperienced man. Who knows about such things? I am a fixer."

"You can deny it all you want, we know the truth," Grubeshov shouted. "The Jews dominate the world and we feel ourselves under their yoke. I personally consider myself under the power of the Jews; under the power of Jewish thought, under the power of the Jewish press. To speak against the crimes of the Jews means to evoke the charge that one is either a Black Hundred, an obscurantist, or a reactionary. I am none of these things. I am a Russian patriot! I love the Russian Tsar!"

Yakov stared miserably at the indictment papers.

Grubeshov grabbed them and locked them in the drawer.

"If you come to your senses, let me know through the warden. Until then you will continue to give off your stink in prison."

Before Yakov was permitted to leave the office, the Prosecuting Attorney, his face darkened by blood, reading from his notebook, asked the prisoner if he was related to Baal Shem Tov or Rabbi Zalman Schneur of Ladi, and whether there had ever been a shochet in his family. To each question Yakov, shivering uncontrollably, replied no, and Grubeshov painstakingly recorded his answers.

9

He sat in his prison clothes in the dark cell, his beard tormented, eyes red, head burning, the acid cold cracking his bones. The snow hissed on the window. The wind seeping through the split glass sank on him like an evil bird, gnawing his head and hands. He ran in the cell, his breath visible, beating his chest, waving his arms, slapping blue hands together, crying anguish. He sighed, he wailed, called to the sky for help, until Zhitnyak, one nervous eye at the spy hole, ordered him to shut up. When the guard lit the evening fire the fixer sat at the smoky stove with its door open, the collar of his greatcoat raised above his ears, the light of the flames heatless on his face. Except for the glowing, crackling, moaning fire the cell was black, dank, heavy with wet stink. He could smell the rotten odor of himself in the enduring stench of all the prisoners who had lived and died in this miserable cell.

The fixer shivered for hours, plunged in the deepest gloom. Who would believe it? The Tsar himself knew of him. The Tsar was convinced of his guilt. The Tsar wanted him convicted and punished. Yakov saw himself locked in combat with the Russian Emperor. They wrestled, beard to beard, in the dark until Nicholas proclaimed himself an angel of God and ascended into the sky.

"It's all a fantasy," the fixer muttered. "He doesn't need me and I don't need him. Why don't they let me alone? What have I truly done to them?"

His fate nauseated him. Escaping from the Pale he had at once been entrapped in prison. From birth a black horse had followed him, a Jewish nightmare. What was being a Jew but an everlasting curse? He was sick of their history, destiny, blood guilt.

VII

He waits.

The snow turned to rain.

Nothing happened.

Nothing but the long winter; not the indictment.

He felt the change of weather in his head. Spring came but stayed outside the bars. Through the window he heard the shrilling of swallows.

The seasons came faster than the indictment. The indictment was very slow. The thought that it might sometime come made it so slow.

In the spring it rained heavily. He listened to the sound of the rain and liked the thought of the outside wet, but he didn't like the inside wet. Water seeped through the wall on the prison yard side. Lines of wet formed on the cement between the exposed bricks. From an eroded part of the ceiling above the window, water dripped after the rain had stopped. After the rain there was always a puddle on the floor. Sometimes the dripping went on for days. He awakened at night listening to it. Sometimes it stopped for a few minutes and he slept. When the dripping began again he awoke.

I used to sleep through thunder.

He was so nervous, irritable, so oppressed by imprisonment he feared for his sanity. What will I confess to them if I go mad? Each day's oppressive boredom terrified him. The boredom and the nervousness made him think he might go insane.

One day, out of hunger for something to do, for a word to read, he cracked open one of the phylacteries that had been left in the cell. Holding it by the thongs he hit the box against the wall till it burst with a puff of dust. The inside of the phylactery box smelled of old parchment and leather, yet there was a curious human odor to it. It smelled a little like the sweat of the body. The fixer held the broken phylactery to his nose and greedily sucked in the smell. The small black box was divided into four compartments, each containing a tightly rolled little scroll, two with verses from Exodus and two from Deuteronomy. Yakov puzzled out the script, remembering the words faster than he could read. The bondage in Egypt was over, and in one scroll Moses proclaimed the celebration of Passover. Another scroll was the Sh'ma Yisroël. Another enumerated the rewards for loving and serving God and the punishment for not: the loss of heaven, rain, and the fruit of that rain; even life. In each of the four scrolls the people were commanded to obey God and teach his words. "Therefore you shall lay up these my words in your heart and in your soul, and bind them for a sign upon your hand, that they may be frontlets between your eyes." The sign was the phylactery and it was the phylactery that Yakov had broken. He read the scrolls with excitement and sadness and hid them deep in the mattress straw. But one day Zhitnyak, his eye roving at the peephole, caught the fixer absorbed in reading them. He entered the cell and forced him to give them up. The appearance of the four scrolls puzzled the guard, although Yakov showed him the broken phylactery; and Zhitnyak turned them over to the Deputy Warden, who was greatly excited to have this "new evidence."

A few weeks later, Zhitnyak, while in the cell, sneaked the fixer a small green paper-covered New Testament in Russian. The pages were worn and soiled with use. "It's from my old woman," Zhitnyak whispered. "She said to give it to you so you could repent for the wrong you did. Besides, you're always complaining you have nothing to read. Take it but don't tell anyone who gave it to you or I will break your ass. If they ask you say that one of the prisoners in the kitchen slipped it in your pocket without you knowing it, or maybe one of those who empty the shit cans."

"But why the New Testament, why not the Old?" Yakov said.

"The Old won't do you any good at all," Zhitnyak said. "It's long been used out and full of old graybeard Jews crawling around from one mess to the other. Also there's a lot of fucking in the Old Testament, so how is that religious? If you want to read the true word of God, read the gospels. My old woman told me to tell you that."

Yakov would at first not open the book, having from childhood feared Jesus Christ, as stranger, apostate, mysterious enemy of the Jews. But with the book there his boredom grew deeper and his curiosity stronger. At last he opened it and began to read. He sat at the table reading through the darkness on the page, though not for long periods because he found it hard to concentrate. Yet the story of Jesus fascinated him and he read it in the four gospels. He was a strange Jew, humorless and fanatic, but the fixer liked his teachings and read with pleasure of the healing of lame, blind, and of the epileptics who fell into fire and water. He enjoyed the loaves and fishes and the raising of the dead. In the end he was deeply moved when he read how they spat on him and beat him with sticks; and how he hung on the cross at night. Jesus cried out help to God but God gave no help. There was a man crying out in anguish in the dark, but God was on the other side of his mountain. He heard but he had heard everything. What was there to hear that he hadn't heard before? Christ died and they took him down. The fixer wiped his eyes. Afterwards he thought if that's how it happened and it's part of the Christian religion, and they believe it, how can they keep me in prison, knowing I am innocent? Why don't they have pity and let me go?

Though his memory gave him trouble he tried to learn by heart some of the verses he liked in the gospels. It was a way to keep his mind occupied and his memory alert. Then he would recite to himself what he had learned. One day he began to say verses aloud through the peephole. Zhitnyak, sitting in his chair in the corridor, hacking at a stick with his knife, heard the fixer recite the Beatitudes, listened to the end, then told him to shut his mouth. When Yakov could not sleep at night; or when he had slept a little and was waked by some dream or noise, he passed part of his waking time reciting in the cell, and Kogin as usual kept his ear to the spy hole, breathing audibly. One night, the guard, lately morose with worry, remarked through the door in his deep voice, "How is it that a Jew who killed a Christian child goes around reciting the words of Christ?"

"I never even touched that boy," said the fixer.

"Everybody says you did. They say you had a secret dispensation from a rabbi to go ahead and do it and your conscience wouldn't hurt you. I've heard it said you were a hardworking man, Yakov Bok, but you still could have committed the crime because in your thinking it was no crime to murder a Christian. All that blood and matzo business is an old part of your religion. I've heard about it ever since I was a small boy."

"In the Old Testament we're not allowed to eat blood. It's forbidden," said Yakov. "But what about these words: 'Truly, truly, I say to you, unless you eat the flesh of the Son of man and drink His blood, you have no life in you; he who eats My flesh and drinks My blood has eternal life, and I will raise him up on the last day. For My flesh is good indeed, and My blood is drink indeed. He who eats My flesh and drinks My blood, abides in Me, and I in him.' "

"Ah, that's a different load of fish altogether," said Kogin. "It means the bread and wine and not the real flesh and blood. Besides, how do you know those words that you just said? When the Devil teaches scripture to a Jew they both get it wrong."

"Blood is blood. I said it the way it was written."

"How do you know it?"

"I read it in the Gospel of John."

"What's a Jew doing reading the gospels?"

"I read them to find out what a Christian is."

"A Christian is a man who loves Christ."

"How can anyone love Christ and keep an innocent man suffering in prison?"

"There is no innocent Christ-killer," Kogin said, shutting the disk over the spy hole.

But the next night as the rain droned steadily in the prison yard and drops of water dripped from the ceiling, the guard came to hear what else Yakov had memorized.

"I haven't been in a church in years," Kogin said. "I'm not

much of a body for incense and priests but I like to hear the words of Christ."

" 'Which of you convicts me of sin?' " said Yakov. " 'If I tell the truth, why do you not believe me?' "

"Did he say that?"

"Yes."

"Go on to another one."

" 'But it is easier for heaven and earth to pass away, than for one dot of the law to become void.' "

"When you say the words they sound different than I remember them."

"They're the same words."

"Go on to another one."

" 'Judge not, that you be not judged. For with the judgment you pronounce you will be judged and the measure you give will be the measure you get.' "

"That's enough," said Kogin. "I've had enough."

But the next night he brought a candle stub and match.

"Look, Yakov Bok, I know you're hiding a book of the gospels in your cell. How did you get it?"

Yakov said someone had slipped it into his pocket when he went to get his rations in the kitchen.

"Well, maybe, and maybe not," said Kogin, "but since you have the book in there you might as well read me something. I'm bored to my ass out here all alone night after night. What I really am is a family man."

Yakov lit the candle and read to Kogin through the hole in the door. He read him of the trial and suffering of Christ, as the yellow candle flame dipped and sputtered in the damp cell. When he came to where the soldiers pressed a crown of thorns on Jesus' head, the guard sighed.

Then the fixer spoke in an anxious whisper. "Listen, Kogin, could I ask you for a small favor? It isn't much of one. I would like a piece of paper and a pencil stub to write a few words to an acquaintance of mine. Could you lend them to me?"

"You better go fuck yourself, Bok," said Kogin. "I'm onto your Jew tricks."

He took the candle, blew it out, and did not again come to hear the verses of the gospels.

2

Sometimes he caught the scent of spring through the broken window when a breeze that had passed through the flowering bushes and trees left him with a remembrance of green things growing on earth, and his heart ached beyond belief.

One late afternoon in May, or possibly June, after the fixer had been imprisoned more than a year, a priest in gray vestments and a black hat appeared in the dark cell, a pale-faced young man with stringy hair, wet lips, and haunted, dark eyes.

Yakov, thinking himself hallucinated, retreated to the wall. "Who are you? Where do you come from?"

"Your guard opened the door for me," said the priest, nodding, blinking. He coughed, a complex fit it took him a while to get through. "I've been ill," he said, "and once as I lay in bed in a fever I had an extraordinary vision of a man suffering in this prison. Who can it be? I thought, and at once it came to me, it must be the Jew who was arrested for killing the Christian child. I was covered with perspiration and cried out, 'Heavenly Father, I thank you for this sign, for I understand you wish me to be of service to the imprisoned Jew.' When I had recovered from my illness, I wrote at once to your warden asking him to permit me to see you. At first it seemed impossible, but after I had prayed and fasted, it was finally arranged with the Metropolitan's assistance."

Seeing the ragged, bearded fixer in the gloom, standing with his back to the sweating wall, the priest fell to his knees.

"Dear Lord," he prayed, "forgive this poor Hebrew for his sins, and let him forgive us for sinning against him. 'For if you forgive men their trespasses, your heavenly father also will forgive you; but if you do not forgive men their trespasses, neither will your father forgive your trespasses.' "

"I forgive no one."

Approaching the prisoner on his knees, the priest tried to kiss his hand but the fixer snatched it away and retreated into the shadows of the cell.

Groaning, the priest rose, breathing heavily.

"I beg you to listen to me, Yakov Shepsovitch Bok," he wheezed. "I am told by the guard Zhitnyak that you religiously read the gospels. And the guard Kogin says that you have memorized many passages of the words of the true Christ. This is an excellent sign, for if you embrace Christ, you will have truly repented. He will save you from damnation. And if you are converted to the Orthodox faith, your captors will be compelled to reconsider their accusations and ultimately to release you as one of our brothers. Believe me, there is none so dear in the eyes of God as a Jew who admits he is in error and comes willingly to the true faith. If you agree I will begin to instruct you in the Orthodox dogma. The warden has given his permission. He is a broadminded man."

The fixer stood mute.

"Are you there?" said the priest, peering into the shadows. "Where are you?" he called, blinking uneasily. He coughed with a heavy rasp.

Yakov stood in the dim light, motionless at the table, the prayer shawl covering his head, the phylactery for the arm bound to his brow.

The priest, coughing thickly, his handkerchief held to his mouth, retreated to the metal door and banged on it with his fist. It was quickly opened and he hurried out.

"You'll get yours," said Zhitnyak to the fixer, from the hall.

Afterwards a lamp was brought into the cell and Yakov was stripped of his clothes and searched for the fourth time that day. The Deputy Warden, in a foul mood, kicked at the mattress and found the New Testament in the straw.

"Where the hell did you get this?"

"Somebody must've slipped it to him in the kitchen," said Zhitnyak.

The Deputy Warden floored the fixer with a blow.

He confiscated the phylacteries and Zhitnyak's New Testament but returned in the morning and flung at Yakov a handful of pages that flew all over the cell. They were pages from the Old Testament in Hebrew, and Yakov collected them and patiently put them together. Half the book was missing and some of the pages were covered with muddy brown stains that looked like dry blood.

3

The birch twig broom came apart. He had used it for months and the twigs had worn out on the stone floor. Some had snapped off in the sweeping and he was given nothing to replace them with. Then the frayed cord that bound the twigs wore away and that was the end of the broom. Zhitnyak would not supply twigs or a new cord. Yakov had asked for them, but he took the broomstick away instead.

"That's so you won't hurt yourself, Bok, or try any more of your dirty tricks on anybody else. Some say you clubbed the poor boy unconscious before you stuck him with your knife."

The fixer talked less with the guards, it was less wearying; they said little to him, once in a while a gruff command, or a curse if he was slow. Without the broom his thin routine began to collapse. He tried to hang on to it but now there was no stove to make or tend, or wait to be lit, and he was no longer permitted to go to the kitchen to get his rations. The food was brought to him in the cell, as it had been before. They said he had stolen things from the kitchen. The New Testament Bible, for instance. And a knife had been "found" during an inspection of his cell. That ended the excursions he had looked forward to, sometimes with excited eagerness, twice a day. "It's only right," said the warden. "We can't have a Jew going around flouting the rules. There have been mutterings among some of the other prisoners." What was left of the routine was to be waked by the prison bell in the morning, to eat meagerly not once but twice a day, and three times each day to be searched to desperation.

He had stopped keeping track of time with the long and short splinters. Beyond a year he couldn't go. Time was summer now, when the hot cell stank heavily and the walls sweated. There were mosquitoes, and bugs hitting the walls. Yet, better summer; he feared another winter. And if there was a spring after the winter it would mean two years in prison. And after that? Time blew like a steppe wind into an empty future. There was no end, no event, indictment, trial. The waiting withered him. He was worn thin by the struggle to wait, by the knowledge of his innocence against the fact of his imprisonment; that nothing had been done in a whole year to free him. He was stricken to be so absolutely alone. Oppressed by the heat, eaten by damp cold, eroded by the expectation of an indictment that never came, were his gray bones visible through his skin? His nerves were threads stretched to the instant before snapping. He cried out of the deepest part of him, a narrow pit, but no one appeared or answered, or looked at him or spoke to him, neither friend nor stranger. Nothing changed but his age. If he were tried, convicted, and sentenced to Siberia, that at least would be something to do. He combed his hair and beard until the teeth of the comb fell out. No one would give him another although he begged, wheedled; so he combed with his fingers. He picked his nose obsessively. His flesh, containing girls who had never become women, tempted him, but that upset his stomach. He tried unsuccessfully to keep himself clean.

Yakov read the Old Testament through the stained and muddied pages, chapter by fragmentary chapter. He read each squat letter with care, although often the words were incomprehensible to him. He had forgotten many he once knew, but in the reading and rereading some came back; some were lost forever. The passages he could not understand and the missing pages of the book did not bother him; he knew the sense of the story. What wasn't there he guessed at, or afterwards recalled. At first he read only for a few minutes at a time. The light was bad. His eyes watered and head swam. Then he read longer and faster, gripped by the narrative of the joyous and frenzied Hebrews, doing business, fighting wars, sinning and worshipping—whatever they were doing always engaged in talk with the huffing-puffing God who tried to sound, maybe out of envy, like a human being.

God talks. He has chosen, he says, the Hebrews to preserve him. He covenants, therefore he is. He offers and Israel accepts, or when will history begin? Abraham, Moses, Noah, Jeremiah, Hosea, Ezra, even Job, make their personal covenant with the talking God. But Israel accepts the covenant in order to break it. That's the mysterious purpose: they need the experience. So they worship false Gods; and this brings Yahweh up out of his golden throne with a flaming sword in both hands. When he talks loud history boils. Assyria, Babylonia, Greece, Rome, become the rod of his anger, the rod that breaks the heads of the Chosen People. Having betrayed the covenant with God they have to pay: war, destruction, death, exile—and they take what goes with it. Suffering, they say, awakens repentance, at least in those who can repent. Thus the people of the covenant wear out their sins against the Lord. He then forgives them and offers a new covenant. Why not? This is his nature, everything must begin again, don't ask him why. Israel, changed yet unchanged, accepts the new covenant in order to break it by worshipping false gods so that they will ultimately suffer and repent, which they do endlessly. The purpose of the covenant, Yakov thinks, is to create human experience, although human experience baffles God. God is after all God; what he is is what he is: God. What does he know about such things? Has he ever worshipped God? Has he ever suffered? How much, after all, has he experienced? God envies the Jews: it's a rich life. Maybe he would like to be human, it's possible, nobody knows. That's this God, Yahweh, the one who appears out of clouds, cyclones, burning bushes; talking. With Spinoza's God it's different. He is the eternal infinite idea of God as discovered in all of Nature. This one says nothing; either he can't talk or has no need to. If you're an idea what can you say? One has to find him in the machinations of his own mind. Spinoza had reasoned him out but Yakov Bok can't. He is, after all, no philosopher. So he suffers without either the intellectual idea of God, or the God of the covenant; he had broken the phylactery. Nobody suffers for him and he suffers for no one except himself. The rod of God's anger against the fixer is Nicholas II, the Russian Tsar. He punishes the suffering servant for being godless.

It's a hard life.

Zhitnyak watched him as he read. "Rock back and forth like they do in the synagogue," he said through the spy hole. The fixer rocked back and forth. The Deputy Warden was called to see. "What else would you expect?" he said as he spat.

Sometimes Yakov lost sight of the words. They were black birds with white wings, white birds with black wings. He was falling in thoughtless thought, a stupefying whiteness. The fixer lost track of where he was, a forgetting so profound he ached on coming out of it. This occurred often now and went on for hours. Once he fell into this state in the morning, sitting at the table reading the Old Testament, and came back to the present in the late afternoon, standing naked in the cell, being searched by the Deputy Warden and Zhitnyak. And he sometimes walked across Russia without knowing it. It was hard on the feet and had to be controlled because he wore out the soles of his bast shoes and nobody wanted to give him another pair. He walked in his bare feet over a long rocky road and afterwards found both feet battered and blistered. He awoke to find himself walking and it frightened him when he recalled the pain of the surgeon's scalpel. He willed himself to attention when he began to walk. He took a step or two on the long road and awoke in fright.

Yakov reveried the past; the shtetl, the mistakes and failures of his life. One white-mooned night, after a bitter quarrel about something he couldn't remember now, Raisl had left the hut and run in the dark to her father. The fixer, sitting alone, thinking over his bitterness and the falseness of his accusations, had thought of going after her but had gone to sleep instead. After all, he was dead tired doing nothing. The next year the accusations against her had come true, although it wasn't true then. Who had made it come true? If he had run after her then, would he be sitting here now?

He turned often to pages of Hosea and read with fascination the story of this man God had commanded to marry a harlot. The harlot, he had heard it said, was Israel, but the jealousy and anguish Hosea felt was that of a man whose wife had left his bed and board and gone whoring after strangers.

> "And let her put away her harlotries from her face, and her
> adulteries from between her breasts;
> Lest I strip her naked,
> And set her as in the day that she was born,
> And make her as the wilderness,
> And set her like dry land,
> And stay her with thirst.
> And I will not have compassion on her children;
> For they are the children of harlotry.

For their mother hath played the harlot,
She that conceived them hath done shamefully;
For she said: 'I will go after my lovers,
That give me bread and my water.
My wool and my flax, mine oil and my drink!'
Therefore, behold, I will hedge up thy way with thorns,
And I will make a wall against her,
That she will not find her paths.
And she shall run after her lovers, but she shall not
  overtake them,
And she shall seek them, but shall not find them;
Then shall she say: 'I will go and return to my first
  husband:
For then was it better with me than now.' "

4

One morning Zhitnyak brought the prisoner a thick letter in a soiled white envelope with a long row of red stamps. The stamps were portraits of the Tsar in military tunic, wearing a medallion of the royal coat of arms, the double-headed eagle. The letter had been opened by the censor and resealed with a strip of gummed paper. It was addressed to "The Murderer of Zhenia Golov" and sent in care of the Prosecuting Attorney of the Superior Court, Plossky District, Kiev.

Yakov's heart palpitated when he took the letter. "Who is it from?"

"The Queen of Sheba," said the guard. "Open and see."

The fixer waited until the guard had gone. He put the letter down on the table to get it out of his hand. He stared at it for five minutes. Could it be the indictment? Would they address it like that? Yakov clumsily ripped open the envelope, tearing it across, and found in it a sixteen-page letter written in Russian in a woman's spidery handwriting. There were blots of ink on every page, many words misspelled, and some heavily crossed out and rewritten.

"Sir," it began, "I am the bereaved and unfortunate mother

of the martyred Zhenia Golov, and I take my pen in my hand to beg you to do the right and decent thing. In God's name give an ear to a mother's pleas. I am worn out by the wicked insults and insinuations that have been wrongfully cast on myself by certain worthless people—including certain neighbors I have now cut myself off from, without any proof whatsoever. *On the contrary* with all the proof directed against you, and I beg you to clear the air up by a complete and candid confession. Although I admit your face, when I saw it in my household, didn't look too Jewish, and maybe you really wouldn't commit such a dreadful crime murdering a child and taking out his precious lifeblood if you hadn't been egged on to do it by fanatical Jews—you know the kind I mean. Still you probably did it because they threatened you with death, although maybe you didn't want to, I don't know. But now I know for a certainty that it was these old Jews with long black coats and nasty beards that warned you you had to make the kill and they would hide my child's corpse in the cave when you did. Just the same night before Zheniushka disappeared I dreamed of one of them carrying a satchel, with wild glaring eyes and bright red spots in his beard, and my former neighbor Sofya Shiskovsky told me she had dreamed the same dream that I had on the same night.

"I am asking you to own up because the evidence is all against you. One thing you might not know is that after Zheniushka confided to me you had chased him with a knife in the cemetery, I had you followed by a gentleman friend of mine to find out what other criminal activities you were engaged in. It is a known fact that you were involved in certain illegal acts in secretly dealing with other Jews in the brickyard who pretended they were not Jews, and also in the cellar of the synagogue, where you all met in the Podol District. You smuggled, robbed, and traded in goods that didn't belong to you. Zheniushka found out all about this and other of your illegalities, and that's another reason why you bore him such a violent hatred, and why you had him in your mind as the victim as soon as you were chosen to find one and drain his blood for the Jewish Easter. You also acted as a fence for this gang of Jews who broke into the homes of the Gentry as well as in certain commercial stores, and houses in the Lipki District, where the aristocratic houses are, and took out all sorts of loot in money, furs and jewels, not to mention other precious objects of different kinds. Also you paid your gang only a part of the real price the goods were worth because as the saying is, each Jew cheats the other. Which is nothing new to anybody because the whole world knows they are born criminals. A Jew wanted to lend a friend of mine money to build a house, but she went to the priest for advice and he began to tremble and advised her to take nothing from a cursed Jew, in Christ's name, because they will defraud and cheat you because it is their nature and they can't do otherwise. This priest said their Jewish blood itches when they aren't engaged in evil. If it weren't for that maybe you would have resisted the murder of a saintly boy when they egged you to do it. And I suppose you know there have been attempts to bribe me not to testify against you when your trial comes. One fat Jew in silk clothes offered me the sum of 40,000 rubles to leave Russia and he would pay me the sum of another 10,000 rubles, on arriving in Austria, but even if he and your fellow Jews had offered me 400,000 rubles, I would still spit in their faces and say *absolutely no* because I prefer the honor of my good name to 400,000 rubles of Jewish blood money.

"My gentleman friend also saw you spit on the ground one day when you walked around on the outside of St. Sophia's Cathedral after spying out the school in the courtyard where Zhenia went. He saw you turn your head as though you might go blind if you didn't, when you looked up on the golden crosses on top of the green domes, and you spat fast so none should see you, but my friend saw you. I was also told you practice black magic religious ceremonies and certain cabalistic superstitions.

"Also, don't think I don't know the sordid part of the story. Zhenia told me about the times you enticed him to come to your room in the stable and there with the promise of bonbons and sweets you got him to open the buttons of his pants and with your hand caused him intense excitement. There were other lewd things you performed which I can't even write because I get very faint. He told me that after you did those awful things you were afraid he would tell me and I would denounce you to the police, so you used to give him ten kopeks not to say anything to anybody. He never did at the time this all happened, although once he told me about what went on up there, because he was worried and frightened, but I haven't breathed a word of it to anyone, not even to my closest neighbors because I was ashamed to say anything, and also because your crime of murder is enough to answer for, and you will probably suffer the tortures of the cursed for that alone. Yet I will honestly and frankly tell you that if people go on making suspicious and vile remarks about me behind my back, I will tell all the facts of the case whether I blush or not to the Prosecuting Attorney who is first of all a gentleman. I will also tell everybody the sordid things you did to my child.

"I will petition the Tsar to defend my good name. Besides losing my child I have led an irreproachable life of toil. I have been an honest person and a pure woman. I have been the best of mothers even though I was a working woman with no time to herself and two people to support. Those who say I didn't weep for my poor boy at his funeral are saying a filthy lie and I will some day sue someone for libel and character assassination. I looked after my Zhenia as though he were a prince. I attended to his clothes and all of his other needs. I cooked special dishes that he liked most of all, all sorts of pastries and expensive treats. I was a mother and also a father to him since his own weakling of a father deserted me. I helped him with his lessons where I could and encouraged him and said yes when he wanted to be a priest. He was already in a preparatory church school to prepare for the priesthood when he was murdered. He felt to me the way I felt to him—he loved me passionately. Rest assured of that. Mamashka, he said, I only love you. Please, Zheniushka, I begged him, stay away from those evil Jews. To my sorrow he did not follow his mother's advice. You are my son's murderer. I urge you as the martyred mother of a martyred child to confess *the whole truth* at once and clear the evil out of the air so that we can breathe again. If you do, at least you won't have to suffer so much in the afterworld.

"Marfa Vladimirovna Golov"

The excitement of receiving the letter had increased in the reading and Yakov's head throbbed at the questions that ran through his mind. Was the trial she had mentioned already on its way or only assumed to be by her? Probably assumed, yet how could he be sure? Anyway the indictment would still have to come, and where was the indictment? What had caused her to write the letter? What were the "wicked insults and insinuations," and the "suspicious and vile remarks" she referred to? And who was making them? Could it be she was being investigated, yet by whom if not Bibikov? Certainly not Grubeshov, yet why had he let the letter, mad as it was, go through to him? Had she written it with his help? Was it to demonstrate the quality of the witness, to show Yakov what he was up against and thus again to warn or threaten him? To say we assure you she will say these things and more you can never guess, and she will convince a jury of people like her, so why not confess now? They were multiplying the accusations and disgusting motives, and would not rest until they had trapped him like a fly in a gluepot; therefore he had better confess before other means of escape were impossible.

Whatever her reason for sending it the letter seemed close to a confession by her, maybe a sign something else was going on. Would he ever know what? The fixer felt his heartbeat in his ears. He looked around for a place to hide the letter, hoping to pass it on to the lawyer, if he ever had one. But the next morning after he had finished eating, the letter was missing from his coat pocket and he suspected he had been doped, or they had got it some other way, possibly while he was being searched. Anyway the letter was gone.

"Can't I send her an answer?" he asked the Deputy Warden before the next search, and the Deputy Warden said he could if he was willing to admit the wrongs he had done.

That night the fixer saw Marfa, a tallish, scrawny-necked woman with a figure something like Raisl's, enter the cell and without so much as a word begin to undress—the white hat with cherries, the red rose scarf, green skirt, flowery blouse, cotton petticoat, pointed button shoes, red garters, black stockings and soiled frilly drawers. Lying naked on the fixer's mattress, her legs spread apart, she promised many goyish delights if he would confess to the priest at the peephole.

5

One night he awoke hearing someone singing in the cell and when he listened with his whole being the song was in a boy's high sweet voice. Yakov got up to see where the singing was coming from. The child's pale, shrunken, bony face, corroded copper and black, shone from a pit in the corner of the cell. He was dead yet sang how he had been murdered by a black-bearded Jew. He had gone on an errand for his mother and was on his way home through the Jewish section when this hairy, bent-back rabbi caught up with him and offered him a lozenge. The instant the boy put the candy into his mouth he fell to the ground. The Jew lifted him onto his shoulder and hurried to the brickworks. There the boy was laid on the stable floor, tied up, and stabbed until the blood spouted from the orifices of his body. Yakov listened to the end of the song and cried, "Again! Sing it again!" Again he heard the same sweet song the dead child was singing in his grave.

Afterwards the boy, appearing to him naked, his stigmata brightly bleeding, begged, "Please give me back my clothes."

They're trying to unhinge me, the fixer thought, and then they'll say I went mad because I committed the crime. He feared what he might confess if he went crazy; his suffering to defend his innocence would come to nothing as he babbled his guilt and the blood guilt of those who had put him up to it. He strove with himself, struggled, shouted at him to hold tight to sanity, to keep in the dark unsettled center of the mind a candle burning.

A bloody horse with frantic eyes appeared: Shmuel's nag.

"Murderer!" the horse neighed. "Horsekiller! Childkiller! You deserve what you get!"

He beat the nag's head with a log.

Yakov slept often during the day but badly. Sleep left him limp, depressed. He was being watched by many eyes through the spy hole for the minute he went mad. The air throbbed with voices from afar. There was a plot afoot to save him. He had visions of being rescued by the International Jewish Army. They were laying siege to the outer walls. Among the familiar faces he recognized Berele Margolis, Leib Rosenbach, Dudye Bont, Itzik Shulman, Kalman Kohler, Shloime Pincus, Yose-Moishe Magadov, Pinye Apfelbaum, and Benya Merpetz, all from the orphans' home, although it seemed to him they were long since gone, some dead, some fled—he should have gone with them.

"Wait," he shouted. "Wait."

Then the streets around the prison were noisy, the crowds roaring, chanting, wailing; animals mooing, clucking, grunting. Everyone ran in several directions, feathers floating in the air, *gevalt* they were killing the Jews! A horde of thick-booted, baggy-trousered, sword-swinging Cossacks were galloping in on small ferocious ponies. In the yard the double-eagled banners were unfurled and fluttered in the wind. Nicholas the Second drove in in a coach drawn by six white horses, saluting from both sides the hundreds of Black Hundreds aching to get at the prisoner and hammer nails into his head. Yakov hid in his cell with chest pains and heartburn. The guards were planning to murder him with rat poison. He planned to murder them first. A Zhid shits on Zhitnyak. Kog on Kogin. He barricaded the door with the table and stool, then smashed them against the wall. While they were battering the door down to get at him he sat cross-legged on the floor, mixing blood with unleavened flour. He kicked savagely as the guards lugged him through the corridor, raining blows on his head.

The fixer crouched in a dark place trying to hold his mind together with a piece of string so he wouldn't confess. But it exploded into a fountain of rotting fruit, one-eyed herrings, birds of Paradise. It exploded into a million stinking words but when he confessed he confessed in Yiddish so the goyim couldn't understand. In Hebrew he recited the Psalms. In Russian he was silent. He slept in fear and waked in fright. In dreams he heard the voices of screaming children. Dressed in a long caftan and round fur hat he hid behind trees, and when a Christian child approached, compulsively chased him. One small-faced boy, a consumptive type, ran from him frantically, his eyes rolling in fright.

"Stop, I love you," the fixer called to him, but the child never looked back.

"Once is enough, Yakov Bok."

Nicholas II appeared in the white uniform of an admiral of the Russian Navy.

"Little Father," said the fixer on both knees, "you'll never meet a more patriotic Jew. Tears fill my eyes when I see the flag. Also I'm not interested in politics, I want to make a living. Those accusations are all wrong or you've got the wrong man. Live and let live, if you don't mind me saying so. It's a short life when you think of it."

"My dear fellow," said the blue-eyed, pale-faced Tsar in a gentle voice, "don't envy me my throne. Uneasy lies the et cetera. The Zhidy would do well to understand and stop complaining in a whining tongue. The simple fact is there are too many Jews—my how you procreate! Why should Russia be burdened with teeming millions of you? You yourselves are to blame for your troubles, and the pogroms of 1905–6 *outside* the Pale of Settlement, mind you, were proof positive, if proof is needed, that you aren't staying where you were put. The ingestion of this tribe has poisoned Russia. Who ever wanted it? Our revered ancestor Peter the Great, when asked to admit them into Russia, said, 'They are rogues and cheats. I am trying to eradicate evil, not increase it.' Our revered ancestor, the Tsarina Elizabeth Petrovna, said, 'From the enemies of Christ I wish neither gain nor profit.' Hordes of Jews were expelled from one or another part of the Motherland in 1727, 1739, 1742, but still they crawled back and we have been unable to delouse ourselves of them. The worst of it happened, our greatest error, when Catherine the Great took over half of Poland and inherited the whole filthy lot, a million poisoners of wells, spies against us all, cowardly traitors. I always said it was the Poles' plot to ruin Russia."

"Have mercy on me, your Majesty. So far as I'm concerned, I am an innocent man. What have I seen of the world? Please have mercy."

"The Tsar's heart is in God's hands." He stepped into his white sailboat and sailed away on the Black Sea.

Nikolai Maximovitch had lost weight, the girl limped badly and would not look at the fixer. Proshko, Serdiuk and Richter came in on three skittish horses whose droppings were full of oats he longed to get at. Father Anastasy sought to convert him to Roman Catholicism. Marfa Golov, wept dry-eyed and haggard, offered him a bribe to testify against himself; and the Deputy Warden, in the uniform of a naval officer, for personal reasons insisted on continuing the searches. The guards promised the fixer anything if he would open up and name names, and Yakov said he might for a heated cell in wintertime, a daily bowl of noodles and cheese, and a firm clean hair mattress.

Shots were fired.

He passed through time he had no memory of and one day awoke to find himself in the same cell, not a new one with six doors and windows he had dreamed of. It was still hot but he couldn't be sure it was the same summer. The cell seemed the same, possibly a bit smaller, with the same scabby sweating walls. The same wet stone floor. The same stinking straw mattress; its smell had never killed the bugs. The table and three-legged stool were gone. Scattered over the wet floor were pages of the Old Testament, stained and muddied. He could not find the phylacteries but still wore the ragged prayer shawl. And the last of the firewood had been removed and the cell hosed down as though to make it fit for him to stay forever.

"How long was I gone?" he asked Zhitnyak.

"You weren't gone. Who says you were gone?"

"Was I sick then?"

"They say you ran a fever."

"What did I say when I ranted and raved?" he asked uneasily.

"Who the hell knows," said the guard impatiently. "I have my own troubles. Try and live on the lousy wages they pay you here. The Deputy Warden listened to you twice a day but couldn't make heads or tails. He says you have a filthy mind but nobody expected otherwise."

"Am I better now?"

"That's up to you, but if you break another piece of furniture, we'll smash your head."

Though his legs trembled, he stood at the peephole, looking out. Moving the disk aside with his finger, he stared out into the corridor. A yellow bulb lit the windowless wall. The cells on both sides of him, he remembered, were empty. He had more than once hit a log against the walls but there was never any response. Once an official passing by in the corridor saw his eye staring out and ordered him to shut the hole and move away from the door. After the man had gone Yakov looked out again. All he could see on the left was the chair the guards sat on, Zhitnyak whittling a stick, Kogan sighing, worrying. The other way a dusty bulb lit up a broken barrel against the wall. The fixer stood for hours staring into the corridor. When Zhitnyak came over to look in, he saw the fixer's eye staring out.

6

One midsummer night, long past midnight, Yakov, too long imprisoned to sleep, was staring out the peephole when his eye throbbed as if it had been touched, and slowly filled with the pained sight of Shmuel.

The fixer cursed himself, withdrew his eye, and tried the other. Whether vision or visitor it looked like Shmuel, though older, shrunken, grayer, a scarecrow with a frightened beard.

The prisoner, in disbelief, heard a whisper. "Yakov, it's you? Here is Shmuel, your father-in-law."

First the Tsar and now Shmuel. Either I'm still crazy or it's another mad dream. Next comes the Prophet Elijah or Jesus Christ.

But the figure of the fragile old man in shirt-sleeves and a head hat, standing in the yellow light, his fringed garment hanging out under his shirt, persisted.

"Shmuel, don't lie, is it really you?"

"Who else?" said the peddler hoarsely.

"God forbid you're not a prisoner, are you?" the fixer asked in anguish.

"God forbid. I came to see you though I almost didn't. It's erev shabbos but God will forgive me."

Yakov wiped his eyes. "I've dreamed of everybody so why not you? But how did you get in? How did you come here?"

The old man shrugged his thin shoulders.

"We came in circles. I did what they told me. Yakov, for more than a year I tried to find you but nobody knew where. I thought to myself he's gone for good, I'll never see him again. Then one day I bought for a few kopeks a hill of rotting sugar beets from a sick Russian. Don't ask me why but for the first time in my life what I bought for rotten was not all rotten. More than half the beets turned out good. God's gift to a poor man. The sugar company sent some wagons and took them away. Anyway, I sold the beets for forty rubles, my biggest profit since I'm in business. Also I met Fyodor Zhitnyak, the brother of the one here—he peddles in the Kiev market. We got to talking and he knew your name. He told me that for forty rubles he could arrange it so I could speak to you. He spoke to the brother and the brother said yes if I came late at night and wasn't too ambitious. Who's ambitious, so here I am. For forty rubles they will let me stand here just ten minutes, so we must talk fast. Time I've had like dirt my whole life but now it's worth money. Zhitnyak, the brother who's the guard here, changed shifts with another one who took the night off because his son got arrested. That's how it goes, I wish him luck. Anyway, Zhitnyak will wait for ten minutes down the hall by the outside door but he warned me if somebody comes he might have to shoot. He might as well, if they see me I'm lost."

"Shmuel, before I faint from excitement, how did you know I was in prison?"

Shmuel moved his feet restlessly. It wasn't a dance though it looked like one.

"How I know, he asks. I knew because I knew. I know. When it came out in the Yiddish papers last year that a Jew was arrested in Kiev for murdering a Christian child, I thought to myself who can this poor Jew be, it must be my son-in-law Yakov. Then after a year I saw your name in the newspaper. A counterfeiter by the name of Gronfein got sick from his nerves and went around saying that Yakov Bok was in the

Kiev prison for killing a Russian child. He saw him there. I tried to find this man but he disappeared and those who are hopeful hope he's alive. Maybe he went to America, that's what they hope. Yakov, maybe you don't know, it's a terrible tumult now all over Russia, and to tell you the truth, the Jews are frightened to death. Only a few know who you are, and some say it's a fake, there's nobody by that name, the goyim made it up to cast suspicion on the Jews. In the shtetl those who never liked you say it serves you right. Some have pity and would like to help you but we can't do a thing till they give you an indictment. When I saw your name in the Jewish paper I wrote you right away a letter and they sent it back—'No such prisoner.' I also sent you a little package, not much in it, just a few little things, but did you ever get it?"

"Poison I got but no package."

"I tried to get in here to see you and nobody would let me till I made my profit on the sugar beets and I met the brother Zhitnyak."

"Shmuel, I'm sorry for your forty rubles. It's a lot of money and what are you getting for it?"

"Money is nothing. I came to see you, but if it paves my way a foot into Paradise it's a fine investment."

"Run, Shmuel," the fixer said, agitated, "get out while you can or they'll shoot you in cold blood and call it a Jewish conspiracy. If that happens I'm doomed forever."

"I'm running," said Shmuel, cracking his knuckles against his bony chest, "but tell me first why they blame you for this terrible crime?"

"Why they blame me? Because I was a stupid ass. I worked for a Russian factory owner in a forbidden district. Also I lived there without telling him my papers were Jewish."

"You see, Yakov, what happens when you shave your beard and forget your God?"

"Don't talk to me about God," Yakov said bitterly. "I want no part of God. When you need him most he's farthest away. Enough is enough. My past I don't have to tell you, but if you knew what I've lived through since I saw you last." He began to say but his voice cracked.

"Yakov," said Shmuel, clasping and unclasping his excitable hands, "we're not Jews for nothing. Without God we can't live. Without the covenant we would have disappeared out of history. Let that be a lesson to you. He's all we have but who wants more?"

"Me. I'll take misery but not forever."

"For misery don't blame God. He gives the food but we cook it."

"I blame him for not existing. Or if he does it's on the moon or stars but not here. The thing is not to believe or the waiting becomes unbearable. I can't hear his voice and never have. I don't need him unless he appears."

"Who are you, Yakov, Moses himself? If you don't hear His voice so let Him hear yours. 'When prayers go up blessings descend.' "

"Scorpions descend, hail, fire, sharp rocks, excrement. For that I don't need God's help, the Russians are enough. All right, once I used to talk to him and answer myself, but what good does it do if I know so little in the first place? I used to mention once in a while the conditions of my life, my struggles, misfortunes, mistakes. On rare occasions I gave him a little good news, but whatever I said he never answered me. Silence I now give back."

"A proud man is deaf and blind. How can he hear God? How can he see Him?"

"Who's proud if I ever was? What have I got to be proud of? That I was born without parents? I never made a decent living? My barren wife ran off with a goy? When a boy was murdered in Kiev, out of three million Jews in Russia they arrested me? So I'm not proud. If God exists I'll gladly listen to him. If he doesn't feel like talking let him open the door so I can walk out. I have nothing. From nothing you get nothing. If he wants from me he has to give first. If not a favor at least a sign."

"Don't ask for signs, ask for mercy."

"I've asked for everything and got nothing." The fixer, after a sigh, spoke close to the peephole. " 'In the beginning was the word,' but it wasn't his. That's the way I look at it now. Nature invented itself and also man. Whatever was there was there to begin with. Spinoza said so. It sounds fantastic but it must be true. When it comes down to basic facts, either God is our invention and can't do anything about it, or he's a force in Nature but not in history. A force is not a father. He's a cold wind and try and keep warm. To tell the truth, I've written him off as a dead loss."

"Yakov," said Shmuel, squeezing both hands, "don't talk so fast. Don't look for God in the wrong place, look in the Torah, the law. That's where to look, not in bad books that poison your thoughts."

"As for the law it was invented by man, is far from perfect, and what good is it to me if the Tsar has no use for it? If God can't give me simple respect I'll settle for justice. Uphold the Law! Destroy the Tsar with a thunderbolt! Free me from prison!"

"God's justice is for the end of time."

"I'm not so young any more, I can't wait that long. Neither can the Jews running from pogroms. We're dealing nowadays with the slaughter of large numbers and it's getting worse. God counts in astronomy but where men are concerned all I know is one plus one. Shmuel, let's drop this useless subject. What's the sense of arguing through a little hole where you can barely see part of my face in the dark? Besides, it's a short visit and we're eating up time."

"Yakov," said Shmuel, "He invented light. He created the world. He made us both. The true miracle is belief. I believe in Him. Job said, 'Though he slay me, yet will I trust in Him.' He said more but that's enough."

"To win a lousy bet with the devil he killed off all the servants and innocent children of Job. For that alone I hate him, not to mention ten thousand pogroms. Ach, why do you make me talk fairy tales? Job is an invention and so is God. Let's let it go at that." He stared at the peddler with one eye. "I'm sorry I'm making you feel bad on your expensive time, Shmuel, but take my word for it, it's not easy to be a freethinker in this terrible cell. I say this without pride or joy. Still, whatever reason a man has, he's got to depend on."

"Yakov," said Shmuel, mopping his face with his blue handkerchief, "do me a favor, don't close your heart. Nobody is lost to God if his heart is open."

"What's left of my heart is pure rock."

"Also don't forget repentance," said Shmuel. "This comes first."

Zhitnyak appeared in a great hurry. "That's enough now, it's time to go. Ten minutes is up but you talked longer."

"It felt like two," Shmuel said. "I was just about to say what's on my heart."

"Run, Shmuel," Yakov urged, his mouth pressed to the peephole. "Do whatever you can to help me. Run to the newspapers and tell them the police have imprisoned an innocent man. Run to the rich Jews, to Rothschild if necessary. Ask for help, money, mercy, a good lawyer to defend me. Get me out of here before they lay me in my grave."

Shmuel pulled a cucumber out of his pants pocket. "Here's a little pickle I brought you." He attempted to thrust it through the spy hole but Zhitnyak grabbed it.

"None of that," the guard loudly whispered. "Don't try any Jew tricks on me. Also you shut up," he said to Yakov. "You've had your say and that's enough now."

He grabbed Shmuel by the arm. "Hurry up, it's getting towards morning."

"Goodbye, Yakov, remember what I told you."

"Raisl," Yakov called after him. "I forgot to ask. Whatever happened to her?"

"I'm running," said Shmuel, holding on to his hat.

VIII

Shmuel's visit left the fixer with a heavy burden of excitement. Something must happen now, he thought. He will run to people on my behalf. He will say this is my son-in-law Yakov and look what happened to him. He will tell them I'm in prison in Kiev and what for. He will cry out my innocence and beg for help. Maybe a lawyer will then go to Grubeshov and ask for the indictment. He will say, "You must give it to us before this man dies in his cell." Maybe he will even petition the Minister of Justice. If he's a good lawyer he will think of other things to do. He won't neglect me here.

Instead the warden appeared in the cell, tense and agitated. His good eye gleamed. His mouth was loose with anger. "We'll give you escape, you bastard. We'll give you conspiracy."

A prisoner in strict confinement nearby had heard voices that night and had informed on Zhitnyak. The guard was arrested and after a while confessed that he had let an old Jew in to talk to the murderer.

"This time you overreached yourself, Bok. You'll wish you had never laid eyes on this other conspirator. We'll show you what good outside agitation will do. You'll wish you had never been born."

He demanded to know who the conspirator was, and the fixer excitedly answered, "Nobody. He was a stranger to me. He didn't tell me his name. A poor man. He met Zhitnyak by accident."

"What did he say to you? Come out with it."

"He asked me if I was hungry."

"What did you answer?"

"I said yes."

"We'll give you hunger," shouted the warden.

Early the next day two workmen entered the cell with boxes of tools, and after laboring all morning with steel hammers and long metal spikes, drilled four deep holes in the inner wall, in which they cemented heavy bolts with attached rings. The workmen also constructed a bed-size platform with four short wooden legs. The foot of the "bed" was a stock for enclosing the prisoner's legs, that would be padlocked at night. The window bars were strengthened and two more were added, reducing the meager light in the cell. But the cracked window was left cracked, and six additional bolts were fastened to the outside of the iron door, making twelve altogether, plus the lock that had to be opened by key. There was a rumor, the Deputy Warden said, that the Jews were planning a ruse to free him. He warned the fixer a lookout tower was being constructed on the high wall directly opposite his cell, and the number of guards patrolling the yard had been increased.

"If you try to escape out of this prison we'll slaughter the whole goddamn gang of you. We'll get every last one."

In Zhitnyak's place a new guard was stationed at the cell door during the day, Berezhinsky, an ex-soldier, a dark-faced man with pouched, expressionless eyes, swollen knuckles and a broken nose. There were patches of hair on his cheekbones and neck even after he had shaved. At times, out of boredom, he thrust a rifle barrel through the spy hole and sighted along it at the prisoner's heart.

"Bang!"

The fixer was chained to the wall all day, and at night he lay on the bedplank, his legs locked in the stocks. The leg holes were tight and chafed his flesh if he tried to turn a little. The straw mattress had been removed from the cell. At least that smell was gone, and the bedbugs, though some still inhabited his clothes. Since the fixer slept on his side when he slept, it took a while before he could begin to fall asleep on his back. He lay awake until he could no longer stand it, then seemed to faint into sleep. He slept heavily for an hour or two and woke. If he slept again the slightest movement of his body awakened him.

Now in chains, he thought the searches of his body would end, but they were increased to six a day, three in the morning and three in the afternoon. If the Deputy Warden went off duty early, the six searches were carried out in the morning. Berezhinsky went in with him in place of Zhitnyak. Six times a day his key grated in the lock, and one by one the twelve bolts were snapped back, each with a noise like a pistol shot. Yakov put his hands to his head, obsessed by the thought that someone was hitting him repeatedly. When the searchers appeared he was unchained and ordered to strip quickly. Though he tried to hurry, his fingers were like lead; he could not open his few buttons, and the guard booted him for not moving fast enough. He begged them to examine half his body at a time, with his jacket and shirt on and pants off; then with his pants on and the other clothes off, but they wouldn't. All he was allowed to keep on was his undershirt. It was as though, if that were not removed, the search could not be such a bad thing whatever else they did to him. During the search Berezhinsky grabbed the fixer's beard in his fist and tugged. When Yakov complained, he yanked his penis.

"Ding-dong, giddyap. A Jew's cock's in the devil's hock."

The Deputy Warden's color heightened. He laughed with a gasp and during the search his mouth wore a smile.

After each search, Yakov, exhausted, bleak, fell into depression. At first he had waited with hope that *anyway* something might come of Shmuel's visit. Then he began to fear that the peddler had been arrested. At times he wondered whether Shmuel had really come to see him, and if he had, he now wished he hadn't. If he had not come, there would now be no chains. For the chains he cursed him.

The second winter in prison was worse than the first. The outside weather was worse, less snow and sleet but more clear freezing days, especially cold when a wind was blowing. The wind bayed at the window like starving wolves. And the inside weather was worse. The cold glowed in the cell. It sometimes struck him with pain, pressing his chest so hard it hurt to breathe. He wore his cap with earflaps, the ragged prayer shawl looped around it, twice around the head, and knotted on top. He wore it until it fell apart and then kept a piece of it for a handkerchief. He tried to get his coat sleeves under the manacles but couldn't. The icy shackles encircled his bare legs. They threw him a horse blanket which he wore over his shoulders in the worst of winter, for though there were now a few bundles of wood in the cell, Berezhinsky was never in a hurry to light the stove, and most of the day the fixer's bones were like ice-covered branches of a tree in the winter woods. The searches in the freezing cold were terrible; the cold plunged knives into his chest, armpits, anus. His body shriveled and teeth chattered. But when Kogin came in, in the late afternoon, he built a fire. Sometimes he lit one late at night. Since the arrest of his son, the guard's eyes were almost glazed. He usually said nothing, puffed on a dead butt. After Yakov had cleaned out his supper bowl and lain down, Kogin locked his feet in the bed stocks and left.

During the day the fixer sat in chains on a low stool they had given him. The Old Testament pages had been taken from the cell the day he was chained to the wall, and the Deputy Warden said they had been burned. "They went up like a fart in the breeze." Yakov had nothing to do but sit and not think. To keep his blood from freezing he would often get up, move one step to the right, then two to the left; or one to the left and two to the right. He could also move a step back to the frozen wall, then one step forward. This was as far as he could go, and whichever way he moved he dragged the clanking chains with him. He did this for hours during the day. Sometimes he sobbed as he strained to pull the chains out of their sockets.

He was allowed to do nothing for himself. To urinate he had to call the guard and ask for the can. If Berezhinsky was not at the door, or was too lazy to hear, or Yakov could not stand the sound of the bolts hitting his head, he held his water till it cut like a knife. When he could no longer hold it he pissed on the floor. Once he held it so long the stream burst forth, wetting his pants and shoes. When Berezhinsky came in and saw what had happened he slapped the fixer's face with one hand, then with the other until the day blotted out.

"You cocksucker Zhid, I ought to make you lick it up off the floor."

When Berezhinsky delivered the gruel, Yakov often begged him to remove the manacles for a few minutes while he ate, but the guard refused. Once after eating, while the guard was gone, Yakov turned sideways, used the spoon handle to dig a little at the cement around one of the bolts. But the guard saw this through the spy hole, entered the cell, and bloodied the prisoner's mouth. After that Berezhinsky had the cell searched by a detail of five guards. Nothing was turned up at first, but they came again later in the week and found the blackened needle Yakov had long ago borrowed from Zhitnyak and carefully hidden in a crevice in the stove. To punish the fixer, his stool was removed for a week. He stood in chains all day and at night slept the sleep of the dead.

Thus the days went by. Each day went by alone. It crawled along like a dying thing. Sometimes, if he thought about it, three days went by, but the third was the same as the first. It was the first day because he could not say that three single days, counted, came to something they did not come to if they were not counted. One day crawled by. Then one day. Then one day. Never three. Nor five or seven. There was no such thing as a week if there was no end to his time in prison. If he were in Siberia serving twenty years at hard labor, a week might mean something. It would be twenty years less a week. But for a man who might be in prison for countless days, there were only first days following one another. The third was the first, the fourth was the first, the seventy-first was the first. The first day was the three thousandth.

Yakov thought how it used to be before he was chained to the wall. He remembered sweeping the floor with the birch broom. He remembered reading Zhitnyak's gospels, and the Old Testament pages. He had saved and counted the wood splinters and kept track of the days and months when it seemed a sort of reward to add up time. He thought of the minutes of light on the scabby wall. He thought of the table he had once had to sit at reading before he smashed it in a fit of madness. He thought of being free to walk back and forth in the cell, or in circles, until he was too tired to think. He thought of being able to urinate without having to call the guard; and of only two searches a day instead of a terrifying six. He thought of lying down on the straw mattress any time he wanted to; but now he could not even lie down on the wooden bed except when they released him to. And he also thought of the time he was allowed to go to the kitchen to fill his bowl; and also of tending the stove in winter, and Zhitnyak, who was not too bad, coming in twice a day to light it. The guard had permitted him a good fire. He allowed Yakov to put in plenty of wood; then before leaving the cell he lit it with a match and watched until it really blazed. Yakov thought he would be glad if things went back to how they had once been. He wished he had enjoyed the bit of comfort, in a way of freedom, he had had then. In chains all that was left of freedom was life, just existence; but to exist without choice was the same as death.

He had secret, almost pleasurable thoughts of death, had had from the time he had stolen Zhitnyak's needle. He had thought, if I want to die sometime I can use the needle to cut my veins. He could do it after Kogin left, and bleed all night. In the morning they would find a corpse. He had these thoughts more intensely now. After a while all he thought of was death. He was terribly weary, hungry to rid himself of the hard chains and the devilishly freezing cell. He hoped to die quickly, to end his suffering for once and all, to get rid of all he was and had been. His death would mean there was one last choice, there always is, and he had taken it. He had taken his fate in his hands. How will I do it? He thought of a hunger strike but that would take too long, slowly starving. He had no belt but could tear up his clothes and the blanket, braid the strips together, and if he did not first freeze to death, hang himself from the window bars. But he couldn't reach the window bars, and even if he found some way to get the rope behind them and down to him, hanging himself was not what he wanted. It would leave them out of it. He wanted them involved. He thought of Fetyukov shot by the guard. That's how I have to do it. They want me to die but not directly by their hand. They'll keep me in chains, making searches until my heart gives out. Then they can say I died of natural causes "while awaiting trial." I'll make it unnatural causes. I'll make it by their hand. I'll provoke them to kill me. He had made up his mind. He planned to do it during the sixth search of the next day, when they were at their most irritable, so they would react without thought, mechanically, instantly. He would refuse to undress, and when they ordered him to, he would spit into the Deputy Warden's eye. If he were not at once shot he would try to wrestle a gun out of one of his holsters. By then Berezhinsky would have shot him through the head. It would be over in minutes, and the guard would later receive five or ten rubles for meritorious service. The Tsar would read about it in the St. Petersburg newspapers and at once sit down at his desk to write out a telegram to Grubeshov. "I heartily congratulate you for paying back in his own coin the Jewish murderer of Zhenia Golov. You will hear from me soon regarding advancement. Nicholas." But then the officials would have to explain his death, and whatever they said, they could never say they had proved his guilt. Who would believe them? It might even create a tumult on the outside.

Let the Tsar jig on his polished floor. I shit my death on him.

2

It is late afternoon. The sun is sinking behind the cold treetops. A black carriage appears in the distance (coming from what city?) drawn by four black horses. He loses it amid traffic on the Kreshchatik, among other carriages, droshkies, trolleys, wagon-trucks, a few motorcars. The trees are now black. It is night again. Kogin is restlessly pacing back and forth in the corridor. He has often stood by Yakov's cell door, the spy hole open, listening to his noisy wheezing, the guard's breathing audible as he wets his pencil and writes in the notebook what Yakov cries out in his sleep. But tonight, a blizzarding night, the snow swirling thickly around the prison, after hours of walking back and forth past Yakov's cell door, knowing the prisoner is awake, the guard stops and sighs through the spy hole, "Ah, Yakov Bok, don't think you're the only one with troubles. They're piled on my head like snows on a mountain top."

He walks away and then returns to say that his son Trofim has murdered an old man while robbing a house in the Podol. "That's what it comes to, you see."

After a long silence he says, "I had trouble enough with my daughter, who got herself pregnant by a man of my age, a goddamn drunk, but no sooner do I get her married off to someone," Kogin says through the spy hole, "than the boy takes to robbing a house, a thing that never entered his mind before. He stole from me but never from anybody else until this night he went into a house by the Dnieper, and while he was in there, killed the old man who lived in it. He was a harmless old man, and anyone in his right mind could see from the outside of the house that there wasn't likely to be anything of any value in it, not a thing. He knew it, but in that case why did he do it, Yakov Bok? Was there anything on his mind but to pay me back with worries for the years of love I gave him? When the old man caught him in his house he grabbed Trofim's coat and hung on to it, and he, in fright, he says, beat the old man on the head with his fists until he let go, but by that time it was too late—the old man had had some kind of stroke and died. That was the end of him. Trofim came in, as you might say, to partake of his hospitality, and he stayed on there to light the funeral candles and maybe say a prayer over the remains. He returned to the house that morning as I was taking my boots off after a night's work and told me what he had done. So I put my boots on again, and we went together to the District Police and there inscribed him for murder. A few months ago he was tried in a court and sentenced to the highest penalty, twenty years at forced labor in Siberia. He's on his way there now. They started out across the Nicholas Bridge on a freezing day in December, and God only knows where they are now in all this snow and wind. Just imagine, twenty years—it's a lifetime."

"It's only twenty years," says Yakov.

"I won't see him, if we both live that long, till he's fifty-two, which is the age I am now."

The guard's low voice rumbles in the cell so he goes on in a thick whisper.

"I asked him why he had done that thing, and he said he had no particular reason. Can you imagine a more ridiculous statement, Bok? He came to the end I had predicted for him, all of a father's love gone for nothing. That's how it goes. You plan one thing and get another. Life plays no favorites and what's the use of hoping for it? The children were ruined by their mother, a woman of unsettled character and lax ways. My son was always hard to control because of her ways with him, and I thought for a time he would murder one of us in spite of all the love I had for him, but it turned out that he murdered somebody else."

Kogin sighs, pauses a minute, and asks Yakov if he wants a cigarette.

Yakov says no. He breathes deeply so the guard can hear the whine in his chest. A cigarette would make him sick.

"But if you open the stocks for a minute," he says, "it would ease my stiff legs."

Kogin says he can't do that. He stands silently at the spy hole for a few minutes, then whispers heavily, "Don't think I am not aware of your misfortunes, Bok, because I am. It's a terrible thing to see a man in chains, whoever he is, and have to lock his feet in stocks every night, but to be frank with you I don't allow myself to dwell on it much. I try not to think of you there in chains all day long. The nerves can take just so much, and I already have all the worry I can stand. I think you know what I mean by that."

Yakov says he does.

"You're sure about a cigarette? It's a small infraction of the rules. Some of the guards sell them to prisoners here, and if you ask me the warden knows it. But if I opened your stocks I could get myself shot."

After a while Yakov thinks the guard has gone away but he hasn't.

"Do you still have the gospels in there?" Kogin asks.

"No, they're gone."

"What about the sayings you used to say by memory? Why don't you say any of them any more?"

"I've forgotten them."

"This is one I remember," says the guard. " 'But he who endures to the end will be saved.' It's either from Matthew or Luke, one or the other."

Yakov is moved so deeply he laughs.

The guard walks away. Tonight he is restless and in a half hour returns to the cell door, holding a lamp to the hole, peering above it to see what he can see. The light falls on the fixer's imprisoned feet, waking him again. Kogin is about to say something but doesn't. The light goes out. Yakov moves restlessly, lying awake listening to the guard walking back and forth in the corridor as though he were walking to Siberia along with his son. The prisoner listens until exhaustion overtakes him, then goes on with the dream he was having.

He locates the black carriage once again, only it is a rickety wagon coming from the provinces, carrying a coffin made of weatherbeaten pine boards. For me or who else? he thinks. Afraid to name names he struggles to wake up and instead finds himself in an empty room standing by a small black coffin, like a trunk locked with chains.

It's Zhenia's coffin, he thinks. Marfa Golov has sent it to me as a present. But when he unlocks the rusty chains and raises the coffin lid, there lies Shmuel, his father-in-law, with a prayer shawl covering his head, a purple hole in his forehead and one eye still wet with blood.

"Shmuel, are you dead?" the fixer cries, and the old man, if not in peace, at least in repose, for once has nothing to say.

The fixer awakens, grieving, his beard damp with salt tears.

"Live, Shmuel," he sighs, "live. Let me die for you."

Then he thinks in the dark, how can I die for him if I take my life? If I die I die to fuck them and end my suffering. As for Shmuel, he's already out in the cold. He may even die for my death if they work up a pogrom in celebration of it. If so what do I get by dying, outside of release from pain? What have I earned if a single Jew dies because I did? Suffering I can gladly live without, I hate the taste of it, but if I must suffer let it be for something. Let it be for Shmuel.

The next day he is searched six times in the bitterly cold cell, standing barefoot on the floor, each stone like a block of ice, as they poke their filthy fingers into his private parts. The sixth search, when he has planned to die, is the most dreadful of all. He struggles with himself to keep from leaping on the Deputy Warden, to murder him a little with his bare hands before he is shot to death.

He tells himself he mustn't die. Why should I take from

myself what they are destroying me to take? Why should I help them kill me?

Who, for instance, would know if he dies now? They'll sweep his remains off the bloody floor and throw them into a wet hole. A year or two later they'd say he died attempting to escape. Who would question it after a year or two? It was a natural thing for prisoners to die in prison. They died like flies all over Russia. It was a vast country and there were many prisons. There were more prisoners than there were Jews. And what difference if the Jews said they didn't believe he had died naturally? They would have other headaches then.

Not that he is afraid to die because he is afraid of suicide, but because there is no way of keeping the consequences of his death to himself. To the goyim what one Jew is is what they all are. If the fixer stands accused of murdering one of their children, so does the rest of the tribe. Since the crucifixion the crime of the Christkiller is the crime of all Jews. "His blood be on us and our children."

He pities their fate in history. After a short time of sunlight you awake in a black and bloody world. Overnight a madman is born who thinks Jewish blood is water. Overnight life becomes worthless. The innocent are born without innocence. The human body is worth less than its substance. A person is shit. Those Jews who escape with their lives live in memory's eternal pain. So what can Yakov Bok do about it? All he can do is not make things worse. He's half a Jew himself, yet enough of one to protect them. After all, he knows the people; and he believes in their right to be Jews and live in the world like men. He is against those who are against them. He will protect them to the extent that he can. This is his covenant with himself. If God's not a man he has to be. Therefore he must endure to the trial and let them confirm his innocence by their lies. He has no future but to hold on, wait it out.

He is enraged by what has happened—is happening to him—a whole society has set itself against Yakov Bok, a poor man with a few grains of education, but in any case innocent of the crime they accuse him of. What a strange and extraordinary thing for someone like himself, a fixer by trade, who had never in his life done a thing to them but live for a few months in a forbidden district, to have as his sworn and bitter enemies the Russian State, through its officials and Tsar, for no better reason than that he was born a Jew, therefore their appointed enemy, though the truth of it is he is in his heart no one's enemy but his own.

Where's reason? Where's justice? What does Spinoza say—that it's the purpose of the state to preserve a man's peace and security so he can do his day's work. To help him live out his few poor years, against circumstance, sickness, the frights of the universe. So at least don't make it any worse than it is. But the Russian State denies Yakov Bok the most elemental justice, and to show its fear and contempt of humankind, has chained him to the wall like an animal.

"Dogs," he cries out.

He beats his chains against the wall, his neck cords thick. He is in a rage to be free, has at times glimmerings of hope, as though imagining creates it, thinks of it as close by, about to happen if he breathes right, or thinks the one right thought. Maybe a wall will collapse, or sunrise burn through it and make an opening as large as a man's body. Or he will remember where he has hidden a book that will tell him how to walk with ease through a locked-and-twelve-times-bolted door.

"I'll live," he shouts in his cell, "I'll wait, I'll come to my trial."

Berezhinsky opens the spy hole, inserts his rifle, and sights along the barrel at the fixer's genitals.

Yakov sits in the pit. An angelic voice, or so he thinks, calls his name, but he isn't sure he has heard right; his hearing is dulled in the right ear since Berezhinsky hit him there. The sky rains and snows on him. Or it may be bits of wood or frozen time. He doesn't reply. His hair is matted and long. His nails grow until they break. He has dysentery, dirties himself, stinks.

Berezhinsky douses him with a bucket of cold water. "It's no secret why Jews won't eat pig. You're blood brothers and both live on shit."

He sits on the grass under a leafy tree. The fields are full of flowers. He talks to himself not to forget. Some things he remembers astonish him. Are they memories or thoughts of things he had hoped to do? He is shrouded in thick clouds of yellow fog. Sometimes in painful stretches of light. Memories thin out and fall away. Events of the past he has difficulty recalling. He remembers having gone mad once. Where do you look if you lose your mind? That's the end of it. He would, in his mind, be forever locked in prison, no longer knowing why or what he is locked in. Locked in his final fate, the last unknowing.

"Die," says Berezhinsky. "For Christ's sake, die."

He dies. He dies.

Kogin says he has received a letter that his son is dead. He has drowned himself in a river in Irkutsk on the way to Novorosiisk.

3

"Remove your cap," said the warden, standing in his cell.

He removed his cap, and the warden handed him a sheaf of papers.

"It's your indictment, Bok, but that doesn't mean your trial is necessarily on its way."

Afterwards, crouched on his stool in chains, Yakov very slowly read the papers. His heart raced as he read but the mind ran ahead of the heart; this Jew they were talking about had committed a terrible crime and then stepped into a trap, and at once the prisoner saw him dead and buried in a thin grave. Sometimes the words on the paper grew blurred and disappeared under water. When they rose to the surface he read them one by one, saying each aloud. After reading three pages he hadn't the strength to concentrate longer. The papers weighed like oakwood and he had to put them down. Soon, though the barred window was still lit, it was too dark to read. At night he awoke famished to devour the words. He thought of begging Kogin for a candle but had visions of the paper catching fire and burning. So he waited for morning, once dreaming he was trying to read the indictment but the language was Turkish. Then he awoke and frantically felt for the papers. They were in his greatcoat pocket. He waited impatiently for daylight. In the morning, when there was enough light the fixer avidly read through the whole document. It seemed to him that the story had changed from how he read it yesterday, but then he realized it had changed from how he knew it as he had pieced it together from the questions he had been asked, and the accusations that had been made. The crime was the same but there were details that he had not heard before, some fantastic ones; and some of the old ones had been altered and a new mystery created. Yakov read, straining to find a combination of facts that would make them, by virtue of this arrangement, truer than they were when he first heard them; or as though, if he comprehended them in some way others did not, he would at once establish his innocence. And once he established it they would have to release him from his chains and open the prison doors.

This "Court Indictment," typed on long sheets of blue paper, retold the murder of Zhenia Golov, much as Yakov knew it, but now the number of wounds was unaccountably forty-five, "3 groups of 13, plus 2 additional groups of 3." There were wounds, the paper said, on the boy's chest, throat, face, and skull—"around the ears"; and the autopsy, performed by Professor M. Zagreb of the Medical Faculty of Kiev University, indicated that all the wounds had been inflicted on the body when the boy's heart was still strong. "But those in the principal veins of the neck had been inflicted when the heart was weakening."

On the day the boy was found murdered in the cave, his mother, when she heard the news, fainted. This had been noted on the police record of the case. Then came some details Yakov read quickly but had to go back and read slowly. The collapse of Marfa Golov, the indictment said, "was noted here with particular interest" because it was later observed that she was composed at the funeral and did not weep at her son's burial, although others, "mere strangers," had wept without restraint. Some "well-meaning spectators" and others "perhaps not so well-meaning," were disturbed by this, and "foolish rumors" began at once to circulate "concerning the possible involvement of this good woman, through a former and seriously incapacitated friend, in the murder of her own child." Because of this baseless rumor, but in the interests of arriving at the truth, she was arrested and thoroughly investigated by the police. They searched her house more than once and found "nothing in the least incriminating." Thus, after days of painstaking investigation she was released with the apologies of the police and other officials. The Chief of Police concluded that the rumors previously referred to were false and unfounded, "probably the invention of the enemies of Marfa Golov, or possibly of certain sinister forces," for Marfa Golov was a devoted mother, "blameless of any crime against her child." Such suspicion was contemptible. Her composed behavior at her son's funeral was the "behavior of a dignified person in control of her sentiments although involved in a profound personal loss." For "not all who are sad, weep" and "guilt is not a matter of facial expression but of evidence." "How much this unfortunate woman had mourned and endured *prior* to the child's funeral no one had inquired." However, witnesses had testified that Marfa Golov had been a more than ordinarily conscientious mother, and a "hard-working virtuous woman of unstained character, who without any assistance to speak of, had provided for her child since the desertion and death of the irresponsible father." It was therefore concluded that the attempts to destroy her reputation were "the work of unknown subversive alien groups" for the purpose of "concealing the guilt of one of its members, the true murderer of Zhenia Golov, the jack-of-all-trades, Yakov Bok."

"Vey is mir," said Yakov.

The fixer had been suspected from the beginning. Even before the funeral, rumors had begun to fly through the city that "the real culprit responsible for the murder of the boy was a member of the Hebrew faith." Then came a summary of reasons why Bok had come to the attention of the police "as a suspicious person": First, because it had come out he was a Hebrew using a false name and living in the Lukianovsky District, a district forbidden by special law to all members of his faith except Merchants of the First Guild and some professionals. Second, while representing himself as a Russian, one Yakov Ivanovitch Dologushev, this same Yakov Bok had made improper advances, and even attempted physical assault of Zinaida Nikolaevna, the daughter of Bok's employer, Nikolai Maximovitch Lebedev. "By good fortune she thwarted his nefarious purposes." Third, Yakov Bok was suspected by certain of his fellow employees at the brickworks, in particular "the observant foreman Proshko," of systematically peculating from funds belonging to the business enterprise of Nikolai Maximovitch Lebedev. Fourth, he was seen on certain occasions by the yardkeeper Skobeliev, the foreman Proshko, and "other witnesses," chasing boys in the brickyard, near the kilns. These were Vasya Shiskovsky, Andrei Khototov, the deceased Zhenia Golov, and other even younger children, all of them boys. And fifth, Zhenia Golov had one night been pursued among the tombstones in the cemetery close to the brickyard by the same Yakov Bok "clasping in his hand a long thin carpenter's knife." The frightened boy had related this to his mother. In Bok's living quarters in the stable the police had unearthed his bag of tools, which included "certain bloodstained awls and knives." Some bloody rags also were recovered in this room.

The fixer sighed and went on reading.

"In addition to the above-listed evidence, Marfa Golov has testified that Zhenia complained Yakov Bok had interfered with him sexually and had feared the boy would expose him to the authorities." "Zhenia, a bright and perceptive lad," had "on certain occasions" followed Bok and discovered that he sometimes met "with a group of other Hebrews, suspected smugglers, house-breakers, and other criminal elements, in the cellar of the synagogue." Her son, according to the mother, threatened to report these illegal activities to the police. Furthermore, Vasya Shiskovsky and Zhenia Golov had once or twice "in the manner of boys," angered Bok by flinging rocks at him and taunting him about his race, and he was determined to take revenge on them. "Zhenia Golov, to his great misfortune, was the one who had fallen into Bok's evil hands, but by great good luck Vasya Shiskovsky had escaped his poor friend's fate."

He read quickly through the section where he had killed the boy. ("Skobeliev testified that he had seen Bok carrying something heavy in his arms, a large squirming package of some sort that resembled a human body, up the stairs to his quarters. There, the evidence is clear, the boy was tortured and then murdered by Yakov Bok, probably with the assistance of one or two of his co-religionists.") "While in prison," the indictment went on, "the said Yakov Bok had attempted to influence the counterfeiter Gronfein, a friend and fellow religionist, to bribe Marfa Golov not to testify against him. The sum of money for that purpose was to be raised by subscription in the Hebrew communities of the Jewish Pale of Settlement. Another bribe was offered to Marfa Golov herself at a later date, the large sum of 40,000 rubles if she would flee across the Austrian border, but she indignantly refused."

The last paragraph read: "It is therefore the fully considered opinion of the Investigating Magistrate, the Prosecuting Attorney, and the President of the Superior Court of the Kiev Province, where the Court Indictment is this day filed, that Yakov Bok, an admitted Hebrew, had with premeditation, and for purposes of torture and murder, stabbed to death Yevgeny Golov, age 12, the beloved son of Marfa Vladimirovna Golov, for the reasons stated above; in sum, an overweening and abnormal desire for revenge against an innocent child who had discovered his participation in criminal activities. However, the crime was so wicked and debased that an additional element may be said to have been present. Only a criminal of the worst sadistic instincts could have engaged in such an unnatural act of unprovoked hostility and degraded bestiality."

The indictment was signed by Yehm Balik, Investigating Magistrate; V. G. Grubeshov, Prosecuting Attorney; and P. F. Furmanov, President of the Superior Court.

Yakov squeezed his throbbing head after reading the papers. Though his eyes ached—he felt as though he had read the words through sand and glue—he at once reread them, and again, in increasing astonishment and disbelief. What had happened to the charge of ritual murder? Holding each sheet up for better light he searched in vain. There was no such charge. Every reference to a religious crime, though hinted at, led up to, had in the end been omitted. The Jews had become Hebrews. Why? The only reason he could think of was that they could not prove a charge of ritual murder. And if they couldn't prove that, what could they prove? Not these stupid lies, vile, ridiculous, some snipped directly out of Marfa's insane letter. They can't prove a thing, he thought, that's why they've kept me in solitary imprisonment for almost two years. They know the mother and her lover murdered the boy. He fought a deepening depression. With this "evidence" they'll never bring me to trial. The weakness of the indictment showed they had no intention to.

Still it was an indictment and he was wondering if they would now let him see a lawyer, when the warden appeared again in the cell and ordered him to hand over the papers.

"You may not believe this, Bok, but they were issued through an administrative error. I was supposed to look them over but not give them to you."

They're afraid of the trial, the fixer thought bitterly, after the warden had left. Maybe people arc asking when it will begin. Maybe this has them worried. If I live, sooner or later they'll have to bring me to trial. If not Nicholas the Second, then Nicholas the Third will.

4

When his chains were unlocked and he was permitted to lie on his bedbench as long as he liked with his legs free, or to walk around, he could not comprehend what had happened and for a while suffered from excitement. Yakov limped around the cell but mostly lay, breathing through his mouth, on the wooden bed. "Is it another indictment, or maybe is the trial coming?" he asked Berezhinsky, but the guard wouldn't say. One day the fixer's hair was trimmed a bit and the beard combed. The barber, glancing stealthily at a yellowed photograph in his tunic pocket, combed out curls over his ears. He was then given another suit of prison clothes, permitted to wash his hands and face with soap, and called to the warden's office.

Berezhinsky pushed him out into the hall and commanded

him to move along, but the prisoner limped slowly, stopping often to recover his breath. The guard prodded him with his rifle butt, then the fixer ran a step and limped two. He worried how he would make it back to the cell.

"Your wife is here," said Warden Grizitskoy, in his office. "You can see her in the visitors' room. There'll be a guard present, so don't presume any privileges.

He felt, in towering astonishment, this could not be true, they were deceiving him to extend the torture. And when, as he watched the warden and guard, he believed it, the fixer gasped as though fire had scorched his lungs. When he could breathe he was frightened.

"My wife?"

"Raisl Bok?"

"It's true."

"You'll be allowed to speak to her for several minutes in the visitors' room, but watch your step."

"Please, not now," said Yakov wearily. "Some other time."

"That'll do," said the warden.

The fixer, shaken, upset, his thoughts in turmoil, was led in a limping trot by Berezhinsky through a series of narrow corridors to the prisoners' pen in the visitors' room. At the door Yakov tried to straighten himself, entered, and was locked in. It's a trick, he thought, it's not her, it's a spy. I must be careful.

She sat on a bench, separated from him by a heavy wire grating. On the far side of the bare-walled boxlike room, a uniformed guard stood behind her, his rifle resting against the wall, slowly rolling a cigarette.

Yakov sat stiffly opposite her, hunched cold, his throat aching, palms clammy. He felt a dread of cracking up, going mad in front of her—of will failing him once they talked and how would he go on after that?

"Get along with your business," said the guard in Russian.

Though the visitors' room was dimly lit it was brighter than his cell, and the light hurt his eyes before he could get used to it. The woman sat motionless, her coat threadbare, a wool shawl covering her head, her fingers clasped like spikes in her lap. She was watching him mutely, eyes stricken. He had expected a hag, but though she was worn, tensely embarrassed, and had abandoned the wig she had never liked to wear, she looked otherwise the same, surprising how young though he knew she was thirty, and not bad as a woman. It's at my expense, he thought bitterly.

"Yakov?"

"Raisl?"

"Yes."

As she unwound her shawl—her own dark hair cut short, the hairline damp—and he looked fully into her face, at the long exposed neck, both eyes sad, she was staring at him with fright and feeling. He tried twice to speak and could not. His face ached and mouth trembled.

"I know, Yakov," Raisl said. "What more can I say? I know."

Emotion blinded him.

My God, what have I forgotten? I've forgotten nothing. He experienced a depth of loss and shame, overwhelming—that the feelings of the past could still be alive after so long and terrible an imprisonment. The deepest wounds never die.

"Yakov, is it really you?"

He shook away the beginning of tears and turned his good ear to her.

"It's me. Who else could it be?"

"How strange you look in earlocks and long beard."

"That's their evidence against me."

"How thin you are, how withered."

"I'm thin," he said, "I'm withered. What do you want from me?"

"They forbade me to ask you any questions about your conditions in this prison," Raisl said in Yiddish, "and I promised not to but who has to ask? I have eyes and can see. I wish I couldn't. Oh, Yakov, what have they done to you? What did you do to yourself? How did such a terrible thing happen?"

"You stinking whore, what did *you* do to me? It wasn't enough we were poor as dirt and childless. On top of that you had to be a whore."

She said tonelessly, "It's not what I alone did, it's what we did to each other. Did you love me? Did I love you? I say yes and I say no. As for being a whore, if I was I'm not. I've had my ups and downs, the same as you, Yakov, but if you're going to judge me you'll have to judge me as I am."

"What are you?"

"Whatever I am I'm not what I was."

"Why did you marry me for I'd like to know? 'Love,' she says. If you didn't love me why didn't you leave me alone?"

"You can believe me I was afraid to marry you, but you were affectionate then, and when a person is lonely it's easy to lean toward a tender word. Also I thought you loved me although you found it hard to say so."

"What can a man say if he's afraid of a trap? I was afraid of you. I never met anybody so dissatisfied. I am a limited man. What could I promise you? Besides that, your father was behind me, pushing with both hands: If I married you the world would change, everyday a rainbow. Then you got me in the woods that day."

"We were to the woods more than once. You wanted what I wanted. It takes two to lie down, one on top of the other."

"So we got married," he said bitterly. "Still, we had a chance. Once we were married you should have been faithful. A contract is a contract. A wife is a wife. Married is married."

"Were you such a fine husband?" Raisl said. "Yes, you always tried to make a living, I won't say no, though you never did. And if you wanted to stay up all night reading Spinoza I had nothing against that either, though it wasn't Torah, except when it was at my expense, and you know what I mean. What bothered me most were the curses and dirty names. Because I slept with you before we were married you were convinced I was sleeping with the world. I slept with no one but you until you stopped sleeping with me. At twenty-eight I was too young for the grave. So, as you advised, I stopped being superstitious and at last took a chance. Otherwise I would soon have been dead. I was barren. I ran in every direction. I flung myself against trees. I tore at my dry breasts and cursed my empty womb. Whether I stayed or left I was useless to you, so I decided to leave. You wouldn't so I had to. I left in desperation to change my life. I got out the only way I could. It was either that or death, one sin or worse. I chose the lesser sin. If you want to know the truth, Yakov, one reason I left was to make you move. Whoever thought it would come to this?"

She cracked her white knuckles against her chest, "Yakov, I didn't come here to fight about the past. Forgive me, forgive the past."

"Why did you come?"

"Papa said he saw you in prison, it's all he talks about. I went back to the shtetl last November. I was first in Kharkov, then in Moscow, but couldn't get along any more, so I had to go back. When I found out you were in Kiev Prison I came to see you but they wouldn't let me in. Then I went to the Prosecuting Attorney and showed him the papers that I was your wife. He said I couldn't see you except under the most extraordinary circumstances, and I said the circumstances were extraordinary enough when an innocent man is kept in prison. I went to see him at least five times and finally he said he would let me in if I brought you a paper to sign. He told me to urge you to sign it."

"A black year on his papers to sign. A black year on you for bringing it."

"Yakov, if you sign you can go free tomorrow. It's at least something to think about."

"I've thought," he shouted. "It's nothing to think about. I'm innocent."

Raisl stared at him mutely.

The guard came over with his rifle. "Nobody's supposed to be talking Yiddish here," he said. "You're supposed to be talking Russian. This prison is a Russian institution."

"It takes longer in Russian," she said. "I speak very slowly in Russian."

"Hurry up with the paper you're supposed to give him."

"The paper has to be explained. There are advantages but there are also disadvantages. I have to tell him what the Prosecuting Attorney said."

"Then tell him, for Christ's sake, and be done with it."

Taking a small key out of his pants pocket, he unlocked a small wire door in the grating.

"Don't try to pass anything but the paper he has to sign or it'll go hard on you both. I've got my eyes wide open."

Raisl unclasped a grayed cloth handbag and took out a folded envelope.

"This is the paper I promised I would give you," she said in Russian to Yakov. "The Prosecuting Attorney says it's your last chance."

"So that's why you came," he said in vehement Yiddish, "to get me to confess lies I've resisted for two years. To betray me again."

"It was the only way I could get in," Raisl said. "But it's not why I came, I came to cry." She gasped a little. Her mouth fell open, the lips contorted; she wept. Tears flowed through her fingers as she pressed them to her eyes. Her shoulders shook.

He felt, as he watched her, the weight of the blood in his heart.

The guard rolled another cigarette, lit it, and smoked slowly.

This is where we left off, thought Yakov. The last time I saw her she was crying like this, and here she is still crying. In the meantime I've been two years in prison without cause, in solitary confinement, and chains. I've suffered freezing cold, filth, lice, the degradation of those searches, and she's still crying.

"What are you crying for?" he asked.

"For you, for me, for the world."

She was as she wept, a frail woman, lanky, small-breasted, worn and sad. Who would have thought so frail? As she wept she moved him. He had learned about tears.

"What's there to do here but think, so I've thought," Yakov said after a while. "I've thought about our life from beginning to end and I can't blame you for more than I blame myself. If you give little you get less, though of some things I got more than I deserved. Also, it takes me a long time to learn. Some people have to make the same mistake seven times before they know they've made it. That's my type and I'm sorry. I'm also sorry I stopped sleeping with you. I was out to stab myself, so I stabbed you. Who else was so close to me? Still I've suffered in this prison and I'm not the same man I once was. What more can I say, Raisl? If I had my life to live over, you'd have less to cry about, so stop crying."

"Yakov," she said, when she had wiped her eyes with her fingers, "I brought this confession paper here so they would let me talk to you, not because I want you to sign it. I don't. Still, if you wanted to what could I say? Should I say stay in prison? What I also came to tell you is maybe not such good news. I came to say I've given birth to a child. After I ran away I found out I was pregnant. I was ashamed and frightened, but at the same time I was happy I was no longer barren and could have a baby."

There's no bottom to my bitterness, he thought.

He flailed at the wooden walls of the pen with both fists. The guard sternly ordered him to stop, so he beat himself instead, his face and head. She looked on with shut eyes.

Afterwards, when it was over, except what was left of his anguish, he said, "So if you weren't barren, what was the matter?"

She looked away, then at him. "Who knows? Some women conceive later. With conception you need luck."

Luck I was short of, he thought, so I blamed her.

"Boy or girl?" Yakov asked.

She smiled at her hands. "A boy, Chaiml, after my grandfather."

"How old now?"

"Almost a year and a half."

"It couldn't be mine?"

"How could it be?"

"Too bad," he sighed. "Where is he now?"

"With Papa. That's why I went back, I couldn't take care of him alone any more. Ah, Yakov, it's not all raisins and almonds. I've gone back to the shtetl but they blame me for your fate. I tried to take up my little dairy business but I might just as well be selling pork. The rabbi calls me to my face, pariah. The child will think his name is bastard."

"So what do you want from me?"

"Yakov," she said, "I'm sorry for what you're suffering. When I heard it was you I tore my hair; but I figured you'd also be sorry for me. Please, it might make things easier if you wouldn't mind saying you are my son's father. Still, if you can't you can't. I don't want to add to your burden."

"Who's the father, some goy I'll bet."

"If it makes you feel better he was a Jew, a musician. He came, he went, I forgot him. He fathered the child but he's not his father. Whoever acts the father is the father. My father's the father but he's only two steps from death's door. One knock and I'm twice widowed."

"What's the matter with him?"

"Diabetes, though he drags himself around. He worries about you, he worries about me and the child. He wakes up cursing himself for not having been born rich. He prays every time he thinks of it. I take care of him the best I can. He sleeps on a bag of rags pushed to the wall. He needs food, rest, medicine. The little we get comes from charity. One or two of the rich send their servants over with this or that, but when they see me they hold their noses."

"Has he talked to anybody about me?"

"To everybody. He runs everywhere, sick as he is."

"What do they say?"

"They tear their hair. They beat their chests. They thank God it wasn't them. Some collect money. Some say they will make protests. Some are afraid to do anything because it may annoy the Christians and make things worse. Some are pessimistic but a few have hope. Still, there's more going on than I know."

"If it doesn't go faster I won't be here to find out what."

"Don't say that, Yakov. I went myself to see some lawyers in Kiev. Two of them swear they will help you but nobody can move without an indictment."

"So I'll wait," said Yakov. Before her eyes he shrank in size.

"I've brought you some haleh and cheese and an apple in a little pack," Raisl said, "But they made me leave it at the warden's office. Don't forget to ask for it. It's goat's cheese but I don't think you'll notice."

"Thanks," said Yakov wearily. He said, after a sigh, "Listen, Raisl, I'll write you a paper that the child's mine."

Her eyes glistened, "God will bless you."

"Never mind God. Have you got a piece of paper, I'll write something down. Show it to the rabbi's father, the old melamed. He knows my handwriting and he's a kinder man than his son."

"I have paper and pencil," she whispered nervously, "but

I'm afraid to give them to you with this guard in the room. They warned me not to hand you anything but the confession and to take nothing but that from you or they would arrest me for attempting to help you escape."

The guard was restless and again came forward. "There's nothing more to talk about. Either sign the paper or go back to your cell."

"Have you got a pencil?" the fixer asked.

The guard took a fat fountain pen from his tunic pocket, and gave it to him through the opening in the grating.

He stayed to watch but Yakov waited until he had withdrawn.

"Give me the confession," he said to Raisl in Russian.

Raisl handed him the envelope. Yakov removed the paper, unfolded it, and read: "I, Yakov Bok, confess that I witnessed the murder of Zhenia Golov, the son of Marfa Golov, by my Jewish compatriots. They killed him on the night of March 20, 1911, upstairs in the stable in the brickyard belonging to Nikolai Maximovitch Lebedev, merchant of the Lukianovsky District."

Under that a heavy line was drawn on which to sign his name.

Yakov placed the paper on the shelf before him and wrote in Russian on the line for his name: "Every word is a lie."

On the envelope, pausing between words to remember the letters for the next, he wrote in Yiddish, "I declare myself to be the father of Chaim, the infant son of my wife, Raisl Bok. He was conceived before she left me. Please help the mother and child, and for this, amid all my troubles, I'll be grateful. Yakov Bok."

She told him the date and he wrote it down. "February 27, 1913." Yakov passed it to her through the opening in the grating.

Raisl slipped the envelope into her coat sleeve and handed the guard the confession paper. He folded it at once, and thrust it into his tunic pocket. After examining the contents of Raisl's handbag and tapping her coat pockets he told her to go.

"Yakov," she wept, "come home."

IX

He was chained to the wall again. Things went badly. Better not have been unchained, the getting back was so bad. He beat the clanking chains against the wall until it was scarred white where he stood. They let him beat the wall. Otherwise he slept. But for the searches he would have slept through the day. He slept through the end of winter and into spring. Kogin said it was April. Two years. The searches went on except when he was sick with dysentery. The Deputy Warden did not come near him then, though Berezhinsky sometimes searched him alone. Once after the fixer was sick the cell was hosed down and a fire started in the stove. An old pink-faced man came into the cell dressed in winter clothes. He wore a black cape and black gaiters and grasped a gnarled cane. Berezhinsky followed him in, carrying a slender chair with a delicate back, and the old man sat in it erectly, several feet from the fixer, holding the cane with gray-mittened hands. His watery eyes wandered. He told Yakov he was a former jurist of high repute, and that he came with good news. An excitement so thick it felt like sickness surged through the fixer. He asked what good news. The former jurist said this was the year of the three-hundredth anniversary of the rule of the House of Romanov and that the Tsar, in celebration, would issue a ukase amnestying certain classes of criminals. Yakov's name would be listed among them. He was to be pardoned and permitted to return to his village. The old man's face flushed with pleasure. The prisoner clung to the wall, too burdened to speak. Then he asked, Pardoned as a criminal or pardoned as innocent? The former jurist testily said what difference did it make so long as he was let out of prison. It was impossible to erase the sins of the past, but it was not impossible for a humane ruler, a Christian gentleman, to forgive an evil act. The old man sneezed without snuff and peered at his silver watch. Yakov said he wanted a fair trial, not a pardon. If they ordered him to leave the prison without a trial they would have to shoot him first. Don't be foolish, said the former jurist, how can you go on suffering like this, caked in filth? The fixer moved his chains restlessly. I have no choice, he said. I have just offered you one. That's not choice, said Yakov. The former jurist tried to convince the prisoner, then gave up in irritation. It's easier to reason with a peasant. He rose and shook his cane at the fixer. How can we help you, he shouted, if you are so pigheaded? Berezhinsky, who had been listening at the spy hole, opened the door and the old man left the cell. The guard came in for the chair but before taking it, he let Yakov urinate in the can, then dumped the contents on his head. The fixer was left in chains that night. He thought that whenever he had been through the worst, there was always worse.

One day, during Yakov's third summer in prison, his manacles and shackles were unlocked. Immediately his heart beat heavily and when he touched it with his hand the hand beat like his heart. In an hour the warden, who had aged since the fixer had last seen him and walked with shorter steps, brought in a new indictment in a brown envelope, a sheaf of papers twice thicker than the last. The fixer took the papers and read them slowly and frantically, fearing he would never get to the end of them; but he had discovered at once what he had expected: that the blood murder charge had been violently revived. Now they are serious again, he thought. The reference to sexual experiences with the boy, and to activities with a gang of Jewish housebreakers and smugglers operating out of the cellar of the Kiev synagogue—all the insane lies from Marfa Golov's letter—were omitted. Once again Yakov Bok was accused of murdering the innocent boy in order to drain his body of blood necessary for the baking of Passover matzos and cakes.

This was affirmed by Professor Manilius Zagreb, who with his distinguished colleague, the surgeon Dr. Sergei Bul, had twice performed the autopsy of Zhenia's remains. Both categorically stated that the vicious wounds had been inflicted in prearranged clusters with a time interval between each cluster in order to prolong the torture and facilitate the bleeding. It was estimated that one litre of blood was collected from each set of wounds, and that a total of five litres of blood was collected in bottles. Such was also the conclusion of Father Anastasy, the well-known specialist in Jewish affairs, who had made a close study of the Talmud, his reasons given in minute detail for eight single-spaced pages. And it was also the conclusion of Yefim Balik, the Investigating Magistrate. He had carefully reviewed the entire evidence and agreed with its "direction and findings."

How the bloodthirsty crime was committed was described in this indictment much as it had been by Grubeshov at the cave, more than two years ago, "with careful note taken of the fanatic Hasidic tsadik, seen in the brickyard by the foreman Proshko; who had no doubt helped the accused drain the necessary blood from the boy's still living body, and also assisted him in transporting the corpse to the cave where two horrified boys had found it." And related evidence omitted from the previous indictment was included in this. It was stated that half a bag of matzo flour was "hidden away" in Yakov Bok's stable room, together with certain hard pieces of already baked matzo no doubt containing the innocent blood, which both the Jews "in all probability" had eaten. And the usual bloodstained rag, "admitted by the accused to be a piece of his shirt" had been uncovered in the same room. According to the testimony of Vasya Shiskovsky, a bottle of bright-red blood was seen by him and Zhenia on a table in Bok's stable room, but it had disappeared when the police searched for it. And a sack of carpenter's tools containing bloodstained awls and knives had been found in the same room after the fixer's arrest, "despite a plot later carried out by Jewish co-conspirators to destroy this and other significant evidence by burning down the brickyard stable, a plot which they ultimately achieved."

Towards the end of this wearying, terrifying document a new subject was introduced, "the matter of Yakov Bok's self-proclaimed atheism." It was noted that although the accused, when first examined by the authorities, had confessed he was a Jew "by birth and nationality," he had however claimed for himself "an atheistic status; to wit, that he was a freethinker and not a religious Jew." Why he should make "such an odious self-description" was understandable to anyone who reflected for a moment on the matter. It was done to create "extenuating circumstances" and "obfuscating details" in order "to deflect the legal investigation by hiding the motive for this dastardly crime." However this assertion of atheism could not be defended, for it was observed by reliable witnesses, including prison guards and officials, that Yakov Bok, while incarcerated and awaiting trial, "though persisting in his false claim of irreligion, had in his cell secretly prayed daily in the manner of Orthodox Jews, wrapped in a prayer shawl, with black phylacteries entwined around his brow and left arm." He was also seen piously reading an Old Testament Bible, "which, like the previously mentioned Orthodox religious instruments, had been smuggled into his cell by fellow Jews of the synagogue." It was clear to all who observed him that he was engaged in the performance of a devout religious rite. He had continued to use the prayer shawl until he had worn it out, and "even now he kept a remnant of this sacred garment in his coat pocket."

It was the opinion of investigators and other officials that this self-incriminating atheism "was a fabrication of Yakov Bok's, in order to hide from the legal authorities that he had committed a vile religious murder of a child for the sole and evil purpose of providing his Hasidic compatriots with the uncorrupted human blood needed to bake the Passover matzos and unleavened cakes."

After he had finished reading the document the fixer, in exhaustion, thought, there's no getting rid of the blood any more. It's stained every word of the indictment and can't be washed out. When they try me it will be for the crucifixion.

The fixer grew more intensely worried. Now that he had this paper would they withdraw it and later issue another? Was this the newest torture? Would they hand him indictments, time after time, for the next twenty years? He would read them till he died of frustration or his dry brain exploded. Or would they, after this indictment, or the third, seventh, or thirteenth *at last* bring him to trial? Could they make a strong enough circumstantial case against him? He hoped they could. Anyway, just barely. If not, would they keep him in chains forever? Or were they planning a worse fate? One day as he was about to clean himself with a scrap of newspaper he read on it, "THE JEW IS DOOMED." Yakov frantically read on to find out why, but that part was torn off.

2

He had been told a lawyer was on his way to the prison, but when the cell door was opened on a hot July night, it was not the lawyer, it was Grubeshov, in evening dress. The fixer awoke when Kogin, holding a dripping candle, unlocked his feet. "Wake up," said the guard, shaking him, "his honor is here." Yakov awoke as though coming up out of deep dirty water. He beheld Grubeshov's moist fleshy face, his sidewhiskers limp, his red-shot eyes, lit, restless. The public prosecutor's chest rose and fell. He began pacing in the cell, unsteadily, then sat down on the stool, one hand on the table, an enormous shadow on the wall behind him. He stared for a moment at the lamp, blinked at it, and gazed at Yakov. When he talked, the stink of rich food and alcohol on his breath drifted across to the fixer, nauseating him.

"I am on my way home from a civic banquet in honor of the Tsar," Grubeshov, breathing with a whistle, said to the prisoner. "Since my motorcar happened to be in this district, I ordered the driver to go on to the prison. I thought I would speak to you. You are a stubborn man, Bok, but perhaps not yet beyond reason. I thought I would talk to you one last time. Please stand up while I am speaking."

Yakov, sitting on the wooden bed with his bony bare feet on the clammy floor, slowly got up. Grubeshov, gazing at his face, shuddered. The fixer felt a violent hatred of him.

"First of all," said Grubeshov, patting the back of his flushed neck with a large humid handkerchief, "you oughtn't to let your expectations rise too high, Yakov Bok. You will be disappointed if they do. Don't think just because an indictment has been issued that your worries are over. On the contrary—now begin your worst troubles. I warn you, you will be publicly unmasked and seen for what you are."

"What do you want from me here, Mr. Grubeshov? It's late at night. I need my little rest for the chains in the morning."

"As for the chains, that's your fault; learn to follow orders. It's none of my affair, I came on other business. Marfa Golov, the victim's mother, visited me in my office today. She knelt before me with holy tears streaming from her eyes, and swore before God that she had told the absolute truth regarding Zhenia and his experiences with you that led to the murder. She is a totally sincere woman and I was deeply affected by her. I am more than ever convinced that a jury will believe what she says, and so much the worse for you. Her testimony and the sincerity of her appearance will demolish whatever case you think you can make."

"Then let her give her testimony," Yakov said. "Why don't you begin the trial?"

Grubeshov, who squirmed on the stool as though it were the top of a hot stove, answered, "I have no intention of engaging in an argument with a criminal. I came to tell you that if you and your fellow Jews continue to press me to bring you to trial before I have gathered every last grain of evidence, or investigated all courses of action, then you ought to know what dangers you are creating for yourself. There can be too much of a good thing, Bok, if you understand my meaning. The kettle may steam but don't be surprised if the water is boiled off."

"Mr. Grubeshov," said Yakov, "I can't stand up any more. I'm tired and must sit down. If you want to shoot me call the guard, he has a gun."

Yakov sat down on the bedplank.

"You're a cheeky one," Grubeshov said, his voice emotional. "The Russian people are sick to their souls of your Jewish tricks and deceptions. That holds also for your investigators, your complaints, your libels from all over. What is happening, Bok, obviously reveals the underground involvement of the Jewish conspiracy in Russian affairs, and I warn you to take rational notice that there is bound to be a tumultuous reprisal against the enemies of the state. Even if by some trickery you were to succeed in swaying a jury to render a judgment against the weight of the true evidence, then you can believe me that the Russian people in justifiable wrath will avenge this poor Zhenia for the pain and torture that you inflicted on him. You may wish for the trial now, but remember this: even the judgment that you are guilty will set off a bloodbath in this city that will outdo the ferocity of the so-called Kishinev massacres. A trial will not save you nor your fellow Jews. You would be better off confessing, and after a period of time when the public has settled down, we could announce your death in prison, or something of the sort, and spirit you out of Russia. If you insist on the trial, then don't be surprised if bearded heads roll in the street. Feathers fly. Cossack steel invades the tender flesh of young Jewesses."

Grubeshov had risen from the hot stool and was pacing again, his shadow going one way on the wall as he went the other.

"A government has to protect itself from subversion, by force if it can't persuade."

Yakov stared at his white crooked feet.

The public prosecutor, in the grip of his excitement, went on: "My father once described to me an incident involving a synagogue cellar full of Jews, men and women, who attempted to hide from the Cossacks during a raid on their village. The sergeant ordered them to come up one by one and at first none of them stirred, but then a few came up the steps holding their arms over their heads. This did do them not the least good as they were clubbed to death with rifle butts. The rest of them, though they were like herrings stuck together in a stinking barrel, would not move although they had been warned it would go worse with them. And so it did. The impatient Cossacks rushed into the cellar, bayoneting and shooting every last Jew. Those who were dragged out still alive were later thrown from speeding trains. A few, beginning with their benzine-soaked beards, were burned alive, and some of the women were dropped in their underclothes into wells to drown. You can take my word for it that in less than a week after your trial, there will be a quarter-million fewer Zhidy in the Pale."

He paused to breathe, then went on thickly. "Don't think we don't know that you wish to provoke just such a pogrom. We know from Secret Police reports that you are plotting to bring down on yourselves a violent reaction for revolutionary purposes—to stimulate active subversion among Socialist revolutionaries. The Tsar is informed of this, you can be sure, and is prepared to give you increased doses of the medicine I have described if you persist in trying to destroy his authority. I warn you, there is already a detachment of Ural Cossacks quartered in Kiev."

Yakov spat on the floor.

Either Grubeshov did not see or pretended he hadn't. Now, as though he had spent his anger, his voice became calm. "I am here to tell you this for your own good, Yakov Bok, and for the ultimate good of your fellow Jews. It's all I will say now, absolutely all. I leave the rest to your contemplation and judgment. Have you any suggestions on how to forestall such an appalling, catastrophic—and I say frankly—useless tragedy? I appeal to your humanitarian impulses. One can imagine all sorts of compromises a person in your situation might be willing to make to tip the balance against disaster. I'm very serious. Have you something to say? If so, speak up."

"Mr. Grubeshov, bring me to trial. I will wait for the trial, even to my death."

"And death is what you will get. It's on your head, Bok."

"On yours," said Yakov. "And for what you did to Bibikov."

Grubeshov stared at the fixer with white eyes. The shadow of a huge bird flew off the wall. The lamps went out and the cell door clanged.

Kogin, in a foul mood, slammed the stocks on the fixer's feet.

3

The lawyer had come and gone, Julius Ostrovsky.

He had appeared one day a few weeks after the Prosecuting Attorney's visit, whispered with the prisoner an hour, filling his ear with what was going on, some that the fixer already had guessed, much that astonished him. He was astonished that strangers knew more than he of the public cause of his suffering and that the complications were so fantastic and endless.

"Tell me the worst," Yakov had begged, "do you think I will ever get out of here?"

"The worst is that we don't know the worst," Ostrovsky had answered. "We know you didn't do it, the worst is they know it too but say you did. This is the worst."

"Do you know when my trial is coming—if ever?"

"What can I answer you? They won't tell us what's happening today, so what can we expect to find out about tomorrow? Tomorrow they also hide from us. They hide even the most basic facts. They're afraid that anything we might know is a Jewish trick. What else can you expect if you are fighting a deadly war and everybody pretends, who's fighting? it's peace. It's a war, believe me."

The lawyer had risen when Yakov had limped into the room. This time there was no screen separating the prisoner from his visitor. Ostrovsky had at once cautioned him with a gesture, then whispered in his ear, "Speak quietly—to the floor. They say there's no guard outside the door but speak as if Grubeshov stands there if not the devil."

He was past sixty, a stocky man with a lined face and baldish head from which a few gray hairs rose like stubble. He had bent legs, wore two-toned button shoes, a black cravat and a short beard.

He had, when the prisoner appeared, stared at Yakov as though unable to believe this was the one. Finally he believed and his eyes changed from surprise to concern. He spoke in intense whispered Yiddish with more than one emotion. "I will introduce myself, Mr. Bok, Julius Ostrovsky of the Kiev bar. I'm glad I'm here at last but don't cheer yet, it's a long way to go. Anyway, some friends sent me."

"I'm thankful."

"You have friends though not all Jews, I'm sorry to say, are your friends. What I mean is that if a man hides his head in a bucket, whose friend is he? To my great regret some of our people shiver in every weather. We have organized a committee to help you but their caution is excessive. They're afraid to 'meddle' or there'll be another calamity. That's in itself a calamity. They shoot with popguns and run from the noise. Still, who has all friends?"

"Then who are my friends?"

"I am one and there are others. Take my word, you're not alone."

"Can you do anything for me? I'm sick of prison."

"What we can do we'll do. It's a long fight, I don't have to tell you, and the odds are against us. Still, anyway, calm, calm, calm. As the sages say, there are always two possibilities. One we know from too long experience; the other—the miracle—we will hope for. It's easy to hope, it's the waiting that spoils it. But two possibilities make the odds even. So enough philosophy. At this minute there's not much good news; finally we squeezed out an indictment, which means they will now have to schedule the case for trial, though when I leave to Rashi. But first, if you'll excuse me, I'll give you the bad news." Ostrovsky sighed. "I'm sorry that your father-in-law, Shmuel Rabinovitch, who I had the pleasure to meet and talk to last summer—a gifted man—is now, I'm sorry to tell you, dead from diabetes. This your wife wrote me in a letter."

"Ah," said Yakov.

Death had preceded itself. Poor Shmuel, the fixer thought, now I'll never see him again. That's what happens when you say goodbye to a friend and ride out into the world.

He covered his face with his hands and wept.

"He was a good man, he tried to educate me."

"The thing about life is how fast it goes," Ostrovsky said.

"Faster than that."

"You suffer for us all," the lawyer said huskily. "I would be honored to be in your place."

"It's without honor," Yakov said, wiping his eyes with his fingers, and rubbing his hands together. "It's a dirty suffering."

"You've got my respect."

"If you don't mind tell me how my case stands. Tell me the truth."

"The truth is that things are bad though how bad I don't

know myself. The case is clear enough—it's a bad joke from top to bottom—but it's mixed up in the worst way with the political situation. Kiev, you understand, is a medieval city full of wild superstition and mysticism. It has always been the heart of Russian reaction. The Black Hundreds, may they sink into their graves, have aroused against you the most ignorant and brutal of the masses. They are deathly afraid of Jews and at the same time frighten them to death. This reveals to you something about the human condition. Rich or poor, those of our brethren who can run out of here are running. Some who can't are already mourning. They sniff at the air and it stinks of pogrom. What's going on, as I say, nobody can say precisely. There's on the one hand a rumor that everything that happens, including your indictment, is another delay, and your trial, if you'll excuse me for saying it, will never take place; but on the other hand we hear it might start right after the Duma elections in September. Yes or no, they have no case against you. The civilized world knows this, including the Pope and his cardinals. If Grubeshov 'proves' anything it will be by the lies of 'the experts.' But we have our experts against them, for instance a Russian professor of theology, and I've written to Pavlov, the Tsar's surgeon, to testify on the medical report of the boy's autopsy and he hasn't said no yet. Grubeshov knows who the real murderers are but he shuts both eyes and stares at you. He went to law school with my oldest son and was famous for his socks and vests. Now he's famous for his anti-Semitic socks and vests. Out of Marfa Golov, that piece of trash, he tries to make if not a new saint, at least a persecuted heroine. Her blind lover tried last week to take his life but thank God, he's still alive. Also a clever journalist—may the Lord make more like him!—Pitirim Mirsky, discovered recently that Zhenia's father left him a life insurance legacy of five hundred rubles that the two murderers coveted, got, and at once spent. Two hogs, as they say, are worse than one. Mirsky printed this last week in *Poslednie Novosti,* and for that the publisher was fined and the press shut down by the police for three months. They must now discontinue all items about Golov. This is black reaction, but I'm not here to frighten you. You have enough to worry about."

"What else can frighten me?"

"If you feel bad think of Dreyfus. He went through the same thing with the script in French. We're persecuted in the most civilized languages."

"I've thought of him. It doesn't help."

"He was in prison many years, much longer than you."

"So far."

Ostrovsky, nodding absently as he gazed at the door, softened his whisper. "We also have an affidavit from Sofya Shiskovsky. One night she went into the toilet in Marfa's house to relieve herself, and there in the bathtub lay the naked corpse covered with wounds. So she screamed and ran out of the house. Marfa, who had gone for a minute upstairs to get a letter to prove a lie, ran after her and caught her in the street. That one—a madwoman of the First Guild—threatened to murder the whole Shiskovsky family if they breathed a word to anybody. They were afraid for Vasya, so they packed the furniture and moved on. When we finally located them, in a log hut in a back street in Moscow, she threatened to kill herself if we interfered with her, but with luck we got at least a short affidavit. She wouldn't let us question Vasya, but we will try to have them both in court when the trial starts, if they aren't by that time in Asia. So this is another reason why the prosecution drags its feet: they can't prove a ritual murder but they won't stop trying, and the longer they take the more dangerous the situation becomes. It's dangerous because it's irrational, complex, secret. And it grows more dangerous as they get more desperate."

"Then what will I do?" said Yakov in despair. "How much more can I stand if I'm already half dead?"

"Patience, calm, calm, calm," Ostrovsky counseled, clasping his hands and squeezing. Then he looked at the fixer in a new light and struck his head with his palm.

"For God's sake, why are we standing yet? Come sit down. Forgive me, I'm blind in both eyes."

They sat then on a narrow bench in the far corner of the room away from the door, the lawyer still whispering. "Your case is tied up with the frustrations of recent Russian history. The Russo-Japanese War, I don't have to tell you, was a terrible disaster but it brought on the Revolution of 1905, which was coming anyway. 'War,' as Marx says, 'is the locomotive of history.' This was good for Russia but bad for the Jews. The government, as usual, blamed us for their troubles and not more than one day after the Tsar's concessions pogroms started simultaneously in three hundred towns. Of course you know this, what Jew doesn't?"

"Tell me anyway, what harm can it do?"

"The Tsar was frightened by the rising agitation—strikes, riots, assassinations. The country was paralyzed. After the Winter Palace massacre he reluctantly gave out a ukase promising the basic freedoms. He granted a Constitution, the Imperial Duma was established, and for a short time it looked—for Russia, you understand—like the beginning of a liberal period. The Jews cried hurray for the Tsar and wished him luck. Imagine, in the first Duma we had twelve deputies! Right away they brought up the question of equal rights for all and the abolition of the Pale of Settlement. Like a new world, no?"

"Yes, but go on."

"I'll go on but what can I say? In a sick country every step to health is an insult to those who live on its sickness. The imperial absolutists, the rightist elements, warned the Tsar his crown was slipping. He was already regretting the concessions and began to try to cancel them. In other words, for ten minutes he put on the lights and what he saw frightened him so much, since then he has been putting them out one by one so nobody will notice. As much as he could he changed back to an autocratic regime. The reactionary groups—the Union of Russian People, the Society of the Double-headed Eagle, the Union of the Archangel Michael—oppose worker and peasant movements, liberalism, socialism, any kind of reform, which also meant, naturally, the common enemy, the Jews. At the thought of a constitutional monarch their bones rattled. Organized together, they became the Black Hundreds, which means in gangs of a hundred for what disgusting purposes I don't have to tell you. They gnaw like rats to destroy the independence of the courts, the liberal press, the prestige of the Duma. To distract popular attention from the breaches of the Russian Constitution they incite nationalism against non-Orthodox Russians. They persecute every minority—Poles, Finns, Germans, us—but especially us. Popular discontent they divert into anti-Semitic outbreaks. It's a simple solution to their problems. Also they enjoy themselves because with the government's help they murder Jews and it's good for business."

"I'm only one man, what do they want from me?"

"One man is all they need so long as they can hold him up as an example of Jewish bloodthirst and criminality. To prove a point it's best to have a victim. In 1905 and 1906 thousands of innocent people were butchered, property damage in the millions of rubles. These pogroms were planned in the office of the Minister of Interior. We know that the anti-Jewish proclamations were printed on Police Department presses. And there are rumors that the Tsar himself contributes from the royal treasury for anti-Semitic books and pamphlets. We got all we need to frighten us but we're also frightened by rumors."

"By the wind," said Yakov.

"If you're frightened everything frightens you," Ostrovsky said. "Anyway, it's a long story but I'm making it short. Now I come direct to your door. When Premier Stolypin, no friend of ours, wanted, before the election of the second Duma, to throw a few bones to the Jews, a few little rights to stop their big complaints, the reactionaries ran to the Tsar and right away he changed the Electoral Laws, taking away the vote from a large part of the population to reduce Jewish and liberal representation in the Duma and cut down opposition to the government. We now have maybe three deputies for three and a half million Jews and these too they want to get rid of. A year ago they assassinated one right in the street. But now I come to you. An atmosphere of hysteria developed all over the country. Still, there was some progress, don't ask me how, and the Imperial Duma was once more discussing whether, yes or no, to abolish the Pale of Jewish Settlement when right at this minute, when the Black Hundreds were frantic, one day a Christian boy was found dead in a cave and there appeared on the scene, Yakov Bok."

The fixer sat numbed. He waited for Ostrovsky to spit, but the lawyer sighed deeply and went on talking. "Where you came from nobody knew, or who you were, but you came just in time. I understand you came on a horse. When they saw you they pounced, and that's why we're sitting here now. But don't feel too bad, if it weren't you there'd be another in your place."

"Yes," said Yakov. "Somebody like me. I've thought it all out."

"So that's your bag of history," Ostrovsky said.

"In that case, what difference does it make if my trial comes or it doesn't?"

Ostrovsky got up, tiptoed to the door and abruptly opened it. Then he returned to the bench. "No one there but this way they'll know we're alert to them. I told you the worst," he said as he sat down, "now I'll tell you the best: You have a chance. What kind of chance? A chance. A chance is a chance, it's better than no chance. Anyway, hear me out so I can stop talking. First of all, not every Russian is your enemy. God forbid. The intelligentsia is disturbed by this case. Many luminaries of literature, science, and the professions have objected against the blood ritual slander. Not so long ago the Kharkov Medical Society passed a resolution protesting your imprisonment, and the next thing that happened the society was dissolved by the government authorities. I told you already about *Poslednie Novosti.* Other newspapers have been fined for their probing articles and editorials. I know members of the bar who openly say that Marfa Golov and her lover committed the murder. Some say she wrote the original letter to the Black Hundreds, accusing the Jews of the crime. My theory is they came to her and asked her to write such a letter. Anyway, an opposition exists, which is good and it's bad. Where there's opposition to reaction there's also repression; but better repression than public sanction of injustice. So a chance you've got."

"Not more?"

"More. Freedom exists in the cracks of the state. Even in Russia a little justice can be found. It's a strange world. On the one hand we have the strictest autocracy; on the other we are approaching anarchy; in between courts exist and justice is possible. The law lives in the minds of men. If a judge is honest the law is protected. If that's the case, so are you. Also a jury is a jury—human beings—they could free you in five minutes."

"Should I hope?" said the fixer.

"If it doesn't hurt, hope. Still, since I'm telling the truth let me tell it all. Once we're on trial some witnesses will lie because they're frightened, and others because they're liars. Also you can expect that the Minister of Justice will appoint a presiding judge who is favorable to the prosecution. If the verdict is guilty his career will advance. And we also suspect that intellectuals and liberals will be eliminated from the jury lists and there's nothing we can do about it. With those that are left we will have to contend. So if you must hope, hope. I'm sure Grubeshov isn't confident of his case. What's more important he's not confident of himself. He's ambitious but limited. In the end he will need better evidence than he has now. The trouble with resting your case on experts is that there are other experts. So I come back to the jury. In our favor is that although they may be ignorant peasants and shopkeepers, simple folk, as a rule they have little love for state officials, and when it comes to facts they can smell when they stink. For instance they know that Jewish roosters don't lay eggs. If Grubeshov strains he will make serious mistakes and your lawyer will know how to take advantage of them. He's an outstanding man from Moscow, Suslov-Smirnov, a Ukrainian by birth."

"Not you?" said Yakov in astonishment. "You aren't my lawyer?"

"I was," said Ostrovsky with an apologetic smile, "but not any more. Now I'm a witness."

"What kind of witness?"

"They accuse me of attempting to bribe Marfa Golov not to testify against you. Of course she swears to it. I talked to her, naturally, but the accusation is ridiculous, it's to keep me from defending you. I don't know if you've heard my name before, Mr. Bok? Probably not," he sighed, "but I have a little reputation in criminal cases. Still I don't want you to worry. Suslov-Smirnov I would use myself if I were in your place. He will be chief of your defense. He was in his youth anti-Semitic but he has now become a vigorous defender of the rights of Jews."

Yakov groaned. "Who needs a former anti-Semite?"

"You can take my word," Ostrovsky said quickly. "He is a brilliant lawyer, and his conversion is sincere. Next time I come I will bring him to you. Believe me, he will know how to deal with these people."

He glanced at his ticking watch, tucked it into his vest pocket, then hurried to the door and opened it. A guard with a rifle was standing there. Without surprise the lawyer shut the door and returned to the prisoner.

"I will speak what's on my mind," he said in Russian. "I say this against my will, Mr. Bok, and with a heavy heart. You have suffered much and I don't want to add to your burdens but the prosecution is desperate and this makes me fear for your life. If you should die, naturally an unproved case will help the government more than a verdict against them, no matter how much they are suspected of or criticized for your death. I think you know what I mean. So all I will say to you is be careful. Don't allow yourself to be provoked. Remember—patience, calm, you have a few friends."

Yakov said he wanted to live.

"Please," said Ostrovsky.

4

He was not, on his return to the cell, locked in chains. They had been torn out of the wall and the holes cemented. The fixer, all but weightless, sat on the edge of the wooden bed, his head in rarefied air, his body roaring with excitement. He listened to the noise for half an hour before he knew he was listening to his swarming clanking thoughts. Shmuel was dead, let him rest in peace. He had deserved better than he had got. A lawyer, Ostrovsky, had been to see him. He had spoken of the trial; there was a chance. Another lawyer, a reformed Ukrainian anti-Semite, would defend him in court before a prejudiced judge and ignorant jury. But that was all in the future, when, nobody could say. Now he was at least no longer anonymous to all but his prosecutors and jailers.

He was not unknown. There had blown up from somewhere a public opinion. Not every Russian believed him guilty. The fog was thinning a little. Newspapers were printing articles casting doubt on the accusation. Some lawyers were openly blaming Marfa Golov. A doctors' society had protested his imprisonment. He had become—who would have thought it?—a public person. Yakov laughed and wept a little. It was fantastic to believe. He tried to be hopeful but was immersed in fears of all there was still to live through.

"Why me?" he asked himself for the ten thousandth time. Why did it happen to a poor, half-ignorant fixer? Who needed this kind of education? Education he would have been satisfied to get from books. Each time he answered his question he answered it differently. He saw it as part personal fate—his various shortcomings and mistakes—but also as force of circumstance, though how you separated one from the other—if one really could—was beyond him. Who, for instance, *had* to go find Nikolai Maximovitch lying drunk in the snow and drag him home to start off an endless series of miserable events? Was that the word of God, inexorable Necessity? Go find your fate—try first the fat Russian with his face in the snow. Go be kind to an anti-Semite and suffer for it. And from him to his daughter with the crippled leg was only one crippled step, and then another into the brickyard. And a crippled hop into prison. If he had stayed in the shtetl it would never have happened. At least not this. Something else would have happened, better not think what.

Once you leave you're out in the open; it rains and snows. It snows history, which means what happens to somebody starts in a web of events outside the personal. It starts of course before he gets there. We're all in history, that's sure, but some are more than others, Jews more than some. If it snows not everybody is out in it getting wet. He had been doused. He had, to his painful surprise, stepped into history more deeply than others—it had worked out so. Why he would never know. Because he had taken to reading Spinoza? An idea makes you adventurous? Maybe, who knows? Anyway, if he hadn't been Yakov Bok, a born Jew, he would not have been, to start with, an outlaw in the Lukianovsky when they were looking for one; he would never have been arrested.

They might still be looking. It was, you could say, history's doing, it was full of all sorts of barriers and limitations, as though certain doors had been boarded up in a house and to get out you had to jump out of a window. If you jumped you might land on your head. In history, thicker at times than at others, too much happens. Ostrovsky had explained this to him. If conditions were ripe whatever was likely to happen was waiting for you to come along so it could happen. With less history around you might walk by or through it: it looked like rain but the sun was shining. In the snow he had once come upon Nikolai Maximovitch Lebedev wearing his Black Hundreds button. Nobody lived in Eden any more.

Yet though his young mother and father had remained all their poor lives in the shtetl, the historical evil had galloped in to murder them there. So the "open," he thought, was anywhere. In or out, it was history that counted—the world's bad memory. It remembered the wrong things. So for a Jew it was the same wherever he went, he carried a remembered pack on his back—a condition of servitude, diminished opportunity, vulnerability. No, there was no need to go to Kiev, or Moscow, or any place else. You could stay in the shtetl and trade in air or beans, dance at weddings or funerals, spend your life in the synagogue, die in bed and pretend you had died in peace, but a Jew wasn't free. Because the government destroyed his freedom by reducing his worth. Therefore wherever he was or went and whatever happened was perilous. A door swung open at his approach. A hand reached forth and plucked him in by his Jewish beard—Yakov Bok, a freethinking Jew in a brick factory in Kiev, yet any Jew, any plausible Jew—to be the Tsar's adversary and victim; chosen to murder the corpse His Majesty had furnished free; to be imprisoned, starved, degraded, chained like an animal to a wall although he was innocent. Why? Because no Jew was innocent in a corrupt state, the most visible sign of its corruption its fear and hatred of those it persecuted. Ostrovsky had reminded him that there was much more wrong with Russia than its anti-Semitism. Those who persecute the innocent were themselves never free. Instead of satisfying him this thought filled him with rage.

It had happened—he was back to this again—because he

was Yakov Bok and had an extraordinary amount to learn. He had learned, it wasn't easy; the experience was his; it was worse than that, it was he. He was the experience. It also meant that now he was somebody else than he had been, who would have thought it? So I learned a little, he thought, I learned this but what good will it do me? Will it open the prison doors? Will it allow me to go out and take up my poor life again? Will it free me a little once I am free? Or have I only learned to know what my condition is—that the ocean is salty as you are drowning, and though you knew it you are drowned? Still, it was better than not knowing. A man had to learn, it was his nature.

Being without chains goaded impatience, what could he do with himself? Time began to move again, like a locomotive with two cars, three cars, four cars, a cluster of days, then two weeks gone, and to his horror, another season. It was autumn and he trembled at the thought of winter. The cold thought hurt his head. Suslov-Smirnov, an excitable, loose-boned long man with thick-lensed eyeglasses on a thin nose, and a bushy head of blond hair, had come four times to ask questions and take voluminous notes on thin sheets of paper—Ostrovsky had been forbidden to return. The lawyer had embraced the prisoner and promised—"Although we are hindered by stupid officials dragging their feet"—to move with all possible dispatch. "But in the meantime you must be careful of every step you take. Walk, as they say, on eggs, Mr. Bok. On eggs." He nodded, winked with both eyes, and pressed four fingers to his lips.

"Do you know," Yakov said, "that they killed Bibikov?"

"We know," whispered Suslov-Smirnov, looking around in fright, "but we can't prove it. Say nothing or you'll make your situation worse."

"I've already said it," the fixer said, "to Grubeshov."

Suslov-Smirnov wrote it down quickly, then erased it and left. He said he would return but didn't, and no one would tell the fixer why. Have I made still another mistake? Again the indictment withdrawn? Yakov slowly tore at his flesh with his nails. The rest of another month leaked by. He again kept count of the days with bits of paper torn from the toilet paper strips. He weighed, he thought, a ton, all grief. His little hope—the hope he had foolishly dared—flickered, waned, withered. His legs were swollen and his back teeth loose. He was at the lowest ebb of his life when the warden appeared with an immaculate paper, saluted, and said his trial was about to begin.

5

All night the cell was crowded with prisoners who had lived and died there. They were broken-faced, greenish-gray men, with haunted eyes, scarred shaved heads and ragged bodies, crowding the cell. Many stared wordlessly at the fixer and he at them, their eyes lit with longing for life. If one disappeared two appeared in his place. So many prisoners, thought the prisoner, it's a country of prisoners. They've freed the serfs, or so they say, but not the innocent prisoners. He beheld long lines of them, gaunt-eyed men with starved mouths, lines stretching through the thick walls to impoverished cities, the vast empty steppe, great snowy virgin forests, to the shabby wooden work camps in Siberia. Trofim Kogin was among them. He had broken his leg and lay in the snow as the long lines slowly moved past him. He lay with his eyes shut and mouth twitching but did not call for help.

"Help!" cried Yakov in the dark.

This night before his trial, the fixer was oppressed by fear of death and though he was deathly sleepy he would not sleep. When his heavy eyes shut momentarily he saw someone standing over him with a knife raised to rip his throat. So the fixer forced himself to stay awake. He threw aside his blanket to make it too cold to sleep. Yakov pinched his arms and thighs. If anyone attempted to sneak into the cell he would shout when the door opened. To cry out was his only defense. It might scare the assassins if they thought any of the prisoners in the cells down the corridor would hear, and guess the Jew was being murdered. If they heard, after a while it would get to the outside that the officials had assassinated him rather than bring him to trial.

The wind wailed mutely in the prison yard. His heart was like a rusted chain, his muscles taut, as though each had been bound with wire. Even in the cold air he sweated. Amid the darkly luminous prisoners he saw spies waiting to kill him. One was the gray-haired warden with a gleaming two-headed ax. He tried to hide his crossed eye behind his hand but it shone like a jewel through his fingers. The Deputy Warden, his fly open, held a black bullwhip behind his back. And though the Tsar wore a white mask over his face and a black on the back of his head, Yakov recognized him standing in the far corner of the cell, dropping green drops into a glass of hot milk.

"It will make you sleep, Yakov Shepsovitch."

"After you, Your Majesty."

The Tsar faded in the dark. The spies disappeared but the lines of prisoners were endless.

What's next, the fixer thought, and when will it happen? Will the trial begin, or will they call it off at the last minute? Suppose they withdraw the Act of Indictment in the morning, hoping I collapse or go insane before they give me another. Many men have lived in prison longer and some under worse conditions, but if I have to live another year in this cell I would rather die. Then the sad-eyed prisoners who crowded the cell began to disappear. First those who were standing around the wooden bed, then those squeezed together in the center, then those at the walls, and finally the long lines of sunken-faced men, moaning women, and ghostly children with glazed eyes in purple sockets, extending through the prison walls into the snowy distance.

"Are you Jews or Russians?" the fixer asked them.

"We are Russian prisoners."

"You look like Jews," he said.

Yakov fell asleep. Knowing he had, he frantically strove to awake, hearing himself sob as he slept, but it was growing lighter in the cell and he soon saw Bibikov sitting at a table in his white summer suit, stirring a spoonful of strawberry jelly in his tea.

"This would hardly be the time for them to kill you, Yakov Shepsovitch," he said. "Anyone would know it was a put-up job, and it would arouse an outcry. What you must watch out for is the sudden and unexpected peril, the apparently accidental. So sleep now, without fear for your life, and if you should ever manage to get out of prison, keep in mind that the purpose of freedom is to create it for others."

"Your honor," said Yakov, "I've had an extraordinary insight."

"You don't say? What is it?"

"Something in myself has changed. I'm not the same man I was. I fear less and hate more."

Before daylight Zhenia came to him with his punctured face and bleeding chest and begged for the return of his life. Yakov laid both hands on the boy and tried to raise him from the dead but it wouldn't work.

In the morning the fixer was still alive. He had awakened in astonishment, his mood mixed, anticipation with depression. It was the end of October, two and a half years after his arrest in Nikolai Maximovitch's brickyard. Kogin told him the date when he came in with the prisoner's breakfast. This morning the gruel was boiled rice in hot milk, eight ounces of black bread, a yellow piece of butter, and an enamel pot of sweet-smelling tea, with a chunk of lemon and two lumps of sugar. There was also a cucumber and a small onion to chew on to strengthen his teeth and reduce the swelling of his legs. Kogin wasn't feeling well. His hands trembled when he put down the food. He looked flushed and said he wanted to get home to bed but the warden had ordered him to stay on till the prisoner had left for the courthouse.

"Full security regulations, the warden said."

Yakov did not touch the food.

"You'd better eat it," Kogin said.

"I'm not hungry."

"Eat anyway, it'll be a long day in court."

"I'm too nervous. If I ate now I'd vomit."

Berezhinsky entered the cell. He seemed uneasy, not knowing whether to smile or mourn. He smiled uneasily.

"Well, your day has come. Here's the trial now."

"What about my clothes?" Yakov asked. "Will I have to wear the prison ones or can I have my own?"

He wondered whether they were going to hand him a silken caftan and a round Hasidic fur hat.

"You'll find out about that," said Berezhinsky.

Both guards accompanied the prisoner to the bathhouse. He undressed and was allowed to soap and wash himself from a bucket of warm water. The warmth of the water brought secret tears to his eyes. He washed slowly with handfuls of water from the bucket. He washed the smells and dirt away.

Yakov was given a comb and carefully combed the long hair and beard, but then the prison barber appeared and said he must shave his head.

"No," the fixer shouted. "Why should I look like a prisoner now when I didn't before?"

"Because you are a prisoner," said Berezhinsky. "The gate's not open yet."

"Why now and not before?"

"Orders," said the prison barber, "so sit still and keep your mouth shut."

"Why does he cut my hair?" Yakov, angered, asked Kogin. He felt, then, the pangs of hunger.

"Orders must be obeyed," said the guard. "It's to show you had no special privileges and were treated like the others."

"I was treated worse than the others."

"If you know all the answers, then don't ask any questions," Kogin said in irritation.

"That's right," said Berezhinsky. "Keep your mouth shut."

When the hair clipping was done, Kogin went out and returned with the fixer's own clothes and told him to put them on.

Yakov got dressed in the bathhouse. He blessed his clothes though they hung on his bony body loosely and limply. The baggy pants were held up by a thin cord. The dank sheepskin coat hung almost to his knees. But the boots, though stiff, were comfortable.

Back in the cell, strangely lit in the light of two lamps, Kogin said, "Listen, Bok, I advise you to eat. I give you my word there's nothing to be afraid of in that food. You better eat."

"That's right," said Berezhinsky. "Do what you're told."

"I don't want to eat," said the fixer, "I want to fast."

"What the hell for?" said Kogin.

"For God's world."

"I thought you didn't believe in God."

"I don't."

"The hell with you," said Kogin.

"Well, good luck and no hard feelings," Berezhinsky said uneasily. "Duty is duty. The prisoner's the prisoner, the guard's the guard."

From the window came the sound of a troop of horses clattering into the prison yard.

"It's the Cossacks," said Berezhinsky.

"Will I have to walk in the middle of the street?"

"You'll find that out. The warden's waiting so hurry up or it will go hard on you."

As Yakov came out of the cell an escort of six Cossack guards with crossed bandoliers were lined up in the corridor. The captain, a burly man with a black mustache, ordered the guard to surround the prisoner.

"Forward march," commanded the escort captain.

The Cossacks marched the prisoner along the corridor toward the warden's office. Though Yakov tried to straighten his leg he walked with a limp. He went as quickly as he could to keep up with the guard. Kogin and Berezhinsky remained behind.

In the warden's inner office the captain carefully searched the prisoner; he wrote out a receipt for him and handed it to the warden.

"Just a minute, young man," said the warden. "I want to have a word of my own with the prisoner."

The captain saluted. "We leave at 8 A.M., sir." He went to wait in the outer office.

The old man wiped the corners of his mouth with a handkerchief. His eye was tearing so he wiped that too. He took out his snuffbox, then put it away.

Yakov watched him nervously. If he withdraws the indictment now I'll choke him to death.

"Well, Bok," said Warden Grizitskoy, "if you had had the sense to follow the Prosecuting Attorney's advice you'd be a free man today and out of the country. As it is now, you'll probably be convicted on the evidence and will spend the rest of your natural life in the strictest confinement."

The fixer scratched his palms.

The warden got his glasses out of a drawer, adjusted them on his nose, and read aloud an item from a newspaper lying on his desk. It was about a tailor in Odessa, Markovitch, a Jew, the father of five children, accused by the police of murdering a nine-year-old boy in a waterfront street late at night. He had then carried the child's body to his tailor shop and drained the still-warm corpse of its lifeblood. The police, suspicious of the tailor, who walked alone in the streets at night, had discovered bloodstains on the floor and had at once arrested him.

The warden put down the newspaper and removed his glasses.

"I'll tell you this, Bok: if we don't convict one of you we'll convict the other. We'll teach you all a lesson."

The fixer remained mute.

The warden, his mouth wet with anger, threw open the door and signaled the escort captain.

But then the Deputy Warden entered from the hall. He came in in a hurry, paying no attention to the escort captain.

"Warden," he said, "I have here a telegram that forbids special privileges for the Jewish prisoner Bok just because he happens to be going on trial. He hasn't been searched this morning through no fault of mine. Please have him returned to his cell to be searched in the usual way."

A sick pressure burdened the fixer's chest.

"Why should I be searched now? What will you find if you search me? Only my miseries. This man doesn't know where to stop."

"I've already searched him," said the Cossack captain to the Deputy Warden. "The prisoner is now in my custody. I've given the warden my personal receipt."

"It's on my desk," said the warden.

The Deputy Warden drew a folded white paper out of his tunic pocket. "This telegram is from his Imperial Majesty in St. Petersburg. It orders us to search the Jew most carefully to prevent any possible dangerous incident."

"Why wasn't the telegram sent to me?" asked the warden.

"I notified you it might come," said the Deputy Warden.

"That's right," said the warden, flustered.

"Why should I be insulted again?" Yakov shouted, the

blood burning in his face. "The guards saw me naked in the bathhouse and watched me dress. Also this captain searched me a few minutes ago in front of the warden. Why should I be further humiliated on the day of my trial?"

The warden banged his fist on the desk. "That will do. Be still, I warn you."

"No one wants your opinion," said the black-mustached captain coldly. "Forward march. Back to the cell."

There's more to this than it says in the telegram, Yakov thought. If they're trying to provoke me I'd better be careful.

Sick to his soul, he was marched to his cell by the Cossack guard.

"Welcome home," Berezhinsky laughed.

Kogin stared at the fixer in frightened surprise.

"Hurry it up," said the Cossack captain to the Deputy Warden.

"Please, friend, don't tell me how to do my job and I won't tell you how to do yours," said the Deputy Warden, coldly. His boots smelled as though he had freshly stepped in excrement.

"Inside and undress," he ordered Yakov.

The prisoner, the Deputy Warden, and the two guards entered the cell, leaving the captain and the escort guard waiting in the corridor. The Deputy Warden slammed the cell door shut.

Inside the cell Kogin crossed himself.

Yakov slowly undressed, shivering. He stood there naked, except for his undershirt. I must be careful, he thought, or it will go hard on me. Ostrovsky warned me. Yet as he told himself this he felt his rage growing. The blood roared in his ears. It was as though he had dug a hole, then put the shovel aside but the hole was still growing. It grew into a grave. He imagined himself tearing the Deputy Warden's face apart and kicking him to death.

"Open your mouth," Berezhinsky ran a dirty finger under his tongue.

"Now spread your ass apart."

Kogin stared at the wall.

"Take off that stinking undershirt," ordered the Deputy Warden.

I must calm my anger, thought the fixer, seeing the world black. Instead, his anger grew.

"Why should I?" he shouted. "I have never taken it off before. Why should I take it off now? Why do you insult me?"

"Take it off before I tear it off."

Yakov felt the cell tremble and dip. I should have eaten, he thought. It was a mistake not to. He saw a bald-headed thin naked man in a freezing prison cell ripping off his undershirt and to his horror watched him fling it into the face of the Deputy Warden.

A solemn silence filled the cell.

Though his wet eyes were lit, murderous, the Deputy Warden spoke calmly. "I am within my rights to punish you for interfering with and insulting a prison official in the performance of his duty."

He drew his revolver.

My dirty luck. Yakov thought of the way his life had gone. Now Shmuel is dead and Raisl has nothing to eat. I've never been of use to anybody and I'll never be.

"Hold on a minute, your honor," said Kogin to the Deputy Warden. His deep voice broke. "I've listened to this man night after night, I know his sorrows. Enough is enough, and anyway it's time for his trial to begin."

"Get out of my way or I'll cite you for insubordination, you son-of-a-bitch."

Kogin pressed the muzzle of his revolver against the Deputy Warden's neck.

Berezhinsky reached for his gun but before he could draw, Kogin fired.

He fired at the ceiling and after a while dust drifted to the floor.

A whistle sounded shrilly in the corridor. The prison bell clanged. The iron cell door was slammed open and the white-faced captain and his Cossack guards rushed into the cell.

"I've given my personal receipt," he roared.

"My head aches," Kogin muttered. He sank to his knees with blood on his face. The Deputy Warden had shot him.

6

A church bell tolled.

A black bird flew out of the sky. Crow? Hawk? Or the black egg of a black eagle falling towards the carriage? If it isn't that what is it? If it's a bomb, thought Yakov, what can I do? I'll duck, what else can I do? If it's a bomb why was I ever born?

The prisoner, watched in silence by a crowd of officials, guests, and the mounted Cossacks in the yard, had limped amid the guard from the prison door to the massive black armored carriage drawn by four thick-necked, heavy-rumped horses at the gate. On the driver's seat a hawk-eyed coachman in a long coat and visored cap, whip in his hand.

The fixer was boosted up the metal step by two Cossacks and locked in the large-wheeled coach by the Chief of Police and his assistant. Inside it was dark and musty. An unlit lamp hung in the corner; the windows were round and small. Yakov put his eye to one of them, saw nothing he wanted to see—Warden Grizitskoy in military cap and coat rubbing a bloodshot eye—and sat back in the gloom.

The coachman shouted to the horses; a whip snapped and the huge carriage with its escort of fur-capped, gray-coated Cossack riders, a platoon in front with glittering lances, another in the rear with swords unsheathed, lumbered through the gate and rattled out on the cobblestone street. The coach moved quickly up the street, turned a corner and then went along an avenue with fields on one side and occasional factories and houses on the other.

I'm off, thought the fixer, for better or worse, and if it's worse it'll be worse than it was.

He sat for a while shrunken in loneliness, then through a window he saw a bird in the sky and watched with emotion until he could no longer see it. The weak sun stained the thin drifting clouds and for a minute snow flurried in different directions. In a wood not far from the road the oaks retained their bronze leaves but the large chestnut trees were black and barren. Yakov, seeing them in memory in full bloom, regretted the seasons he had missed and the years of his youth lost in prison.

Though still stunned by Kogin's death he felt, finally, the relief of motion, though to what fate who could say? Yet on the move at last to the courthouse, his trial about to take place, they said, a full three years from the time he had left the shtetl and ridden to Kiev. Then as they passed the brick wall of the factory, its chimneys pouring out coal smoke whipped by the wind into the sky, he caught a reflected glimpse of a faded shrunken Jew in the circle of window and hid from him, but could not, a minute later, from the memory of his gaunt face, its darkened stringy beard white around the bitter mouth, and though he would not weep for himself, his palms, when he rubbed his eyes, were wet.

At the factory gate five or six workers had turned to watch the procession; but when it had gone a verst into the business district, the fixer looked up in astonishment at the masses of people gathered on both sides of the street. Though it was early morning the crowds stretched along, five and six deep, laborers and civil servants on their way to work, shopkeepers, peasants in sheepskin coats, women in shawls and a few in hats, a scattering of military cadets and soldiers, and here and there a gray-robed monk or priest staring at the carriage. The trolleys were stopped, passengers rising from their seats to look out the windows as the Cossack riders and lumbering coach passed by. In the sidestreets the police held up carriages and motorcars, and bullock carts from the provinces, piled high with vegetables and grains, or loaded with cans of milk. Along the route to the courthouse mounted police were stationed at intervals to keep order. Yakov moved from one window to another to see the crowds.

"Yakov Bok!" he called out. "Yakov Bok!"

The Cossack riding on the left side of the carriage, a thick-shouldered man with overhanging brows and a mustache turning gray, gazed impassively ahead; but the rider cantering along on the door side, a youth of twenty or so on a gray mare, from time to time stole a glance at Yakov when he was staring out the window, as though trying to measure his guilt or innocence.

"Innocent!" the fixer cried out to him. "Innocent!" And though he had no reason to, he smiled a little at the Cossack for his youth and good looks, and for being, as such things go, a free man, give or take a little. The Cossack then rode forward as the mare, raising her tail, dropped a steaming load on the street at which a schoolboy pointed.

Amid the crowd were a few Jews watching with commiseration or fear. Most of the Russian faces were impassive, though some showed hostility and some loathing. A shopkeeper in a smock spat at the carriage. Two boys hooted. Some of the men in the crowd wore Black Hundreds buttons and when Yakov, out of one window then quickly the other, saw how many of them there were at this place, he grew apprehensive. Where there was one there were a hundred. A man with a strained face and deadly eyes threw his hand into the air as though it had caught on fire. The fixer's scrotum shrank painfully and he tore at his chest with his fingers as a black bird seemed to fly out of the white hand clawing the air.

Yakov frantically ducked. If this is my death I've endured for nothing.

"You might have waited a bit, Yakov Bok," the chairman of the jury said. "None of us are gentry or educated folk, but neither are we without a bit of experience in the world. A man learns to recognize the truth even if he doesn't always live by it. And there are times he does that if it suits his fancy. The officials may not want us to know what the truth is but it comes in, you might say, through the chinks in the walls. They may try to deceive us, as they do often enough, but we will sift the evidence and if the facts are not as they say, then let them look to their consciences."

"They have none."

"So much the worse for them, in that case. You aren't born human for nothing, I say."

"I'm innocent," said Yakov, "you can look at me and see. Look in my face and say whether a man like me, whatever else he might do, could kill a boy and drain the blood out of his body. If I have any humanity in my heart and you are men you must know it. Tell me do I look like a murderer?"

The chairman was about to say but a violent explosion rocked the coach.

Yakov waited for death. He wandered for a while in a cemetery reading the names on the tombstones. Then he ran from grave to grave, searching them frantically, one after another, but could not find his name. After a while he stopped looking. He had waited a long time but maybe he had longer to wait. If you were a certain type death stayed its distance. Your afflictions were from life—a poor living, mistakes with people, the blows of fate. You lived, you suffered, but you lived.

He heard screams, shouts, commotion, the frightened whinnying of horses. The carriage rattled and seemed to leap up, then struck the ground and stopped dead, shuddering, but remained upright. The stench of gunpowder bored through his nostrils. A door lock snapped and the door fell ajar. He felt an overwhelming hunger to be back home, to see Raisl and set things straight, to decide what to do. "Raisl," he said, "dress the boy and pack the few things we need, we'll have to hide." He was about to kick the door open but warned himself not to. Through the cracked right window he saw people on the run. A squad of Cossacks with lances raised galloped away from the carriage. A squad with uplifted sabers galloped towards it, risen in their saddles. The gray mare lay dead on the cobblestones. Three policemen were lifting the young Cossack rider. His foot had been torn off by the bomb. The boot had been blown away and his leg was shattered and bloody. As they carried him past the carriage his eyes opened and he looked in horror and anguish at Yakov as though to say, "What has my foot got to do with it?"

The fixer shrank from the sight. The Cossack had fainted but his torn leg shook, spattering blood on the policeman. Then a Cossack colonel galloped up to the carriage, holding a sword aloft, shouting to the coachman, 'Go on, go on!" He dismounted and tried to slam the door shut but it wouldn't lock. "Go on, go on!" he shouted. The carriage rumbled on, the horses picked up speed and broke into a fast trot. The colonel, on a white horse, cantered along beside the coach in place of the wounded Cossack.

Yakov sat in the gloomy coach overcome by hatred so intense his chest heaved as though the carriage were airless. He saw himself, after a while, sitting at a table somewhere, opposite the Tsar, a lit candle between them, in a cell or cellar, whatever it was. Nicholas the Second, of medium height, with frank blue eyes and neatly trimmed beard a little too large for his face, sat there naked, holding in his hand a small silver ikon of the Virgin Mary. Though distraught and pale, afflicted with a bad cough he had recently developed, he spoke in a gentle voice and with moving eloquence.

"Though you have me at a disadvantage, Yakov Shepsovitch, I will speak the truth to you. It isn't only that the Jews are freemasons and revolutionaries who make a shambles of our laws and demoralize our police by systematic bribery for social exemptions—I can forgive that a bit but not the other things, in particular the terrible crime you are accused of, which is so repellent to me personally. I refer to the draining of his lifeblood out of Zhenia Golov's body. I don't know whether you are aware that my own child, the Tsarevitch Alexis, is a hemophiliac? The newspapers, out of courtesy to the royal family, and the Tsarina in particular, do not, of course, mention it. We are fortunate in having four healthy daughters, the princess Olga, the studious one; Tatyana, the prettiest, and something of a coquette—I say this with amusement; Maria, shy and sweet-tempered; and Anastasya, the youngest and liveliest of them; but when after many prayers an heir to the throne was born at last—it pleased God to make this joy our greatest trial—his blood unfortunately was deficient in that substance which is necessary for coagulation and healing. A small cut, the most trivial, and he may bleed to death. We look after him, as you can expect, with the greatest care, on tenterhooks every minute because even a quite ordinary fall may mean extreme peril. Alexei's veins are fragile, brittle, and in the slightest mishap internal bleeding causes him unbearable pain and torment. My dear wife and I—and I may add, the girls—live through death with this poor child. Permit me to ask, Yakov Shepsovitch, are you a father?"

"With all my heart."

"Then you can imagine our anguish," sighed the sad-eyed Tsar.

His hands trembled a little as he lit a green-papered Turkish cigarette from an enameled box on the table. He offered the box to Yakov but the fixer shook his head.

"I never wanted the crown, it kept me from being my true self, but I was not permitted to refuse. To rule is to bear a heavy cross. I've made mistakes, but not, I assure you, out of malice to anyone. My nature is not resolute, not like my late father's—we lived in terror of him—but what can a man do beyond the best he can? One is born as he is born and that's all there is to it. I thank God for my good qualities. To tell you the truth, Yakov Shepsovitch, I don't like to dwell on these things. But I am—I can truthfully say—a kind person and love my people. Though the Jews cause me a great deal of trouble, and we must sometimes suppress them to maintain order, believe me, I wish them well. As for you, if you permit me, I consider you a decent but mistaken man—I insist on honesty—and I must ask you to take note of my obligations and burdens. After all, it isn't as though you yourself are aware of what suffering is. Surely it has taught you the meaning of mercy?"

He was coughing insistently now and his voice, when he finished, was unsteady.

Yakov moved uneasily in his chair. "Excuse me, Your Majesty, but what suffering has taught me is the uselessness of suffering, if you don't mind me saying so. Anyway, there's enough of that to live with naturally without piling a mountain of injustice on top. Rachmones, we say in Hebrew—mercy, one oughtn't to forget it, but one must also think how oppressed, ignorant and miserable most of us are in this country, gentiles as well as Jews, under your government and ministers. What it amounts to, Little Father, is that whether you wanted it or not you had your chance; in fact many chances, but the best you could give us with all good intentions is the poorest and most reactionary state in Europe. In other words, you've made out of this country a valley of bones. You had your chances and pissed them away. There's no argument against that. It's not easy to twist events by the tail but you might have done something for a better life for us all—for the future of Russia, one might say, but you didn't."

The Tsar rose, his phallus meager, coughing still, disturbed and angered. "I'm only one man though ruler yet you blame me for our whole history."

"For what you don't know. Your Majesty, and what you haven't learned. Your poor boy is hemophiliac, something missing in the blood. In you, in spite of certain sentimental feelings, it is missing somewhere else—the sort of insight, you might call it, that creates in a man charity, respect for the most miserable. You say you are kind and prove it with pogroms."

"As for those," said the Tsar, "don't blame me. Water can't be prevented from flowing. They are a genuine expression of the will of the people."

"Then in that case there's no more to say." On the table at the fixer's hand lay a revolver. Yakov pushed a bullet into the rusty cylinder chamber.

The Tsar sat down, watching without apparent emotion, though his face had grown white and his beard darker. "I am the victim, the sufferer for my poor people. What will be will be." He stubbed out his cigarette in the candle saucer. The light flickered but burnt on.

"Don't expect me to beg."

"This is also for the prison, the poison, the six daily searches. It's for Bibikov and Kogin and for a lot more that I won't even mention."

Pointing the gun at the Tsar's heart (though Bibikov, flailing his white arms, cried no no no no), Yakov pressed the trigger. Nicholas, in the act of crossing himself, overturned his chair, and fell, to his surprise, to the floor, the stain spreading on his breast.

The horses clopped on over the cobblestones.

As for history, Yakov thought, there are ways to reverse it. What the Tsar deserves is a bullet in the gut. Better him than us.

The left rear wheel of the carriage seemed to be wobbling.

One thing I've learned, he thought, there's no such thing as an unpolitical man, especially a Jew. You can't be one without the other, that's clear enough. You can't sit still and see yourself destroyed.

Afterwards he thought, Where there's no fight for it there's no freedom. What is it Spinoza says? If the state acts in ways that are abhorrent to human nature it's the lesser evil to destroy it. Death to the anti-Semites! Long live revolution! Long live liberty!

The crowds lining both sides of the streets were dense

again, packed tight between curb and housefront. There were faces at every window and people standing on rooftops along the way. Among those in the street were Jews of the Plossky District. Some, as the carriage clattered by and they glimpsed the fixer, were openly weeping, wringing their hands. One thinly bearded man clawed his face. One or two waved at Yakov. Some shouted his name.

THE NATURAL

For my Father

Pre-game

Roy Hobbs pawed at the glass before thinking to prick a match with his thumbnail and hold the spurting flame in his cupped palm close to the lower berth window, but by then he had figured it was a tunnel they were passing through and was no longer surprised at the bright sight of himself holding a yellow light over his head, peering back in. As the train yanked its long tail out of the thundering tunnel, the kneeling reflection dissolved and he felt a splurge of freedom at the view of the moon-hazed Western hills bulked against night broken by sprays of summer lightning, although the season was early spring. Lying back, elbowed up on his long side, sleepless still despite the lulling train, he watched the land flowing and waited with suppressed expectancy for a sight of the Mississippi, a thousand miles away.

Having no timepiece he appraised the night and decided it was moving toward dawn. As he was looking, there flowed along this bone-white farmhouse with sagging skeletal porch, alone in untold miles of moonlight, and before it this white-faced, long-boned boy whipped with train-whistle yowl a glowing ball to someone hidden under a dark oak, who shot it back without thought, and the kid once more wound and returned. Roy shut his eyes to the sight because if it wasn't real it was a way he sometimes had of observing himself, just as in this dream he could never shake off—that had hours ago waked him out of sound sleep—of him standing at night in a strange field with a golden baseball in his palm that all the time grew heavier as he sweated to settle whether to hold on or fling it away. But when he had made his decision it was too heavy to lift or let fall (who wanted a hole that deep?) so he changed his mind to keep it and the thing grew fluffy light, a white rose breaking out of its hide, and all but soared off by itself, but he had already sworn to hang on forever.

As dawn tilted the night, a gust of windblown rain blinded him—no, there was a window—but the sliding drops made him thirsty and from thirst sprang hunger. He reached into the hammock for his underwear to be first at breakfast in the dining car and make his blunders of ordering and eating more or less in private, since it was doubtful Sam would be up to tell him what to do. Roy peeled his gray sweatshirt and bunched down the white ducks he was wearing for pajamas in case there was a wreck and he didn't have time to dress. He acrobated into a shirt, pulled up the pants of his good suit, arching to draw them high, but he had crammed both feet into one leg and was trapped so tight wriggling got him nowhere. He worried because here he was straitjacketed in the berth without much room to twist around in and might bust his pants or have to buzz the porter, which he dreaded. Grunting, he contorted himself this way and that till he was at last able to grab and pull down the cuff and with a gasp loosened his feet and got the caught one where it belonged. Sitting up, he gartered his socks, tied laces, got on a necktie and even squirmed into a suit coat so that when he parted the curtains to step out he was fully dressed.

Dropping to all fours, he peered under the berth for his bassoon case. Though it was there he thought he had better open it and did but quickly snapped it shut as Eddie, the porter, came walking by.

"Morning, maestro, what's the tune today?"

"It ain't a musical instrument." Roy explained it was something he had made himself.

"Animal, vegetable, or mineral?"

"Just a practical thing."

"A pogo stick?"

"No."

"Foolproof lance?"

"No."

"Lemme guess," Eddie said, covering his eyes with his

long-fingered hand and pawing the air with the other. "I have it—combination fishing rod, gun, and shovel."

Roy laughed. "How far to Chicago, Eddie?"

"Chi? Oh, a long, long ways. I wouldn't walk."

"I don't intend to."

"Why Chi?" Eddie asked. "Why not New Orleans? That's a lush and Frenchy city."

"Never been there."

"Or that hot and hilly town, San Francisco?

Roy shook his head.

"Why not New York, colossus of colossuses?"

"Some day I'll visit there."

"Where have you visited?"

Roy was embarrassed. "Boise."

"That dusty sandstone quarry."

"Portland too when I was small."

"In Maine?"

"No, Oregon—where they hold the Festival of Roses."

"Oregon—where the refugees from Minnesota and the Dakotas go?"

"I wouldn't know," Roy said. "I'm going to Chicago, where the Cubs are."

"Lions and tigers in the zoo?"

"No, the ballplayers."

"Oh, the ball—" Eddie clapped a hand to his mouth. "Are you one of them?"

"I hope to be."

The porter bowed low. "My hero. Let me kiss your hand."

Roy couldn't help but smile yet the porter annoyed and worried him a little. He had forgotten to ask Sam when to tip him, morning or night, and how much? Roy had made it a point, since their funds were so low, not to ask for anything at all but last night Eddie had insisted on fixing a pillow behind his back, and once when he was trying to locate the men's room Eddie practically took him by the hand and led him to it. Did you hand him a dime after that or grunt a foolish thanks as he had done? He'd personally be glad when the trip was over, though he certainly hated to be left alone in a place like Chicago. Without Sam he'd feel shaky-kneed and unable to say or do simple things like ask for directions or know where to go once you had dropped a nickel into the subway.

After a troublesome shave in which he twice drew blood he used one thin towel to dry his hands, face, and neck, clean his razor and wipe up the wet of his toothbrush so as not to have to ask for another and this way keep the bill down. From the flaring sky out the window it looked around half-past five, but he couldn't be sure because somewhere near they left Mountain Time and lost—no, picked up—yes, it was lost an hour, what Sam called the twenty-three hour day. He packed his razor, toothbrush, and pocket comb into a chamois drawstring bag, rolled it up small and kept it handy in his coat pocket. Passing through the long sleeper, he entered the diner and would gladly have sat down to breakfast, for his stomach had contracted into a bean at the smell of food, but the shirt-sleeved waiters in stocking caps were joshing around as they gobbled fried kippers and potatoes. Roy hurried through the large-windowed club car, empty for once, through several sleepers, coaches, a lounge and another long line of coaches, till he came to the last one, where amid the gloom of drawn shades and sleeping people tossed every which way, Sam Simpson also slept although Roy had last night begged him to take the berth but the soft-voiced Sam had insisted, "You take the bed, kiddo, you're the one that has to show what you have got on the ball when we pull into the city. It don't matter where I sleep."

Sam lay very still on his back, looking as if the breath of life had departed from him except that it was audible in the ripe snore that could be chased without waking him, Roy had discovered, if you hissed scat. His lean head was held up by a folded pillow and his scrawny legs, shoeless, hung limp over the arm of the double seat he had managed to acquire, for he had started out with a seat partner. He was an expert conniver where his comfort was concerned, and since that revolved mostly around the filled flat bottle his ability to raise them up was this side of amazing. He often said he would not die of thirst though he never failed to add, in Roy's presence, that he wished for nobody the drunkard's death. He seemed now to be dreaming, and his sharp nose was pointed in the direction of a scent that led perhaps to the perfumed presence of Dame Fortune, long past due in his bed. With dry lips puckered, he smiled in expectation of a spectacular kiss though he looked less like a lover than an old scarecrow with his comical, seamed face sprouting prickly stubble in the dark glow of the expiring bulb overhead. A trainman passed who, seeing Sam sniff in his sleep, pretended it was at his own reek and humorously held his nose. Roy frowned, but Sam, who had a moment before been getting in good licks against fate, saw in his sleep, and his expression changed. A tear broke from his eye and slowly slid down his cheek. Roy concluded not to wake Sam and left.

He returned to the vacant club car and sat there with a magazine on his knee, worrying whether the trip wasn't a mistake, when a puzzled Eddie came into the car and handed him a pair of red dice.

"Mate them," he said. "I can't believe my eyes."

Roy paired the dice. "They mate."

"Now roll them."

He rolled past his shoe. "Snake eyes."

"Try again," said Eddie, interested.

Roy rattled the red cubes. "Snake eyes once more."

"Amazing. Again, please."

Again he rolled on the rug. Roy whistled. "Holy cow, three in a row."

"Fantastic."

"Did they do the same for you?"

"No, for me they did sevens."

"Are they loaded?"

"Bewitched," Eddie muttered. "I found them in the washroom and I'm gonna get rid of them pronto."

"Why?—if you could win all the time?"

"I don't crave any outside assistance in games of chance."

The train had begun to slow down.

"Oh oh, duty." Eddie hurried out.

Watching through the double-paned glass, Roy saw the porter swing himself off the train and jog along with it a few paces as it pulled to a stop. The morning was high and bright but the desolate station—wherever they were—gave up a single passenger, a girl in a dressy black dress, who despite the morning chill waited with a coat over her arm, and two suitcases and a zippered golf bag at her feet. Hatless, too, her hair a froth of dark curls, she held by a loose cord a shiny black hat box which she wouldn't let Eddie touch when he gathered up her things. Her face was striking, a little drawn and pale, and when she stepped up into the train her nyloned legs made Roy's pulses dance. When he could no longer see her, he watched Eddie set down her bags, take the red dice out of his pocket, spit on them and fling them over the depot roof. He hurriedly grabbed the bags and hopped on the moving train.

The girl entered the club car and directed Eddie to carry her suitcases to her compartment and she would stay and have a cigarette. He mentioned the hat box again but she giggled nervously and said no.

"Never lost a female hat yet," Eddie muttered.

"Thank you but I'll carry it myself."

He shrugged and left.

She had dropped a flower. Roy thought it was a gardenia but it turned out to be a white rose she had worn pinned to her dress.

When he handed it to her, her eyes widened with fascination, as if she had recognized him from somewhere, but when she found she hadn't, to his horror her expression changed instantly to one of boredom. Sitting across the aisle from him she fished out of her purse a pack of cigarettes and a lighter. She lit up, and crossing her heartbreaking legs, began to flip through a copy of *Life*.

He figured she was his own age, maybe a year or so older. She looked to him like one of those high-class college girls, only with more zip than most of them, and dressed for 6 A.M. as the girls back home never would. He was marvelously interested in her, so much had her first glance into his eyes meant to him, and already felt a great longing in his life. Anxious to get acquainted, he was flabbergasted how to begin. If she hadn't yet eaten breakfast and he could work up the nerve, he could talk to her in the diner—only he didn't dare.

People were sitting around now and the steward came out and said first call for breakfast.

She snubbed out her cigarette with a wriggling motion of

the wrist—her bracelets tinkled—picked up the hat box and went into the diner. Her crumpled white rose lay in the ashtray. He took it out and quickly stuck it in his pants pocket. Though his hunger bit sharp he waited till everyone was maybe served, and then he entered.

Although he had tried to avoid it, for fear she would see how unsure he was of these things, he was put at the same table with her and her black hat box, which now occupied a seat of its own. She glanced up furtively when he sat down but went wordlessly back to her coffee. When the waiter handed Roy the pad, he absently printed his name and date of birth but the waiter imperceptibly nudged him (hey, hayseed) and indicated it was for ordering. He pointed on the menu with his yellow pencil (this is the buck breakfast) but the blushing ballplayer, squinting through the blur, could only think he was sitting on the lone four-bit piece he had in his back pocket. He tried to squelch the impulse but something forced him to look up at her as he attempted to pour water into his ice-filled (this'll kill the fever) glass, spilling some on the tablecloth (whose diapers you wetting, boy?), then all thumbs and butter fingers, the pitcher thumped the pitcher down, fished the fifty cents out of his pants, and after scratching out the vital statistics on the pad, plunked the coin down on the table.

"That's for you," he told the (what did I do to deserve this?) waiter, and though the silver-eyed mermaid was about to speak, he did not stay to listen but beat it fast out of the accursed car.

Tramping highways and byways, wandering everywhere bird dogging the sandlots for months without spotting so much as a fifth-rater he could telegraph about to the head scout of the Cubs, and maybe pick up a hundred bucks in the mail as a token of their appreciation, with also a word of thanks for his good bird dogging and maybe they would sometime again employ him as a scout on the regular payroll—well, after a disheartening long time in which he was not able to roust up a single specimen worthy to be called by the name of ballplayer, Sam had one day lost his way along a dusty country road and when he finally found out where he was, too weary to turn back, he crossed over to an old, dry barn and sat against the haypile in front, to drown his sorrows with a swig. On the verge of dozing he heard these shouts and opened his eyes, shielding them from the hot sun, and as he lived, a game of ball was being played in a pasture by twelve blond-bearded players, six on each side, and even from where Sam sat he could tell they were terrific the way they smacked the pill—one blow banging it so far out the fielder had to run a mile before he could jump high and snag it smack in his bare hand. Sam's mouth popped open, he got up whoozy and watched, finding it hard to believe his eyes, as the teams changed sides and the first hitter that batted the ball did so for a far-reaching distance before it was caught, and the same with the second, a wicked clout, but then the third came up, the one who had made the bare-handed catch, and he really laid on and powdered the pellet a thundering crack so that even the one who ran for it, his beard parted in the wind, before long looked like a pygmy chasing it and quit running, seeing the thing was a speck on the horizon.

Sweating and shivering by turns, Sam muttered if I could ketch the whole twelve of them—and staggered out on the field to cry out the good news but when they saw him they gathered bats and balls and ran in a dozen directions, and though Sam was smart enough to hang on to the fellow who had banged the sphere out to the horizon, frantically shouting to him, "Whoa—whoa," his lungs bursting with the effort to call a giant—he wouldn't stop so Sam never caught him.

He woke with a sob in his throat but swallowed before he could sound it, for by then Roy had come to mind and he mumbled, "Got someone just as good," so that for once waking was better than dreaming.

He yawned. His mouth felt unholy dry and his underclothes were crawling. Reaching down his battered valise from the rack, he pulled out a used bath towel and cake of white soap, and to the surprise of those who saw him go out that way, went through the baggage cars to the car between them and the tender. Once inside there, he peeled to the skin and stepped into the shower stall, where he enjoyed himself for ten minutes, soaping and resoaping his bony body under warm water. But then a trainman happened to come through and after sniffing around Sam's clothes yelled in to him, "Hey, bud, come outa there."

Sam stopped off the shower and poked out his head.

"What's that?"

"I said come outa there, that's only for the train crew."

"Excuse me," Sam said, and he began quickly to rub himself dry.

"You don't have to hurry. Just wanted you to know you made a mistake."

"Thought it went with the ticket."

"Not in the coaches it don't."

Sam sat on a metal stool and laced up his high brown shoes. Pointing to the cracked mirror on the wall, he said, "Mind if I use your glass?"

"Go ahead."

He parted his sandy hair, combed behind the ears, and managed to work in a shave and brushing of his yellow teeth before he apologized again to the trainman and left.

Going up a few cars to the lounge, he ordered a cup of hot coffee and a sandwich, ate quickly, and made for the club car. It was semi-officially out of bounds for coach travelers but Sam had told the passenger agent last night that he had a nephew riding on a sleeper, and the passenger agent had mentioned to the conductor not to bother him.

When he entered the club car, after making sure Roy was elsewhere Sam headed for the bar, already in a fluid state for the train was moving through wet territory, but then he changed his mind and sat down to size up the congregation over a newspaper and spot who looked particularly amiable. The headlines caught his eye at the same time as they did this short, somewhat popeyed gent's sitting next to him, who had just been greedily questioning the husky, massive-shouldered man on his right, who was wearing sun glasses. Popeyes nudged the big one and they all three stared at Sam's paper.

WEST COAST OLYMPIC ATHLETE SHOT

FOLLOWS 24 HOURS AFTER SLAYING OF
ALL-AMERICAN FOOTBALL ACE

The article went on to relate that both of these men had been shot under mysterious circumstances with silver bullets from a .22 caliber pistol by an unknown woman that police were on the hunt for.

"That makes the second sucker," the short man said.

"But why with silver bullets, Max?"

"Beats me. Maybe she set out after a ghost but couldn't find him."

The other fingered his tie knot. "Why do you suppose she goes around pickin' on atheletes for?"

"Not only athletes but also the cream of the crop. She's knocked off a crack football boy, and now an Olympic runner. Better watch out, Whammer, she may be heading for a baseball player for the third victim." Max chuckled.

Sam looked up and almost hopped out of his seat as he recognized them both.

Hiding his hesitation, he touched the short one on the arm. "Excuse me, mister, but ain't you Max Mercy, the sportswriter? I know your face from your photo in the articles you write."

But the sportswriter, who wore a comical mustache and dressed in stripes that crisscrossed three ways—suit, shirt, and tie—a nervous man with voracious eyes, also had a sharp sense of smell and despite Sam's shower and toothbrushing nosed out an alcoholic fragrance that slowed his usual speedy response in acknowledging the spread of his fame.

"That's right," he finally said.

"Well, I'm happy to have the chance to say a few words to you. You're maybe a little after my time, but I am Sam Simpson—Bub Simpson, that is—who played for the St. Louis Browns in the season of 1919 to 1921."

Sam spoke with a grin though his insides were afry at the mention of his professional baseball career.

"Believe I've heard the name," Mercy said nervously. After a minute he nodded toward the man Sam knew all along as the leading hitter of the American League, three times winner of the Most Valuable Player award, and announced, "This is Walter (the Whammer) Wambold." It had been in the papers that he was a holdout for $75,000 and was coming East to squeeze it out of his boss.

"Howdy," Sam said. "You sure look different in street clothes."

The Whammer, whose yellow hair was slicked flat, with tie and socks to match, grunted.

Sam's ears reddened. He laughed embarrassedly and then remarked sideways to Mercy that he was traveling with a slam-bang young pitcher who'd soon be laying them low in the big leagues. "Spoke to you because I thought you might want to know about him."

"What's his name?"

"Roy Hobbs."

"Where'd he play?"

"Well, he's not exactly been in organized baseball."

"Where'd he learn to pitch?"

"His daddy taught him years ago—he was once a semi-pro—and I have been polishin' him up."

"Where's he been pitching?"

"Well, like I said, he's young, but he certainly mowed them down in the Northwest High School League last year. Thought you might of heard of his eight no-hitters."

"Class D is as far down as I go," Mercy laughed. He lit one of the cigars Sam had been looking at in his breast pocket.

"I'm personally taking him to Clarence Mulligan of the Cubs for a tryout. They will probably pay me a few grand for uncovering the coming pitcher of the century but the condition is—and Roy is backing me on this because he is more devoted to me than a son—that I am to go back as a regular scout, like I was in 1925."

Roy popped his head into the car and searched around for the girl with the black hat box (Miss Harriet Bird, Eddie had gratuitously told him, making a black fluttering of wings), and seeing her seated near the card tables restlessly thumbing through a magazine, popped out.

"That's him," said Sam. "Wait'll I bring him back." He got up and chased after Roy.

"Who's the gabber?" said the Whammer.

"Guy named Simpson who once caught for the Brownies. Funny thing, last night I was doing a Sunday piece on drunks in baseball and I had occasion to look up his record. He was in the game three years, batted .340, .260, and .198, but his catching was terrific—not one error listed."

"Get rid of him, he jaws too much."

"Sh, here he comes."

Sam returned with Roy in tow, gazing uncomfortably ahead.

"Max," said Sam, "this is Roy Hobbs that I mentioned to you. Say hello to Max Mercy, the syndicated sportswriter, kiddo."

"Hello," Roy nodded.

"This is the Whammer," Max said.

Roy extended his hand but the Whammer looked through him with no expression whatsoever. Seeing he had his eye hooked on Harriet, Roy conceived a strong dislike for the guy.

The Whammer got up. "Come on, Max, I wanna play cards."

Max rose. "Well, hang onto the water wagon, Bub," he said to Sam.

Sam turned red.

Roy shot the sportswriter a dirty look.

"Keep up with the no-hitters, kid," Max laughed.

Roy didn't answer. He took the Whammer's chair and Sam sat where he was, brooding.

"What'll it be?" they heard Mercy ask as he shuffled the cards. They had joined two men at one of the card tables.

The Whammer, who looked to Sam like an overgrown side of beef wrapped in gabardine, said, "Hearts." He stared at Harriet until she looked up from her magazine, and after a moment of doubt, smiled.

The Whammer fingered his necktie knot. As he scooped up the cards his diamond ring glinted in the sunlight.

"Goddamned millionaire," Sam thought.

"The hell with her," thought Roy.

"I dealt rummy," Max said, and though no one had called him, Sam promptly looked around.

Toward late afternoon the Whammer, droning on about his deeds on the playing field, got very chummy with Harriet Bird and before long had slipped his fat fingers around the back of her chair so Roy left the club car and sat in the sleeper, looking out of the window, across the aisle from where Eddie slept sitting up. Gosh, the size of the forest. He thought they had left it for good yesterday and here it still was. As he watched, the trees flowed together and so did the hills and clouds. He felt a kind of sadness, because he had lost the feeling of a particular place. Yesterday he had come from somewhere, a place he knew was there, but today it had thinned away in space—how vast he could not have guessed—and he felt like he would never see it again.

The forest stayed with them, climbing hills like an army, shooting down like waterfalls. As the train skirted close in, the trees leveled out and he could see within the woodland the only place he had been truly intimate with in his wanderings, a green world shot through with weird light and strange bird cries, muffled in silence that made the privacy so complete his inmost self had no shame of anything he thought there, and it eased the body-shaking beat of his ambitions. Then he thought of here and now and for the thousandth time wondered why they had come so far and for what. Did Sam really know what he was doing? Sometimes Roy had his doubts. Sometimes he wanted to turn around and go back home, where he could at least predict what tomorrow would be like. Remembering the white rose in his pants pocket, he decided to get rid of it. But then the pine trees flowed away from the train and slowly swerved behind blue hills; all at once there was this beaten gold, snow-capped mountain in the distance, and on the plain several miles from its base lay a small city gleaming in the rays of the declining sun. Approaching it, the long train slowly pulled to a stop.

Eddie woke with a jump and stared out the window.

"Oh oh, trouble, we never stop here."

He looked again and called Roy.

"What do you make out of that?"

About a hundred yards ahead, where two dirt roads crossed, a moth-eaten model-T Ford was parked on the farther side of the road from town, and a fat old man wearing a broad-brimmed black hat and cowboy boots, who they could see was carring a squat doctor's satchel, climbed down from it. To the conductor, who had impatiently swung off the train with a lit red lamp, he flourished a yellow telegram. They argued a minute, then the conductor, snapping open his watch, beckoned him along and they boarded the train. When they passed through Eddie's car the conductor's face was sizzling with irritation but the doctor was unruffled. Before disappearing through the door, the conductor called to Eddie, "Half hour."

"Half hour," Eddie yodeled and he got out the stool and set it outside the car so that anyone who wanted to stretch, could.

Only about a dozen passengers got off the train, including Harriet Bird, still hanging on to her precious hat box, the Whammer, and Max Mercy, all as thick as thieves. Roy hunted up the bassoon case just if the train should decide to take off without him, and when he had located Sam they both got off.

"Well, I'll be jiggered." Sam pointed down about a block beyond where the locomotive had halted. There, sprawled out at the outskirts of the city, a carnival was on. It was made up of try-your-skill booths, kiddie rides, a freak show and a gigantic Ferris wheel that looked like a stopped clock. Though there was still plenty of daylight, the carnival was lit up by twisted ropes of blinking bulbs, and many banners streamed in the breeze as the calliope played.

"Come on," said Roy, and they went along with the people from the train who were going toward the tents.

Once they had got there and fooled around a while, Sam stopped to have a crushed cocoanut drink which he privately spiked with a shot from a new bottle, while Roy wandered over to a place where you could throw three baseballs for a dime at three wooden pins, shaped like pint-size milk bottles and set in pyramids of one on top of two, on small raised platforms about twenty feet back from the counter. He changed the fifty-cent piece Sam had slipped him on leaving the train, and this pretty girl in yellow, a little hefty but with a sweet face and nice ways, who with her peanut of a father was waiting on trade, handed him three balls. Lobbing one of them, Roy easily knocked off the pyramid and won himself a naked kewpie doll. Enjoying the game, he laid down another dime, again clattering the pins to the floor in a single shot and now collecting an alarm clock. With the other three dimes he won a brand-new boxed baseball, a washboard, and baby potty, which he traded in for a six-inch harmonica. A few kids came over to watch and Sam, wandering by, indulgently changed another half into dimes for Roy. And Roy won a fine leather cigar case for Sam, a "God Bless America" banner, a flashlight, can of coffee, and a two-pound box of sweets. To the kids' delight, Sam, after a slight hesitation, flipped Roy another half dollar, but this time the little man behind the counter nudged his daughter and she asked Roy if he would now take a kiss for every three pins he tumbled.

Roy glanced at her breasts and she blushed. He got embarrassed too. "What do you say, Sam, it's your four bits?"

Sam bowed low to the girl. "Ma'am," he said, "now you see how dang foolish it is to be a young feller."

The girl laughed and Roy began to throw for kisses, flushing each pyramid in a shot or two while the girl counted aloud the kisses she owed him.

Some of the people from the train passed by and stayed to watch when they learned from the mocking kids what Roy was throwing for.

The girl, pretending to be unconcerned, tolled off the third and fourth kisses.

As Roy fingered the ball for the last throw the Whammer came by holding over his shoulder a Louisville Slugger that he had won for himself in the batting cage down a way. Harriet, her pretty face flushed, had a kewpie doll, and Max Mercy carried a box of cigars. The Whammer had discarded his sun glasses and all but strutted over his performance and the prizes he had won.

Roy raised his arm to throw for the fifth kiss and a clean sweep when the Whammer called out to him in a loud voice, "Pitch it here, busher, and I will knock it into the moon."

Roy shot for the last kiss and missed. He missed with the second and third balls. The crowd oohed its disappointment.

"Only four," said the girl in yellow as if she mourned the fifth.

Angered at what had happened, Sam hoarsely piped, "I got ten dollars that says he can strike you out with three pitched balls, Wambold."

The Whammer looked at Sam with contempt.

"What d'ye say, Max?" he said.

Mercy shrugged.

"Oh, I love contests of skill," Harriet said excitedly. Roy's face went pale.

"What's the matter, hayfoot, you scared?" the Whammer taunted.

"Not of you," Roy said.

"Let's go across the tracks where nobody'll get hurt," Mercy suggested.

"Nobody but the busher and his bazooka. What's in it, busher?"

"None of your business." Roy picked up the bassoon case.

The crowd moved in a body across the tracks, the kids circling around to get a good view, and the engineer and fireman watching from their cab window.

Sam cornered one of the kids who lived nearby and sent him home for a fielder's glove and his friend's catcher's mitt. While they were waiting, for protection he buttoned underneath his coat the washboard Roy had won. Max drew a batter's box alongside a piece of slate. He said he would call the throws and they would count as one of the three pitches only if they were over or if the Whammer swung and missed.

When the boy returned with the gloves, the sun was going down, and though the sky was aflame with light all the way to the snowy mountain peak, it was chilly on the ground.

Breaking the seal, Sam squeezed the baseball box and the pill shot up like a greased egg. He tossed it to Mercy, who inspected the hide and stitches, then rubbed the shine off and flipped it to Roy.

"Better throw a couple of warm-ups."

"My arm is loose," said Roy.

"It's your funeral."

Placing his bassoon case out of the way in the grass, Roy shed his coat. One of the boys came forth to hold it.

"Be careful you don't spill the pockets," Roy told him.

Sam came forward with the catcher's glove on. It was too small for his big hand but he said it would do all right.

"Sam, I wish you hadn't bet that money on me," Roy said.

"I won't take it if we win, kiddo, but just let it stand if we lose," Sam said, embarrassed.

"We came by it too hard."

"Just let it stand so."

He cautioned Roy to keep his pitches inside, for the Whammer was known to gobble them on the outside corner.

Sam returned to the plate and crouched behind the batter, his knees spread wide because of the washboard. Roy drew on his glove and palmed the ball behind it. Mercy, rubbing his hands to warm them, edged back about six feet behind Sam.

The onlookers retreated to the other side of the tracks, except Harriet, who stood without fear of fouls up close. Her eyes shone at the sight of the two men facing one another.

Mercy called, "Batter up."

The Whammer crowded the left side of the plate, gripping the heavy bat low on the neck, his hands jammed together and legs plunked evenly apart. He hadn't bothered to take off his coat. His eye on Roy said it spied a left-handed monkey.

"Throw it, Rube, it won't get no lighter."

Though he stood about sixty feet away, he loomed up gigantic to Roy, with the wood held like a caveman's ax on his shoulder. His rocklike frame was motionless, his face impassive, unsmiling, dark.

Roy's heart skipped a beat. He turned to gaze at the mountain.

Sam whacked the leather with his fist. "Come on, kiddo, wham it down his whammy."

The Whammer out of the corner of his mouth told the drunk to keep his mouth shut.

"Burn it across his button."

"Close your trap," Mercy said.

"Cut his throat with it."

"If he tries to dust me, so help me I will smash his skull," the Whammer threatened.

Roy stretched loosely, rocked back on his left leg, twirling the right a little like a dancer, then strode forward and threw with such force his knuckles all but scraped the ground on the follow-through.

At thirty-three the Whammer still enjoyed exceptional eyesight. He saw the ball spin off Roy's fingertips and it reminded him of a white pigeon he had kept as a boy, that he would send into flight by flipping it into the air. The ball flew at him and he was conscious of its bird-form and white flapping wings, until it suddenly disappeared from view. He heard a noise like the bang of a firecracker at his feet and Sam had the ball in his mitt. Unable to believe his ears he heard Mercy intone a reluctant strike.

Sam flung off the glove and was wringing his hand.

"Hurt you, Sam?" Roy called.

"No, it's this dang glove."

Though he did not show it, the pitch had bothered the Whammer no end. Not just the speed of it but the sensation of surprise and strangeness that went with it—him batting here on the railroad tracks, the crazy carnival, the drunk catching and a clown pitching, and that queer dame Harriet, who had five minutes ago been patting him on the back for his skill in the batting cage, now eyeing him coldly for letting one pitch go by.

He noticed Max had moved farther back.

"How the hell you expect to call them out there?"

"He looks wild to me." Max moved in.

"Your knees are knockin'," Sam tittered.

"Mind your business, rednose," Max said.

"You better watch your talk, mister," Roy called to Mercy.

"Pitch it, greenhorn," warned the Whammer.

Sam crouched with his glove on. "Do it again, Roy. Give him something simular."

"Do it again," mimicked the Whammer. To the crowd, maybe to Harriet, he held up a vaunting finger showing there were other pitches to come.

Roy pumped, reared and flung.

The ball appeared to the batter to be a slow spinning planet looming toward the earth. For a long light-year he waited for this globe to whirl into the orbit of his swing so he could bust it to smithereens that would settle with dust and dead leaves into some distant cosmos. At last the unseeing eye, maybe a fortuneteller's lit crystal ball—anyway, a curious combination of circles—drifted within range of his weapon, or so he thought, because he lunged at it ferociously, twisting round like a top. He landed on both knees as the world floated by over his head and hit with a *whup* into the cave of Sam's glove.

"Hey, Max," Sam said, as he chased the ball after it had bounced out of the glove, "how do they pernounce Whammer if you leave out the W?"

"Strike," Mercy called long after a cheer (was it a jeer?) had burst from the crowd.

"What's he throwing," the Whammer howled, "spitters?"

"In the pig's poop." Sam thrust the ball at him. "It's drier than your granddaddy's scalp."

"I'm warning him not to try any dirty business."

Yet the Whammer felt oddly relieved. He liked to have his back crowding the wall, when there was a single pitch to worry about and a single pitch to hit. Then the sweat began to leak out of his pores as he stared at the hard, lanky figure of the pitiless pitcher, moving, despite his years and a few waste motions, like a veteran undertaker of the diamond, and he experienced a moment of depression.

Sam must have sensed it, because he discovered an unexpected pity in his heart and even for a split second hoped the idol would not be tumbled. But only for a second, for the Whammer had regained confidence in his known talent and experience and was taunting the greenhorn to throw.

Someone in the crowd hooted and the Whammer raised aloft two fat fingers and pointed where he would murder the ball, where the gleaming rails converged on the horizon and beyond was invisible.

Roy raised his leg. He smelled the Whammer's blood and wanted it, and through him the worm's he had with him, for the way he had insulted Sam.

The third ball slithered at the batter like a meteor, the flame swallowing itself. He lifted his club to crush it into a universe of sparks but the heavy wood dragged, and though he willed to destroy the sound he heard a gong bong and realized with sadness that the ball he had expected to hit had long since been part of the past; and though Max could not cough the fatal word out of his throat, the Whammer understood he was, in the truest sense of it, out.

The crowd was silent as the violet evening fell on their shoulders.

For a night game, the Whammer harshly shouted, it was customary to turn on lights. Dropping the bat, he trotted off to the train, an old man.

The ball had caught Sam smack in the washboard and lifted him off his feet. He lay on the ground, extended on his back. Roy pushed everybody aside to get him air. Unbuttoning Sam's coat, he removed the dented washboard.

"Never meant to hurt you, Sam."

"Just knocked the wind outa me," Sam gasped. "Feel better now." He was pulled to his feet and stood steady.

The train whistle wailed, the echo banging far out against the black mountain.

Then the doctor in the broadbrimmed black hat appeared, flustered and morose, the conductor trying to pacify him, and Eddie hopping along behind.

The doctor waved the crumpled yellow paper around. "Got a telegram says somebody on this train took sick. Anybody out here?"

Roy tugged at Sam's sleeve.

"Ixnay."

"What's that?"

"Not me," said Roy.

The doctor stomped off. He climbed into his Ford, whipped it up and drove away.

The conductor popped open his watch. "Be a good hour late into the city."

"All aboard," he called.

"Aboard," Eddie echoed, carrying the bassoon case.

The buxom girl in yellow broke through the crowd and threw her arms around Roy's neck. He ducked but she hit him quick with her pucker four times upon the right eye, yet he could see with the other that Harriet Bird (certainly a snappy goddess) had her gaze fastened on him.

They sat, after dinner, in Eddie's dimmed and empty Pullman, Roy floating through drifts of clouds on his triumph as Harriet went on about the recent tourney, she put it, and the unreal forest outside swung forward like a gate shutting. The odd way she saw things interested him, yet he was aware of the tormented trees fronting the snaky lake they were passing, trees bent and clawing, plucked white by icy blasts from the black water, their bony branches twisting in many a broken direction.

Harriet's face was flushed, her eyes gleaming with new insights. Occasionally she stopped and giggled at herself for the breathless volume of words that flowed forth, to his growing astonishment, but after a pause was on her galloping way again—a girl on horseback—reviewing the inspiring sight (she said it was) of David jawboning the Goliath-Whammer, or was it Sir Percy lancing Sir Maldemer, or the first son (with a rock in his paw) ranged against the primitive papa?

Roy gulped. "My father? Well, maybe I did want to skull him sometimes. After my grandma died, the old man dumped me in one orphan home after the other, wherever he happened to be working—when he did—though he did used to take me out of there summers and teach me how to toss a ball."

No, that wasn't what she meant, Harriet said. Had he ever read Homer?

Try as he would he could only think of four bases and not a book. His head spun at her allusions. He found her lingo strange with all the college stuff and hoped she would stop it because he wanted to talk about baseball.

Then she took a breather. "My friends say I have a fantastic imagination."

He quickly remarked he wouldn't say that. "But the only thing I had on my mind when I was throwing out there was that Sam had bet this ten spot we couldn't afford to lose out on, so I had to make him whiff."

"To whiff—oh, Roy, how droll," and she laughed again.

He grinned, carried away by the memory of how he had done it, the hero, who with three pitched balls had nailed the best the American League had to offer. What didn't that say about the future? He felt himself falling into sentiment in his thoughts and tried to steady himself but couldn't before he had come forth with a pronouncement: "You have to have the right stuff to play good ball and I have it. I bet some day I'll break every record in the book for throwing and hitting."

Harriet appeared startled then gasped, hiding it like a cough behind her tense fist, and vigorously applauded, her bracelets bouncing on her wrists. "Bravo, Roy, how wonderful."

"What I mean," he insisted, "is I feel that I have got it in me—that I am due for something very big. I have to do it. I mean," he said modestly, "that's of course when I get in the game."

Her mouth opened. "You mean you're not—" She seemed, to his surprise, disappointed, almost on the verge of crying.

"No," he said, ashamed. "Sam's taking me for a tryout."

Her eyes grew vacant as she stared out the window. Then she asked, "But Walter—*he* is a successful professional player, isn't he?"

"The Whammer?" Roy nodded.

"And he has won that award three times—what was it?"

"The Most Valuable Player." He had a panicky feeling he was losing her to the Whammer.

She bit her lip. "Yet you defeated him," she murmured.

He admitted it. "He won't last much longer I don't think—the most a year or two. By then he'll be too old for the game. Myself, I've got my whole life ahead of me."

Harriet brightened, saying sympathetically, "What will you hope to accomplish, Roy?"

He had already told her but after a minute remarked, "Sometimes when I walk down the street I bet people will say there goes Roy Hobbs, the best there ever was in the game."

She gazed at him with touched and troubled eyes. "Is that all?"

He tried to penetrate her question. Twice he had answered it and still she was unsatisfied. He couldn't be sure what she expected him to say. "Is that all?" he repeated. "What more is there?"

"Don't you know?" she said kindly.

Then he had an idea. "You mean the bucks? I'll get them too."

She slowly shook her head. "Isn't there something over and above earthly things—some more glorious meaning to one's life and activities?"

"In baseball?"

"Yes."

He racked his brain—

"Maybe I've not made myself clear, but surely you can see (I was saying this to Walter just before the train stopped) that yourself alone—alone in the sense that we are all terribly alone no matter what people say—I mean by that perhaps if you understood that our values must derive from—oh, I really suppose—" She dropped her hand futilely. "Please forgive me. I sometimes confuse myself with the little I know."

Her eyes were sad. He felt a curious tenderness for her, a little as if she might be his mother (That bird.) and tried very hard to come up with the answer she wanted—something you said about LIFE.

"I think I know what you mean," he said. "You mean the fun and satisfaction you get out of playing the best way that you know how?"

She did not respond to that.

Roy worried out some other things he might have said but had no confidence to put them into words. He felt curiously deflated and a little lost, as if he had just flunked a test. The worst of it was he still didn't know what she'd been driving at.

Harriet yawned. Never before had he felt so tongue-tied in front of a girl, a looker too. Now if he had her in bed—

Almost as if she had guessed what he was thinking and her mood had changed to something more practical than asking nutty questions that didn't count, she sighed and edged closer to him, concealing the move behind a query about his bassoon case. "Do you play?"

"Not any music," he answered, glad they were talking about something different. "There's a thing in it that I made for myself."

"What, for instance?"

He hesitated. "A baseball bat."

She was herself again, laughed merrily. "Roy, you are priceless."

"I got the case because I don't want to get the stick all banged up before I got the chance to use it."

"Oh, Roy." Her laughter grew. He smiled broadly.

She was now so close he felt bold. Reaching down he lifted the hat box by the string and lightly hefted it.

"What's in it?"

She seemed breathless. "In it?" Then she mimicked, "—Something I made for myself."

"Feels like a hat."

"Maybe a head?" Harriet shook a finger at him.

"Feels more like a hat." A little embarrassed, he set the box down. "Will you come and see me play sometime?" he asked.

She nodded and then he was aware of her leg against his and that she was all but on his lap. His heart slapped against his ribs and he took it all to mean that she had dropped the last of her interest in the Whammer and was putting it on the guy who had buried him.

As they went through a tunnel, Roy placed his arm around her shoulders, and when the train lurched on a curve, casually let his hand fall upon her full breast. The nipple rose between his fingers and before he could resist the impulse he had tweaked it.

Her high-pitched scream lifted her up and twirling like a dancer down the aisle.

Stricken, he rose—had gone too far.

Crooking her arms like broken branches she whirled back to him, her head turned so far around her face hung between her shoulders.

"Look, I'm a twisted tree."

Sam had sneaked out on the squirming, apologetic Mercy, who, with his back to the Whammer—he with a newspaper raised in front of his sullen eyes—had kept up a leech-like prodding about Roy, asking where he had come from (oh, he's just a home town boy), how it was no major league scout had got at him (they did but he turned them down for me) even with the bonus cash that they are tossing around these days (yep), who's his father (like I said, just an old semipro who wanted awful bad to be in the big leagues) and what, for God's sake, does he carry around in that case (that's his bat, Wonderboy). The sportswriter was greedy to know more, hinting he could do great things for the kid, but Sam, rubbing his side where it pained, at last put him off and escaped into the coach to get some shuteye before they hit Chicago, sometime past 1 A.M.

After a long time trying to settle himself comfortably, he fell snoring asleep flat on his back and was at once sucked into a long dream that he had gone thirsty mad for a drink and was threatening the slickers in the car get him a bottle or else. Then this weasel of a Mercy, pretending he was writing on a pad, pointed him out with his pencil and the conductor snapped him up by the seat of his pants and ran his free-wheeling feet lickity-split through the sawdust, giving him the merry heave-ho off the train through the air on a floating trapeze, ploop into a bog where it rained buckets. He thought he better get across the foaming river before it flooded the bridge away so he set out, all bespattered, to cross it, only this queer duck of a doctor in oilskins, an old man with a washable white mustache and a yellow lamp he thrust straight into your eyeballs, swore to him the bridge was gone. You're plumb tootin' crazy, Sam shouted in the storm, I saw it standin' with me own eyes, and he scuffled to get past the geezer, who dropped the light setting the rails afire. They wrestled in the rain until Sam slyly tripped and threw him, and helter-skeltered for the bridge, to find to his crawling horror it was truly down and here he was scratching space till he landed with a splishity-splash in the whirling waters, sobbing (whoa whoa) and the white watchman on the embankment flung him a flare but it was all too late because he heard the roar of the falls below (and restless shifting of the sea) and felt with his red hand where the knife had stabbed him . . .

Roy was dreaming of an enormous mountain—Christ, the size of it—when he felt himself roughly shaken—Sam, he thought, because they were there—only it was Eddie holding a lit candle.

"The fuse blew and I've had no chance to fix it."

"What's the matter?"

"Trou-ble. Your friend has collapsed."

Roy hopped out of the berth, stepped into moccasins and ran, with Eddie flying after him with the snuffed wax, into a darkened car where a pool of people under a blue light hovered over Sam, unconscious.

"What happened?" Roy cried.

"Sh," said the conductor, "he's got a raging fever."

"What from?"

"Can't say. We're picking up a doctor."

Sam was lying on a bench, wrapped in blankets with a

pillow tucked under his head, his gaunt face broken out in sweat. When Roy bent over him, his eyes opened.

"Hello, kiddo," he said in a cracked voice.

"What hurts you, Sam?"

"Where the washboard banged me—but it don't hurt so much now."

"Oh, Jesus."

"Don't take it so, Roy. I'll be better."

"Save his strength, son," the conductor said. "Don't talk now."

Roy got up. Sam shut his eyes.

The train whistled and ran slow at the next town then came to a draggy halt. The trainman brought a half-dressed doctor in. He examined Sam and straightened up. "We got to get him off and to the hospital."

Roy was wild with anxiety but Sam opened his eyes and told him to bend down.

Everyone moved away and Roy bent low.

"Take my wallet outa my rear pocket."

Roy pulled out the stuffed cowhide wallet.

"Now you go to the Stevens Hotel—"

"No, oh no, Sam, not without you."

"Go on, kiddo, you got to. See Clarence Mulligan tomorrow and say I sent you—they are expecting you. Give them everything you have got on the ball—that'll make me happy."

"But Sam—"

"You got to. Bend lower."

Roy bent lower and Sam stretched his withered neck and kissed him on the chin.

"Do like I say."

"Yes, Sam."

A tear splashed on Sam's nose.

Sam had something more in his eyes to say but though he tried, agitated, couldn't say it. Then the trainmen came in with a stretcher and they lifted the catcher and handed him down the steps, and overhead the stars were bright but he knew he was dead.

Roy trailed the anonymous crowd out of Northwest Station and clung to the shadowy part of the wall till he had the courage to call a cab.

"Do you go to the Stevens Hotel?" he asked, and the driver without a word shot off before he could rightly be seated, passed a red light and scuttled a cripple across the deserted street. They drove for miles in a shadow-infested, street-lamped jungle.

He had once seen some stereopticon pictures of Chicago and it was a boxed-up ant heap of stone and crumbling wood buildings in a many-miled spreading checkerboard of streets without much open space to speak of except the railroads, stockyards, and the shore of a windy lake. In the Loop, the offices went up high and the streets were jam-packed with people, and he wondered how so many of them could live together in any one place. Suppose there was a fire or something and they all ran out of their houses to see—how could they help but trample all over themselves? And Sam had warned him against strangers, because there were so many bums, sharpers, and gangsters around, people you were dirt to, who didn't know you and didn't want to, and for a dime they would slit your throat and leave you dying in the streets.

"Why did I come here?" he muttered and felt sick for home.

The cab swung into Michigan Avenue, which gave a view of the lake and a white-lit building spiring into the sky, then before he knew it he was standing flatfooted (Christ, the size of it) in front of the hotel, an enormous four-sectioned fortress. He hadn't the nerve to go through the whirling doors but had to because this bellhop grabbed his things—he wrested the bassoon case loose—and led him across the thick-carpeted lobby to a desk where he signed a card and had to count out five of the wallet's pulpy dollars for a room he would give up as soon as he found a house to board in.

But his cubbyhole on the seventeenth floor was neat and private, so after he had stored everything in the closet he lost his nervousness. Unlatching the window brought in the lake breeze. He stared down at the lit sprawl of Chicago, standing higher than he ever had in his life except for a night or two on a mountain. Gazing down upon the city, he felt as if bolts in his knees, wrists, and neck had loosened and he had spread up in height. Here, so high in the world, with the earth laid out in small squares so far below, he knew he would go in tomorrow and wow them with his fast one, and they would know him for the splendid pitcher he was.

The telephone rang. He was at first scared to answer it. In a strange place, so far from everybody he knew, it couldn't possibly be for him.

It rang again. He picked up the phone and listened.

"Hello, Roy? This is Harriet."

He wasn't sure he had got it right. "Excuse me?"

"Harriet Bird, silly."

"Oh, Harriet." He had completely forgotten her.

"Come down to my room," she giggled, "and let me say welcome to the city."

"You mean now?"

"Right away." She gave him the room number.

"Sure." He meant to ask her how she knew he was here but she had hung up.

Then he was elated. So that's how they did it in the city. He combed his hair and got out his bassoon case. In the elevator a drunk tried to take it away from him but Roy was too strong for him.

He walked—it seemed ages because he was impatient—through a long corridor till he found her number and knocked.

"Come on in."

Opening the door, he was astonished at the enormous room. Through the white-curtained window the sight of the endless dark lake sent a shiver down his spine.

Then he saw her standing shyly in the far corner of the room, naked under the gossamer thing she wore, held up on her risen nipples and the puffed wedge of hair beneath her white belly. A great weight went off his mind.

As he shut the door she reached into the hat box which lay open next to a vase of white roses on the table and fitted the black feathered hat on her head. A thick veil fell to her breasts. In her hand she held a squat, shining pistol.

He was greatly confused and thought she was kidding but

a grating lump formed in his throat and his blood shed ice. He cried out in a gruff voice, "What's wrong here?"

She said sweetly, "Roy, will you be the best there ever was in the game?"

"That's right."

She pulled the trigger (thrum of bull fiddle). The bullet cut a silver line across the water. He sought with his bare hands to catch it, but it eluded him and, to his horror, bounced into his gut. A twisted dagger of smoke drifted up from the gun barrel. Fallen on one knee he groped for the bullet, sickened as it moved, and fell over as the forest flew upward, and she, making muted noises of triumph and despair, danced on her toes around the stricken hero.

Batter Up!

"I shoulda been a farmer," Pop Fisher said bitterly. "I shoulda farmed since the day I was born. I like cows, sheep, and those hornless goats—I am partial to nanny goats, my daddy wore a beard—I like to feed animals and milk 'em. I like fixing things, weeding poison oak out of the pasture, and seeing to the watering of the crops. I like to be by myself on a farm. I like to stand out in the fields, tending the vegetables, the corn, the winter wheat—greenest looking stuff you ever saw. When Ma was alive she kept urging me to leave baseball and take up farming, and I always meant to but after she died I had no heart for it." Pop's voice all but broke and Red Blow shifted nervously on the bench but Pop didn't cry. He took out his handkerchief, flipped it, and blew his nose. "I have that green thumb," he said huskily, "and I shoulda farmed instead of playing wet nurse to a last place, dead-to-the-neck ball team."

They were sitting in the New York Knights' dugout, scanning the dusty field, the listless game and half-empty stands.

"Tough," said Red. He kept his eye on the pitcher.

Removing his cap, Pop rubbed his bald head with his bandaged fingers. "It's been a blasted dry season. No rains at all. The grass is worn scabby in the outfield and the infield is cracking. My heart feels as dry as dirt for the little I have to show for all my years in the game."

He got up, stooped at the fountain and spat the warm, rusty water into the dust. "When the hell they going to fix this thing so we can have a decent drink of water? Did you speak to that bastard partner I have, like I said to?"

"Says he's working on it."

"Working on it," Pop grunted. "He's so tight that if he was any tighter he'd be too stiff to move. It was one of the darkest days of my life when that snake crawled into this club. He's done me out of more dough than I can count."

"Kid's weakening again," Red said. "He passed two."

Pop watched Fowler for a minute but let him stay. "If those boy scouts could bring in a couple runs once in a while I'd change pitchers, but they couldn't bring their own grandmother in from across the street. What a butchering we took from the Pirates in the first game and here we are six runs behind in this. It's Memorial Day, all right, but not for the soldiers."

"Should've had some runs. Bump had four for four in the first, and two hits before he got himself chucked out of this."

Pop's face burned. "Don't mention that ape man to me—getting hisself bounced out of the game the only time we had runners on the bases when he come up."

"I'd've thrown him out too if I was the ump and he slid dry ice down my pants."

"I'd like to stuff him with ice. I never saw such a disgusting screwball for practical jokes."

Pop scratched violently under his loosely bandaged fingers. "And to top it off I have to go catch athlete's foot on my hands. Now ain't that one for the books? Everybody I have ever heard of have got it on their feet but I have to go and get it on both of my hands and be itchy and bandaged in this goshdarn hot weather. No wonder I am always asking myself is life worth the living of it."

"Tough," Red said. "He's passed Feeber, bases loaded."

Pop fumed. "My best pitcher and he blows up every time I put him against a first place team. Yank him."

The coach, a lean and freckled man, got nimbly up on the dugout steps and signaled to the bullpen in right field. He sauntered out to the mound just as somebody in street clothes came up the stairs of the tunnel leading from the clubhouse and asked the player at the end of the bench, "Who's Fisher?" The player jerked his thumb toward the opposite side of the dugout, and the man, dragging a large, beat-up valise and a bassoon case, treaded his way to Pop.

When Pop saw him coming he exclaimed, "Oh, my eight-foot uncle, what have we got here, the Salvation Army band?"

The man set his things on the floor and sat down on a concrete step, facing Pop. He beheld an old geezer of sixty-five with watery blue eyes, a thin red neck and a bitter mouth, who looked like a lost banana in the overgrown baseball suit he wore, especially his skinny legs in loose blue-and-white stockings.

And Pop saw a tall, husky, dark-bearded fellow with old eyes but not bad features. His face was strong-boned, if a trifle meaty, and his mouth seemed pleasant though its expression was grim. For his bulk he looked lithe, and he appeared calmer than he felt, for although he was sitting here on this step he was still in motion. He was traveling (on the train that never stopped). His self, his mind, raced on and he felt he hadn't stopped going wherever he was going because he hadn't yet arrived. Where hadn't he arrived? Here. But now it was time to calm down, ease up on the old scooter, sit still and be quiet, though the inside of him was still streaming through towns and cities, across forests and fields, over long years.

"The only music I make," he answered Pop, patting the bassoon case, "is with my bat." Searching through the pockets of his frayed and baggy suit, worn to threads at the knees and elbows, he located a folded letter that he reached over to the manager. "I'm your new left fielder, Roy Hobbs."

"My what!" Pop exploded.

"It says in the letter."

Red, who had returned from the mound, took the letter, unfolded it, and handed it to Pop. He read it in a single swoop then shook his head in disbelief.

"Scotty Carson sent you?"

"That's right."

"He must be daffy."

Roy wet his dry lips.

Pop shot him a shrewd look. "You're thirty-five if you're a day."

"Thirty-four, but I'm good for ten years."

"Thirty-four—Holy Jupiter, mister, you belong in an old man's home, not baseball."

The players along the bench were looking at him. Roy licked his lips.

"Where'd he pick you up?" Pop asked.

"I was with the Oomoo Oilers."

"In what league?"

"They're semipros."

"Ever been in organized baseball?"

"I only recently got back in the game."

"What do you mean got back?"

"Used to play in high school."

Pop snorted. "Well, it's a helluva mess." He slapped the letter with the back of his fingers. "Scotty signed him and the Judge okayed it. Neither of them consulted me. They can't do that," he said to Red. "That thief in the tower might have sixty per cent of the stock but I have it in writing that I am to manage this team and approve all player deals *as long as I live*."

"I got a contract," said Roy.

Roy pulled a blue-backed paper out of his inside coat pocket.

"Lemme see it."

Pop scanned it. "Where in blazes did he get the figure of three thousand dollars?"

"It was for five thousand minimum but the Judge said I already missed one-third of the season."

Pop burst into scornful laughter. "Sure, but that entitles you to about thirty-three hundred. Just like that godawful deadbeat. He'd skin his dead father if he could get into the grave."

He returned the contract to Roy. "It's illegal."

"Scotty's your chief scout?" Roy asked.

"That's right."

"He signed me to a contract with an open figure and the Judge filled it in. I asked about that and Scotty said he had the authority to sign me."

"He has," Red said to Pop. "You said so yourself if he found anybody decent."

"That's right, that's what I said, but who needs a fielder old enough to be my son? I got a left fielder," he said to Roy, "a darn good one when he feels like it and ain't playing practical jokes on everybody."

Roy stood up. "If you don't want me, Merry Christmas."

"Wait a second," said Red. He fingered Pop up close to the fountain and spoke to him privately.

Pop calmed down. "I'm sorry, son," he apologized to Roy when he returned to the bench, "but you came across me at a bad time. Also thirty-four years for a rookie is starting with one foot in the grave. But like Red says, if our best scout sent you, you musta showed him something. Go on in the clubhouse and have Dizzy fit you up with a monkey suit. Then report back here and I will locate you a place on this bench with the rest of my All-Stars." He threw the players a withering look and they quickly turned away.

"Listen, mister," Roy said, "I know my way out of this jungle if you can't use me. I don't want any second pickings."

"Do as he told you," Red said.

Roy rose, got his valise and bassoon case together, and headed into the tunnel. His heart was thumping like a noisy barrel.

"I shoulda bought a farm," Pop muttered.

The pitcher in the shower had left the door wide open so the locker room was clouded with steam when Roy came in. Unable to find anybody he yelled into the shower room where was the prop man, and the one in the shower yelled back in the equipment room and close the door it was drafty. When the steam had thinned out and Roy could see his way around he located the manager's office, so labeled in black letters on the door, but not the equipment room. In the diagonally opposite corner were the trainer's quarters, and here the door was ajar and gave forth an oil of wintergreen smell that crawled up his nose. He could see the trainer, in a gray sweatshirt with KNIGHTS stenciled across his chest, working on a man mountain on the rubbing table. Catching sight of Roy, the trainer called out in an Irish brogue who was he looking for?

"Prop man," Roy said.

"That's Dizzy—down the hall." The trainer made with his eyes to the left so Roy opened the door there and went down the hall. He located a sign, "Equipment," and through the window under it saw the prop man in a baseball jersey sitting on a uniform trunk with his back to the wall. He was reading the sports page of the *Mirror*.

Roy rapped on the ledge and Dizzy, a former utility pitcher, hastily put the paper down. "Caught me at an interesting moment," he grinned. "I was reading about this catcher that got beaned in Boston yesterday. Broke the side of his skull."

"The name's Roy Hobbs, new hand here. Fisher told me to get outfitted."

"New man—fielder, eh?"

Roy nodded.

"Yeah, we been one man short on the roster for two weeks. One of our guys went and got himself hit on the head with a fly ball and both of his legs are now paralyzed."

Roy winked.

"Honest to God. And just before that our regular third baseman stepped on a bat and rolled down the dugout steps. Snapped his spine in two places." Dizzy grimaced. "We sure been enjoying an unlucky season."

He came forth with a tape measure and took Roy's measurements, then he went back and collected a pile of stuff from the shelves.

"Try this for size." He handed him a blue cap with a white K stitched on the front of it.

Roy tried it. "Too small."

"You sure got some size noggin there."

"Seven and a half." Roy looked at him.

"Just a social remark. No offense meant or intended." He gave Roy a size that fitted.

"How's it look?" Roy asked.

"A dream but why the tears?"

"I have a cold." He turned away.

Dizzy asked him to sign for the stuff—Judge Banner insisted. He helped Roy carry it to his locker.

"Keep anything you like inside of here but for goodness' sakes no booze. Pop throws fits if any of the players drink."

Roy stood the bassoon case in upright. "Got a lock for the door?"

"Nobody locks their doors here. Before the game you deposit your valuables in that trunk there and I will lock them up."

"Okay, skip it."

Dizzy excused himself to get back to his paper and Roy began to undress.

The locker room was tomblike quiet. The pitcher who had been in the showers—his footsteps were still wet on the floor—had dressed rapidly and vanished. As he put his things away, Roy found himself looking around every so often to make sure he was here. He was, all right, yet in all his imagining of how it would be when he finally hit the majors, he had not expected to feel so down in the dumps. It was different than walking out, jumping back on a train, and going wherever people went when they were running out on something. Maybe for a long rest in one of those towns he had lived in as a kid. Like the place where he had that shaggy mutt that used to scamper through the woods, drawing him after it to the deepest, stillest part, till the silence was so pure you could crack it if you threw a rock. Roy remained lost in the silence till the dog's yapping woke him, though as he came out of it, it was not barking he heard but the sound of voices through the trainer's half-open door.

He listened closely because he had the weird impression that he knew all the voices in there, and as he sorted them he recognized first the trainer's brogue and then a big voice that he did not so much recall, as remember having heard throughout his life—a strong, rawboned voice, familiar from his boyhood and some of the jobs he had worked at later, and the different places he had bummed around in, slop joints, third-rate hotels, prize fight gyms and such; the big voice of a heavy, bull-necked, strong-muscled guy, the kind of gorilla he had more than once fought half to death for no reason he could think of. Oh, the Whammer, he thought, and quickly ducked but straightened up when he remembered the Whammer was almost fifty and long since retired out of the game. But what made him most uneasy was a third voice, higher than the other two, a greedy, penetrating, ass-kissing voice he had definitely heard before. He strained his ears to hear it again but the big voice was talking about this gag he had pulled on Pop Fisher, in particular, spraying white pepper in

Pop's handkerchief, which made him sneeze and constantly blow his beak. That commenced an epidemic of base stealing, to Pop's fury, because the signal to steal that day was for him to raise his handkerchief to his schnozzle.

At the end of the story there was a guffaw and a yelp of laughter, then the trainer remarked something and this other voice, one that stood on stilts, commented that Bump certainly got a kick out of his jokes, and Bump, he must have been, said Pop wouldn't agree to his release, so if he was going to be stuck in this swamp he would at least have a little fun.

He laughed loudly and said, "Here's one for your colyum, kid. We were in Cincy in April and had a free day on our hands because this exhibition game was called off, so in the Plaza lobby that morning we get to bulling about players and records, and you know Pop and this line of his about how lousy the modern player is compared to those mustached freaks he played with in the time of King Tut. He was saying that the average fielder nowadays could maybe hit the kangaroo ball we got—he was looking at me—but you couldn't count on him to catch a high fly. 'How high'? I asked him, innocent, and he points up and says, 'Any decent height. They either lose them in the sun or misjudge them in the wind.' So I say, 'Could you catch the real high ones, Pop? And he pipes up, 'As high as they went up I could catch them.' He thinks a minute and says, 'I bet I could catch a ball that is dropped from the top of the Empire State Building.' 'No,' I says, like I was surprised, and 'Yes,' he says. So I say, 'We have nothing on for today, and although there isn't any Empire State Building in Cincinnati, yet I do have this friend of mine at the airport who owns a Piper Cub. I will give him a National League baseball and he will drop it at the height of the building if you will catch it.' 'Done,' he says, as perky as a turkey, so I call up this guy I know and arrange it and off we go across the bridge to the Kentucky side of the river, where there is plenty of room to move around in. Well, sir, soon this yellow plane comes over and circles a couple of times till he has the right height, and then he lets go with something that I didn't tell Pop, but which the boys are onto, is a grapefruit so that if it hits him it will not crack his skull open and kill him. Down the thing comes like a cannonball and Pop, in his black two-piece bathing suit, in case he has to go a little in the water, and wearing a mitt the size of a basket, circles under it like a dizzy duck, holding the sun out of his eyes as he gets a line on where it is coming down. Faster it falls, getting bigger by the second, then Pop, who is now set for the catch, suddenly lets out a howl, 'My Christ, the moon is falling on me,' and the next second, bong—the grapefruit busts him on the conk and we have all we can do to keep him from drowning in the juice."

Now there was a loud cackle of laughter in the trainer's room. The voice Roy didn't like—the frightening thought dawned on him that the voice *knew* what he was hiding—it changed the subject and wanted to know from Bump if there was any truth to the rumor about him and Pop's niece.

"Naw," Bump said, and cagily asked, "What rumor?"

"That you and Memo are getting hitched."

Bump laughed. "She must've started that one herself."

"Then you deny it?"

The door was shoved open and Bump waltzed out in his shorts, as husky, broadbacked, and big-shouldered as Roy had thought, followed by the trainer and a slightly popeyed gent dressed in an expensive striped suit, whose appearance gave Roy a shooting pain in the pit of his stomach—Max Mercy.

Ashamed to be recognized, to have his past revealed like an egg spattered on the floor, Roy turned away, tucking his jersey into his pants.

But Bump paraded over with his hairy arm outstretched. "Hiya, Buster, you the latest victim they have trapped?"

Roy felt an irritable urge to pitch his fist at the loudmouth, but he nodded and shook hands.

"Welcome to the lousiest team in the world, barring none," Bump said. "And this is ol' Doc Casey, the trainer, who has got nobody but cripples on his hands except me. And the hawkshaw with the eyes is Max Mercy, the famous sports colyumist. Most newspaper guys are your pals and know when to keep their traps shut, but to Max a private life is a personal insult. Before you are here a week he will tell the public how much of your salary you send to your grandma and how good is your sex life."

Max, whose mustache and sideboards were graying, laughed hollowly. He said to Roy, "Didn't catch the name."

"Roy Hobbs," he said stiffly, but no one seemed to think it mattered very much.

The game was over and the players hoofed through the tunnel into the locker room. They tore out of their uniforms and piled into the showers. Some stayed in only long enough to wet their skins. Wiping themselves dry, they tumbled into street clothes. Their speed, however, did them no good, for Red, after courteously asking Mercy to leave, posted himself and Earl Wilson, the third base coach, at the door and they let nobody else out. The players waited nervously, except Bump, who slapped backs and advised everybody to cheer up. A few of the boys were working the strategy of staying in the showers so long they hoped Pop would grow sick and tired and leave. But Pop, a self-sustaining torch in the shut managerial office, outwaited them, and when he got the quiet knock from Red that the lobsters were in the pot, yanked open the door and strode sulphurously forth. The team shriveled.

Pop stepped up on a chair where for once, a bald, bristling figure, he towered over them. Waving his bandaged hands he began to berate them but immediately stopped, choked by his rage into silence.

"If he coughs now," Bump boomed, "he will bust into dust."

Pop glared at him, his head glowing like a red sun. He savagely burst out that not a single blasted one of them here was a true ballplayer. They were sick monkeys, broken-down mules, pigeon-chested toads, slimy horned worms, but not real honest-to-god baseball players.

"How's about flatfooted fish?" Bump wisecracked. "Get it, boys, fish—Fisher," and he fell into a deep gargle of laughter at his wit, but the semi-frozen players in the room did not react.

"How's he get away with it?" Roy asked the ghost standing next to him. The pale player whispered out of the corner of his mouth that Bump was presently the leading hitter in the league.

Pop ignored Bump and continued to give the team the rough side of his tongue. "What beats me is that I have spent thousands of dollars for the best players I could lay my hands on. I hired two of the finest coaches in the game. I sweat myself sick trying to direct you, and all you can deliver is those goddamn goose eggs." His voice rose. "Do you dimwits realize that we have been skunked for the last forty-five innings in a row?"

"Not Bumpsy," the big voice said, "I am terrific."

"You now hold the record of the most consecutive games lost in the whole league history, the most strikeouts, the most errors—"

"Not Bumpsy—"

"—the most foolishness and colossal stupidities. In plain words you all stink. I am tempted to take pity on those poor dopes who spend a buck and a half to watch you play and trade the whole lousy lot of you away."

Bump dropped down on his knees and raised his clasped hands. "Me first, Lawdy, me first."

"—and start from scratch to build up a team that will know how to play together and has guts and will fight the other guy to death before they drop seventeen games in the cellar."

The players in the locker room were worn out but Bump was singing, "Many brave hearts are asleep in the deep."

"Beware," he croaked low in his throat, "bewaaare—"

Pop shook a furious finger at him that looked as if it would fly off and strike him in the face. "As for you, Bump Baily, high and mighty though you are, some day you'll pay for your sassifras. Remember that lightning cuts down the tallest tree too."

Bump didn't like warnings of retribution. His face turned surly.

"Lightning, maybe, but no burnt out old fuse."

Pop tottered. "Practice at eight in the morning," he said brokenly. But for Red he would have tumbled off the chair. In his office behind the slammed and smoking door they could hear him sobbing, "Sometimes I could cut my own throat."

It took the Knights a while to grow bones and crawl out

after Bump. But when everybody had gone, including the coaches and Dizzy, Roy remained behind. His face was flaming hot, his clothes soaked in sweat and shame, as if the man's accusations had been leveled at his head.

When Pop came out in his street clothes, a yellowed Panama and a loud sport jacket, he was startled to see Roy sitting there in the gloom and asked what he was waiting for.

"No place to go," Roy said.

"Whyn't you get a room?"

"Ain't got what it takes."

Pop looked at him. "Scotty paid you your bonus cash, didn't he?"

"Two hundred, but I had debts."

"You shoulda drawn an advance on your first two week's pay from the office when you came in today. It's too late now, they quit at five, so I will write you out my personal check for twenty-five dollars and you can pay me back when you get the money."

Pop balanced his checkbook on his knee. "You married?"

"No."

"Whyn't you ask around among the married players to see who has got a spare room? That way you'd have a more regular life. Either that, or in a respectable boarding house. Some of the boys who have their homes out of town prefer to stay at a moderate-priced hotel, which I myself have done since my wife passed away, but a boarding house is more homelike and cheaper. Anyway," Pop advised, "tonight you better come along with me to the hotel and tomorrow you can find a place to suit your needs."

Roy remarked he wasn't particularly crazy about hotels.

They left the ball park, got into a cab and drove downtown. The sky over the Hudson was orange. Once Pop broke out of his reverie to point out Grant's Tomb.

At the Midtown Hotel, Pop spoke to the desk clerk and he assigned Roy a room on the ninth floor, facing toward the Empire State Building. Pop went up with him and pumped the mattress.

"Not bad," he said.

After the bellhop had left he said he hoped Roy wasn't the shenanigan type.

"What kind?" Roy asked.

"There are all sorts of nuts in this game and I remember one of my players—seems to me it was close to twenty years ago—who used to walk out on the fifteenth floor ledge and scare fits out of people in the other rooms. One day when he was walking out there he fell and broke his leg and only the darndest luck kept him from rolling right overboard. It was beginning to rain and he pulled himself around from window to window, begging for help, and everybody went into stitches at his acting but kept their windows closed. He finally rolled off and hit bottom."

Roy had unpacked his valise and was washing up.

"Lemme tell you one practical piece of advice, son," Pop went on. "You're staying way late—I was finished after fifteen years as an active player one year after the age you're coming in, but if you want to get along the best way, behave and give the game all you have got, and when you can't do that, quit. We don't need any more goldbrickers or fourflushers or practical jokers around. One Bump Baily is too much for any team."

He left the room wretched.

The phone jangled and after a minute Roy got around to lifting it.

"What's the matter?" Red Blow barked. "Don't you answer your telephone?"

"I like it to ring a little, gives 'em a chance to change their mind."

"Who?"

"Anybody."

Red paused. "Pop asked me to show you around. When are you eating?"

"I am hungry now."

"Meet me in the lobby, half past six."

As Roy hung up there was a loud dum-diddy-um-dum on the door and Bump Baily in a red-flowered Hollywood shirt breezed in.

"Hiya, buster. Saw you pull in with the old geezer and tracked you down. I would like for you to do me a favor."

"Roy is the name."

"Roy is fine. Listen, I got my room on the fourth floor, which is a damn sight classier than this mouse trap. I would like you to borrow it and I will borrow this for tonight."

"What's the pitch?"

"I am having a lady friend visit me and there are too many nosy people on my floor."

Roy considered and said okay. He unconsciously wet his lips.

Bump slapped him between the shoulders. "Stick around buster, you will get yours."

Roy knew he would never like the guy.

Bump told him his room number and they exchanged keys, then Roy put a few things into his valise and went downstairs.

Coming along the fourth floor hall he saw a door half open and figured this was it. As he pulled the knob he froze, for there with her back to him stood a slim, red-headed girl in black panties and brassiere. She was combing her hair before a mirror on the wall as the light streamed in around her through the billowy curtains. When she saw him in the mirror she let out a scream. He stepped back as if he had been kicked in the face. Then the door slammed and he had a splitting headache.

Bump's room was next door so Roy went in and lay down on the bed, amid four purple walls traced through with leaves flying among white baskets of fruit, some loaded high and some spilled over. He lay there till the pain in his brain eased.

At 6:30 he went down and met Red, in a droopy linen suit, and they had steaks in a nearby chophouse. Roy had two and plenty of mashed potatoes. Afterwards they walked up Fifth Avenue. He felt better after the meal.

"Want to see the Village?" Red said.

"What's in it?"

Red picked his teeth. "Beats me. Whatever they got I can't find it. How about a picture?"

Roy was agreeable so they dropped into a movie. It was a picture about a city guy who came to the country, where he had a satisfying love affair with a girl he met. Roy enjoyed it. As they walked back to the hotel the night was soft and summery. He thought about the black-brassiered girl in the next room.

Red talked about the Knights. "They are not a bad bunch of players, but they aren't playing together and it's mostly Bump's fault. He is for Bump and not for the team. Fowler, Schultz, Hinkle, and Hill are all good pitchers and could maybe be fifteen or twenty game winners if they got some support in the clutches, which they don't, and whatever Bump gives them in hitting he takes away with his lousy fielding."

"How's that?"

"He's just so damn lazy. Pop has thrown many a fine and suspension at him, but after that he will go into a slump on purpose and we don't win a one. If I was Pop I'da had his ass long ago, but Pop thinks a hitter like him could be a bell cow and lead the rest ahead, so he keeps hoping he will reform. If we could get the team rolling we'd be out of the cellar in no time."

They were approaching the hotel and Roy counted with his eyes up to the fourth floor and watched the curtains in the windows.

"I read Scotty's report on you," Red said. "He says you are a terrific hitter. How come you didn't start playing when you were younger?"

"I did but I flopped." Roy was evasive. Red cringed. "Don't say that word around here."

"What word?"

"Flopped—at least not anywhere near Pop. He starts to cry when he hears it."

"What for?"

"Didn't you ever hear about Fisher's Flop?"

"Seems to me I did but I am not sure."

Red told him the story. "About forty years ago Pop was the third sacker for the old Sox when they got into their first World Series after twenty years. They sure wanted to take the flag that year but so did the Athletics, who they were playing, and it was a rough contest all the way into the seventh game. That one was played at Philly and from the first inning the score stood at 3-3, until the Athletics drove the tie-breaker across in the last of the eighth. In the ninth the Sox's power was due up but they started out bad. The leadoffer hit a blooper to short, the second struck out, and the third was Pop. It was up to him. He let one go for a strike, then he slammed a low, inside pitch for a tremendous knock.

"The ball sailed out to deep center," Red said, "where the center fielder came in too fast and it rolled through him to the fence and looked good for an inside-the-park homer, or at least a triple. Meanwhile, Pop, who is of course a young guy at this time, was ripping around the bags, and the crowd was howling for him to score and tie up the game, when in some crazy way as he was heading for home, his legs got tangled under him and he fell flat on his stomach, the living bejesus knocked out of him. By the time he was up again the ball was in the catcher's glove and he ran up the baseline after Pop. In the rundown that followed, the third baseman tagged him on the behind and the game was over."

Red spat into the street. Roy tried to say something but couldn't.

"That night Fisher's Flop, or as they mostly call it, 'Fisher's Famous Flop,' was in every newspaper in the country and was talked about by everybody. Naturally Pop felt like hell. I understand that Ma Fisher had the phone out and hid him up in the attic. He stayed there two weeks, till the roof caught fire and he had to come out or burn. After that they went to Florida for a vacation but it didn't help much. His picture was known to all and wherever he went they yelled after him, 'Flippity-flop, flippity-flop.' It was at this time that Pop lost his hair. After a while people no longer recognized him, except on the ball field, yet though the kidding died down, Pop was a marked man."

Roy mopped his face. "Hot," he said.

"But he had his guts in him," Red said, "and stayed in the game for ten years more and made a fine record. Then he retired from baseball for a couple of years, which was a good thing but he didn't know it. Soon one of Ma's rich relatives died and left them a pile of dough that Pop used to buy himself a half share of the Knights. He was made field manager and the flop was forgotten by now except for a few wise-egg sportswriters that, when they are too drunk to do an honest day's work, would raise up the old story and call it

Fisher's Fizzle, or Farce, or Fandango—you wouldn't guess there are so many funny words beginning with an f—which some of them do to this day when the Knights look foolish. The result is that Pop has the feeling he has been jinxed since the time of his flop, and he has spent twenty-five years and practically all of his pile trying to break the jinx, which he thinks he can do by making the Knights into the world champs that the old Sox never did become. Eight times he had finished in second place, five in third, and the rest in fourth or fifth, but last season when the Judge bought into the club and then took advantage of Pop's financial necessity to get hold of ten per cent of his shares and make himself the majority stockholder, was our worst season. We ended up in the sewer and this year it looks like a repeat."

"How come?"

"The Judge is trying to push Pop out of his job although he has a contract to manage for life—that's what the judge had to promise to get that ten per cent of stock. Anyway, he's been trying everything he can think of to make things tough for Pop. He has by his sly ways forced all sorts of trades on us which make money all right but hurt the team. It burns me up," Red said, "because I would give my right arm if I could get Pop the pennant. I am sure that if he took one and the Series after that, he would feel satisfied, quit baseball, and live in peace. He is one helluva white guy and deserves better than he got. That's why I am asking you to give him the best you have in you."

"Let him play me," Roy said, "and he will get the best."

In the lobby Red said he had enjoyed Roy's company and they should eat together more. Before he left he warned Roy to be careful with his earnings. They weren't much, he knew, but if in the future Roy had a chance to invest in something good, he advised him to do so. "There is a short life in baseball and we have to think of the future. Anything can happen to you in this game. Today you are on top and tomorrow you will be on your way out to Dubuque. Try to protect your old age. It don't pay to waste what you earn." To his surprise, Roy answered, "To hell with my old age. I will be in this game a long time."

Red rubbed his chin. "How are you so sure?"

"It wasn't for nothing it took me fifteen years to get here. I came for more than the ride and I will leave my mark around here."

Red waited to hear more but Roy shut up.

Red shrugged, "Well, each to their choice."

Roy said good night and went upstairs. Entering Bump's room, he picked up a gilt hairpin from the carpet and put it into his wallet because some claimed it brought luck. For a while he stood at the window and watched the lit Empire State Building. It was a great big city, all right. He undressed, thinking of Pop's flop that changed his whole life, and got into bed.

In the dark the bed was in motion, going round in wide, sweeping circles. He didn't like the feeling so he lay deathly still and let everything go by—the trees, mountains, states. Then he felt he was headed into a place where he did not want to go and tried urgently to think of ways to stop the bed. But he couldn't and it went on, a roaring locomotive now, screaming into the night, so that he was tensed and sweating and groaned aloud why did it have to be me? what did I do to deserve it? seeing himself again walking down the long, lonely corridor, carrying the bassoon case, the knock, the crazy Harriet (less and more than human) with the pistol, and him, cut down in the very flower of his youth, lying in a red pool of his own blood.

No, he cried, oh no, and lashed at his pillow, as he had a thousand times before.

Finally, as the sight of him through the long long years of suffering faded away, he quieted down. The noise of the train eased off as it came to a stop, and Roy found himself set down in a field somewhere in the country, where he had a long and satisfying love affair with this girl he had seen in the picture tonight.

He thought of her till he had fallen all but deep asleep, when a door seemed to open in the mind and this naked redheaded lovely slid out of a momentary flash of light, and the room was dark again. He thought he was still dreaming of the picture but the funny part of it was when she got into bed with him he almost cried out in pain as her icy hands and feet, in immediate embrace, slashed his hot body, but there among the apples, grapes, and melons, he found what he wanted and had it.

At the clubhouse the next morning the unshaven Knights were glum and redeyed. They moved around listlessly and cursed each step. Angry fist fights broke out among them. They were sore at themselves and the world, yet when Roy came in and headed for his locker they looked up and watched with interest. He opened the door and found his new uniform knotted up dripping wet on a hook. His sanitary socks and woolen stocking were slashed to shreds and all the other things were smeared black with shoe polish. He located his jock, with two red apples in it, swinging from a cord attached to the light globe, and both his shoes were nailed to the ceiling. The boys let out a bellow of laughter. Bump just about doubled up howling, but Roy yanked the wet pants off the hook and caught him with it smack in the face. The players let out another howl.

Bump comically dried himself with a bath towel, digging deep into his ears, wiping under the arms, and shimmying as he rubbed it across his fat behind.

"Fast guesswork, buster, and to show you there's no hard feelings, how's about a Camel?"

Roy wanted nothing from the bastard but took the cigarette because everyone was looking on. When he lit it, someone in the rear yelled, "Fire!" and ducked as it burst in Roy's face. Bump had disappeared. The players fell into each other's arms. Tears streamed down their cheeks. Some of them could not unbend and limped around from laughing so.

Roy flipped the ragged butt away and began to mop up his wet locker.

Allie Stubbs, the second baseman, danced around the room in imitation of a naked nature dancer. He pretended to discover a trombone at the foot of a tree and marched around blowing oompah, oompah, oompah.

Roy then realized the bassoon case was missing. It startled him that he hadn't thought of it before.

"Who's got it, boys?"—but no one answered. Allie now made out like he was flinging handfuls of rose petals into the trainer's office.

Going in there, Roy saw that Bump had broken open the bassoon case and was about to attack Wonderboy with a hacksaw.

"Lay off of that, you goon."

Bump turned and stepped back with the bat raised. Roy grabbed it and with a quick twist tore it out of his sweaty hands, turning him around as he did and booting him hard with his knee. Bump grunted and swung but Roy ducked. The team crowded into the trainer's office, roaring with delight.

But Doc Casey pushed his way through them and stepped between Roy and Bump. "That'll do, boys. We want no trouble here. Go on outside or Pop will have your hides."

Bump was sweaty and sore. "You're a lousy sport, alfalfa."

"I don't like the scummy tricks you play on people you have asked for a favor," Roy said.

"I hear you had a swell time, wonderboy."

Again they grappled for each other, but Doc, shouting for help, kept them apart until the players pinned Roy's arms and held on to Bump.

"Lemme at him," Bump roared, "and I will skin the skunk."

Held back by the team, they glared at one another over the trainer's head.

"What's going on in there?" Pop's shrill blast came from inside the locker room. Earl Wilson poked his gray-haired, sunburned head in and quickly called, "All out, men, on the double." The players scurried past Pop and through the tunnel. They felt better.

Dizzy hustled up a makeshift rig for Roy. He dressed and polished his bat, a little sorry he had lost his temper, because he had wanted to speak quietly to the guy and find out whether he was expecting the redhead in his room last night.

Thinking about her made him uneasy. He reported to Pop in the dugout.

"What was the trouble in there between Bump and you?" Pop asked.

Roy didn't say and Pop got annoyed. "I won't stand for any

ructions between players so cut it out or you will find yourself chopping wood back in the sticks. Now report to Red."

Roy went over to where Red was catching Chet Schultz, today's pitcher, and Red said to wait his turn at the batting cage.

The field was overrun with droopy players. Half a dozen were bunched near the gate of the cage, waiting to be pitched to by Al Fowler, whom Pop had ordered to throw batting practice for not bearing down in the clutches yesterday. Some of the men were at the sidelines, throwing catch. A few were shagging flies in the field, a group was playing pepper. On the line between home and first Earl Wilson was hacking out grounders to Allie Stubbs, Cal Baker at short, Hank Benz, the third baseman, and Emil Lajong, who played first. At the edge of the outfield, Hinkle and Hill, two of the regular starters, and McGee, the reliefer, were doing a weak walk-run-walk routine. No one seemed to be thoroughly awake, but when Roy went into the batting cage they came to life and observed him.

Fowler, a southpaw, was in a nasty mood. He didn't like having his ears burned by Pop, called a showboat in front of the other men, and then shoved into batting practice the day after he had pitched. Fowler was twenty-three but looked thirty. He was built rangy, with very light hair and eyelashes, and small blue eyes. As a pitcher he had the stuff and knew it, but all season long he had been erratic and did a great amount of griping. He was palsy with Bump, who as a rule had no friends.

When Roy came up with Wonderboy, he hugged the plate too close to suit Fowler, who was in there anyway only to help the batters find their timing. In annoyance Fowler pitched the ball at Roy's head. Roy hit the dirt.

Pop shrieked, "Cut that out, you blasted fool." Fowler mumbled something about the ball slipping. Yet he wanted to make Roy look silly and burned the next one in. Roy swung and the ball sailed over the right field fence. Redfaced, Fowler tried a hard, sharp-breaking curve. Roy caught it at the end of his bat and pulled it into the left field stands.

"Try this one, grandpa." Fowler flung a stiff-wrist knuckler that hung in the air without spin before it took a sudden dip, but Roy scooped it up with the stick and lifted it twenty rows up into the center field stands. Then he quit. Fowler was scowling at his feet. Everybody else stared at Roy.

Pop called out, "Lemme see that bat, son."

Both he and Red examined it, hefting it and rubbing along the grain with their fingers.

"Where'd you get it?" Pop asked.

Roy cleared his throat. He said he had made it himself.

"Did you brand this name Wonderboy on it?"

"That's right."

"What's it mean?"

"I made it long ago," Roy said, "when I was a kid. I wanted it to be a very good bat and that's why I gave it that name."

"A bat's cheap to buy," Red said.

"I know it but this tree near the river where I lived was split by lightning. I liked the wood inside of it so I cut me out a bat. Hadn't used it much until I played semipro ball, but I always kept it oiled with sweet oil and boned it so it wouldn't chip."

"Sure is white. Did you bleach the wood?"

"No, that's the true color."

"How long ago d'you make it?" Pop asked.

"A long time—I don't remember."

"Whyn't you get into the game then?"

Roy couldn't answer for a minute. "I sorta got sidetracked."

But Pop was all smiles. "Red'll measure and weigh it. If there's no filler and it meets specifications you'll be allowed to use it."

"There's nothing in it but wood."

Red clapped him on the back. "I feel it in my bones that you will have luck with it." He said to Pop, "Maybe we can start Roy in the line-up soon?"

Pop said they would see how it worked out.

But he sent Roy out to left field and Earl hit fungos to him all over the lot. Roy ran them down well. He took one shot over his shoulder and two caroming off the wall below the stands. His throwing was quick, strong, and bull's eye.

When Bump got around to his turn in the cage, though he did not as a rule exert himself in practice, he now whammed five of Fowler's fast pitches into the stands. Then he trotted out to his regular spot in the sun field and Earl hit him some long flies, all of which he ran for and caught with gusto, even those that went close to the wall, which was unusual for him because he didn't like to go too near it.

Practice picked up. The men worked faster and harder than they had in a long time. Pop suddenly felt so good, tears came to his eyes and he had to blow his nose.

In the clubhouse about an hour and a half before game time, the boys were sitting around in their underwear after showers. They were bulling, working crossword puzzles, shaving and writing letters. Two were playing checkers, surrounded by a circle of others, and the rest were drinking soda, looking at the *Sporting News,* or just resting their eyes. Though they tried to hide it they were all nervous, always glancing up whenever someone came into the room. Roy couldn't make sense of it.

Red took him around to meet some of the boys and Roy spoke a few words to Dave Olson, the squat catcher, also to the shy Mexican center fielder, Juan Flores, and to Gabby Laslow, who patrolled right field. They sidestepped Bump, sitting in front of his locker with a bath towel around his rump, as he worked a red thread across the yellowed foot of a sanitary sock.

"Changes that thread from sock to sock every day," Red said in a low voice. "Claims it keeps him hitting."

As the players began to get into clean uniforms, Pop, wearing halfmoon specs, stepped out of his office. He read aloud the batting order, then flipping through his dogeared, yellow-paged notebook he read the names of the players opposing them and reminded them how the pitchers were to pitch and the fielders field them. This information was scribbled all over the book and Pop had to thumb around a lot before he had covered everybody. Roy then expected him to lay on with a blistering mustard plaster for all, but he only glanced anxiously at the door and urged them all to be on their toes and for gosh sakes get some runs.

Just as Pop finished his pep talk the door squeaked open and a short and tubby man in a green suit peeked in. Seeing they were ready, he straightened up and entered briskly, carrying a briefcase in his hand. He beamed at the players and without a word from anybody they moved chairs and benches and arranged themselves in rows before him. Roy joined the rest, expecting to hear some kind of talk. Only Pop and the coaches sat behind the man, and Dizzy lounged, half open-mouthed, at the door leading to the hall.

"What's the act?" Roy asked Olson.

"It's Doc Knobb." The catcher looked sleepy.

"What's he do?"

"Pacifies us."

The players were attentive, sitting as if they were going to have their pictures snapped. The nervousness Roy had sensed among them was all but gone. They looked like men whose worries had been lifted, and even Bump gave forth a soft grunt of contentment.

The doctor removed his coat and rolled up his shirtsleeves. "Got to hurry today," he told Pop, "got a polo team to cheer up in Brooklyn."

He smiled at the men and then spoke so softly, at first they couldn't hear him. When he raised his voice it exuded calm.

"Now, men," he purred, "all of you relax and let me have your complete attention. Don't think of a thing but me." He laughed, brushed a spot off his pants, and continued. "You know what my purpose is. You're familiar with that. It's to help you get rid of the fears and personal inferiorities that tie you into knots and keep you from being aces in this game. Who are the Pirates? Not supermen, only mortals. What have they got that you haven't got? I can't think of a thing, absolutely not one. It's the attitude that's licking you—your own, not the Pirates'. What do you mean to yourselves? Are you a flock of bats flying around in a coffin, or the sun shining calmly on a blue lake? Are you sardines being swallowed up in the sea, or the whale that does the swallowing? That's why I'm here, to help you answer that question in the affirmative, to help you by mesmerism and autosuggestion, meaning you do the suggesting, not I. I only assist by making you receptive to your own basic thoughts. If you think you are winners, you will be. If you don't, you won't. That's psychology. That's the way the world works. Give me your whole attention and look straight into my eyes. What do you see there? You see sleep. That's right, sleep. So relax, sleep, relax . . ."

His voice was soft, lulling, peaceful. He had raised his pudgy arms and with stubby fingers was making ripples on a vast calm sea. Already Olson was gently snoring. Flores, with the tip of his tongue protruding, Bump, and some of the other players were fast asleep. Pop looked on, absorbed.

Staring at the light gleaming on Pop's bald bean, Roy felt himself going off . . . way way down, drifting through the tides into golden water as he searched for this fish, or mermaid, or whatever you called her. His eyes grew big in the seeking, first fish eyes, then bulbous frog eyes. Sailing lower into the pale green sea, he sought everywhere for the reddish glint of her scales, until the water became dense and dark green and then everything gradually got so black he lost all sight of where he was. When he tried to rise up into the light he couldn't find it. He darted in all directions, and though there were times he saw flashes of her green tail, it was dark everywhere. He threshed up a storm of luminous bubbles but they gave out little light and he did not know where in all the glass to go.

Roy ripped open his lids and sprang up. He shoved his way out from between the benches.

The doctor was startled but made no attempt to stop him. Pop called out, "Hey, where do you think you're going?"

"Out."

"Sit down, dammit, you're on the team."

"I might be on the team but no medicine man is going to hypnotize me."

"You signed a contract to obey orders," Pop snapped shrilly.

"Yes, but not to let anybody monkey around in my mind."

As he headed into the tunnel he heard Pop swear by his eight-foot uncle that nobody by the name of Roy Hobbs would ever play ball for him as long as he lived.

He had waited before . . . and he waited now, on a spike-scuffed bench in the dugout, hidden from sky, wind and weather, from all but the dust that blew up from Knights Field and lodged dry in the throat, as the grass grew browner. And from time ticking off balls and strikes, batters up and out, halves and full innings, games won and (mostly) lost, days and nights, and the endless train miles from Philly, with in-between stops, along the arc to St. Louis, and circling back by way of Chi, Boston, Brooklyn . . . still waiting.

"C'mon, Roy," Red had urged, "apologize to Pop, then the next time Knobb comes around, join the boys and everything will be okay."

"Nix on that," said Roy, "I don't need a shyster quack to shoot me full of confidence juice. I want to go through on my own steam."

"He only wants everybody to relax and be able to do their best."

Roy shook his head. "I been a long time getting here and now that I am, I want to do it by myself, not with that kind of bunk."

"Do what?" Red asked.

"What I have to do."

Red shrugged and gave him up as too stubborn. Roy sat around, and though it said on his chest he was one of the team, he sat among them alone; at the train window, gazing at the moving trees, in front of his locker, absorbed in an untied shoe lace, in the dugout, squinting at the great glare of the game. He traveled in their company and dressed where they did but he joined them in nothing, except maybe batting practice, entering the cage with the lumber on his shoulder glistening like a leg bone in the sun and taking his chops at the pill. Almost always he hammered the swift, often murderous throws (the practice pitchers dumped their bag of tricks on him) deep into the stands, as the players watched and muttered at the swift flight of the balls, then forgot him when the game started. But there were days when the waiting got him. He could feel the strength draining from his bones, weakening him so he could hardly lift Wonderboy. He was unwilling to move then, for fear he would fall over on his puss and have to crawl away on all fours. Nobody noticed he did not bat when he felt this way except Pop; and Bump, seeing how white his face was, squirted contemptuous tobacco juice in the dust. Then when Roy's strength ebbed back, he would once again go into the batters' cage and do all sorts of marvelous things that made them watch in wonder.

He watched *them* and bad as he felt he had to laugh. They were a nutty bunch to begin with but when they were losing they were impossible. It was like some kind of sickness. They threw to the wrong bases, bumped heads together in the outfield, passed each other on the baselines, sometimes batted out of order, throwing both Pop and the ump into fits, and cussed everybody else for their mistakes. It was not uncommon to see them pile three men on a bag, or behold a catcher on the opposing team, in a single skip and jump, lay the tag on two of them as they came thundering together into home plate. Or watch Gabby Laslow, in a tight spot, freeze onto the ball, or Allie Stubbs get socked with it in the jaw, thrown by Olson on a steal as Allie admired a lady in the stands. Doc Knobb's hypnotism cut down their jitters but it didn't much help their coordination, yet when they were left unhypnotized for a few days, they were afflicted with more than the usual number of hexes and whammies and practiced all sorts of magic to undo them. To a man they crossed their fingers over spilled salt, or coffee or tea, or at the sight of a hearse. Emil Lajong did a backward flip whenever he located a cross-eyed fan in the stands. Olson hated a woman who wore the same drab brown-feathered hat every time she showed up. He spat through two fingers whenever he spotted her in the crowd. Bump went through his ritual with the colored threads in his socks and shorts. Pop sometimes stroked a rabbit's foot. Red Blow never changed his clothes during a "winning streak," and Flores secretly touched his genitals whenever a bird flew over his head.

They were not much different from the fans in the patched and peeling stands. On weekdays the stadium usually looked like a haunted house but over the weekend crowds developed. The place often resembled a zoo full of oddballs, including gamblers, bums, drunks, and some ugly crackpots. Many of them came just to get a laugh out of the bonehead plays. Some, when the boys were losing, cursed and jeered, showering them—whenever they came close enough—with rotten cabbages, tomatoes, blackened bananas and occasionally an eggplant. Yet let the umpire call a close play against the Knights and he became a target for pop bottles, beer cans, old shoes or anything that happened to be lying around loose.

Surprisingly, however, a few players were chosen for affection and even admiration by their fans. Sadie Sutter, a girl of sixty-plus, who wore large flowered hats, bobby sox, and short skirts, showed her undying love for Dave Olson every time he came up to the plate by banging with all her might on a Chinese gong she dragged into the stadium every day. A Hungarian cook, a hearty man with a hard yellow straw hat jammed tight on his skull, hopped up on his seat and crowed like a rooster whenever Emil Lajong originated a double play. And there was a girl named Gloria from Mississippi, a washed-out flower of the vestibules, who between innings when her eyes were not on the game, lined up a customer or two for a quickie later. She gave her heart to Gabby, yelling, "Get a move on, mo-lasses," to set him in motion after a fly ball. Besides these, there had appeared early in the present season, a pompous Otto P. Zipp, whose peevish loudspeaker could be heard all over the park, his self-chosen mission to rout the critics of Bump Baily, most of whom razzed the big boy for short legging on the other fielders. The dwarf honked a loud horn at the end of a two-foot walking stick, and it sounded as if a flock of geese had been let loose at the offenders, driving them—his purple curses ringing in their ears—to seek some hidden hole in the stands or altogether out of the ballpark. Zipp was present at every home game, sitting at the rail in short left field, and Bump made it his much publicized business, as he trotted out to his position at the start of the game, to greet him with a loud kiss on the forehead, leaving Otto in a state of creamy bliss.

Roy got to know them all as he waited, all one if you looked long enough through the haze of cigarette smoke, except one . . . Memo Paris, Pop's redheaded niece, sad, spurned lady, who sat without wifehood in the wive's box behind third base. He could, if she would let him, find her with his eyes shut, with his hands alone as he had in the dark. Always in the act of love she lived in his mind, the only way he knew her, because she would not otherwise suffer his approach. *He* was to blame, she had wept one bitter midnight, so she hated his putrid guts. Since the team's return to the city (the phone banged in his ear and she ripped up his letters when they were delivered) whenever he got up from his seat in the hotel lobby as she stepped out of the elevator, to say how sorry he was for beginning at the wrong end, she tugged at her summer fur-piece and breezed past him in greeneyed scorn, withering in the process Bump at the cigar stand, who had laughed aloud at Roy's rout. ("Honeybunch," he had explained, "it was out of the pity of my heart that I took that shmo into my room, because they didn't have one for him and I was intending to pass the night at the apartment of my he cousin from Mobile. How'd I know you'd go in there when you said you weren't speaking to me?" He swore it hadn't been a gag—had he ever pulled one on her?—but Memo punished him in silence, punishing herself, and he knew it because she still came every day to see him play.) She walked out of the lobby, with her silver bracelets tinkling, swaying a little on her high heels, as if she had not too long ago learned to walk on them, and went with her beautiful body away, for which Roy everlastingly fried Bump Baily in the deep fat of abomination.

It was for her he waited.

On the morning of the twenty-first of June Pop told Roy that as of tomorrow he was being shipped to a Class B team in the Great Lakes Association. Roy said he was quitting baseball anyway, but that same day, in answer to an angry question of Pop's as to why the team continued to flop, Doc Knobb said that the manager's hysterical behavior was undoing all the good he had done, and he offered to hypnotize Pop along with the others without hiking his fee. Pop shrilly told the psychologist he was too old for such bamboozlement, and Knobb retorted that his attitude was not only ridiculous but stupid. Pop got redfaced and told him to go to perdition with his hocus pocus and as of right then the doctor was canned.

That afternoon the Knights began a series with the second-place Phils. Instead of falling into a swoon when they learned there was to be no further hypnosis, the team played its best ball in weeks. Against superior pitching, in the sixth they bunched three singles for a run, and though Schultz had already given up five hits to the Phils, they were scattered and came to nothing. The Phils couldn't score till the top of the eighth, when with two out Schultz weakened, walking one man and handing the next a good enough throw to hit for a sharp single, so that there were now men on first and third. Up came Rogers, the Phils' slugger, and hit a fast curve for what looked like no more than a long fly ball, a routine catch, to left center. Now it happened that Bump was nearer to the ball than Flores, who was shifted to the right, but he was feeling horny in the sun and casting about in his mind for who to invite to his bed tonight, when he looked up and noticed this ball coming. He still had time to get under it but then saw Flores going for it like a galloping horse, and the anguished look on the Mexican's face, his black eyes popping, neck like a thick rope, and mouth haunted, fascinated Bump so, he decided to let him have it if he wanted it that bad. At the last minute he tried to take it away from the Mex, risking a head-on collision, but the wind whipped the ball closer to the wall than he had bargained for, so Bump fell back to cover Flores in case he misplayed it.

The ball fell between them, good for a double, and scoring two of the Phils. Pop tore at what was left of his gray hair but couldn't grip it with his oily, bandaged fingers so he pulled at his ears till they were lit like red lamps. Luckily the next Phil smothered the fire by rolling to first, which kept the score at 2–1. When Bump returned to the dugout Pop cursed him from the cradle to the grave and for once Bump had no sassy answers. When it came his time to go out on deck, Pop snarled for him to stay where he was. Flores found a ripe one and landed on first but Pop stuck to his guns and looked down the line past Bump. His eye lit on Roy at the far end of the bench, and he called his name to go out there and hit. Bump turned purple. He grabbed a bat and headed for Roy but half the team jumped on him. Roy just sat there without moving and it looked to everyone like he wouldn't get up. The umpire roared in for a batter to come out, and after a while, as the players fidgeted and Pop fumed, Roy sighed and picked up Wonderboy. He slowly walked up the steps.

"Knock the cover off of it," Pop yelled.

"Attention, please," the P.A. man announced. "Roy Hobbs, number forty-five, batting for Baily."

A groan rose from the stands and turned into a roar of protest.

Otto Zipp jumped up and down on his seat, shaking his furious little fist at home plate.

"Throw him to the dogs," he shouted, and filled the air with his piercing curses.

Glancing at the wives' box, Roy saw that Memo had her head turned away. He set his jaw and advanced to the plate. His impulse was to knock the dirt out of his cleats but he refrained because he did not want to harm his bat in any way. Waiting for the pitcher to get set, Roy wiped his palms on his pants and twitched his cap. He lifted Wonderboy and waited rocklike for the throw.

He couldn't tell the color of the pitch that came at him. All he could think of was that he was sick to death of waiting, and tongue-out thirsty to begin. The ball was now a dew drop staring him in the eye so he stepped back and swung from the toes.

Wonderboy flashed in the sun. It caught the sphere where it was biggest. A noise like a twenty-one gun salute cracked the sky. There was a straining, ripping sound and a few drops of rain spattered to the ground. The ball screamed toward the pitcher and seemed suddenly to dive down at his feet. He grabbed it to throw to first and realized to his horror that he held only the cover. The rest of it, unraveling cotton thread as it rode, was headed into the outfield.

Roy was rounding first when the ball plummeted like a dead bird into center field. Attempting to retrieve and throw, the Philly fielder got tangled in thread. The second baseman rushed up, bit the cord and heaved the ball to the catcher but Roy had passed third and made home, standing. The umpire called him safe and immediately a rhubarb boiled. The Phils' manager and his players charged out of the dugout and were joined by the nine men on the field. At the same time, Pop, shouting in defense of the ump, rushed forth with all the Knights but Bump. The umpire, caught between both teams, had a troublesome time of it and was shoved this way and that. He tossed out two men on each side but by then came to the decision that the hit was a ground rules double. Flores had scored and the game was tied up. Roy was ordered back to second, and Pop announced he was finishing the game under protest. Somebody then shouted it was raining cats and dogs. The stands emptied like a yawn and the players piled into the dugouts. By the time Roy got in from second he was wading in water ankle deep. Pop sent him into the clubhouse for a change of uniform but he could have saved himself the trouble because it rained steadily for three days. The game was recorded as a 2–2 tie, to be replayed later in the season.

In the locker room Pop asked Roy to explain why he thought the cover had come off the ball.

"That's what you said to do, wasn't it?"

"That's right," said Pop, scratching his bean.

The next day he told Roy he was withdrawing his release and would hereafter use him as a pinch hitter and substitute fielder.

The rain had washed out the Phils' series but the Knights were starting another with the seventh-place Redbirds. In batting practice, Roy, who was exciting some curiosity for his freak hit of yesterday, looked tremendous but so did Bump. For the first time in a long while Roy went out to left field to limber up. Bump was out there too and Earl swatted fungos to both.

As they were changing into clean uniforms before the start of the game, Bump warned Roy in front of everybody, "Stay out of my way, busher, or you will get your head bashed."

Roy squirted spit on the floor.

When Pop later handed the batting order to Stuffy Briggs, the plate umpire, it had Bump's name scribbled on it as usual in the fourth slot, but Pop had already warned him that if he didn't hustle his behind when a ball was hit out to his field, he would rest it a long time on the bench.

Bump made no reply but it was obvious that he took Pop's words to heart, because he was a bang-up fielder that day. He accepted eight chances, twice chasing into center field to take them from Flores. He caught them to his left and right, dove for and came up with a breathtaking shoestringer, and running as if on fire, speared a fantastic catch over his shoulder. Still not satisfied, he pounded like a bull after his ninth try, again in Flores' territory, a smoking ball that sailed up high, headed for the wall. As Bump ran for it he could feel fear leaking through his stomach, and his legs unwillingly slowed down, but then he had this vision of himself as the league's best outfielder, acknowledged so by fans and players alike, even Pop, whom he'd be nothing less than forever respectful to, and in love with and married to Memo. Thinking this way he ran harder, though Zipp's geese honked madly at his back, and with a magnificent twisting jump, he trapped the ball in his iron fingers. Yet the wall continued to advance, and though the redheaded lady of his choice was on her feet shrieking, Bump bumped it with a skull-breaking bang, and the wall embraced his broken body.

Though Bump was on the critical list in the hospital, many newspapers continued to speculate about that ball whose cover Roy had knocked off. It was explained as everything from an optical illusion (neither the ball nor the cover was ever found, the remnant caught by the catcher disappeared, and it was thought some fan had snatched the cover) to a feat of prodigious strength. Baseball records and newspaper files were combed but no one could find any evidence that it had happened before, although some of the older scribes swore it had. Then it leaked out that Pop had ordered Roy to skin the ball and Roy had obliged, but no one took that very seriously. One of the sportswriters suggested that a hard downward chop could shear off the outer covering. He had tried it in his cellar and had split the horsehide. Another pointed out that such a blow would have produced an infield grounder, therefore maybe a tremendous upward slash? The first man proved that would have uncorked a sure pop fly whereas the ball, as everyone knew, had sailed straight out over the pitcher's head. So it had probably resulted from a very very forceful sock. But many a hitter had plastered the ball forcefully before, still another argued, and his idea was that it was defective to begin with, a fact the company that manufactured the ball vigorously denied. Max Mercy had his own theory. He wrote in his column, "My Eye in the Knot Hole" (the year he'd done the Broadway stint for his paper his eye was in the key hole), that Roy's bat was a suspicious one and hinted it might be filled with something a helluva lot stronger than wood. Red Blow publicly denied this. He said the bat had been examined by league authorities and was found to be less than forty-two inches long, less than two and three-quarters inches thick at its fattest part, and in weight less than two pounds, which made it a legal weapon. Mercy then demanded that the wood be X-rayed but Roy turned thumbs down on that proposition and kept Wonderboy hidden away when the sports columnist was nosing around in the clubhouse.

On the day after the accident Pop soberly gave Roy the nod to play in Bump's place. As Roy trotted out to left, Otto Zipp was in his usual seat but looking worn and aged. His face, tilted to the warming rays of the sun, was like a pancake with a cherry nose, and tears were streaming through slits where the eyes would be. He seemed to be waiting for his pre-game kiss on the brow but Roy passed without looking at him.

The long rain had turned the grass green and Roy romped in it like a happy calf in its pasture. The Redbirds, probing his armor, belted the ball to him whenever they could, which was often, because Hill was not too happy on the mound, but Roy took everything they aimed at him. He seemed to know the soft, hard, and bumpy places in the field and just how high a ball would bounce on them. From the flags on the stadium roof he noted the way the wind would blow the ball, and he was quick at fishing it out of the tricky undercurrents on the ground. Not sun, shadow, nor smoke-haze bothered him, and when a ball was knocked against the wall he estimated the angle of rebound and speared it as if its course had been plotted on a chart. He was good at gauging slices and knew when to charge the pill to save on the throw. Once he put his head down and ran ahead of a shot going into the concrete. Though the crowd rose with a thunderous warning, he caught it with his back to the wall and did a little jig to show he was alive. Everyone laughed in relief, and they liked his long-legged loping and that he resembled an acrobat the way he tumbled and came up with the ball in his glove. For his performance that day there was much whistling and applause, except where he would have liked to hear it, an empty seat in the wives' box.

His batting was no less successful. He stood at the plate lean and loose, right-handed with an open stance, knees relaxed and shoulders squared. The bat he held in a curious position, lifted slightly above his head as if prepared to beat a rattlesnake to death, but it didn't harm his smooth stride into the pitch, nor the easy way he met the ball and slashed it out with a flick of the wrists. The pitchers tried something different every time he came up, sliders, sinkers, knucklers, but he swung and connected, spraying them to all fields. He was, Red Blow said to Pop, a natural, though somewhat less than perfect because he sometimes hit at bad ones, which caused Pop to frown.

"I mistrust a bad ball hitter."

"There are all kinds of hitters," Red answered. "Some are bucket foots, and some go for bad throws but none of them bother me as long as they naturally connect with anything that gets in their way."

Pop spat up over the dugout steps. "They sometimes make some harmful mistakes."

"Who don't?" Red asked.

Pop then muttered something about this bad ball hitter he knew who had reached for a lemon and cracked his spine.

But the only thing Roy cracked that day was the record for the number of triples hit in a major league debut and also the one for chances accepted in the outfield. Everybody agreed that in him the Knights had uncovered something special. One reporter wrote, "He can catch everything in creation," and Roy just about proved it. It happened that a woman who lived on the sixth floor of an apartment house overlooking the stadium was cleaning out her bird cage, near the end of the game, which the Knights took handily, when her canary flew out of the window and darted down across the field. Roy, who was waiting for the last out, saw something coming at him in the low rays of the sun, and leaping high, bagged it in his glove.

He got rid of the bloody mess in the clubhouse can.

When Bump died Memo went wild with grief. Bump, Bump, she wailed, pounding on the wall. Pop, who hovered over her at first, found her in bed clutching strands of red hair. Her cheeks were scratched where the tears rolled down. He was frightened and urged her to have the doctor but her piercing screams drove him away. She wept for days. Clad in black pajamas she lay across the white bed like a broken candle still lit. In her mind she planted kisses all over the corpse and when she kissed his mouthless mouth blew back the breath of life, her womb stirring at the image of his restoration. Yet she saw down a dark corridor that he was laid out dead, gripping in his fingers the glowing ball he had caught, and that there were too many locked doors to go through to return. She stopped trying to think of him alive and thought of him dead. Then she really hit the wall.

She could not stop weeping, as if the faucet were broken. Or she were a fountain they had forgotten to turn off. There was no end to her tears. They flowed on as if she had never wept before. Wherever she turned she cried, the world was wet. Her thoughts dripped on flowers, dark, stained ones in night fields. She moved among them, tasting their many darknesses, could not tell them from the rocks on the ground. His shade was there. She saw it drifting before her and recognized it by the broken places. Bump, oh Bump, but her voice was drowned in water. She heard a gurgle and the bubbles breaking and felt the tears go searing down a hurt face (hers) and though she wanted always to be with him she was (here) weeping.

After unnumbered days she dragged herself out of bed, disturbed by all the space, her bare feet with lacquered nails, her shaky presence among changeless things. She sought in the hollow closet souvenirs of him, an autographed baseball "to my Honey from her Bump" (tears), a cigarette lighter shaped like a bat, click-open-light. She blew it out and searching further found an old kewpie doll he had won for her and a pressed, yellowed gardenia, but couldn't with her wept-out nose detect the faintest odor; also a pair of purple shorts she herself had laundered and placed in the drawer among her soft (and useless) underthings. Going through her scrapbook, only rarely could she find menus (Sardi's, Toots Shor, and once the Diamond Horseshoe) or movie ticket stubs (Palace, Paramount, Capitol) and other such things of them both that one could paste in, but most were pictures she had clipped from the sports pages, showing Bump at bat, on the basepaths, and crossing the plate. She idly turned the pages, sighed deeply and put the book away, then picked up the old picture album, and here was her sadeyed mother, and the torn up, patched together one was of Daddy grinning, who with a grin had (forever) exited dancing with his dancing partner, and here she was herself, a little girl weeping, as if nothing ever changed . . . The heartbreak was always present—he had not been truly hers when he died (she tried not to think whose, in many cities, he had been) so that she now mourned someone who even before his death had made her a mourner. That was the thorn in her grief.

When the July stifle drove her out of her room she appeared in the hotel lobby in black, her hair turned a lighter, golden shade as though some of the fire had burned out of it, and Roy was moved by her appearance. He had imagined how she would look when he saw her again but both the black and red, though predictable, surprised him. They told him with thunderclap quickness what he wanted to be sure of, that she, despite green eyes brimming for Bump, was the one for him, the ever desirable only. Occasionally he reflected what if the red were black and ditto the other way? Here, for example, was this blackhaired dame in red and what about it? He could take her or leave her, though there was a time in his life when a red dress would excite his fancy, but with Memo, flaming above and dark below, there was no choice—he was chosen so why not admit it though it brought pain? He had tried lately to forget her but had a long memory for what he wanted so there was only this to do, wait till she came in out of the rain.

Sometimes it was tough to, even for one used to waiting. Once a hungry desire sent him down to knock at her door but she shut it in his face although he was standing there with his hat in his embarrassed hands. He thought of asking Pop to put in a good word for him—how long was life anyhow?—but something told him to wait. And from other cities, when the team was on the road, he sent her cards, candies, little presents, which were all stuffed in his mailbox when he returned. It took the heart out of him. Yet each morning when she came out of the elevator he would look up at her as she walked by on her high heels, although she never seemed to see him. Then one day she shed black and put on white but still looked as if she were wearing black, so he waited. Only, now, when he looked at her she sometimes glanced at him. He watched her dislike of him fade to something neutral which he slowly became confident he could beat.

"One thing I hafta tell you not to do, son," Pop said to Roy in the hotel lobby one rainy morning not long after Bump's funeral, "and that is to blame yourself about what happened to Bump. He had a tough break but it wasn't your fault."

"What do you mean my fault?"

Pop looked up. "All I mean to say was he did it himself."

"Never thought anything but."

"Some have said maybe it wouldn't happen if you didn't join the team, and maybe so, but I believe such things are outside of yours and my control and I wouldn't want you to worry that you had caused it in any way."

"I won't because I didn't. Bump didn't have to go to the wall for that shot, did he? We were ahead in runs and the bases were clear. He could've taken it when it came off the wall without losing a thing, couldn't he?"

Pop scratched his baldy. "I guess so."

"Who are the people who said I did it?"

"Well, nobody exactly. My niece said you coulda wanted it to happen but that don't mean a thing. She was hysterical then."

Roy felt uneasy. Had he arranged Bump's run into the wall? No. Had he wished the guy would drop dead? Only once, after the night with Memo. But he had never consciously hoped he would crack up against the wall. That was none of his doing and he told Pop to tell it to Memo. But Pop was embarrassed now and said to drop the whole thing, it was a lot of foolishness.

Though Roy denied wishing Bump's fate on him or having been in any way involved in it, he continued to be unwillingly concerned with him even after his death. He was conscious that he was filling Bump's shoes, not only because he batted in the clean-up slot and fielded in the sun field (often watched his shadow fly across the very spot Bump had dived into) and became, in no time to speak of, one of the leading hitters in the league and at present certainly the most sensational, but also because the crowds made no attempt to separate his identity from Bump's. To his annoyance, when he made a hot catch, the kind Bump in all his glory would have left alone, he could hear through the curtain of applause, "Nice work, Bumpsy, 'at's grabbin' th' old apple," or "Leave it to Bump, he will be where they drop." It was goddamn stupid. The same fans who a month ago were hissing Bump for short legging on the other fielders now praised his name so high Roy felt like painting up a sandwich sign to wear out on the field, that said, ROY HOBBS PLAYING.

Even Otto Zipp made no effort to distinguish him from his predecessor and used the honker to applaud his doings, though there were some who said the dwarf sounded half-hearted in his honking. And Roy also shared the limelight with Bump on the sports page, where the writers were constantly comparing them for everything under the sun. One of them went so far as to keep a tally of their batting averages—Roy's total after his first, second, and third weeks of play, as compared with Bump's at the beginning of the season. One paper even printed pictures showing the living and dead facing each other with bats held high, as white arrows pointed at various places in their anatomies to show how much alike their measurements and stances were.

All this irritated Roy no end until he happened to notice Memo walk into the lobby one night with a paper turned to the sports page. From having read the same paper he knew she had seen a column about Bump and him as batsmen, so he decided there might be some percentage to all these comparisons. He came to feel more kindly to the memory of Bump and thought he was not such a bad egg after all, even if he did go in for too many screwball gags. Thinking back on him, he could sort of understand why Memo had been interested in him, and he felt that, though he was superior to Bump as an athlete, they were both money players, both showmen in the game. He figured it was through these resemblances that Memo would gradually get used to him and then come over all the way, although once she did, it would have to be for Hobbsie himself and not for some ghost by another name.

So he blazed away for her with his golden bat. It was not really golden, it was white, but in the sun it sometimes flashed gold and some of the opposing pitchers complained it shone in their eyes. Stuffy Briggs told Roy to put it away and use some other club but he stood on his rights and wouldn't. There was a hot rhubarb about that until Roy promised to rub some of the shine off Wonderboy. This he did with a hambone, and though the pitchers shut up, the bat still shone a dull gold. It brought him some wondrous averages in hits, runs, RBI's and total bases, and for the period of his few weeks in the game he led the league in homers and triples. (He was quoted in an interview as saying his singles were "mistakes." And he never bunted. "There is no percentage in bunts." Pop shook his head over that, but Red chuckled and said it was true for a wonderful hitter like Roy.) He also destroyed many short-term records, calling down on his performance tons of newspaper comment. However, his accomplishments were not entirely satisfying to him. He was gnawed by a nagging impatience—so much more to do, so much of the world to win for himself. He felt he had nothing of value yet to show for what he was accomplishing, and in his dreams he still sped over endless miles of monotonous rail toward something he desperately wanted. Memo, he sighed.

Pop couldn't believe his amazed eyes. "Beginner's luck," he muttered. Many a rookie had he seen come out blasting them in the breeze only to blow out in it with his tail between his legs. "The boy's having hisself a shower of luck. Usually they end up with a loud bust, so let's wait and see," he cautioned. Yet Roy continued on as before, by his own efforts winning many a ball game. The team too were doubtful he could go on like this, and doubtful of their doubt. They often discussed him when he wasn't around, compared him to Bump, and argued whether he was for the team or for himself. Olson said he was for the team. Cal Baker insisted no. When asked for a reason he could give none except to say, "Those big guys are always for themselves. They are not for the little guy. If he was for us why don't he come around more? Why does he hang out so much by himself?" "Yeah," answered Olson, "but we're outa the cellar now and who done that—the wind? That's what counts, not if he sits around chewin' his ass with us." Most of them agreed with Olson. Even if Roy wasn't actively interested in them he was a slick ballplayer and his example was having a good effect on them. In the course of three weeks they had achieved a coordination of fielding, hitting and pitching (Fowler and Schultz were whipping the opposition, and Hinkle and Hill, with an assist here and there from McGee, were at least breaking even) such as they had not for seasons known. Like a rusty locomotive pulling out of the roundhouse for the first time in years, they ground down the tracks, puffing, wheezing, belching smoke and shooting sparks. And before long they had dislodged the Reds, who had been living on the floor above them since the season started. When, near the end of July, they caught up with the Cubs and, twelve games behind the league-leading Pirates, took possession of sixth place, Pop rubbed his unbelieving eyes. The players thought now that the team is on its way up he will change his crabby ways and give us a smile once in a while, but Pop surprised them by growing sad, then actually melancholy at the thought that but for kis keeping Roy out of the line-up for three weeks they might now be in first division.

A new day dawned on Knights Field. Looking down upon the crowds from his office in the curious tower he inhabited that rose on a slight tilt above the main entrance of the ball park, Judge Goodwill Banner was at first made uneasy by what he saw, for every rise in attendance would make it more difficult for him to get Pop to give up the managerial reins, a feat he hoped to accomplish by next season. However, the sound of the merry, clicking turnstiles was more than he could resist, so, although reluctantly, he put on extra help to sweep the stand and ramps and dust off seats that hadn't been sat in for years but were now almost always occupied.

The original Knights "fans," those who had come to see them suffer, were snowed under by this new breed here to cheer the boys on. Vegetables were abolished, even at the umps, and the crowd assisted the boys by working on the nerves of the visiting team with whammy words, catcalls, wisecracks, the kind of sustained jockeying that exhausted the rival pitchers and sometimes drove them out of the game. Now the old faithful were spouting steam—the Hungarian cook outcrowed a flock of healthy roosters, Gloria, the vestibule lady, acquired a better type customer, and Sadie Sutter gave up Dave Olson and now beat her hectic gong for the man of the hour. "Oh, you Roy," she screeched in her yolky cackle, "embracez moy," and the stands went wild with laughter. Victory was sweet, except for Otto Zipp, who no longer attended the games. Someone who met him waddling out of a subway station in Canarsie asked how come, but the dwarf only waved a pudgy palm in disgust. Nobody could guess what he meant by that and his honker lay dusty and silent on a shelf in the attic.

Even the weather was better, more temperate after the insulting early heat, with just enough rain to keep the grass a bright green and yet not pile up future double headers. Pop soon got into the spirit of winning, lowered the boom on his dismal thoughts, and showed he had a lighter side. He unwound the oily rags on his fingers and flushed them down the bowl. His hands healed and so did his heart, for even during the tensest struggle he looked a picture of contentment. And he was patient now, extraordinarily so, giving people the impression he had never been otherwise. Let a man bobble a hot one, opening the gate for a worrisome run, and he no longer jumped down his throat but wagged his head in silent sympathy. And sometimes he patted the offender on the surprised back. Formerly his strident yell was everywhere, on the field, in the dugout, clubhouse, players' duffle bags, also in their dreams, but now you never heard it because he no longer raised his voice, not even to Dizzy's cat when it wet on his shoes. Nobody teased him or played jokes on him any more and every tactic he ordered on the field was acted on, usually successfully. He was in the driver's seat. His muscles eased, the apoplexy went out of his system, and for his star fielder a love-light shone in his eyes.

As Roy's fame grew, Bump was gradually forgotten. The fans no longer confused talent with genius. When they cheered, they cheered for Roy Hobbs alone. People wondered about him, wanted news of his life and career. Reporters kept after him for information and Max Mercy, who for some reason felt he ought to know a lot more about Roy than he did, worked a sharp pickax over his shadow but gathered no usable nugget. All that was known was that Roy had first played ball on an orphan asylum team, that his father was a restless itinerant worker and his mother rumored to have been a burlesque actress. Stingy with facts, Roy wouldn't confirm a thing. Mercy sent a questionnaire to one thousand country papers in the West but there were no towns or cities that claimed the hero as their own.

It came about that Roy discovered Memo at one of the home games, though not, as formerly, sitting in the wives' box. Happening to meet her later in the hotel elevator, where they were pressed close together because of the crowd, he got off at her floor. Taking her arm he said, "Memo, I don't know what more I can do to show you how sorry I am about that time and tell you how I feel in my heart for you now."

But Memo stared at him through a veil of tears and said, "I'm strictly a dead man's girl."

He figured she had to be made to forget. If she would go out with him he would give her a good time at the night clubs and musical shows. But to do that and buy her some decent presents a guy needed cash, and on the meager three thousand he got he had beans—barely enough to pay his hotel bill. He considered selling his name for endorsements and approached a sporting goods concern but they paid him only fifty dollars. Elsewhere he got a suit and a pair of shoes but no cash. An agent he consulted advised him that the companies were suspicious he might be a flash in the pan. "Lay low now," he advised. "By the end of the season, if you keep on like you're going, they'll be ready to talk turkey, then we'll put the heat on."

The newspaper boys supplied him with the cue for what to do next. They pointed out how he filled up Knights Field; and on the road, as soon as the Knights blew into town the game was a sellout and the customers weren't exactly coming to see a strip-tease. One of the columnists (not Mercy) wrote an open letter to the Judge, saying it was a crying shame that a man as good as Roy should get a rock-bottom salary when he was playing better ball than some of the so-called stars who drew up to a hundred grand. Roy was being gypped, the columnist wrote, and he called on the Judge to burn up his old contract and write a decent one instead. Why, even Bump had earned thirty-five thousand. That decided Roy. He figured for himself a flat forty-five thousand for the rest of the season, plus a guarantee of a percentage of the gate. He thought that if he got this sort of arrangement and really piled in the dough, it would do him no harm with Memo.

So one day after a long double header, both ends of which the Knights finally took, Roy climbed the slippery stairs up the tower to the Judge's office. The Judge's male secretary said he was busy but Roy sat down to wait so they soon let him in. The huge office was half dark, though lit on the double-windowed street side (the Judge counted the customers going in and from the opposite window he counted them in the stands) by the greenish evening sky. The Judge, a massive rumpled figure in a large chair before an empty mahogany desk, was wearing a black fedora with a round pot crown and smoking, under grizzled eyebrows, a fat, black King Oscar I. This always looked to be the same size in the rare newspaper photographs of the Judge, and many people maintained it was the same picture of him all the time, because it was a known fact that the Judge never left the tower and no photographer ever got in. Roy noted a shellacked half of stuffed shark, mounted on pine board on the faded green wall, and a framed motto piece that read:

"Be it ever so humble, there is no place like home"
"Nihil nisi bonum"
"All is not gold that glitters"
"The dog is turned to his vomit again"

The floor of the office was, of course, slanted—because of the way the tower, an addition to the stadium structure, had settled—and to level it the Judge had a rug made a quarter of an inch thick on one side and a good inch on the other, but the few visitors to the place noticed they were not standing strictly on keel so they quickly sat down, which was what Roy did too. He had heard that the door on the opposite side of the room led up to the Judge's apartment. Pop said that though the Judge was a sluggish man with a buck it was a lavish place, and the bathroom had a television set and a sunken bathtub inlaid with mother of pearl. It was also rumored that he kept in there two enormous medicine cabinets loaded with laxatives and cathartics.

The Judge looked Roy over, struck a match under the top of his desk and drew a flame into his dead King Oscar. He blew out a smelly cloud of yellow smoke that hid his face a full minute.

"Nice of you to come," he rumbled. "To what good cause may I attribute this pleasant surprise?"

"I guess you know, Judge," said Roy, trying to make himself comfortable.

The Judge rumbled in his belly.

"I'm reminded of a case that came before me once. 'What do you plead?' I asked the defendant. 'I leave it to you, Judge, take your choice,' he responded. I did and sent him to the penitentiary for twenty years."

The Judge coughed and cackled over that. Roy regarded him closely. Everybody had warned him he was a slick trader, especially Pop who had poured out a hot earful about his partner. "He will peel the skin off of your behind without you knowing it if you don't watch out." That was what happened to him, he said, and he went on to tell Roy that not long after the Judge had bought into the club—after working up Charlie Gulch, Pop's old-time partner, against him and getting him to sell out—he had taken advantage of some financial troubles Pop was having with his two brothers who owned a paint factory, and also because of his own sickness that kept him in a hospital under expensive medical care all winter long, and the Judge put the squeeze on him to get ten per cent of his stock for a pittance, which had then looked like a life saver because Pop was overdrawn at the bank and they wouldn't lend him another cent on his share of the Knights. Later, when he realized how much of a say in things he had lost to the Judge he kicked himself all over the lot, for the Judge, as Red Blow had told Roy, drummed up all sorts of player deals to turn a buck, and though Pop fought him on these, he showed on paper that they were losing money at the gate and this was the only way to cover their losses and keep the team going, so Pop had to give in on most of them although he had fought the Judge to a standstill when he wanted to sell Bump and would do the same if he tried it with Roy. It beat Pop where Goodie Banner, as he called him, had got the money to operate with in the first place. He had known him years ago as an impoverished shyster but once he got on the bench his fortunes improved. Yet his salary was only twelve thousand a year for the three years he had served so he must have had backing to buy into the club and later—the dratted nerve of the worm—to offer to buy Pop out altogether. He said he wouldn't exactly call the Judge a thief but he wouldn't exactly call him honest either. For instance, the Judge had once casually asked Pop if he wanted to go in for any sideline activities over what they had already contracted for, meaning concessions and the like. Pop said no, he was only interested in the game end of it, so the Judge drew up an agreement offering Pop five per cent of all receipts from enterprises initiated by himself, and he began to rent the place to miniature auto races, meetings, conventions, and dog races. Making all sorts of money for himself, while things necessary to the team were being neglected. "When triple talk is invented," Pop said bitterly, "he will own the copyright."

It was dark in the office but the Judge made no attempt to switch on the lights. He sat there motionless, a lumpy figure aglow around the edges against the darkening sky.

Roy thought he better get down to brass tacks. "Well, Judge," he said, shifting in his chair, "I thought you might be expecting me to drop in and see you. You know what I am doing to the ball both here and on the road. The papers have been writing that you might be considering a new contract for me."

The Judge blew at the ash of his cigar.

Roy grew restless. "I figure forty-five thousand is a fair price for my work. That's only ten grand more than Bump was getting—and you can subtract off the three thousand in my contract now." This last was an afterthought and he had decided to leave out the percentage of the gate till next year.

The Judge rumbled, Roy couldn't tell if it was in his throat or belly.

"I was thinking of Olaf Jespersen." The Judge's eyes took

on a faraway, slightly glazed look. "He was a farmer I knew in my youth—terrible life. Yet as farmers often do, he managed to live comfortably because he owned a plot of ground with a house on it and had come into possession of an extraordinary cow, Sieglinde. She was a splendid animal with soft and silky front and well-shaped hooves. Her milk yield was some nine gallons per diem, altogether exceptional. In a word she was a superior creature and had the nicest ways with children—her own of course; but Olaf was deeply disturbed by an ugly skin discoloration that ran across her rump. For a long while he had been eyeing Gussie, an albino cow of his neighbor down the road. One day he approached the man and asked if Gussie was for sale. The neighbor said yes, frankly admitting she gave very little milk although she consumed more than her share of fodder. Olaf said he was willing to trade Sieglinde for her and the neighbor readily agreed. Olaf went back for the cow but on the way to the neighbor's she stepped into a rut in the road and keeled over as if struck dead. Olaf suffered a heart attack. Thus they were found but Sieglinde recovered and became, before very long, her splendid nine-gallon self, whereas Olaf was incapacitated for the remainder of his days. I often drove past this place and saw him sitting on the moldy front porch, a doddering cripple starving to death with his tubercular albino cow."

Roy worked the fable around in his mind and got the point. It was not an impressive argument: be satisfied with what you have, and he said so to the Judge.

" 'The love of money is the root of all evil,' " intoned the Judge.

"I do not love it, Judge. I have not been near enough to it to build up any affection to speak of."

"Think, on the one hand, of the almost indigent Abraham Lincoln, and on the other of Judas Iscariot. What I am saying is that emphasis upon money will pervert your values. One cannot begin to imagine how one's life may alter for the worse under the impetus of wealth-seeking."

Roy saw how the land lay. "I will drop it to thirty-five thousand, the same as Bump, but not a cent less."

The Judge struck a match, throwing shadows on the wall. It was not night. He sucked a flame into his cigar. It went in like a slug, out like a moth—in and out, then forever in and the match was out. The cigar glowed, the Judge blew out a black fog of smoke, then they were once more in the dark.

Lights on, you stingy bastard, Roy thought.

"Pardon the absence of light," the Judge said, almost making him jump. "As a youngster I was frightened of the dark—used to wake up sobbing in it, as if it were water and I were drowning—but you will observe that I have disciplined myself so thoroughly against that fear, that I much prefer a dark to a lit room, and water is my favorite beverage. Will you have some?"

"No."

"There is in the darkness a unity, if you will, that cannot be achieved in any other environment, a blending of self with what the self perceives, an exquisite mystical experience. I intend some day to write a disquisition 'On the Harmony of Darkness; Can Evil Exist in Harmony?' It may profit you to ponder the question."

"All I know about the dark is that you can't see in it."

"A pure canard. You know you can."

"Not good enough."

"You see me, don't you?"

"Maybe I do and maybe I don't."

"What do you mean?"

"I see somebody but I am not sure if it is you or a guy who sneaked in and took your chair."

The cigar glowed just enough to light up the Judge's rubbery lips. It was him all right.

"Twenty-five thousand," Roy said in a low voice. "Ten less than Bump."

The cigar lit for a long pull then went out. Its smell was giving Roy a headache. The Judge was silent so long Roy wasn't sure he would ever hear from him again. He wasn't even sure he was there anymore but then he thought yes he is, I can smell him. He is here in the dark and if I come back tomorrow he will still be here and also the year after that.

" 'He that maketh haste to be rich shall not be innocent,' " spoke the Judge.

"Judge," said Roy, "I am thirty-four, going on thirty-five. That's not haste, that's downright slow."

"I hear that you bet money on horse races?"

"In moderation, not more than a deuce on the daily double."

"Avoid gambling like a plague. It will cause your downfall. And stay away from loose ladies. 'Put a knife to thy throat if thou be a man given to appetite.' "

Roy could hear him open a drawer and take something out. Handing it to him, he lit a match over it and Roy read: "The Curse of Venereal Disease."

He tossed the pamphlet on the desk.

"Yes or no?" he said.

"Yes or no what?" The Judge's voice was edged with anger.

"Fifteen thousand."

The Judge rose. "I shall have to ask you to fulfill the obligations of your contract."

Roy got up. "I wouldn't exactly say you were building up my good will for next year."

"I have learned to let the future take care of itself."

The Judge took some other papers out of the drawer. "I presume these are your signatures?" He scratched up another match.

"That's right."

"The first acknowledging the receipt of two uniforms and sundry articles?"

"Right."

"And the second indicating the receipt of a third uniform?"

"That's what it says."

"You were entitled to only two. I understand that some of the other clubs issue four, but that is an extravagance. Here, therefore, is a bill to the amount of fifty-one dollars for property destroyed. Will you remit or shall I deduct the sum from your next check?"

"I didn't destroy them, Bump did."

"They were your responsibility."

Roy picked up the receipts and bill and tore them to pieces. He did the same with the VD pamphlet, then blew the whole business over the Judge's head. The scraps of paper fluttered down like snow on his round hat.

"The interview is ended," snapped the Judge. He scratched up a match and with it led Roy to the stairs. He stood on the landing, his oily shadow dripping down the steps as Roy descended.

"Mr. Hobbs."

Roy stopped.

"Resist all evil—"

The match sputtered and went out. Roy went the rest of the way down in the pitch black.

"How'd you make out, kid?"

It was Max Mercy lurking under a foggy street lamp at the corner. He had tailed Roy from the dressing room and had spent a frustrated hour thinking I know the guy but who is he? It was on the tip of his tongue but he couldn't spit it out. He saw the face as he thought he had seen it before somewhere, but what team, where, in what league, and doing what that caused him to be remembered? The mystery was like an itch. The more he scratched the more he drew his own blood. At times the situation infuriated him. Once he dreamed he had the big s.o.b. by the throat and was forcing him to talk. Then he told the world Mercy knew.

The sight of the columnist did not calm Roy as he came out of the tower. Why does he haunt me? He thought he knew what Max sensed and he knew that he didn't want him to know. I don't want his dirty eyes peeking into my past. What luck for me that I had Sam's wallet in my pocket that night, and they wrote down his name. This creep will never find that out, or anything else about me unless I tell him, and the only time I'll do that is when I am dead.

"Listen, El Smearo," he said, "why don't you stay home in bed?"

Max laughed hollowly.

"Who has ever seen the like of it?" he said, trying to put some warmth into his voice. "Here's the public following everything a man does with their tongue hanging out and all he gives out with is little balls of nothing. What are you hiding? If it was something serious you woulda been caught long ago—your picture has been in the papers every day for weeks."

"I ain't hiding a thing."

"Who says you are? But what's all the mystery about?

Where were you born? Why'd you stay out of the game so long? What was your life like before this? My paper will guarantee you five grand in cash for five three-thousand word articles on your past life. I'll help you write them. What do you say?"

"I say no. My life is my own business."

"Think of your public."

"All they're entitled to is to pay a buck and watch me play."

"Answer me this—is it true you once tried out with another major league team?"

"I got nothing to say."

"Then you don't deny it?"

"I got nothing to say."

"Were you once an acrobat or something in a circus?"

"Same answer as before."

Max scratched in his mustache. "Hobbs, the man nobody knows. Say, kid, you're not doing it on purpose, are you?"

"What do you mean?"

"To raise speculation and get publicity?"

"Nuts I am."

"I don't catch. You're a public figure. You got to give the fans something once in a while to keep up their good will to you."

Roy thought a second. "Okay, tell them my cheapskate of a boss has turned me down flat on a raise and I am still his slave for a lousy three thousand bucks."

Max wrote a hasty note in his black book.

"Listen, Roy, let's you and I have a little chin-chin. You'll like me better once you get to know me. Have you had your supper yet?"

"No."

"Then have a steak with me at the Pot of Fire. Know the place?"

"I have never been there."

"It's a night club with a nice girlie show. All the hotshot celebrities like yourself hang out there. They have a good kitchen and a first class bar."

"Okay with me." He was in a mood for something for nothing.

In the cab Max said, "You know, I sometimes get the funny feeling that I have met you some place before. Is that right?"

Roy thrust his head forward. "Where?"

Max contemplated his eyes and solid chin.

"It musta been somebody else."

At the entrance to the Pot of Fire a beggar accosted them.

"Jesus," Max said, "can't I ever get rid of you?"

"All I ask is a buck."

"Go to hell."

The beggar was hurt. "You'll get yours," he said.

"You'll get yours," said Max. "I'll call a cop."

"You'll get yours," the beggar said. "You too," he said to Roy and spat on the sidewalk.

"Friend of yours?" Roy asked as they went down the stairs into the nightspot.

Max's face was inflamed. "I can't get rid of that scurvy bastard. Picks this place to hang around and they can't flush him outa here."

Inside the club the audience was in an uproar. The show was on and some screaming, half-naked girls were being chased by masked devils with tin pitchforks. Then the lights went out and the devils ran around poking at the customers. Roy was jabbed in the rear end. He grabbed at the devil but missed, then he heard a giggle and realized it was a girl. He grabbed for her again but the devil jabbed him and ran. When the lights went on all the girls and devils were gone. The customers guffawed and applauded.

"Come on," Max said.

The captain had recognized him and was beckoning them to a ringside table. Roy sat down. Max looked around and bounced up.

"See a party I know. Be right back."

The band struck up a number and the chorus wriggled out amid weaving spotlights for the finale. They were wearing red spangled briefs and brassieres and looked so pretty that Roy felt lonely.

Max was back.

"We're changing tables. Gus Sands wants us with him."

"Who's he?"

Max looked to see if Roy was kidding.

"You don't know Gus Sands?"

"Never heard of him."

"What d'ye read, the Podunk Pipsqueak? They call him the Supreme Bookie, he nets at least ten million a year. Awfully nice guy and he will give you the silk shirt off his back. Also somebody you know is with him."

"Who's that?"

"Memo Paris."

Roy got up. What's she doing here? He followed Max across the floor to Gus Sands's table. Memo was sitting there alone in a black strapless gown and wearing her hair up. The sight of her, so beautiful, hit him hard. He had been picturing her alone in her room nights. She said hello evasively. At first he thought she was still sore at him, but then he heard voices coming from the floor at thc other side of the table and understood that was where she was looking.

A surprising semi-bald dome rose up above the table and Roy found himself staring into a pair of strange eyes, a mournful blue one and the other glowing weirdly golden. His scalp prickled as the bookie, a long stretch of bone, rose to his full height. The angle at which the spotlight had caught his glass eye, lighting it like a Christmas tree, changed, and the eye became just a ball of ice.

"S'matter, Gus?" Mercy said.

"Memo lost two bits." His voice was sugar soft. "Find it yet?" he asked the waiter, still down on all fours.

"Not yet, sir." He got up, "No, sir."

"Forget it." Sands flicked a deft fiver into the man's loose fist.

He shook hands with Roy. "Glad to meet you, slugger. Whyn't you sit down?"

"Tough luck, babyface," he said, giving Memo a smile. Roy sat down facing her but she barely glanced at him. Though dressed up she was not entirely herself. The blue eye shadow she had on could not hide the dark circles around her eyes and she looked tired. Her chair was close to Gus's. Once he chucked her under the chin and she giggled. It sickened Roy because it didn't make sense.

The busboy cleaned up the remains of two lobsters. Gus slipped him a fiver.

"Nice kid," he said softly. Reaching for the menu, he handed it to Roy.

Roy read it and although he was hungry couldn't concentrate on food. What did this glass-eye bookie, a good fifty years if not more, mean to a lively girl like Memo, a girl who was, after all, just out of mourning for a young fellow like Bump? Over the top of the menu he noticed Gus's soft-boned hands and the thick, yellow-nailed fingers. He had pouches under both the good and fake eyes, and though he smiled a lot, his expression was melancholy. Roy disliked him right off. There was something wormy about him. He belonged in the dark with the Judge. Let them both haunt themselves there.

"Order, guys," Gus said.

Roy did just to have something to do.

The captain came over and asked was everything all right.

"Check and double check." Gus pressed two folded fives into his palm. Roy didn't like the way he threw out the bucks. He thought of the raise he didn't get and felt bad about it.

"Lemme buy you a drink, slugger," Gus said, pointing to his own Scotch.

"No, thanks."

"Clean living, eh?"

"The eyes," Roy said, pointing to his. "Got to keep 'em clear."

Gus smiled. "Nice goin', slugger."

"He needs a drink," Max said. "The Judge gave him nix on a raise."

Roy could have bopped him for telling it in front of Memo.

Gus was interested.

"Y'mean he didn't pull out his pouch and shake you out some rusty two-dollar gold pieces?"

Everybody laughed but Roy.

"I see you met him," Max said.

Gus winked the glass eye. "We had some dealings."

"How'd you make out?"

"No evidence. We were acquitted." He chuckled softly.

Max made a note in his book.

"Don't write that, Max," said Gus.

Max quickly tore out the page. "Whatever you say, Gus."

Gus beamed. He turned to Roy. "How'd it go today, slugger?"

"Fine," Roy said.

"He got five for five in the first, and four hits in the nightcap," Max explained.

"Say, what d'ye know?" Gus whistled softly. "That'll cost me a pretty penny." He focused his good eye on Roy. "I was betting against you today, slugger."

"You mean the Knights?"

"No, just you."

"Didn't know you bet on any special player."

"On anybody or anything. We bet on strikes, balls, hits, runs, innings, and full games. If a good team plays a lousy team we will bet on the spread of runs. We cover anything anyone wants to bet on. Once in a Series game I bet a hundred grand on three pitched balls."

"How'd you make out on that?"

"Guess."

"I guess you didn't."

"Right, I didn't." Gus chuckled. "But it don't matter. The next week I ruined the guy in a different deal. Sometimes we win, sometimes we don't but the percentage is for us. Today we lost on you, some other time we will clean up double."

"How'll you do that?"

"When you are not hitting so good."

"How'll you know when to bet on that?"

Gus pointed to his glass eye. "The Magic Eye," he said. "It sees everything and tells me."

The steaks came and Roy cut into his.

"Wanna see how it works, slugger? Let's you and I bet on something."

"I got nothing I want to bet on," Roy said, his mouth full of meat and potatoes.

"Bet on any old thing and I will come up with the opposite even though your luck is running high now."

"It's a helluva lot more than luck."

"I will bet anyway."

Memo looked interested. Roy decided to take a chance.

"How about that I will get four hits in tomorrow's game?"

Gus paused. "Don't bet on baseball now," he said. "Bet on something we can settle here."

"Well, you pick it and I'll bet against you."

"Done," said Gus. "Tell you what, see the bar over by the entrance?"

Roy nodded.

"We will bet on the next order. You see Harry there, don't you? He's just resting now. In a minute somebody's gonna order drinks and Harry will make them. We'll wait till a waiter goes over and gives him an order—any one of them in the joint any time you say, so nobody thinks it's rigged. Then I will name you one of the drinks that will go on the waiter's tray, before Harry makes them. If there is only one drink there I will have to name it exactly—for a grand."

Roy hesitated. "Make it a hundred."

Max tittered.

"A 'C' it is," Gus said. "Say when."

"Now."

Gus shut his eyes and rubbed his brow with his left hand. "One of the drinks on the tray will be a Pink Lady."

The way they were seated everybody but Mercy could see the bar, so he turned his chair around to watch.

"Your steak might get cold, Max."

"This I got to see."

Memo looked on, amused.

They waited a minute, then a waiter went over to the bar and said something to the bartender. Harry nodded and turned around for a bottle, but they couldn't see what he was mixing because a customer was standing in front of him. When he left, Roy saw a tall pink drink standing on the counter. He felt sick but then he thought maybe it's a sloe gin fizz. Harry poured a Scotch and soda for the same tray and the waiter came for it.

As he passed by, Gus called him over to the table.

"What is that red drink that you have got there?"

"This one?" said the waiter. "A Pink Lady, Mr. Sands."

Gus slipped him a fiver.

Everybody laughed.

"Nothing to it," said Gus.

"It never fails." Max had turned his chair and was eating. "Nice work, Gus."

Gus beamed. Memo patted his hand. Roy felt annoyed.

"That's a hundred," he said.

"It was a freak win," Gus said, "so we will write it off."

"No, I owe it to you but give me a chance to win it back."

He thought Memo was mocking him and it made him stubborn.

"Anything you say," Gus shrugged.

"You can say it," said Roy. "I'll cover you for two hundred."

Gus concentrated a minute. Everybody watched him, Roy tensely. It wasn't the money he was afraid of. He wanted to win in front of Memo.

"Let's play on some kind of a number," Gus said.

"What kind?"

"Of the amount of bills you are carrying on you."

A slow flush crept up Roy's cheeks.

"I will bet I can guess by one buck either way how much you have got on you now," Gus said.

"You're on." Roy's voice was husky.

Gus covered his good eye and pretended he was a mind reader trying to fathom the number. His glass eye stared unblinking.

"Ten bucks," he announced.

Roy's throat went dry. He drew his wallet out of his pants pocket. Max took it from him and loudly counted up a five and four single dollar bills. "Nine." He slapped the table and guffawed.

"Wonderful," Memo murmured.

"Three hundred I owe to you."

"Don't mention it."

"It was a bet. Will you take my IOU?"

"Wanna try again?"

"Sure."

"You'll lose your panties," Max warned.

"On what?" Gus asked.

Roy thought. "What about another number?"

"Righto. What kind?"

"I'll pick out a number from one to ten. You tell me what it is."

Gus considered. "For the three hundred?"

"Yes."

"Okay."

"Do you want me to write the number?"

"Keep it in your head."

"Go ahead."

"Got the number?"

"I have it."

Again Gus eclipsed his good eye and took a slow breath. He made it seem like a kind of magic he was doing. Memo was fascinated.

"Deuce," Gus quickly announced.

Roy felt as if he had been struck on the conk. He considered lying but knew they could tell if he did.

"That's right, how'd you do it?" He felt foolish.

Gus winked.

Max was all but coming apart with laughter. Memo looked away.

Gus swallowed his Scotch. "Two is a magic number," he crooned at Memo. "Two makes the world go around." She smiled slightly, watching Roy.

He tried to eat but felt numbed.

Max just couldn't stop cackling. Roy felt like busting him one in the snoot.

Gus put his long arm around Memo's bare shoulders. "I have lots of luck, don't I, babyface?"

She nodded and sipped her drink.

The lights went on. The m.c. bobbed up from a table he had been sitting at and went into his routine.

"Six hundred I owe to you," Roy said, throwing Max into another whoop of laughter.

"Forget it, slugger. Maybe some day you might be able to do me a favor."

They were all suddenly silent.

"What kind of favor?" Roy asked.

"When I am down and out you can buy me a cup o' coffee."

They laughed, except Roy.

"I'll pay you now." He left the table and disappeared.

In a few minutes he returned with a white tablecloth over his arm.

Roy flapped out the cloth and one of the spotlights happened to catch it in the air. It turned red, then gold.

"What's going on?" Max said.

Roy whisked the cloth over Gus's head.

"The first installment."

He grabbed the bookie's nose and yanked. A stream of silver dollars clattered into his plate.

Gus stared at the money. Memo looked at Roy in intense surprise.

People at the nearby tables turned to see what was going on. Those in the rear craned and got up. The m.c. gave up his jokes and waved both spots to Roy.

"For Pete's sake, sit down," Max hissed.

Roy rippled the green cloth in front of Max's face and dragged out of his astonished mouth a dead herring.

Everybody in the place applauded.

From Memo's bosom, he plucked a duck egg.

Gus got red in the face. Roy grabbed his beak again and twisted—it shed more cartwheels.

"Second installment."

"What the hell is this?" Gus sputtered.

The color wheels spun. Roy turned purple, red, and yellow. From the glum Mercy's pocket he extracted a long salami. Gus's ears ran a third installment of silver. A whirl of the cloth and a white bunny hopped out of Memo's purse. From Max's size sixteen shirt collar, he teased out a pig's tail.

As the customers howled, Max pulled out his black book and furiously scribbled in it. Gus's blue, depressed eye hunted around for a way out but his glass one gleamed like a lamp in a graveyard. And Memo laughed and laughed till the tears streamed down her cheeks.

"Maybe I might break my back while I am at it," Roy spoke into the microphone at home plate before a hushed sellout crowd jampacked into Knights Field, "but I will do my best—the best I am able—to be the greatest there ever was in the game.

"I thank you." He finished with a gulp that echoed like an electric hiccup through the loudspeakers and sat down, not quite happy with himself despite the celebration, because when called on to speak he had meant to begin with a joke, then thank them for their favor and say what a good team the Knights were and how he enjoyed working for Pop Fisher, but it had come out this other way. On the other hand, so what the hell if they knew what was on his mind?

It was "Roy Hobbs Day," that had been in the making since two weeks ago, when Max Mercy printed in his column: "Roy Hobbs, El Swatto, has been ixnayed on a pay raise. Trying to kill the bird that lays the golden baseball, Judge?" A grass roots movement developed among the loyal fans to put the Judge to shame (if possible) and they had quickly arranged a Day for Roy, which was held after the Knights had bounced into third place, following a night game win over the Phils, who now led them by only four games, themselves two behind the first-place Pirates.

The whole thing was kept a surprise, and after batting practice was over on this particular Saturday afternoon in early August, the right field gate had swung open and a whole caravan of cars, led by a limousine full of officials and American Legionnaires, and followed by a gorgeous, under-slung white Mercedes-Benz and a lumbering warehouse van loaded with stuff, drove in and slowly circled the field to the music of a band playing "Yankee Doodle," while the crowd cheered shrilly. Someone then tapped Roy and said it was all for him.

"Who, me?" he said, rising . . .

When he had made his speech and retired to the dugout, after a quick, unbelieving glance at the mountain of gifts they were unpacking for him, the fans sat back in frozen silence, some quickly crossing their fingers, some spitting over their left shoulders, onto the steps so they wouldn't get anyone wet, almost all hoping he had not jinxed himself forever by saying what he had said. "The best there ever was in the game" might tempt the wrath of some mighty powerful ghosts. But they quickly recovered from the shock of his audacity and clapped up a thick thunder of applause.

It was everyman's party and they were determined to enjoy it. No one knew exactly who had supplied the big dough, but the loyal everyday fans had contributed all sorts of small change and single bucks to buy enough merchandise to furnish a fair-sized general store. When everything was unloaded from the van, Roy posed in front of it, fiddling with a gadget or two for the benefit of the photographers, though he later tipped off Dizzy to sell whatever he could to whoever had the cash. Mercy himself counted two television sets, a baby tractor, five hundred feet of pink plastic garden hose, a nanny goat, lifetime pass to the Paramount, one dozen hand-painted neckties offering different views of the Grand Canyon, six aluminum traveling cases, and a credit for seventy-five taxi rides in Philadelphia. Also three hundred pounds of a New Jersey brand Swiss cheese, a set of andirons and tongs, forty gallons of pistachio ice cream, six crates of lemons, a frozen side of hog, hunting knife, bearskin rug, snowshoes, four burner electric range, deed to a lot in Florida, twelve pairs of monogrammed blue shorts, movie camera and projector, a Chris-Craft motor boat—and, because everybody thought the Judge (unashamedly looking on from his window in the tower) was too cheap to live—a certified check for thirty-six hundred dollars. Although the committee had tried to keep out all oddball contributions, a few slippped in, including a smelly package of Limburger cheese, one human skull, bundle of comic books, can of rat exterminator, and a package of dull razor blades, this last with a card attached in the crabbed handwriting of Otto Zipp: "Here, cut your throat," but Roy did not take it to heart.

When he was told, to his amazement, that the Mercedes-Benz was his too, he could only say, "This is the happiest day of my life." Getting in, he drove around the park to the frenzied waving and whistling of the fans and whirring of movie cameras. The gleaming white job was light to the touch of hand and foot and he felt he could float off in it over the stadium wall. But he stopped before Memo's box and asked if she would go with him for a jaunt after the game, to which she, lowering her eyes, replied she was agreeable.

Memo said she longed to see the ocean so they drove over the bridge and down into Long Island toward Jones Beach, stopping when she was hungry, for charcoal-broiled steaks at a roadside tavern. Afterwards it was night, lit up by a full moon swimming in lemon juice, but at intervals eclipsed by rain clouds that gathered in dark blots and shuttered the yellow light off the fields and tree tops.

She spoke little, once remarking it looked like rain.

He didn't answer. Though he had started off riding high (he had paid back the patrons of his Day by walloping a homer that drove in the winning run) he now felt somewhat heavy hearted. For the past two weeks he had been seeing Memo most every day but had made little headway. There were times when he thought yes, I am on my way up in her affections, but no sooner did he think that when something she did or said, or didn't do or didn't say, made him think no, I am not. It was a confusing proposition to want a girl you'd already had and couldn't get because you had; a situation common in his life, of having first and then wanting what he had had, as if he hadn't had it but just heard about it, and it had, in the hearing, aroused his appetite. He even wished he had not had her that night, and wondered—say he hadn't—whether he would be in the least interested in her today.

In another sense it wasn't a bad evening. He was with her, at least, and they were traveling together, relaxed, to the ocean. He didn't exactly know where it was and though he liked the water, tonight he did not much care if they never came to it. He felt contentment in moving. It rested him by cutting down the inside motion—that which got him nowhere, which was where he was and she was not, or where his ambitions were and he was chasing after. Sometimes he wished he had no ambitions—often wondered where they had come from in his life, because he remembered how satisfied he had been as a youngster, and that with the little he had had—a dog, a stick, an aloneness he loved (which did not bleed him like his later loneliness), and he wished he could have lived longer in his boyhood. This was an old thought with him.

Hoping for a better fate in the future he stepped on the gas and was at once seized by an uneasy fear they were being followed. Since the mirror showed nobody behind them, he wondered at his suspicions and then recalled a black sedan that had been on their tail, he thought, all the way down from the city, only they had lost it a while back in turning off the highway. Yet he continued to watch in the mirror, though it showed only the lifeless moonlit road.

Memo said Jones Beach was too far and told him to stop the next time they came to a brook or pond where she could take off her shoes and go wading in the water. When he spied a small stream running along the edge of a wooded section between two towns, he slowed down. They parked across the shoulder of the asphalt and got out but as they crossed this wooden bridge to the grassy side of the stream, they were confronted by a sign: DANGER. POLLUTED WATER. NO SWIMMING. Roy was all for getting into the car to find another place, but Memo said no, they could watch the water from the bridge. She lit a cigarette, all in light, her hair and green summer dress, and her naked legs and even the slave bracelet around her left ankle gleaming in the light of the moon. Smoking, she watched the water flowing under the bridge, its movement reflected on her face.

After a while, seeing how silent she was, Roy said, "I bet I got enough today to furnish a house."

Memo said, "Bump was coming up for a Day just before he died."

He felt anger rise in his heart and asked coldly, "Well," Memo, what did he have that I haven't got?" He stood to his full height, strong and handsome.

Without looking at him she spoke Bump's name thoughtfully, then shook her head to snap out of it, as if it didn't pay to be thoughtful about Bump. "Oh," she answered, "he was carefree and full of life. He did the craziest things and always kept everybody in stitches. Even when he played ball, there was something carefree and playful about it. Maybe he went all the way after a fly ball or maybe he didn't, but once he made up his mind to catch it, it was exciting how he ran and exciting how he caught it. He made you think you had been wishing for a thing to happen for a long time and then he made it happen. And the same with his hitting. When you catch one, Roy, or go up to hit, everybody knows before hand that it will land up in your glove, or be a hit. You work at it so—sometimes you even look desperate—but to him it was a playful game and so was his life. Nobody could ever tell what would happen next with Bump, and that was the wonderful thing of it."

Roy thought this is how she sees him now that he is dead. She forgets how hopping sore she was at him after that time in bed with me.

But Bump was dead, he thought, dead and buried in his new box, an inescapable six feet under, so he subtly changed the subject to Gus.

"Gus?" Memo said. At first her face was expressionless. "Oh, he's just like a daddy to me."

He asked her in what way but she laughed and said, "That was a funny business you did with him in the Pot of Fire. How did you do all those tricks?"

"Easy. They had a magic act all laid out to go on. I walked into the guy's dressing room and when they saw who I was they let me use his stuff just for the laughs."

"Who showed you how to use it?"

"Nobody. I have done some different things in my time, Memo."

"Such as what other ones?"

"You name it, I did it."

"What you did to Max was a scream."

A black cloud rolled like a slow wave across the moon.

"It's so strange," she murmured, looking at the moving water.

"What is?"

For a time she didn't speak, then she sighed and said she meant her life. "It's been strange ever since I can remember except for a year or two—mostly the part with Bump. That was the good part only it didn't last very long, not much of the good part ever did. When I was little my daddy walked out on us and I don't ever remember being happy again till the time I got to go to Hollywood when I was nineteen."

He waited.

"I won a beauty contest where they picked a winner from each state and she was sent to Hollywood to be a starlet. For a few weeks I felt like the Queen of the May, then they took a screen test and though I had the looks and figure my test did not come out so good in acting and they practically told me to go home. I couldn't stand the thought of that so I stayed there for three more years, doing night club work and going to an acting school besides, hoping that I would some day be a good enough actress but it didn't take. I knew what I was supposed to do but I couldn't make myself, in my thoughts, into somebody else. You're supposed to forget who you are but I couldn't. Then I came east and had some more bad times after my mother died, till I met Bump."

He thought she would cry but she didn't.

Memo watched the pebbles in the flowing water. "After Bump I realized I could never be happy any more."

"How do you know that?" Roy asked slowly.

"Oh, I know. I can tell from the way I feel. Sometimes in the morning I never want to wake up."

He felt a dreary emptiness at her words.

"What about yourself?" she asked, wanting to change the subject.

"What about me?" he said gloomily.

"Max says you are sort of a mystery."

"Max is a jerk. My past life is nobody's business."

"What was it like?"

"Like yours, for years I took it on the chin." He sounded as if he had caught a cold, took out his handkerchief and blew his nose.

"What happened?"

He wanted to tell her everything, match her story and go her a couple better but couldn't bring himself to. It wasn't, he thought, that he was afraid to tell her what had happened to him that first time (though the thought of doing that raised a hot blush on his pan, for he had never told anybody about it yet), but about the miserable years after that, when everything, everything he tried somehow went to the post as if that was its destiny in the first place, a thing he couldn't understand.

"What happened?" she asked again.

"The hell with it," he said.

"I told you about myself."

He watched the water.

"I have knocked around a lot and been hard hurt in plenty of ways," he said huskily. "There were times I thought I would never get anywhere and it made me eat my guts, but all that is gone now. I know I have the stuff and will get there."

"Get where?"

"Where I am going. Where I will be the champ and have what goes with it."

She drew back but he had caught her arm and tugged her to him.

"Don't."

"You got to live, Memo."

He trapped her lips, tasting of lemon drops, kissing hard. Happening to open his eyes, he saw her staring at him in the middle of the kiss. Shutting them, he dived deep down again. Then she caught his passion, opened her mouth for his tongue and went limp around the knees.

They swayed together and he turned his hand and slipped it through the top of her dress into her loose brassiere, cupping her warm small breast in his palm.

Her legs stiffened. She pushed at him, sobbing, "Don't touch it."

He was slow to react.

She wailed, "Don't, please don't."

He pulled his hand out, angrily disappointed.

She was crying now, rubbing her hand across her bosom.

"Did I hurt you?"

"Yes."

"How the hell did I do that? I was nice with it."

"It's sick," she wept.

He felt like he had had an icy shave and haircut. "Who says so?"

"It hurts. I know."

She could be lying, only her eyes were crisscrossed with fear and her arms goosefleshed.

"Did you go to a doctor?"

"I don't like them."

"You ought to go."

Memo ran off the bridge. He followed her to the car. She sat at the wheel and started the motor. Figuring she would calm down quicker this way he let her.

She backed the car onto the road and drove off. The moon

sank into an enormous cloud-sea. Memo sped along the asphalt and turned at a fork down a hard dirt road.

"Put on the lights."

"I like it dark." Her white arms were stiff on the wheel.

He knew she didn't but figured she was still nervous.

Dripping dark cloud spray, the moon bobbed up and flooded the road ahead with bright light. Memo pressed her foot on the gas.

A thundering wind beat across his skull. Let her, he thought. Whatever she has got on her mind, let her get it off, especially if it is still Bump.

He thought about what she had said on the bridge about never being happy again and wondered what it meant. In a way he was tired of her—she was too complicated—but in a different way he desired her more than ever. He could not decide what to say or do next. Maybe wait, but he didn't want to any more. Yet what else was there to do?

The white moonlight shot through a stretch of woods ahead. He found himself wishing he could go back somewhere, go home, whenever that was. As he was thinking this, he looked up and saw in the moonlight a boy coming out of the woods, followed by his dog. Squinting through the windshield, he was unable to tell if the kid was an illusion thrown forth by the trees or someone really alive. After fifteen seconds he was still there. Roy yelled to Memo to slow down in case he wanted to cross the road. Instead, the car shot forward so fast the woods blurred, the trees racing along like shadows in weak light, then skipping into black and white, finally all black and the moon was gone.

"Lights!"

She sat there stiffly so he reached over and switched them on.

As the road flared up, Memo screamed and tugged at the wheel. He felt a thud and his heart sickened. It was a full minute before he realized they hadn't stopped.

"For Christ sake, stop—we hit somebody."

"No." Her face was bloodless.

He reached for the brake.

"Don't, it was just something on the road."

"I heard somebody groan."

"That was yourself."

He couldn't remember that he had.

"I want to go back and see."

"If you do, the cops will get us."

"What cops?"

"They have been after us since we started. I've been doing ninety."

He looked back and saw a black car with dimmed headlights speeding after them.

"Turn at the next bend," he ordered her, "and I will take over.

They were nearer to the Sound than he had suspected, and when a white pea-souper crawled in off the water Roy headed into it. Though the Mercedes showed no lights the whiteness of it was enough to keep it in the sedan's eye, so he welcomed the fog and within it easily ditched those who chased them.

On the way back he attempted to find the road along the woods to see if they had hit somebody. Memo had little patience with him. She was sure, despite Roy's insistence of an outside groan, that they had hit a rock or log in the road. If they went back the cops might be laying for them and they'd be arrested, which would cause no end of trouble.

He said he was going back anyway.

Roy had the feeling that the sedan was still at his shoulder—he could see it wasn't—as he tried to locate the bridge and then the road along the woods. He wasn't convinced they had not hit somebody and if he could do anything for the kid, even this late, he wanted to. So he turned the lights on bright, illuminating the swirling fog, and as they went by the fog-shrouded woods—he couldn't be sure it was the right woods—he searched the road intently for signs of a body or its blood but found nothing. Memo dozed off but was awakened when Roy, paying no heed to what lay ahead, ran off a low embankment, crashing the car into a tree. Though shaken up, neither of them was much hurt. Roy had a black eye and Memo bruised her sick breast. The car was a wreck.

Helping Memo out of a cab that same morning before dawn, Roy glanced into the hotel lobby just as Pop Fisher bounced up out of a couch and came charging at them like a runaway trolley. Memo said to run, so they raced down the street and ducked into the hotel by the side entrance, but they were barely to the stairs when Pop, who had doubled back on his tracks, came at them smoking with anger.

Memo sobbed she had taken all she could tonight and ran up the stairs. Roy had hoped to have another chance at a kiss but when Pop flew at him like a batty, loose-feathered fowl, killing the stillness of the place with his shrill crowing, he figured it best to keep him away from Memo.

He turned to Pop, who then got a closeup of Roy's rainbow eye and all but blew apart. He called him everything from a dadblamed sonovagun to a blankety blank Judas traitor for breaking training, hurting his eye, and blowing in at almost 5 A.M. on the day of an important twin bill with the Phils.

"You damn near drove me wild," he shouted. "I just about had heart failure when Red told me you weren't in your room at midnight."

He then and there fined Roy two hundred and fifty dollars, but reduced it to an even hundred when Roy sarcastically mentioned how much the Knights were paying him.

"And nothing is wrong with my eye," he said. "It don't hurt but a little and I can see out of it as clear as day, but if you want me to get some sleep before the game don't stand there jawing my head off."

Pop was quickly pacified. "I admit you are entitled to a good time on your Day but you have no idea of all that I have suffered in those hours I was waiting up for you. All kinds of terrible things ran through my mind. I don't hafta tell you it don't take much to kill off a man nowadays."

Roy laughed. "Nothing is going to kill me before my time. I am the type that will die a natural death."

Seeing the affectionate smile this raised up on Pop's puss, he felt sorry for the old man and said, "Even with one eye I will wow them for you today."

"I know you will, son," Pop almost purred. "You're the one I'm depending on to get us up there. We're hot now and I figure, barring any serious accidents, that we will catch up with the Pirates in less than two weeks. Then once we are first we should stay there till we take the flag. My God, when

I think of that my legs get dizzy. I guess you know what that would mean to me after all of these years. Sometimes I feel I have been waiting for it my whole life. So take care of yourself. When all is said and done, you ain't a kid any more. At your age the body will often act up, so be wise and avoid any trouble."

"I am young in my mind and healthy in my body," Roy said. "You don't have to worry about me."

"Only be careful," Pop said.

Roy said good night but couldn't move because Pop had gripped his elbow. Leading him to the corner, he whispered to Roy not to have too much to do with Memo.

Roy stiffened.

"Don't get me wrong, son, she's not a bad girl—"

Roy glared.

Pop gulped. "I am the one who is really bad. It was me who introduced her to Bump." He looked sick. "I hoped she would straighten him out and sorta hold him in the team—but—well, you know how these things are. Bump was not the marrying kind and she sorta—well, you know what I mean."

"So what?" said Roy.

"Nothing," he answered brokenly. "Only I was wrong for encouraging them to get together with maybe in the back of my mind the idea of how they would do so—without getting married, that is—and I have suffered from it since."

Roy said nothing and Pop wouldn't look him in the eye. "What I started to say," he went on, "is that although she is not really a bad person, yet she is unlucky and always has been and I think that there is some kind of whammy in her that carries her luck to other people. That's why I would like you to watch out and not get too tied up with her."

"You're a lousy uncle."

"I am considering you."

"I will consider myself."

"Don't mistake me, son. She was my sister's girl and I do love her, but she is always dissatisfied and will snarl you up in her trouble in a way that will weaken your strength if you don't watch out."

"You might as well know that I love her."

Pop listened gloomily. "Does she feel the same to you?"

"Not yet but I think she will."

"Well, you are on your own." He looked so forlorn that Roy said, "Don't worry yourself about her. I will change her luck too."

"You might at that." Pop took out his billfold and extracted a pink paper that he handed to Roy.

Roy inspected it through his good eye. It was a check for two thousand dollars, made out to him. "What's it for?"

"The balance of your salary for the time you missed before you got here. I figure that you are entitled to at least the minimum pay for the year."

"Did the Judge send it?"

"That worm? He wouldn't send you his bad breath. It's my personal check." Pop was blushing.

Roy handed it back. "I am making out okay. If the Judge wants to raise my pay, all right, but I don't want your personal money."

"My boy, if you knew what you mean to me—"

"Don't say it." Roy's throat was thick with sentiment. "Wait till I get you the pennant."

He turned to go and bumped into Max Mercy at his elbow. Max's sleepy popeyes goggled when he saw Roy's shiner. He sped back into the lobby.

"That slob is up to no good," Roy said.

"He was sleeping on the couch next to where I was waiting for you to come home. He heard Red tell me you hadn't showed up. Kept a camera with him back there."

"He better not take a picture of my eye," Roy said.

He beat it up the back stairs with Max on his tail. Though the columnist carried a camera and a pocketful of flashbulbs he ran faster than Roy had expected, so to ditch him he shot through the second-floor door and sped down the corridor. Seeing over his shoulder that Max was still after him he ducked through a pair of open glass doors into an enormous black ballroom, strewn with chairs, potted palms, and music stands from a dance last night. The lingering odor of perfume mixed with cigarette smoke reminded him of the smell of Memo's hair and haunted him even now. He thought of hiding behind something but that would make him a ridiculous sitting duck for a chance shot of Max's, so since his good eye had become accustomed to the dark he nimbly picked his way among the obstacles, hoping the four-eyed monstrosity behind him would break his camera or maybe a leg. But Max seemed to smell his way around in the dark and hung tight. Reaching the glass doors at the other end of the ballroom, Roy sidestepped out just as a bulb lit in a wavering flash that would leave Max with a snapshot of nothing but a deserted ballroom. The columnist stuck like glue to Roy's shadow, spiraling after him up the stairs and through the long empty ninth-floor corridor (broad and soft-carpeted so that their footsteps were silent) which stretched ahead, it seemed to Roy, like an endless highway.

He felt he had been running for ages, then this blurred black forest slid past him, and as he slowed down, each black tree followed a white, and then all the trees were lit in somber light till the moon burst forth through the leaves and the woods glowed. Out of it appeared this boy and his dog, and Roy in his heart whispered him a confidential message: watch out when you cross the road, kid, but he had spoken too late, for the boy lay brokenboned and bleeding in a puddle of light, with no one to care for him or whisper a benediction upon his lost youth. A groan rose in Roy's throat (he holding a flashlight over the remains) for not having forced Memo to stop and go back to undo some of the harm. A sudden dark glare flashed over his head, eerily catapulting his shadow forward, and erasing in its incandescence the boy in the road. Roy felt a burning pain in his gut, yet simultaneously remembered there had been no sign of blood on the bumper or fender, and Memo said she had screamed because she saw in the mirror that they were being chased by cops. The black sedan that trailed them had not stopped either, which it would have done if there were cops in it and somebody was dying in the road. So Memo must've been right—either it was a rock, or maybe the kid's hound, probably not even that, for it did not appear there ever was any kid in those woods, except in his mind.

Ahead was his door. Max was panting after him. As Roy shoved the key into the lock, poking his eye close to do the job quick, Max from fifteen feet away aimed the camera and snapped the shutter. The flashbulb burst in the reflector. The door slammed. Max swore blue bloody murder as Roy, inside, howled with laughing.

He had a whopping good time at the ball game. Doc Casey had squeezed the swelling of his eye down and painted out the black with a flesh-tone color, and Roy led the attack against the Phils that sank them twice that afternoon, sweeping the series for the Knights and raising them into second place, only three games behind the Pirates. Pop was hilarious. The fans went wild. The newspapers called the Knights "the wonder team of the age" and said they were headed for the pennant.

On his way to Memo's after the game, Roy met her, wearing her summer furpiece, coming along the fourth-floor hall.

"I thought I would drop around and see how you are, Memo."

She continued her slightly swaying walk to the elevator.

"I am all right," she said.

He paused. "See the doctor yet?"

Memo blushed and said quickly, "He says it's neuritis—nothing serious."

She pressed the elevator button.

"Nothing serious?"

"That's what he said." She was looking up the elevator shaft and he sensed she had not been to the doctor. He guessed her breast was not sick. He guessed she had said that to get him to slow down. Though he did not care for her technique, he controlled his anger and asked her to go to the movies.

"Sorry. Gus is picking me up."

Back in his room he felt restless. He thought he'd be better off without her but the thought only made him bitter. Red Blow called him to go to the pictures but Roy said he had a headache. Later he went out by himself. That night he dreamed of her all night long. The sick breast had turned green yet he was anxious to have a feel of it.

The next day, against the Braves, Roy got exactly no hits. The Knights won, but against the Dodgers in Brooklyn on Tuesday he went hitless once more and they lost. Since he had never before gone without a hit more than six times in a row there was talk now of a slump. That made him uneasy but he tried not to think of it, concerning himself with Memo and continuing his search through the papers for news of a hit-and-run accident on Long Island. Finding no mention of one he blamed the whole thing on his imagination and thought he'd better forget it. And he told himself not to worry about the slump—it happened to the very best—but after a third day without even a bingle he couldn't help but worry.

As his hitlessness persisted everyone was astonished. It didn't seem possible this could happen to a miracle man like Roy. Enemy pitchers were the last to believe the news. They pitched him warily, fearing an eruption of his wrath, but before long they saw the worry in his eyes and would no longer yield those free and easy walks of yore. They straightened out their curves and whizzed them over the gut of the plate, counting on him either to top a slow roller to the infield or strike himself out. True, he was the same majestic-looking figure up there, well back in the box, legs spread wide, and with Wonderboy gleaming in the sun, raised over his shoulder (he had lowered it from his head). He swung with such power you could see a circle of dust lift off the ground as the bat passed over it, yet all it amounted to was breeze. It made many a pitcher feel like a pretty tough hombre to see Roy drag himself away from the plate and with lowered head enter the dugout.

"What's the matter with me?" he thought with irritation. He didn't feel himself (wondered if he could possibly be sick). He felt blunt and dull—all thumbs, muscles, and joints, Charley horse all over. He missed the sensation of the sock—the moment the stomach galloped just before the wood hit the ball, and the satisfying sting that sped through his arms and shoulders as he belted one. Though there was plenty of fielding to do—the Knights' pitchers were getting to be loose with the hits—he missed the special exercise of running the bases, whirling round them with the speed of a race horse as nine frantic men tried to cut him down. Most of all he missed the gloating that blew up his lungs when he crossed the plate and they ran up another tally opposite his name in the record book. A whole apparatus of physical and mental pleasures was on the kibosh and without them he felt like the Hobbs he thought he had left behind dead and buried.

"What am I doing that's wrong?" he asked himself. No one on the bench or in the clubhouse had offered any advice or information on the subject or even so much as mentioned slump. Not even Pop, also worried, but hoping it would fade as suddenly as it had appeared. Roy realized that he was overanxious and pressing—either hitting impatiently in front of the ball or swinging too late—so that Wonderboy only got little bites of it or went hungry. Thinking he was maybe overstriding and getting his feet too far apart so that he could not pivot freely, he shifted his stride but that didn't help. He tried a new stance and attempted, by counting to himself, to alter his timing. It did no good. To save his eyesight he cut out all reading and going to the pictures. At bat his expression was so dark and foreboding it gave the opposing pitchers the shakes, but still they had his number.

He spent hours fretting whether to ask for help or wait it out. Some day the slump was bound to go, but when? Not that he was ashamed to ask for help but once you had come this far you felt you had learned the game and could afford to give out with the advice instead of being forced to ask for it. He was, as they say, established and it was like breaking up the establishment to go around panhandling an earful. Like making a new beginning and he was sick up to here of new beginnings. But as he continued to whiff he felt a little panicky. In the end he sought out Red Blow, drew him out to center field and asked in an embarrassed voice, "Red, what is the matter with me that I am not hitting them?" He gazed over the right field wall as he asked the question.

Red squirted tobacco juice into the grass.

"Well," he said, rubbing his freckled nose, "what's worrying your mind?"

Roy was slow to reply. "I am worrying that I am missing so many and can't get back in the groove."

"I mean besides that. You haven't knocked up a dame maybe?"

"No."

"Any financial worries about money?"

"Not right now."

"Are you doing something you don't like to do?"

"Such as what?"

"Once we had a guy here whose wife made him empty the garbage pail in the barrel every night and believe it or not it began to depress him. After that he fanned the breeze a whole month until one night he told her to take the damn garbage out herself, and the next day he hit again."

"No, nothing like that."

Red smiled. "Thought I'd get a laugh out of you, Roy. A good belly laugh has more than once broke up a slump."

"I would be glad to laugh but I don't feel much like it. I hate to say it but I feel more like crying."

Red was sympathetic. "I have seen lots of slumps in my time, Roy, and if I could tell you why they come I could make a fortune, buy a saloon and retire. All I know about them is you have to relax to beat 'em. I know how you feel now and I realize that every game we lose hurts us, but if you can take it easy and get rid of the nervousness that is for some reason in your system, you will soon snap into your form. From there on in you will hit like a house on fire."

"I might be dead by then," Roy said gloomily.

Red removed his cap and with the hand that held it scratched his head.

"All I can say is that you have got to figure this out for yourself, Roy."

Pop's advice was more practical. Roy visited the manager in his office after the next (fruitless) game. Pop was sitting at his roll top desk, compiling player averages in a looseleaf notebook. On the desk were a pair of sneakers, a picture of Ma Fisher, and an old clipping from the *Sporting News* saying how sensational the Knights were going. Pop closed the average book but not before Roy had seen a large red zero for the day's work opposite his name. The Knights had dropped back to third place, only a game higher than the Cardinals, and Pop's athlete's foot on his hands was acting up.

"What do I have to do to get out of this?" Roy asked moodily.

Pop looked at him over his half-moon specs.

"Nobody can tell you exactly, son, but I'd say right off stop climbing up after those bad balls."

Roy shook his head. "I don't think that's it. I can tell when they're bad but the reason I reach for them sometimes is that the pitchers don't throw me any good ones, which hasn't been so lately. Lately, they're almost all good but not for me."

"Danged if I know just what to tell you," Pop said, scratching at his reddened fingers. He too felt a little frightened. But he recommended bunting and trying to beat them out. He said Roy had a fast pair of legs and getting on base, in which ever way, might act to restore his confidence.

But Roy, who was not much of a bunter—never had his heart in letting the ball hit the bat and roll, when he could just as well lash out and send the same pitch over the fence—could not master the art of it overnight. He looked foolish trying to bunt, and soon gave it up.

Pop then recommended hitting at fast straight ones thrown by different pitchers for thirty minutes every morning, and to do this till he had got his timing back, because it was timing that was lost in a slump. Roy practiced diligently and got so he could connect, yet he couldn't seem to touch the same pitches during the game.

Then Pop advised him to drop all batting practice and to bat cold. That didn't help either.

"How is your eye that got hurt?" Pop asked.

"Doc tested it, he says I see perfect."

Pop looked grimly at Wonderboy. "Don't you think you ought to try another stick for a change? Sometimes that will end up a slump."

Roy wouldn't hear of it. "Wonderboy made all of my records with me and I am staying with him. Whatever is wrong is wrong with me and not my bat.

Pop looked miserable but didn't argue.

Only rarely he saw Memo. She was not around much, never at the games, though she had begun to come quite often a while back. Roy had the morbid feeling she couldn't stand him while he was in this slump. He knew that other people's worries bothered her and that she liked to be where everybody was merry. Maybe she thought the slump proved he was not as good a player as Bump. Whatever it was, she found excuses not to see him and he got only an occasional glimpse of her here and there in the building. One morning when he ran into her in the hotel grill room, Memo reddened and said she was sorry to read he was having a tough time.

Roy just nodded but she went on to say that Bump used to ease his nerves when he wasn't hitting by consulting a fortune-teller named Lola who lived in Jersey City.

"What for?" Roy asked.

"She used to tell him things that gave him a lift, like the time she said he was going to be left money by someone, and he felt so good it raised him clean out of his slump."

"Did he get the dough that she said?"

"Yes. Around Christmas his father died and left him a garage and a new Pontiac. Bump cleared nine thousand cash when he sold the property."

Roy thought it over afterwards. He had little faith that any fortuneteller could help him out of his trouble but the failure of each remedy he tried sank him deeper into the dumps and he was now clutching for any straw. Borrowing a car, he hunted up Lola in Jersey City, locating her in a two-story shack near the river. She was a fat woman of fifty, and wore black felt slippers broken at the seams, and a kitchen towel wrapped around her head.

"Step right inside the parlor," she said, holding aside the braded curtain leading into a dark and smelly room, "and I will be with you in a jiffy, just as soon as I get rid of this loud mouth on the back porch."

Feeling ill at east and foolish, Roy waited for her.

Lola finally came in with a Spanish shawl twisted around her. She lit up the crystal ball, passed her gnarled hands over it and peered nearsightedly into the glass. After watching for a minute she told Roy he would soon meet and fall in love with a darkhaired lady.

"Anything else?" he said impatiently.

Lola looked. A blank expression came over her face and she

slowly shook her head. "Funny," she said, "there ain't a thing more."

"Nothing about me getting out of a slump in baseball?"

"Nothing. The future has closed down on me."

Roy stood up. "The trouble with what you said is that I am already in love with a swell-looking redhead."

Because of the shortness of the sitting Lola charged him a buck instead of the usual two.

After his visit to her, though Roy was as a rule not superstitious, he tried one or two things he had heard about to see how they would work. He put his socks on inside out, ran a red thread through his underpants, spat between two fingers when he met a black cat, and daily searched the stands for some crosseyed whammy who might be hexing him. He also ate less meat, though he was always hungry, and he arranged for a physical check-up. The doctor told him he was in good shape except for some high blood pressure that was caused by worrying and would diminish as soon as he relaxed. He practiced different grips on Wonderboy before his bureau mirror and sewed miraculous medals and evil-eye amulets of fish, goats, clenched fists, open scissors, and hunchbacks all over the inside of his clothes.

Little of this escaped the other Knights. While the going was good they had abandoned this sort of thing, but now that they were on the skids they felt the need of some extra assistance. So Dave Olson renewed his feud with the lady in the brown-feathered hat, Emil Lajong spun his protective backflips, and Flores revived the business with the birds. Clothes were put on from down up, gloves were arranged to point south when the players left the field to go to bat, and everybody, including Dizzy, owned at least one rabbit's foot. Despite these precautions the boys were once more afflicted by bonehead plays—failing to step on base on a simple force, walking off the field with two out as the winning run scored from first, attempting to stretch singles into triples, and fearing to leave first when the ball was good for at least two. And they were not ashamed to blame it all on Roy.

It didn't take the fans very long to grow disgusted with their antics. Some of them agreed it was Roy's fault, for jinxing himself and the team on his Day by promising the impossible out of his big mouth. Others, including a group of sportswriters, claimed the big boy had all the while been living on borrowed time, a large bag of wind burst by the law of averages. Sadie, dabbing at her eyes with the edge of her petticoat, kept her gong in storage, and Gloria disgustedly swore off men. And Otto Zipp had reappeared like a bad dream with his loud voice and pesky tooter venomously hooting Roy into oblivion. A few of the fans were ashamed that Otto was picking on somebody obviously down, but the majority approved his sentiments. The oldtimers began once again to heave vegetables and oddments around, and following the dwarf's lead they heckled the players, especially Roy, calling him everything from a coward to a son of a bitch. Since Roy had always had rabbit ears, every taunt and barb hit its mark. He changed color and muttered at his tormentors. Once in a spasm of weakness he went slowly after a fly ball (lately he had to push himself to catch shots he had palmed with ease before), compelling Flores to rush into his territory to take it. The meatheads rose to a man and hissed. Roy shook his fist at their stupid faces. They booed. He thumbed his nose. "You'll get yours," they howled in chorus.

He had, a vile powerlessness seized him.

Seeing all this, Pop was darkly furious. He all but ripped the recently restored bandages off his pusing fingers. His temper flared wild and red, his voice tore, he ladled out fines like soup to breadline beggars, and he was vicious to Roy.

"It's that goshdamn bat," he roared one forenoon in the club house. "When will you get rid of that danged Wonderboy and try some other stick?"

"Never," said Roy.

"Then rest your ass on the bench."

So Roy sat out the game on the far corner of the bench, from where he could watch Memo, lovelier than ever in a box up front, in the company of two undertakers, the smiling, one-eye Gus, and Mercy, catlike contented, whose lead that night would read: "Hobbs is benched. The All-American Out has sunk the Knights into second division."

He woke in the locker room, stretched out on a bench. He remembered lying down to dry out before dressing but he was still wet with sweat, and a lit match over his wristwatch told him it was past midnight. He sat up stiffly, groaned and rubbed his hard palms over his bearded face. The thinking started up and stunned him. He sat there paralyzed though his innards were in flight—the double-winged lungs, followed by the boat-shaped heart, trailing a long string of guts. He longed for a friend, a father, a home to return to—saw himself packing his duds in a suitcase, buying a ticket, and running for a train. Beyond the first station he'd fling Wonderboy out the window. (Years later, an old man returning to the city for a visit, he would scan the flats to see if it was there, glowing in the mud.) The train sped through the night across the country. In it he felt safe. He tittered.

The mousy laughter irritated him. "Am I outa my mind?" He fell to brooding and mumbled, "What am I doing that's wrong?" Now he shouted the question and it boomed back at him off the walls. Lighting matches, he hurriedly dressed. Before leaving, he remembered to wrap Wonderboy in flannel. In the street he breathed easier momentarily, till he suspected someone was following him. Stopping suddenly, he wheeled about. A woman, walking alone in the glare of the street lamp, noticed him. She went faster, her heels clicking down the street. He hugged the stadium wall, occasionally casting stealthy glances behind. In the tower burned a dark light, the Judge counting his shekels. He cursed him and dragged his carcass on.

A cabbie with a broken nose and cauliflower ear stared but did not recognize him. The hotel lobby was deserted. An old elevator man mumbled to himself. The ninth-floor hall was long and empty. Silent. He felt a driblet of fear . . . like a glug of water backing up the momentarily opened drain and polluting the bath with a dead spider, three lice, a rat turd, and things he couldn't stand to name or look at. For the first time in years he felt afraid to enter his room. The telephone rang. It rang and rang. He waited for it to stop. Finally it did. He warned himself he was acting like a crazy fool. Twisting the key in the lock, he pushed open the door. In the far corner of the room, something moved. His blood changed to falling snow.

Bracing himself to fight without strength he snapped on

the light. A white shadow flew into the bathroom. Rushing in, he kicked the door open. An ancient hoary face stared at him. "Bump!" He groaned and shuddered. An age passed . . . His own face gazed back at him from the bathroom mirror, his past, his youth, the fleeting years. He all but blacked out in relief. His head, a jagged rock on aching shoulders, throbbed from its rocky interior. An oppressive sadness weighed like a live pain on his heart. Gasping for air, he stood at the open window and looked down at the dreary city till his legs and arms were drugged with heaviness. He shut the hall door and flopped into bed. In the dark he was lost in an overwhelming weakness . . . I am finished, he muttered. The pages of the record book fell apart and fluttered away in the wind. He slept and woke, finished. All night long he waited for the bloody silver bullet.

On the road Pop was in a foul mood. He cracked down on team privileges: no more traveling wives, no signing of food checks—Red dispensed the cash for meals every morning before breakfast—curfew at eleven and bed check every night. But Roy had discovered that the old boy had invited Memo to come along with them anyway. He went on the theory that Roy had taken to heart his advice to stay away from her and it was making a wreck out of him. Memo had declined the invitation and Pop guiltily kicked himself for asking her.

Roy was thinking about her the morning they came into Chicago and were on their way to the hotel in a cab—Pop, Red, and him. For a time he had succeeded in keeping her out of his thoughts but now, because of the renewed disappointment, she was back in again. He wondered whether Pop was right and she had maybe jinxed him into a slump. If so, would he do better out here, so far away from her?

The taxi turned up Michigan Avenue, where they had a clear view of the lake. Roy was silent. Red happened to glance out the back window. He stared at something and then said, "Have either of you guys noticed the black Cadillac that is following us around? I've seen that damn auto most everywhere we go."

Roy turned to see. His heart jumped. It looked like the car that had chased them halfway across Long Island.

"Drat 'em," Pop said. "I fired those guys a week ago. Guess they didn't get my postcard."

Red asked who they were.

"A private eye and his partner," Pop explained. "I hired them about a month back to watch the Great Man here and keep him outa trouble but it's a waste of good money now." He gazed back and fumed. "Those goshdarn saps."

Roy didn't say anything but he threw Pop a hard look and the manager was embarrassed.

As the cab pulled up before the hotel, a wild-eyed man in shirtsleeves, hairy-looking and frantic, rushed up to them.

"Any of you guys Roy Hobbs?"

"That's him," Pop said grimly, heading into the hotel with Red. He pointed back to where Roy was getting out of the cab.

"No autographs." Roy ducked past the man.

"Jesus God, Roy," he cried in a broken voice. He caught Roy's arm and held on to it. "Don't pass me by, for the love of God."

"What d'you want?" Roy stared, suspicious.

"Roy, you don't know me," the man sobbed. "My name's Mike Barney and I drive a truck for Cudahy's. I don't want a thing for myself, only a favor for my boy Pete. He was hurt in an accident, playin' in the street. They operated him for a broken skull a couple days ago and he ain't doin' so good. The doctor says he ain't fightin' much."

Mike Barney's mouth twisted and he wept.

"What has that got to do with me?" Roy asked, white-faced.

The truck driver wiped his eyes on his sleeve. "Pete's a fan of yours, Roy. He got a scrapbook that thick fulla pictures of you. Yesterday they lemme go in and see him and I said to Pete you told me you'd sock a homer for him in the game tonight. After that he sorta smiled and looked better. They gonna let him listen a little tonight, and I know if you will hit one it will save him."

"Why did you say that for?" Roy said bitterly. "The way I am now I couldn't hit the side of a barn."

Holding to Roy's sleeve, Mike Barney fell to his knees. "Please, you gotta do it."

"Get up," Roy said. He pitied the guy and wanted to help him yet was afraid what would happen if he couldn't. He didn't want that responsibility.

Mike Barney stayed on his knees, sobbing. A crowd had collected and was watching them.

"I will do the best I can if I get the chance." Roy wrenched his sleeve free and hurried into the lobby.

"A father's blessing on you," the truck driver called after him in a cracked voice.

Dressing in the visitors' clubhouse for the game that night, Roy thought about the kid in the hospital. He had been thinking of him on and off and was anxious to do something for him. He could see himself walking up to the plate and clobbering a long one into the stands and then he imagined the boy, healed and whole, thanking him for saving his life. The picture was unusually vivid, and as he polished Wonderboy, his fingers itched to carry it into the batter's box and let go at a fat one.

But Pop had other plans. "You are still on the bench, Roy, unless you put that Wonderboy away and use a different stick."

Roy shook his head and Pop gave the line-up card to the ump without his name on it. When Mike Barney, sitting a few rows behind a box above third base, heard the announcement of the Knights' line-up without Roy in it, his face broke out in a sickish sweat.

The game began, Roy taking his non-playing position on the far corner of the bench and holding Wonderboy between his knees. It was a clear, warm night and the stands were just about full. The floods on the roof lit up the stadium brighter than day. Above the globe of light lay the dark night, and high in the sky the stars glittered. Though unhappy not to be playing, Roy, for no reason he could think of, felt better in his body than he had in a week. He had a hunch things could go well for him tonight, which was why he especially regretted not being in the game. Furthermore, Mike Barney was directly in his line of vision and sometimes stared at him. Roy's gaze went past him, farther down the stands, to where a young black-haired woman, wearing a red dress, was sitting at an aisle seat in short left. He could clearly see the white flower she wore pinned on her bosom and that she seemed to spend more time craning to get a look into the Knights' dugout—at him, he could swear—than in watching the game. She interested him, in that red dress, and he would have liked a close gander at her but he couldn't get out there without arousing attention.

Pop was pitching Fowler, who had kept going pretty well during the two dismal weeks of Roy's slump, only he was very crabby at everybody—especially Roy—for not getting him any runs, and causing him to lose two well-pitched games. As a result Pop had to keep after him in the late innings, because when Fowler felt disgusted he wouldn't bear down on the opposing batters.

Up through the fifth he had kept the Cubs bottled up but he eased off the next inning and they reached him for two runs with only one out. Pop gave him a fierce glaring at and Fowler then tightened and finished off the side with a pop fly and strikeout. In the Knights' half of the seventh, Cal Baker came through with a stinging triple, scoring Stubbs, and was himself driven in by Flores' single. That tied the score but it became untied when, in their part of the inning, the Cubs placed two doubles back to back, to produce another run.

As the game went on Roy grew tense. He considered telling Pop about the kid and asking for a chance to hit. But Pop was a stubborn cuss and Roy knew he'd continue to insist on him laying Wonderboy aside. This he was afraid to do. Much as he wanted to help the boy—and it really troubled him now—he felt he didn't stand a Chinaman's chance at a hit without his own club. And if he once abandoned Wonderboy there was no telling what would happen to him. Probably it would finish his career for keeps, because never since he had made the bat had he swung at a ball with any other.

In the eighth on a double and sacrifice, Pop worked a runner around to third. The squeeze failed so he looked around anxiously for a pinch hitter. Catching Roy's eye, he said, as Roy had thought he would, "Take a decent stick and go on up there."

Roy didn't move. He was sweating heavily and it cost him a great effort to stay put. He could see the truck driver suffering in his seat, wiping his face, cracking his knuckles, and sighing. Roy averted his glance.

There was a commotion in the lower left field stands. This lady in the red dress, whoever she was, had risen, and standing in a sea of gaping faces, seemed to be searching for someone. Then she looked toward the Knights' dugout and sort of half bowed her head. A murmur went up from the crowd. Some of them explained it that she had got mixed up about the seventh inning stretch and others answered how could she when the scoreboard showed the seventh inning was over? As she stood there, so cleanly etched in light, as if trying to communicate something she couldn't express, some of the fans were embarrassed. And the stranger sitting next to her felt a strong sexual urge which he concealed behind an impatient cigarette. Roy scarcely noticed her because he was lost in worry, seriously considering whether he ought to give up on Wonderboy.

Pop of course had no idea what was going on in Roy's head, so he gave the nod to Ed Simmons, a substitute infielder. Ed picked a bat out of the rack and as he approached the plate the standing lady slowly sat down. Everyone seemed to forget her then. Ed flied out. Pop looked scornfully at Roy and shot a stream of snuff into the dust.

Fowler had a little more trouble in the Cubs half of the eighth but a double play saved him, and the score was still 3-2. The ninth opened. Pop appeared worn out. Roy had his eyes shut. It was Fowler's turn to bat. The second guessers were certain Pop would yank him for a pinch hitter but Fowler was a pretty fair hitter for a pitcher, and if the Knights could tie the score, his pitching tonight was too good to waste. He swung at the first ball, connecting for a line drive single, to Pop's satisfaction. Allie Stubbs tried to lay one away but his hard-hit fly ball to center was caught. To everybody's surprise Fowler went down the white line on the next pitch and dove safe into second under a cloud of dust. A long single could tie the score, but Cal Baker, to his disgust, struck out and flung his bat away. Pop again searched the bench for a pinch hitter. He fastened his gaze on Roy but Roy was unapproachable. Pop turned bitterly away.

Mike Barney, a picture of despair, was doing exercises of

grief. He stretched forth his long hairy arms, his knobby hands clasped, pleading. Roy felt as though they were reaching right into the dugout to throttle him.

He couldn't stand it any longer. "I give up." Placing Wonderboy on the bench he rose and stood abjectly in front of Pop.

Pop looked up at him sadly. "You win," he said. "Go on in."

Roy gulped. "With my own bat?"

Pop nodded and gazed away.

Roy got Wonderboy and walked out into the light. A roar of recognition drowned the announcement of his name but not the loud beating of his heart. Though he'd been at bat only three days ago, it felt like years—an ageless time. He almost wept at how long it had been.

Lon Toomey, the hulking Cub hurler, who had twice in the last two weeks handed Roy his lumps, smiled behind his glove. He shot a quick glance at Fowler on second, fingered the ball, reared and threw. Roy, at the plate, watched it streak by.

"Stuh-rike."

He toed in, his fear returning. What if the slump did not give way? How much longer could it go on without destroying him?

Toomey lifted his right leg high and threw. Roy swung from his heels at a bad ball and the umpire sneezed in the breeze.

Wonderboy resembled a sagging baloney. Pop cursed the bat and some of the Knights' rooters among the fans booed. Mike Barney's harrowed puss looked yellow.

Roy felt sick with remorse that he hadn't laid aside Wonderboy in the beginning and gone into the game with four licks at bat instead of only three miserable strikes, two of which he already used up. How could he explain to Barney that he had traded his kid's life away out of loyalty to a hunk of wood?

The lady in the stands hesitantly rose for the second time. A photographer who had stationed himself nearby snapped a clear shot of her. She was an attractive woman, around thirty, maybe more, and built solid but not too big. Her bosom was neat, and her dark hair, parted on the side, hung loose and soft. A reporter approached her and asked her name but she wouldn't give it to him, nor would she, blushing, say why she was standing now. The fans behind her hooted, "Down in front," but though her eyes showed she was troubled she remained standing.

Noticing Toomey watching her, Roy stole a quick look. He caught the red dress and a white rose, turned away, then came quickly back for another take, drawn by the feeling that her smile was for him. Now why would she do that for? She seemed to be wanting to say something, and then it flashed on him the reason she was standing was to show her confidence in him. He felt surprised that anybody would want to do that for him. At the same time he became aware that the night had spread out in all directions and was filled with an unbelievable fragrance.

A pitch streaked toward him. Toomey had pulled a fast one. With a sob Roy fell back and swung.

Part of the crowd broke for the exits. Mike Barney wept freely now, and the lady who had stood up for Roy absently pulled on her white gloves and left.

The ball shot through Toomey's astounded legs and began to climb. The second baseman, laying back on the grass on a hunch, stabbed high for it but it leaped over his straining fingers, sailed through the light and up into the dark, like a white star seeking an old constellation.

Toomey, shrunk to a pygmy, stared into the vast sky.

Roy circled the bases like a Mississippi steamboat, lights lit, flags fluttering, whistle banging, coming around the bend. The Knights poured out of their dugout to pound his back, and hundreds of their rooters hopped about in the field. He stood on the home base, lifting his cap to the lady's empty seat.

And though Fowler goose-egged the Cubs in the last of the ninth and got credit for the win, everybody knew it was Roy alone who had saved the boy's life.

It seemed perfectly natural to Iris to be waiting for him, with her shoes off to ease her feet, here on the park grass. He had been in her mind so often in the past month she could not conceive of him as a stranger, though he certainly was. She remembered having fallen asleep thinking of him last night. She had been gazing at the stars through her window, unaware just when they dissolved into summer rain, although she remembered opening a brown eye in time to see the two-pronged lightning plunge through a cloud and spread its running fire in all directions. And though she was sometimes afraid she would be hurt by it (this was her particular fear) she did not get up to shut the window but watched the writhing flame roll across the sky, until it disappeared over the horizon. The night was drenched and fragrant. Without the others knowing, she had slipped on a dress and gone across the road to walk in a field of daisies whose white stars lit up her bare feet as she thought of tomorrow in much the way she had at sixteen.

Tonight was a high, free evening, still green and gold above the white fortress of buildings on Michigan Avenue, yet fading over the lake, from violet to the first blue of night. A breeze with a breath of autumn in it, despite that afternoon's heat in the city, blew at intervals through the trees. From time to time she caught herself glancing, sometimes frowning, at her wristwatch although it was her own fault she had come so early. Her arms showed gooseflesh and she wondered if she had been rash to wear a thin dress at night but that was silly because the night was warm. It did not take her long to comprehend that the gooseflesh was not for now but another time, long ago, a time she was, however, no longer afraid to remember.

Half her life ago, just out of childhood it seemed, but that couldn't be because she was too strangely ready for the irrevocable change that followed, she had one night alone in the movies met a man twice her age, with whom she had gone walking in the park. Sensing at once what he so unyieldingly desired, she felt instead of fright, amazement at her willingness to respond, considering she was not, like some she later met, starved of affection. But a mother's love was one thing, and his, when he embraced her under the thick-leaved tree that covered them, was something else again. She had all she could do to tear herself away from him, and rushed through the branches, scratching her face and arms in the bargain. But he would not let her go, leading her always into dark places, hidden from all but the light of the stars, and taught her with his kisses that she could race without running. All but bursting with motion she cried don't look, and when he restlessly turned away, undressed the bottom half of her. She offered herself in a white dress and bare feet and was considerably surprised when he pounced like a tiger.

A horn hooted.

It was Roy driving a hired car. He looked around for a parking place but she had slipped on her shoes and waved she was coming.

He had come across her picture in one of the morning papers the day after he had knocked out the homer for the kid. Slicing it out carefully with his knife, he folded it without creasing the face and kept it in his wallet. Whenever he had a minute to himself (he was a smashing success at bat—five for five, three home runs—and was lionized by all) he took the picture out and studied it, trying to figure out why she had done that for him; nobody else ever had. Usually when he was down he was down alone, without flowers or mourners. He suspected she might be batty or a grownup bobby soxer gone nuts over him for having his name and picture in the papers. But from the intelligent look of her it didn't seem likely. There were some players the ladies might fall for through seeing their pictures but not him—not that he was bad-looking or anything, just that he was no dream boy—nor was she the type to do it. In her wide eyes he saw something which caused him to believe she knew what life was like, though you really couldn't be sure.

He made up his mind and telephoned the photographer who had taken this shot of her, for any information he might have as to where she lived, but at his office they said he was covering a forest fire in Minnesota. During the game that afternoon Roy scanned the stands around him and in the fifth frame located her practically at his elbow in deep left. He got one of the ushers to take her a note saying could she meet him tonight? She wrote back not tonight but enclosed her phone number. After a shot of Scotch he called her. Her voice was interesting but she said frankly she wondered if their acquaintance ought to end now, because these things could be disillusioning when they dragged past their time. He said he didn't think she would disappoint him. After some coaxing she yielded, chiefly because Roy insisted he wanted to thank her in person for her support of him.

He held the door open and she stepped in.

"I'm Iris Lemon," she said with a blush.

"Roy Hobbs." He felt foolish for of course she knew his name. Despite his good intentions he was disappointed right off, because she was heavier than he had thought—the picture didn't show that so much or if it did he hadn't noticed—and she had lost something, in this soft brown dress, that she'd had in the red. He didn't like them hefty, yet on second thought it couldn't be said she really was. Big, yes, but shapely too. Her face and hair were pretty and her body—she knew what to wear on her feet—was well proportioned. He admitted she was attractive although as a rule he never thought so unless they were slim like Memo.

So he asked her right out was she married.

She seemed startled, then smiled and said, "No, are you?"

"Nope."

"How is it the girls missed you?"

Though tempted to go into a long explanation about that, he let it pass with a shrug. Neither of them was looking at the other. They both stared at the road ahead. The car hadn't moved.

Iris felt she had been mistaken to come. He seemed so big and bulky next to her, and close up looked disappointingly different from what she had expected. In street clothes he gained little and lost more, a warrior's quality he showed in his uniform. Now he looked like any big-muscled mechanic or bartender on his night off. Whatever difference could it have made to her that this particular one had slumped? She was amazed at her sentimentality.

Roy was thinking about Memo. If not for her he wouldn't be here trying to make himself at ease with this one. She hadn't treated him right. For a while things had looked good between them but no sooner had he gone into a slump when she began again to avoid him. Had she been nice to him instead, he'd have got out of his trouble sooner. However, he wasn't bitter, because Memo was remote, even unreal. Strange how quick he forgot what she was like, though he couldn't what she looked like. Yet with that thought even her image went up in smoke. Iris, a stranger, had done for him what the other wouldn't, in public view what's more. He felt for her a gratitude it was hard to hold in.

"When you get to know me better you will like me more." He surprised himself with that—the hoarse remark echoed within him—and she, sure she had misjudged him, felt a catch in her throat as she replied, "I like you now."

He stepped on the starter and they drove off in the lilac dusk. Where to? he had asked and she had said it made no difference, she liked to ride. He felt, once they started, as if he had been sprung from the coop, and only now, as the white moon popped into the sky, did he begin to appreciate how bad it had been with him during the time of his slump.

They drove so they could almost always see the lake. The new moon climbed higher in the blue night, shedding light like rain. They drove along the lit highway to where the lake turned up into Indiana and they could see the lumpy yellow dunes along the shore. Elsewhere the land was shadowless and flat except for a few trees here and there. Roy turned into a winding dirt road and before long they came to this deserted beach, enclosed in a broken arc of white birches. The wind here was balmy and the water lit on its surface.

He shut off the motor. In the silence—everything but the lapping of the lake water—they too were silent. He hesitated at what next move to make and she prayed it would be the right one although she was not quite sure what she meant.

Roy asked did she want to get out. She understood he wanted her to so she said yes. But she surprised him by saying she had been here before.

"How's the water?" he asked.

"Cold. The whole lake is, but you get used to it soon."

They walked along the shore and then to a cluster of birches. Iris sat on the ground under one of the trees and slipped off her shoes. Her movements were graceful, she made her big feet seem small.

He sat nearby, his eyes on her. She sensed he wanted to

talk but now felt curiously unconcerned with his problems. She had not expected the night to be this beautiful. Since it was, she asked no more than to be allowed to enjoy it.

But Roy impatiently asked her why she had stood up for him the other night.

She did not immediately reply.

After a minute he asked again.

"I don't know," Iris sighed.

That was not the answer he had expected.

"How come?"

"I've been trying to explain it to myself." She lit a cigarette.

He was now a little in awe of her, something he had not foreseen, though he pretended not to be.

"You're a Knights fan, ain't you?"

"No."

"Then how come—I don't get it."

"I'm not a baseball fan but I like to read about the different players. That's how I became interested in you—your career."

"You read about my slump?" His throat tightened at the word.

"Yes, and before that of your triumphs."

"Ever see me play—before the other night?"

She shook her head. "Once then and again yesterday."

"Why'd you come—the first time?"

She rubbed her cigarette into the dirt. "Because I hate to see a hero fail. There are so few of them."

She said it seriously and he felt she meant it.

"Without heroes we're all plain people and don't know how far we can go."

"You mean the big guys set the records and the little buggers try and bust them?"

"Yes, it's their function to be the best and for the rest of us to understand what they represent and guide ourselves accordingly."

He hadn't thought of it that way but it sounded all right.

"There are so many young boys you influence."

"That's right," said Roy.

"You've got to give them your best."

"I try to do that."

"I mean as a man too."

He nodded.

"I felt that if you knew people believed in you, you'd regain your power. That's why I stood up in the grandstand. I hadn't meant to before I came. It happened naturally. Of course I was embarrassed but I don't think you can do anything for anyone without giving up something of your own. What I gave up was my privacy among all those people. I hope you weren't ashamed of me?"

He shook his head. "Were you praying for me to smack one over the roof?"

"I hoped you might become yourself again."

"I was jinxed," Roy explained to her. "Something was keeping me out of my true form. Up at the plate I was blind as a bat and Wonderboy had the heebie jeebies. But when you stood up and I saw you with that red dress on and thought to myself she is with me even if nobody else is, it broke the whammy."

Iris laughed.

Roy crawled over to her and laid his head in her lap. She let him. Her dress was scented with lilac and clean laundry smell. Her thighs were firm under his head. He got a cigar out of his pocket and lit it but it stank up the night so he flung it away.

"I sure am glad you didn't stand me up," he sighed.

"Who would?" she smiled.

"You don't know the half of it."

She softly said she was willing to.

Roy struggled with himself. The urge to tell her was strong. On the other hand, talk about his inner self was always like plowing up a graveyard.

She saw the sweat gleaming on his brow. "Don't if you don't feel like it."

"Everything came out different than I thought." His eyes were clouded.

"In what sense?"

"Different."

"I don't understand."

He coughed, tore his voice clear and blurted, "My goddamn life didn't turn out like I wanted it to."

"Whose does?" she said cruelly. He looked up. Her expression was tender.

The sweat oozed out of him. "I wanted everything." His voice boomed out in the silence.

She waited.

"I had a lot to give to this game."

"Life?"

"Baseball. If I had started out fifteen years ago like I tried to, I'da been the king of them all by now."

"The king of what?"

"The best in the game," he said impatiently.

She sighed deeply. "You're so good now."

"I'da been better. I'da broke most every record there was."

"Does that mean so much to you?"

"Sure," he answered. "It's like what you said before. You break the records and everybody else tries to catch up with you if they can."

"Couldn't you be satisfied with just breaking a few?"

Her pinpricking was beginning to annoy him. "Not if I could break most of them," he insisted.

"But I don't understand why you should make so much of that. Are your values so—"

He heard a train hoot and went freezing cold.

"Where's that train?" he cried, jumping to his feet.

"What train?"

He stared into the night.

"The one I just heard."

"It must have been a bird cry. There are no trains here."

He gazed at her suspiciously but then relaxed and sat down.

"That way," he continued with what he had been saying, "if you leave all those records that nobody else can beat—they'll always remember you. You sorta never die."

"Are you afraid of death?"

Roy stared at her listening face. "Now what has that got to do with it?"

She didn't answer. Finally he laid his head back on her lap, his eyes shut.

She stroked his brow slowly with her fingers.

"What happened fifteen years ago, Roy?"

Roy felt like crying, yet he told her—the first one he ever

had. "I was just a kid and I got shot by this batty dame on the night before my tryout, and after that I just couldn't get started again. I lost my confidence and everything I did flopped."

He said this was the shame of his life, that his fate, somehow, had always been the same (on the train going nowhere)—defeat in sight of his goal.

"Always?"

"Always the same."

"Always with a woman?"

He laughed harshly. "I sure met some honeys in my time. They burned me good."

"Why do you pick that type?"

"It's like I say—they picked me. It's the breaks."

"You could say no, couldn't you?"

"Not to that dame I always fell for—they weren't like you."

She smiled.

"I mean you are a different kind."

"Does that finish me?"

"No," he said seriously.

"I won't ever hurt you, Roy."

"No."

"Don't ever hurt me."

"No."

"What beats me," he said with a trembling voice, "is why did it always have to happen to me? What did I do to deserve it?"

"Being stopped before you started?"

He nodded.

"Perhaps it was because you were a good person?"

"How's that?"

"Experience makes good people better."

She was staring at the lake.

"How does it do that?"

"Through their suffering."

"I had enough of that," he said in disgust.

"We have two lives, Roy, the life we learn with and the life we live with after that. Suffering is what brings us toward happiness."

"I had it up to here." He ran a finger across his windpipe.

"Had what?"

"What I suffered—and I don't want any more."

"It teaches us to want the right things."

"All it taught me is to stay away from it. I am sick of all I have suffered."

She shrank away a little.

He shut his eyes.

Afterwards, sighing, she began to rub his brow, and then his lips.

"And is that the mystery about you, Roy?"

"What mystery?"

"I don't know. Everyone seems to think there is one."

"I told you everything."

"Then there really isn't?"

"Nope."

Her cool fingers touched his eyelids. It was unaccountably sweet to him.

"You broke my jinx," he muttered.

"I'm thirty-three," she said, looking at the moonlit water.

He whistled but said, "I am no spring chicken either, honey."

"Iris."

"Iris, honey."

"That won't come between us?"

"What?"

"My age?"

"No."

"Nothing?"

"If you are not married?"

"No."

"Divorced?"

"No."

"A widow?"

"No," said Iris.

He opened his eyes. "How come with all your sex appeal that you never got hitched?"

She gazed away.

Roy suddenly sat up and bounced to his feet. "Jesus, will you look at that water. What are we waiting for?" He tore at his tie.

Iris was saying that she had, however, brought a child into the world, a girl now grown, but Roy seemed not to hear, he was so busy getting out of his clothes. In no time to speak of he stood before her stripped to his shorts.

"Get undressed."

The thought of standing naked before him frightened her. She told herself not to be—she was no longer a child about the naked body. But she couldn't bring herself to remove her clothes in front of him so she went back to the car and undressed there. He waited impatiently, then before he expected her, she stepped out without a thing on and ran in the moonlight straight into the water, through the shallow part, and dived where it was deep.

Hopping high through the cold water, Roy plunged in after her. He dived neatly, kicked hard underwater and came up almost under her. Iris fell back out of his reach and swam away. He pursued her with less skill than she had but more strength. At first he damn near froze but as he swam his blood warmed. She would not stop and before long the white birches near the beach looked to be the size of match sticks.

Though they were only a dozen strokes apart she wouldn't let him gain, and after another fifty tiring yards he wondered how long this would go on. He called to her but she didn't answer and wouldn't stop. He was beginning to be winded and considered quitting, only he didn't want to give up. Then just about when his lungs were frying in live coals, she stopped swimming. As she trod water, the light on the surface hid all but her head from him.

He caught up with her at last and attempted to get his arms around her waist. "Give us a kiss, honey."

She was repelled and shoved him away.

He saw she meant it, realized he had made a mistake, and felt terrible.

Roy turned tail, kicking himself down into the dark water. As he sank lower it got darker and colder but he kept going down. Before long the water turned murky yet there was no bottom he could feel with his hands. Though his legs and arms were numb he continued to work his way down, filled with icy apprehensions and weird thoughts.

Iris couldn't believe it when he did not quickly rise. Before long she felt frightened. She looked everywhere but he was still under water. A sense of abandonment gripped her. She remembered standing up in the crowd that night, and said to herself that she had really stood up because he was a man whose life she wanted to share . . . a man who had suffered. She thought distractedly of a home, children, and him coming home every night to supper. But he had already left her . . .

. . . At last in the murk he touched the liquid mud at the bottom. He dimly thought he ought to feel proud to have done that but his mind was crammed with old memories flitting back and forth like ghostly sardines, and there wasn't a one of them that roused his pride or gave him any comfort.

So he forced himself, though sleepily, to somersault up and begin the slow task of climbing through all the iron bars of the currents . . . too slow, too tasteless, and he wondered was it worth it.

Opening his bloodshot eyes he was surprised how far down the moonlight had filtered. It dripped down like oil in the black water, and then, unexpectedly, there came into his sight this pair of golden arms searching, and a golden head with a frantic face. Even her hair sought him.

He felt relieved no end.

I am a lucky bastard.

He was climbing a long, slow ladder, broad at the base and narrowing on top, and she, trailing clusters of white bubbles, was weaving her way to him. She had golden breasts and when he looked to see, the hair between her legs was golden too.

With a watery howl bubbling from his blistered lungs he shot past her inverted eyes and bobbed up on the surface, inhaling the soothing coolness of the whole sky.

She rose beside him, gasping, her hair plastered to her naked skull, and kissed him full on the lips. He tore off his shorts and held her tight. She stayed in his arms.

"Why did you do it?" she wept.

"To see if I could touch the bottom."

They swam in together, taking their time. As they dragged themselves out of the water, she said, "Go make a fire, otherwise we will have nothing to dry ourselves with."

He covered her shoulders with his shirt and went hunting for wood. Under the trees he collected an armload of branches. Near the dunes he located some heavy boxwood. Then he came back to where she was sitting and began to build a fire. He set an even row of birch sticks down flat and with his knife shaved up a thick branch till he had a pile of dry shavings. These he lit with the only match he had. When they were burning he added some dry birch pieces he had cut up. He split the boxwood against a rock and when the fire was crackling added that, hunk by hunk, to the flames. Before long he had a roaring blaze going. The fire reddened the water and the lacy birches.

It reddened her naked body. Her thighs and rump were broad but her waist was narrow and virginal. Her breasts were hard, shapely. From above her hips she looked like a girl but the lower half of her looked like a woman.

Watching her, he thought he would wait for the fire to die down, when she was warm and dry and felt not rushed.

She was sitting close to the fire with her hair pulled over her head so the inside would dry first. She was thinking why did he go down? Did he touch the bottom of the lake out of pride, because he wants to make records, or did he do it in disappointment, because I wouldn't let him kiss me?

Roy was rubbing his hands before the fire. She looked up and said in a tremulous voice, "Roy, I have a confession to you. I was never married, but I am the mother of a grown girl."

He said he had heard her the first time.

She brushed her hair back with her fingers. "I don't often talk about it, but I want to tell you I made a mistake long ago and had a hard time afterwards. Anyway, the child meant everything to me and made me happy. I gave her a good upbringing and now she is grown and on her own, I am free to think of myself and young enough to want to."

That was the end of it because Roy asked no questions.

He watched the fire. The flames sank low. When they had just about been sucked into the ashes he crept toward her and took her in his arms. Her breasts beat like hearts against him.

"You are really the first," she whispered.

He smiled, never so relaxed in sex.

But while he was in the middle of loving her she spoke: "I forgot to tell you I am a grandmother."

He stopped. Holy Jesus.

Then she remembered something else and tried, in fright, to raise herself.

"Roy, are you—"

But he shoved her back and went on from where he had left off.

After a hilarious celebration in the dining car (which they roused to uproar by tossing baked potatoes and ketchup bottles around) and later in the Pullman, where a wild bunch led by Roy stripped the pajamas off players already sound asleep in their berths, peeled Red Blow out of his long underwear, and totally demolished the pants of a new summer suit of Pop's, who was anyway not sold on premature celebrations, Roy slept restlessly. In his sleep he knew he was restless and blamed it (in his sleep) on all he had eaten. The Knights had come out of Sportsman's Park after trouncing the Cards in a double header and making it an even dozen in a row without a loss, and the whole club had gone gay on the train, including, mildly, Pop himself, considerably thawed out now that the team had leap-frogged over the backs of the Dodgers and Cards into third place. They were again hot on the heels of the Phils and not too distant from the Pirates, with a whole month to go before the end of the season, and about sixty per cent of their remaining games on home grounds. Roy was of course in fine fettle, the acknowledged King of Klouters, whose sensational hitting, pulverizing every kind of pitching, more than made up for his slump. Yet no matter how many bangs he collected, he was ravenously hungry for more and all he could eat besides. The Knights had boarded the train at dinner time but he had stopped off at the station to devour half a dozen franks smothered in sauerkraut and he guzzled down six bottles of pop before his meal on the train, which consisted of two oversize sirloins, at least a dozen rolls, four orders of mashed, and three (some said five) slabs of apple pie. Still that didn't do the trick, for while they were all at cards that evening, he sneaked off the train as it was being hosed and oiled and hustled up another three wieners, and later secretly arranged with the steward for a midnight snack of a long T-bone with trimmings, although that did not keep him from waking several times during the night with pangs of hunger.

When the diner opened in the morning he put away an enormous breakfast and afterwards escaped those who were up, and found himself some privacy in a half-empty coach near the engine, where nobody bothered him because he was not too recognizable in gabardine, behind dark glasses. For a while he stared at the scattered outskirts of the city they were passing through, but in reality he was wondering whether to read the fat letter from Iris Lemon he had been carrying around in his suit pocket. Roy recalled the night on the lake shore, the long swim, the fire and after. The memory of all was not unpleasant, but what for the love of mud had made her take him for a sucker who would be interested in a grandmother? He found that still terrifying to think of, and although she was a nice enough girl, it had changed her in his mind from Iris more to lemon. To do her justice he concentrated on her good looks and the pleasures of her body but when her kid's kid came to mind, despite grandma's age of only thirty-three, that was asking too much and spoiled the appetizing part of her. It was simple enough to him: if he got serious with her it could only lead to one thing—him being a grandfather. God save him from that for he personally felt as young and frisky as a colt. That was what he told himself as the train sped east, and though he had a slight bellyache he fell into a sound sleep and dreamed how on frosty mornings when he was a kid the white grass stood up prickly stiff and the frozen air deep-cleaned his insides.

He awoke with Memo on his mind. To his wonder she turned up in his room in Boston the next night. It was after supper and he was sitting in a rocker near the window reading about himself in the paper when she knocked. He opened the door and she could have thrown him with a breath, so great was his surprise (and sadness) at seeing her. Memo laughingly said she had been visiting a girl friend's summer place on the Cape, and on her way back to New York had heard the boys were in town so she stopped off to say hello, and here she was. Her face and arms were tanned and she looked better than she had in a long while. He felt too that she had changed somehow in the weeks he hadn't seen her. That made him uneasy, as if any change in her would automatically be to his hurt. He searched her face but could not uncover anything new so explained it as the five pounds she said she had put on since he had seen her last.

He felt he still held it against her for giving him very little support at a time when he could use a lot, and also for turning Pop down when he had invited her to join them on the Western trip. Yet here, alone with her in his room, she so close and inevitably desirable—this struck him with the force of an unforgettable truth: the one he had had and always wanted—he thought it wouldn't do to put on a sourpuss and make complaints. True, there was something about her, like all the food he had lately been eating, that left him, after the having of it, unsatisfied, sometimes even with a greater hunger than before. Yet she was a truly beautiful doll with a form like Miss America, and despite the bumps and bruises he had taken, he was sure that once he got an armlock on her things would go better.

His face must have shown more than he intended, because she turned moodily to the window and said, "Roy, don't bawl me out for not seeing you for a while. There are some things I just can't take and one of them is being with people who are blue. I had too much of that in my life with my mother and it really makes me desperate." More tenderly she said, "That's why I had to stand off to the side, though I didn't like to, and wait till you had worked out of it, which I knew you would do. Now here I am the first chance I got and that is the way it used to be between Bump and me."

Roy said soberly, "When are you going to find out that I ain't Bump, Memo?"

"Don't be mad," she said, lifting her face to him. "All I meant to say is that I treat all my friends the same." She was close and warm-breathed. He caught her in his arms and she snuggled tight, and let him feel the "sick" breast without complaining. But when he tried to edge her to the bed, she broke for air and said no.

"Why not?" he demanded.

"I'm not well," said Memo.

He was suspicious. "What's wrong?"

Memo laughed. "Sometimes you are very innocent, Roy. When a girl says she is not well, does she have to draw you a map?"

Then he understood and was embarrassed for being so dimwitted. He did not insist on any more necking and thought it a good sign that she had talked to him so intimately.

The Knights took their three in Boston and the next day won a twi-night double header in Ebbets Field, making it seventeen straight wins on the comeback climb. Before Roy ended his slump they had fallen into fifth place, twelve games behind, then they slowly rose to third, and after this twin bill with Brooklyn, were within two of the Phils, who had been nip and tucking it all season with the Cards and Dodgers. The Pirates, though beaten three in a row by the Knights on their Western swing (the first Knight wins over them this season) were still in first place, two games ahead of the Phils in a tight National League race.

When the Knights returned to their home grounds for a three-game set with the cellar-dwelling Reds, the city awakened in a stampede. The fans, recovered from their stunned surprise at the brilliant progress of the team, turned out in droves. They piled into the stands with foolish smiles, for most of them had sworn off the Knights during the time of Roy's slump. Now for blocks around the field, the neighborhood was in an uproar as hordes fought their way out of subways, trolleys and buses, and along the packed streets to ticket windows that had been boarded up (to Judge Banner's heartfelt regret) from early that morning, while grunting lines of red-faced cops, reinforced by sweating mounties, tried to shove everybody back where they had come from. After many amused years at the expense of the laughingstock Knights, a scorching pennant fever blew through the city. Everywhere people were bent close to their radios or stretching their necks in bars to have a look at the miracle boys (so named by sportswriters from all over the U.S. who now crammed into the once deserted press boxes) whose every move aroused their fanatic supporters to a frenzy of excitement which whirled out of them in concentric rings around the figure of Roy Hobbs, hero and undeniable man of destiny. He, it was said by everyone, would lead the Knights to it.

The fans dearly loved Roy but Roy did not love the fans. He hadn't forgotten the dirty treatment they had dished out during the time of his trouble. Often he felt he would like to ram their cheers down their throats. Instead he took it out on the ball, pounding it to a pulp, as if the best way to get even with the fans, the pitchers who had mocked him, and the statisticians who had recorded (forever) the kind and quantity of his failures, was to smash every conceivable record. He was like a hunter stalking a bear, a whale, or maybe the sight of a single fleeing star the way he went after that ball. He gave it no rest (Wonderboy, after its long famine, chopping, chewing, devouring) and was not satisfied unless he lifted it (one eye cocked as he swung) over the roof and spinning toward the horizon. Often, for no accountable reason, he hated the pill, which represented more of himself than he was willing to give away for nothing to whoever found it one dull day in a dirty lot. Sometimes as he watched the ball soar, it seemed to him all circles, and he was mystified at his devotion to hacking at it, for he had never really liked the sight of a circle. They got you nowhere but back to the place you were to begin with, yet here he stood banging them like smoke rings out of Wonderboy and everybody cheered like crazy. The more they cheered the colder he got to them. He couldn't stop hitting and every hit made him hungry for the next (a doctor said he had no tapeworm but ate like that because he worked so hard), yet he craved no cheers from the slobs in the stands. Only once he momentarily forgave them—when reaching for a fly, he almost cracked into the wall and they gasped their fright and shrieked warnings. After he caught the ball he doffed his cap and they rocked the rafters with their thunder.

The press, generally snotty to him during his slump, also changed its tune. To a man (except one) they showered him with praise, whooped him on, and in their columns unofficially accoladed him Rookie of the Year (although they agreed he resembled nothing so much as an old hand, a toughened veteran of baseball wars) and Most Valuable Player, and years before it was time talked of nominating him for a permanent niche in the Cooperstown Hall of Fame. He belonged, they wrote, with the other immortals, a giant in performance, who resembled the burly boys of the eighties and nineties more than the streamlined kids of today. He was a throwback to a time of true heroes, not of the brittle, razzle dazzle boys that had sprung up around the jack rabbit ball—a natural not seen in a dog's age, and weren't they the lucky ones he had appeared here and now to work his wonders before them? More than one writer held his aching head when he speculated on all Roy might have accomplished had he come into the game at twenty.

The exception was of course Mercy, who continued to concern himself with Roy's past rather than his accomplishments. He spent hours in the morgue, trying to dredge up possible clues to possible crimes (What's he hiding from me?), wrote for information to prison wardens, sheriffs, county truant officers, heads of orphan asylums, and semipro managers in many cities in the West and Northwest, and by offering rewards, spurred all sorts of research on Roy by small-town sportswriters. His efforts proved fruitless until one day, to his surprise, he got a letter from a man who block printed on a sheet of notebook paper that for two hundred bucks he might be tempted to tell a thing or two about the new champ. Max hastily promised the dough and got his first break. Here was an old sideshow freak who swore that Roy had worked as a clown in a small traveling carnival. For proof he sent a poster showing the clown's face—in his white and red warpaint—bursting through a paper hoop. Roy was recognizable as the snubnose Bobo, who despite the painted laugh on his pan, seemed sadeyed and unhappy. Certain the picture would create a sensation, Max had it printed on the first page above the legend, "Roy Hobbs, Clown Prince of Baseball," but most of those who bought the paper refused to believe it was Roy and those who did, didn't give a hoot.

Roy was burned about the picture and vowed to kick the

blabbermouth in the teeth. But he didn't exactly do that, for when they met the next evening, in the Midtown lobby, Max made a handsome apology. He said he had to hand it to Roy for beating everybody else in the game ten different ways, and he was sorry about the picture. Roy nodded but didn't show up on time at the chophouse down the block, where he was awaited by Pop, Red, and Max—to Pop's uneasiness, because Roy was prompt for his meals these days.

The waiter, a heavyset German with a schmaltzy accent and handlebar mustaches, approached for their orders. He started the meal by spilling soup on Max's back, then serving him a steak that looked like the charcoal it had been broiled on. When Max loudly complained he brought him, after fifteen minutes, another, a bleeding beauty, but this the waiter snatched from under the columnist's knife because he had already collected Pop's and Red's finished plates and wanted the third. Max let out a yawp, the frightened waiter dropped the dishes on his lap, and while stooping to collect the pieces, lurched against the table and spilled Max's beer all over his pants.

Pop sprang up and took an angry swipe at the man but Red hauled him down. Meanwhile the waiter was trying to wipe Max's pants with a wet towel and Max was swearing bloody murder at him. This got the waiter sore. Seizing the columnist by his coat collar he shook him and said he would teach him to talk like a "shentleman und nod a slob." He laid Max across his knee, and as the customers in the chophouse looked on in disbelief, smacked his rear with a heavy hand. Max managed to twist himself free. Slapping frantically at the German's face, he knocked off his mustache. In a minute everybody in the place was shrieking with laughter, and even Pop had to smile though he said to Red he was not at all surprised it had turned out to be Roy.

Roy had a Saturday date with Memo coming up but he was lonely for her that night so he went up to the fourth floor and rang her buzzer. She opened the door, dressed in black lounging pajamas with a black ribbon tied around her horsetail of red hair, which had a stunning effect on him.

Memo's face lit in a slow blush. "Why, Roy," she said, and seemed not to know what else to say.

"Shut the door," came a man's annoyed voice from inside, "or I might catch a cold."

"Gus is here," Memo quickly explained. "Come on in."

Roy entered, greatly disappointed.

Memo lived in a large and airy one-room apartment with a kitchenette, and a Murphy bed out of sight. Gus Sands, smoking a Between-the-Acts little cigar, was sitting at a table near the curtained window, examining a hand of double solitaire he and Memo had been playing. His coat was hanging on the chair and a hand-painted tie that Roy didn't like, showing a naked lady dancing with a red rose, hung like a tongue out of his unbuttoned vest, over a heavy gold watch chain.

Seeing who it was, Gus said, "Welcome home, slugger. I see you have climbed out of the hole that you were in."

"I suppose it cost you a couple of bucks," said Roy.

Gus was forced to laugh. He had extended his hand but Roy didn't shake. Memo glanced at Roy as if to say be nice to Gus.

Roy couldn't get rid of his irritation that he had found Gus here, and he felt doubly annoyed that she was still seeing him. He had heard nothing from her about Gus and had hoped the bookie was out of the picture, but here he was as shifty-eyed as ever. What she saw in this half-bald apology for a cigar store Indian had him beat, yet he was conscious of a fear in his chest that maybe Gus meant more to her than he had guessed. The thought of them sitting peacefully together playing cards gave him the uneasy feeling they might even be married or something. But that couldn't be because it didn't make sense. In the first place why would she marry a freak like Gus? Sure he had the bucks but Memo was a hot kid and she couldn't take them to bed with her. And how could she stand what he looked like in the morning without the glass eye in the slot? In the second place Gus wouldn't let *his* wife walk around without a potato-sized diamond, and the only piece of jewelry Memo wore was a ring with small jade stone. Besides, what would they be doing here in this one-room box when Gus owned a penthouse apartment on Central Park West?

No. He blamed these fantastic thoughts on the fact that he was still not sure of her. And he kept wishing he could have her to himself tonight. Memo caught on because, when he looked at her, she shrugged.

Gus got suspicious. He stared at them with the baleful eye, the glass one frosty.

They were sitting around uncomfortably until Memo suggested they play cards. Gus cheered up at once.

"What'll it be, slugger?" he said, collecting the cards.

"Pinochle is the game for three."

"I hate pinochle," Memo said. "Let's play poker but not the open kind."

"Poker is not wise now," Gus said. "The one in the middle gets squeezed. Anybody like to shoot crap?"

He brought forth a pair of green dominoes. Roy said he was agreeable and Memo nodded. Gus wanted to roll on the table but Roy said the rug was better, with the dice bouncing against the wall.

They moved the table and squatted on the floor. Memo, kneeling, rolled first. Gus told her to fade high and in a few minutes she picked up two hundred dollars. Roy hit snake eyes right off, then sevened out after that. Gus shot, teasing Roy to cover the three one-hundred dollar bills he had put down. Memo took twenty-five of it and Roy had the rest. Gus made his point and on the next roll took another two hundred from Roy. That was more than he was carrying in cash but Gus said he could play the rest of the game on credit. The bookie continued to roll passes. In no time he was twelve hundred in on Roy, not counting the cash he had lost. Roy was irritated because he didn't like to lose to Gus in front of Memo. He watched Gus's hands to make sure he wasn't palming another pair of dice. What made him suspicious was that Gus seemed to be uncomfortable. His glass eye was fastened on the dice but the good one roamed restlessly about. And he was now fading three hundred a throw and sidebetting high. Since Memo was taking only a ten spot here and there, Roy was covering the rest. By the end of Gus's second streak Roy was thirty-five hundred behind and his underwear was sweating. Gus finally went out, Memo quickly lost, then Roy, to his surprise, started off on a string of passes.

Now he was hot and rolled the cubes for a long haul, growing merrier by the minute as Gus grew glummer. Before Roy was through, Gus had returned the cash he had taken from him and owed him eleven hundred besides. When Roy finally hit seven, Memo got up and said she had to make coffee. Gus and Roy played on but Roy was still the lucky one. Gus said the dice ought never to be played with less than four and gave up in disgust. He dusted off his knees.

"You sure had luck in your pants tonight, slugger."

"Some call it that."

Memo added the figures. She owed Roy two ten but Gus owed him twenty-one hundred. Roy laughed out loud.

Gus wrote out a check, his eye still restless.

Memo said she would write one too.

"Forget it," Roy said.

"I have covered hers in mine," said Gus, circling his pen around before signing.

Memo flushed. "I like to pay my own way."

Gus tore up the check and wrote another. Seeing how she felt about it, Roy took Memo's, figuring he would return it in the form of some present or other.

Gus handed him a check for twenty-one hundred. "Chicken feed," he said.

Roy gave the paper a loud smack with his lips. "I love it."

Gus dropped his guard and pinned his restless eye on Roy. "Say the word, slugger, and you can make yourself a nice pile of dough quick."

Roy wasn't sure he had heard right. Gus repeated the offer.

This time Roy was sure. "Say it again and I will spit in your good eye."

Gus's grayish complexion turned blue.

"Boys," Memo said uneasily.

Gus stalked into the bathroom.

Memo's face was pale. "Help me with the sandwiches, Roy."

"Did you hear what that bastard said to me?"

"Sometimes he talks through his hat."

"Why do you invite him here?"

She turned away. "He invited himself."

As she was slicing meat for the sandwiches Roy felt tender

toward her. He slipped his arm around her waist. She looked up a little unhappily but when he kissed her she kissed back. They broke apart as Gus unlocked the bathroom door and came out glaring at them.

While they were all drinking coffee Roy was in good spirits and no longer minded that Gus was around. Memo kidded him about the way he wolfed the sandwiches, but she showed her affection by also serving him half a cold chicken which he picked to the bone. He demolished a large slab of chocolate cake and made a mental note for a hamburger or two before he went to bed. Though Gus had only had a cup of coffee he was thoughtfully picking his teeth. After a while he looked at his gold watch, buttoned his vest, and said he was going. Roy glanced at Memo but she yawned and said she had to get up very very early in the morning.

To everybody's disgust the Reds, as if contemptuous of the bums who had so long lived in the basement below them, snapped the Knights' streak at seventeen and the next day again beat them over a barrel. A great groan went up from the faithful. Stand back everybody, here they go again. Timber! As if by magic, attendance for a single game with the Phils sank to a handful. The Phils gave them another spanking. The press tipped their hats and turned their respectful attention to the Pirates, pointing out again how superb they were. It was beyond everybody how the half-baked Knights could ever hope to win the N.L. pennant. With twenty-one games left to play they were six behind the Pirates and four in back of the Phils. And to make matters worse, they'd fallen into a third-place tie with the Cards. Pop's boys still retained a mathematical chance all right but they were at best a first-rate third-place team, one writer put it, and ended his piece, "Wait till next year."

Pop held his suffering head. The players stole guilty looks at one another. Even the Great Man himself was in a rut, though not exactly a slump. Still, he was held by inferior pitching to three constipated singles in three days. Everyone on the team was conscious something drastic had to be done but none could say what. Time was after them with a bludgeon. Any game they lost was the last to lose. It was autumn almost. They saw leaves falling and shivered at the thought of the barren winds of winter.

The Pirates blew into town for their last games of the year with the Knights, a series of four. Thus far during the season they had trounced the Knights a fantastic 15–3 and despite the loss of their last three to the Knights (fool's luck) were prepared to blast them out of their field. Watching the way the Pirates cut up the pea patch with their merciless hitting and precision fielding, the New Yorkers grew more dejected. Here was a team that was really a team, not a Rube Goldberg contraption. Every man jack was a fine player and no one guy outstanding. The Knights' fans were embarrassed . . . Yet their boys managed to tease the first away from the Pirates. No one quite knew how, here a lucky bingle, there a lucky error. Opposite the first-place slickers they looked like hayseeds yet the harvest was theirs. But tomorrow was another day. Wait'll the boys from the smoky city had got the stiffness of the train ride out of their legs. Yet the Knights won again in the same, inept way. Their own rooters, seeping back into the stands, whistled and cheered. By some freak of nature they took the third too. The last game was sold out before 10 A.M. Again the cops had trouble with the ticketless hordes that descended on them.

Walt Wickitt, the peerless Pirate manager, pitched his ace hurler, Dutch Vogelman, in the last game. Vogelman was a terrific pitcher, a twenty-three game winner, the only specimen in either league that season. He was poison to the Knights who had beat him only once in the past two years. Facing Roy in some six games, he had held him to a single in four, and crippled him altogether in the last two, during Roy's slump. Most everyone kissed this game goodbye, although Roy started with a homer his first time up. Schultz then gave up two runs to the Pirates. Roy hit another round tripper. Schultz made it three for the Pirates. Roy ended by slamming two more homers and that did it, 4–3. High and mighty to begin with, Vogelman looked like a drowned dog at the end, and the Pirates hurriedly packed their duffel bags and slunk out of the stadium. The Phils were now in first place by a game, the Pirates second, and the Knights were one behind them and coming up like a rocket. Again pennant fever raged through the city and there was cheering in the streets.

Now all that was left for the Knights in this nerve-racking race were four games in Brooklyn, including a Sunday double header, four with Boston and two more with the Reds, these at home. Then three away with the Phils, one of which was the playoff of the washed-out game in June when Roy had knocked the cover off the ball. Their schedule called for the wind-up in the last week of September, against the Reds in another three-game tilt at home, a soft finish, considering the fact that the Pirates and Phils had each other to contend with. If, God willing, the Knights made it (and were still functioning), the World Series was scheduled to begin on Tuesday, October first, at the Yankee Stadium, for the Yanks had already cinched the American League pennant.

The race went touch and go. To begin with the Knights dropped a squeaker (Roy went absolutely hitless) to the Dodgers as the Pirates won and the Phils lost—both now running neck and neck for first, the Knights two behind. Just as the boys were again despairing of themselves, Roy got after the ball again. He did not let on to anyone, but he had undergone a terrible day after his slaughter of the Pirates, a day of great physical weakness, a strange draining of strength from his arms and legs, followed by a splitting headache that whooshed in his ears. However, in the second game at Ebbets Field, he took hold of himself, gripped Wonderboy, and bashed the first pitch into the clock on the right field wall. The clock spattered minutes all over the place, and after that the Dodgers never knew what time it was. All they knew was that Roy Hobbs collected a phenomenal fourteen straight hits that shot them dead three times. Carried on by the momentum, the Knights ripped the Braves and brutally trounced the Reds, taking revenge on them for having ended their recent streak of seventeen.

With only six games to play, a triple first-place tie resulted. The Knights' fans beat themselves delirious, and it became almost unbearable when the Phils lost a heartbreaker to the Cards and dropped into second place, leaving the Pirates and Knights in the tie. Before the Phils could recover, the Knights descended upon Shibe Park, followed by wild trainloads of fans who had to be there to see. They saw their loveboys take the crucial playoff (Roy was terrific), squeak through the second game (he had a poor day), and thoroughly wipe the stunned Phils off the map in the last (again stupendous). At this point of highest tension the Pirate mechanism burst. To the insane cheering of the population of the City of New York, the Cubs pounded them twice, and the Reds came in with a surprise haymaker. A pall of silence descended upon Pennsylvania. Then a roar rose in Manhattan and leaped across the country. When the shouting stopped the Knights were undeniably on top by three over the Pirates, the Phils third by one more, and therefore mathematically out of the race. With three last ones to play against the lowly Reds, the Knights looked *in.* The worst that could possibly happen to them was a first-place tie with the Pirates—if the Pirates won their three from the Phils as the Knights lost theirs to the Reds—a fantastic impossibility the way Roy was mauling them.

The ride home from Philadelphia usually took a little more than an hour but it was a bughouse nightmare because of the way the fans on the train pummeled the players. Hearing that a mob had gathered at Penn Station to welcome the team, Pop ordered everyone off at Newark and into cabs. But as they approached the tunnel they were greeted by a deafening roar as every craft in the Hudson, and all the way down the bay, opened up with whistles and foghorns . . .

In their locker room after the last game at Philly, some of the boys had started chucking wet towels around but Pop, who had privately wept tears of joy, put the squelch on that.

"Cut out all that danged foolishness when we still need one more to win," he had sternly yelled.

When they protested that it looked at last that they were in, he turned lobster red and bellowed did they want to jinx themselves and cook their own gooses? As a result, despite all the attention they were receiving, the boys were a glum bunch going home. Some had secretly talked of celebrating once they had ditched the old fusspot but they were afraid to. Even Roy had fallen into low spirits, only he was thinking of Memo.

His heart ached the way he yearned for her (sometimes seeing her in a house they had bought, with a redheaded baby on her lap, and himself going fishing in a way that made it satisfying to fish, knowing that everything was all right behind him, and the home-cooked meal would be hot and plentiful, and the kid would carry the name of Roy Hobbs into generations his old man would never know. With this in mind he fished the stream in peace and later, sitting around the supper table, they ate the fish he had caught), yearning so deep that the depth ran through ever since he could remember, remembering the countless things he had wanted and missed out on, wondering, now that he was famous, if the intensity of his desires would ever go down. The only way that could happen (he relived that time in bed with her) was to have her always. That would end the dissatisfactions that ate him, no matter how great were his triumphs, and made his life still wanting and not having.

It later struck him that the picture he had drawn of Memo sitting domestically home wasn't exactly the girl she was. The kind he had in mind, though it bothered him to admit it, was more like Iris seemed to be, only she didn't suit him. Yet he could not help but wonder what was in her letter and he made up his mind he would read it once he got back in his room. Not that he would bother to answer, but he ought at least to know what she said.

He felt better, at the hotel, to find a note from Memo in his mailbox, saying to come up and celebrate with a drink. She greeted him at the door with a fresh kiss, her face flushed with how glad she was, saying, "Well, Roy, you've really done it. Everybody is talking about what a wonderful marvel you are."

"We still got this last one to take," he said modestly, though tickled at her praise. "I am not counting my onions till that."

"Oh, the Knights are sure to win. All the papers are saying it all depends what you do. You're the big boy, Roy."

He grabbed both her palms. "Bigger than Bump?"

Her eyelids fluttered but she said yes.

He pulled her close. She kissed for kiss with her warm wet mouth. Now is the time, he thought. Backing her against the wall, he slowly rubbed his hand up between her thighs.

She broke away, breathing heavily. He caught her and pressed his lips against her nippled blouse.

There were tears in her eyes.

He groaned, "Honey, we are the ones that are alive, not him."

"Don't say his name."

"You will forget him when I love you."

"Please let's not talk."

He lifted her in his arms and laid her down on the couch. She sat bolt upright.

"For Christ sakes, Memo, I am a grown guy and not a kid. When are you gonna be nice to me?"

"I am, Roy."

"Not the way I want it."

"I will." She was breathing quietly now.

"When?" he demanded.

She thought, distracted, then said, "Tomorrow—tomorrow night."

"That's too long."

"Later." She sighed, "Tonight."

"You are my sugar honey." He kissed her.

Her mood quickly changed. "Come on, let's celebrate."

"Celebrate what?"

"About the team."

Surprised she wanted to do that now, he said he was shaved and ready to go.

"I don't mean to go out." What she meant, she explained, was that she had prepared a snack in one of the party rooms upstairs. "They're bringing it all up from the kitchen-buffet with cold meats and lots of other things. I thought it'd be fun to get some girls together with the boys and all enjoy ourselves."

Though he had on his mind what he was going to do to her later, and anything in between was a waste of time, still she had gone to all the trouble, and he wanted to please her. Nor was the mention of food exactly distasteful to him. He had made a double steak disappear on the train, but that was hours ago.

Memo served him a drink and finished telephoning the men she couldn't reach before. Though on the whole the players said they wanted to come, some, still remembering Pop, were doubtful they ought to, but Memo convinced them by saying that Roy and others were coming. She didn't ask the married players to bring their wives and they didn't mention the oversight to her.

At ten o'clock Memo went into the bathroom and put on a flaming yellow strapless gown. Roy got the idea that she was wearing nothing underneath and it gave him a tense pleasure. They rode up to the eighteenth floor. The party was already on. There were about a dozen men around but only four or five girls. Memo said more were coming later. Most of the players did not exactly look happy. A few were self-consciously talking to the girls, and the others were sitting on chairs gabbing among themselves. Flores stood in a corner with a melancholy expression on his phiz. Al Fowler, one of those having himself a fine time, called to him when was the wake.

Someone was pounding the keys of the upright piano against the wall. On the other side of the room, a brisk, pint-size chef with a tall puffed cap on, half again as big as him, stood behind a long cloth-covered table, dishing out the delicatessen.

"Sure is some snack," Roy marveled. "You must've hocked your fur coat."

"Gus chipped in," Memo said absently.

He was immediately annoyed. "Is that ape coming up here?"

She looked hurt. "Don't call him dirty names. He is a fine, generous guy."

"Two bits he had the grub poisoned."

"That's not funny." Memo walked away but Roy went after her and apologized, though her concern for the bookie—even on the night they were going to sleep together—unsettled and irritated him. Furthermore, he was now worried how Pop would take it if he found out about the players at this shindig despite his warning against celebrating too soon.

He asked Memo if the manager knew what was going on.

She was sweet again. "Don't worry about him, Roy. I'd've invited him but he wouldn't fit in at all here because we are all young people. Don't get anxious about the party, because Gus said not to serve any hard liquor."

"Nice kid, Gus. Must be laying his paper on us for a change."

Memo made no reply.

Everybody was there by then. Dave Olson had a cheerful blonde on his arm. Allie, Lajong, Hinkle, and Hill were harmonizing "Down by the Old Mill Stream." Fowler was showing some of the boys how to do a buck and wing. The cigar smoke was thick. To Roy things did still not sit just right. Everybody was watching everybody else, as if they were all waiting for a signal to get up and leave, and some of the players looked up nervously every time the door opened, as if they were expecting Doc Knobb, who used to hypnotize them before the games. Flores, from across the room, stared at Roy with black, mournful eyes, but Roy turned away. He couldn't walk out on Memo.

"Some blowout," Fowler said to him.

"Watch yourself, kid," Roy warned him in an undertone.

"Watch yourself yourself."

Roy threw him a hard look but Memo said, "Just let Roy head over to the table. He is dying for a bite."

It was true. Though the thought of having her tonight was on the top of his mind, he could not entirely forget the appetizing food. She led him to the table and he was surprised and slightly trembly at all there was of it—different kinds of delicatessen meat, appetizing fish, shrimp, crab and lobster, also caviar, salads, cheeses of all sorts, bread, rolls, and three flavors of ice cream. It made his belly ache, as if it had an existence apart from himself.

"What'll it be?" said the little chef. He had a large fork and plate poised but Roy took them from him, to his annoyance, and said he would fix what he wanted himself.

Memo helped. "Don't be stingy, Roy."

"Pile it on, honey."

"You sure are a scream the way you eat."

"I am a picnic." He kidded to ease the embarrassment his appetite caused him.

"Bump liked to shovel it down—" She caught herself.

After his plate was loaded, Memo placed a slice of ham and a roll on her own and they sat at a table in the far corner of the room—away from where Flores was standing—so Roy could concentrate on the food without having to bother with anybody.

Memo watched him, fascinated. She shredded the ham on her plate and nibbled on a roll.

"That all you're eating?" he asked.

"I guess I haven't got much appetite."

He was gobbling it down and it gave him a feeling of both having something and wanting it the same minute he was having it. And every mouthful seemed to have the effect of increasing his desire for her. He thought how satisfying it would be to lift that yellow dress over her bare thighs.

Roy didn't realize it till she mentioned it that his plate was empty. "Let me get you some more, hon."

"I will get it myself."

"Food is a woman's work." She took his plate to the table and the busy little chef heaped it high with corned beef, pastrami, turkey, potato salad, cheese, and pickles.

"You sure are nice to me," he said.

"You are a nice guy."

"Why did you get so much of it?"

"It's good for you, silly."

Roy laughed. "You sound like my grandma."

Memo was interested. "Weren't you brought up in an orphan's home, Roy?"

"I went there after grandma died."

"Didn't you ever live with your mother?"

He was suddenly thoughtful. "Seven years."

"What was she like? Do you remember?"

"A whore. She spoiled my old man's life. He was a good guy but died young."

A group of girls flocked through the door and Memo hastily excused herself. They were her showgirl friends from a Broadway musical that had just let out. She welcomed them and introduced them around. Dancing started and the party got livelier.

Roy polished his plate with a crust of bread. He felt as if he had hardly eaten anything—it was sliced so thin you could hardly chew your teeth into it.

Memo returned. "How about having something different

now?" But Roy said no and got up. "Lemme say hello to some of the gals that came in."

"You are all alike." He thought she sounded jealous and it was all right if she was. The girls she brought him around to were tickled to meet him. They felt his muscles and wanted to know how he belted the ball so hard.

"Clean living," Roy told them.

The girls laughed out loud. He looked them over. The best of the bunch was a slightly chubby one with an appealing face, but in her body she did not compare to Memo.

When he told Memo she had more of what it took than the rest of them put together, she giggled nervously. He looked at her and felt she was different tonight in a way he could not figure out. He worried about Gus, but then he thought that after tonight he would be getting it steady, and then he would tell her he did not want that glass-eye monkey tailing her around.

Memo led him back to the table. She pointed out what she wanted for Roy and the chef ladled it into the plate. Her own came back with a slice of ham and a roll on it. He followed her to the corner table. He wondered if Flores was still standing in the opposite corner, watching, but he didn't look.

Gazing at the mountain of stuff Memo handed him, he said, "I am getting tired of eating."

Memo had returned to the subject of his mother. "But didn't you love her, Roy?"

He stared at her through one eye. "Who wants to know?"

"Just me."

"I don't remember." He helped himself to a forkful of food. "No."

"Didn't she love you?"

"She didn't love anybody."

Memo said, "Let's try some new combinations with the buffet. Sometimes when you eat things that you didn't know could mix together but they do, you satisfy your appetite all at once. Now let's mix this lobster meat with hidden treats of anchovies, and here we will lay it on this tasty pumpernickel and spread Greek salad over it, then smear this other slice of bread with nice sharp cheese and put it on top of the rest."

"All it needs now is a shovel of manure and a forest will grow out of it."

"Now don't get dirty, Roy."

"It looks like it could blow a man apart."

"All the food is very fresh."

After making the sandwich she went to the ladies' room. He felt depressed. Now why the hell did she have to go and ask him questions about his old lady? Thinking about her, he chewed on the sandwich. With the help of three bottles of lemon pop he downed it but had to guzzle three more of lime to get rid of the artificial lemon taste. He felt a little drunk and snickered because it was a food and pop drunk. He had the old feeling he was down on his hands and knees searching for something that he couldn't find.

Flores stood at the table.

"If you tell them to go home," he hissed, "they weel."

Roy stared. "Tell who?"

"The players. They are afraid to stay here but they don't go because you stay."

"Go ahead and tell them to go."

"You tell them," Flores urged. "They weel leesten to your word."

"Right," said Roy.

Memo returned and Flores left him. Roy struggled to his feet, broke into a sweat, and sat down again. Fowler grabbed Memo and they whirled around. Roy didn't like them pressed so close together.

His face was damp. He reached into his pocket for a handkerchief and felt Iris' letter. For a second he thought he had found what he was looking for. More clearly than ever he remembered her pretty face and the brown eyes you could look into and see yourself as something more satisfying than you were, and he remembered telling her everything, the first time he had ever told anybody about it, and the relieved feeling he had afterward, and the long swim and Iris swimming down in the moonlit water searching for him, and the fire on the beach, she naked, and finally him banging her. For some reason this was the only thing he was ashamed of, though it could be said she hadn't asked for it.

Roy pushed himself up and headed for the table. The chef shined up a fast plate and with delight lifted the serving fork.

"I've had a snootful," Roy said.

The chef tittered. "It's all fresh food."

Roy looked into his button eyes. They were small pig's eyes. "Who says so?"

"It's the best there is."

"It stinks." He turned and walked stiffly to the door. Memo saw him. She waved gaily and kept on dancing.

He dragged his belly through the hall. When the elevator came it dropped him down in the lobby. He went along the corridor into the grill room. Carefully sitting down at the table, he ordered six hamburgers and two tall glasses of milk—clean food to kill the pangs of hunger.

The waiter told the cook to order, who got six red meat patties out of the refrigerator and pressed them on the grill. They softly sputtered. He thought he oughtn't to eat any more, but then he thought I am hungry. No, I am not hungry, I am hungry, whatever that means . . . What must I do not to be hungry? He considered fasting but he hadn't fasted since he was a kid. Besides, it made him hungry. He tried hard to recapture how it felt when he was hungry after a day of fishing and was sizzling lake bass over an open fire and boiling coffee in a tin can. All around his head were the sharp-pointed stars.

He was about to lift himself out of the chair but remembered his date with Memo and stayed put. There was time to kill before that so he might as well have a bite.

A hand whacked him across the shoulders.

It was Red Blow . . . Roy slowly sat down.

"Looked for a minute like you were gonna murder me," said Red.

"I thought it was somebody else."

"Who, for instance?"

Roy thought. "I am not sure. Maybe the Mex."

"Flores?"

"Sometimes he gets on my nerves."

"He is really a nice guy."

"I guess so."

Red sat down. "Don't eat too much crap. We have a big day comin' up."

"I am just taking a bite."

"Better get to bed and have plenty of sleep."

"Yes."

Red looked glum. "Can't sleep myself. Don't know what's the matter with me." He yawned and twitched his shoulders. "You all right?"

"Fine and dandy. Have a hamburger."

"Not for me, thanks. Guess I will go for a little walk. Best thing when you can't sleep."

Roy nodded.

"Take care of yourself, feller. Tomorrow's our day. Pop'll dance a jig after tomorrow. You'll be his hero."

Roy didn't answer.

Red smiled a little sadly. "I'm gonna be sorry when it's over."

The waiter brought the six hamburgers. Red looked at them absently. "It's all up to you." He got up and left.

Through the window Roy watched him go down the street.

"I'll be the hero."

The hamburgers looked like six dead birds. He took up the first one and gobbled it down. It was warm but dry. No more dead birds, he thought . . . not without ketchup. He poured a blop on three of the birds. Then he shuffled them up with the other two so as not to know which three had the ketchup and which two hadn't. Eating them, he could not tell the difference except that they all tasted like dead birds. They were not satisfying but the milk was. He made a mental note to drink more milk.

He paid and left. The elevator went up like a greased shot. As it stopped he felt a ripping pain on the floor of the stomach. The wax-faced elevator man watched him with big eyes. He stared at the old scarecrow, then stumbled out. He stood alone in the hall, trying to figure it out. Something was happening that he didn't understand. He roused himself to do battle, wishing for Wonderboy, but no enemy was visible. He rested and the pain left him.

The party was quiet. Flores had disappeared. The lights were dimmed and there was some preliminary sex work going on. Olson had his blonde backed into a corner. A group near the piano were passing a secret bottle around. In the center of the darkened room one of the girls held her dress over her pink panties and was doing bumps and grinds. A silent circle watched her.

Roy buttonholed Fowler. "Stay off the rotgut, kid."

"Stay away from the stuffin's, big shot."

Roy swiped at him but Fowler was gone. He wiped his sweaty face with his sleeve and searched for Memo to tell her it was time. He couldn't find her in the fog that had blown up, so he left the party and reeled down the stairs to the fourth floor. Feeling for her buzzer, he found the key left in the lock and softly turned it.

She was lying naked in bed, chewing a turkey drumstick as she looked at the pictures in a large scrapbook. Not till he was quite close did she see him. She let out a scream.

"You frightened me, Roy." Memo shut the scrapbook.

He had caught a glimpse of Bump's face. I'll take care of that bastard. He unzipped his fly.

Her green eyes closely watched him, her belly heaving above the red flame.

Undressing caused him great distress. Inside him they were tearing up a street. The sweat dripped from his face . . . Yet there was music, the sweetest piping he had ever heard. Dropping his pants he approached for the piping fulfillment.

She drew her legs back. Her expression puzzled him. It was not—the lights were wavering, blinking on and off. A thundering locomotive roared through the mountain. As it burst out of the rock with a whistle howl he felt on the verge of an extraordinary insight, but a bolt of shuddering lightning came at him from some unknown place. He threw up his arms for protection and it socked him, yowling, in the shattered gut. He lived a pain he could not believe existed. Agonized at the extent of it, Roy thudded to his knees as a picture he had long carried in his mind broke into pieces. He keeled over.

The raft with the singing green-eyed siren guarding the forbidden flame gave off into the rotting flood a scuttering one-eyed rat. In the distance though quite near, a toilet flushed, and though the hero braced himself against it, a rush of dirty water got a good grip and sucked him under.

Judge Banner had a money-saving contract with a small maternity hospital near Knights Field (it was there Bump had died) to treat all player emergencies, so that was where they had rushed Roy. The flustered obstetrician on duty decided to deliver the hero of his appendix. However he fought them deliriously and his strength was too much for the surgeon, anesthetist, attendant, and two mild maternity nurses. They subdued him with a hypo only to uncover a scar snaking down his belly. Investigation showed he had no appendix—it had long ago been removed along with some other stuff. (All were surprised at his scarred and battered body.) The doctors considered cutting out the gall bladder or maybe part of the stomach but nobody wanted to be responsible for the effect of the operation upon the Knights and the general public. (The city was aghast. Crowds gathered outside the hospital, waiting for bulletins. The Japanese government issued an Edict of Sorrow.) So they used the stomach pump instead and dredged up unbelievable quantities of bilge. The patient moaned along with thc ladies in labor on the floor, but the doctors adopted a policy of watchful waiting and held off anything drastic.

His belly racked his mind. Icy streams coursed through the fiery desert. He chattered and steamed, rarely conscious, tormented by his dreams. In them he waxed to gigantic heights then abruptly fell miles to be a little Roy dwarf (Hey, mister, you're stepping on my feet). He was caught in roaring gales amid loose, glaring lights, so bright they smothered the eyeballs. Iris' sad head topped Memo's dancing body, with Memo's vice versa upon the shimmying rest of Iris, a confused fusion that dizzied him. He hungered in nightmare for quantities of exotic food—wondrous fowl stuffed with fruit, and the multitudinous roe of tropical fish. When he bent his toothy head to devour, every last morsel vanished. So they served him a prime hunk of beef and he found it enormously delicious only to discover it was himself he was chewing. His thunderous roars sent nurses running from all directions. They were powerless before his flailing fists.

In delirium he hopped out of bed and hunted through the corridors in a nightgown—frightening the newly delivered mothers—for a mop or broom that he snatched back to his aseptic chamber and practiced vicious cuts with before the dresser mirror . . . They found him on the floor . . . At dawn he warily rose and ferreted a plumber's plunger out of the utility closet but this time he was caught by three attendants and dragged back to bed. They strapped him down and there he lay a prisoner, as the frightened Knights dropped the third of three hot potatoes to the scarred and embittered last-place Reds. Since the resurgent Pirates had scattered the brains of the Phils, three in a bloody row, the season ended in a dead heat. A single playoff game in Knights Field was arranged for Monday next, the day before the World Series.

Late that afternoon the fever abated. He returned, unstrapped, to consciousness and recognized a harried Memo at his bedside. From her he learned what had happened to the team, and groaned in anguish. When she left, with a hankie pressed to her reddened nostrils, he discovered his troubles had only just begun. The specialist in the case, a tall stoop-shouldered man with a white mustache with sad eyes, who absently hefted a heavy gold watch as he spoke, gave Roy a bill of particulars. He began almost merrily by telling him there wasn't much doubt he would participate in the Monday playoff (Roy just about leaped out of the bed but the doctor held him back with a gesture). He could play, yes, though he'd not feel at his best, nor would he be able to extend himself so far as he would like, but he would certainly be present and in the game, which, as the doctor understood it, was the big thing for both Roy and his public. (Interest in the matter was so great, he said, that he had permitted release of this news to the press.) Public clamor has compelled his reluctant yielding, though it was his considered opinion that, ideally, Roy ought to rest a good deal longer before getting back to his—ah—normal activities. But someone had explained to him that baseball players were in a way like soldiers, and since he knew that the body's response to duty sometimes achieved many of the good results of prolonged care and medication, he had agreed to let him play.

However, all good news has its counterpart of bad, he almost sadly said, and to prove the point let it come out that it would be best for Roy to say goodbye forever to baseball—if he hoped to stay alive. His blood pressure—at times amazingly high—complicated by an athlete's heart—could conceivably cause his sudden death if he were to attempt to play next season, whereas if he worked at something light and relaxing, one might say he could go on for years, as many had. The doctor slipped the gold watch into his vest pocket, and nodding to the patient, departed. Roy felt that this giant hand holding a club had broken through the clouds and with a single blow crushed his skull.

The hours that followed were the most terrifying of his life (more so than fifteen years ago). He lived in the thought of death, would not move, speak, take food or receive visitors. Yet all the while he fanatically fought the doctor's revelation, wrestled it every waking second, though something in him said the old boy with the white mustache was right. He felt he had for years suspected something wrong, and this was it. Too much pressure in the pipes—blew your conk off. (He saw it blown sky high.) He was through—finished. Only he couldn't—just couldn't believe it. Me. I. Roy Hobbs forever out of the game? Inconceivable. He thought of the fantastic hundreds of records he had broken in so short a time, which had made him a hero to the people, and he thought of the thousands—tens of thousands—that he had pledged himself to break. A moan escaped him.

Still a doubt existed. Maybe white mustache was wrong? They could misjudge them too. Maybe there was a mite less wind behind the ball than he thought, and it would hit the ground at his feet rather than land in the glove. Mistakes could happen in everything. Wouldn't be the first time a sawbones was wrong. *Maybe he was a hundred per cent dead wrong.*

The next evening, amid a procession of fathers leaving the hospital at baby-feeding time, he sneaked out of the building. A cab got him to Knights Field, and Happy Pellers, the astonished groundskeeper, let him in. A phone call brought

Dizzy to the scene. Roy changed into uniform (he almost wept to behold Wonderboy so forlorn in the locker) and Happy donned catcher's gear. Dizzy prepared to pitch. It was just to practice, Roy said, so he would have his eye and timing alert for the playoff Monday. Happy switched on the night floods to make things clearer. Dizzy practiced a few pitches and then with Roy standing at the plate, served one over the middle. As he swung, Roy felt a jet stream blow through the center of his skull. They gathered him up, bundled him into a cab, and got him back to the hospital, where nobody had missed him.

It was a storm on and Roy out in it. Not exactly true, it was Sam Simpson who was lost and Roy outsearching him. He tracked up and down the hills, leaving his white tracks, till he come to this shack with the white on the roof.

Anybody in here? he calls.

Nope.

You don't know my friend Sam?

Nope.

He wept and try to go away.

Come on in, kiddo, I was only foolin'.

Roy dry his eyes and went in. Sam was settin' at the table under the open bulb, his collar and tie off, playing solitaire with all spades.

Roy sit by the fire till Sam finish. Sam looked up wearing his half-moon specs, glinting moonlight.

Well, son, said Sam, lightin' up on his cigar.

I swear I didn't do it, Sam.

Didn't do what?

Didn't do nothin'.

Who said you did?

Roy wouldn't answer, shut tight as a clam.

Sam stayed awhile, then he say to Roy, Take my advice, kiddo.

Yes, Sam.

Don't do it.

No, said Roy, I won't. He rose and stood headbent before Sam's chair.

Let's go back home, Sam, let's now.

Sam peered out the window.

I would like to, kiddo, honest, but we can't go out there now. Heck, it's snowin' baseballs.

When he came to, Roy made the specialist promise to tell no one about his condition just in case he had the slightest chance of improving enough to play for maybe another season. The specialist frankly said he didn't see that chance, but he was willing to keep mum because he believed in the principle of freedom of action. So he told no one and neither did Roy—not even Memo. (No one had even mentioned the subject of his playing in the Series but Roy had already privately decided to take his chances in that.)

But mostly his thoughts were dismal. That frightened feeling: bust before beginning. On the merry-go-round again about his failure to complete his mission in the game. About this he suffered most. He lay for hours staring at the window. Often the glass looked wet though it wasn't raining. A man who had been walking in bright sunshine limped away into a mist. This broke the heart . . . When the feeling passed, if it ever did, there was the necessity of making new choices. Since it was already the end of the season, he had about four months in which to cash in on testimonials, endorsements, ghost-written articles, personal appearances, and such like. But what after that, when spring training time came and he disappeared into the backwoods? He recalled a sickening procession of jobs—as cook, well-driller, mechanic, logger, bean-picker, and for whatever odd change, semipro ballplayer. He dared not think further.

And the loneliness too, from job to job, never some place in particular for any decent length of time because of the dissatisfaction that grew, after a short while, out of anything he did . . . But supposing he could collect around twenty-five G's—could that amount, to begin with, satisfy a girl like Memo if she married him? He tried to think of ways of investing twenty-five thousand—maybe in a restaurant or tavern—to build it up to fifty, and then somehow to double that. His mind skipped from money to Memo, the only one who came to see him every day. He remembered the excitement he felt for her in that strapless yellow dress the night of the party.

And bad as he felt now he couldn't help but think how desirable she had looked, waiting for him naked in bed.

Such thoughts occupied him much of the time as he sat in the armchair, thumbing through old magazines, or resting in bed. He sometimes considered suicide but the thought was too oppressive to stay long in his mind. He dozed a good deal and usually woke feeling lonely. (Except for Red, once, nobody from the team had come to see him, though small knots of fans still gathered in the street and argued whether he would really be in Monday's game.) Saturday night he awoke from an after supper nap more gloomy than ever, so he reached under his pillow for Iris' letter. But just then Memo came into the room with an armful of flowers so he gladly let it lay where it was.

Despite how attractive she usually managed to keep herself (he could appreciate that in spite of a momentary return of the nausea) she appeared worn out now, with bluish shadows under her eyes. And he noticed, as she stuffed the flowers and red autumn leaves into the vase, that she was wearing the same black dress she had worn all week, a thing she never did before, and that her hair was lusterless and not well kept. She had days ago sorrowed it was her fault that this had happened to the team. How stupid not to have waited just a day or two more. (Pop, she wept, had called her filthy names.) She had despaired every minute—really despaired—up to the time she heard he was going to be in the playoff. At least she did not have it on her conscience that he would be out of that, so she felt better now. Not better enough, he worried, or she wouldn't be so lost and lonely-looking.

After she had arranged the flowers, Memo stood mutely at the open window, gazing down into the darkening street. When he least expected it, she sobbed out in a voice full of misery, "Oh, Roy, I can't stand it any longer, I can't."

He sat up. "What's wrong?"

Her voice was choked. "I can't go on with my life as it is." Memo dropped into the armchair and began to weep. In a minute everything around her was wet.

Tossing aside the blanket he swung his legs out of bed. She looked up, attempting to smile. "Don't get up, hon. I'll be all right."

Roy sat uneasily at the edge of the bed. He never knew what to do when they cried.

"It's just that I'm fed up," she wept. "Fed up. Pop is terrible to me and I don't want to go on living off him, even if he is my uncle. I have to get a job or something, or go somewhere.

"What did that bastard shrimp say to you?"

She found a handkerchief in her purse and blew her nose.

"It isn't his words," she said sadly. "Words can't kill. It's that I'm sick of this kind of life. I want to get away."

Then she let go again and looked like a little lost bird beating around in a cage. He was moved, and hovered over her like an old maid aunt trying to stop a leak.

"Don't cry, Memo. Just say the word and I will take care of you." In a cracked voice he said, "Just marry me."

She sobbed for the longest time. So long he grew jumpy with doubts about their future relations, but then she stopped crying and said in a damp voice, "Would you have me, Roy?"

He swayed with emotion as he got out thickly, "Would I?" To keep from hitting the ground he hopped into bed and sprawled out.

She came to him, her white hands clasped, her wet eyelids like sparkling flowers. "There's one thing you have to understand, Roy, and then maybe you won't want me. That is that I am afraid to be poor." She said it with intensity, her face turning dark at her words. "Maybe I am weak or spoiled, but I am the type who has to have somebody who can support her in a decent way. I'm sick of living like a slave. I got to have a house of my own, a maid to help me with the hard work, a decent car to shop with and a fur coat for winter time when it's cold. I don't want to have to worry every time a can of beans jumps a nickel. I suppose it's wrong to want all of that but I can't help it. I've been around too long and seen too much. I saw how my mother lived and I know it killed her. I made up my mind to have certain things. You understand that, don't you, Roy?"

He nodded.

"We have to face it," she said. "You're thirty-five now and that don't give you much time left as a ball player."

"What d'ye mean?" he asked. Deadpan.

But it wasn't his blood pressure she was referring to. For a minute he was afraid she had found out.

"I'm sorry to say this, Roy, but I have to be practical. Suppose the next one is your last season, or that you will have one more after that? Sure, you'll probably get a good contract till then, but it costs money to live, and then what'll we do for the rest of our lives?"

It was dark in the room now. He could scarcely see her.

"Turn on the lights."

She smeared powder over her nose and under her eyes, then pressed the button.

He stared at her.

She grew restless. "Roy—"

"I was just thinking, even if I had to quit right now I could still scrounge up about twenty-five grand in the next few months. That's a lotta dough."

She seemed doubtful. "What would you do with it?"

"We'd get hitched and I would invest in a business. Everybody does that. My name is famous already. We will make out okay. You will have what you want."

"What kind of business?" Memo asked.

"I can't say for sure—maybe a restaurant."

She made a face.

"What do you have in mind?" Roy asked.

"Oh, something big, Roy. I would like you to buy into a company where you could have an executive job and won't have to go poking your nose into the stew in a smelly restaurant."

A jet of nausea shot up from his gizzard. He admitted to himself he wanted nothing to do with restaurants.

"How much dough do we need to get in on one of those big companies?"

"I should think more than twenty-five thousand."

He gulped. "Around thirty-five?"

"More like fifty."

Roy frowned. Talk of that kind of dough gave him a bellyache. But Memo was right. It had to be something big or it wouldn't pay back enough. And if it was a big company he could take it a little easy, to protect his health, without anybody kicking. He pondered where to get another twenty-five thousand, and it had to be before the start of the next baseball season because as soon as everybody saw he wasn't playing, it wouldn't be easy to cash in on his name. People had no use for a has been. He had to be married and have the dough, both before next spring—in case he never did get to play. He thought of other means to earn some money fast—selling the story of his life to the papers, barnstorming a bit this fall and winter, not too strenuously. But neither of these things added up to much—not twenty-five grand. Roy lay back with his eyes shut.

Memo whispered something. His lids flew open. What was she doing with an old black dress on, her hair uncombed, looking like Lola, the Jersey City fortuneteller? Yet her voice was calm . . .

"Who sent you," he spoke harshly, "—that bastard Gus?"

She turned flame-faced but answered quietly, "The Judge."

"Banner?" Somebody inside of him—this nervous character lately hanging around—crashed a glass to the floor. Roy's pulses banged.

"He said he'd pay you fifteen thousand now and more next season. He says it would depend on you."

"I thought I smelled skunk."

"He asked me to deliver the message. I have nothing to do with it."

"Who else is in on this?"

"I don't know."

"Pop?"

"No."

He lay motionless for an age. She said no more, did not plead or prod. It grew late. An announcement was made for visitors to leave. She rose and tiredly put on her coat.

"I was thinking of all the years you would be out of the game."

"What does he want me to do?"

"It's something about the playoff—I don't know."

"They want me to drop it?"

She didn't answer.

"No," he said out loud.

She shrugged. "I told them you wouldn't."

She was thin and haggard-looking. Her shoulders drooped,

her hands were bloodless. To refuse her just about broke his heart.

He fell into a deep slumber but had not slept very long before this rat-eyed vulture, black against the ceiling, began to flap around the room and dripping deep fat spiraled down toward his face. Wrestling together, they knocked over the tables and chairs, when the lights went on and waked him. Roy grabbed under the pillow for a gun he thought was there, only it wasn't. Awake, he saw through the glare that Judge Goodwill Banner, in dark glasses and hairy black fedora, was staring at him from the foot of the bed.

"What the hell do you want here?"

"Don't be alarmed," the Judge rumbled. "Miss Paris informed me you were not asleep, and the authorities granted me a few minutes to visit with you."

"I got nothing to say to you." The nightmare had weakened him. Not wanting the Judge to see that, he pulled himself into a sitting position.

The Judge, yellow-skinned in the electric light, and rumpled-looking, sat in the armchair with his potlike hat on. He sucked an unwilling flame into his King Oscar and tossed the burnt-out match on the floor.

"How is your health, young man?"

"Skip it. I am all right now."

The Judge scrutinized him.

"Wanna bet?" Roy said.

The Judge's rubbery lips tightened around his cigar. After a minute he removed it from his mouth and said cautiously, "I assume that Miss Paris has acquainted you with the terms of a certain proposal?"

"Leave her name out of it."

"An admirable suggestion—a proposal, you understand, made by persons unknown."

"Don't make me laugh. I got a good mind to sick the FBI on you."

The Judge examined his cigar. "I rely on your honor. You might consider, however, that there is no witness other than Miss Paris, and I assume you would be solicitous of her?"

"I said to leave her name out."

"Quite so. I believe she erred concerning the emolument offered—fifteen thousand, was it? My understanding is that twenty thousand, payable in cash in one sum, is closer to the correct amount. I'm sure you know the prevailing rate for this sort of thing is ten thousand dollars. We offer twice that. Any larger sum is unqualifiedly out of the question because it will impair the profitableness of the venture. I urge you to consider carefully. You know as well as I that you are in no condition to play."

"Then what are you offering me twenty thousand smackers for—to show your gratitude for how I have built up your bank account?"

"I see no reason for sarcasm. You were paid for your services as contracted. As for this offer, I frankly confess it is insurance. There is the possibility that you may get into the game and unexpectedly wreck it with a single blow. I personally doubt this will occur, but we prefer to take no chances."

"Don't kid yourself that I am too weak to play. You know that the doctor himself said I'll be in there Monday."

The Judge hesitated. "Twenty-five thousand," he finally said. "Absolutely my last offer."

"I hear the bookies collect ten million a day on baseball bets."

"Ridiculous."

"That's what I hear."

"It makes no difference, I am not a bookie. What is your answer?"

"I say no."

The judge bit his lip.

Roy said, "Ain't you ashamed that you are selling a club down the river that hasn't won a pennant in twenty-five years and now they have a chance to?"

"We'll have substantially the same team next year," the Judge answered, "and I have no doubt that we will make a better job of the entire season, supported as we shall be by new players and possibly another manager. If we take on the Yankees now—that is, if we are foolish enough to win the playoff match—they will beat us a merciless four in a row, despite your presence. You are not strong enough to withstand the strain of a World Series, and you know it. We'd be ground to pulp, made the laughingstock of organized baseball, and your foolish friend, Pop Fisher, would this time destroy himself in his humiliation."

"What about all the jack you'd miss out on, even if we only played four Series games and lost every one?"

"I have calculated the amount and am certain I can do better, on the whole, in the way I suggest. I have reason to believe that, although we are considered to be the underdogs, certain gambling interests have been betting heavily on the Knights to win. Now it is my purpose, via the uncontested—so to speak—game, to teach these parasites a lesson they will never forget. After that they will not dare to infest our stands again."

"Pardon me while I throw up."

The Judge looked hurt.

"The odds favor us," Roy said. "I saw it in tonight's paper."

"In one only. The others quote odds against us."

Roy laughed out loud.

The Judge flushed through his yellow skin. "Honi soit qui mal y pense."

"Double to you," Roy said.

"Twenty-five thousand," said the Judge with an angry gesture. "The rest is silence."

"Though Roy had a splitting headache he tried to think the situation out. The way he now felt, he wouldn't be able to stand at the plate with a feather duster on his shoulder, let alone a bat. Maybe the Judge's hunch was right, and he might not be able to do a single thing to help the Knights win their game. On the other hand—maybe he'd be himself, his real self. If he helped them win the playoff—no matter if they later dropped the Series four in a row—there would still be all sorts of endorsement offers and maybe even a contract to do a baseball movie. Then he'd have the dough to take care of Memo in proper style. Yet suppose he played and because of his weakness flopped as miserably as he had during his slump? That might sour the endorsements and everything else, and he'd end up with nothing—or very little. His mind went around in drunken circles.

All this time the Judge's voice was droning on. "I have observed," he was saying, "how one moral condition may lead to or become its opposite. I recall an occasion on the bench when out of the goodness of my heart and a warm belief in humanity I resolved to save a boy from serving a prison sentence. Though his guilt was clear, because of his age I suspended sentence and paroled him for a period of five years. That afternoon as I walked down the courthouse steps, I felt I could surely face my maker without a blush. However, not one week later the boy stood before me, arraigned as a most wicked parricide. I asked myself can any action—no matter what its origin or motive—which ends so evilly—can such an action possibly be designated as good?"

He took out a clotted handkerchief, spat into it, folded it and thrust it into his pocket. "Contrarily," he went on, "a deed of apparently evil significance may come to pure and beautiful flower. I have in mind a later case tried before me in which a physician swindled his patient, a paralytic, out of almost a quarter of a million dollars. So well did he contrive to hide the loot that it has till this day not been recovered. Nevertheless, the documentary evidence was strong enough to convict the embezzler and I sentenced him to a term of from forty to fifty years in prison, thus insuring he would not emerge from the penitentiary to enjoy his ill-gotten gains before he is eighty-three years of age. Yet, while testifying from his wheel chair at the trial, the paralytic astonished himself and all present by rising in righteous wrath against the malcontent and, indeed, tottered across the floor to wreak upon him his vengeance. Naturally, the bailiff restrained him, but would you have guessed that he was, from that day on, sound in wind and limb, and as active as you or I? He wrote me afterwards that the return of his power of locomotion more than compensated him for the loss of his fortune."

Roy frowned. "Come out of the bushes."

The Judge paused. "I was trying to help you assess this action in terms of the future."

"You mean if I sell out?"

"Put it that way if you like."

"And that maybe some good might come out of it?"

"That is my assumption."

"For me, you mean?"

"For others too. It is impossible to predict who will be benefited."

"I thought you said you were doing this to get rid of the gamblers—that's good right off, ain't it?"

The Judge cleared his throat. "Indeed it is. However, one might consider, despite the difficulty of the personal situation—that is to say, within the context of one's own compunctions—that it is impossible to predict what further good may accrue to one, and others, in the future, as a result of an initially difficult decision."

Roy laughed. "You should be selling snake oil."

He had thought there might be something to the argument. He was now sure there wasn't, for as the Judge had talked he recalled an experience he had had when he was a kid. He and his dog were following an old skid road into the heart of a spooky forest when the hound suddenly let out a yelp, ran on ahead, and got lost. It was late in the afternoon and he couldn't stand the thought of leaving the dog there alone all night, so he went into the wood after it. At first he could see daylight between the trees—to this minute he remembered how still the trunks were, as the tree tops circled around in the breeze—and in sight of daylight it wasn't so bad, nor a little deeper in, despite the green gloom, but just at about the time the darkness got so thick he was conscious of having to shove against it as he hallooed for the dog, he got this scared and lonely feeling that he was impossibly lost. With his heart whamming against his ribs he looked around but could recognize no direction in the darkness, let alone discover the right one. It was cold and he shivered. Only, the payoff of it was that the mutt found him and led him out of the woods. That was good out of good.

Roy pulled the covers over his head. "Go home."

The Judge didn't move. "There is also the matter of next season's contract."

Roy listened. Would there ever be a next season? He uncovered his head. "How much?"

"I shall offer—provided we agree on the other matter—a substantial raise."

"Talk figures."

"Forty-five thousand for the season. We might also work out some small percentage on the gate."

"Twenty-five thousand for dropping the game is not enough," said Roy. As he spoke an icicle of fright punctured his spine.

The Judge scowled and drew on his half-gone cigar. "Thirty," he said, "and no more."

"Thirty-five," Roy got out. "Don't forget I stand to lose a couple of thousand on the pay I could get in the Series."

"Utterly outrageous," snapped the Judge.

"Don't slam the door on your way out."

The Judge rose, brushed his wrinkled pants and left.

Roy stared at the ceiling—relieved.

The Judge returned. He removed his hat and wiped his perspiring face with his dirty handkerchief. His head was covered with a thick black wig. You never got to the bottom of that creep.

"You are impossible to deal with—but I accept." His voice was flat. He covered his head with his hat.

But Roy said he had changed his mind when the Judge was out of the room. He had thought it over and decided the boys wanted to win that game and he wanted to help them. That was good. He couldn't betray his own team and manager. That was bad.

The Judge then hissed, "You may lose Miss Paris to someone else if you are not careful."

Roy bolted up. "To who for instance?"

"A better provider."

"You mean Gus Sands?"

The Judge did not directly reply. "A word to the wise—"

"That's none of your business," said Roy. He lay back. Then he asked, "What if I couldn't lose the game by myself? The Pirates ain't exactly world beaters. We roasted them the last seven times. The boys might do it again even if I didn't hit a thing."

The Judge rubbed his scaly hands. "The Knights are demoralized. Without you, I doubt they can win over a sandlot team, contrary opinion notwithstanding. As for the contingency of the flat failure of the opposing team, we have made the necessary arrangements to take care of that."

Roy was up again. "You mean there's somebody else in on this deal?"

The Judge smiled around his cigar.

"Somebody on our team?"

"A key man."

"In that case—" Roy said slowly.

"The thirty-five thousand is final. There'll be no changing that."

"With forty-five for the contract—"

"Agreed. You understand you are not under any circumstances to hit the ball safely?"

After a minute Roy said slowly, "I will take the pitch."

"I beg your pardon?"

"The fix is on."

The Judge caught on and said with a laugh, "I see you share my philological interests." He lit his dead King Oscar.

Through the nausea Roy remembered an old saying. He quoted, "Woe unto him who calls evil good and good evil."

The Judge glared at him.

Memo returned and covered his face with wet kisses. She tweaked his nose, mussed his hair, and called him wonderful. After she left he couldn't sleep so he reached under his pillow and got out Iris' letter.

". . . After my baby was born, the women of the home where my father had brought me to save himself further shame were after me to give it up. They said it would be bad for her to be brought up by an unmarried mother, and that I would have no time to myself or opportunity to take up my normal life. I tried, as they said, to be sensible and offer her for adoption, but I had been nursing her—although warned against it, nursing shrinks the breasts you know, and they were afraid for my figure—and the thought of tearing myself away from her forever was too much for me. Since Papa wouldn't have her in his house I decided to find a job and bring her up myself. That turned out to be a lot harder than I had expected, because I earned not very much and had to pay for baby's care all day, her things, the rent of course, and the clothes I had to have for work. At night I had supper to think of, bathing her, laundry, house cleaning, and preparing for the next day, which never changed from any other.

"Except for my baby I was nearly always alone, reading, mostly, to improve myself, although sometimes it was unbearable, especially before I was twenty and just after. It also took quite a while until I got rid of my guilt, or could look upon her as innocent of it, but eventually I did, and soon her loveliness and gaiety and all the tender feelings I had in my heart for her made up for a lot I had suffered. Yet I was tied to time—not so much to the past—nor to the expectations of the future, which was really too far away—only to here and now, day after day, until suddenly the years unrolled and a change came—more a reward of standing it so long than any sudden magic—and more quickly than I could believe, she had grown into a young woman, and almost as if I had wished it on her, fell in love with a wonderful boy and married him. Like me she was a mother before she was seventeen. Suddenly everywhere I looked seemed to be tomorrow, and I was at last free to take up my life where I had left it off one summer night when I went for a walk in the park with a stranger . . ."

He read down to the last page, where she once more mentioned herself as a grandmother. Roy crumpled the letter and pitched it against the wall.

On the morning of the game fist fights broke out all over the stands in Knights Field. Hats, bottles, apple cores, bananas, and the mushy contents of sack lunches were thrown around. A fan in one of the boxes had a rock bounced off his skull, opening a bleeding gash. Two special cops rushed up the steps and got hold of an innocent-looking guy with glasses, whose pockets were stuffed with odd-shaped rocks. They dragged him forth, although he was hollering he had collected them for his rock garden, and flung him headlong out of the park. He was from Pittsburgh and cursed the Knights into the ground. A disappointed truck driver who couldn't get in to see the game tackled him from behind, knocking the rock collector's head against the sidewalk and smashing his glasses. He spat out two bloody teeth and sat there sobbing till the ambulance came.

The sun hid behind the clouds for the most part. The day was chilly, football weather, but the stands were decorated with colored bunting, the flags on the grandstand roof rode high in the breeze and the crowd was raucous. The PA man tried to calm them but they were packed together too tight to be peaceful, for the Judge had sold hundreds of extra tickets and the standees raced for any seat that was vacant for a second. Besides, the Knights' fans were jumpy, their nerves ragged from following the ups and downs of the team. Some glum-face gents bitterly cursed Roy out, calling him welsher, fool, pig-horse for eating himself into that colossal bellyache. But he had his defenders, who claimed the Big Man's body burned food so fast he needed every bit he ate. They blamed the damage on ptomaine. The accusers wanted to know why no one else at the party had come down sick. They were answered where would the Knights be without Roy—at the bottom of the heap. The one who spoke got a rap on the ear for his trouble. The rapper was grabbed by a cop, run down the catwalk, and pitched into the rotunda. Yet though the fans were out of sorts and crabbing at each other, they presented a solid front when it came to laying bets. Many pessimistically shook their heads, but they counted up the seven straight wins over the Pirates, figured in that Hobbs was back, and reached into their pockets. Although there were not too many Pirate rooters around, the bets were quickly covered for every hard-earned buck.

Otto Zipp was above all this. He sat like a small mountain behind the rail in short left, reading the sports page of his newspaper. He looked neither right nor left, and if somebody tried to talk to him Otto gave him short shrift. Then when they least expected it, he would honk his horn and cry out in shrill tones, "Throw him to the hawks." After that he went back to the sports page.

When the players began drifting into the clubhouse they were surprised to see Roy there. He was wearing his uniform and slowly polishing Wonderboy. The boys said hello and not much more. Flores looked at his feet. Some of them were embarrassed that they hadn't gone to see him in the hospital. Secretly they were pleased he was here. Allie Stubbs even began to kid around with Olson. Roy thought they would not act so chipper if they knew he felt weak as piss and was dreading the game. The Judge was absolutely crazy to pay him thirty-five grand not to hit when he didn't feel able to even lift a stick. He hoped Pop would guess how shaky he was and bench him. What a laugh that would be on the Judge—serve the bastard right. But when Pop came in, he didn't so much as glance in Roy's direction. He walked straight into his office and slammed the door, which suited Roy fine.

Pop had ordered everybody kept out of the clubhouse until after the game but Mercy weaseled in. All smiles, he approached Roy, asking for the true story of what went on at the party that night, but Red Blow saw him and told him to stay outside. Max had tried the same act in the hospital last week. The floor nurse caught him sneaking toward Roy's room and had him dropped out on the front steps. After leaving the clubhouse Max sent in a note, inviting Roy to come out and make a statement. People were calling him a filthy coward and what did he intend to say to that? Roy gave out a one-word unprintable reply. Mercy shot in a second note. "You'll get yours—M.M." Roy tore it up and told the usher to take no more slop from him.

Pop poked his baldy out of his door and called for Roy. The players looked around uneasily. Roy got up and finally went into the office. For an unsufferable time Pop failed to speak. He was unshaven, his face exuding gray stubble that made him look eighty years old. His thin frame seemed shrunken and his left eye was a little crossed with fatigue. Pop leaned back in his creaking swivel chair, staring with tears in his eyes over his half moons at the picture of Ma on his desk. Roy examined his fingernails.

Pop sighed, "Roy, it's my own fault."

It made Roy edgy. "What is?"

"This mess that we are now in. I am not forgetting I kept you on the bench for three solid weeks in June. If I hadn't done that foolish thing we'da finished the season at least half a dozen games out in front."

Roy offered no reply.

"But your own mistake was a bad one too."

Roy nodded.

"A bad one, with the team right on top of hooking the pennant." Pop shook his head. Yet he said he wouldn't blame Roy too much because it wasn't entirely of his own doing. He then apologized for not coming to see him in the hospital. He had twice set out to but felt too grumpy to be fit company for a sick man, so he hadn't come. "It's not you that I am mad at, Roy—it's that blasted Memo. I shoulda pitched her out on her ass the first day she showed up at my door."

Roy got up.

"Sit down." Pop bent forward. "We can win today." His cold breath smelled bad. Roy drew his head back.

"Well, we can, can't we?"

He nodded.

"What's the matter with you?"

"I feel weak," Roy said, "and I am not betting how I will hit today."

Pop's voice got kindly again. "I say we can win it whichever way you feel. Once you begin to play you will feel stronger. And if the rest of those birds see you hustling they will break their backs to win. All they got to feel is there is somebody on this team who thinks they can."

Pop then related a story about a rookie third baseman he once knew, a lad named Mulligan. He was a fine hitter and thrower but full of hard luck all his life. Once he was beaned at the plate and had his skull cracked. He returned for spring practice the following year and the first day out he crashed into another fielder and broke his arm. On the return from that he was on first running to second on a hit and run play and the batter smacked the ball straight at him, breaking two ribs and dislocating a disc in his spine. After that he quit baseball, to everybody's relief.

"He was just unlucky," Pop said, "and there wasn't a thing anybody could do to take the whammy off of him and change his hard luck. You know, Roy, I been lately thinking that a whole lot of people are like him, and for one reason or the other their lives will go the same way all the time, without them getting what they want, no matter what. I for one."

Then to Roy's surprise he said he never hoped to have a

World Series flag. Pop swiveled his chair closer. "It ain't in the cards for me—that's all. I am wise to admit it to myself. It took a long time but I finally saw which way the arrow has been pointing." He sighed deeply. "But that don't hold true about our league pennant, Roy. That's the next best thing and I feel I am entitled to it. I feel if I win it just this once—I will be satisfied. I will be satisfied, and win or lose in the Series, I will quit baseball forever." He lowered his voice. "You see what it means to me, son?"

"I see."

"Roy, I would give my whole life to win this game and take the pennant. Promise me that you will go in there and do your damndest."

"I will go in," Roy sighed.

After the practice bell had rung, when he reluctantly climbed up out of the dugout and shoved himself toward the batting cage with his bat in his hand, as soon as the crowd got a look at him the boo birds opened up, alternating with shrill whistles and brassy catcalls. Roy hardened his jaws, but then a rumble erupted that sounded like bubbling tubfuls of people laughing and sobbing. The noise grew to a roar, boiled over, and to his astonishment, drowned out the disapprovers in an ovation of cheering. Men flung their hats into the air, scaling straws and limp felts, pounded each other's skulls, and cried themselves hoarse. Women screeched and ended up weeping. The shouting grew, piling reverberation upon reverberation, till it reached blast proportions. When it momentarily wore thin, Sadie Sutter's solemn gong could be heard, but as the roar rose again, the gonging grew faint and died in the distance. Roy felt feverish. The applause was about over when he removed his cap to clean the sweat off his brow, and once more thunder rolled across the field, continuing in waves as he entered the cage. With teeth clenched to stop the chattering, he took three swipes at the ball, driving each a decent distance. At Pop's urging he also went out onto the field to shag some flies. Again the cheers resounded, although he wished they wouldn't. He speared a few flies in his tracks, dropped his glove and walked to the dugout. The cheers trailed him in a foaming billow, but above the surflike roar and the renewed tolling of Sadie's gong, he could hear Otto Zipp's shrill curses. The dwarf drew down on his head a chorus of hisses but thumbed his cherry nose as Roy passed by. Roy paid him no heed whatsoever, infuriating Otto.

The Pirates flipped through their practice and the game began. Pop had picked Fowler to start for the Knights. Roy figured then that he knew who was in this deal with him. Leave it to the Judge to tie the bag in the most economical way—with the best hitter and pitcher. He had probably asked Pop who he was intending to pitch and then went out and bought him, though no doubt paying a good deal less than the price Roy was getting. What surprised and shocked him was that Fowler could be so corrupt though so young and in the best of health. If he only had half the promise of the future Fowler had, he would never have dirtied his paws in this business. However, as he watched Fowler pitch during the first inning he wasn't certain he was the one. His fast ball hopped today and he got rid of the first two Pirates with ease. Maybe he was playing it cagey first off, time would tell. Roy's thoughts were broken up by the sound, and echo behind him, of the crack of a bat. The third man up had taken hold of one and it was arcing into deep left. Already Flores was hot footing it in from center. It occurred to Roy that although he had promised the Judge he wouldn't hit, he had made no commitments as to catching them. Waving Flores aside, he ran several shaky steps and made a throbbing stab at the ball, spearing it on the half run for the third out. As he did so he noticed a movement up in the tower window and saw the Judge's stout figure pressed against the window. He then recollected he hadn't seen Memo since Saturday.

To nobody's surprise, Dutch Vogelman went to the mound for the Pirates. In a few minutes it was clear to all he was working with championship stuff, because he knocked the first three Knights off without half trying, including Flores, who was no easy victim. Roy had no chance to bat, for which he felt relieved. But after Fowler had also rubbed out the opposition, he was first up in the second inning. As he dragged Wonderboy up to the plate, the stands, after a short outburst, were hushed. Everybody remembered the four homers he had got off Vogelman the last time he had faced him. In the dugout

Pop and the boys were peppering it up for him to give the ball a big ride, and so were Red Blow and Earl Wilson, on the baselines. What they didn't know was that Roy had been struck giddy with weakness. His heart whammed like a wheezing steam engine, his head felt nailed to a pole, his eardrums throbbed as if he were listening to the bottom of the sea, and his arms hung like dead weights. It was with the greatest effort that he raised Wonderboy. As he was slowly getting set, he sneaked a cautious glance up at the tower, and it did not exactly surprise him that Memo, still in black, was standing at the window next to the Judge, blankly gazing down at him. Anyway, he knew where she was now.

Vogelman had been taking his time. For a pitcher he was a comparatively short duck, with a long beak, powerful arms and legs, red sleeves leaking out of a battered jersey, and a nervous delivery. Despite the fact that he had ended the regular season as a twenty-five game winner, he worried to bursting beads of sweat at the thought of pitching to Roy. Every time he recalled those four gopher balls, one after the other landing in the stands, he cringed with embarrassment. And he knew, although there was nobody on base at the moment, that if he served one of them up now, it could conceivably ice the game for the Knights and louse up the very peak of his year of triumph. So Vogelman delayed by wiping the shine off the ball, inspecting the stitches, fumbling for the resin bag, scuffing his cleats in the dirt, and removing his cap to rub away the sweat he had worked up. When the boos of the crowd got good and loud, Stuffy Briggs bellowed for him to throw and Vogelman reluctantly let go with a pitch.

The ball was a whizzer but dripping lard. Weak as he felt, Roy had to smile at what he could really do to that baby if he had his heart set on it, but he swung the slightest bit too late, grunting as the ball shot past Wonderboy—which almost broke his wrists to get at it—and plunked in the pocket of the catcher's glove.

. . . Where had she been since Saturday? Sunday was the first day she hadn't come to the hospital, the day she knew he was getting out of the joint. He had left alone, followed by some reporters he wouldn't talk to, and had taken a cab to the hotel. Once in his room he got into pajamas, and wondering why she hadn't at least called him, fell asleep. He had then had this dream of her—seeing her in some city, it looked like Boston—and she didn't recognize him when they passed but walked on fast in her swaying walk. He chased after her and she was (he remembered) swallowed up in the crowd. But he saw the red hair and followed after that, only it turned out to be a dyed redhead with a mean mouth and dirty eyes. Where's Memo? he called, and woke thinking she was here in the room, but she wasn't, and he hadn't seen her till he located her up there in the tower.

Roy gazed at the empty bases. Striking out with nobody on was the least harm he could do the team, yet his fingers itched to sock it a little. He couldn't trust himself to because—who could tell? it might go over the fence, the way Wonderboy was tugging at his muscles. Vogelman then tried a low-breaking curve that Roy had to "take" for ball one. The pitcher came back with a foolish floater that he pretended to almost break his back reaching after.

Strike two. There were only three.

. . . He was remembering the time his old lady drowned the black tom cat in the tub. It had gotten into the bathroom with her and bit at her bare ankles. She once and for all grabbed the cursed thing and dropped it into the hot tub. The cat fought to get out, but she shrilly beat it back and though it yowled mournfully, gave it no mercy. Yet it managed in its hysterical cat-way to stay afloat in the scalding water that she bathed in to cut her weight down, until she shoved its dirty biting head under, from which her hand bled all over. But when the water was drained, and the cat, all glossy wet, with its pink tongue caught between its teeth, lay there dead, the whole thing got to be too much for her and she couldn't lift it out of the tub.

He closed his eyes before the next pitch in the hope it would be quickly called against him, but it curved out for a ripe ball two. Opening his lids, he saw Mercy in a nearby seat, gazing at him with a malevolent sneer. You too, Max, Roy thought, tightening his hold on the bat. Vogelman was beginning to act more confident. You too, Vogelman, and he shut his eyes again, thinking how, after that time with Iris on the beach, when they were driving home, she rested her head against his arm. She was frightened, wanted him to comfort her but he wouldn't. "When will you grow up, Roy?" she said.

Vogelman blistered across a hot, somewhat high one, not too bad to miss, and that made it three and out. Otto Zipp held his nose and pulled the chain, and Roy, quivering, remained for a few seconds with the stick raised over his head, shriveling the dwarf into the silence and immobility that prevailed elsewhere. He threw Wonderboy aside—some in the front boxes let out a gasp—and returned empty-handed to the bench. The Judge and Memo had gone from the tower window.

As the Pirates came to bat for their half of the third (there were no Knight hits after Roy struck out) a breeze blew dust all over the place. Some of the fans with nothing better to do were shoveling the rotten fruit and slices of buttered sandwich bread into paper sacks, or kicking it under their seats. Nobody seemed to be hungry and the Stevens boys, despite all their barking, sold only a few hot coffees. Nor was there much talk of the past half inning. A few complained that Roy had never looked so bad—like a sloppy walrus. Others reminded them the game was young yet.

Neither team scored in either the third or fourth. The way the Knights fanned made Roy wonder if they had all been bought off by the Judge. Yet it didn't seem likely. He was too stingy. In the fifth came his next turn, again first up, a small break.

The stands awoke and began a rhythmic clapping. "Lift 'at pill, Roy. Bust its guts. Make it bleed. You can do it, kid."

"You can do it," Pop hollered from the dugout steps.

With a heavy heart Roy pulled himself up to the plate. He had shooting pains in back muscles that had never bothered him before and a crick in his neck. He couldn't comfortably straighten up and the weight of Wonderboy crouched him further. But Vogelman, despite Roy's strikeout, was burdened with worry over what he still *might* do. He wiped his face with his red sleeve but failed to calm down. By wide margins his first two throws were balls. To help him out, Roy swung under the third pitch. Otto Zipp then let out a string of boos, bahs, and bums. Roy thought he better foul the next one for strike two but Vogelman wouldn't let him, throwing almost over his head. Remembering he could walk if he wanted to, Roy waited. There was no harm to anybody in that and it would look better for him. The next pitch came in too close, and that was how he got to first and the Judge again to the window. But it made no difference one way or the other, for though Lajong sacrificed him to second, Gabby slashed a high one across the diamond which the second baseman jumped for, and he tagged Roy for an unassisted double play. Nobody could blame *him* for that, Roy thought, as he headed out to the field. He stole a look back at Pop and the manager was muttering to himself out of loose lips in a bony face. It seemed to Roy he had known the old man all his life long.

He found himself thinking of maybe quitting the deal with the Judge. He could send a note up there saying the fix was off. But he couldn't think what to write Memo. He tried to imagine what it would be like living without her and couldn't stand the thought of the loneliness.

Dave Olson opened the sixth with the Knights' first hit, a thumping double. The stands sounded like a gigantic drawerful of voices that had suddenly been pulled open. But Benz went down swinging, then Fowler bunted into another quick d.p. and the drawerful of voices was shut. Roy wondered about that bunt. He had a notion Fowler would commit himself soon because time was on the go. But Fowler didn't, making it another sweep of three Pirates. He had thus far given up only two safeties. In the seventh, the Knights, sensing Vogelman was tiring, found their way to him. Allie Stubbs chopped a grass cutter through a hole in the infield for a single. Baker, attempting to lay down a bunt, was overanxious and struck out. Then Flores lifted one just above the first baseman's frantic fingers, and Stubbs, running with his head down, sprang safely into third. Roy was on deck but with two on base his heart misgave him. The crowd jumped to its feet, roaring for him to come through.

As he approached the plate, the sun, that had been plumbing the clouds since the game began, at last broke through and bathed the stadium in a golden glow that caused the crowd to murmur. As the warmth fell upon him, Roy felt a sob break in his throat. The weakness left his legs, his heart beat steadily, his giddy gut tightened, and he stood firm and strong upon the earth. Though it startled him to find it so, he had regained a sense of his own well-being. A thousand springlike thoughts crowded through his mind, blotting out the dark diagnosis of the white-mustached specialist. He felt almost happy, and that he could do anything he wanted, if he wanted. His eyes scanned the forward rows in left field but stopped at Zipp's surly face. He felt suddenly anguished at what he had promised the Judge.

On his first swing—at a bad pitch—Otto let out a stream of jeers, oaths, and horn hoots that burned Roy to his bones. I will get that little ass-faced bastard. On the next pitch he shortened his hold on Wonderboy, stepped in front of the ball, and pulled it sharply foul. The ball whizzed past Otto's nose and boomed down an entrance way. The dwarf turned into flour, then as the blood rushed back to his face, grew furious. He jumped up and down on his seat, shook his fist, and screeched curses.

"Carrion, offal, turd—flush the bowl."

Roy tried to send the next ball through his teeth. It hit the rail with a bong and bounced into the air. A fan behind Otto caught it in his straw hat. Though the crowd laughed, the boos at Roy grew louder. Red Blow held up two warning fingers. Roy chopped a third foul at the dwarf. With a shriek he covered his face with his arms and ducked.

Several rows up from Otto, a dark-haired woman in a white dress had risen and was standing alone amid the crowd. Christ, another one, Roy thought. At the last split second he had tried to hold his swing but couldn't. The ball spun like a shot at Otto, struck his hard skull with a thud, and was deflected upward. It caught the lady in the face, and to the crowd's horror, she went soundlessly down.

A commotion rose in the stands. Fans by the hundreds piled out of their seats to get at her but the cops and ushers blocked their way, warning them not to crush her to death. Stuffy Briggs called time. Roy dropped his bat, hopped into the boxes and ran up the stairs—his clacking cleats shooting sparks—and along the aisle to where she lay. Many of the fans were standing on their seats to see and there was a crowd pressed around her. Murmuring lynch threats, they let Roy through. A doctor was attending her but she was stretched out unconscious.

Roy already knew who it was. "Iris," he groaned.

Iris woke, opened her good eye and sighed, "Roy."

Lifting her in his arms, he carried her to the clubhouse. Doc Casey and Dizzy kept everybody out. Max Mercy, hot for news, jammed his foot in the door but Dizzy crushed it hard, and Max danced as he cursed.

Roy gently laid her on the trainer's table. The left side of her face was hurt, bruised and rainbow-colored. Her eye was black and the lid thick. But the right side was still calm and lovely.

What have I done, he thought, and why did I do it? And he thought of all the wrong things he had done in his life and tried to undo them but who could?

The doctor went out to call an ambulance. Roy closed the door after him.

"Oh, Roy," sighed Iris.

"Iris, I am sorry."

"Roy, you must win—"

He groaned. "Why didn't you come here before?"

"My letter—you never answered."

He bowed his head.

The doctor entered. "Contusions and lacerations. Not much to worry about, but to be on the safe side she ought to be X-rayed."

"Don't spare any expenses," Roy said.

"She'll be fine. You can go back to the game now."

"You must win, Roy," said Iris.

Seeing there was more to this than he had thought, the doctor left.

Roy turned to her trying to keep in mind that she was a grandmother but when he scanned the fine shape of her body, he couldn't. Instead there rose in him an odd disgust for Memo. It came quickly, nauseating him.

"Darling," whispered Iris, "win for our boy."

He stared at her. "What boy?"

"I am pregnant." There were tears in her eyes.

Her belly was slender . . . then the impact hit him.

"Holy Jesus."

Iris smiled with quivering lips.

Bending over, he kissed her mouth and tasted blood. He kissed her breasts, they smelled of roses. He kissed her hard belly, wild with love for her and the child.

"Win for us, you were meant to."

She took his head in her hands and drew it to her bosom. How like the one who jumped me in the park that night he looks, she thought, and to drive the thought away pressed his head deeper into her breasts, thinking, this will be different. Oh, Roy, be my love and protect me. But by then the ambulance had come so they took her away.

In the dugout Pop confronted him with withering curses. "Get in there and attend to business. No more monkey shines or I will pitch you out on your banana."

Roy nodded. Climbing out of the dugout, to his dismay he found Wonderboy lying near the water fountain, in the mud. He tenderly wiped it dry. Stuffy called time in and the Pirates, furious at the long delay (Wickitt had demanded the forfeit of the game, but Pop had scared Stuffy into waiting for Roy by threatening to go to court), returned to their positions, Allie and Flores to third and first, and Roy stepped into the batter's box to face a storm of Bronx cheers. They came in wind-driven sheets until Vogelman reared and threw, then they stopped.

It was 0 and 2 on him because, except for the one he had purposely missed, Roy had turned each pitch into a foul. He watched Vogelman with burning eyes. Vogelman was almost hypnotized. He saw a different man and didn't like what he saw. His next throw was wide of the plate. Ball one. Then a quick ball two, and the pitcher was nervous again. He took a very long time with the next throw but to his horror the pellet slipped away from him and hit the dirt just short of the plate. Allie broke for home but the catcher quickly trapped it and threw to third. Flopping back, Allie made it with his fingers. Flores, in the meantime, had taken second.

And that was ball three. Roy now prayed for a decent throw.

Vogelman glanced at Allie edging into a lead again, kicked, and threw almost in desperation. Roy swung from his cleats.

Thunder crashed. The pitcher stuffed his maimed fingers into his ears. His eyes were blinded. Pop rose and crowed himself hoarse. Otto Zipp, carrying a dark lump on his noodle, cowered beneath the ledge. Some of the fans had seen lightning, thought it was going to rain, and raised their coat collars. Most of them were on their feet, raving at the flight of the ball. Allie had raced in to score, so had Flores, and Roy was heading into second, when the umpire waved them all back. The ball had landed clearly foul. The fans groaned in shuddering tones.

Wonderboy lay on the ground split lengthwise, one half pointing to first, the other to third.

The Knights' bat boy nervously collected both the pieces and thrust a Louisville Slugger into Roy's limp hand. The crowd sat in raw silence as the nerveless Vogelman delivered his next pitch. It floated in, perfect for pickling, but Roy failed to lift the bat.

Lajong, who followed, also struck out.

With the Knights back in the field, Fowler quickly gave up a whacking triple to the first Pirate hitter. This was followed by a hard double, and almost before any of the stunned fans could realize it, the first run of the game was in. Pop bounced off the bench as if electrocuted and signaled the bullpen into hot activity. Red Blow sauntered out to the mound to quiet Fowler down but Fowler said he was all right so Red left.

The next Pirate laced a long hopper to left. The shouting of the crowd woke Roy out of his grief for Wonderboy. He tore in for the ball, made a running jab for it and held it. With an effort he heaved to third, holding both runners to one bag. He knew now he was right about Fowler. The pitcher had pulled the plug. Roy signaled time and drifted in to talk to him. Both Red and Dave Olson also walked forward for a mound conference but Roy waved them back. As he approached the dark-faced Fowler, he saw the Judge up at the window, puffing his cigar.

Roy spoke in a low voice. "Watch out, kid, we don't want to lose the game."

Fowler studied him craftily. "Cut the crap, big shot. A lotta winning you been doing."

"Throw the ball good," Roy advised him.

"I will, when you start hitting it."

"Listen," Roy said patiently. "This might be my last season in the game for I am already thirty-five. You want it to be yours?"

Fowler paled. "You wouldn't dare open your trap."

"Try something funny again and you will see."

Fowler turned angrily away. The fans began to whistle and stamp. "Set 'em up," called Stuffy Briggs. Roy returned to left but after that, Fowler somehow managed to keep the next two men from connecting, and everybody said too bad that Roy hadn't given him that pep talk after the first hit. Some of the fans remarked had anybody noticed that Roy had thumbed his nose up to the tower at the end of the inning?

Every time Vogelman put Roy away, he felt infinitely better, consequently his pitching improved as the game progressed. Though he was surprised in the eighth to have Gabby Laslow touch him for a sharp single, he forced Olson to pop to short, Benz to line to him, and Fowler obliged by biting at three gamey ones for the last out. Counting up who he would have to throw to in the ninth, Vogelman discovered that if he got Stubbs, Baker, and the more difficult Flores out, there would be no Roy Hobbs to pitch to. The idea so excited him he determined to beat his brains out trying. Fowler, on the other hand, despite Roy's good advice to him, got sloppier in his throwing, although subtly, so that nobody could be sure why, only his support was a whole lot better than he had hoped for, and neither of the first two Pirates up in the ninth, though they had walloped the ball hard, could land on base. Flores, the Mexican jumping bean, had nailed both shots. The third Pirate then caught a juicy pitch and poled out a high looping beauty to left, but Roy, running back—back—back, speared it against the wall. Though he was winded and cursed Fowler through his teeth, he couldn't help but smile, picturing the pitcher's disgust. And he felt confident that the boys would hold him a turn at bat and he would destroy Vogelman and save the game, the most important thing he ever had to do in his life.

Pop, on the other hand, was losing hope. His hands trembled and his false teeth felt like rocks in his mouth, so he plucked them out and dropped them into his shirt pocket. Instead of Allie, he called Ed Simmons to pinch hit, but Vogelman, working with renewed speed and canniness, got Ed to hit a soft one to center field. Pop swayed on the bench, drooling a little out of the corners of his puckered mouth. Red was a ghost, even his freckles were pale. The stands were shrouded in darkening silence. Baker spat and approached the plate. Remembering he hadn't once hit safely today, Pop called him back and substituted Hank Kelly, another pinch hitter.

Vogelman struck him out. He dried his mouth on his sleeve, smiling faintly to himself for the first time since the game began. One more—the Mex. To finish him meant slamming the door on Hobbs, a clean shut-out, and tomorrow the World Series. The sun fell back in the sky and a hush hung like a smell in the air. Flores, with a crazed look in his eye, faced the pitcher. Fouling the first throw, he took for a ball, and swung savagely at the third pitch. He missed. Two strikes, there were only three . . . Roy felt himself slowly dying. You died alone. At least if he were up there batting . . . The Mexican's face was lit in anguish. With bulging eyes he rushed at the next throw, and cursing in Spanish, swung. The ball wobbled crazily in the air, took off, and leaped for the right field wall. Running as though death dogged him, Flores made it, sliding headlong into third. Vogelman, drained of his heart's blood, stared at him through glazed eyes.

The silence shattered into insane, raucous noise.

Roy rose from the bench. When he saw Pop searching among the other faces, his heart flopped and froze. He would gladly get down on his knees and kiss the old man's skinny, crooked feet, do anything to get up there this last time. Pop's haunted gleam settled on him, wavered, traveled down the line of grim faces . . . and came back to Roy. He called his name.

Up close he had black rings around his eyes, and when he spoke his voice broke.

"See what we have come to, Roy."

Roy stared at the dugout floor. "Let me go in."

"What would you expect to do?"

"Murder it."

"Murder which?"

"The ball—I swear."

Pop's eyes wavered to the men on the bench. Reluctantly his gaze returned to Roy. "If you weren't so damn busy gunning fouls into the stands that last time, you woulda straightened out that big one, and with three scoring, that woulda been the game."

"Now I understand why they call them fouls."

"Go on in," Pop said. He added in afterthought, "Keep us alive."

Roy selected out of the rack a bat that looked something like Wonderboy. He swung it once and advanced to the plate. Flores was dancing on the bag, beating his body as if it were burning, and jabbering in Spanish that if by the mercy of St. Christopher he was allowed to make the voyage home from third, he would forever after light candles before the saint.

The blank-faced crowd was almost hidden by the darkness crouching in the stands. Home plate lay under a deepening dusty shadow but Roy saw things with more light than he ever had before. A hit, tying up the game, would cure what ailed him. Only a homer, with himself scoring the winning run, would truly redeem him.

Vogelman was contemplating how close he had come to paradise. If the Mex had missed that pitch, the game would now be over. All night long he'd've felt eight foot tall, and when he got into bed with his wife, she'd've given it to him the way they do to heroes.

The sight of his nemesis crouched low in the brooding darkness around the plate filled him with fear.

Sighing, he brought himself, without conviction, to throw.

"Bo-ool one."

The staring faces in the stands broke into a cry that stayed till the end of the game.

Vogelman was drenched in sweat. He could have thrown a spitter without half trying but didn't know how and was afraid to monkey with them.

The next went in cap high.

"Eee bo-ool."

Wickitt, the Pirate manager, ambled out to the mound.

"S'matter, Dutch?"

"Take me outa here," Vogelman moaned.

"What the hell for? You got that bastard three times so far and you can do it again."

"He gives me the shits, Walt. Look at him standing there like a goddamn gorilla. Look at his burning eyes. He ain't human."

Wickitt talked low as he studied Roy. "That ain't what I see. He looks old and beat up. Last week he had a mile-high bellyache in a ladies' hospital. They say he could drop dead any minute. Bear up and curve 'em low. I don't think he can bend to his knees. Get one strike on him and he will be your nookie."

He left the mound.

Vogelman threw the next ball with his flesh screaming.

"Bo-ool three."

He sought for Wickitt but the manager kept his face hidden. In that case, the pitcher thought, I will walk him. They could yank him after that—he was a sick man.

Roy was also considering a walk. It would relieve him of responsibility but not make up for all the harm he had done. He discarded the idea. Vogelman made a bony steeple with his arms. Gazing at the plate, he found his eyes were misty and he couldn't read the catcher's sign. He looked again and saw Roy, in full armor, mounted on a black charger. Vogelman stared hard, his arms held high so as not to balk. Yes, there he was coming at him with a long lance as thick as a young tree. He rubbed his arm across his eyes and keeled over in a dead faint.

A roar ascended skywards.

The sun slid behind the clouds. It got cold again. Wickitt, leaning darkly out of the dugout, raised his arm aloft to the center field bullpen. The boy who had been pitching flipped the ball to the bullpen catcher, straightened his cap, and began the long trek in. He was twenty, a scrawny youth with light eyes.

"Herman Youngberry, number sixty-six, pitching for the Pirates."

Few in the stands had heard of him, but before his long trek to the mound was finished his life was common knowledge. He was a six-footer but weighed a skinny one fifty-eight. One day about two years ago a Pirate scout watching him pitching for his home town team had written on a card, "This boy has a fluid delivery of a blinding fast ball and an exploding curve." Though he offered him a contract then and there, Youngberry refused to sign because it was his lifelong ambition to be a farmer. Everybody, including the girl he was engaged to, argued him into signing. He didn't say so but he had it in mind to earn enough money to buy a three hundred acre farm and then quit baseball forever. Sometimes when he pitched, he saw fields of golden wheat gleaming in the sun.

He had come to the Pirates on the first of September from one of their class A clubs, to help in the pennant drive. Since then he'd worked up a three won, two lost record. He'd seen what Roy had done to Vogelman the day he hit the four homers, and just now, and wasn't anxious to face him. After throwing his warm-ups he stepped off the mound and looked away as Roy got back into the box.

Despite the rest he had had, Roy's armpits were creepy with sweat. He felt a bulk of heaviness around his middle and that the individual hairs on his legs and chest were bristling.

Youngberry gazed around to see how they were playing Roy. It was straightaway and deep, with the infield pulled back too. Flores, though hopping about, was on the bag. The pitcher took a full wind-up and became aware the Knights were yelling dirty names to rattle him.

Roy had considered and decided against a surprise bunt. As things were, it was best to take three good swings.

He felt the shadow of the Judge and Memo fouling the air around him and turned to shake his fist at them but they had left the window.

The ball lit its own path.

The speed of the pitch surprised Stuffy Briggs and it was a little time before he could work his tongue free.

"Stuh-rike."

Roy's nose was full of the dust he had raised.

"Throw him to the pigs," shrilled Otto Zipp.

If he bunted, the surprise could get him to first, and Flores home for the tying run. The only trouble was he had not much confidence in his ability to bunt. Roy stared at the kid, trying to hook his eye, but Youngberry wouldn't look at him. As Roy stared a fog blew up around the young pitcher, full of old ghosts and snowy scenes. The fog shot forth a snaky finger and Roy carefully searched under it for the ball but it was already in the catcher's mitt.

"Strike two."

"Off with his head," Otto shrieked.

It felt like winter. He wished for fire to warm his frozen fingers. Too late for the bunt now. He wished he had tried it. He would never give up, he swore. Flores had fallen to his knees on third and was imploring the sky.

Roy caught the pitcher's eye. His own had blood in them. Youngberry shuddered. He threw—a bad ball—but the batter leaped at it.

He struck out with a roar.

Bump Baily's form glowed red on the wall. There was a wail in the wind. He feared the mob would swarm all over him, tear him apart, and strew his polluted remains over the field, but they had vanished. Only O. Zipp climbed down out of his seat. He waddled to the plate, picked up the bat and took a vicious cut at something. He must've connected, because his dumpy bow legs went like pistons around the bases. Thundering down from third he slid into the plate and called himself safe.

Otto dusted himself off, lit a cigar and went home.

When it was night he dragged the two halves of the bat into left field, and with his jackknife cut a long rectangular slash into the turf and dug out the earth. With his hands he deepened the grave in the dry earth and packed the sides tight. He then placed the broken bat in it. He couldn't stand seeing it in two pieces so he removed them and tried squeezing them together in the hope they would stick but the split was smooth, as if the bat had willed its own brokenness, and the two parts would not stay together. Roy undid his shoelaces and wound one around the slender handle of the bat, and the other he tied around the hitting part of the wood, so that except for the knotted laces and the split he knew was there it looked like a whole bat. And this was the way he buried it, wishing it would take root and become a tree. He poured back the earth, carefully pressing it down, and replaced the grass. He trod on it in his stocking feet, and after a last long look around, walked off the field. At the fountain he considered whether to carry out a few handfuls of water to wet the earth above Wonderboy but they would only leak through his fingers before he got there, and since he doubted he could find the exact spot in the dark he went down the dugout steps and into the tunnel.

He felt afraid to go in the clubhouse and so was glad the lights were left on with nobody there. From the looks of things everybody had got their clothes on and torn out. All was silence except the drip drop of the shower and he did not want to go in there. He got rid of his uniform in the soiled clothes can, then dressed in street clothes. He felt something thick against his chest and brought out a sealed envelope. Tearing it open, he discovered a package of thousand dollar bills. He had never seen one before and here were thirty-five. In with the bills was a typewritten note: "The contract will have to wait. There are grave doubts that your cooperation was wholehearted." Roy burned the paper with a match. He considered burning the bills but didn't. He tried to stuff them into his wallet. The wad was too thick so he put them back in the envelope and slipped it into his pocket.

The street was chill and its swaying lights, dark. He shivered as he went to the corner. At the tower he pulled himself up the unlit stairs.

The Judge's secretary was gone but his private door was unlocked so Roy let himself in. The office was pitch black. He located the apartment door and stumbled up the narrow stairs. When he came into the Judge's overstuffed apartment, they were all sitting around a table, the red-headed Memo, the Judge with a green eyeshade over his black wig, and the Supreme Bookie, enjoying a little cigar. They were counting piles of betting slips and a mass of bills. Memo was adding the figures with an adding machine.

Gus got up quickly when he saw Roy. "Nice goin', slugger," he said softly. Smiling, he advanced with his arm extended. "That was some fine show you put on today."

Roy slugged the slug and he went down in open-mouthed wonder. His head hit the floor and the glass eye dropped out and rolled into a mousehole.

Memo was furious. "Don't touch him, you big bastard. He's worth a million of your kind."

Roy said, "You act all right, Memo, but only like a whore."

"Tut," said the Judge.

She ran to him and tried to scratch his eyes but he pushed her aside and she fell over Gus. With a cry she lifted the bookie's head on her lap and made mothering noises over him.

Roy took the envelope out of his pocket. He slapped the Judge's wig and eyeshade off and showered the thousand dollar bills on his wormy head.

The Judge raised a revolver.

"That will do, Hobbs. Another move and I shall be forced to defend myself."

Roy snatched the gun and dropped it in the wastebasket. He twisted the Judge's nose till he screamed. Then he lifted him onto the table and pounded his back with his fists. The Judge made groans and pig squeals. With his foot Roy shoved the carcass off the table. He hit the floor with a crash and had a bowel movement in his pants. He lay moaning amid the betting slips and bills.

Memo had let Gus's head fall and ran around the table to the basket. Raising the pistol, she shot at Roy's back. The bullet grazed his shoulder and broke the Judge's bathroom mirror. The glass clattered to the floor.

Roy turned to her.

"Don't come any nearer or I'll shoot."

He slowly moved forward.

"You filthy scum, I hate your guts and always have since the day you murdered Bump."

Her finger tightened on the trigger but when he came very close she sobbed aloud and thrust the muzzle into her mouth. He gently took the gun from her, opened the cylinder, and shook the cartridges into his palm. He pocketed them and again dumped the gun into the basket.

She was sobbing hysterically as he left.

Going down the tower stairs he fought his overwhelming self-hatred. In each stinking wave of it he remembered some disgusting happening of his life.

He thought, I never did learn anything out of my past life, now I have to suffer again.

When he hit the street he was exhausted. He had not shaved, and a black beard gripped his face. He felt old and grimy.

He stared into faces of people he passed along the street but nobody recognized him.

"He coulda been a king," a woman remarked to a man.

At the corner near some stores he watched the comings and goings of the night traffic. He felt the insides of him beginning to take off (chug chug choo choo . . .). Pretty soon they were in fast flight. A boy thrust a newspaper at him. He wanted to say no but had no voice. The headline screamed, "Suspicion of Hobbs's Sellout—Max Mercy." Under this was a photo Mercy had triumphantly discovered, showing Roy on his back, an obscene bullet imbedded in his gut. Around him danced a naked lady: "Hobbs at nineteen."

And there was also a statement by the baseball commissioner. "If this alleged report is true, that is the last of Roy Hobbs in organized baseball. He will be excluded from the game and all his records forever destroyed."

Roy handed the paper back to the kid.

"Say it ain't true, Roy."

When Roy looked into the boy's eyes he wanted to say it wasn't but couldn't, and he lifted his hands to his face and wept many bitter tears.

THE ASSISTANT

For Ann with love

The early November street was dark though night had ended, but the wind, to the grocer's surprise, already clawed. It flung his apron into his face as he bent for the two milk cases at the curb. Morris Bober dragged the heavy boxes to the door, panting. A large brown bag of hard rolls stood in the doorway along with the sour-faced, gray-haired Poilisheh huddled there, who wanted one.

"What's the matter so late?"

"Ten after six," said the grocer.

"Is cold," she complained.

Turning the key in the lock he let her in. Usually he lugged in the milk and lit the gas radiators, but the Polish woman was impatient. Morris poured the bag of rolls into a wire basket on the counter and found an unseeded one for her. Slicing it in halves, he wrapped it in white store paper. She tucked the roll into her cord market bag and left three pennies on the counter. He rang up the sale on an old noisy cash register, smoothed and put away the bag the rolls had come in, finished pulling in the milk, and stored the bottles at the bottom of the refrigerator. He lit the gas radiator at the front of the store and went into the back to light the one there.

He boiled up coffee in a blackened enamel pot and sipped it, chewing on a roll, not tasting what he was eating. After he had cleaned up he waited; he waited for Nick Fuso, the upstairs tenant, a young mechanic who worked in a garage in the neighborhood. Nick came in every morning around seven for twenty cents' worth of ham and a loaf of bread.

But the front door opened and a girl of ten entered, her face pinched and eyes excited. His heart held no welcome for her.

"My mother says," she said quickly, "can you trust her till tomorrow for a pound of butter, loaf of rye bread and a small bottle of cider vinegar?"

He knew the mother. "No more trust."

The girl burst into tears.

Morris gave her a quarter-pound of butter, the bread and vinegar. He found a penciled spot on the worn counter, near the cash register, and wrote a sum under "Drunk Woman." The total now came to $2.03, which he never hoped to see. But Ida would nag if she noticed a new figure, so he reduced the amount to $1.61. His peace—the little he lived with—was worth forty-two cents.

He sat in a chair at the round wooden table in the rear of the store and scanned, with raised brows, yesterday's Jewish paper that he had already thoroughly read. From time to time he looked absently through the square windowless window cut through the wall, to see if anybody had by chance come into the store. Sometimes when he looked up from his newspaper, he was startled to see a customer standing silently at the counter.

Now the store looked like a long dark tunnel.

The grocer sighed and waited. Waiting he did poorly. When times were bad time was bad. It died as he waited, stinking in his nose.

A workman came in for a fifteen-cent can of King Oscar Norwegian sardines.

Morris went back to waiting. In twenty-one years the store had changed little. Twice he had painted all over, once added new shelving. The old-fashioned double windows at the front a carpenter had made into a large single one. Ten years ago the sign hanging outside fell to the ground but he had never replaced it. Once, when business hit a long good spell, he had had the wooden icebox ripped out and a new white refrigerated showcase put in. The showcase stood at the front in line with the old counter and he often leaned against it as he stared out of the window. Otherwise the store was the same. Years ago it was more a delicatessen; now, though he still sold a little delicatessen, it was more a poor grocery.

A half-hour passed. When Nick Fuso failed to appear, Morris got up and stationed himself at the front window, behind a large cardboard display sign the beer people had rigged up in an otherwise empty window. After a while the hall door opened, and Nick came out in a thick, handknitted green sweater. He trotted around the corner and soon returned carrying a bag of groceries. Morris was now visible at the window. Nick saw the look on his face but didn't look long. He ran into the house, trying to make it seem it was the wind that was chasing him. The door slammed behind him, a loud door.

The grocer gazed into the street. He wished fleetingly that he could once more be out in the open as when he was a boy—never in the house, but the sound of the blustery wind frightened him. He thought again of selling the store but who would buy? Ida still hoped to sell. Every day she hoped. The thought caused him grimly to smile, although he did not feel like smiling. It was an impossible idea so he tried to put it out of his mind. Still, there were times when he went into the back, poured himself a spout of coffee and pleasantly thought of selling. Yet if he miraculously did, where would he go, where? He had a moment of uneasiness as he pictured himself without a roof over his head. There he stood in all kinds of weather, drenched in rain, and the snow froze on his head. No, not for an age had he lived a whole day in the open. As a boy, always running in the muddy, rutted streets of the village, or across the fields, or bathing with the other boys in the river; but as a man, in America, he rarely saw the sky. In the early days when he drove a horse and wagon, yes, but not since his first store. In a store you were entombed.

The milkman drove up to the door in his truck and hurried in, a bull, for his empties. He lugged out a caseful and returned with two half-pints of light cream. Then Otto Vogel, the meat provisions man, entered, a bush-mustached German carrying a smoked liverwurst and string of wieners in his oily meat basket. Morris paid cash for the liverwurst; from a German he wanted no favors. Otto left with the wieners. The bread driver, new on the route, exchanged three fresh loaves for three stale and walked out without a word. Leo, the cake man, glanced hastily at the package cake on top of the refrigerator and called, "See you Monday, Morris."

Morris didn't answer.

Leo hesitated. "Bad all over, Morris."

"Here is the worst."

"See you Monday."

A young housewife from close by bought sixty-three cents' worth; another came in for forty-one cents'. He had earned his first cash dollar for the day.

Breitbart, the bulb peddler, laid down his two enormous cartons of light bulbs and diffidently entered the back.

"Go in," Morris urged. He boiled up some tea and served it in a thick glass, with a slice of lemon. The peddler eased himself into a chair, derby hat and coat on, and gulped the hot tea, his Adam's apple bobbing.

"So how goes now?" asked the grocer.

"Slow," shrugged Breitbart.

Morris sighed. "How is your boy?"

Breitbart nodded absently, then picked up the Jewish paper and read. After ten minutes he got up, scratched all over, lifted across his thin shoulders the two large cartons tied together with clothesline and left.

Morris watched him go.

The world suffers. *He* felt every schmerz.

At lunchtime Ida came down. She had cleaned the whole house.

Morris was standing before the faded couch, looking out of the rear window at the back yards. He had been thinking of Ephraim.

His wife saw his wet eyes.

"So stop sometime, please." Her own grew wet.

He went to the sink, caught cold water in his cupped palms and dipped his face into it.

"The Italyener," he said, drying himself, "bought this morning across the street."

She was irritated. "Give him for twenty-nine dollars five rooms so he should spit in your face."

"A cold water flat," he reminded her.

"You put in gas radiators."

"Who says he spits? This I didn't say."

"You said something to him not nice?"

"Me?"

"Then why he went across the street?"

"Why? Go ask him," he said angrily.

"How much you took in till now?"

"Dirt."

She turned away.

He absent-mindedly scratched a match and lit a cigarette.

"Stop with the smoking," she nagged.

He took a quick drag, clipped the butt with his thumb nail and quickly thrust it under his apron into his pants pocket. The smoke made him cough. He coughed harshly, his face lit like a tomato. Ida held her hands over her ears. Finally he brought up a gob of phlegm and wiped his mouth with his handkerchief, then his eyes.

"Cigarettes," she said bitterly. "Why don't you listen what the doctor tells you?"

"Doctors," he remarked.

Afterward he noticed the dress she was wearing. "What is the picnic?"

Ida said, embarrassed, "I thought to myself maybe will come today the buyer."

She was fifty-one, nine years younger than he, her thick hair still almost all black. But her face was lined, and her legs hurt when she stood too long on them, although she now wore shoes with arch supports. She had waked that morning resenting the grocer for having dragged her, so many years ago, out of a Jewish neighborhood into this. She missed to this day their old friends and landsleit—lost for parnusseh unrealized. That was bad enough, but on top of their isolation, the endless worry about money embittered her. She shared unwillingly the grocer's fate though she did not show it and her dissatisfaction went no farther than nagging—her guilt that she had talked him into a grocery store when he was in the first year of evening high school, preparing, he had said, for pharmacy. He was, through the years, a hard man to move. In the past she could sometimes resist him, but the weight of his endurance was too much for her now.

"A buyer," Morris grunted, "will come next Purim."

"Don't be so smart. Karp telephoned him."

"Karp," he said in disgust. "Where he telephoned—the cheapskate?"

"Here."

"When?"

"Yesterday. You were sleeping."

"What did he told him?"

"For sale a store—yours, cheap."

"What do you mean cheap?"

"The key is worth now nothing. For the stock and the fixtures that they are worth also nothing, maybe three thousand, maybe less."

"I paid four."

"Twenty-one years ago," she said irritably. "So don't sell, go in auction."

"He wants the house too?"

"Karp don't know. Maybe."

"Big mouth. Imagine a man that they held him up four times in the last three years and he still don't take in a telephone. What he says ain't worth a cent. He promised me he wouldn't put in a grocery around the corner, but what did he put?—a grocery. Why does he bring me buyers? Why didn't he keep out the German around the corner?"

She sighed. "He tries to help you now because he feels sorry for you."

"Who needs his sorrow?" Morris said. "Who needs him?"

"So why *you* didn't have the sense to make out of your grocery a wine and liquor store when came out the licenses?"

"Who had cash for stock?"

"So if you don't have, don't talk."

"A business for drunken bums."

"A business is a business. What Julius Karp takes in next door in a day we don't take in in two weeks."

But Ida saw he was annoyed and changed the subject.

"I told you to oil the floor."

"I forgot."

"I asked you special. By now would be dry."

"I will do later."

"Later the customers will walk in the oil and make everything dirty."

"What customers?" he shouted. "Who customers? Who comes in here?"

"Go," she said quietly. "Go upstairs and sleep. I will oil myself."

But he got out the oil can and mop and oiled the floor until the wood shone darkly. No one had come in.

She had prepared his soup. "Helen left this morning without breakfast."

"She wasn't hungry."

"Something worries her."

He said with sarcasm, "What worries her?" Meaning: the store, his health, that most of her meager wages went to keep up payments on the house; that she had wanted a college education but had got instead a job she disliked. Her father's daughter, no wonder she didn't feel like eating.

"If she will only get married," Ida murmured.

"She will get."

"Soon." She was on the verge of tears.

He grunted.

"I don't understand why she don't see Nat Pearl anymore. All summer they went together like lovers."

"A showoff."

"He'll be someday a rich lawyer."

"I don't like him."

"Louis Karp also likes her. I wish she will give him a chance."

"A stupe," Morris said, "like the father."

"Everybody is a stupe but not Morris Bober."

He was staring out at the back yards.

"Eat already and go to sleep," she said impatiently.

He finished the soup and went upstairs. The going up was easier than coming down. In the bedroom, sighing, he drew down the black window shades. He was half asleep, so pleasant was the anticipation. Sleep was his one true refreshment: it excited him to go to sleep. Morris took off his apron, tie and trousers, and laid them on a chair. Sitting at the edge of the sagging wide bed, he unlaced his misshapen shoes and slid under the cold covers in shirt, long underwear and white socks. He nudged his eye into the pillow and waited to grow warm. He crawled toward sleep. But upstairs Tessie Fuso was running the vacuum cleaner, and though the grocer tried to blot the incident out of his mind, he remembered Nick's visit to the German and on the verge of sleep felt bad.

He recalled the bad times he had lived through, but now times were worse than in the past; now they were impossible. His store was always a marginal one, up today, down tomorrow—as the wind blew. Overnight business could go down enough to hurt; yet as a rule it slowly recovered—sometimes it seemed to take forever—went up, not high enough to be really *up*, only not down. When he had first bought the grocery it was all right for the neighborhood; it had got worse as the neighborhood had. Yet even a year ago, staying open seven days a week, sixteen hours a day, he could still eke out a living. What kind of living?—a living; you lived. Now, though he toiled the same hard hours, he was close to bankruptcy, his patience torn. In the past when bad times came he had somehow lived through them, and when good times returned, they more or less returned to him. But now, since the appearance of H. Schmitz across the street ten months ago, all times were bad.

Last year a broken tailor, a poor man with a sick wife, had locked up his shop and gone away, and from the minute of the store's emptiness Morris had felt a gnawing anxiety. He went with hesitation to Karp, who owned the building, and asked him to please keep out another grocery. In this kind of neighborhood one was more than enough. If another squeezed in they would both starve. Karp answered that the neighborhood was better than Morris gave it credit (for schnapps, thought the grocer), but he promised he would look for another tailor or maybe a shoemaker, to rent to. He said so but the grocer didn't believe him. Yet weeks went by and the store stayed empty. Though Ida pooh-poohed his worries, Morris could not overcome his underlying dread. Then one day, as he daily expected, there appeared a sign in the empty store window, announcing the coming of a new fancy delicatessen and grocery.

Morris ran to Karp. "What did you do to me?"

The liquor dealer said with a one-shouldered shrug. "You saw how long stayed empty the store. Who will pay my taxes? But don't worry," he added, "he'll sell more delicatessen but you'll sell more groceries. Wait, you'll see he'll bring you in customers."

Morris groaned; he knew his fate.

Yet as the days went by, the store still sitting empty—emptier, he found himself thinking maybe the new business would never materialize. Maybe the man had changed his mind. It was possible he had seen how poor the neighborhood was and would not attempt to open the new place. Morris wanted to ask Karp if he had guessed right but could not bear to humiliate himself further.

Often after he had locked his grocery at night, he would go secretly around the corner and cross the quiet street. The empty store, dark and deserted, was one door to the left of the corner drugstore; and if no one was looking the grocer would peer through its dusty window, trying to see through shadows whether the emptiness had changed. For two months it stayed the same, and every night he went away reprieved. Then one time—after he saw that Karp was, for once, avoiding him—he spied a web of shelves sprouting from the rear wall, and that shattered the hope he had climbed into.

In a few days the shelves stretched many arms along the other walls, and soon the whole tiered and layered place glowed with new paint. Morris told himself to stay away but he could not help coming nightly to inspect, appraise, then guess the damage, in dollars, to himself. Each night as he looked, in his mind he destroyed what had been built, tried to make of it nothing, but the growth was too quick. Every day the place flowered with new fixtures streamlined counters, the latest refrigerator, fluorescent lights, a fruit stall, a chromium cash register; then from the wholesalers arrived a mountain of cartons and wooden boxes of all sizes, and one night there appeared in the white light a stranger, a gaunt German with a German pompadour, who spent the silent night hours, a dead cigar stuck in his teeth, packing out symmetrical rows of brightly labeled cans, jars, gleaming bottles. Though Morris hated the new store, in a curious way he loved it too, so that sometimes as he entered his own old-fashioned place of business, he could not stand the sight of it; and now he understood why Nick Fuso had that morning run around the corner and crossed the street—to taste the newness of the place and be waited on by Heinrich Schmitz, an energetic German dressed like a doctor, in a white duck jacket. And that was where many of his other customers had gone, and stayed, so that his own poor living was cut in impossible half.

Morris tried hard to sleep but couldn't and grew restless in bed. After another quarter of an hour he decided to dress and go downstairs, but there drifted into his mind, with ease and no sorrow, the form and image of his boy Ephraim, gone so long from him, and he fell deeply and calmly asleep.

Helen Bober squeezed into a subway seat between two women and was on the last page of a chapter when a man dissolved in front of her and another appeared; she knew without looking that Nat Pearl was standing there. She thought she would go on reading, but couldn't, and shut her book.

"Hello, Helen." Nat touched a gloved hand to a new hat. He was cordial but as usual held back something—his future. He carried a fat law book, so she was glad to be protected with a book of her own. But not enough protected, for her hat and coat felt suddenly shabby, a trick of the mind, because on her they would still do.

"*Don Quixote*"?

She nodded.

He seemed respectful, then said in an undertone, "I haven't seen you a long time. Where've you been keeping yourself?"

She blushed under her clothes.

"Did I offend you in some way or other?"

Both of the women beside her seemed stolidly deaf. One held a rosary in her heavy hand.

"No." The offense was hers against herself.

"So what's the score?" Nat's voice was low, his gray eyes annoyed.

"No score," she murmured.

"How so?"

"You're you, I'm me."

This he considered a minute, then remarked, "I haven't much of a head for oracles."

But she felt she had said enough.

He tried another way. "Betty asks for you."

"Give her my best." She had not meant it but this sounded funny because they all lived on the same block, separated by one house.

Tight-jawed, he opened his book. She returned to hers, hiding her thoughts behind the antics of a madman until memory overthrew him and she found herself ensnared in scenes of summer that she would gladly undo, although she loved the season; but how could you undo what you had done again in the fall, unwillingly willing? Virginity she thought she had parted with without sorrow, yet was surprised by torments of conscience, or was it disappointment at being valued under her expectations? Nat Pearl, handsome, cleft-chinned, gifted, ambitious, had wanted without too much trouble a lay and she, half in love, had obliged and regretted. Not the loving, but that it had taken her so long to realize how little he wanted. Not her, Helen Bober.

Why should he?—magna cum laude, Columbia, now in his second year at law school, she only a high school graduate with a year's evening college credit mostly in lit; he with first-rate prospects, also rich friends he had never bothered to introduce her to; she as poor as her name sounded, with little promise of a better future. She had more than once asked herself if she had meant by her favors to work up a claim on him. Always she denied it. She had wanted, admittedly, satisfaction, but more than that—respect for the giver of what she had to give, had hoped desire would become more than just that. She wanted, simply, a future in love. Enjoyment she had somehow had, felt very moving the freedom of fundamental intimacy with a man. Though she wished for more of the same, she wanted it without aftermath of conscience, or pride, or sense of waste. So she promised herself next time it would go the other way; first mutual love, then loving, harder maybe on the nerves, but easier in memory. Thus she had reasoned, until one night in September, when coming up to see his sister Betty, she had found herself alone in the house with Nat and had done again what she had promised herself she wouldn't. Afterward she fought self-hatred. Since then, to this day, without telling him why, she had avoided Nat Pearl.

Two stations before their stop, Helen shut her book, got up in silence and left the train. On the platform, as the train moved away, she caught a glimpse of Nat standing before her empty seat, calmly reading. She walked on, lacking, wanting, not wanting, not happy.

Coming up the subway steps, she went into the park by a side entrance, and despite the sharp wind and her threadbare coat, took the long way home. The leafless trees left her with unearned sadness. She mourned the long age before spring and feared loneliness in winter. Wishing she hadn't come, she left the park, searching the faces of strangers although she couldn't stand their stares. She went quickly along the Parkway, glancing with envy into the lighted depths of private houses that were, for no reason she could give, except experience, not for her. She promised herself she would save every cent possible and register next fall for a full program at NYU, night.

When she reached her block, a row of faded yellow brick houses, two stories squatting on ancient stores, Sam Pearl, stifling a yawn, was reaching into his corner candy store window to put on the lamp. He snapped the string and the dull glow from the fly-specked globe fell upon her. Helen quickened her step. Sam, always sociable, a former cabbie, bulky, wearing bifocals and chewing gum, beamed at her but she pretended no see. Most of the day he sat hunched over dope sheets spread out on the soda fountain counter, smoking as he chewed gum, making smeary marks with a pencil stub under horses' names. He neglected the store; his wife Goldie was the broad-backed one, yet she did not much complain, because Sam's luck with the nags were exceptional and he had nicely supported Nat in college until the scholarships started rolling in.

Around the corner, through the many-bottled window that blinked in neon "KARP wines and liquors," she glimpsed paunchy Julius Karp, with bushy eyebrows and an ambitious mouth, blowing imaginary dust off a bottle as he slipped a deft fifth of something into a paper bag, while Louis, slightly popeyed son and heir, looking up from clipping to the quick his poor fingernails, smiled amiably upon a sale. The Karps, Pearls and Bobers, representing attached houses and stores, but otherwise detachment, made up the small Jewish segment of this gentile community. They had somehow, her father first, then Karp, later Pearl, drifted together here where no other Jews dwelt, except on the far fringes of the neighborhood. None of them did well and were too poor to move elsewhere until Karp, who was with a shoe store that barely made him a living, got the brilliant idea after Prohibition gurgled down the drain and liquor licenses were offered to the public, to borrow cash from a white-bearded rich uncle and put in for one. To everybody's surprise he got the license, though Karp, when asked how, winked a heavy-lidded eye and answered nothing. Within a short time after cheap shoes had become expensive bottles, in spite of the poor neighborhood—or maybe because of it, Helen supposed—he became astonishingly successful and retired his overweight wife from the meager railroad flat above the store to a big house on the Parkway—from which she hardly ever stepped forth—the house complete with two-car garage and Mercury; and at the same time as Karp changed his luck—to hear her father tell it—he became wise without brains.

The grocer, on the other hand, had never altered his fortune, unless degrees of poverty meant alteration, for luck and he were, if not natural enemies, not good friends. He labored long hours, was the soul of honesty—he could not escape his honesty, it was bedrock; to cheat would cause an explosion in him, yet he trusted cheaters—coveted nobody's nothing and always got poorer. The harder he worked—his toil was a form of time devouring time—the less he seemed to have. He was Morris Bober and could be nobody more fortunate. With that name you had no sure sense of property, as if it were in your blood and history not to possess, or if by some miracle to own something, to do so on the verge of loss. At the end you were sixty and had less than at thirty. It was, she thought, surely a talent.

Helen removed her hat as she entered the grocery. "Me," she called, as she had from childhood. It meant that whoever was sitting in the back should sit and not suddenly think he was going to get rich.

Morris awoke, soured by the long afternoon sleep. He dressed, combed his hair with a broken comb and trudged downstairs, a heavy-bodied man with sloping shoulders and bushy gray hair in need of a haircut. He came down with his apron on. Although he felt chilly he poured out a cup of cold coffee, and backed against the radiator, slowly sipped it. Ida sat at the table, reading.

"Why you let me sleep so long?" the grocer complained.

She didn't answer.

"Yesterday or today's paper?"

"Yesterday."

He rinsed the cup and set it on the top of the gas range. In the store he rang up "no sale" and took a nickel out of the drawer. Morris lifted the lid of the cash register, struck a match on the underside of the counter, and holding the flame cupped in his palm, peered at the figure of his earnings. Ida had taken in three dollars. Who could afford a paper?

Nevertheless he went for one, doubting the small pleasure he would get from it. What was so worth reading about the world? Through Karp's window, as he passed, he saw Louis waiting on a customer while four others crowded the counter. Der oilem iz a goilem. Morris took the *Forward* from the newsstand and dropped a nickel into the cigar box. Sam Pearl, working over a green racing sheet, gave him a wave of his hammy hand. They never bothered to talk. What did he know about race horses? What did the other know of the tragic quality of life? Wisdom flew over his hard head.

The grocer returned to the rear of his store and sat on the couch, letting the diminishing light in the yard fall upon the paper. He read nearsightedly, with eyes stretched wide, but his thoughts would not let him read long. He put down the newspaper.

"So where is your buyer?" he asked Ida.

Looking absently into the store she did not reply.

"You should sell long ago the store," she remarked after a minute.

"When the store was good, who wanted to sell? After came bad times, who wanted to buy?"

"Everything we did too late. The store we didn't sell in time. I said, 'Morris, sell now the store.' You said, 'Wait.' What for? The house we bought too late, so we have still a big mortgage that it's hard to pay every month. 'Don't buy,' I said, 'times are bad.' 'Buy,' you said, 'will get better. We will save rent.' "

He answered nothing. If you had failed to do the right thing, talk was useless.

When Helen entered, she asked if the buyer had come. She had forgotten about him but remembered when she saw her mother's dress.

Opening her purse, she took out her pay check and handed it to her father. The grocer, without a word, slipped it under his apron into his pants pocket.

"Not yet," Ida answered, also embarrassed. "Maybe later."

"Nobody goes in the night to buy a store," Morris said. "The time to go is in the day to see how many customers. If this man comes here he will see with one eye the store is dead, then he will run home."

"Did you eat lunch?" Ida asked Helen.

"Yes."

"What did you eat?"

"I don't save menus, Mama."

"Your supper is ready." Ida lit the flame under the pot on the gas range.

"What makes you think he'll come today?" Helen asked her.

"Karp told me yesterday. He knows a refugee that he looks to buy a grocery. He works in the Bronx, so he will be here late."

Morris shook his head.

"He's a young man," Ida went on, "maybe thirty—thirty-two. Karp says he saved a little cash. He can make alterations, buy new goods, fix up modern, advertise a little and make here a nice business."

"Karp should live so long," the grocer said.

"Let's eat." Helen sat at the table.

Ida said she would eat later.

"What about you, Papa?"

"I am not hungry." He picked up his paper.

She ate alone. It would be wonderful to sell out and move but the possibility struck her as remote. If you had lived so long in one place, all but two years of your life, you didn't move out overnight.

Afterward she got up to help with the dishes but Ida wouldn't let her. "Go rest," she said.

Helen took her things and went upstairs.

She hated the drab five-room flat; a gray kitchen she used for breakfast so she could quickly get out to work in the morning. The living room was colorless and cramped; for all its overstuffed furniture of twenty years ago it seemed barren because it was lived in so little, her parents being seven days out of seven in the store; even their rare visitors, when invited upstairs, preferred to remain in the back. Sometimes Helen asked a friend up, but she went to other people's houses if she had a choice. Her bedroom was another impossibility, tiny, dark, despite the two by three foot opening in the wall, through which she could see the living room windows; and at night Morris and Ida had to pass through her room to get to theirs, and from their bedroom back to the bathroom. They had several times talked of giving her the big room, the only comfortable one in the house, but there was no place else that would hold their double bed. The fifth room was a small icebox off the second floor stairs, in which Ida stored a few odds and ends of clothes and furniture. Such was home. Helen had once in anger remarked that the place was awful to live in, and it had made her feel bad that her father had felt so bad.

She heard Morris's slow footsteps on the stairs. He came aimlessly into the living room and tried to relax in a stiff armchair. He sat with sad eyes, saying nothing, which was how he began when he wanted to say something.

When she and her brother were kids, at least on Jewish holidays Morris would close the store and venture forth to Second Avenue to see a Yiddish play, or take the family visiting; but after Ephraim died he rarely went beyond the corner. Thinking about his life always left her with a sense of the waste of her own.

She looks like a little bird, Morris thought. Why should she be lonely? Look how pretty she looks. Whoever saw such blue eyes?

He reached into his pants pocket and took out a five-dollar bill.

"Take," he said, rising and embarrassedly handing her the money. "You will need for shoes."

"You just gave me five dollars downstairs."

"Here is five more."

"Wednesday was the first of the month, Pa."

"I can't take away from you all your pay."

"You're not taking, I'm giving."

She made him put the five away. He did, with renewed shame. "What did I ever give you? Even your college education I took away."

"It was my own decision not to go, yet maybe I will yet. You can never tell."

"How can you go? You are twenty-three years old."

"Aren't you always saying a person's never too old to go to school?"

"My child," he sighed, "for myself I don't care, for you I want the best but what did I give you?"

"I'll give myself," she smiled. "There's hope."

With this he had to be satisfied. He still conceded her a future.

But before he went down, he said gently, "What's the matter you stay home so much lately? You had a fight with Nat?"

"No." Blushing, she answered, "I don't think we see things in the same way."

He hadn't the heart to ask more.

Going down, he met Ida on the stairs and knew she would cover the same ground.

In the evening there was a flurry of business. Morris's mood quickened and he exchanged pleasantries with the customers. Carl Johnsen, the Swedish painter, whom he hadn't seen in weeks, came in with a wet smile and bought two dollars' worth of beer, cold cuts and sliced Swiss cheese. The grocer was at first worried he would ask to charge—he had never paid what he owed on the books before Morris had stopped giving trust—but the painter had the cash. Mrs. Anderson, an old loyal customer, bought for a dollar. A stranger then came in and left eighty-eight cents. After him two more customers appeared. Morris felt a little surge of hope. Maybe things were picking up. But after half-past eight his hands grew heavy with nothing to do. For years he had been the only one for miles around who stayed open at night and had just about made a living from it, but now Schmitz matched him hour for hour. Morris sneaked a little smoke, then began to cough. Ida pounded on the floor upstairs, so he clipped the butt and put it away. He felt restless and stood at the front window, watching the street. He watched a trolley go by. Mr. Lawler, formerly a customer, good for at least a fiver on Friday nights, passed the store. Morris hadn't seen him for months but knew where he was going. Mr. Lawler averted his gaze and hurried along. Morris watched him disappear around the corner. He lit a match and again checked the register—nine and a half dollars, not even expenses.

Julius Karp opened the front door and poked his foolish head in.

"Podolsky came?"

"Who Podolsky?"

"The refugee."

Morris said in annoyance, "What refugee?"

With a grunt Karp shut the door behind him. He was short, pompous, a natty dresser in his advanced age. In the past, like Morris, he had toiled long hours in his shoe store, now he stayed all day in silk pajamas until it came time to relieve Louis before supper. Though the little man was insensitive and a blunderer, Morris had got along fairly well with him, but since Karp had rented the tailor shop to another grocer, sometimes they did not speak. Years ago Karp had spent much time in the back of the grocery, complaining of his poverty as if it were a new invention and he its first victim. Since his success with wines and liquors he came in less often, but he still visited Morris more than his welcome entitled him to, usually to run down the grocery and spout unwanted advice. His ticket of admission was his luck, which he gathered wherever he reached, at a loss, Morris thought, to somebody else. Once a drunk had heaved a rock at Karp's window, but it had shattered his. Another time, Sam Pearl gave the liquor dealer a tip on a horse, then forgot to place a bet himself. Karp collected five hundred for his ten-dollar bill. For years the grocer had escaped resenting the man's good luck, but lately he had caught himself wishing on him some small misfortune.

"Podolsky is the one I called up to take a look at your gesheft," Karp answered.

"Who is this refugee, tell me, an enemy yours?"

Karp stared at him unpleasantly.

"Does a man," Morris insisted, "send a friend he should buy such a store that you yourself took away from it the best business?"

"Podolsky ain't you," the liquor dealer replied. "I told him about this place. I said, 'the neighborhood is improving. You can buy cheap and build up this store. It's run down for years, nobody changed anything there for twenty years.' "

"You should live so long how much I changed—" Morris began but he didn't finish, for Karp was at the window, peering nervously into the dark street.

"You saw that gray car that just passed," the liquor dealer said. "This is the third time I saw it in the last twenty minutes." His eyes were restless.

Morris knew what worried him. "Put in a telephone in your store," he advised, "so you will feel better."

Karp watched the street for another minute and worriedly replied, "Not for a liquor store in this neighborhood. If I had a telephone, every drunken bum would call me to make deliveries, and when you go there they don't have a cent."

He opened the door but shut it in afterthought. "Listen, Morris," he said, lowering his voice, "if they come back again, I will lock my front door and put out my lights. Then I will call you from the back window so you can telephone the police."

"This will cost you five cents," Morris said grimly.

"My credit is class A."

Karp left the grocery, disturbed.

God bless Julius Karp, the grocer thought. Without him I would have my life too easy. God made Karp so a poor grocery man will not forget his life is hard. For Karp, he thought, it was miraculously not so hard, but what was there to envy?

He would allow the liquor dealer his bottles and gelt just not to be him. Life was bad enough.

At nine-thirty a stranger came in for a box of matches. Fifteen minutes later Morris put out the lights in his window. The street was deserted except for an automobile parked in front of the laundry across the car tracks. Morris peered at it sharply but could see nobody in it. He considered locking up and going to bed, then decided to stay open the last few minutes. Sometimes a person came in at a minute to ten. A dime was a dime.

A noise at the side door which led into the hall frightened him.

"Ida?"

The door opened slowly. Tessie Fuso came in in her housecoat, a homely Italian girl with a big face.

"Are you closed, Mr. Bober?" she asked embarrassedly.

"Come in," said Morris.

"I'm sorry I came through the back way but I was undressed and didn't want to go out in the street."

"Don't worry."

"Please give me twenty cents' ham for Nick's lunch tomorrow."

He understood. She was making amends for Nick's trip around the corner that morning. He cut her an extra slice of ham.

Tessie bought also a quart of milk, package of paper napkins and loaf of bread. When she had gone he lifted the register lid. Ten dollars. He thought he had long ago touched bottom but now knew there was none.

I slaved my whole life for nothing, he thought.

Then he heard Karp calling him from the rear. The grocer went inside, worn out.

Raising the window he called harshly, "What's the matter there?"

"Telephone the police," cried Karp. "The car is parked across the street."

"What car?"

"The holdupniks."

"There is nobody in this car, I saw myself."

"For God's sake, I tell you call the police. I will pay for the telephone."

Morris shut the window. He looked up the phone number and was about to dial the police when the store door opened and he hurried inside.

Two men were standing at the other side of the counter, with handkerchiefs over their faces. One wore a dirty yellow clotted one, the other's was white. The one with the white one began pulling out the store lights. It took the grocer a half-minute to comprehend that he, not Karp, was their victim.

Morris sat at the table, the dark light of the dusty bulb falling on his head, gazing dully at the few crumpled bills before him, including Helen's check, and the small pile of silver. The gunman with the dirty handkerchief, fleshy, wearing a fuzzy black hat, waved a pistol at the grocer's head. His pimply brow was thick with sweat; from time to time with furtive eyes he glanced into the darkened store. The other, a taller man in an old cap and torn sneakers, to control his trembling leaned against the sink, cleaning his fingernails with a matchstick. A cracked mirror hung behind him on the wall above the sink and every so often he turned to stare into it.

"I know damn well this ain't everything you took in," said the heavy one to Morris, in a hoarse, unnatural voice. "Where've you got the rest hid?"

Morris, sick to his stomach, couldn't speak.

"Tell the goddam truth." He aimed the gun at the grocer's mouth.

"Times are bad," Morris muttered.

"You're a Jew liar."

The man at the sink fluttered his hand, catching the other's attention. They met in the center of the room, the other with the cap hunched awkwardly over the one in the fuzzy hat, whispering into his ear.

"No," snapped the heavy one sullenly.

His partner bent lower, whispering earnestly through his handkerchief.

"I say he hid it," the heavy one snarled, "and I'm gonna get it if I have to crack his goddam head."

At the table he whacked the grocer across the face.

Morris moaned.

The one at the sink hastily rinsed a cup and filled it with water. He brought it to the grocer, spilling some on his apron as he raised the cup to his lips.

Morris tried to swallow but managed only a dry sip. His frightened eyes sought the man's but he was looking elsewhere.

"Please," murmured the grocer.

"Hurry up," warned the one with the gun.

The tall one straightened up and gulped down the water. He rinsed the cup and placed it on a cupboard shelf.

He then began to hunt among the cups and dishes there and pulled out the pots on the bottom. Next, he went hurriedly through the drawers of an old bureau in the room, and on hands and knees searched under the couch. He ducked into the store, removed the empty cash drawer from the register and thrust his hand into the slot, but came up with nothing.

"The heavy one elbowed him aside.

"We better scram out of here."

"Are you gonna go chicken on me?"

"That's all the dough he has, let's beat it."

"Business is bad," Morris muttered.

"Your Jew ass is bad, you understand?"

"Don't hurt me."

"I will give you your last chance. Where have you got it hid?"

"I am a poor man." He spoke through cracked lips.

The one in the dirty handkerchief raised his gun. The other, staring into the mirror, waved frantically, his black eyes bulging, but Morris saw the blow descend and felt sick of himself, of soured expectations, endless frustration, the years gone up in smoke, he could not begin to count how many. He had hoped for much in America and got little. And because of him Helen and Ida had less. He had defrauded them, he and the bloodsucking store.

He fell without a cry. The end fitted the day. It was his luck, others had better.

During the week that Morris lay in bed with a thickly bandaged head, Ida tended the store fitfully. She went up and down twenty times a day until her bones ached and her head hurt with all her worries. Helen stayed home Satuday, a half-day in her place, and Monday, to help her mother, but she could not risk longer than that, so Ida, who ate in snatches and worked up a massive nervousness, had to shut the store for a full day, although Morris angrily protested. He needed no attention, he insisted, and urged her to keep open at least half the day or he would lose his remaining few customers; but Ida, short of breath, said she hadn't the strength, her legs hurt. The grocer attempted to get up and pull on his pants but was struck by a violent headache and had to drag himself back to bed.

On the Tuesday the store was closed a man appeared in the neighborhood, a stranger who spent much of his time standing on Sam Pearl's corner with a toothpick in his teeth, intently observing the people who passed by; or he would drift down the long block of stores, some empty, from Pearl's to the bar at the far end of the street. Beyond that was a freight yard, and in the distance, a bulky warehouse. After an occasional slow beer in the tavern, the stranger turned the corner and wandered past the high-fenced coal yard; he would go around the block until he got back to Sam's candy store. Once in a while the man would walk over to Morris's closed grocery, and with both hands shading his brow, stare through the window; sighing, he went back to Sam's. When he had as much as he could take of the corner he walked around the block again, or elsewhere in the neighborhood.

Helen had pasted a paper on the window of the front door, that said her father wasn't well but the store would open on Wednesday. The man spent a good deal of time studying this paper. He was young, dark-bearded, wore an old brown rain-stained hat, cracked patent leather shoes and a long black overcoat that looked as if it had been lived in. He was tall and not bad looking, except for a nose that had been broken and badly set, unbalancing his face. His eyes were melancholy. Sometimes he sat at the fountain with Sam Pearl, lost in his thoughts, smoking from a crumpled pack of cigarettes he had bought with pennies. Sam, who was used to all kinds of people, and had in his time seen many strangers appear in the neighborhood and as quickly disappear, showed no special concern for the man, though Goldie, after a full day of his presence complained that too much was too much; he didn't pay rent. Sam did notice that the stranger sometimes seemed to be under stress, sighed much and muttered inaudibly to himself. However, he paid the man scant attention—everybody to their own troubles. Other times the stranger, as if he had somehow squared himself with himself, seemed relaxed, even satisfied with his existence. He read through Sam's magazines, strolled around in the neighborhood and when he returned, lit a fresh cigarette as he opened a paperbound book from the rack in the store. Sam served him coffee when he asked for it, and the stranger, squinting from the smoke of the butt in his mouth, carefully counted out five pennies to pay. Though nobody had asked him he said his name was Frank Alpine and he had lately come from the West, looking for a better opportunity. Sam advised if he could qualify for a chauffeur's license, to try for work as a hack driver. It wasn't a bad life. The man agreed but stayed around as if he was expecting something else to open up.

The day Ida reopened the grocery the stranger disappeared but he returned to the candy store the next morning, and seating himself at the fountain, asked for coffee. He looked bleary, unhappy, his beard hard, dark, contrasting with the pallor of his face; his nostrils were inflamed and his voice was husky. He looks half in his grave, Sam thought. God knows what hole he slept in last night.

As Frank Alpine was stirring his coffee, with his free hand he opened a magazine lying on the counter, and his eye was caught by a picture in color of a monk. He lifted the coffee cup to drink but had to put it down, and he stared at the picture for five minutes.

Sam, out of curiosity, went behind him with a broom, to see what he was looking at. The picture was of a thin-faced, dark-bearded monk in a coarse brown garment, standing barefooted on a sunny country road. His skinny, hairy arms were raised to a flock of birds that dipped over his head. In the background was a grove of leafy trees; and in the far distance a church in sunlight.

"He looks like some kind of a priest," Sam said cautiously.

"No, it's St. Francis of Assisi. You can tell from that brown robe he's wearing and all those birds in the air. That's the time he was preaching to them. When I was a kid, an old priest used to come to the orphans' home where I was raised, and every time he came he read us a different story about St. Francis. They are clear in my mind to this day."

"Stories are stories," Sam said.

"Don't ask me why I never forgot them."

Sam took a closer squint at the picture. "Talking to the birds? What was he—crazy? I don't say this out of any harm."

The stranger smiled at the Jew. "He was a great man. The way I look at it, it takes a certain kind of a nerve to preach to birds."

"That makes him great, because he talked to birds?"

"Also for other things. For instance, he gave everything away that he owned, every cent, all his clothes off his back. He enjoyed to be poor. He said poverty was a queen and he loved her like she was a beautiful woman."

Sam shook his head. "It ain't beautiful, kiddo. To be poor is dirty work."

"He took a fresh view of things."

The candy store owner glanced again at St. Francis, then poked his broom into a dirty corner. Frank, as he drank his coffee, continued to study the picture. He said to Sam, "Every time I read about somebody like him I get a feeling inside of me I have to fight to keep from crying. He was born good, which is a talent if you have it."

He spoke with embarrassment, embarrassing Sam.

Frank drained his cup and left.

That night as he was wandering past Morris's store he glanced through the door and saw Helen inside, relieving her mother. She looked up and noticed him staring at her through the plate glass. His appearance startled her; his eyes were haunted, hungry, sad; she got the impression he would come in and ask for a handout and had made up her mind to give him a dime, but instead he disappeared.

On Friday Morris weakly descended the stairs at six A.M., and Ida, nagging, came after him. She had been opening at eight o'clock and had begged him to stay in bed until then, but he had refused, saying he had to give the Poilisheh her roll.

"Why does three cents for a lousy roll mean more to you than another hour sleep?" Ida complained.

"Who can sleep?"

"You need rest, the doctor said."

"Rest I will take in my grave."

She shuddered. Morris said, "For fifteen years she gets here her roll, so let her get."

"All right, but let me open up. I will give her and you go back to bed."

"I stayed in bed too long. Makes me feel weak."

But the woman wasn't there and Morris feared he had lost her to the German. Ida insisted on dragging in the milk boxes, threatening to shout if he made a move for them. She packed the bottles into the refrigerator. After Nick Fuso they waited hours for another customer. Morris sat at the table, reading the paper, occasionally raising his hand gently to feel the bandage around his head. When he shut his eyes he still experienced moments of weakness. By noon he was glad to go upstairs and crawl into bed and he didn't get up until Helen came home.

The next morning he insisted on opening alone. The Poilisheh was there. He did not know her name. She worked somewhere in a laundry and had a little dog called Polaschaya. When she came home at night she took the little Polish dog for a walk around the block. He liked to run loose in the coal yard. She lived in one of the stucco houses nearby. Ida called her die antisemitke, but that part of her didn't bother Morris. She had come with it from the old country, a different kind of anti-Semitism from in America. Sometimes he suspected she needled him a little by asking for a "Jewish roll," and once or twice, with an odd smile, she wanted a "Jewish pickle." Generally she said nothing at all. This morning Morris handed her her roll and she said nothing. She didn't ask him about his bandaged head though her quick beady eyes stared at it, nor why he had not been there for a week; but she put six pennies on the counter instead of three. He figured she had taken a roll from the bag one of the days the store hadn't opened on time. He rang up the six-cent sale.

Morris went outside to pull in the two milk cases. He gripped the boxes but they were like rocks, so he let one go and tugged at the other. A storm cloud formed in his head and blew up to the size of a house. Morris reeled and almost fell into the gutter, but he was caught by Frank Alpine, in his long coat, steadied and led back into the store. Frank then hauled in the milk cases and refrigerated the bottles. He quickly swept up behind the counter and went into the back. Morris, recovered, warmly thanked him.

Frank said huskily, his eyes on his scarred and heavy hands, that he was new to the neighborhood but living here now with a married sister. He had lately come from the West and was looking for a better job.

The grocer offered him a cup of coffee, which he at once accepted. As he sat down Frank placed his hat on the floor at his feet, and he drank the coffee with three heaping spoonfuls of sugar, to get warm quick, he said. When Morris offered him a seeded hard roll, he bit into it hungrily. "Jesus, this is good bread." After he had finished he wiped his mouth with his handkerchief, then swept the crumbs off the table with one hand into the other, and though Morris protested, he rinsed the cup and saucer at the sink, dried them and set them on top of the gas range, where the grocer had got them.

"Much obliged for everything." He had picked up his hat but made no move to leave.

"Once in San Francisco I worked in a grocery for a couple

of months," he remarked after a minute, "only it was one of those supermarket chain store deals."

"The chain store kills the small man."

"Personally I like a small store myself. I might someday have one."

"A store is a prison. Look for something better."

"At least you're your own boss."

"To be a boss of nothing is nothing."

"Still and all, the idea of it appeals to me. The only thing is I would need experience on what goods to order. I mean about brand names, et cetera. I guess I ought to look for a job in a store and get more experience."

"Try the A&P," advised the grocer.

"I might."

Morris dropped the subject. The man put on his hat.

"What's the matter," he said, staring at the grocer's bandage, "did you have some kind of an accident to your head?"

Morris nodded. He didn't care to talk about it, so the stranger, somehow disappointed, left.

He happened to be in the street very early on Monday when Morris was again struggling with the milk cases. The stranger tipped his hat and said he was off to the city to find a job but he had time to help him pull in the milk. This he did and quickly left. However, the grocer thought he saw him pass by in the other direction about an hour later. That afternoon when he went for his *Forward* he noticed him sitting at the fountain with Sam Pearl. The next morning, just after six, Frank was there to help him haul in the milk bottles and he willingly accepted when Morris, who knew a poor man when he saw one, invited him for coffee.

"How is going now the job?" Morris asked as they were eating.

"So-so," said Frank, his glance shifting. He seemed preoccupied, nervous. Every few minutes he would set down his cup and uneasily look around. His lips parted as if to speak, his eyes took on a tormented expression, but then he shut his jaw as if he had decided it was better never to say what he intended. He seemed to need to talk, broke into sweat—his brow gleamed with it—his pupils widening as he struggled. He looked to Morris like someone who had to retch—no matter where; but after a brutal interval his eyes grew dull. He sighed heavily and gulped down the last of his coffee. After, he brought up a belch. This for a moment satisfied him.

Whatever he wants to say, Morris thought, let him say it to somebody else. I am only a grocer. He shifted in his chair, fearing to catch some illness.

Again the tall man leaned forward, drew a breath and once more was at the point of speaking, but now a shudder passed through him, followed by a fit of shivering.

The grocer hastened to the stove and poured out a cup of steaming coffee. Frank swallowed it in two terrible gulps. He soon stopped shaking, but looked defeated, humiliated, like somebody, the grocer felt, who had lost out on something he had wanted badly.

"You caught a cold?" he asked sympathetically.

The stranger nodded, scratched up a match on the sole of his cracked shoe, lit a cigarette and sat there, listless.

"I had a rough life," he muttered, and lapsed into silence.

Neither of them spoke. Then the grocer, to ease the other's mood, casually inquired, "Where in the neighborhood lives your sister? Maybe I know her."

Frank answered in a monotone. "I forget the exact address. Near the park somewheres."

"What is her name?"

"Mrs. Garibaldi."

"What kind name is this?"

"What do you mean?" Frank stared at him.

"I mean the nationality?"

"Italian. I am of Italian extraction. My name is Frank Alpine—Alpino in Italian."

The smell of Frank Alpine's cigarette compelled Morris to light his butt. He thought he could control his cough and tried but couldn't. He coughed till he feared his head would pop off. Frank watched with interest. Ida banged on the floor upstairs, and the grocer ashamedly pinched his cigarette and dropped it into the garbage pail.

"She don't like me to smoke," he explained between coughs. "My lungs ain't so healthy."

"Who don't?"

"My wife. It's a catarrh some kind. My mother had it all

her life and lived till eighty-four. But they took a picture of my chest last year and found two dried spots. This frightened my wife."

Frank slowly put out his cigarette. "What I started out to say before about my life," he said heavily, "is that I have had a funny one, only I don't mean funny. I mean I've been through a lot. I've been close to some wonderful things—jobs, for instance, education, women, but close is as far as I go." His hands were tightly clasped between his knees. "Don't ask me why, but sooner or later everything I think is worth having gets away from me in some way or another. I work like a mule for what I want, and just when it looks like I am going to get it I make some kind of a stupid move, and everything that is just about nailed down tight blows up in my face."

"Don't throw away your chance for education," Morris advised. "It's the best thing for a young man."

"I could've been a college graduate by now, but when the time came to start going, I missed out because something else turned up that I took instead. With me one wrong thing leads to another and it ends in a trap. I want the moon so all I get is cheese."

"You are young yet."

"Twenty-five," he said bitterly.

"You look older."

"I feel old—damn old."

Morris shook his head.

"Sometimes I think your life keeps going the way it starts out on you," Frank went on. "The week after I was born my mother was dead and buried. I never saw her face, not even a picture. When I was five years old, one day my old man leaves this furnished room where we were staying, to get a pack of butts. He takes off and that was the last I ever saw of him. They traced him years later but by then he was dead. I was raised in an orphans' home and when I was eight they farmed me out to a tough family. I ran away ten times, also from the next people I lived with. I think about my life a lot. I say to myself, 'What do you expect to happen after all of that?' Of course, every now and again, you understand, I hit some nice good spots in between, but they are few and far, and usually I end up like I started out, with nothing."

The grocer was moved. Poor boy.

"I've often tried to change the way things work out for me but I don't know how, even when I think I do. I have it in my heart to do more than I can remember." He paused, cleared his throat and said, "That makes me sound stupid but it's not as easy as that. What I mean to say is that when I need it most something is missing in me, in me or on account of me. I always have this dream where I want to tell somebody something on the telephone so bad it hurts, but then when I am in the booth, instead of a phone being there, a bunch of bananas is hanging on a hook."

He gazed at the grocer then at the floor. "All my life I wanted to accomplish something worthwhile—a thing people will say took a little doing, but I don't. I am too restless—six months in any one place is too much for me. Also I grab at everything too quick—too impatient. I don't do what I have to—that's what I mean. The result is I move into a place with nothing, and I move out with nothing. You understand me?"

"Yes," said Morris.

Frank fell into silence. After a while he said, "I don't understand myself. I don't really know what I'm saying to you or why I am saying it."

"Rest yourself," said Morris.

"What kind of a life is that for a man my age?"

He waited for the grocer to reply—to tell him how to live his life, but Morris was thinking, I am sixty and he talks like me.

"Take some more coffee," he said.

"No, thanks." Frank lit another cigarette and smoked it to the tip. He seemed eased yet not eased, as though he had accomplished something (What? wondered the grocer) yet had not. His face was relaxed, almost sleepy, but he cracked the knuckles of both hands and silently sighed.

Why don't he go home? the grocer thought. I am a working man.

"I'm going." Frank got up but stayed.

"What happened to your head?" he asked again.

Morris felt the bandage. "This Friday before last I had here a holdup."

"You mean they slugged you?"

The grocer nodded.

"Bastards like that ought to die." Frank spoke vehemently.

Morris stared at him.

Frank brushed his sleeve. "You people are Jews, aren't you?"

"Yes," said the grocer, still watching him.

"I always liked Jews." His eyes were downcast.

Morris did not speak.

"I suppose you have some kids?" Frank asked.

"Me?"

"Excuse me for being curious."

"A girl." Morris sighed. "I had once a wonderful boy but he died from an ear sickness that they had in those days."

"Too bad." Frank blew his nose.

A gentleman, Morris thought with a watery eye.

"Is the girl the one that was here behind the counter a couple of nights last week?"

"Yes," the grocer replied, a little uneasily.

"Well, thanks for all the coffee."

"Let me make you a sandwich. Maybe you'll be hungry later."

"No thanks."

The Jew insisted, but Frank felt he had all he wanted from him at the moment.

Left alone, Morris began to worry about his health. He felt dizzy at times, often headachy. Murderers, he thought. Standing before the cracked and faded mirror at the sink he unwound the bandage from his head. He wanted to leave it off but the scar was still ugly, not nice for the customers, so he tied a fresh bandage around his skull. As he did this he thought of that night with bitterness, recalling the buyer who hadn't come, nor had since then, nor ever would. Since his recovery, Morris had not spoken to Karp. Against words the liquor dealer had other words, but silence silenced him.

Afterward the grocer looked up from his paper and was startled to see somebody out front washing his window with a brush on a stick. He ran out with a roar to drive the intruder away, for there were nervy window cleaners who did the job without asking permission, then held out their palms to collect. But when Morris came out of the store he saw the window washer was Frank Alpine.

"Just to show my thanks and appreciation." Frank explained he had borrowed the pail from Sam Pearl and the brush and squeegee from the butcher next door.

Ida then entered the store by the inside door, and seeing the window being washed, hurried outside.

"You got rich all of a sudden?" she asked Morris, her face inflamed.

"He does me a favor," the grocer replied.

"That's right," said Frank, bearing down on the squeegee.

"Come inside, it's cold." In the store Ida asked, "Who is this goy?"

"A poor boy, an Italyener he looks for a job. He gives me a help in the morning with the cases milk."

"If you sold containers like I told you a thousand times, you wouldn't need help."

"Containers leak. I like bottles."

"Talk to the wind," Ida said.

Frank came in blowing his breath on water-reddened fists. "How's it look now, folks, though you can't really tell till I do the inside."

Ida remarked under her breath, "Pay now for your favor."

"Fine," Morris said to Frank. He went to the register and rang up "no sale."

"No, thanks," Frank said, holding up his hand. "For services already rendered."

Ida reddened.

"Another cup coffee?" Morris asked.

"Thanks. Not as of now."

"Let me make you a sandwich?"

"I just ate."

He walked out, threw the dirty water into the gutter, returned the pail and brush, then came back to the grocery. He went behind the counter and into the rear, pausing to rap on the doorjamb.

"How do you like the clean window?" he asked Ida.

"Clean is clean." She was cool.

"I don't want to intrude here but your husband was nice to me, so I just thought maybe I could ask for one more small favor. I am looking for work and I want to try some kind of a grocery job just for size. Maybe I might like it, who knows? It happens I forgot some of the things about cutting and weighing and such, so I am wondering if you would mind me working around here for a couple-three weeks without wages just so I could learn again? It won't cost you a red cent. I know I am a stranger but I am an honest guy. Whoever keeps an eye on me will find that out in no time. That's fair enough, isn't it?"

Ida said, "Mister, isn't here a school."

"What do you say, pop?" Frank asked Morris.

"Because somebody is a stranger don't mean they ain't honest," answered the grocer. "This subject don't interest me. Interests me what you can learn here. Only one thing"—he pressed his hand to his chest—"a heartache."

"You got nothing to lose on my proposition, has he now, Mrs?" Frank said. "I understand he don't feel so hot yet, and if I helped him out a short week or two it would be good for his health, wouldn't it?"

Ida didn't answer.

But Morris said flatly, "No. It's a small, poor store. Three people would be too much."

Frank flipped an apron off a hook behind the door and before either of them could say a word, removed his hat and dropped the loop over his head. He tied the apron strings around him.

"How's that for fit?"

Ida flushed, and Morris ordered him to take it off and put it back on the hook.

"No bad feelings, I hope," Frank said on his way out.

Helen Bober and Louis Karp walked, no hands touching, in the windy dark on the Coney Island boardwalk.

Louis had, on his way home for supper that evening, stopped her in front of the liquor store, on her way in from work.

"How's about a ride in the Mercury, Helen? I never see you much anymore. Things were better in the bygone days in high school."

Helen smiled. "Honestly, Louis, that's so far away." A sense of mourning at once oppressed her, which she fought to a practiced draw.

"Near or far, it's all the same for me." He was built with broad back and narrow head, and despite prominent eyes was presentable. In high school, before he quit, he had worn his wet hair slicked straight back. One day, after studying a picture of a movie actor in the *Daily News,* he had run a part across his head. This was as much change as she had known in him. If Nat Pearl was ambitious, Louis made a relaxed living letting the fruit of his father's investment fall into his lap.

"Anyway," he said, "why not a ride for old-times' sake?"

She thought a minute, a gloved finger pressed into her cheek; but it was a fake gesture because she was lonely.

"For old-times' sake, where?"

"Name your scenery—continuous performance."

"The Island?"

He raised his coat collar. "Brr, it's a cold, windy night. You wanna freeze?"

Seeing her hesitation, he said, "But I'll die game. When'll I pick you up?"

"Ring my bell after eight and I'll come down."

"Check," Louis said. "Eight bells."

They walked to Seagate, where the boardwalk ended. She gazed with envy through a wire fence at the large lit houses fronting the ocean. The Island was deserted, except here and there an open hamburger joint or pinball machine concession. Gone from the sky was the umbrella of rosy light that glowed over the place in summertime. A few cold stars gleamed down. In the distance a dark Ferris wheel looked like a stopped clock. They stood at the rail of the boardwalk, watching the black, restless sea.

All during their walk she had been thinking about her life, the difference between her aloneness now and the fun when she was young and spending every day of summer in a lively crowd of kids on the beach. But as her high school friends had got married, she had one by one given them up; and as others of them graduated from college, envious, ashamed of how little she was accomplishing, she stopped seeing them too. At first it hurt to drop people but after a time it became a not too difficult habit. Now she saw almost no one, occasionally Betty Pearl, who understood, but not enough to make much difference.

Louis, his face reddened by the wind, sensed her mood.

"What's got in you, Helen?" he said, putting his arm around her.

"I can't really explain it. All night I've been thinking of the swell times we had on this beach when we were kids. And do you remember the parties? I suppose I'm blue that I'm no longer seventeen."

"What's so wrong about twenty-three?"

"It's old, Louis. Our lives change so quickly. You know what youth means?"

"Sure I know. You don't catch me giving away nothing for nothing. I got my youth yet."

"When a person is young he's privileged, " Helen said, "with all kinds of possibilities. Wonderful things might happen, and when you get up in the morning you feel they will. That's what youth means, and that's what I've lost. Nowadays I feel that every day is like the day before, and what's worse, like the day after."

"So now you're a grandmother?"

"The world has shrunk for me."

"What do you wanna be—Miss Rheingold?"

"I want a larger and better life. I want the return of my possibilities."

"Such as which ones?"

She clutched the rail, cold through her gloves. "Education," she said, "prospects. Things I've wanted but never had."

"Also a man?"

"Also a man."

His arm tightened around her waist. "Talk is too cold, baby, how's about a kiss?"

She brushed his cold lips, then averted her head. He did not press her.

"Louis," she said, watching a far-off light on the water, "what do you want out of your life?"

He kept his arm around her. "The same thing I got—plus."

"Plus what?"

"Plus more, so my wife and family can have also."

"What if she wanted something different than you do?"

"Whatever she wanted I would gladly give her."

"But what if she wanted to make herself a better person, have bigger ideas, live a more worthwhile life? We die so quickly, so helplessly. Life *has* to have some meaning."

"I ain't gonna stop anybody from being better," Louis said, "That's up to them."

"I suppose," she said.

"Say, baby, let's drop this deep philosophy and go trap a hamburger. My stomach complains."

"Just a little longer. It's been ages since I came here this late in the year."

He pumped his arms. "Jesus, this wind, it flies up my pants. At least gimme another kiss." He unbuttoned his overcoat.

She let him kiss her. He felt her breast. Helen stepped back out of his embrace. "Don't, Louis."

"Why not?" He stood there awkwardly, annoyed.

"It gives me no pleasure."

"I suppose I'm the first guy that ever gave it a nip?"

"Are you collecting statistics?"

"Okay," he said, "I'm sorry. You know I ain't a bad guy, Helen."

"I know you're not, but please don't do what I don't like."

"There was a time you treated me a whole lot better."

"That was the past, we were kids."

It's funny, she remembered, how necking made glorious dreams.

"We were older than that, up till the time Nat Pearl started in college, then you got interested in him. I suppose you got him in mind for the future?"

"If I do, I don't know it."

"But he's the one you want, ain't he? I like to know what that stuck up has got beside a college education? I work for my living."

"No, I don't want him, Louis." But she thought, Suppose Nat said I love you? For magic words a girl might do magic tricks.

"So if that's so, what's wrong with me?"

"Nothing. We're friends."

"Friends I got all I need."

"What do you need, Louis?"

"Cut out the wisecracks, Helen. Would it interest you that I would honestly like to marry you?" He paled at his nerve.

She was surprised, touched.

"Thank you," she murmured.

"Thank you ain't good enough. Give me yes or no."

"No, Louis."

"That's what I thought." He gazed blankly at the ocean.

"I never guessed you were at all remotely interested. You go with girls who are so different from me."

"Please, when I go with them you can't see my thoughts."

"No," she admitted.

"I can give you a whole lot better than you got."

"I know you can, but I want a different life from mine now, or yours. I don't want a storekeeper for a husband."

"Wines and liquors ain't exactly pisher groceries."

"I know."

"It ain't because your old man don't like mine?"

"No."

She listened to the wind-driven, sobbing surf.

Louis said, "Let's go get the hamburgers."

"Gladly." She took his arm but could tell from the stiff way he walked that he was hurt.

As they drove home on the Parkway, Louis said, "If you can't have everything you want, at least take something. Don't be so goddam proud."

Touché. "What shall I take, Louis?"

He paused. "Take less."

"Less I'll never take."

"People got to compromise."

"I won't with my ideals."

"So what'll you be then, a dried-up prune of an old maid? What's the percentage of that?"

"None."

"So what'll you do?"

"I'll wait. I'll dream. Something will happen."

"Nuts," he said.

He let her off in front of the grocery.

"Thanks for everything."

"You'll make me laugh." Louis drove off.

The store was closed, upstairs dark. She pictured her father asleep after his long day, dreaming of Ephraim. What am I saving myself for? she asked herself. What unhappy Bober fate?

It snowed lightly the next day—too early in the year, complained Ida, and when the snow had melted it snowed again. The grocer remarked, as he was dressing in the dark, that he would shovel after he had opened the store. He enjoyed shoveling snow. It reminded him that he had practically lived in it in his boyhood; but Ida forbade him to exert himself because he still complained of dizziness. Later, when he tried to lug the milk cases through the snow, he found it all but impossible. And there was no Frank Alpine to help him, for he had disappeared after washing the window.

Ida came down shortly after her husband, in a heavy cloth coat, a woolen scarf pinned around her head and wearing galoshes. She shoveled a path through the snow and together they pulled in the milk. Only then did Morris notice that a quart bottle was missing from one of the cases.

"Who took it?" Ida cried.

"How do I know?"

"Did you count yet the rolls?"

"No."

"I told you always to count right away."

"The baker will steal from me? I know him twenty years."

"Count what everybody delivers, I told you a thousand times."

He dumped the rolls out of the basket and counted them. Three were missing and he had sold only one to the Poilisheh. To appease Ida he said they were all there.

The next morning another quart of milk and two rolls were gone. He was worried but didn't tell Ida the truth when she asked him if anything else was missing. He often hid unpleasant news from her because she made it worse. He mentioned the missing bottle to the milkman, who answered, "Morris, I swear I left every bottle in that case. Am I responsible for this lousy neighborhood?"

He promised to cart the milk cases into the vestibule for a

few days. Maybe whoever was stealing the bottles would be afraid to go in there. Morris considered asking the milk company for a storage box. Years ago he had had one at the curb, a large wooden box in which the milk was padlocked; but he had given it up after developing a hernia lifting the heavy cases out, so he decided against a box.

On the third day, when a quart of milk and two rolls had again been taken, the grocer, much disturbed, considered calling the police. It wasn't the first time he had lost milk and rolls in this neighborhood. That had happened more than once—usually some poor person stealing a breakfast. For this reason Morris preferred not to call the police but to get rid of the thief by himself. To do it, he would usually wake up very early and wait at his bedroom window in the dark. Then when the man—sometimes it was a woman—showed up and was helping himself to the milk, Morris would quickly raise the window and shout down, "Get outa here, you thief you." The thief, startled—sometimes it was a customer who could afford to buy the milk he was stealing—would drop the bottle and run. Usually he never appeared again—a lost customer cut another way—and the next goniff was somebody else.

So this morning Morris arose at four-thirty, a little before the milk was delivered, and sat in the cold in his long underwear, to wait. The street was heavy with darkness as he peered down. Soon the milk truck came, and the milkman, his breath foggy, lugged the two cases of milk into the vestibule. Then the street was silent again, the night dark, the snow white. One or two people trudged by. An hour later, Witzig, the baker, delivered the rolls, but no one else stopped at the door. Just before six Morris dressed hastily and went downstairs. A bottle of milk was gone, and when he counted the rolls, so were two of them.

He still kept the truth from Ida. The next night she awoke and found him at the window in the dark.

"What's the matter?" she asked, sitting up in bed.

"I can't sleep."

"So don't sit in your underwear in the cold. Come back to bed."

He did as she said. Later, the milk and rolls were missing.

In the store he asked the Poilisheh whether she had seen

anyone sneak into the vestibule and steal a quart of milk. She stared at him with small eyes, grabbed the sliced roll and slammed the door.

Morris had a theory that the thief lived on the block. Nick Fuso wouldn't do such a thing; if he did Morris would have heard him going down the stairs, then coming up again. The thief was somebody from outside. He sneaked along the street close to the houses, where Morris couldn't see him because of the cornice that hung over the store; then he softly opened the hall door, took the milk, two rolls from the bag, and stole away, hugging the house fronts.

The grocer suspected Mike Papadopolous, the Greek boy who lived on the floor above Karp's store. He had served a reformatory sentence at eighteen. A year later he had in the dead of night climbed down the fire escape overhanging Karp's back yard, boosted himself up on the fence and forced a window into the grocery. There he stole three cartons of cigarettes, and a roll of dimes that Morris had left in the cash register. In the morning, as the grocer was opening the store, Mike's mother, a thin, old-looking woman, returned the cigarettes and dimes to him. She had caught her son coming in with them and had walloped his head with a shoe. She clawed his face, making him confess what he had done. Returning the cigarettes and dimes, she had begged Morris not to have the boy arrested and he had assured her he wouldn't do such a thing.

On this day that he had guessed it might be Mike taking the milk and rolls, shortly after eight A.M., Morris went up the stairs and knocked reluctantly on Mrs. Papadopolous' door.

"Excuse me that I bother you," he said, and told her what had been happening to his milk and rolls.

"Mike work all nights in restaurants," she said. "No come home till nine o'clock in mornings. Sleep all days." Her eyes smoldered. The grocer left.

Now he was greatly troubled. Should he tell Ida and let her call the police? They were bothering him at least once a week with questions about the holdup but had produced nobody. Still, maybe it would be best to call them, for this stealing had gone on for almost a week. Who could afford it? Yet he waited, and that night as he was leaving the store by the side door, which he always padlocked after shutting the front door from inside, he flicked on the cellar light and as he peered down the stairs, his nightly habit, his heart tightened with foreboding that somebody was down there. Morris unlocked the lock, went back into the store and got a hatchet. Forcing his courage, he slowly descended the wooden steps. The cellar was empty. He searched in the dusty storage bins, poked around all over, but there was no sign of anybody.

In the morning he told Ida what was going on and she, calling him big fool, telephoned the police. A stocky, red-faced detective came, Mr. Minogue, from a nearby precinct, who was in charge of investigating Morris's holdup. He was a soft-spoken, unsmiling man, bald, a widower who had once lived in this neighborhood. He had a son Ward, who had gone to Helen's junior high school, a wild boy, always in trouble for manhandling girls. When he saw one he knew playing in front of her house, or on the stoop, he would come swooping down and chase her into the hall. There, no matter how desperately the girl struggled, or tenderly begged him to stop, Ward forced his hand down her dress and squeezed her breast till she screamed. Then by the time her mother came running down the stairs he had ducked out of the hall, leaving the girl sobbing. The detective, when he heard of these happenings, regularly beat up his son, but it didn't do much good. Then one day, about eight years ago, Ward was canned from his job for stealing from the company. His father beat him sick and bloody with his billy and drove him out of the neighborhood. After that, Ward disappeared and nobody knew where he had gone. People felt sorry for the detective, for he was a strict man and they knew what it meant to him to have such a son.

Mr. Minogue seated himself at the table in the rear and listened to Ida's complaint. He slipped on his glasses and wrote in a little black notebook. The detective said he would have a cop watch the store mornings after the milk was delivered, and if there was any more trouble to let him know.

As he was leaving, he said, "Morris, would you recognize Ward Minogue if you happened to see him again? I hear he's been seen around but whereabouts I don't know."

"I don't know," said Morris. "Maybe yes or maybe no. I didn't see him for years."

"If I ever meet up with him," said the detective, "I might bring him in to you for identification."

"What for?"

"I don't know myself—just for possible identification."

Ida said afterward that if Morris had called the police in the first place, he might have saved himself a few bottles of milk that they could hardly afford to lose.

That night, on an impulse, the grocer closed the store an hour later than usual. He snapped on the cellar light and cautiously descended the stairs, gripping his hatchet. Near the bottom he uttered a cry and the hatchet fell from his hands. A man's drawn and haggard face stared up at him in dismay. It was Frank Alpine, gray and unshaven. He had been asleep with his hat and coat on, sitting on a box against the wall. The light had awakened him.

"What do you want here?" Morris cried out.

"Nothing," Frank said dully. "I have just been sleeping in the cellar. No harm done."

"Did you steal from me my milk and rolls?"

"Yes," he confessed. "On account of I was hungry."

"Why didn't you ask me?"

Frank got up. "Nobody has any responsibility to take care of me but myself. I couldn't find any job. I used up every last cent I had. My coat is too thin for this cold and lousy climate. The snow and the rain get in my shoes so I am always shivering. Also, I had no place to sleep. That's why I came down here."

"Don't you stay any more with your sister?"

"I have no sister. That was a lie I told you. I am alone by myself."

"Why you told me you had a sister?"

"I didn't want you to think I was a bum."

Morris regarded the man silently. "Were you ever in prison sometimes?"

"Never, I swear to Christ."

"How you came to me in my cellar?"

"By accident. One night I was walking around in the snow so I tried the cellar door and found out you left it unlocked, then I started coming down at night about an hour after you closed the store. In the morning, when they delivered the milk and rolls, I sneaked up through the hall, opened the door and took what I needed for breakfast. That's practically all I ate all day. After you came down and got busy with some customer or a salesman, I left by the hallway with the empty milk bottle under my coat. Later I threw it away in a lot. That's all there is to it. Tonight I took a chance and came in while you were still in the back of the store, because I have a cold and don't feel too good."

"How can you sleep in such a cold and drafty cellar?"

"I slept in worse."

"Are you hungry now?"

"I'm always hungry."

"Come upstairs."

Morris picked up his hatchet, and Frank, blowing his nose in his damp handkerchief, followed him up the stairs.

Morris lit a light in the store and made two fat liverwurst sandwiches with mustard, and in the back heated up a can of bean soup. Frank sat at the table in his coat, his hat lying at his feet. He ate with great hunger, his hand trembling as he brought the spoon to his mouth. The grocer had to look away.

As the man was finishing his meal, with coffee and cup cakes, Ida came down in felt slippers and bathrobe.

"What happened?" she asked in fright, when she saw Frank Alpine.

"He's hungry," Morris said.

She guessed at once. "He stole the milk!"

"He was hungry," explained Morris. "He slept in the cellar."

"I was practically starving," said Frank.

"Why didn't you look for a job?" Ida asked.

"I looked all over."

After, Ida said to Frank, "When you finish, please go someplace else." She turned to her husband. "Morris, tell him to go someplace else. We are poor people."

"This he knows."

"I'll go away," Frank said, "as the lady wishes."

"Tonight is already too late," Morris said. "Who wants he should walk all night in the streets?"

"I don't want him here." She was tense.

"Where you want him to go?"

Frank set his coffee cup on the saucer and listened with interest.

"This ain't my business," Ida answered.

"Don't anybody worry," said Frank. "I'll leave in ten minutes' time. You got a cigarette, Morris?"

The grocer went to the bureau and took out of the drawer a crumpled pack of cigarettes.

"It's stale," he apologized.

"Don't make any difference." Frank lit a stale cigarette, inhaling with pleasure.

"I'll go after a short while," he said to Ida.

"I don't like trouble," she explained.

"I won't make any. I might look like a bum in these clothes, but I am not. All my life I lived with good people."

"Let him stay here tonight on the couch," Morris said to Ida.

"No. Give him better a dollar he should go someplace else."

"The cellar would be fine," Frank remarked.

"It's too damp. Also rats."

"If you let me stay there one more night I promise I will get out the first thing in the morning. You don't have to be afraid to trust me. I am an honest man."

"You can sleep here," Morris said.

"Morris, you crazy," shouted Ida.

"I'll work it off for you," Frank said. "Whatever I cost you I'll pay you back. Anything you want me to do, I'll do it."

"We will see," Morris said.

"No," insisted Ida.

But Morris won out, and they went up, leaving Frank in the back, the gas radiator left lit.

"He will clean out the store," Ida said wrathfully.

"Where is his truck?" Morris asked, smiling. Seriously he said, "He's a poor boy. I feel sorry for him."

They went to bed. Ida slept badly. Sometimes she was racked by awful dreams. Then she awoke and sat up in bed, straining to hear noises in the store—of Frank packing huge bags of groceries to steal. But there was no sound. She dreamed she came down in the morning and all the stock was gone, the shelves as barren as the picked bones of dead birds. She dreamed, too, that the Italyener had sneaked up into the house and was peeking through the keyhole of Helen's door. Only when Morris got up to open the store did Ida fall fitfully asleep.

The grocer trudged down the stairs with a dull pain in his head. His legs felt weak. His sleep had not been refreshing.

The snow was gone from the streets and the milk boxes were again lying on the sidewalk near the curb. None of the bottles were missing. The grocer was about to drag in the milk cases when the Poilisheh came by. She went inside and placed three pennies on the counter. He entered with a brown bag of rolls, cut up and wrapped it. She took it wordlessly and left.

Morris looked through the window in the wall. Frank was asleep on the couch in his clothes, his coat covering him. His beard was black, his mouth loosely opened.

The grocer went out into the street, grabbed both milk boxes and yanked. The shape of a black hat blew up in his head, flared into hissing light, and exploded. He thought he was rising but felt himself fall.

Frank dragged him in and laid him on the couch. He ran upstairs and banged on the door. Helen, holding a housecoat over her nightdress, opened it. She suppressed a cry.

"Tell your mother your father just passed out. I called the ambulance."

She screamed. As he ran down the stairs he could hear Ida moaning. Frank hurried into the back of the store. The Jew lay white and motionless on the couch. Frank gently removed his apron. Draping the loop over his own head, he tied the tapes around him.

"I need the experience," he muttered.

Morris had reopened the wound on his head. The ambulance doctor, the same who had treated him after the holdup, said he had got up too soon last time and worn himself out. He again bandaged the grocer's head, saying to Ida, "This time let him lay in bed a good couple of weeks till his strength comes back." "You tell him, doctor," she begged, "he don't listen to me." So the doctor told Morris, and Morris weakly nodded. Ida, in a gray state of collapse, remained with the patient all day. So did Helen, after calling the ladies' underthings concern where she worked. Frank Alpine stayed competently downstairs in the store. At noon Ida remembered him and came down to tell him to leave. Recalling her dreams, she connected him with their new misfortune. She felt that if he had not stayed the night, this might not have happened.

Frank was clean-shaven in the back, having borrowed Morris's safety razor, his thick hair neatly combed, and when she appeared he hopped up to ring open the cash register, showing her a pile of puffy bills.

"Fifteen," he said, "count every one."

She was astonished. "How is so much?"

He explained, "We had a busy morning. A lot of people stopped in to ask about Morris's accident.

Ida had planned to replace him with Helen for the time being, until she herself could take over, but she was now of two minds.

"Maybe you can stay," she faltered, "if you want to, till tomorrow."

"I'll sleep in the cellar, Mrs. You don't have to worry about me. I am as honest as the day."

"Don't sleep in the cellar," she said with a tremble to her voice, "my husband said on the couch. What can anybody steal here? We have nothing."

"How is he now?" Frank asked in a low voice.

She blew her nose.

The next morning Helen went reluctantly to work. Ida came down at ten to see how things were. This time there were only eight dollars in the drawer, but still better than lately. He apologized, "Not so good today, but I wrote down every article I sold so you'll know nothing stuck to my fingers." He produced a list of goods sold, written on wrapping paper. She happened to notice that it began with three cents for a roll. Glancing around, Ida saw he had packed out the few cartons delivered yesterday, swept up, washed the window from the inside and had straightened the cans on the shelves.

The place looked a little less dreary.

During the day he also kept himself busy with odd jobs. He cleaned the trap of the kitchen sink, which swallowed water slowly, and in the store fixed a light whose chain wouldn't pull, making useless one lamp. Neither of them mentioned his leaving. Ida, still uneasy, wanted to tell him to go but she couldn't ask Helen to stay home any more, and the prospect of two weeks alone in the store, with her feet and a sick man in the bargain to attend upstairs, was too much for her. Maybe she would let the Italian stay ten days or so. With Morris fairly well recovered there would be no reason to keep him after that. In the meantime he would have three good meals a day and a bed, for being little more than a watchman. What business, after all, did they do here? And while Morris was not around she would change a thing or two she should have done before. So when the milkman stopped by for yesterday's empties, she ordered containers brought from now on. Frank Alpine heartily approved. "Why should we bother with bottles?" he said.

Despite all she had to do upstairs, and her recent good impressions of him, Ida haunted the store, watching his every move. She was worried because, now, not Morris but she was responsible for the man's presence in the store. If something bad happened, it would be her fault. Therefore, though she climbed the stairs often to tend to her husband's needs, she hurried back down, arriving pale and breathless to see what Frank was up to. But anything he happened to be doing was helpful. Her suspicions died slowly, though they never wholly died.

She tried not to be too friendly to him, to make him feel that a distant relationship meant a short one. When they were in the back or for a few minutes together behind the counter she discouraged conversation, took up something to do, or clean, or her paper to read. And in the matter of teaching him the business there was also little to say. Morris had price tags displayed under all items on the shelves, and Ida supplied Frank with a list of prices for meats and salads and for the miscellaneous unmarked things like loose coffee, rice or beans. She taught him how to wrap neatly and efficiently, as Morris had long ago taught her, how to read the scale and to set and handle the electric meat slicer. He caught on quickly; she suspected he knew more than he said he did. He added rapidly and accurately, did not overcut meats or overload the scale on bulk items, as she had urged him not to do, and judged well the length of paper needed to wrap with, and what number bag to pack goods into, conserving the larger bags which cost more money. Since he learned so fast, and since she had seen in him not the least evidence of dishonesty (a hungry man who took milk and rolls, though not above suspicion, was not the same as a thief), Ida forced herself to remain upstairs with more calm, in order to give Morris his medicine, bathe her aching feet and keep up the house, which was always dusty from the coal yard. Yet she felt, whenever she thought of it, always a little troubled at the thought of a stranger's presence below, a goy, after all, and she looked forward to the time when he was gone.

Although his hours were long—six to six, at which time she served him his supper—Frank was content. In the store he was quits with the outside world, safe from cold, hunger and a damp bed. He had cigarettes when he wanted them and was comfortable in clean clothes Morris had sent down, even a pair of pants that fitted him after Ida lengthened and pressed the cuffs. The store was fixed, a cave, motionless. He had all his life been on the move, no matter where he was; here he somehow couldn't be. Here he could stand at the window and watch the world go by, content to be here.

It wasn't a bad life. He woke before dawn. The Polish dame was planted at the door like a statue, distrusting him with beady eyes to open the place in time for her to get to work. Her he didn't like; he would gladly have slept longer. To get up in the middle of the night for three lousy cents was a joke but he did it for the Jew. After packing away the milk containers, turning bottomside up the occasional one that leaked, he swept the store and then the sidewalk. In the back he washed, shaved, had coffee and a sandwich, at first made with meat from a ham or roast pork butt, then after a few days, from the best cut. As he smoked after coffee he thought of everything he could do to improve this dump if it were his. When somebody came into the store he was up with a bound, offering service with a smile. Nick Fuso, on Frank's first day, was surprised to see him there, knowing Morris could not afford a clerk. But Frank said that though the pay was scarce there were other advantages. They spoke about this and that, and when the upstairs tenant learned Frank Alpine was a paisan, he told him to come up and meet Tessie. She cordially invited him for macaroni that same night, and he said he would come if they let him bring the macs.

Ida, after the first few days, began to go down at her regular hour, around ten, after she had finished the housework; and she busied herself with writing in a notebook which bills they had got and which paid. She also wrote out, in a halting hand, a few meager special-account checks for bills that could not be paid in cash directly to the drivers, mopped the kitchen floor, emptied the garbage pail into the metal can on the curb outside and prepared salad if it was needed. Frank watched her shred cabbage on the meat slicer for coleslaw, which she made in careful quantity, because if it turned sour it had to be dumped into the garbage. Potato salad was a bigger job, and she cooked up a large pot of new potatoes, which Frank helped her peel hot in their steaming jackets. Every Friday she prepared fish cakes and a panful of homemade baked beans, first soaking the little beans overnight, pouring out the water, then spreading brown sugar on top before baking. Her expression as she dipped in among the soggy beans pieces of ham from a butt she had cut up caught his eye, and he felt for her repugnance for hating to touch the ham, and some for himself because he had never lived this close to Jews before. At lunchtime there was a little "rush," which meant that a few dirty-faced laborers from the coal yard and a couple of store clerks from on the block wanted sandwiches and containers of hot coffee. But the "rush," for which they both went behind the counter, petered out in a matter of minutes and then came the dead hours of the afternoon. Ida said he ought to take some time off, but he answered that he had nowhere special to go and stayed in the back, reading the *Daily News* on the couch, or flipping through some magazines that he had got out of the public library, which he had discovered during one of his solitary walks in the neighborhood.

At three, when Ida departed for an hour or so to see if Morris needed something, and to rest, Frank felt relieved. Alone, he did a lot of casual eating, sometimes with unexpected pleasure. He sampled nuts, raisins, and small boxes of stale dates or dried figs, which he liked anyway; he also opened packages of crackers, macaroons, cupcakes and doughnuts, tearing up their wrappers into small pieces and flushing them down the toilet. Sometimes in the middle of eating sweets he would get very hungry for something more substantial, so he made a thick meat and Swiss cheese sandwich on a seeded hard roll spread with mustard, and swallowed it down with a bottle of ice-cold beer. Satisfied, he stopped roaming in the store.

Now and then there were sudden unlooked-for flurries of customers, mostly women, whom he waited on attentively, talking to them about all kinds of things. The drivers, too, liked his sociability and cheery manner and stayed to chew the fat. Otto Vogel, once when he was weighing a ham, warned him in a low voice, "Don't work for a Yid, kiddo. They will steal your ass while you are sitting on it." Frank, though he said he didn't expect to stay long, felt embarrassed for being there; then, to his surprise, he got another warning, from an apologetic Jew salesman of paper products, Al Marcus, a prosperous, yet very sick and solemn character who wouldn't stop working. "This kind of a store is a death tomb, positive,"

Al Marcus said. "Run out while you can. Take my word, if you stay six months, you'll stay forever."

"Don't worry about that," answered Frank.

Alone afterward, he stood at the window, thinking thoughts about his past, and wanting a new life. Would he ever get what he wanted? Sometimes he stared out of the back yard window at nothing at all, or at the clothesline above, moving idly in the wind, flying Morris's scarecrow union suits, Ida's hefty bloomers, modestly folded lengthwise, and her housedresses guarding her daughter's flower-like panties and restless brasières.

In the evening, whether he wanted to or not, he was "off." Ida insisted, fair was fair. She fed him a quick supper and allowed him, with apologies because she couldn't afford more, fifty cents spending money. He occasionally passed the time upstairs with the Fusos or went with them to a picture at the local movie house. Sometimes he walked, in spite of the cold, and stopped off at a poolroom he knew, about a mile and a half from the grocery store. When he got back, always before closing, for Ida wouldn't let him keep a key to the store in his pocket, she counted up the day's receipts, put most of the cash into a small paper bag and took it with her, leaving Frank five dollars to open up with in the morning. After she had gone, he turned the key in the front door lock, hooked the side door through which she had left, put out the store lights and sat in his undershirt in the rear, reading tomorrow's pink-sheeted paper that he had picked off Sam Pearl's stand on his way home. Then he undressed and went restlessly to bed in a pair of Morris's bulky, rarely used, flannel pajamas.

The old dame, he thought with disgust, always hurried him out of the joint before her daughter came down for supper.

The girl was in his mind a lot. He couldn't help it, imagined seeing her in the things that were hanging on the line—he had always had a good imagination. He pictured her as she came down the stairs in the morning; also saw himself standing in the hall after she came home, watching her skirts go flying as she ran up the stairs. He rarely saw her around, had never spoken to her but twice, on the day her father had passed out. She had kept her distance—who could blame her, dressed as he was and what he looked like then? He had the feeling as he spoke to her, a few hurried words, that he knew more about her than anybody would give him credit for. He had got this thought the first time he had ever laid eyes on her, that night he saw her through the grocery window. When she had looked at him he was at once aware of something starved about her, a hunger in her eyes he couldn't forget because it made him remember his own, so he knew how wide open she must be. But he wouldn't try to push anything, for he had heard that these Jewish babes could be troublemakers and he was not looking for any of that now—at least no more than usual; besides, he didn't want to spoil anything before it got started. There were some dames you had to wait for—for them to come to you.

His desire grew to get to know her, he supposed because she had never once come into the store in all the time he was there except after he left at night. There was no way to see and talk to her to her face, and this increased his curiosity. He felt they were both lonely but her old lady kept her away from him as if he had a dirty disease; the result was he grew more impatient to find out what she was like, get to be friends with her for whatever it was worth. So, since she was never around, he listened and watched for her. When he heard her walking down the stairs he went to the front window and stood there waiting for her to come out; he tried to look casual, as if he weren't watching, just in case she happened to glance back and see him; but she never did, as if she liked nothing about the place enough to look back on. She had a pretty face and a good figure, small-breasted, neat, as if she had meant herself to look that way. He liked to watch her brisk, awkward walk till she turned the corner. It was a sexy walk, with a wobble in it, a strange movement, as though she might dart sideways although she was walking forward. Her legs were just a bit bowed, and maybe that was the sexy part of it. She stayed in his mind after she had turned the corner; her legs and small breasts and the pink brassières that covered them. He would be reading something or lying on his back on the couch, smoking, and she would appear in his mind, walking to the corner. He did not have to shut his eyes to see her. Turn around, he said out loud, but in his thoughts she wouldn't.

To see her coming toward him he stood at the lit grocery window at night, but often before he could catch sight of her she was on her way upstairs, or already changing her dress in her room, and his chance was over for the day. She came home about a quarter to six, sometimes a little earlier, so he tried to be at the window around them, which wasn't so easy because that was the time for Morris's few supper customers to come in. So he rarely saw her come home from work, though he always heard her on the stairs. One day things were slower than usual in the store, it was dead at five-thirty, and Frank said to himself, Today I will see her. He combed his hair in the toilet so that Ida wouldn't notice, changed into a clean apron, lit a cigarette, and stood at the window, visible in its light. At twenty to six, just after he had practically shoved a woman out of the joint, a dame who had happened to walk in off the trolley, he saw Helen turn Sam Pearl's corner. Her face was prettier than he had remembered and his throat tightened as she walked to within a couple of feet of him, her eyes blue, her hair, which she wore fairly long, brown, and she had an absent-minded way of smoothing it back off the side of her face. He thought she didn't look Jewish, which was all to the good. But her expression was discontented, and her mouth a little drawn. She seemed to be thinking of something she had no hope of ever getting. This moved him, so that when she glanced up and saw his eyes on her, his face plainly showed his emotion. It must have bothered her because she quickly walked, without noticing him further, to the hall and disappeared inside.

The next morning he didn't see her—as if she had sneaked out on him—and at night he was waiting on somebody when she returned from work; regretfully he heard the door slam behind her. Afterward he felt downhearted; every sight lost to a guy who lived with his eyes was lost for all time. He thought up different ways to meet her and exchange a few words. What he had on his mind to say to her about himself was beginning to weigh on him, though he hadn't clearly figured out the words. Once he thought of coming in on her unexpectedly while she was eating her supper, but then he would have Ida to deal with. He also had the idea of opening the door the next time he saw her and calling her into the store; he could say that some guy had telephoned her, and after that talk about something else, but nobody did call her. She was in her way a lone bird, which suited him fine, though why she should be with her looks he couldn't figure out. He got the feeling that she wanted something big out of life, and this scared him. Still, he tried to think of schemes of getting her inside the store, even planning to ask her something like did she know where her old man kept his saw; only she mightn't like that, her mother being around all day to tell him. He had to watch out not to scare her any farther away than the old dame had done.

For a couple of nights after work he stood in a hallway next door to the laundry across the street in the hope that she would come out to do some errand, then he would cross over, tip his hat and ask if he could keep her company to where she was going. But this did not pay off either, because she didn't leave the house. The second night he waited fruitlessly until Ida put out the lights in the grocery window.

One evening toward the end of the second week after Morris's accident, Frank's loneliness burdened him to the point of irritation. He was eating his supper a few minutes after Helen had returned from work, while Ida happened to be upstairs with Morris. He had seen Helen come round the corner and had nodded to her as she approached the house. Caught by surprise, she half-smiled, then entered the hall. It was then the lonely feeling gripped him. While he was eating, he felt he had to get her into the store before her old lady came down and it was time for him to leave. The only excuse he could think of was to call Helen to answer the phone and after he would say that the guy must've hung up. It was a trick but he had to do it. He warned himself not to, because it would be starting out the wrong way with her and he might someday regret it. He tried to think of a better way but time was pressing him and he couldn't.

Frank got up, went over to the bureau, and took the phone off its cradle. He then walked out into the hall, opened the vestibule door, and holding his breath, pressed the Bober bell.

Ida looked over the banister. "What's the matter?"

"Telephone for Helen."

He could see her hesitate, so he returned quickly to the store. He sat down, pretending to be eating, his heart whamming so hard it hurt. All he wanted, he told himself, was to talk to her a minute so the next time would be easier.

Helen eagerly entered the kitchen. On the stairs she had noticed the excitement that flowed through her. My God, it's gotten to be that a phone call is an event.

If it's Nat, she thought, I might give him another chance.

Frank half-rose as she entered, then sat down.

"Thanks," she said to him as she picked up the phone.

"Hello." While she waited he could hear the buzz in the receiver.

"There's nobody there," she said mystified.

He laid down his fork. "This girl called you," he said gently.

But when he saw the disappointment in her eyes, how bad she felt, he felt bad.

"You must've been cut off."

She gave him a long look. She was wearing a white blouse that showed the firmness of her small breasts. He wet his dry lips, trying to figure out some quick way to square himself, but his mind, usually crowded with all sorts of schemes, had gone blank. He felt very bad, as he had known he would, that he had done what he had. If he had it to do over he wouldn't do it this way.

"Did she leave you her name?" Helen asked.

"No."

"It wasn't Betty Pearl?"

"No."

She absently brushed back her hair. "Did she say anything to you?"

"Only to call you." He paused. "Her voice was nice—like yours. Maybe she didn't get me straight when I said you were upstairs but I would ring your doorbell, and that's why she hung up."

"I don't know why anybody would do that."

Neither did he. He wanted to step clear of his mess but saw no way other than to keep on lying. But lying made their talk useless. When he lied he was somebody else lying to somebody else. It wasn't the two of them as they were. He should have kept that in his mind.

She stood at the bureau, holding the telephone in her hand as if still expecting the buzz to become a voice; so he waited for the same thing, a voice to speak and say he had been telling the truth, that he was a man of fine character. Only that didn't happen either.

He gazed at her with dignity as he considered saying the simple truth, starting from there, come what would, but the thought of confessing what he had done almost panicked him.

"I'm sorry," he said brokenly, but by then she was gone, and he was attempting to fix in his memory what she had looked like so close.

Helen too was troubled. Not only could she not explain why she believed yet did not fully believe him, nor why she had lately become so curious of his presence among them, though he never strayed from the store, but she was also disturbed by her mother's efforts to keep her away from him. "Eat when he leaves," Ida had said. "I am not used to goyim in my house." This annoyed Helen because of the assumption that she would keel over for somebody just because he happened to be a gentile. It meant, obviously, her mother didn't trust her. If she had been casual about him, Helen doubted she would have paid him any attention to speak of. He was interesting looking, true, but what except a poor grocery clerk? Out of nothing Ida was trying to make something.

Though Ida was still concerned at having the young Italian around the place, she observed with pleased surprise how practically from the day of his appearance, the store had improved. During the first week there were days when they had taken in from five to seven dollars more than they were averaging daily in the months since summer. And the same held for the second week. The store was of course still a poor store, but with this forty to fifty a week more they might at least limp along until a buyer appeared. She could at first not understand why more people were coming in, why more goods were being sold. True, the same thing had happened before. Without warning, after a long season of dearth, three or four customers, lost faces, straggled in one day, as if they had been let out of their poor rooms with a few pennies in their pockets. And others, who had skimped on food, began to buy more. A storekeeper could tell almost at once when times were getting better. People seemed less worried and irritable, less in competition for the little sunlight in the world. Yet the curious thing was that business, according to most of the drivers, had not very much improved anywhere. One of them said that Schmitz around the corner was having his troubles too; furthermore he wasn't feeling so good. So the sudden pickup of business in the store, Ida thought, would not have happened without Frank Alpine. It took her a while to admit this to herself.

The customers seemed to like him. He talked a lot as he waited on them, sometimes saying things that embarrassed Ida but made the customers, the gentile housewives, laugh. He somehow drew in people she had never before seen in the neighborhood, not only women, men too. Frank tried things that Morris and she could never do, such as attempting to sell people more than they asked for, and usually he succeeded. "What can you do with a quarter of a pound?" he would say. "A quarter is for the birds—not even a mouthful. Better make it a half." So they would make it a half. Or he would say, "Here's a new brand of mustard that we just got in today. It weighs two ounces more than the stuff they sell you in the supermarkets for the same price. Why don't you give it a try? If you don't like it, bring it back and I will gargle it." And they laughed and bought it. This made Ida wonder if Morris and she were really suited to the grocery business. They had never been salesmen.

One of the women customers called Frank a supersalesman, a word that brought a pleased smile to his lips. He was clever and worked hard. Ida's respect for him reluctantly grew; graudally she became more relaxed in his presence. Morris was right in recognizing that he was not a bum but a boy who had gone through bad times. She pitied him for having lived in an orphan asylum. He did his work quickly, never complained, kept himself neat and clean now that he had soap and water around, and answered her politely. The one or two times, just lately, that he had briefly talked to Helen in her presence, he had spoken like a gentleman and didn't try to stretch a word into a mouthful. Ida discussed the situation with Morris and they raised his "spending money" from fifty cents a day to five dollars for the week. Despite her good will to him, this worried Ida, but, after all, he was bringing more money into the store, the place looked spic and span—let him keep five dollars of their poor profit. Bad as things still were, he willingly did so much extra around the store—how could they not pay him a little something? Besides, she thought, he would soon be leaving.

Frank accepted the little raise with an embarrassed smile. "You don't have to pay me anything more, Mrs, I said I would work for nothing to make up for past favors from your husband and also to learn the business. Besides that, you give me my bed and board, so you don't owe me a thing."

"Take," she said, handing him a crumpled five-dollar bill. He let the money lie on the counter till she urged him to put it into his pocket. Frank felt troubled about the raise because he was earning something for his labor that Ida knew nothing of, for business was a little better than she thought. During the day, while she was not around, he sold at least a buck's worth, or a buck and a half, that he made no attempt to ring up on the register. Ida guessed nothing; the list of sold items he had supplied her with in the beginning they had discontinued as impractical. It wasn't hard for him to scrape up here a bit of change, there a bit. At the end of the second week he had ten dollars in his pocket. With this and the five she gave him he bought a shaving kit, a pair of cheap brown suede shoes, a couple of shirts and a tie or two; he figured that if he stayed around two more weeks he would own an inexpensive suit. He had nothing to be ashamed of, he thought—it was practically his own dough he was taking. The grocer and his wife wouldn't miss it because they didn't know they had it, and they wouldn't have it if it wasn't for his hard work. If he weren't working there, they would have less than they had with him taking what he took.

Thus he settled it in his mind only to find himself remorseful. He groaned, scratching the backs of his hands with his thick nails. Sometimes he felt short of breath and sweated profusely. He talked aloud to himself when he was alone, usually when he was shaving or in the toilet, exhorted himself to be honest. Yet he felt a curious pleasure in his misery, as he had at times in the past when he was doing something he knew he oughtn't to, so he kept on dropping quarters into his pants pocket.

One night he felt very bad about all the wrong he was doing and vowed to set himself straight. If I could do one right thing, he thought, maybe that would start me off; then he thought if he could get the gun and get rid of it he would at least feel better. He left the grocery after supper and wandered restlessly in the foggy streets, feeling cramped in the chest from his long days in the store and because his life hadn't changed much since he had come here. As he passed by the cemetery, he tried to keep out of his mind the memory of the holdup but it kept coming back in. He saw himself sitting with Ward Minogue in the parked car, waiting for Karp to come out of the grocery, but when he did his store lights went out and he hid in the back among the bottles. Ward said to drive quick around the block so they would flush the Jew out, and he would slug him on the sidewalk and take his fat wallet away; but when they got back, Karp's car was gone with him in it, and Ward cursed him into an early grave. Frank said Karp had beat it, so they ought to scram, but Ward sat there with heartburn, watching with his small eyes, the grocery store, the one lit place on the block besides the candy store on the corner.

"No," Frank urged, "it's just a little joint, I got my doubts if they took in thirty bucks today."

"Thirty is thirty," Ward said. "I don't care if it's Karp or Bober, a Jew is a Jew."

"Why not the candy store?"

Ward made a face. "I can't stand penny candy."

"How do you know his name?" asked Frank.

"Who?"

"The Jew grocer."

"I used to go to school with his daughter. She has a nice ass."

"Then if that's so, he will recognize you."

"Not with a rag around my snoot, and I will rough up my

voice. He aint' seen me for eight or nine years. I was a skinny kid then."

"Have it your way. I will keep the car running."

"Come in with me," Ward said. "The block is dead. Nobody will expect a stickup in this dump."

But Frank hesitated. "I thought you said Karp was the one you were out after?"

"I will take Karp some other time. Come on."

Frank put on his cap and crossed the car tracks with Ward Minogue. "It's your funeral," he said, but it was really his own.

He remembered thinking as they went into the store, a Jew is a Jew, what difference does it make? Now he thought, I held him up because he was a Jew. What the hell are they to me so that I gave them credit for it?

But he didn't know the answer and walked faster, from time to time glancing through the spiked iron fence at the shrouded gravestones. Once he felt he was being followed and his heart picked up a hard beat. He hurried past the cemetery and turned right on the first street after it, hugging the stoops of the stone houses as he went quickly down the dark street. When he reached the poolroom he felt relieved.

Pop's poolroom was a dreary four-table joint, owned by a glum old Italian with a blue-veined bald head and droopy hands, who sat close to his cash register.

"Seen Ward yet?" Frank said.

Pop pointed to the rear where Ward Minogue, in his fuzzy black hat and a bulky overcoat, was practicing shots alone at a table. Frank watched him place a black ball at a corner pocket and aim a white at it. Ward leaned tensely forward, his face strained, a dead butt hanging from his sick mouth. He shot but missed. He banged his cue on the floor.

Frank had drifted past the players at the other tables. When Ward looked up and saw him, his eyes lit with fear. The fear drained after he recognized who it was. But his pimply face was covered with sweat.

He spat his butt to the floor. "What have you got on your feet, you bastard, gumshoes?"

"I didn't want to spoil your shot."

"Anyway you did."

"I've been looking for you about a week."

"I was on my vacation." Ward smiled in the corner of his mouth.

"On a drunk?"

Ward put his hand to his chest and brought up a belch. "I wish to hell it was. Somebody tipped my old man I was around here, so I hid out for a while. I had a rough time. My heartburn is acting up." He hung up his cue, then wiped his face with a dirty handkerchief.

"Why don't you go to a doctor?" Frank said.

"The hell with them."

"Some medicine might help you."

"What will help me is if my goddam father drops dead."

"I want to talk to you, Ward," Frank said in a low voice.

"So talk."

Frank nodded toward the players at the next table.

"Come out in the yard," Ward said. "I got something I want to say to you."

Frank followed him out the rear door into a small enclosed back yard with a wooden bench against the building. A weak bulb shone down on them from the top of the doorjamb.

Ward sat down on the bench and lit a cigarette. Frank did the same, from his own pack. He puffed but got no pleasure from the butt, so he threw it away.

"Sit down," said Ward.

Frank sat on the bench. Even in the fog he stinks, he thought.

"What do you want me for?" Ward asked, his small eyes restless.

"I want my gun, Ward. Where is it?"

"What for?"

"I want to throw it in the ocean."

Ward snickered. "Cat got your nuts?"

"I don't want some dick coming around and asking me do I own it."

"I thought you said you bought the rod off a fence."

"That's right."

"Then nobody's got a record of it, so what are you scared of?"

"If you lost it," Frank said, "they trace them even without a record."

"I won't lose it," Ward said. After a minute he ground his cigarette into the dirt. "I will give it back to you after we do this job I have on my mind."

Frank looked at him. "What kind of a job?"

"Karp. I want to stick him up."

"Why Karp?—there are bigger liquor stores."

"I hate that Jew son of a bitch and his popeyed Louis. When I was a kid all I had to do was go near banjo eyes and they would complain to my old man and get me beat up."

"They would recognize you if you go in there."

"Bober didn't. I will use a handkerchief and wear some different clothes. Tomorrow I will go out and pick up a car. All you got to do is drive and I will make the heist."

"You better stay away from that block," Frank warned. "Somebody might recognize you."

Ward moodily rubbed his chest. "All right, you sold me. We will go somewheres else."

"Not with me," Frank said.

"Think it over."

"I've had all I want."

Ward showed his disgust. "The minute I saw you I knew you would puke all over."

Frank didn't answer.

"Don't act so innocent," Ward said angrily. "You're hot, the same as me."

"I know," Frank said.

"I slugged him because he was lying where he hid the rest of the dough," Ward argued.

"He didn't hide it. It's a poor, lousy store."

"I guess you know all about that."

"What do you mean?"

"Can the crud. I know you been working there."

Frank drew a breath. "You following me again, Ward?"

Ward smiled. "I followed you one night after you left the poolroom. I found out you were working for a Jew and living on bird crap."

Frank slowly got up. "I felt sorry for him after you slugged him, so I went back to give him a hand while he was in a weak condition. But I won't be staying there long."

"That was real sweet of you. I suppose you gave him back the lousy seven and a half bucks that was your part of the take?"

"I put it back in the cash register. I told the Mrs. the business was getting better."

"I never thought I would meet up with a goddam Salvation Army soldier."

"I did it to quiet my conscience," Frank said.

Ward rose. "That ain't your conscience you are worried about."

"No?"

"It's something else. I hear those Jew girls make nice ripe lays."

Frank went back without his gun.

Helen was with her mother as Ida counted the cash.

Frank stood behind the counter, cleaning his fingernails with his jackknife blade, waiting for them to leave so he could close up.

"I think I'll take a hot shower before I go to bed," Helen said to her mother. "I've felt chilled all night."

"Good night," Ida said to Frank. "I left five dollars change for the morning."

"Good night," said Frank.

They left by the rear door and he heard them go up the stairs. Frank closed the store and went into the back. He thumbed through tomorrow's *News*, then got restless.

After a while he went into the store and listened at the side door; he unlatched the lock, snapped on the cellar light, closed the cellar door behind him so no light would leak out into the hall, then quietly descended the stairs.

He found the air shaft where an old unused dumb-waiter stood, pushed the dusty box back and gazed up the vertical shaft. It was pitch-dark. Neither the Bobers' bathroom window nor the Fusos' showed any light.

Frank struggled against himself but not for long. Shoving the dumb-waiter back as far as it would go, he squeezed into the shaft and then boosted himself up on top of the box. His heart shook him with its beating.

When his eyes got used to the dark he saw that her bathroom window was only a couple of feet above his head. He felt along the wall as high as he could reach and touched a narrow ledge around the air shaft. He thought he could anchor himself on it and see into the bathroom.

But if you do it, he told himself, you will suffer.

Though his throat hurt and his clothes were drenched in sweat, the excitement of what he might see forced him to go up.

Crossing himself, Frank grabbed both of the dumb-waiter ropes and slowly pulled himself up, praying the pulley at the skylight wouldn't squeak too much.

A light went on over his head.

Holding his breath, he crouched motionless, clinging to the swaying ropes. Then the bathroom window was shut with a bang. For a while he couldn't move, the strength gone out of him. He thought he might lose his grip and fall, and he thought of her opening the bathroom window and seeing him lying at the bottom of the shaft in a broken, filthy heap.

It was a mistake to do it, he thought.

But she might be in the shower before he could get a look at her, so, trembling, he began again to pull himself up. In a few minutes he was stradding the ledge, holding onto the ropes to steady himself yet keep his full weight off the wood.

Leaning forward, though not too far, he could see through the uncurtained crossed sash window into the old-fashioned bathroom. Helen was there looking with sad eyes at herself in the mirror. He thought she would stand there forever, but at last she unzippered her housecoat, stepping out of it.

He felt a throb of pain at her nakedness, an overwhelming desire to love her, at the same time an awareness of loss, of never having had what he had wanted most, and other such memories he didn't care to recall.

Her body was young, soft, lovely, the breasts like small birds in flight, her ass like a flower. Yet it was a lonely body in spite of its lovely form, lonelier. Bodies are lonely, he thought, but in bed she wouldn't be. She seemed realer to him now than she had been, revealed without clothes, personal, possible. He felt greedy as he gazed, all eyes at a banquet, hungry so long as he must look. But in looking he was forcing her out of reach, making her into a thing only of his seeing, her eyes reflecting his sins, rotten past, spoiled ideals, his passion poisoned by his shame.

Frank's eyes grew moist and he wiped them with one hand. When he gazed up again she seemed, to his horror, to be staring at him through the window, a mocking smile on her lips, her eyes filled with scorn, pitiless. He thought wildly of jumping, bolting, broken-boned, out of the house; but she turned on the shower and stepped into the tub, drawing the flowered plastic curtain around her.

The window was quickly covered with steam. For this he was relieved, grateful. He let himself down silently. In the cellar, instead of the grinding remorse he had expected to suffer, he felt a moving joy.

On a Saturday morning in December, Morris, after a little more than two impatient weeks upstairs, came down with his head healed. The night before, Ida told Frank he would have to leave in the morning, but when Morris later learned this they had an argument. Although he hadn't said so to Ida, the grocer, after his long layoff, was depressed at the prospect of having to take up his dreary existence in the store. He dreaded the deadweight of hours, mostly sad memories of his lost years of youth. That business was better gave him some comfort but not enough, for he was convinced from all Ida had told him that business was better only because of their assistant, whom he remembered as a stranger with hungry eyes, a man to be pitied. Yet the why of it was simple enough—the store had improved not because this cellar dweller was a magician, but because he was not Jewish. The goyim in the neighborhood were happier with one of their own. A Jew stuck in their throats. Yes, they had, on and off, patronized his store, called him by his first name and asked for credit as if he were obliged to give it, which he had, in the past, often foolishly done; but in their hearts they hated him. If it weren't so, Frank's presence could not have made such a quick difference in income. He was afraid that the extra forty-five dollars weekly would melt away overnight if the Italian left and he vehemently said so to Ida. She, though she feared he was right, still argued that Frank must be let go. How could they, she asked, keep him working seven days a week, twelve hours a day, for a miserable five dollars? It was unjust. The grocer agreed, but why push the boy into the street if he wanted to stay longer? The five dollars, he admitted, was nothing, but what of the bed and board, the free packs of cigarettes, the bottles of beer she said he guzzled in the store? If things went on well, he would offer him more, maybe even a small commission, very small—maybe on all they took in over a hundred and fifty a week, a sum they had not realized since Schmitz had opened up around the corner; meantime he would give him his Sundays off and otherwise reduce his hours. Since Morris was now able to open the store, Frank could stay in bed till nine. This proposition was no great bargain but the grocer insisted that the man have the chance to take or refuse it.

Ida, a red flush spreading on her neck, said, "Are you crazy, Morris? Even with the forty more that comes in, which we give him away five dollars, our little profit, who can afford to keep him here? Look what he eats. It's impossible."

"We can't afford to keep him but we can't afford to lose him, on account he might improve more the business if he stays," Morris answered.

"How can three people work in such a small store?" she cried.

"Rest your sick feet," he answered. "Sleep longer in the morning and stay more upstairs in the house. Who needs you should be so tired every night?"

"Also," Ida argued, "who wants him in the back all night so we can't go inside after the store is closed when we forget something?"

"This I thought about also. I think I will take off from Nick's rent upstairs a couple dollars and tell him he should give Frank the little room to sleep in. They don't use it for nothing, only storage. There, with plenty blankets he will be comfortable, with a door which it goes right in the hall so he can come in and go out with his own key without bothering anybody. He can wash himself here in the store."

"A couple dollars less from the rent comes also from our poor pocket," Ida replied, pressing her clasped hands to her bosom. "But the most important is I don't want him here on account of Helen. I don't like the way he looks on her."

Morris gazed at her. "So you like maybe how Nat looks on

her, or Louis Karp? That's the way they look, the boys. Tell me better, how does she look on him."

She shrugged stiffly.

"This is what I thought. You know yourself Helen wouldn't be interested in such a boy. A grocery clerk don't interest her. Does she go out with the salesmen where she works, that they ask her? No. She wants better—so let her have better."

"Will be trouble," she murmured.

He belittled her fears, and when he came down on Saturday morning, spoke to Frank about staying on for a while. Frank had arisen before six and was sitting dejectedly on the couch when the grocer came in. He agreed at once to continue on in the store under the conditions Morris offered.

More animated now, the clerk said he liked the idea of living upstairs near Nick and Tessie; and Morris that day arranged it, in spite of Ida's misgivings, by promising three dollars off their rent. Tessie lugged out of the room a trunk, garment bags and a few odds and ends of furniture; after, she dusted and vacuumed. Between what she offered, and what Morris got out of his bin in the cellar, they supplied a bed with a fairly good mattress, a usable chest of drawers, chair, small table, electric heater and even an old radio Nick had around. Although the room was cold, because it had no radiator and was locked off from the Fusos' gas-heated bedroom, Frank was satisfied. Tessie worried about what would happen if he had to go to the bathroom at night, and Nick talked the matter over with Frank, saying apologetically that she was ashamed to have him go through their bedroom, but Frank said he never woke up at night. Anyway, Nick had a key made to the front door patent lock. He said if Frank ever had to get up he could walk across the hall and let himself in through the front without waking them. And he could also use their bathtub, just so long as he told them when he would want it.

This arrangement suited Tessie. Everyone was satisfied but Ida, who was unhappy with herself for having kept Frank on. She made the grocer promise he would send the clerk away before the summer. Business was always more active in the summertime, so Morris agreed. She asked him to tell Frank at once that he would be let go then, and when the grocer did, the clerk smiled amiably and said the summer was a long ways off but anyway it was all right with him.

The grocer felt his mood change. It was a better mood than he had expected. A few of his old customers had returned. One woman told him that Schmitz was not giving as good service as he once did; he was having trouble with his health and was thinking of selling the store. Let him sell, thought Morris. He thought, let him die, then severely struck his chest.

Ida stayed upstairs most of the day, reluctantly at first, less so as time went by. She came down to prepare lunch and supper—Frank still ate before Helen—or to make a salad when it was needed. She attended to little else in the store; Frank did the cleaning and mopping. Upstairs, Ida took care of the house, read a bit, listened to the Jewish programs on the radio and knitted. Helen bought some wool and Ida knitted her a sweater. In the night, after Frank had gone, Ida spent her time in the store, added up the accounts in her notebook and left with Morris when he closed up.

The grocer got alone well with his assistant. They divided tasks and waited on alternate customers, though the waiting in between was still much too long. Morris went up for naps to forget the store. He too urged Frank to take some time off in the afternoon, to break the monotony of the day. Frank, somewhat restless, finally began to. Sometimes he went up to his room and lay on the bed, listening to the radio. Usually he put his coat on over his apron and visited one of the other stores on the block. He liked Giannola, the Italian barber across the street, an old man who had recently lost his wife and sat in the shop all day, even when it was long past time to go home; the old barber gave a fine haircut. Occasionally Frank dropped in on Louis Karp and gassed with him, but generally Louis bored him. Sometimes he went into the butcher store, next door to Morris, and talked in the back room with Artie, the butcher's son, a blond fellow with a bad complexion who was interested in riding horses. Frank said he might go riding with him sometime but he never did though Artie invited him. Once in a while he drank a beer in the bar on the corner, where he liked Earl, the bartender. Yet when the clerk got back to the grocery he was glad to go in.

When he and Morris were together in the back they spent a lot of time talking. Morris liked Frank's company; he liked to hear about strange places, and Frank told him about some of the cities he had been to, in his long wandering, and some of the different jobs he had worked at. He had passed part of his early life in Oakland, California, but most of it across the bay in a home in San Francisco. He told Morris stories about his hard times as a kid. In this second family the home had sent him to, the man used to work him hard in his machine shop. "I wasn't twelve," Frank said, "and he kept me out of school as long as he could get away with."

After staying with that family for three years, he took off. "Then began my long period of travels." The clerk fell silent, and the ticking clock, on the shelf above the sink, sounded flat and heavy. "I am mostly self-educated," he ended.

Morris told Frank about life in the old country. They were poor and there were pogroms. So when he was about to be conscripted into the czar's army his father said, "Run to America." A landsman, a friend of his father, had sent money for his passage. But he waited for the Russians to call him up, because if you left the district before they had conscripted you, then your father was arrested, fined and imprisoned. If the son got away after induction, then the father could not be blamed; it was the army's responsibility. Morris and his father, a peddler in butter and eggs, planned that he would try to get away on his first day in the barracks.

So on that day, Morris said, he told the sergeant, a peasant with red eyes and a bushy mustache which smelled of tobacco, that he wanted to buy some cigarettes in the town. He felt scared but was doing what his father had advised him to do. The half-drunk sergeant agreed he could go, but since Morris was not yet in uniform he would have to go along with him. It was a September day and had just rained. They walked along a muddy road till they reached the town. There, in an inn, Morris bought cigarettes for himself and the sergeant; then, as he had planned it with his father, he invited the soldier to drink some vodka with him. His stomach became rigid at the chance he was taking. He had never drunk in an inn before, and he had never before tried to deceive anybody to this extent. The sergeant, filling his glass often, told Morris the story of his life, crying when he came to the part where, through forgetfulness, he had not attended his mother's funeral. Then he blew his nose, and wagging a thick finger in Morris's face, warned him if he had any plans to skip, he had better forget them if he expected to live. A dead Jew was of less consequence than a live one. Morris felt a heavy gloom descend on him. In his heart he surrendered his freedom for years to come. Yet once they had left the inn and were trudging in the mud back to the barracks, his hopes rose as the sergeant, in his stupor, kept falling behind. Morris walked slowly on, then the sergeant would cup his hands to his mouth, and cursing, haloo for him to wait. Morris waited. They would go on together, the sergeant muttering to himself, Morris uncertain what would happen next. Then the soldier stopped to urinate into a ditch in the road. Morris pretended to wait but he walked on, every minute expecting a bullet to crash through his shoulders and leave him lying in the dirt, his future with the worms. But then, as if seized by his fate, he began to run. The halooing and cursing grew louder as the red-faced sergeant, waving a revolver, stumbled after him; but when he reached the bend of the tree-lined road where he had last seen Morris, nobody was there but a yellow-bearded peasant driving a nag pulling a load of hay.

Telling this story excited the grocer. He lit a cigarette and smoked without coughing. But when he had finished, when there was no more to say, a sadness settled on him. Sitting in his chair, he seemed a small, lonely man. All the time he had been upstairs his hair had grown bushier and he wore a thick pelt of it at the back of his neck. His face was thinner than before.

Frank thought about the story Morris had just told him. That was the big jig in his life but where had it got him? He had escaped out of the Russian Army to the U.S.A., but once in a store he was like a fish fried in deep fat.

"After I came here I wanted to be a druggist," Morris said. "I went for a year in night school. I took algebra, also German and English. ' "Come," said the wind to the leaves one day, "come over the meadow with me and play." ' This is a poem I learned. But I didn't have the patience to stay in night school, so when I met my wife I gave up my chances." Sighing, he said, "Without education you are lost."

Frank nodded.

"You're still young," Morris said. "A young man without a family is free. Don't do what I did."

"I won't," Frank said.

But the grocer didn't seem to believe him. It made the clerk uncomfortable to see the wet-eyed old bird brooding over him. His pity leaks out of his pants, he thought, but he would get used to it.

When they were behind the counter together, Morris kept an eye on Frank and tried to improve some of the things Ida had taught him. The clerk did very well what he was supposed to. As if ashamed somebody could learn the business so easily, Morris explained to him how different it had been to be a grocer only a few years ago. In those days one was more of a macher, a craftsman. Who was ever called on nowadays to slice up a loaf of bread for a customer, or ladle out a quart of milk?

"Now is everything in containers, jars, or packages. Even hard cheeses that they cut them for hundreds of years by hand come now sliced up in cellophane packages. Nobody has to know anything any more."

"I remember the family milk cans," Frank said, "only my family sent me out to get beer in them."

But Morris said it was a good idea that milk wasn't sold loose any more. "I used to know grocers that they took out a quart or two cream from the top of the can, then they put in water. This water-milk they sold at the regular price."

He told Frank about some other tricks he had seen. "In some stores they bought two kinds loose coffee and two kinds tub butter. One was low grade, the other was medium, but the medium they put half in the medium bin and half in the best. So if you bought the best coffee or the best butter you got medium—nothing else."

Frank laughed. "I'll bet some of the customers came back saying that the best butter tasted better than the medium."

"It's easy to fool people," said Morris.

"Why don't you try a couple of those tricks yourself, Morris? Your amount of profit is small."

Morris looked at him in surprise. "Why should I steal from my customers? Do they steal from me?"

"They would if they could."

"When a man is honest he don't worry when he sleeps. This is more important than to steal a nickel."

Frank nodded.

But he continued to steal. He would stop for a few days then almost with relief go back to it. There were times stealing made him feel good. It felt good to have some change in his pocket, and it felt good to pluck a buck from under the Jew's nose. He would slip it into his pants pocket so deftly that he had to keep himself from laughing. With this money, and what he earned, he bought a suit and hat, and got new tubes for Nick's radio. Now and then, through Sam Pearl, who telephoned it in for him, he laid a two-buck bet on a horse, but as a rule he was careful with the dough. He opened a small savings account in a bank near the library and hid the bankbook under his mattress. The money was for future use.

When he felt pepped up about stealing, it was also because he felt he had brought them luck. If he stopped stealing he bet business would fall off again. He was doing them a favor, at the same time making it a little worth his while to stay on and give them a hand. Taking this small cut was his way of showing himself he had something to give. Besides, he planned to return everything sometime or why would he be marking down the figure of what he took? He kept it on a small card in his shoe. He might someday plunk down a tenner or so on some longshot and then have enough to pay back every lousy cent of what he had taken.

For this reason he could not explain why, from one day to another, he should begin to feel bad about snitching the bucks from Morris, but he did. Sometimes he went around with a quiet grief in him, as if he had just buried a friend and was carrying the fresh grave within himself. This was an old feeling of his. He remembered having had something like it for years back. On days he felt this way he sometimes got headaches and went around muttering to himself. He was afraid to look into the mirror for fear it would split apart and drop into the sink. He was wound up so tight he would spin for a week if the spring snapped. He was full of sudden rages at himself. These were his worst days and he suffered trying to hide his feelings. Yet they had a curious way of ending. The rage he felt disappeared like a windstorm that quietly pooped out, and he felt a sort of gentleness creeping in. He felt gentle to the people who came into the store, especially the kids, whom he gave penny crackers to for nothing. He was gentle to Morris, and the Jew was gentle to him. And he was filled with a quiet gentleness for Helen and no longer climbed the air shaft to spy on her, naked in the bathroom.

And there were days when he was sick to death of everything. He had had it, up to here. Going downstairs in the morning he thought he would gladly help the store burn if it caught on fire. Thinking of Morris waiting on the same lousy customers day after day throughout the years, as they picked out with dirty fingers the same cheap items they ate every day of their flea-bitten lives, then when they were gone, waiting for them to come back again, he felt like leaning over the banister and throwing up. What kind of a man did you have to be born to shut yourself up in an overgrown coffin and never once during the day, so help you, outside of going for your Yiddish newspaper, poke your beak out of the door for a snootful of air? The answer wasn't hard to say—you had to be a Jew. They were born prisoners. That was what Morris was, with his deadly patience, or endurance, or whatever the hell it was; and it explained Al Marcus, the paper products salesman, and that skinny rooster Breitbart, who dragged from store to store his two heavy cartons full of bulbs.

Al Marcus, who had once, with an apologetic smile, warned the clerk not to trap himself in a grocery, was a well-dressed man of forty-six, but he looked, whenever you saw him, as if he had just lapped up cyanide. His face was the whitest Frank had ever seen, and what anybody saw in his eyes if he took a good look, would not help his appetite. The truth of it was, the grocer had confided to Frank, that Al had cancer and was supposed to be dead in his grave a year ago, but he fooled the doctors; he stayed alive if you could call it that. Although he had a comfortable pile, he wouldn't quit working and showed up regularly once a month to take orders for paper bags, wrapping paper and containers. No matter how bad business was, Morris tried to have some kind of little order waiting for him. Al would suck on an unlit cigar, scribble an item or two on a pink page in his metal-covered salesbook, then stand around a few minutes, making small talk, his eyes far away from what he was saying; and after that, tip his hat and take off for the next place. Everybody knew how sick he was, and a couple of the storekeepers earnestly advised him to quit working, but Al, smiling apologetically, took his cigar out of his mouth and said, "If I stay home, somebody in a high hat is gonna walk up the stairs and put a knock on my door. This way let him at least move his bony ass around and try and find me."

As for Breitbart, according to Morris, nine years ago he had owned a good business, but his brother ran it into the ground, gambling, then he took off with what was left of the bank account, persuading Breitbart's wife to come along and keep it company. That left him with a drawerful of bills and no credit; also a not too bright five-year-old boy. Breitbart went bankrupt; his creditors plucked every feather. For months he and the boy lived in a small, dirty furnished room, Breitbart not having the heart to go out to look for work. Times were bad. He went on relief and later took to peddling. He was now in his fifties but his hair had turned white and he acted like an old man. He bought electric bulbs at wholesale and carried two cartons of them slung, with clothesline rope, over his shoulder. Every day, in his crooked shoes, he walked miles, looking into stores and calling out in a mournful voice, "Lights for sale." At night he went home and cooked supper for his Hymie, who played hooky whenever he could from the vocational school where they were making him into a shoemaker.

When Breitbart first came to Morris's neighborhood and dropped into the store, the grocer, seeing his fatigue, offered him a glass of tea with lemon. The peddler eased the rope off his shoulder and set his boxes on the floor. In the back he gulped the hot tea in silence, warming both hands on the glass. And though he had, besides his other troubles, the seven-year itch, which kept him awake half the night, he never complained. After ten minutes he got up, thanked the grocer, fitted the rope onto his lean and itchy shoulder and left. One day he told morris the story of his life and they both wept.

That's what they live for, Frank thought, to suffer. And the one that has got the biggest pain in the gut and can hold onto it the longest without running to the toilet is the best Jew. No wonder they got on his nerves.

Winter tormented Helen. She ran from it, hid in the house. In the house she revenged herself on December by crossing off the calendar all its days. If Nat would only call, she thought endlessly, but the telephone was deaf and dumb. She dreamed of him nightly, felt deeply in love, famished for him; would gladly have danced into his warm white bed if only he nodded, or she dared ask him to ask her; but Nat never called. She hadn't for a minute glimpsed him since running into him on the subway early in November. He lived around the corner but it might as well be Paradise. So with a sharp-pointed pencil she scratched out each dead day while it still lived.

Though Frank hungered for her company he rarely spoke to her. Now and then he passed her on the street. She murmured hello and walked on with her books, conscious of his eyes following her. Sometimes in the store, as if in defiance of her mother, she stopped to talk for a minute with the clerk. Once he startled her by abruptly mentioning this book he was reading. He longed to ask her to go out with him, but never dared; the old lady's eyes showed distrust of the goings on. So he waited. Mostly he watched for her at the window. He studied her hidden face, sensed her lacks, which deepened his own, but didn't know what to do about it.

December yielded nothing to spring. She awoke to each frozen, lonely day with dulled feeling. Then one Sunday afternoon winter leaned backward for an hour and she went walking. Suddenly she forgave everyone everything. A warmish breath of air was enough to inspire; she was again grateful for living. But the sun soon sank and it snowed pellets. She returned home, leaden. Frank was standing at Sam Pearl's deserted corner but she seemed not to see him though she brushed by. He felt very bad. He wanted her but the facts made a terrible construction. They were Jews and he was not. If he started going out with Helen her mother would throw a double fit and Morris another. And Helen made him feel, from the way she carried herself, even when she seemed most lonely, that she had plans for something big in her life—nobody like F. Alpine. He had nothing, a backbreaking past, had committed a crime against her old man, and in spite of his touchy conscience, was stealing from him too. How complicated could impossible get?

He saw only one way of squeezing through the stone knot; start by shoveling out the load he was carrying around in his mind by admitting to Morris that he was one of the guys that had held him up. It was a funny thing about that; he wasn't really sorry they had stuck up a Jew but he hadn't expected to be sorry that they had picked on this particular one, Bober; yet now he was. He had not minded, if by mind you meant in expectation, but what he hadn't minded no longer seemed to matter. The matter was how he now felt, and he now felt bad he had done it. And when Helen was around he felt worse.

So the confession had to come first—this stuck like a bone through the neck. From the minute he had he had tailed Ward Minogue into the grocery that night, he had got this sick feeling that he might someday have to vomit up in words, no matter how hard or disgusting it was to do, the thing he was then engaged in doing. He felt he had known this, in some frightful way, a long time before he went into the store, before he had met Minogue, or even come east; that he had really known all his life he would sometime, through throat blistered with shame, his eyes in the dirt, have to tell some poor son of a bitch tht he was the one who had hurt or betrayed him. This thought had lived in him with claws; or like a thirst he could never spit out, a repulsive need to get out of his system all that had happened—for whatever had happened had happened wrong; to clean it out of his self and bring in a little peace, a little order; to change the beginning, beginning with the past that always stupendously stank up the now—to change his life before the smell of it suffocated him.

Yet when the chance came to say it, when he was alone with Morris that November morning in the back of the store, as they were drinking the coffee that the Jew had served him, and the impulse came on him to spill everything now, *now,* he had strained to heave it up, but it was like tearing up your whole life, with the broken roots and blood; and a fear burned in his gut that once he had got started saying the wrongs he had done he never would leave off until he had turned black; so instead he had told him a few hurried things about how ass-backward his life had gone, which didn't even begin to say what he wanted. He had worked on Morris's pity and left halfway satisfied, but not for long, because soon the need to say it returned and he heard himself groaning, but groans weren't words.

He argued with himself that he was smart in not revealing to the grocer more than he had. Enough was enough; besides, how much of a confession was the Jew entitled to for the seven and a half bucks he had taken, then put back into his cash register drawer, and for the knock on the head he had got from Ward, whom he himself had come with unwillingly? Maybe willing, but not to do what had finally been done. That deserved some consideration, didn't it? Furthermore, he had begged the creep not to hurt anybody, and later turned him down when he cooked up another scheme of stickup against Karp, who they were out to get in the first place. That showed his good intentions for the future, didn't it? And who was it, after all was said and done, that had waited around shivering in his pants in the dark cold, to pull in Morris's milk boxes, and had worked his ass to a frazzle twelve hours a day while the Jew lay upstairs resting in his bed? And was even now keeping him from starvation in his little rat hole? All that added up to something too.

That was how he argued with himself, but it didn't help for long, and he was soon again fighting out how to jump free of what he had done. He would someday confess it all—he promised himself. If Morris accepted his explanation and solemn apology, it would clear the rocks out of the road for the next move. As for his present stealing from the cash register, he had decided that once he had told the grocer all there was to say about the holdup, he would at the same time start paying back into the drawer, out of his little salary and the few bucks he had put away in the bank, what he had taken, and that would fix that. It wouldn't necessarily mean that Helen Bober would then and there fall for him—the opposite could happen—but if she did, he wouldn't feel bad about it.

He knew by heart what he would say to the grocer once he got to say it. One day while they were talking in the back, he would begin, as he had once done, about how his life was mostly made up of lost chances, some so promising he could not stand to remember them. Well, after certain bad breaks through various causes, mostly his own mistakes—he was piled high with regrets—after many such failures, though he tried every which way to free himself from them, usually he failed; so after a time he gave up and let himself be a bum. He lived in gutters, cellars if he was lucky, slept in lots, ate what the dogs wouldn't, or couldn't, and what he scrounged out of garbage cans. He wore what he found, slept where he flopped and guzzled anything.

By rights this should have killed him, but he lived on, bearded, smelly, dragging himself through the seasons without a hope to go by. How many months he had existed this way he would never know. Nobody kept the score of it. But one day while he lay in some hole he had crawled into, he had this terrific idea that he was really an important guy, and was torn out of his reverie with the thought that he was living this kind of life only because he hadn't known he was meant for something a whole lot better—to do something big, different. He had not till that minute understood this. In the past he had usually thought of himself as an average guy, but there in this cellar it came to him he was wrong. That was why his luck had so often curdled, because he had the wrong idea of what he really was and had spent all his energy trying to do the wrong things. Then when he had asked himself what should he be doing, he had another powerful idea, that he was meant for crime. He had at times teased himself with this thought, but now it wouldn't let go of him. At crime he would change his luck, make adventure, live like a prince. He shivered with pleasure as he conceived robberies, assaults—murders if it had to be—each violent act helping to satisfy a craving that somebody suffer as his own fortune improved. He felt infinitely relieved, believing that if a person figured for himself something big, something different in his life, he had a better chance to get it than some poor jerk who couldn't think that high up.

So he gave up his outhouse existence. He began to work again, got himself a room, saved and bought a gun. Then he headed east, where he figured he could live the way he wanted—where there was money, nightclubs, babes. After a week of prowling around in Boston, not sure where he ought to start off, he hopped a freight to Brooklyn and a couple of days after he got there met Ward Minogue. As they were shooting pool one night, Ward cannily detected the gun on him and made him the proposition that they do a holdup together. Frank welcomed the idea of some kind of start but said he wanted to think about it more. He went to Coney Island, and while sitting on the boardwalk, worrying about what he ought to do, got this oppressive feeling he was being watched. When he turned around it was Ward Minogue. Ward sat down and told him that it was a Jew he planned to rob, so Frank agreed to go with him.

But on the night of the holdup he found himself nervous. In the car Ward sensed it and cursed him. Frank felt he had to stick it out, but the minute they were both in the grocery and tying handkerchiefs around their mouths, the whole idea seemed senseless. He could feel it poop out in his mind. His plans of crime lay down and died. He could hardly breathe in his unhappiness, wanted to rush out into the street and be swallowed up out of existence, but he couldn't let Ward stay there alone. In the back, nauseated by the sight of the Jew's bloodied head, he realized he had made the worst mistake yet, the hardest to wipe out. And that ended his short life of violent crime, another pipe dream, and he was trapped tighter in the tangle of his failures. All this he thought he would someday tell Morris. He knew the Jew well enough to feel sure of his mercy.

Yet there were times when he imagined himself, instead, telling it all to Helen. He wanted to do something that would open her eyes to his true self, but who could be a hero in a grocery store? Telling her would take guts and guts was something. He continued to feel he deserved a better fate, and he would find it if he only once—*once*—did the right thing—

the thing to do at the right time. Maybe if they were ever together for any decent amount of time, he would ask her to listen. At first she might be embarrassed, but when he started telling her about his life, he knew she would hear him to the end. After that—who knew? With a dame all you needed was a beginning.

But when the clerk caught himself coldly and saw the sentimentality of his thinking—he was a sentimental wop at heart—he knew he was having another of his hopped-up dreams. What kind of a chance did he think he would have with her after he had admitted the stickup of her old man? So he figured the best thing was to keep quiet. At the same time a foreboding crept into him that if he said nothing now, he would someday soon have a dirtier past to reveal.

A few days after Christmas, on the night of a full moon, Frank, dressed in his new clothes, hurried to the library, about a dozen blocks from the grocery. The library was an enlarged store, well lit, with bulging shelves of books that smelled warm on winter nights. In the rear there were a few large reading tables. It was a pleasant place to come to out of the cold. His guess was good, soon Helen arrived. She wore a red woolen scarf on her head, one end thrown over her shoulder. He was at a table reading. She noticed him as she closed the door behind her; he knew it. They had met here, briefly, before. She had wondered what he read at the table, and once in passing, glanced quickly over his shoulder. She had guessed *Popular Mechanics*, but it was the life of somebody or other. Tonight, as usual, she was aware of his eyes on her as she moved about from shelf to shelf. When, after an hour, she left, he caught a tight hidden glance in his direction. Frank got up and checked out a book. She was halfway down the street before he caught up with her.

"Big moon." He reached up to tip his hat and awkwardly discovered he wasn't wearing any.

"It feels like snow," Helen answered.

He glanced at her to see if she was kidding, then at the sky. It was cloudless, flooded with moonlight.

"Maybe." As they approached the street corner, he remarked, "We could take a walk in the park if it's okay with you."

She shivered at the suggestion, yet turned with a nervous laugh at the corner, and walked by his side. She had said almost nothing to him since the night he had called her to answer the empty phone. Who it had been she would never know; the incident still puzzled her.

Helen felt for him, as they walked, an irritation bordering on something worse. She knew what caused it—her mother, in making every gentile, by definition, dangerous; therefore he and she, together, represented some potential evil. She was also annoyed that his eating eyes were always on her, for he saw, she felt, more than his occasionally trapped gaze revealed. She fought her dislike of him, reasoning it wasn't his fault if her mother had made him into an enemy; and if he was always looking at her, it meant at least he saw something attractive or why would he look? Considering her lonely life, for that she owed him gratitude.

The unpleasant feeling passed and she glanced guardedly up at him. He was walking unmarked in moonlight, innocent of her reaction to him. She felt then—this thought had come to her before—that there might be more to him than she had imagined. She felt ashamed she had never thanked him for the help he had given her father.

In the park the moon was smaller, a wanderer in the white sky. He was talking about winter.

"It's funny you mentioned snow before," Frank said. "I was reading about the life of St. Francis in the library, and when you mentioned the snow it made me think about this story where he wakes up one winter night, asking himself did he do the right thing to be a monk. My God, he thought, supposing I met some nice young girl and got married to her and by now I had a wife and a family? That made him feel bad so he couldn't sleep. He got out of his straw bed and went outside of the church or monastery or wherever he was staying. The ground was all covered with snow. Out of it he made this snow woman, and he said. 'There, that's my wife.' Then he made two or three kids out of the snow. After, he kissed them all and went inside and laid down in the straw. He felt a whole lot better and fell asleep."

The story surprised and touched her.

"Did you just read that?"

"No. I remember it from the time I was a kid. My head is full of those stories, don't ask me why. A priest used to read them to the orphans in this home I was in, and I guess I never forgot them. They come into my thoughts for no reason at all."

He had had a haircut and in his new clothes was hardly recognizable as her father's baggy-pants assistant who had slept a week in their cellar. Tonight he looked like somebody she had never seen before. His clothes showed taste, and he was, in his way, interesting looking. Without an apron on he seemed younger.

They passed an empty bench. "What do you say if we sit down?" Frank said.

"I'd rather walk."

"Smoke?"

"No."

He lit a cigarette, then caught up with her.

"Sure is some night."

"I want to say thanks for helping my father," Helen said, "You've been very kind. I should have mentioned it before."

"Nobody has to thank me. Your father did me some good favors." He felt uncomfortable.

"Anyway, don't make a career of a grocery," she said. "There's no future in it."

He puffed with a smile on his lips. "Everybody warns me. Don't worry, my imagination is too big for me to get stuck in a grocery. It's only temporary work."

"It isn't what you usually do?"

"No." He set himself to be honest. "I'm just taking a breather, you could call it. I started out wrong and have to change my direction where I am going. The way it happened I landed up in your father's store, but I'm only staying there till I figure out what's my next move."

He remembered the confession he had considered making to her, but the time wasn't ready yet. You could confess as a stranger, and you could confess as a friend.

"I've tried about everything," he said, "now I got to choose one thing and stick with it. I'm tired of being on the move all the time."

"Isn't it a little late for you to be getting started?"

"I'm twenty-five. There are plenty of guys who start that late and some I have read about started later. Age don't mean a thing. It doesn't make you less than anybody else."

"I never said so." At the next empty bench she paused. "We could sit here for a few minutes if you like."

"Sure." Frank wiped the seat with his handkerchief before she sat down. He offered her his cigarettes.

"I said I don't smoke."

"Sorry, I thought you didn't want to smoke while you were walking. Some girls don't like to." He put his pack away.

She noticed the book he was carrying. "What are you reading?"

He showed it to her.

"The Life of Napoleon"?

"That's right."

"Why him?"

"Why not—he was great, wasn't he?"

"Others were in better ways."

"I'll read about them too," Frank said.

"Do you read a lot?"

"Sure. I am a curious guy. I like to know why people tick. I like to know the reason they do the things they do, if you know what I mean."

She said she did.

He asked her what book she was reading.

"*The Idiot.* Do you know it?"

"No. What's it about?"

"It's a novel."

"I'd rather read the truth," he said.

"It is the truth."

Helen asked, "Are you a high school graduate?"

He laughed. "Sure I am. Education is free in this country."

She blushed. "It was a silly question."

"I didn't mean any wisecrack," he said quickly.

"I didn't take it as such."

"I went to high school in three different states and finally got finished up at night—in a night school. I planned on going to college but this job came along that I couldn't turn down, so I changed my mind, but it was a mistake."

"I had to help my mother and father out," Helen said, "so I couldn't go either. I've taken courses in NYU at night—mostly lit courses—and I've added up about a year's credit, but it's very hard at night. My work doesn't satisfy me. I would still like to go full time in the day."

He flipped his butt away. "I've been thinking about starting in college lately, even if I am this age. I know a guy who did it."

"Would you go at night?" she asked.

"Maybe, maybe in the day if I could get the right kind of a job—in an all-night cafeteria or something like that, for instance. This guy I just mentioned did that—assistant manager or something. After five or six years he graduated an engineer. Now he's making his pile, working all over the country."

"It's hard doing it that way—very hard."

"The hours are rough but you get used to it. When you got something good to do, sleep is a waste of time."

"It takes years at night."

"Time don't mean anything to me."

"It does to me."

"The way I figure, anything is possible. I always think about the different kinds of chances I have. This has stuck in my mind—don't get yourself trapped in one thing, because maybe you can do something else a whole lot better. That's why I guess I never settled down so far. I've been exploring conditions. I still have some very good ambitions which I would like to see come true. The first step to that, I know for sure now, is to get a good education. I didn't use to think like that, but the more I live the more I do. Now it's always on my mind."

"I've always felt that way," Helen said.

He lit another cigarette, throwing the burnt match away. "What kind of work do you do?"

"I'm a secretary."

"You like it?" He smoked with half-closed eyes. She sensed he knew she didn't care for her job and suspected he had heard her father or mother say so.

After a while, she answered, "No, I don't. The job never changes. And I could live happily without seeing some of those characters I have to deal with all day long, the salesmen, I mean."

"They get fresh?"

"They talk a lot. I'd like to be doing something that feels useful—some kind of social work or maybe teaching. I have no sense of accomplishment in what I'm doing now. Five o'clock comes and at last I go home. That's about all I live for, I guess.

She spoke of her daily routine, but after a minute saw he was only half-listening. He was staring at the moon-drenched trees in the distance, his face drawn, his lit eyes elsewhere.

Helen sneezed, unwound her scarf and wrapped it tightly around her head.

"Shall we go now?"

"Just till I finish my cigarette."

Some fat nerve, she thought.

Yet his face, even with the broken nose, was sensitive in the dark light. What makes me so irritable? She had had the wrong idea of him but it was her own fault, the result of staying so long apart from people.

He drew a long jagged breath.

"Is something the matter?" she asked.

Frank cleared his throat but his voice was hoarse. "No, just something popped into my mind when I was looking at the moon. You know how your thoughts are."

"Nature sets you thinking?"

"I like scenery."

"I walk a lot for that reason."

"I like the sky at night, but you see more of it in the West. Out here the sky is too high, there are too many big buildings."

He squashed his cigarette with his heel and wearily rose, looking now like someone who had parted with his youth.

She got up and walked with him, curious about him. The moon moved above them in the homeless sky.

After a long silence, he said as they were walking, "I like to tell you what I was thinking about."

"Please, you don't have to."

"I feel like talking," he said. "I got to thinking about this carnie outfit I worked for one time when I was about twenty-one. Right after I got the job I fell for a girl in an acrobatic act. She was built something like you—on the slim side, I would say. At first I don't think I rated with her. I think she thought I wasn't a serious type of guy. She was kind of a complicated girl, you know, moody, with lots of problems in her mind that she kept to herself. Well, one day we got to talking and she told me she wanted to be a nun. I said, 'I don't think it will suit you.' 'What do you know about me?' she said. I didn't tell her, although I know people pretty well, don't ask me why, I guess you are born with certain things. Anyway, the whole summer long I was nuts about her but she wouldn't give me another look though there was nobody else around that I saw she went with. 'Is it my age?' I asked her. 'No, but you haven't lived,' she answered me. 'If you only could see in my heart all I have lived through,' I said, but I have my doubts if she believed me. All we ever did was talk like that. Once in a while I would ask her for a date, not thinking I would ever get one, and I never did. 'Give up,' I said to myself, 'all she is interested in is herself.'

"Then one morning, when it was getting to be around fall and you could smell the season changing, I said to her I was taking off when the show closed. 'Where are you going?' she asked me. I said I was going to look for a better life. She didn't answer anything to that. I said, 'Do you still want to be a nun?' She got red and looked away, then she answered she wasn't sure about that any more. I could see she had changed but I wasn't fool enough to think it was account of me. But I guess it really was, because by accident our hands sort of touched, and when I saw the way she looked at me, it was hard to breathe. My God, I thought, we are both in love. I said to her, 'Honey, meet me here after the show tonight and let's go where we will be alone.' She said yes. Before she left she gave me a quick kiss.

"Anyway, that same afternoon she took off in her old man's jalopy to buy a blouse she had seen in some store window in the last town, but on the way back it started to rain. Exactly what happened I don't know. I guess she misjudged a curve or something and went flying off the road. The jalopy bounced down the hill, and her neck was broken. . . . That's how it ended."

They walked in silence. Helen was moved. But why, she thought, all the sad music?

"I'm awfully sorry."

"It was years ago."

"It was a tragic thing to happen."

"I couldn't expect better," he said.

"Life renews itself."

"My luck stays the same."

"Go on with your plans for an education."

"That's about it," Frank said. "That's what I got to do."

Their eyes met, she felt her scalp prickle.

Then they left the park and went home.

Outside the dark grocery store she quickly said good night.

"I'll stay out a little longer," Frank said. "I like to see the moon."

She went upstairs.

In bed she thought of their walk, wondering how much to believe of what he had told her about his ambitions and plans for college. He could not have said anything to make a better impression on her. And what was the purpose of the sad tale of the carnival girl "built something like you"? Who was he mixing up with his carnival girls? Yet he had told the story simply, without any visible attempt to work on her sympathy. Probably it was a true memory, recalled because he happened to be feeling lonely. She had had her own moonlit memories to contend with. Thinking about Frank, she tried to see him straight but came up with a confusing image: the grocery clerk with the greedy eyes, on top of the ex-carnival hand and future serious college student, a man of possibilities.

On the verge of sleep she sensed a desire on his part to involve her in his life. The aversion she felt for him before returned but she succeeded without too much effort in dispelling it. Thoroughly awake now, she regretted she could not see the sky from her window in the wall, or look down into the street. Who was he making into a wife out of snowy moonlight?

Earnings in the grocery, especially around Christmas and New Year's, continued to rise. For the last two weeks in December Morris averaged an unusual one hundred and ninety. Ida had a new theory to explain the spurt of business: an apartment house had opened for rentals a few blocks away; furthermore, she had heard that Schmitz was not so attentive to his store as he was before. An unmarried storekeeper was sometimes erratic. Morris didn't deny these things but he still attributed their good fortune mostly to his clerk. For reasons that were clear to him the customers liked Frank, so they brought in their friends. As a result, the grocer could once more meet his running expenses, and with pinching and scrimping, even pay off some outstanding bills. Grateful to Frank—who seemed to take for granted the upswing of business—he planned to pay him more than the measly five dollars they shamefacedly gave him, but cautiously decided to see if the added income would continue in January, when business usually slackened off. Even if he regularly took in two hundred a week, with the slight profit he made he could hardly afford a clerk. Before things were easier they had to take in a minimum of two-fifty or three hundred, an impossibility.

Since, though, the situation was better, Morris told Helen that he wanted her to keep more of her hard-earned twenty-five dollars; he said she must now keep fifteen, and if business stayed as it was maybe he would not need her assistance any more. He hoped so. Helen was overwhelmed at having fifteen a week to spend on herself. She needed shoes badly and could use a new coat—hers was little better than a rag-and a dress or two. And she wanted to put away a few dollars for future tuition at NYU. She felt like her father about Frank—he had changed their luck. Remembering what he had said in the park that night about his ambitions and desire for education, she felt he someday would get what he wanted because he was obviously more than just an ordinary person.

He was often at the library. Almost every time Helen went there she saw him sitting over an open book at one of the tables; she wondered if all he did in his spare time was come here and read. She respected him for it. She herself averaged two weekly visits, each time checking out only a book or two, because it was one of her few pleasures to return for another. Even at her loneliest she liked being among books, although she was sometimes depressed to see how much there was to read that she hadn't. Meeting Frank so often, she was at first uneasy: he haunted the place, for what? But, a library was a library; he came here, as she did, to satisfy certain needs. Like her he read a lot because he was lonely, Helen thought. She thought this after he had told her about the carnival girl. Gradually her uneasiness left her.

Although he left, as a rule, when she did, if she wanted to walk home alone, he did not intrude. Sometimes he rode back on the trolley while she walked. Sometimes she was on the trolley and saw him walking. But generally, so long as the weather was not too bad, they went home together, a couple of times turning off into the park. He told her more about himself. He had lived a different life from most people she had known, and she envied him all the places he had been to. Her own life, she thought, was much like her father's, restricted by his store, his habits, hers. Morris hardly ever journeyed past the corner, except on rare occasions, usually to return something a customer had left on the counter. When Ephraim was alive, when they were kids, her father liked to go bathing Sunday afternoons at Coney Island; and on Jewish holidays they would sometimes see a Yiddish play, or ride on the subway to the Bronx to call on landsleit. But after Ephraim died Morris had for years gone nowhere. Neither had she, for other reasons. Where could she go without a cent? She read with eagerness of far-off places but spent her life close to home. She would have given much to visit Charleston, New Orleans, San Francisco, cities she had heard so much about, but she hardly ever got beyond the borough of Manhattan. Hearing Frank talk of Mexico, Texas, California, other such places, she realized anew the meagerness of her movements: every day but Sunday on the BMT to Thirty-fourth Street and back. Add to that a twice-weekly visit to the library at night. In summer, the same as before, except a few times—usually during her vacation—to Manhattan Beach; also, if she were lucky, to a concert or two at Lewisohn Stadium. Once when she was twenty and worn out, her mother had insisted she go for a week to an inexpensive adult camp in New Jersey. Before that, while in high school, she had traveled to Washington, D.C., with her American history class for a week end of visiting government buildings. So far and no further in the open world. To stick so close to where she had lived her whole life was a crime. His stories made her impatient—she wanted to travel, experience, live.

One night as they were sitting on a bench in an enclosed part of the park beyond the tree-lined plaza, Frank said he had definitely made up his mind to start college in the fall. This excited her, and for hours afterward Helen couldn't stop thinking about it. She imagined all the interesting courses he could take, envied him the worthwhile people he'd meet in his classes, the fun he'd have studying. She pictured him in nice clothes, his hair cut shorter, maybe his nose straightened, speaking a more careful English, interested in music and literature, learning about politics, psychology, philosophy; wanting to know more the more he knew, in this way growing in value to himself and others. She imagined herself invited by him to a campus concert or play, where she would meet his college friends, people of promise. Afterward as they crossed the campus in the dark, Frank would point out the buildings his classes met in, classes taught by distinguished professors. And maybe if she closed her eyes she could see a time—miracle of miracles—when Helen Bober was enrolled here, not just a stranger on the run, pecking at a course or two at night, and tomorrow morning back at Levenspiel's Louisville Panties and Bras. At least he made her dream.

To help him prepare for college Helen said he ought to read

some good novels, some of the great ones. She wanted Frank to like novels, to enjoy in them what she did. So she checked out *Madame Bovary, Anna Karenina* and *Crime and Punishment,* all by writers he had barely heard of, but they were very satisfying books, she said. He noticed she handled each yellow-paged volume as though she were holding in her respectful hands the works of God Almighty. As if—according to her—you could read in them everything you couldn't afford not to know—the Truth about Life. Frank carried the three books up to his room, and huddled in a blanket to escape the cold that seeped in through the loose window frames, had rough going. The stories were hard to get into because the people and places were strange to him, their crazy names difficult to hold in his mind and some of the sentences were so godawful complicated he forgot the beginning before he got to the end. The opening pages irritated him as he pushed through forests of odd facts and actions. Though he stared for hours at the words, starting one book, then another, then the third—in the end, in exasperation, he flung them aside.

But because Helen had read and respected these books, it shamed him that he hadn't, so he picked one up from the floor and went back to it. As he dragged himself through the first chapters, gradually the reading became easier and he got interested in the people—their lives in one way or another wounded—some to death. Frank read, at the start, in snatches, then in bursts of strange hunger, and before too long he had managed to finish the books. He had started *Madame Bovary* with some curiosity, but in the end he felt disgusted, wearied, left cold. He did not know why people would want to write about that kind of a dame. Yet he felt a little sorry for her and the way things had happened, till there was no way out of it but her death. *Anna Karenina* was better; she was more interesting and better in bed. He didn't want her to kill herself under the train in the end. Still, although Frank felt he could also take the book or leave it, he was moved at the deep change that came over Levin in the woods just after he had thought of hanging himself. At least he wanted to live. *Crime and Punishment* repelled yet fascinated him, with everybody in the joint confessing to something every time he opened his yap—to some weakness, or sickness, or crime. Raskolnikov, the student, gave him a pain, with all his miseries. Frank first had the idea he must be a Jew and was surprised when he found he wasn't. He felt, in places in the book, even when it excited him, as if his face had been shoved into dirty water in the gutter; in other places, as if he had been on a drunk for a month. He was glad when he finished with the book, although he liked Sonia, the prostitute, and thought of her for days after he had read it.

Afterward Helen suggested other novels by the same writers, so he would know them better, but Frank balked, saying he wasn't sure that he had understood those he had read. "I'm sure you have," she answered, "if you got to know the people." "I know them," he muttered. But to please her he worked through two more thick books, sometimes tasting nausea on his tongue, his face strained as he read, eyes bright black, frowning, although he usually felt some relief at the end of the book. He wondered what Helen found so satisfying in all this goddamned human misery, and suspected her of knowing he had spied on her in the bathroom and was using the books to punish him for it. But then he thought it was an unlikely idea. Anyway, he could not get out of his thoughts how quick some people's lives went to pot when they couldn't make up their minds what to do when they had to do it; and he was troubled by the thought of how easy it was for a man to wreck his whole life in a single wrong act. After that the guy suffered forever, no matter what he did to make up for the wrong. At times, as the clerk had sat in his room late at night, a book held stiffy in his reddened hands, his head numb although he wore a hat, he felt a strange falling away from the printed page and had this crazy sensation that he was reading about himself. At first this picked him up but then it deeply depressed him.

One rainy night, as Helen was about to go up to Frank's room to ask him to take back something he had given her that she didn't want, before she could go the phone rang, and Ida hastened out into the hall to call her. Frank, lying on his bed in his room, watching the rainy window, heard her go downstairs. Morris was in the store waiting on someone as Helen came in, but her mother sat in the back over a cup of tea.

"It's Nat," Ida whispered, not moving.

She'll tell herself she isn't listening, thought Helen.

Her first feeling was that she didn't want to talk to the law student, but his voice was warm, which for him meant extended effort, and a warm voice on a wet night was a warm voice. She could easily picture what he looked like as he spoke into the phone. Yet she wished he had called her in December, when she had so desperately wanted him, for now she was again aware of a detachment in herself that she couldn't account for.

"Nobody sees you any more, Helen," Nat began. "Where've you disappeared to?"

"Oh, I've been around," she said, trying to hide a slight tremble in her voice. "And you?"

"Is somebody there where you're talking that you sound so restrained?"

"That's right."

"I thought so. So let me make it quick and clean. Helen, it's been a long time. I want to see you. What do you say if we take in a play this Saturday night? I can stop off for tickets on my way uptown tomorrow."

"Thanks, Nat. I don't think so." She heard her mother sigh.

Nat cleared his throat. "Helen, I honestly want to know how somebody's supposed to defend himself when he hasn't any idea what's in the indictment against him? What kind of a crime have I committed? Yield the details."

"I'm not a lawyer—I don't make indictments."

"So call it a cause—what's the cause? One day we're close to each other, the next I'm alone on an island, holding my hat. What did I do, please tell me?"

"Let's drop this subject."

Here Ida rose and went into the store, softly closing the door behind her. Thanks, thought Helen. She kept her voice low so they wouldn't hear her through the window in the wall.

"You're a funny kid," Nat was saying. "You've got some old-fashioned values about some things. I always told you you punish yourself too much. Why should anybody have such a hot and heavy conscience in these times? People are freer in the twentieth century. Pardon me for saying it but it's true."

She blushed. His insight was to his credit. "My values are my values," she replied.

"What," Nat argued, "would people's lives be like if everybody regretted every beautiful minute of all that happened? Where's the poetry of living?"

"I hope you're alone," she said angrily, "where you're so blithely discussing this subject."

He sounded weary, hurt. "Of course I'm alone. My God, Helen, how low have I fallen in your opinion?"

"I told you what was going on at this end. Up to a minute ago my mother was still in the room."

"I'm sorry, I forgot."

"It's all right now."

"Look, girl," he said affectionately, "the telephone is no place to hash out our personal relations. What do you say if I run upstairs and see you right away? We got to come to some kind of a sensible understanding. I'm not exactly a pig, Helen. What you don't want is your privilege, if I may be so frank. So you don't want, but at least let's be friends and go out once in a while. Let me come up and talk to you."

"Some other time, Nat, I have to do something now."

"For instance?"

"Some other time," she said.

"Why not?" Nat answered amiably.

When he had hung up, Helen stood at the phone, wondering if she had done right. She felt she hadn't.

Ida entered the kitchen. "What did he want—Nat?"

"Just to talk."

"He asked you to go out?"

She admitted it.

"What did you answer him?"

"I said I would some other time."

"What do you mean 'some other time?' " Ida said sharply. "What are you already, Helen, an old lady? What good is it to sit so many nights alone upstairs? Who gets rich from reading? What's the matter with you?"

"Nothing's the matter, Mama." She left the store and went into the hall.

"Don't forget you're twenty-three years old," Ida called after her.

"I won't."

Upstairs her nervousness grew. When she thought what she had to do she didn't want to, yet felt she must.

They had met, she and Frank, last night at the library, the third time in eight days. Helen noticed as they were leaving that he clumsily carried a package she took to contain some shirts or underwear, but on the way home Frank flung away his cigarette, and under a stree lamp handed it to her. "Here, this is for you."

"For me? What is it?"

"You'll find out."

She took it half-willingly, and thanked him. Helen carried it awkwardly the rest of the way home, neither of them saying much. She had been caught by surprise. If she had given herself a minute to think, she would have refused it on grounds that it was wise just to stay friends; because, she thought, neither of them really knew the other. But once she had the thing in her hands she hadn't the nerve to ask him to take it back. It was a medium-sized box of some sort with something heavy in it—she guessed a book; yet it seemed too big for a book. As she held it against her breast, she felt a throb of desire for Frank and this disturbed her. About a block from the grocery, nervously saying good night, she went on ahead. This was how they parted when the store window was still lit.

Ida was downstairs with Morris when Helen came into the house, so no questions were asked. She shivered a little as she unwrapped the box on her bed, ready to hide it the minute she heard a footstep on the stairs. Lifting the carton lid, she found two packages in it, each wrapped in white tissue paper and tied with red ribbons with uneven bows, obviously by Frank. When she had untied the first present, Helen gasped at the sight of a long, hand-woven scarf—rich black wool interlaced with gold thread. She was startled to discover that the second present was a red leather copy of Shakespeare's plays. There was no card.

She sat weakly down on the bed. I can't, she told herself. They were expensive things, probably had cost him every penny of the hard-earned money he was saving for college. Even supposing he had enough for that, she still couldn't take his gifts. It wasn't right, and coming from him, it was, somehow, less than not right.

She wanted then and there to go up to his room and leave them at the door with a note, but hadn't the heart to the very night he had given them to her.

The next evening, after a day of worry, she felt she must return them; and now she wished she had done it before Nat had called, then she might have been more relaxed on the phone.

Helen got down on her hands and knees and reached under the bed for the carton with Frank's scarf and book in it. It touched her that he had given her such lovely things—so much nicer than anyone else ever had. Nat, at his best, had produced a half-dozen small pink roses.

For gifts you pay, Helen thought. She drew a deep breath, and taking the box went quietly up the stairs. She tapped hesitantly on Frank's door. He had recognized her step and was waiting behind the door. His fists were clenched, the nails cutting his palms.

When he opened the door and his glance fell on what she was carrying, he frowned as though struck in the face.

Helen stepped awkwardly into the little room, quickly shutting the door behind her. She suppressed a shudder at the smallness and barrenness of the place. On his unmade bed lay a sock he had been trying to mend.

"Are the Fusos home?" she asked in a low voice.

"They went out." He spoke dully, his eyes hopelessly stuck to the things he had given her.

Helen handed him the box with the presents. "Thanks so much, Frank," she said, trying to smile, "but I really don't think I ought to take them. You'll need every cent for your college tuition in the fall."

"That's not the reason you mean," he said.

Her face reddened. She was about to explain that her mother would surely make a scene if she saw his gifts, but instead said, "I can't keep them."

"Why not?"

It wasn't easy to answer and he didn't make it easier, just held the rejected presents in his big hands as if they were living things that had suddenly died.

"I can't," she got out. "Your taste is so nice, I'm sorry."

"Okay," he said wearily. He tossed the box on the bed and the Shakespeare fell to the floor. She stooped quickly to pick it up and was unnerved to see it had opened to "Romeo and Juliet."

"Good night." She left his room and went hastily downstairs. In her room she thought she heard the distant sound of a man crying. She listened tensely, her hand on her throbbing throat, but no longer heard it.

Helen took a shower to relax, then got into a nightgown and housecoat. She picked up a book but couldn't read. She had noticed before signs he might be in love with her, but now she was almost sure of it. Carrying his package as he had walked with her last night, he had been somebody different, though the hat and overcoat were the same. There seemed to be about him a size and potentiality she had not seen before. He did not say love but love was in him. When the insight came to her, at almost the minute he was handing her the package, she had reacted with gooseflesh. That it had gone this far was her own fault. She had warned herself not to get mixed up with him but hadn't obeyed her warning. Out of loneliness she had encouraged him. What else, going so often to the library, knowing he would be there? And she had stopped off with him, on their walks, for pizzas and coffee; had listened to his stories, discussed with him plans for college, talked at length about books he was reading; at the same time she had been concealing these meetings from her father and mother. He knew it, no wonder he had built up hopes.

The strange thing was there were times she felt she liked him very much. He was, in many ways, a worthwhile person, and where a man gave off honest feeling, was she a machine to shut off her own? Yet she knew she mustn't become seriously attracted to him because there would be trouble in buckets. Trouble, thank you, she had had enough of. She wanted now a peaceful life without worry—any more worries. Friends they could be, in a minor key; she might on a moonlit night even hold hands with him, but beyond that nothing. She should have said something of the sort; he would have saved his presents for a better prospect and she would not now be feeling guilt at having hurt him. Yet in a way he had surprised her by his apparent depth of affection. She had not expected anything to happen so quickly, because, for her, things had happened in reverse order. Usually she fell in love first, then the man, if he wasn't Nat Pearl, responded. So the other way around was nice for a change, and she wished it would happen more often, but with the right one. She must go, she decided, less to the library; he would then understand, if he didn't already, and give up any idea of having her love. When he realized what was what he would get over his pain, if he really felt any. But her thoughts gave her no peace, and though she tried often, she could still not concentrate on her books. When Morris and Ida trudged through her room, her light was out and she seemed to be sleeping.

As she left the house for work the next morning, to her dismay she spied the carton containing his presents on top of some greasy garbage bags in the stuffed rubbish can at the curb. The cover of the can apparently had been squeezed down on the box but had fallen off and now lay on the sidewalk. Lifting the carton cover, Helen saw the two gifts, loosely covered with the tissue paper. Angered by the waste, she plucked the scarf and book out of the crushed cardboard box and went quickly into the hall with them. If she took them upstairs Ida would want to know what she had, so she decided to hide them in the cellar. She turned on the light and went quietly down, trying to keep her high heels from clicking on the stairs. Then she removed the tissue paper and hid the presents, neither of which had been harmed, in the bottom drawer of a broken chiffonier in their bin. The dirty tissue paper and red ribbons she rolled up in a sheet of old newspaper, then went upstairs and pressed it into the garbage can. Helen noticed her father at the window, idly watching her. She passed into the store, said good morning, washed her hands and left for work. On the subway she felt despondent.

After supper that night, while Ida was washing dishes, Helen sneaked down into the cellar, got the scarf and book and carried them up to Frank's room. She knocked and nobody answered. She considered leaving them at the door but felt he would throw them away again unless she spoke to him first.

Tessie opened her door. "I heard him go out a while before, Helen." Her eyes were on the things in her hands.

Helen blushed. "Thanks, Tessie."

"Any message?"

"No." She returned to her floor and once more pushed the gifts under her bed. Changing her mind, she put the book and scarf in different bureau drawers, hiding them under her underwear. When her mother came up she was listening to the radio.

"You going someplace tonight, Helen?"

"Maybe, I don't know. Maybe to the library."

"Why so much to the library? You went a couple days ago."

"I go to meet Clark Gable, Mama."

"Helen, don't get fresh."

Sighing, she said she was sorry.

Ida sighed too. "Some people want their children to read more. I want mine to read less."

"That won't get me married any faster."

Ida knitted but soon grew restless and went down to the store again. Helen got out Frank's things, packed them in heavy paper she had bought on her way home, tied the bundle with cord, and took the trolley to the library. He wasn't there.

The next night she tried first his room, then when she was able to slip out of the house, again the library, but found him in neither place.

"Does Frank still work here?" she asked Morris in the morning.

"Of course he works."

"I haven't seen him for a while," she said. "I thought he might be gone."

"In the summer he leaves."

"Did he say that?"

"Mama says."

"Does he know?"

"He knows. Why you ask me?"

She said she was just curious.

As Helen came into the hall that evening she heard the

clerk descending the stairs and waited for him at the landing. Lifting his hat, he was about to pass when she spoke.

"Frank, why did you throw your two presents into the garbage?"

"What good were they to me?"

"It was a terrible waste. You should have got your money back."

He smiled in the corners of his mouth. "Easy come, easy go."

"Don't joke. I took them out of the rubbish and have them in my room for you. They weren't damaged."

"Thanks."

"Please give them back and get your money. You'll need every penny for the fall."

"Since I was a kid I hate to go back with stuff I bought."

"Then let me have the sales checks and I'll return them during my lunch hour."

"I lost them," he answered.

She said gently, "Frank, sometimes things turn out other than we plan. Don't feel hurt."

"When I don't feel hurt, I hope they bury me."

He left the house, she walked up the stairs.

Over the week end Helen went back to crossing off the days on the calendar. She found she had crossed nothing since New Year's. She fixed that. On Sunday the weather turned fair and she grew restless. She wished again for Nat to call her; instead his sister did and they walked, in the early afternoon, on the Parkway.

Betty was twenty-seven and resembled Sam Pearl. She was large-boned and on the plain side but made good use of reddish hair and a nice nature. She was in her ideas, Helen thought, somewhat dull. They had not too much in common and saw each other infrequently, but liked to talk once in a while, or go to a movie together. Recently Betty had become engaged to a CPA in her office and was with him most of the time. Now she sported a prosperous diamond ring on her stylish finger. Helen, for once, envied her, and Betty, as if she had guessed, wished her the same good luck.

"And it should happen soon," she said.

"Many thanks, Betty."

After they had gone a few blocks, Betty said, "Helen, I don't like to butt in somebody else's private business but for a long time I wanted to ask you what happened between you and my brother Nat. I once asked him and he gave me double talk."

"You know how such things go."

"I thought you liked him?"

"I did."

"Then why don't you see him any more? Did you have some kind of a fight?"

"No fights. We didn't have the same things in mind."

Betty asked no more. Later, she remarked, "Sometime give him another chance, Helen. Nat really has the makings of a good person. Shep, my boy friend, thinks so too. His worst fault is he thinks his brains entitle him to certain privileges. You'll see, in time he'll get over it."

"I may," Helen said. "We'll see sometime."

They returned to the candy store, where Shep Hirsch, Betty's stout, eyeglassed, future husband was waiting to take her for a drive in his Pontiac.

"Come along, Helen," said Betty.

"With pleasure." Shep tipped his hat.

"Go, Helen," advised Goldie Pearl.

"Thanks, all, from the bottom of my heart," said Helen, "but I have some of my underthings to iron."

Upstairs, she stood at the window, looking out at the back yards. The remnants of last week's dirty snow. No single blade of green, or flower to light the eye or lift the heart. She felt as if she were made of knots and in desperation got on her coat, tied a yellow kerchief around her head and left the house again, not knowing which way to go. She wandered toward the leafless park.

At the approach to the park's main entrance there was a small island in the street, a concrete triangle formed by intersecting avenues. Here people sat on benches during the day and tossed peanuts or pieces of bread to the noisy pigeons that haunted the place. Coming up the block, Helen saw a man squatting by one of the benches, feeding the birds. Otherwise, the island was deserted. When the man rose, the pigeons fluttered up with him, a few landing on his arms and shoulders, one perched on his fingers, pecking peanuts from his cupped palm. Another fat bird sat on his hat. The man clapped his hands when the peanuts were gone and the birds, beating their wings, scattered.

When she recognized Frank Alpine, Helen hesitated. She felt in no mood to see him, but remembering the package hidden in her bureau drawer, determined once and for all to get rid of it. Reaching the corner, she crossed over to the island.

Frank saw her coming and wasn't sure he cared one way or the other. The return of his presents had collapsed his hopes. He had thought that if she ever fell for him it would change his life in the way he wanted it to happen, although at times the very thought of another change, even in this sense of it, made him miserable. Yet what was the payoff, for instance, of marrying a dame like her and having to do with Jews the rest of his life? So he told himself he didn't care one way or the other.

"Hi," Helen said.

He touched his hat. His face looked tired but his eyes were clear and his gaze steady, as if he had been through something and had beat it. She felt sorry if she had caused him any trouble.

"I had a cold," Frank remarked.

"You should get more sun."

Helen sat down on the edge of the bench, as if she were afraid, he thought, she would be asked to take a lease on it; and he sat a little apart from her. One of the pigeons began to chase another running in circles and landed on its back. Helen looked away but Frank idly watched the birds until they flew off.

"Frank," she said, "I hate to sound like a pest on this subject, but if there's anything I can't stand it's waste. I know you're not Rockefeller, so would you mind giving me the names of the stores where you bought your kind presents so that I can return them? I think I can without the sales checks."

Her eyes, he noticed, were a hard blue, and though he thought it ridiculous, he was a little scared of her, as if she were far too determined, too dead serious for him. At the same time he felt he still liked her. He had not thought so, but with them sitting together like this he thought again that he did. It was in a way a hopeless feeling, yet it was more than that because he did not exactly feel hopeless. He felt, as he sat next to her and saw her worn, unhappy face, that he still had a chance.

Frank cracked his knuckles one by one. He turned to her. "Look, Helen, maybe I try to work too fast. If so, I am sorry. I am the type of a person, who if he likes somebody, has to show it. I like to give her things, if you understand that, though I do know that not everybody likes to take. That's their business. My nature is to give and I couldn't change it even if I wanted. So okay. I am also sorry I got sore and dumped your presents in the can and you had to take them out. But what I want to say is this. Why don't you just go ahead and keep one of those things that I got for you? Let it be a little memory of a guy you once knew that wants to thank you for the good books you told him to read. You don't have to worry that I expect anything for what I give you."

"Frank . . ." she said, reddening.

"Just let me finish. How's this for a deal? If you keep one of those things, I will take the other back to the store and get what I paid for it. What do you say?"

She was not sure what to say, but since she wanted to be finished with it, nodded at his proposal.

"Fine," Frank said. "Now what do you want the most?"

"Well, the scarf is awfully nice, but I'd rather keep the book."

"So keep the book then," he said. "You can give me the scarf anytime you want and I promise I will bring it back."

He lit a cigarette and inhaled deeply.

She considered whether to say good-by, now that the matter had been settled, and go on with her walk.

"You busy now?" he asked.

She guessed a short stroll. "No."

"How about a movie?"

It took her a minute to reply. Was he starting up once more? She felt she must quickly set limits to keep him from again creeping too close. Yet out of respect for his already hurt feelings, she thought it best that she think out exactly what to say and tactfully say it, later on.

"I'll have to be back early."

"So let's go," he said, getting up.

Helen slowly untied her kerchief, then knotted it, and they went off together.

As they walked she kept wondering if she hadn't made a mistake in accepting the book. In spite of what he had said about expecting nothing she felt a gift was a claim, and she wanted none on her. Yet, when, almost without noticing, she once more asked herself if she liked him at all, she had to admit she did a little. But not enough to get worried about; she liked him but not with an eye to the possibility of any deeper feeling. He was not the kind of man she wanted to be in love with. She made that very clear to herself, for among his other disadvantages there was something about him, evasive, hidden. He sometimes appeared to be more than he was, sometimes less. His aspirations, she sensed, were somehow apart from the self he presented normally when he wasn't trying, though he was always more or less trying; therefore when he was trying less. She could not quite explain this to herself, for if he could make himself seem better, broader, wiser when he tried, then he had these things in him because you couldn't make them out of nothing. There was more to him than his appearance. Still, he hid what he had and he hid what he hadn't. With one hand the magician showed his cards, with the other he turned them into smoke. At the very minute he was revealing himself, saying who he was, he made you wonder if it was true. You looked into mirrors and saw mirrors and didn't know what was right or real or important. She had gradually got the feeling that he only pretended to be frank about himself, that in telling so much about his experiences, his trick was to hide his true self. Maybe not purposely—maybe he had no idea he was doing it. She asked herself whether he might have been married already. He had once said he never was. And was there more to the story of the once-kissed, tragic carnival girl? He had said no. If not, what made her feel he had done something—committed himself in a way she couldn't guess?

As they were approaching the movie theater, a thought of

her mother crossed her mind and she heard herself say, "Don't forget I'm Jewish."

"So what?" Frank said.

Inside in the dark, recalling what he had answered her, he felt this elated feeling, as if he had crashed head on through a brick wall but hadn't bruised himself.

She had bitten her tongue but made no reply.

Anyway, by summer he'd be gone.

Ida was very unhappy that she had kept Frank on when she could have got rid of him so easily. She was to blame and she actively worried. Though she had no evidence, she suspected Helen was interested in the clerk. *Something* was going on between them. She did not ask her daughter what, because a denial would shame her. And though she had tried she felt she could not really trust Frank. Yes, he had helped the business, but how much would they have to pay for it? Sometimes when she came upon him alone in the store, his expression, she told herself, was sneaky. He sighed often, muttered to himself, and if he saw he was observed, pretended he hadn't. Whatever he did there was more in it than he was doing. He was like a man with two minds. With one he was here, with the other someplace else. Even while he read he was doing more than reading. And his silence spoke a language she couldn't understand. Something bothered him and Ida suspected it was her daughter. Only when Helen happened to come into the store or the back while he was there, did he seem to relax, become one person. Ida was troubled, although she could not discover in Helen any response to him. Helen was quiet in his presence, detached, almost cold to the clerk. She gave him for his restless eyes, nothing—her back. Yet for this reason, too, Ida worried.

One night after Helen had left the house, when her mother heard the clerk's footsteps going down the stairs, she quickly got into a coat, wrapped a shawl around her head and trudged through a sprinkle of snow after him. He walked to the movie house several blocks away, paid his money, and passed in. Ida was almost certain that Helen was inside, waiting for him. She returned home with nails in her heart and found her daughter upstairs, ironing. Another night she followed Helen to the library. Ida waited across the street, shivering for almost an hour in the cold, until Helen emerged, then followed her home. She chided herself for her suspicions but they would not fly from her mind. Once, listening from the back, she heard her daughter and the clerk talking about a book. This annoyed her. And when Helen later happened to mention that Frank had plans to begin college in the autumn, Ida felt he was saying that only to get her interested in him.

She spoke to Morris and cautiously asked if he had noticed anything developing between Helen and the clerk.

"Don't be foolish," the grocer replied. He had thought about the possibility, at times felt concerned, but after pondering how different they were, had put the idea out of his head.

"Morris, I am afraid."

"You are afraid of everything, even which it don't exist."

"Tell him to leave now—business is better."

"So is better," he muttered, "but who knows how will be next week. We decided he will stay till summer."

"Morris, he will make trouble."

"What kind trouble will he make?"

"Wait," she said, clasping her hands, "a tragedy will happen."

Her remark at first annoyed, then worried him.

The next morning the grocer and his clerk were sitting at the table, peeling hot potatoes. The pot had been drained of water and dumped on its side; they sat close to the steaming pile of potatoes, hunched over, ripping off the salt-stained skins with small knives. Frank seemed ill at ease. He hadn't shaved and had dark blobs under his eyes. Morris wondered if he had been drinking but there was never any smell of liquor about him. They worked without speaking, each lost in his thoughts.

After a half-hour, Frank squirming restlessly in his chair, remarked, "Say, Morris, suppose somebody asked you what do the Jews believe in, what would you tell them?"

The grocer stopped peeling, unable at once to reply.

"What I like to know is what is a Jew anyway?"

Because he was ashamed of his meager education Morris was never comfortable with such questions, yet he felt he must answer.

"My father used to say to be a Jew all you need is a good heart."

"What do you say?"

"The important thing is the Torah. This is the Law—a Jew must believe in the Law."

"Let me ask you this," Frank went on. "Do you consider yourself a real Jew?"

Morris was startled, "What do you mean if I am a real Jew?"

"Don't get sore about this," Frank said. "But I can give you an argument that you aren't. First thing, you don't go to the synagogue—not that I have ever seen. You don't keep your kitchen kosher and you don't eat kosher. You don't even wear one of those little black hats like this tailor I knew in South Chicago. He prayed three times a day. I even hear the Mrs say you kept the store open on Jewish holidays, it makes no difference if she yells her head off."

"Sometimes," Morris answered, flushing, "to have to eat, you must keep open on holidays. On Yom Kippur I don't keep open. But I don't worry about kosher, which is to me old-fashioned. What I worry is to follow the Jewish Law."

"But all those things are the Law, aren't they? And don't the Law say you can't eat any pig, but I have seen you taste ham."

"This is not important to me if I taste pig or if I don't. To some Jews is this important but not to me. Nobody will tell me that I am not Jewish because I put in my mouth once in a while, when my tongue is dry, a piece ham. But they will tell me, and I will believe them, if I forget the Law. This means to do what is right, to be honest, to be good. This means to other people. Our life is hard enough. Why should we hurt somebody else? For everybody should be the best, not only for you or me. We ain't animals. This is why we need the Law. This is what a Jew believes."

"I think other religions have those ideas too," Frank said. "But tell me why it is that the Jews suffer so damn much, Morris? It seems to me that they like to suffer, don't they?"

"Do you like to suffer? They suffer because they are Jews."

"That's what I mean, they suffer more than they have to."

"If you live, you suffer. Some people suffer more, but not

because they want. But I think if a Jew don't suffer for the Law, he will suffer for nothing."

"What do you suffer for, Morris?" Frank said.

"I suffer for you," Morris said calmly.

Frank laid his knife down on the table. His mouth ached. "What do you mean?"

"I mean you suffer for me."

The clerk let it go at that.

"If a Jew forgets the Law," Morris ended, "he is not a good Jew, and not a good man."

Frank picked up his knife and began to tear the skins off the potatoes. The grocer peeled his pile in silence. The clerk asked nothing more.

When the potatoes were cooling, Morris, troubled by their talk, asked himself why Frank had brought up this subject. A thought of Helen, for some reason, crossed his mind.

"Tell me the truth," he said, "why did you ask me such questions?"

Frank shifted in his chair. He answered slowly, "To be truthful to you, Morris, once I didn't have much use for the Jews."

Morris looked at him without moving.

"But that was long ago," said Frank, "before I got to know what they were like. I don't think I understood much about them."

His brow was covered with sweat.

"Happens like this many times," Morris said.

But his confession had not made the clerk any happier.

One afternoon, shortly after lunch, happening to glance at himself in the mirror, Morris saw how bushy his hair was and how thick the pelt on his neck; he felt ashamed. So he said to Frank he was going across the street to the barber. The clerk, studying the racing page of the *Mirror*, nodded. Morris hung up his apron and went into the store to get some change from the cash register. After he took a few quarters out of the drawer, he checked the receipts for the day and was pleased. He left the grocery and crossed the car tracks to the barber shop.

The chair was empty and he didn't have to wait. As Mr.

Giannola, who smelled of olive oil, worked on him and they talked, Morris, though embarrassed at all the hair that had to be cut by the barber, found himself thinking mostly of his store. If it would only stay like this—no Karp's paradise, but at least livable, not the terrible misery of only a few months ago—he would be satisfied. Ida had again been nagging him to sell, but what was the use of selling until things all over got better and he could find a place he would have confidence in? Al Marcus, Breitbart, all the drivers he talked to, still complained about business. The best thing was not to look for trouble but stay where he was. Maybe in the summer, after Frank left, he would sell out and search for a new place.

As he rested in the barber's chair, the grocer, watching through the window his own store, saw with satisfaction that at least three customers had been in since he had sat down. One man left with a large lumpy bag, in which Morris imagined at least six bottles of beer. Also, two women had come out with heavy packages, one carrying a loaded market bag. Figuring, let's say, at least two dollars apiece for the women, he estimated he had taken in a nice fiver and earned his haircut. When the barber unpinned the sheet around him and Morris returned to the grocery, he struck a match over the cash register and peered with anticipation at the figures. To his great surprise he saw that only a little more than three dollars had been added to the sum he had noted on leaving the store. He was stunned. How could it be only three if the bags had been packed tight with groceries? Could it be they contained maybe a couple of boxes of some large item like cornflakes, that came to nothing? He could hardly believe this and felt upset to the point of illness.

In the back he hung up his overcoat, and with fumbling fingers tied his apron strings.

Frank glanced up from the racing page with a smile. "You look different without all the kelp on you, Morris. You look like a sheep that had the wool clipped off it."

The grocer, ashen, nodded.

"What's the matter your face is so pale?"

"I don't feel so good."

"Whyn't you go up then and take your snooze?"

"After."

He shakily poured himself a cup of coffee.

"How's business?" he asked, his back to the clerk.

"So-so," said Frank.

"How many customers you had since I went to the barber?"

"Two or three."

Unable to meet Frank's eye, Morris went into the store and stood at the window, staring at the barber shop, his thoughts in a turmoil, tormented by anxiety. Was the Italyener stealing from the cash register? The customers had come out with stuffed bags, what was there to show for it? Could he have given things on credit? They had told him never to. So what then?

A man entered and Morris waited on him. The man spent forty-one cents. When Morris rang up the sale, he saw it added correctly to the previous total. So the register was not broken. He was now almost certain that Frank had been stealing, and when he asked himself how long, he was numbed.

Frank went into the store and saw the dazed grocer at the window.

"Don't you feel any better, Morris?"

"It will go away."

"Take care of yourself. You don't want to get sick any more."

Morris wet his lips but made no reply. All day he went around, dragging his heart. He had said nothing to Ida, he didn't dare.

For the next few days he carefully watched the clerk. He had decided to give him the benefit of doubt yet not rest till he knew the truth. Sometimes he sat at the table inside, pretending to be reading, but he was carefully listening to each item the customer ordered. He jotted down the prices and when Frank packed the groceries, quickly calculated the approximate sum. After the customer had gone he went idly to the register and secretly examined the amount the clerk had rung up. Always it was near the figure he had figured, a few pennies more or less. So Morris said he would go upstairs for a few minutes, but instead stationed himself in the hall, behind the back door. Peering through a crack in the wood, he could see into the store. Standing here, he added in his head the prices of the items ordered, and later, about fifteen minutes, casually checked the receipts and found totaled there the sum he had estimated. He began to doubt his suspicions. He may have wrongly guessed the contents of customers' bags when he was at the barber's. Yet he could still not believe they had spent only three dollars; maybe Frank had caught on and was being wary.

Morris then thought, yes, the clerk could have been stealing, but if so it was more his fault than Frank's. He was a grown man with a man's needs and all he was paying him, including his meager commission, was about six or seven dollars a week. True, he got his room and meals free, plus cigarettes, but what was six or seven dollars to anybody in times like these, when a decent pair of shoes cost eight to ten? The fault was therefore his for paying slave wages for a workman's services, including the extra things Frank did, like last week cleaning out the stopped sewer pipe in the cellar with a long wire and so saving five or ten dollars that would surely have gone to the plumber, not to mention how his presence alone had improved the store.

So although he worked on a slim markup, one late afternoon when he and Frank were packing out some cartons of goods that had just been delivered, Morris said to his assistant standing on the stepladder, "Frank, I think from now on till it comes summer I will raise you your wages to straight fifteen dollars without any commission. I would like to pay you more, but you know how much we do here business."

Frank looked down at the grocer. "What for, Morris? The store can't afford to pay me any more than I am getting. If I take fifteen your profit will be shot. Let it go the way it is now. I am satisfied."

"A young man needs more and he spends more."

"I got all I want."

"Let it be like I said."

"I don't want it," said the clerk, annoyed.

"Take," insisted the grocer.

Frank finished his packing then got down, saying he was going to Sam Pearl's. His eyes were averted as he went past the grocer.

Morris continued to pack the cans on the shelves. Rather

than admit Frank's raise to Ida and start a fuss, he decided to withhold from the register the money he would need to pay him, a little every day so it would not be noticed. He would privately give it to the clerk sometime on Saturday, before Ida handed him his regular wages.

Helen felt herself, despite the strongest doubts, falling in love with Frank. It was a dizzying dance, she didn't want to. The month was cold—it often snowed—she had a rough time, fighting hesitancies, fears of a disastrous mistake. One night she dreamed their house had burned down and her poor parents had nowhere to go. They stood on the sidewalk, wailing in their underwear. Waking, she fought an old distrust of the broken-faced stranger, without success. The stranger had changed, grown unstrange. That was the clue to what was happening to her. One day he seemed unknown, lurking at the far end of an unlit cellar; the next he was standing in sunlight, a smile on his face, as if all she knew of him and all she didn't, had fused into a healed and easily remembered whole. If he was hiding anything, she thought, it was his past pain, his orphanhood and consequent suffering. His eyes were quieter, wiser. His crooked nose fitted his face and his face fitted him. It stayed on straight. He was gentle, waiting for whatever he awaited with a grace she respected. She felt she had changed him and this affected her. That she had willed to stay free of him made little difference now. She felt tender to him, wanted him close by. She had, she thought, changed in changing him.

After she had accepted his gift of a book their relationship had subtly altered. What else, if whenever she read in her Shakespeare, she thought of Frank Alpine, even heard his voice in the plays? Whatever she read, he crept into her thoughts; in every book he haunted the words, a character in a plot somebody else had invented, as if all associations had only one end. He was, to begin with, everywhere. So, without speaking of it, they met again in the library. That they were meeting among books relieved her doubt, as if she believed, what possible wrong can I do among books, what possible harm can come to me here?

In the library he too seemed surer of himself—though once they were on their way home he became almost remote, strangely watchful, looking back from time to time as though they were being followed, but who or what would follow them? He never took her as far as the store; as before, by mutual consent, she went on ahead, then he walked around the block and entered the hall from the other way so he wouldn't have to go past the grocery window and possibly be seen coming from the direction she had come from. Helen interpreted his caution to mean he sensed victory and didn't want to endanger it. It meant he valued her more than she was altogether sure she wanted to be.

Then one night they walked across a field in the park and turned to one another. She tried to awaken in herself a feeling of danger, but danger was dulled, beyond her, in his arms. Pressed against him, responsive to his touch, she felt the cold ebb out of the night, and a warmth come over her. Her lips parted—she drew from his impassioned kiss all she had long desired. Yet at the moment of sweetest joy she felt again the presence of doubt, almost a touch of illness. This made her sad. The fault was her. It meant she still could not fully accept him. There were still signals signaling no. She had only to think of them and they would work in her, pinching the nerves. On their way home she could not forget the first happiness of their kiss. But why should a kiss become anxiety? Then she saw that his eyes were sad, and she wept when he wasn't looking. Would it never come spring?

She stalled love with arguments, only to be surprised at their swift dissolution; found it difficult to keep her reasons securely nailed down, as they were before. They flew up in the mind, shifted, changed, as if something had altered familiar weights, values, even experience. He wasn't, for instance, Jewish. Not too long ago this was the greatest barrier, her protection against ever taking him seriously; now it no longer seemed such an urgently important thing—how could it in times like these? How could anything be important but love and fulfillment? It had lately come to her that her worry he was a gentile was less for her own sake than for her mother and father. Although she had only loosely been brought up as Jewish she felt loyal to the Jews, more for what they had gone through than what she knew of their history or theology—loved them as a people, thought with pride of herself as one of them; she had never imagined she would marry anybody but a Jew. But she had recently come to think that in such unhappy times—when the odds were so high against personal happiness—to find love was miraculous, and to fulfill it as best two people could was what really mattered. Was it more important to insist a man's religious beliefs be exactly hers (if it was a question of religion), or that the two of them have in common ideals, a desire to keep love in their lives, and to preserve in every possible way what was best in themselves? The less difference among people, the better; thus she settled it for herself yet was dissatisfied for those for whom she hadn't settled it.

But her logic, if it was logic, wouldn't decide a thing for her unhappy parents once they found out what was going on. With Frank enrolled in college maybe some of Ida's doubts of his worth as a person might wither away, but college was not the synagogue, a B.A. not a bar mitzvah; and her mother and even her father with his liberal ideas would insist that Frank had to be what he wasn't. Helen wasn't at all sure she could handle them if it ever came to a showdown. She dreaded the arguments, their tear-stained pleas and her own misery for taking from the small sum of peace they had in the world, adding to the portion of their unhappiness. God knows they had had enough of that. Still, there was just so much time to live, so little of youth among the years; one had to make certain heartbreaking choices. She foresaw the necessity of upholding her own, enduring pain yet keeping to her decisions. Morris and Ida would be grievously hurt, but before too long their pain would grow less and perhaps leave them; yet she could not help but hope her own children would someday marry Jews.

And if she married Frank, her first job would be to help him realize his wish to be somebody. Nat Pearl wanted to be "somebody," but to him this meant making money to lead the life of some of his well-to-do friends at law school. Frank, on the other hand, was struggling to realize himself as a person, a more worthwhile ambition. Though Nat had an excellent formal education, Frank knew more about life and gave the impression of greater potential depth. She wanted him to become what he might, and conceived a plan to support him through college. Maybe she could even see him through a master's degree, once he knew what he wanted to do. She realized this would mean the end of her own vague plans for going to day college, but that was really lost long ago, and she thought she would at last accept the fact once Frank had got what she hadn't. Maybe after he was working, perhaps as an engineer or chemist, she could take a year of college just to slake her thirst. By then she would be almost thirty, but it would be worth postponing having a family to give him a good start and herself a taste of what she had always wanted. She also hoped they would be able to leave New York. She wanted to see more of the country. And if things eventually worked out, maybe Ida and Morris would someday sell the store and come to live near them. They might all live in California, her parents in a little house of their own where they could take life easy and be near their grandchildren. The future offered more in the way of realizable possibilities, Helen thought, if a person dared take a chance with it. The question was, did she?

She postponed making any important decision. She feared most of all the great compromise—she had seen so many of the people she knew settle for so much less than they had always wanted. She feared to be forced to choose beyond a certain point, to accept less of the good life than she had hungered for, appreciably less—to tie up with a fate far short of her ideals. That she mustn't do, whether it meant taking Frank or letting him go. Her constant fear, underlying all others, was that her life would not turn out as she had hoped, or would turn out vastly different. She was willing to change, make substitutions, but she would not part with the substance of her dreams. Well, she would know by summertime what to do. In the meantime Frank went every third night to the library and there she was. But when the old-maid librarian smiled knowingly upon them, Helen felt embarrassed, so they met elsewhere. They met in cafeterias, movie houses, the pizza place—where it was impossible to say much, or hold him or be held. To talk they walked, to kiss they hid.

Frank said he was getting the college bulletins he had written for, and around May he would have a transcript of his high school record sent to whichever place they picked for him to go. He showed he knew she had plans for him. He didn't say much more, for he was always afraid the old jinx would grab hold of him if he opened his mouth a little too wide.

At first he waited patiently. What else was there to do? He had waited and was still waiting. He had been born waiting. But before long, though he tried not to show it, he was beginning to be fed up with his physical loneliness. He grew tired of the frustrations of kissing in doorways, a cold feel on a bench in the park. He thought of her as he had seen her in the bathroom, and the memory became a burden. He was the victim of the sharp edge of his hunger. So he wanted her to the point where he thought up schemes for getting her into his room and in bed. He wanted satisfaction, relief, a stake in the future. She's not yours till she gives it to you, he thought. That's the way they all are. It wasn't always true, but it was true enough. He wanted an end to the torment of coming to a boil, then thank you, no more. He wanted to take her completely.

They met more often now. At a bench on the Parkway, on street corners—in the wide windy world. When it rained or snowed, they stepped into doorways, or went home.

He complained one night, "What a joke. We leave the same warm house to meet out in the cold here."

She said nothing.

"Forget it," Frank said, looking into her troubled eyes, "we will take it the way it is."

"This is our youth," she said bitterly.

He wanted then to ask her to come to his room but felt she wouldn't, so he didn't ask.

One cold, starry night she led him through the trees in the

park near where they usually sat, onto a broad meadow where on summer nights lovers lay in the grass.

"Come on and sit down on the ground for a minute," Frank urged, "there's nobody here now."

But Helen wouldn't.

"Why not?" he asked.

"Not now," she said.

She realized, though he later denied it, that the situation had made him impatient. Sometimes he was moody for hours. She worried, wondering what rusty wound their homelessness had opened in him.

One evening they sat alone on a bench on the Parkway, Frank with his arm around her; but because they were so close to home Helen was jumpy and moved away whenever somebody passed by.

After the third time Frank said, "Listen, Helen, this is no good. Some night we will have to go where we can be inside."

"Where?" she asked.

"Where do you say?"

"I can't say anything, Frank. I don't know."

"How long is this going to keep up like this?"

"As long as we like," she said, smiling faintly, "or as long as we like each other."

"I don't mean it that way. What I am talking about is not having any place private to go to."

She answered nothing.

"Maybe some night we ought to sneak up to my room," he suggested. "We could do it easy enough—I don't mean tonight but maybe Friday, after Nick and Tessie go to the show and your mother is down in the store. I bought a new heater and the room keeps warm. Nobody will know you are there. We would be alone for once. We have never been alone that way."

"I couldn't," Helen said.

"Why?"

"Frank, I can't."

"When will I get a chance to put my arms around you without being an acrobat?"

"Frank," said Helen, "there's one thing I wish to make clear to you. I won't sleep with you now, if that's what you mean.

It'll have to wait till I am really sure I love you, maybe till we're married, if we ever are."

"I never asked you to," Frank said. "All I said was for you to come up to my room so we could spend the time more comfortable, not you bucking away from me every time a shadow passes."

He lit a cigarette and smoked in silence.

"I'm sorry." After a minute she said, "I thought I ought to tell you how I feel on this subject. I was going to sometime anyway."

They got up and walked, Frank gnawing his wound.

A cold rain washed the yellow slush out of the gutters. It rained drearily for two days. Helen had promised to see Frank on Friday night but she didn't like the thought of going out in the wet. When she came home from work, and got the chance, she slipped a note under his door, then went down. The note said that if Nick and Tessie did go to the movies, she would try to come up to his room for a while.

At half past seven Nick knocked on Frank's door and asked him if he wanted to go to the picture. Frank said no, he thought he had seen the picture that was playing. Nick said good-bye and he and Tessie, bundled in raincoats and carrying umbrellas, left the house. Helen waited for her mother to go down to Morris, but Ida complained that her feet hurt, and said she would rest. Helen then went down herself, knowing Frank would hear her on the stairs and figure something had gone wrong. He would understand she could not go up to see him so long as anyone might hear her.

But a few minutes later, Ida came down, saying she felt restless upstairs. Helen then said she intended to drop in on Betty Pearl and might go along with her to the dressmaker who was making her wedding things.

"It's raining," said Ida.

"I know, Mama," Helen answered, hating her deceit.

She went up to her room, got her hat and coat, rubbers and an umbrella; then walked down, letting the door bang, as if she had just left the house. She quietly opened it and went on tiptoe up the stairs.

Frank had guessed what was going on and opened his door to her quick tap. She was pale, obviously troubled, but very lovely. He held her hard and could feel her heartbeat against his chest.

She will let me tonight, he told himself.

Helen was still uneasy. It took her a while to quiet her conscience for having lied to her mother. Frank had put out the light and tuned in the radio to soft dance music; now he lay on the bed, smoking. For a time she sat awkwardly in his chair, watching the glow of his cigarette, and when not that, the drops of lit rain on the window, reflecting the street light. But after he had rubbed his butt into an ash tray on the floor, Helen stepped out of her shoes and lay down beside him on the narrow bed, Frank moving over to the wall.

"This is more like it," he sighed.

She lay with closed eyes in his arms, feeling the warmth of the heater like a hand on her back. For a minute she half-dozed, then woke to his kisses. She lay motionless, a little tense, but when he stopped kissing her, relaxed. She listened to the quiet sound of the rain in the street, making it in her mind into spring rain, though spring was weeks away; and within the rain grew all sorts of flowers; and amid the spring flowers, in this flowering dark—a sweet spring night—she lay with him in the open under new stars and a cry rose to her throat. When he kissed her again, she responded with passion.

"Darling."

"I love you, Helen, you are my girl."

They kissed breathlessly, then he undid the buttons of her blouse. She sat up to unhook her brassière but as she was doing it, felt his fingers under her skirt.

Helen grabbed his hand. "Please, Frank. Let's not get that hot and bothered."

"What are we waiting for, honey?" He tried to move his hand but her legs tightened and she swung her feet off the bed.

He pulled her back, pressing her shoulders down. She felt his body trembling on hers and for a fleeting minute thought he might hurt her; but he didn't.

She lay stiff, unresponsive on the bed. When he kissed her again she didn't move. It took a while before he lay back. She saw by the reflected glow of the heater how unhappy he looked.

Helen sat on the edge of the bed, buttoning her blouse.

His hands covered his face. He said nothing but she could feel his body shivering on the bed.

"Christ," he muttered.

"I'm sorry," she said softly. "I told you I wouldn't."

Five minutes passed. Frank slowly sat up. "Are you a virgin, is that what's eating you?"

"I'm not," she said.

"I thought you were," he said, surprised. "You act like one."

"I said I wasn't."

"Then why do you act like one? Don't you know what it does to people?"

"I'm people."

"Then why do you do it for?"

"Because I believe in what I'm doing."

"I thought you said you weren't a virgin?"

"You don't have to be a virgin to have ideals in sex."

"What I don't understand is if you did it before, what's the difference if we do it now?"

"We can't, just because I did," she said, brushing her hair back. "That's the point. I did it and that's why I can't with you now. I said I wouldn't, that night on the Parkway."

"I don't get it," Frank said.

"Loving should come with love."

"I said I love you, Helen, you heard me say it."

"I mean I have to love you too. I think I do but sometimes I'm not sure."

He fell again into silence. She listened absentmindedly to the radio but nobody was dancing now.

"Don't be hurt, Frank."

"I'm tired of that," he said harshly.

"Frank," said Helen, "I said I slept with somebody before and the truth of it is, if you want to know, I'm sorry I did. I admit I had some pleasure, but after, I thought it wasn't worth it, only I didn't know at the time I would feel that way, because at the time I didn't know what I wanted. I suppose I felt I wanted to be free, so I settled for sex. But if you're not in love sex isn't being free, so I made a promise to myself that

I never would any more unless I really fell in love with somebody. I don't want to dislike myself. I want to be disciplined, and you have to be too if I ask it. I ask it so I might someday love you without reservations."

"Crap," Frank said, but then, to his surprise, the idea seized him. He thought of himself as disciplined, then wished he were. This seemed to him like an old and faraway thought, and he remembered with regret and strange sadness how often he had wished for better control over himself, and how little of it he had achieved.

He said, "I didn't mean to say what I just now did, Helen."

"I know," she answered.

"Helen," he said huskily, "I want you to know I am a very good guy in my heart."

"I don't think otherwise."

"Even when I am bad I am good."

She said she thought she knew what he meant.

They kissed, again and again. He thought there were a whole lot worse things than waiting for something that was going to be good once he got it.

Helen lay back on the bed and dozed, awaking when Nick and Tessie came into their bedroom, talking about the movie they had seen. It was a love story and Tessie had liked it very much. After they undressed and got into bed their double bed creaked. Helen felt bad for Frank but Frank did not seem to feel bad. Nick and Tessie soon fell asleep. Helen, breathing lightly, listened to their heavy breathing, worrying how she was going to get down to her floor, because if Ida was awake she would hear her on the stairs. But Frank said in a low voice that he would carry her to the vestibule, then she could go up after a few minutes, as if she had just come home from some place.

She put on her coat, hat and rubbers, and was careful to remember her umbrella. Frank carried her down the stairs. There were only his slow, heavy steps going down. And not long after they had kissed good night and he had gone for a walk in the rain, Helen opened the hall door and went up.

Then Ida fell asleep.

Thereafter Helen and Frank met outside the house.

It was snowing in the afternoon, when the front door opened and in came Detective Minogue, pushing before him this stocky handcuffed guy, unshaven, and wearing a faded green wind-breaker and denim slacks. He was about twenty-seven, with tired eyes and no hat. In the store, he lifted his manacled hands to wipe the snow off his wet hair.

"Where's Morris?" the detective asked the clerk.

"In the back."

"Go on in," said Detective Minogue to the handcuffed man.

They went into the back. Morris was sitting on the couch, stealing a smoke. He hurriedly put out the butt and dropped it into the garbage pail.

"Morris," said the detective. "I think I have got the one who hit you on the head."

The grocer's face turned white as flour. He stared at the man but didn't approach him.

After a minute he muttered, "I don't know if it's him. He had his face covered with a handkerchief."

"He's a big son of a bitch," the detective said. "The one that hit you was big, wasn't he?"

"Heavy," said Morris. "The other was big."

Frank was standing in the doorway, watching.

Detective Minogue turned to him. "Who're you?"

"He's my clerk," explained Morris.

The detective unbuttoned his overcoat and took a clean handkerchief out of his suit pocket. "Do me a favor," he said to Frank. "Tie this around his puss."

"I would rather not," Frank answered.

"As a favor. To save me the trouble of getting hit on the head with his cuffs."

Frank took the handkerchief, and though not liking to, tied it around the man's face, the suspect holding himself stiffly erect.

"How about it now, Morris?"

"I can't tell you," Morris said, embarrassed. He had to sit down.

"You want some water, Morris?" Frank asked.

"No."

"Take your time," said Detective Minogue, "look him over good."

"I don't recognize him. The other acted more rough. He had a rough voice—not nice."

"Say something, son," the detective said.

"I didn't hold this guy up," said the suspect in a dead voice.

"Is that the voice, Morris?"

"No."

"Does he look like the other one—the heavy guy's partner?"

"No, this is a different man."

"How are you so sure?"

"The helper was a nervous man. He was bigger than this one. Also this one has got small hands. The helper had big heavy hands."

"Are you positive? We grabbed him on a job last night. He held up a grocery with another guy who got away."

The detective pulled the handkerchief off the man's face.

"I don't know him," Morris said with finality.

Detective Minogue folded the handkerchief and tucked it into his pocket. He slipped his eyeglasses into a leather case. "Morris, I think I asked you already if you saw my son Ward Minogue around here. Have you yet?"

"No," said the grocer.

Frank went over to the sink and rinsed his mouth with a cup of water.

"Maybe you know him?" the detective asked him.

"No," said the clerk.

"O.K., then." The detective unbuttoned his overcoat. "By the way, Morris, did you ever find out who was stealing your milk that time?"

"Nobody steals any more," said Morris.

"Come on, son," said the detective to the suspect.

The handcuffed man went out of the store into the snow, the detective following him.

Frank watched them get into the police car, sorry for the guy. What if they arrested me now, he thought, although I am not the same guy I once was?

Morris, thinking of the stolen milk bottles, gazed guiltily at his assistant.

Frank happened to notice the size of his hands, then had to go to the toilet.

As he was lying in his bed after supper, thinking about his

life, Frank heard footsteps coming up the stairs and someone banged on his door. For a minute his head hammered with fear, but he got up and forced himself to open the door. Grinning at him from under his fuzzy hat stood Ward Minogue, his eyes small and smeary. He had lost weight and looked worse.

Frank let him in and turned on the radio. Ward sat on the bed, his shoes dripping from the snow.

"Who told you I lived here?" Frank asked.

"I watched you go in the hall, opened the door and heard you go up the stairs," Ward said.

How am I ever going to get rid of this bastard, Frank thought.

"You better stay away from here," he said with a heavy heart. "If Morris recognizes you in that goddamned hat, we will both go to jail."

"I came to visit my popeyed friend, Louis Karp," said Ward. "I wanted a bottle but he wouldn't give it to me because I am short on cash, so I thought my good-looking friend Frank Alpine will lend me some. He's an honest, hard-working bastard."

"You picked the wrong guy. I am poor."

Ward eyed him craftily. "I was sure you'd have saved up a pile by now, stealing from the Jew."

Frank stared at him but didn't answer.

Ward's glance shifted. "Even if you are stealing his chicken feed, it ain't any skin off me. Why I came is this. I got a new job that we can do without any trouble."

"I told you I am not interested in your jobs, Ward."

"I thought you would like to get your gun back, otherwise it might accidentally get lost with your name on it."

Frank rubbed his hands.

"All you got to do is drive," Ward said amiably. "The job is a cinch, a big liquor joint in Bay Ridge. After nine o'clock they only keep one man on. The take will be over three hundred."

"Ward, you don't look to me in any kind of condition to do a stickup. You look more like you need to be in a hospital."

"All I got is a bad heartburn."

"You better take care of yourself."

"You are making me cry."

"Why don't you start going straight?"

"Why don't you?"

"I am trying to."

"Your Jew girl must be some inspiration."

"Don't talk about her, Ward."

"I tailed you last week when you took her in the park. She's a nice piece. How often do you get it?"

"Get the hell out of here."

Ward got up unsteadily. "Hand over fifty bucks or I will fix you good with your Jew boss and your Jew girl. I will write them a letter who did the stickup last November."

Frank rose, his face hard. Taking his wallet out of his pocket, he emptied it on the bed. There were eight single dollar bills. "That's all I have got."

Ward snatched up the money. "I'll be back for more."

"Ward," Frank said through tight teeth, "if you drag your ass up here any more to make trouble, or if you ever follow me and my girl again, or tell Morris anything, the first thing I will do is telephone your old man at the police station and tell him under which rock he can find you. He was in the grocery asking about you today, and if he ever meets up with you, he looks like he will bust your head off."

Ward with a moan spat at the clerk and missed, the gob of spit trickling down the wall.

"You stinking kike," he snarled. Rushing out into the hall, he all but fell down two flights of stairs.

The grocer and Ida ran out to see who was making the racket, but by then Ward was gone.

Frank lay in bed, his eyes closed.

One dark and windy night when Helen left the house late, Ida followed her through the cold streets and across the plaza into the interior of the deserted park, and saw her meet Frank Alpine. There, in an opening between a semicircle of tall lilac shrubs and a grove of dark maples, were a few benches, dimly lit and private, where they liked to come to be alone. Ida watched them sitting together on one of the benches, kissing. She dragged herself home and went upstairs, half-dead. Morris was asleep and she didn't want to wake him, so she sat in the kitchen, sobbing.

When Helen returned and saw her mother weeping at the kitchen table, she knew Ida knew, and Helen was both moved and frightened.

Out of pity she asked, "Mama, why are you crying?"

Ida at last raised her tear-stained face and said in despair, "Why do I cry? I cry for the world. I cry for my life that it went away wasted. I cry for you."

"What have I done?"

"You have killed me in my heart."

"I've done nothing that's wrong, nothing I'm ashamed of."

"You are not ashamed that you kissed a goy?"

Helen gasped. "Did you follow me, Mama?"

"Yes," Ida wept.

"How could you?"

"How could you kiss a goy?"

"I'm not ashamed that we kissed."

She still hoped to avoid an argument. Everything was unsettled, premature.

Ida said, "If you marry such a man your whole life will be poisoned."

"Mama, you'll have to be satisfied with what I now say. I have no plans to marry anybody."

"What kind plans you got then with a man that he kisses you alone in a place where nobody can find you in the park?"

"I've been kissed before."

"But a goy, Helen, an Italyener."

"A man, a human being like us."

"A man is not good enough. For a Jewish girl must be a Jew."

"Mama, it's very late. I don't wish to argue. Let's not wake Papa."

"Frank is not for you. I don't like him. His eyes don't look at a person when he talks to them."

"His eyes are sad. He's had a hard life."

"Let him go and find someplace a shikse that he likes, not a Jewish girl."

"I have to work in the morning. I'm going to bed."

Ida quieted down. When Helen was undressing she came

into her room. "Helen," she said, holding back her tears, "the only thing I want for you is the best. Don't make my mistake. Don't make worse and spoil your whole life, with a poor man that he is only a grocery clerk which we don't know about him nothing. Marry somebody who can give you a better life, a nice professional boy with a college education. Don't mix up now with a stranger. Helen, I know what I'm talking. Believe me, I know." She was crying again.

"I'll try my best," Helen said.

Ida dabbed at her eyes with a handkerchief. "Helen, darling, do me one favor."

"What is it? I am very tired."

"Please call up Nat tomorrow. Just to speak to him. Say hello, and if he asks you to go out with him, tell him yes. Give him a chance."

"I gave him one."

"Last summer you enjoyed so much with him. You went to the beach, to concerts. What happened?"

"Our tastes are different," Helen said wearily.

"In the summer you said your tastes were the same."

"I learned otherwise."

"He is a Jewish boy, Helen, a college graduate. Give him another chance."

"All right," said Helen, "now will you go to sleep?"

"Also don't go no more with Frank. Don't let him kiss you, it's not nice."

"I can't promise."

"Please, Helen."

"I said I'd call Nat. Let that be an end of it now. Good night, Mama."

"Good night," Ida said sadly.

Though her mother's suggestion depressed her, Helen called Nat from her office the next day. He was cordial, said he had bought a secondhand car from his future brother-in-law and invited her to go for a drive.

She said she would sometime.

"How about Friday night?" Nat asked.

She was seeing Frank on Friday. "Could you make it Saturday?"

"I happen to have an engagement Saturday, also Thursday—something doing at the law school."

"Then Friday is all right." She agreed reluctantly, thinking it would be best to change the date with Frank, to satisfy her mother.

When Morris came up for his nap that afternoon Ida desperately begged him to send Frank away at once.

"Leave me alone on this subject ten minutes."

"Morris," she said, "last night I went out when Helen went, and I saw she met Frank in the park, and they kissed each the other."

Morris frowned. "He kissed her?"

"Yes."

"She kissed him?"

"I saw with my eyes."

But the grocer, after thinking about it, said wearily, "So what is a kiss? A kiss is nothing."

Ida said furiously, "Are you crazy?"

"He will go away soon," he reminded her. "In the summer."

Tears sprang into her eyes. "By summer could happen here ten times a tragedy."

"What kind tragedy you expecting—murder?"

"Worse," she cried.

His heart turned cold, he lost his temper. "Leave me alone on this subject, for God's sakes."

"Wait," Ida bitterly warned.

On Thursday of that week Julius Karp left Louis in the liquor store and stepped outside to peek through the grocery window to see if Morris was alone. Karp had not set foot in Morris's store since the night of the holdup, and he uneasily considered the reception he might meet if her were to go in now. Usually, after a time of not speaking to one another, it was Morris Bober, by nature unable to hold a grudge, who gave in and spoke to Karp; but this time he had put out of his mind the possibility of seeking out the liquor dealer and reestablishing their fruitless relationship. While in bed during his last convalescence he had thought much of Karp—an unwilling and distasteful thinking—and had discovered he disliked him more than he had imagined. He resented him as a crass and stupid person who had fallen through luck into flowing prosperity. His every good fortune spattered others with misfortune, as if there was just so much luck in the world and what Karp left over wasn't fit to eat. Morris was incensed by thoughts of the long years he had toiled without just reward. Though this was not Karp's fault, it *was* that a delicatessen had moved in across the street to make a poor man poorer. Nor could the grocer forgive him the blow he had taken on the head in his place, who could in health and wealth better afford it. Therefore it gave him a certain satisfaction not to have anything to do with the liquor dealer, though he was every day next door.

Karp, on the other hand, had been content to wait for Morris to loosen up first. He pictured the grocer yielding his aloof silence while he enjoyed the signs of its dissolution, meanwhile pitying the poor Jew his hard luck life—in capital letters. Some were born that way. Whereas Karp in whatever he touched now coined pure gold, if Morris Bober found a rotten egg in the street, it was already cracked and leaking. Such a one needed someone with experience to advise him when to stay out of the rain. But Morris, whether he knew how Karp felt, or not, remained rigidly uncommunicative—offering not so much as a flicker of recognition when on his way to the corner for his daily *Forward,* he passed the liquor dealer standing in front of his store or caught his eye peeking into his front window. As a month passed, now, quickly, almost four, Karp came to the uncomfortable conclusion that although Ida was still friendly to him, he would this time get nothing for free from Morris; he wasn't going to give in. He reacted coldly to this insight, would give back what he got—so let it be indifference. But indifference was not a commodity he was pleased to exchange. For some reason that was not clear to him Karp liked Morris to like him, and it soon rankled that his down-at-the-heels neighbor continued to remain distant. So he had been hit on the head in a hold-up, but was the fault Karp's? *He* had taken care—why hadn't Morris, the shlimozel? Why, when he had warned him there were two holdupniks across the street, hadn't he like a sensible person gone first to lock his door, then telephoned the police? Why?—because he was inept, unfortunate.

And because he was, his troubles grew like bananas in bunches. First, in another accident to his hard head, then through employing Frank Alpine. Karp, no fool, knew the makings of a bad situation when he saw it. Frank, whom he had got acquainted with and considered a fly-by-night rolling stone, would soon make trouble—of that he was certain. Morris's fly-specked, worm-eaten shop did not earn half enough to pay for a full-time helper, and it was idiotic extravagance for the grocer, after he was better, to keep the clerk working for him. Karp soon learned from Louis that his estimate of a bad situation was correct. He found out that Frank every so often invested in a bottle of the best stuff, paying, naturally, cash—but whose? Furthermore Sam Pearl, another waster, had mentioned that the clerk would now and then paste a two-dollar bill on some nag's useless nose, from which it blew off in the breeze. This done by a man who was no doubt paid in peanuts added up to only one thing—he stole. Who did he steal from? Naturally from M. Bober, who had anyway nothing—who else? Rockefeller knew how to take care of his millions, but if Morris earned a dime he lost it before he could put it into his torn pocket. It was the nature of clerks to steal from those they were working for. Karp had, as a young man, privately peculated from his employer, a half-blind shoe wholesaler; and Louis, he knew, snitched from him, but by Louis he was not bothered. He was, after all, a son; he worked in the business and would someday—it shouldn't be too soon—own it. Also, by strict warnings and occasional surprise inventories he held Louis down to a bare minimum beans. A stranger stealing money was another matter—slimy. It gave Karp gooseflesh to think of the Italian working for him.

And since misfortune was the grocer's lot, the stranger would shovel on more, not less, for it was always dangerous to have a young goy around where there was a Jewish girl. This worked out by an unchangeable law that Karp would gladly have explained to Morris had they been speaking, and saved him serious trouble. That *this* trouble, too, existed he had confirmed twice in the last week. Once he saw Helen and Frank walking on the Parkway under the trees, and another time while driving home past the local movie house, he had glimpsed them coming out after a show, holding hands. Since then he had often thought about them, indeed with anxiety, and felt he would in some way like to assist the luckless Bober.

Without doubt Morris kept Frank on to make his life easier, and probably, being Bober, he had no idea what was happening behind his back. Well, Julius Karp would warn him of his daughter's danger. Tactfully he would explain him what was what. After, he would put in a plug for Louis, who, Karp was aware, had long liked Helen but was not sure enough of himself to be successful with her. Swat Louis down and he retreated to tenderize his fingernails with his teeth. In some things he needed a push. Karp felt he could ease his son's way to Helen by making Morris a proposition he had had in the back of his head for almost a year. He would describe Louis' prospects after marriage in terms of cold cash and other advantages, and suggest that Morris speak to Helen on the subject of going with him seriously. If they went together a couple of months—Louis would give her an extravagant good time—and the combination worked out, it would benefit not only the daughter, but the grocer as well, for then Karp would take over Morris's sad gesheft and renovate and enlarge it into a self-service market with the latest fixtures and goods. His tenant around the corner he would eliminate when his lease expired—a sacrifice, but worthwhile. After that, with himself as the silent partner giving practical advice, it would take a marvelous catastrophe to keep the grocer from earning a decent living in his old age.

Karp foresaw that the main problem of this matter would be Helen, whom he knew as a strictly independent yet not unworthy girl, even if she had pretensions to marriage with a professional—although she had got no place with Nat Pearl. To be successful, Nat needed what Louis Karp would have plenty of, not a poor girl. So he had acted in his best interests in gently shooing Helen away when her thoughts got too warm—a fact Karp had picked up from Sam Pearl. Louis, on the other hand, could afford a girl like Helen, and Helen, independent and intelligent, would be good for Louis. The liquor store owner decided that when the opportunity came he would talk turkey to her like a Dutch uncle. He would patiently explain that her only future with Frank would be as an outcast, poorer even than her father and sharing his foolish fate; whereas with Louis she could have what she wanted and more—leave it to her father-in-law. Karp felt that once Frank had gone she would listen to reason and appreciate the good life he was offering her. Twenty-three or -four was a dangerous age for a single girl. At that age she would not get younger; at that age even a goy looked good.

Having observed that Frank had gone into Sam Pearl's place, and that Morris was for the moment alone in the back of his store, Karp coughed clear his throat and stepped inside the grocery. When Morris, emerging from the rear, saw who it after all was, he experienced a moment of vindictive triumph, but this was followed by annoyance that the pest was once more present, and at the same time by an uncomfortable remembrance that Karp never entered unaccompanied by bad news. Therefore he stayed silent, waiting for the liquor dealer, in prosperous sport jacket and gabardine slacks which could not camouflage his protrusive belly nor subtract from the foolishness of his face, to speak; but for once Karp's active tongue lay flat on its back as, embarrassed in recalling the results of his very last visit here, he stared at the visible scar on Morris's head.

In pity for him, the grocer spoke, his tone friendlier than he would have guessed. "So how are you, Karp?"

"Thanks. What have I got to complain?" Beaming, he thrust a pudgy hand across the counter and Morris found himself unwillingly weighing the heavy diamond ring that pressed his fingers.

Since it did not seem sensible to Karp, one minute after their reconciliation, to blurt out news of a calamity concerning Morris's daughter, he fiddled around for words to say and came up with, "How's business?"

Morris had hoped he would ask. "Fine, and every day gets better."

Karp contracted his brows; yet it occurred to him that Morris's business might have improved more than he had guessed, when peering at odd moments through the grocery window, he had discovered a customer or two instead of the usual dense emptiness. Now on the inside after several months, he noticed the store seemed better taken care of, the shelves solidly packed with stock. But if business was better he at once knew why.

Yet he casually asked, "How is this possible? You are maybe advertising in the paper?"

Morris smiled at the sad joke. Where there was no wit money couldn't buy it. "By word of mouth," he remarked, "is the best advertising."

"This is according to what the mouth says."

"It says," Morris answered without shame, "that I got a fine clerk who has pepped me up the business. Instead going down in the winter, every day goes up."

"Your clerk did this?" Karp said, thoughtfully scratching under one buttock.

"The customers like him. A goy brings in goyim."

"New customers?"

"New, old."

"Something else helps you also?"

"Also helps a little the new apartment house that it opened in December."

"Hmm," said Karp, "nothing more?"

Morris shrugged. "I don't think so. I hear your Schmitz don't feel so good and he don't give service like he used to give. Came back a few customers from him, but the most important help to me is Frank."

Karp was astonished. Could it be that the man didn't know what had happened practically under his nose? He then and there saw a God-given opportunity to boot the clerk out of the place forever. "That wasn't Frank Alpine who improved you your business," he said decisively. "That was something else."

Morris smiled slightly. As usual the sage knew every reason for every happening.

But Karp persisted. "How long does he work here?"

"You know when he came—in November."

"And right away the business started to pick up?"

"Little by little."

"This happened," Karp announced with excitement, "not because this goy came here. What did he know about the grocery business? Nothing. Your store improved because my tenant Schmitz got sick and had to close his store part of the day. Didn't you know that?"

"I heard he was sick," Morris answered, his throat tightening, "but the drivers said his old father came to give him a help."

"That's right," Karp said, "but in the middle of December he went every morning to the hospital for treatments. First the father stayed in the store, then he got too tired so Schmitz didn't open till maybe nine, ten o'clock, instead of seven. And instead of closing ten o'clock at night, he closed eight. This went on like this till last month, then he couldn't open till eleven o'clock in the morning, and so he lost half a day's business. He tried to sell the store but nobody would buy then. Yesterday he closed up altogether. Didn't somebody mention that to you?"

"One of the customers said," Morris answered, distressed, "but I thought it was temporary."

"He's very sick," said Karp solemnly. "He won't open again."

My God, thought Morris. For months he had watched the store when it was empty and while it was being altered, but never since its opening had he gone past Sam Pearl's corner to look at it. He hadn't the heart to. But why had no one told him that the place had been closing part of the day for more than two months—Ida, Helen? Probably they had gone past it without noticing the door was sometimes closed. In their minds, as in his, it was always open for *his* business.

"I don't say," Karp was saying, "that your clerk didn't help your income, but the real reason things got better is when Schmitz couldn't stay open, some of his customers came here. Naturally, Frank wouldn't tell you that."

Filled with foreboding, Morris reflected on what the liquor dealer had said. "What happened to Schmitz?"

"He has a bad blood disease and lays now in the hospital."

"Poor man," the grocer sighed. Hope wrestled shame as he asked, "Will he give the store in auction?"

Karp was devastating. "What do you mean give in auction? It's a good store. He sold it Wednesday to two up-to-date Norwegian partners and they will open next week a modern fancy grocery and delicatessen. You will see where your business will go."

Morris, with clouded eyes, died slowly.

Karp, to his horror, realized he had shot at the clerk and wounded the grocer. He remarked hastily, "What could I do? I couldn't tell him to go in auction if he had a chance to sell."

The grocer wasn't listening. He was thinking of Frank with a violent sense of outrage, of having been deceived.

"Listen, Morris," Karp said quickly, "I got a proposition for you about your gesheft. Throw out first on his ass this Italyener that he fooled you, then tell Helen that my Louis—"

But when the ghost behind the counter cursed him in a strange tongue for the tidings he had brought, Karp backed out of the store and was swallowed in his own.

After a perilous night at the hands of ancient enemies, Morris escaped from his bed and appeared in the store at five A.M. There he faced the burdensome day alone. The grocer had struggled all night with Karp's terrible news—had tossed around like a red coal why nobody had told him before how sick the German was—maybe one of the salesmen, or Breitbart, or a customer. Probably no one had thought it too important, seeing that Schmitz's store was until yesterday open daily. Sure he was sick, but somebody had already mentioned that, and why should they tell him again if they figured that people got sick but then they got better? Hadn't he himself been sick, but who had talked of it in the neighborhood? Probably nobody. People had their own worries to worry about. As for the news that Schmitz had sold his store, the grocer felt that here he had nothing to complain of—he had been informed at once, like a rock dropped on his skull.

As for what he would do with Frank, after long pondering the situation, thinking how the clerk had acted concerning their increase in business—as if he alone had created their better times—Morris at length decided that Frank had not—as he had assumed when Karp told him the news—tried to trick him into believing that he was responsible for the store's change for the better. The grocer supposed that the clerk, like himself, was probably ignorant of the true reason for their change of luck. Maybe he shouldn't have been, since he at least got out during the day, visited other places on the block, heard news, gossip—maybe he should have known, but Morris felt he didn't, possibly because he wanted to believe he was their benefactor. Maybe that was why he had been too blind to see what he should have seen, too deaf to have heard what he had heard. It was possible.

After his first confusion and fright, Morris had decided he must sell the store—he had by eight o'clock already told a couple of drivers to pass the word around—but he must under no circumstances part with Frank and must keep him here to do all he could to prevent the Norwegian partners, after they had reopened the store, from quickly calling back the customers of Schmitz who were with him now. He couldn't believe that Frank hadn't helped. It had not been proved in the Supreme Court that the German's sickness was the only source of their recent good fortune. Karp said so but since when did Karp speak the word of God? Of course Frank had helped the business—only not so much as they had thought. Ida was not so wrong about that. But maybe Frank could hold onto a few people; the grocer doubted he himself could. He hadn't the energy, the nerve to be alone in the store during another time of change for the worse. The years had eaten away his strength.

When Frank came down he at once noticed that the grocer was not himself, but the clerk was too concerned with his own problems to ask Morris what ailed him. Often since the time Helen had been in his room he had recalled her remark that he must discipline himself and wondered why he had been so moved by the word, why it should now bang around in his head like a stick against a drum. With the idea of self-control came the feeling of the beauty of it—the beauty of a person being able to do things the way he wanted to, to do good if he wanted; and this feeling was followed by regret—of the slow dribbling away, starting long ago, of his character, without him lifting a finger to stop it. But today, as he scraped at his hard beard with a safety razor, he made up his mind to return, bit by bit until all paid up, the hundred and forty-odd bucks he had filched from Morris in the months he had worked for him, the figure of which he had kept for this very purpose written on a card hidden in his shoe.

To clean up the slate in a single swipe, he thought again of telling Morris about his part in the holdup. A week ago he was on the point of getting it past his teeth, had even spoken aloud the grocer's name, but when Morris looked up Frank felt it was useless and said never mind. He was born he thought, with a worrisome conscience that had never done him too much good, although at times he had liked having the acid weight of it in him because it had made him feel he was at least that different from other people. It made him want to set himself straight so he could build his love for Helen right, so it would stay right.

But when he pictured himself confessing, the Jew listening with a fat ear, he still could not stand the thought of it. Why should he make more trouble for himself than he could now handle, and end by defeating his purpose to fix things up and have a better life? The past was the past and the hell with it. He had unwillingly taken part in a holdup, but he was, like Morris, more of a victim of Ward Minogue. If alone, he wouldn't have done it. That didn't excuse him that he did, but it at least showed his true feelings. So what was there to confess if the whole thing had been sort of an accident? Let bygones be gone. He had no control over the past—could only shine it up here and there and shut up as to the rest. From now on he would keep his mind on tomorrow, and tomorrow take up the kind of life that he saw he valued more than how he had been living. He would change and live in a worthwhile way.

Impatient to begin, he waited to empty the contents of his wallet into the cash drawer. He thought he could try it when Morris was napping; but then for some cockeyed reason, although there was nothing for her to do in the store today, Ida came down and sat in the back with him. She was heavy-faced, dispirited; she sighed often but said nothing, although she acted as if she couldn't stand the sight of him. He knew why, Helen had told him, and he felt uncomfortable, as if he were wearing wet clothes she wouldn't let him take off; but the best thing was to keep his trap shut and let Helen handle her end of it.

Ida wouldn't leave, so he couldn't put the dough back although his itch to do so had grown into impatience. Whenever somebody went into the store Ida insisted on waiting on them, but this last time after she came back she said to Frank, stretched out on the couch with a butt in his mouth, that she wasn't feeling so well and was going up.

"Feel better," he said sitting up, but she didn't reply and at last left. He went quickly into the store, once he was sure she was upstairs. His wallet contained a five-dollar bill and a single, and he planned to put it all back in the register, which would leave him only with a few coins in his pocket but tomorrow was payday anyway. After ringing up the six bucks, to erase the evidence of an unlikely sale he rang up "no sale." Frank then felt a surge of joy at what he had done and his eyes misted. In the back he drew off his shoe, got out the card, and substracted six dollars from the total amount he owed, He figured he could pay it all up in a couple-three months, by taking out of the bank the money—about eighty bucks—that was left there, returning it bit by bit, and when that was all used up, giving back part of his weekly salary till he had the debt squared. The trick was to get the money back without arousing anybody's suspicion he was putting in the drawer more than the business was earning.

While he was still in a good mood over what he had done, Helen called up.

"Frank," she said, "are you alone? If not say wrong number and hang up."

"I am alone."

"Have you seen how nice it is today? I went for a walk at lunchtime and it feels like spring has arrived."

"It's still in February. Don't take your coat off too soon."

"After Washington's Birthday winter loses its heart. Do you smell the wonderful air?"

"Not right now."

"Get outside in the sun," she said, "it's warm and wonderful."

"Why did you call me for?" he asked.

"Must I have an excuse to call?" she said softly.

"You never do."

"I called because I wished I were seeing you tonight instead of Nat."

"You don't have to go out with him if you don't want to."

"I'd better, because of my mother."

"Change it to some other time."

She thought a minute then said she had better to get it over with.

"Do it any way you like."

"Frank, do you think we could meet after I see Nat—maybe at half past eleven, or twelve at the latest? Would you like to meet me then?"

"Sure, but what's it all about?"

"I'll tell you when I see you," she said with a little laugh. "Should we meet on the Parkway or our regular place in front of the lilac trees?"

"Wherever you say. The park is okay."

"I really hate to go there since my mother followed us."

"Don't worry about that, honey." He said, "Have you got something nice to tell me?"

"Very nice," Helen said.

He thought he knew what it was. He thought he would carry her like a bride up to his room, then when it was over carry her down so she could go up alone without fear her mother suspected where she had been.

Just then Morris came into the store so he hung up.

The grocer inspected the figure in the cash register and the satisfying sum there set him sighing. By Saturday they would surely have two-forty or fifty, but it wouldn't be that high any more once the Norwegians opened up.

Noticing Morris peering at the register under the yellow flame of his match, Frank remembered that all he had left on him was about seventy cents. He wished Helen had called him before he had put back the six bucks in the drawer. If it rained tonight they might need a cab to get home from the park, or maybe if they went up in his room she would be hungry after and want a pizza or something. Anyway, he could borrow a buck from her if he needed it. He also thought of asking Louis Karp for a little loan but didn't like to.

Morris went out for his *Forward* and spread it before him on the table, but he wasn't reading. He was thinking how distracted he was about the future. While he was upstairs, he had lain in bed trying to think of ways to cut down his expenses. He had thought of the fifteen dollars weekly he paid

Frank and had worried over how large the sum was. He had also thought of Helen being kissed by the clerk, and of Ida's warnings, and all this had worked on his nerves. He seriously considered telling Frank to go but couldn't make the decision to. He wished he had let him go long ago.

Frank had decided he didn't like to ask Helen for any money—it wasn't a nice thing to do with a girl you liked. He thought it was better to take a buck out of the register drawer, out of the amount he had just put back. He wished he had paid back the five and kept himself the one-buck bill.

Morris sneaked a glance at his clerk sitting on the couch. Recalling the time he had sat in the barber's chair, watching the customers coming out of the grocery with big bags, he felt uneasy. I wonder if he steals from me, he thought. The question filled him with dread because he had asked it of himself many times yet had never answered it with certainty.

He saw through the window in the wall that a woman had come into the store. Frank got up from the couch. "I'll take this one, Morris."

Morris spoke to his newspaper. "I got anyway something to clean up in the cellar."

"What have you got there?"

"Something."

When Frank walked behind the counter, Morris went down into the cellar but didn't stay there. He stole up the stairs and stationed himself behind the hall door. Peering through a crack in the wood, he clearly saw the woman and heard her ordering. He added up the prices of the items as she ordered them.

The bill came to $1.81. When Frank rang up the money, the grocer held his breath for a painful second, then stepped inside the store.

The customer, hugging her bag of groceries, was on her way out of the front door. Frank had his hand under his apron, in his pants pocket. He gazed at the grocer with a startled expression. The amount rung up on the cash register was eighty-one cents.

Morris groaned within himself.

Frank, though tense with shame, pretended nothing was

wrong. This enraged Morris. "The bill was a dollar more, why did you ring a dollar less?"

The clerk, after a time of long agony, heard himself say, "It's just a mistake, Morris."

"No," thundered the grocer. "I heard behind the hall door how much you sold her. Don't think I don't know you did many times the same thing before."

Frank could say nothing.

"Give it here the dollar," Morris ordered, extending his trembling hand.

Anguished, the clerk tried lying. "You're making a mistake. The register owes me a buck. I ran short on nickels so I got twenty from Sam Pearl with my own dough. After, I accidentally rang up one buck instead of 'no sale.' That's why I took it back this way. No harm done, I tell you."

"This is a lie," cried Morris. "I left inside a roll of nickels in case anybody needed." He strode behind the counter, rang "no sale" and held up the roll of nickels. "Tell the truth."

Frank thought, This shouldn't be happening to me, for I am a different person now.

"I was short, Morris," he admitted, "that's the truth of it. I figured I would pay you back tomorrow after I got my pay." He took the crumpled dollar out of his pants pocket and Morris snatched it from his hand.

"Why didn't you ask me to lend you a dollar instead to steal it?"

The clerk realized it hadn't occurred to him to borrow from the grocer. The reason was simple—he had never borrowed, he had always stolen.

"I didn't think about it. I made a mistake."

"Always mistakes," the grocer said wrathfully.

"All my life," sighed Frank.

"You stole from me since the day I saw you."

"I confess to it," Frank said, "but for God's sake, Morris, I swear I was paying it back to you. Even today I put back six bucks. That's why you got so much in the drawer from the time you went up to snooze until now. Ask the Mrs if we took in more than two bucks while you were upstairs. The rest I put in."

He thought of taking off his shoe and showing Morris how

carefully he had kept track of the money he had taken, but he didn't want to do that because the amount was so large it might anger the grocer more.

"You put it in," Morris cried, "but it belongs to me. I don't want a thief here." He counted fifteen dollars out of the register. "Here's your week's pay—the last. Please leave now the store."

His anger was gone. He spoke in sadness and fear of tomorrow.

"Give me one last chance," Frank begged, "Morris, please." His face was gaunt, his eyes haunted, his beard like night.

Morris, though moved by the man, thought of Helen.

"No."

Frank stared at the gray and broken Jew and seeing, despite tears in his eyes, that he would not yield, hung up his apron on a hook and left.

The night's new beauty struck Helen with the anguish of loss as she hurried into the lamplit park a half-hour after midnight. That morning as she had stepped into the street, wearing a new dress under her old coat, the fragrant day had moved her to tears and she felt then she was truly in love with Frank. Whatever the future held it couldn't deny her the sense of release and fulfillment she had felt then. Hours later, when she was with Nat Pearl, as they stopped off for a drink at a roadside tavern, then at his insistence drove into Long Island, her thoughts were still on Frank and she was impatient to be with him.

Nat was Nat. He exerted himself tonight, giving out with charm. He talked with charm and was hurt with charm. Unchanged after all the months she hadn't been with him, as they were parked on the dark shore overlooking the starlit Sound, after a few charming preliminaries he had put his arms around her. "Helen, how can we forget what pleasure we had in the past?"

She pushed him away, angered. "It's gone, I've forgotten. If you're so much of a gentleman, Nat, you ought to forget it too. Was a couple of times in bed a mortgage on my future?"

"Helen, don't talk like a stranger. For Pete's sake, be human."

"I *am* human, please remember."

"We were once good friends. My plea is for friendship again."

"Why don't you admit by friendship you mean something different?"

"Helen . . ."

"No."

He sat back at the wheel. "Christ, you have become a suspicious character."

She said, "Things have changed—you must realize."

"Who have they changed for," he asked sullenly, "that dago I hear you go with?"

Her answer was ice.

On the way home he tried to unsay what he had said, but Helen yielded him only a quick good-by. She left him with relief and a poignant sense of all she had wasted of the night.

Worried that Frank had had to wait so long, she hurried across the lit plaza and along a gravel path bordered by tall lilac shrubs, toward their meeting place. As she approached their bench, although she was troubled by a foreboding he would not be there, she couldn't believe it, then was painfully disappointed to find that though others were present—it was true, he wasn't.

Could he have been and gone already? It didn't seem possible; he had always waited before, no matter how late she was. And since she had told him she had something important to say, nothing less than that she now knew she loved him, surely he would want to hear what. She sat down, fearing he had had an accident.

Usually they were alone at this spot, but the almost warmish late-February night had brought out company. On a bench diagonally opposite Helen, in the dark under budding branches, sat two young lovers locked in a long kiss. The bench at her left was empty, but on the one beyond that a man was sleeping under a dim lamp. A cat nosed at his shadow and departed. The man woke with a grunt, squinted at Helen, yawned and went back to sleep. The lovers at last broke apart and left in silence, the boy awkwardly trailing the happy girl. Helen deeply envied her, an awful feeling to end the day with.

Glancing at her watch she saw it was already past one. Shivering, she rose, then sat down to wait five last minutes. She felt the stars clustered like a distant weight above her head. Utterly lonely, she regretted the spring-like loveliness of the night; it had gone, in her hands, to waste. She was tired of anticipation, of waiting for nothing.

A man was standing unsteadily before her, heavy, dirty, stinking of whiskey. Helen half-rose, struck with fright.

He flipped off his hat and said huskily, "Don't be afraid of me, Helen. I'm personally a fine guy—son of a cop. You remember me, don't you—Ward Minogue that went to your school? My old man beat me up once in the girls' yard."

Though it was years since she had seen him she recognized Ward, at once recalling the incident of his following a girl into a lavatory. Instinctively Helen raised her arm to protect herself. She kept herself from screaming, or he might grab her. How stupid, she thought, to wait for this.

"I remember you, Ward."

"Could I sit down?"

She hesitated. "All right."

Helen edged as far away from him as she could. He looked half-stupefied. If he made a move she would run, screaming.

"How did you recognize me in the dark?" she asked, pretending to be casual as she glanced stealthily around to see how best to escape. If she could get past the trees, it was then another twenty feet along the shrub-lined path before she could be out in the open. Once on the plaza there would be people around she could appeal to.

God only help me, she thought.

"I saw you a couple of times lately," Ward answered, rubbing his hand slowly across his chest.

"Where?"

"Around. Once I saw you come out of your old man's grocery and I figured it was you. You have still kept your looks," he grinned.

"Thanks. Don't you feel so well?"

"I got gas pains in my chest and a goddam headache."

"In case you want one I have a box of aspirins in my purse."

"No, they make me puke." She noticed that he was glancing

toward the trees. She grew more anxious, thought of offering him her purse if he only wouldn't touch her.

"How's your boy friend, Frank Alpine?" Ward asked, with a wet wink.

She said in surprise, "Do you know Frank?"

"He's an old friend of mine," he answered. "He was here lookin' for you."

"Is—he all right?"

"Not so hot," said Ward. "He had to go home."

She got up. "I have to leave now."

But he was standing.

"Good night." Helen walked away from him.

"He told me to give you this paper." Ward thrust his hand into his coat pocket.

She didn't believe him but paused long enough for him to move forward. He grabbed her with astonishing swiftness, smothering her scream with his smelly hand, as he dragged her toward the trees.

"All I want is what you give that wop," Ward grunted.

She kicked, clawed, bit his hand, broke loose. He caught her by her coat collar, ripped it off. She screamed again and ran forward but he pounced upon her and got his arm over her mouth. Ward shoved her hard against a tree, knocking the breath out of her. He held her tightly by the throat as with his other hand he ripped open her coat and tore her dress off the shoulder, exposing her brassière.

Struggling, kicking wildly, she caught him between the legs with her knee. He cried out and cracked her across the face. She felt the strength go out of her and fought not to faint. She screamed but heard no sound.

Helen felt his body shuddering against her. I am disgraced, she thought, yet felt curiously freed of his stinking presence, as if he had dissolved into a can of filth and she had kicked it away. Her legs buckled and she slid to the ground. I've fainted, went through her mind, although she felt she was still fighting him.

Dimly she realized that a struggle was going on near her. She heard the noise of a blow, and Ward Minogue cried out in great pain and staggered away.

Frank, she thought with tremulous joy. Helen felt herself

gently lifted and knew she was in his arms. She sobbed in relief. He kissed her eyes and lips and he kissed her half-naked breast. She held him tightly with both arms, weeping, laughing, murmuring she had come to tell him she loved him.

He put her down and they kissed under the dark trees. She tasted whiskey on his tongue and was momentarily afraid.

"I love you, Helen," he murmured, attempting clumsily to cover her breast with the torn dress as he drew her deeper into the dark, and from under the trees onto the star-dark field.

They sank to their knees on the winter earth, Helen urgently whispering, "Please not now, darling," but he spoke of his starved and passionate love, and all the endless heartbreaking waiting. Even as he spoke he thought of her as beyond his reach, forever in the bathroom as he spied, so he stopped her pleas with kisses. . . .

Afterward, she cried, "Dog—uncircumcised dog!"

While Morris was sitting alone in the back the next morning, a boy brought in a pink handbill and left it on the counter. When the grocer picked it up he saw it announced the change of management and reopening on Monday, by Taast and Pederson, of the grocery and fancy delicatessen around the corner. There followed, in large print, a list of specials they were offering during their first week, bargains Morris could never hope to match, because he couldn't afford the loss the Norwegians were planning to take. The grocer felt he was standing in an icy draft blowing from some hidden hole in the store. In the kitchen, though he stood with his legs and buttocks pressed against the gas radiator, it took an age to diminish the chill that had penetrated his bones.

All morning he scanned the crumpled handbill, muttering to himself; he sipped cold coffee, thinking of the future, and off and on, of Frank Alpine. The clerk had left last night without taking his fifteen dollars' wages. Morris thought he would come in for it this morning but, as the hours passed, knew he wouldn't, maybe having left it to make up some of the money he had stolen; yet maybe not. For the thousandth time the grocer wondered if he had done right in ordering Frank to go. True, he had stolen from him, but also true, he was paying it back. His story that he had put six dollars into the register and then found he had left himself without a penny in his pocket was probably the truth, because the sum in the register, when Morris counted it, was more than they usually took in during the dead part of the afternoon when he napped. The clerk was an unfortunate man; yet the grocer was alternately glad and sorry the incident had occurred. He was glad he had finally let him go. For Helen's sake it had had to be done, and for Ida's peace of mind, as well as his own. Still, he felt unhappy to lose his assistant and be by himself when the Norwegians opened up.

Ida came down, puffy-eyed from poor sleep. She felt a hopeless rage against the world. What will become of Helen? she asked herself, and cracked her knuckles against her chest. But when Morris looked up to listen to her complaints, she was afraid to say anything. A half-hour later, aware that something had changed in the store, she thought of the clerk.

"Where is he?" she asked.

"He left," Morris answered.

"Where did he leave?" she said in astonishment.

"He left for good."

She gazed at him. "Morris, what happened, tell me?"

"Nothing," he said, embarrassed. "I told him to leave."

"Why, all of a sudden?"

"Didn't you say you didn't want him here no more?"

"From the first day I saw him, but you always said no."

"Now I said yes."

"A stone falls off my heart." But she was not satisfied. "Did he move out of the house yet?"

"I don't know."

"I will go and ask the upstairske."

"Leave her alone. We will know when he moves."

"When did you tell him to leave?"

"Last night."

"So why didn't you tell me last night?" she said angrily. "Why you told me he went early to the movies?"

"I was nervous."

"Morris," she asked in fright. "Did something else happen? Did Helen—"

"Nothing happened."

"Does she know he left?"

"I didn't tell her. Why she went so early to work this morning?"

"She went early?"

"Yes."

"I don't know," Ida said uneasily.

He produced the handbill. "This is why I feel bad."

She glanced at it, not comprehending.

"The German," he explained. "They bought him out, two Norwegians."

She gasped. "When?"

"This week. Schmitz is sick. He lays now in the hospital."

"I told you," Ida said.

"You told me?"

"Vey is mir. I told you after Christmas—when improved more the business. I told you the drivers said the German was losing customers. You said Frank improved the business. A goy brings in goyim, you said. How much strength I had to argue with you?"

"Did you tell me he kept closed in the morning his store?"

"Who said? I didn't know this."

"Karp told me."

"Karp was here?"

"He came on Thursday to tell me the good news."

"What good news?"

"That Schmitz sold out."

"Is this good news?" she asked.

"Maybe to him but not to me."

"You didn't tell me he came."

"I tell you now," he said irritably. "Schmitz sold out. Monday will open two Norwegians. Our business will go to hell again. We will starve here."

"Some helper you had," she said with bitterness. "Why didn't you listen to me when I said let him go?"

"I listened," he said wearily.

She was silent, then asked, "So when Karp told you Schmitz sold his store you told Frank to leave?"

"The next day."

"Thank God."

"See if you say next week 'Thank God.' "

"What is this got to do with Frank? Did he help us?"

"I don't know."

"You don't know," she said shrilly. "You just told me you said he should leave when you found out where came our business."

"I don't know," he said miserably, "I don't know where it came."

"It didn't come from him."

"Where it came I don't worry any more. Where will it come next week I worry." He read aloud the specials the Norwegians were offering.

She squeezed her hands white. "Morris, we must sell the store."

"So sell." Sighing, Morris removed his apron. "I will take my rest."

"It's only half past eleven."

"I feel cold." He looked depressed.

"Eat something first—your soup."

"Who can eat?"

"Drink a hot glass tea."

"No."

"Morris," she said quietly, "don't worry so much. Something will happen. We will always have to eat."

He made no reply, folded the handbill into a small square and took it upstairs with him.

The rooms were cold. Ida always shut off the radiators when she went down and lit them again in the late afternoon about an hour before Helen returned. Now the house was too cold. Morris turned on the stopcock of the bedroom radiator, then found he had no match in his pocket. He got one in the kitchen.

Under the covers he felt shivery. He lay under two blankets and a quilt yet shivered. He wondered if he was sick but soon fell asleep. He was glad when he felt sleep come over him, although it brought night too quickly. But if you slept it was night, that's how things were. Looking, that same night, from the street into his store, he beheld Taast and Pederson—one with a small blond mustache, the other half-bald, a light shining on his head—standing behind *his* counter, poking into *his* cash register. The grocer rushed in but they were gabbing in German and paid no attention to his gibbering Yiddish. At that moment Frank came out of the back with Helen. Though the clerk spoke a musical Italian, Morris recognized a dirty word. He struck his assistant across the face and they wrestled furiously on the floor, Helen screaming mutely. Frank dumped him heavily on his back and sat on his poor chest. He thought his lungs would burst. He tried hard to cry out but his voice cracked his throat and no one would help. He considered the possibility of dying and would have like to.

Tessie Fuso dreamed of a tree hit by thunder and knocked over; she dreamed she heard someone groan terribly and awoke in fright, listened, then went back to sleep. Frank Alpine, at the dirty end of a long night, awoke groaning. He awoke with a shout—awake, he thought, forever. His impulse was to leap out of bed and rush down to the store; then he remembered that Morris had thrown him out. It was a gray, dreary winter morning. Nick had gone to work and Tessie, in her bathrobe, was sitting in the kitchen, drinking coffee. She heard Frank cry out again but had just discovered that she was pregnant, so did nothing more than wonder at his nightmare.

He lay in bed with the blankets pulled over his head, trying to smother his thoughts but they escaped and stank. The more he smothered them the more they stank. He smelled garbage in the bed and couldn't move out of it. He couldn't because he was it—the stink in his own broken nose. What you did was how bad you smelled. Unable to stand it he flung the covers aside and struggled to dress but couldn't make it. The sight of his bare feet utterly disgusted him. He thirsted for a cigarette but couldn't light one for fear of seeing his hand. He shut his eyes and lit a match. The match burned his nose. He stepped on the lit match with his bare feet and danced in pain.

Oh my God, why did I do it? Why did I ever do it? Why did I do it?

His thoughts were killing him. He couldn't stand them. He sat on the edge of the twisted bed, his thoughtful head ready to bust in his hands. He wanted to run. Part of him was already in flight, he didn't know where. He just wanted to run. But while he was running, he wanted to be back. He wanted to be back with Helen, to be forgiven. It wasn't asking too much. People forgave people—who else? He could explain if she would listen. Explaining was a way of getting close to somebody you had hurt; as if in hurting them you were giving them a reason to love you. He had come, he would say, to the park to wait for her, to hear what she had to tell him. He felt he knew she would say she loved him; it meant they would soon sleep together. This stayed in his mind and he sat there waiting to hear her say it, at the same time in an agony that she never would, that he would lose her the minute she found out why her father had kicked him out of the grocery. What could he tell her about that? He sat for hours trying to think what to say, at last growing famished. At midnight he left to get a pizza but stopped instead in a bar. Then when he saw his face in the mirror he felt a nose-thumbing revulsion. Where have you ever been, he asked the one in the glass, except on the inside of a circle? What have you ever done but always the wrong thing? When he returned to the park, there was Ward Minogue hurting her. He just about killed Ward. Then when he had Helen in his arms, crying, saying at last that she loved him, he had this hopeless feeling it was the end and now he would never see her again. He thought he must love her before she was lost to him. She said no, not to, but he couldn't believe it the same minute she was saying she loved him. He thought, Once I start she will come along with me. So then he did it. He loved her with his love. She should have known that. She should not have gone wild, beat his face with her fists, called him dirty names, run from him, his apologies, pleadings, sorrow.

Oh, Jesus, what did I do?

He moaned; had got instead of a happy ending, a bad smell. If he could root out what he had done, smash and destroy it; but it was done, beyond him to undo. It was where he could never lay hands on it any more—in his stinking mind. His thoughts would forever suffocate him. He had failed once too often. He should somewhere have stopped and changed the way he was going, his luck, himself, stopped hating the world, got a decent education, a job, a nice girl. He had lived without will, betrayed every good intention. Had he ever confessed the holdup to Morris? Hadn't he stolen from the cash register till the minute he was canned? In a single terrible act in the park hadn't he murdered the last of his good hopes, the love he had so long waited for—his chance at a future? His goddamned life had pushed him wherever it went; he had led it nowhere. He was blown around in any breath that blew, owned nothing, not even experience to show for the years he had lived. If you had experience you knew at least when to start and where to quit; all he knew was how to mangle himself more. The self he had secretly considered valuable, for all he could make of it, a dead rat. He stank.

This time his shout frightened Tessie. Frank got up on the run but he had run everywhere. There was no place left to escape to. The room shrank. The bed was flying up at him. He felt trapped—sick, wanted to cry but couldn't. He planned to kill himself, at the same minute had a terrifying insight: that all the while he was acting like he wasn't, he was really a man of stern morality.

Ida had awakened in the night and heard her daughter crying. Nat did something to her, she thought wildly, but was ashamed to go to Helen and beg her to say what. She guessed he had acted like a lout—it was no wonder Helen had stopped seeing him. All night she blamed herself for having urged her to go out with the law student. She fell into an unhappy sleep.

It was growing light when Morris left the flat. Helen dragged herself out of bed and sat with reddened eyes in the bathroom, sewing on her coat collar. Once near the office she would give it to a tailor to fix so the tear couldn't be seen. With her new dress she could do nothing. Rolling it into a hopeless ball, she hid it under some things in her bottom bureau drawer. Monday she would buy one exactly like it and hang it in her closet. Undressing for a shower—her third in hours—she burst into tears at the sight of her body. Every man she drew to her dirtied her. How could she have encouraged him? She felt a violent self-hatred for trusting him, when from the very beginning she had sensed he was untrustable. How could she have allowed herself to fall in love with anybody like him? She was filled with loathing at the fantasy she had created, of making him into what he couldn't be—educable, promising, kind and good, when he was no more than a bum. Where were her wits, her sense of elemental self-preservation?

Under the shower she soaped herself heavily, crying as she

washed. At seven, before her mother awakened, she dressed and left the house, too sickened to eat. She would gladly have forgotten her life, in sleep, but dared not stay home, dared not be questioned. When she returned from her halfday of work, if he was still there, she would order him to leave or would scream him out of the house.

Coming home from the garage, Nick smelled gas in the hall. He inspected the radiators in his flat, saw they were both lit, then knocked on Frank's door.

After a minute the door opened a crack.

"Do you smell anything?" Nick said, staring at the eye in the crack.

"Mind your goddamned business."

"Are you nuts? I smell gas in the house, it's dangerous."

"Gas?" Frank flung open the door. He was in pajamas, haggard.

"What's the matter, you sick?"

"Where do you smell the gas?"

"Don't tell me you can't smell it."

"I got a bad cold," Frank said hoarsely.

"Maybe it's comin' from the cellar," said Nick.

They ran down a flight and then the odor hit Frank, an acrid stench thick enough to wade through.

"It's coming from this floor," Nick said.

Frank pounded on the door. "Helen, there's gas here, let me in, Helen," he cried.

"Shove it," said Nick.

Frank pushed his shoulder against the door. It was unlocked and he fell in. Nick quickly opened the kitchen window while Frank, in his bare feet, roamed through the house. Helen was not there but he found Morris in bed.

The clerk, coughing, dragged the grocer out of bed and carrying him to the living room, laid him on the floor. Nick closed the stopcock of the bedroom radiator and threw open every window. Frank got down on his knees, bent over Morris, clamped his hands to his sides and pumped.

Tessie ran in in fright, and Nick shouted to her to call Ida.

Ida came stumbling up the stairs, moaning, "Oh, my God, oh, my God."

Seeing Morris lying on the floor, his underwear soaked, his face the color of a cooked beet, flecks of foam in the corners of his mouth, she let out a piercing shriek.

Helen, coming dully into the hall, heard her mother's cry. She smelled the gas and ran in terror up the stairs, expecting death.

When she saw Frank in his pajamas bent over her father's back, her throat thickened in disgust. She screamed in fear and hatred.

Frank couldn't look at her, frightened to.

"His eyes just moved," Nick said.

Morris awoke with a massive ache in his chest. His head felt like corroded metal, his mouth horribly dry, his stomach crawling with pain. He was ashamed to find himself stretched out in his long underwear on the floor.

"Morris," cried Ida.

Frank got up, embarrassed at his bare feet and pajamas.

"Papa, Papa." Helen was on her knees.

"Why did you do it for?" Ida yelled in the grocer's ear.

"What happened?" he gasped.

"Why did you do it for?" she wept.

"Are you crazy?" he muttered. "I forgot to light the gas. A mistake."

Helen broke into sobbing. Her lips twisted. Frank had to turn his head.

"The only thing that saved him was he got some air," Nick said. "You're lucky this flat ain't windproof, Morris."

Tessie shivered. "It's cold. Cover him, he's sweating."

"Put him in bed," Ida said.

Frank and Nick lifted the grocer and carried him in to his bed. Ida and Helen covered him with blankets and quilt.

"Thanks," Morris said to them. He stared at Frank. Frank looked at the floor.

"Shut the windows," Tessie said. "The smell is gone."

"Wait a little longer," said Frank. He glanced at Helen but her back was to him. She was still crying.

"Why did he do it?" Ida moaned.

Morris gazed long at her, then shut his eyes.

"Leave him rest," Nick advised.

"Don't light any matches for another hour," Frank told Ida.

Tessie closed all but one window and they left. Ida and Helen remained with Morris in the bedroom.

Frank lingered in Helen's room but nothing welcomed him there.

Later he dressed and went down to the store. Business was brisk. Ida came down, and though he begged her not to, shut the store.

That afternoon Morris developed a fever and the doctor said he had to go to the hospital. An ambulance came and took the grocer away, his wife and daughter riding with him.

From his window upstairs, Frank watched them go.

Sunday morning the store was still shut tight. Though he feared to, Frank considered knocking on Ida's door and asking for the key. But Helen might open the door, and since he would not know what to say to her over the doorsill, he went instead down the cellar, and mounting the dumbwaiter, wriggled through the little window in the air shaft, into the store toilet. Once in the back, the clerk shaved and had his coffee. He thought he would stay in the store till somebody told him to scram; and even if they did, he would try in some way to stay longer. That was his only hope left, if there was any. Turning the front door lock, he carried in the milk and rolls and was ready for business. The register was empty, so he borrowed five dollars in change from Sam Pearl, saying he would put it back from what he took in. Sam wanted to know how Morris was and Frank said he didn't know.

Shortly after half past eight, the clerk was standing at the front window when Ida and her daughter left the house. Helen looked like last year's flower. Observing her, he felt a pang of loss, shame, regret. He felt an unbearable deprivation—that yesterday he had almost had some wonderful thing but today it was gone, all but the misery of remembering it was. Whenever he thought of what he had almost had it made him frantic. He felt like rushing outside, drawing her into a doorway, and declaring the stupendous value of his love for her. But he did nothing. He didn't exactly hide but he didn't show himself, and they soon went away to the subway.

Later he thought he would also go and see Morris in the hospital, as soon as he knew which one he was in—after they got home; but they didn't return till midnight. The store was closed and he saw them from his room, two dark figures getting out of a cab. Monday, the day the Norwegians opened their store, Ida came down at seven A.M. to paste a piece of paper on the door saying Morris Bober was sick and the grocery would be closed till Tuesday or Wednesday. To her amazement, Frank Alpine was standing, in his apron, behind the counter. She entered in anger.

Frank was miserably nervous that Morris or Helen, either or both, had told her all the wrong he had done them, because if they had, he was finished.

"How did you get in here?" Ida asked wrathfully.

He said through the air shaft window. "Thinking of your trouble, I didn't want to bother you about the key, Mrs."

She vigorously forbade him ever to come in that way again. Her face was deeply lined, her eyes weary, mouth bitter, but he could tell that for some miraculous reason she didn't know what he had done.

Frank pulled a handful of dollar bills out of his pants pocket and a little bag of change, laying it all on the counter. "I took in forty-one bucks yesterday."

"You were here yesterday?"

"I got in how I explained you. There was a nice rush around four till about six. We are all out of potato salad."

Her eyes grew tears. He asked how Morris felt.

She touched her wet lids with a handkerchief. "Morris has pneumonia."

"Ah, too bad. Give him my sorrow if you can. How's he coming along out of it?"

"He's a very sick man, he has weak lungs."

"I think I'll go see him in the hospital."

"Not now," Ida said.

"When he's better. How long do you think he'll be there?"

"I don't know. The doctor will telephone today."

"Look, Mrs," Frank said. "Why don't you stop worrying about the store while Morris is sick and let me take care of it? You know I make no demands."

"My husband told you to go out from the store."

He furtively studied her face but there was no sign of accusation.

"I won't stay very long," he answered. "You don't have to worry about that. I'll stay here till Morris gets better. You'll need every cent for the hospital bills. I don't ask a thing for myself."

"Did Morris tell you why you must leave?"

His heart galloped. Did she or didn't she know? If yes, he would say it was a mistake—deny he had touched a red cent in the register. Wasn't the proof of that in the pile of dough that lay right in front of her eyes on the counter? But he answered, "Sure, he didn't want me to hang around Helen any more."

"Yes, she is a Jewish girl. You should look for somebody else. But he also found out that Schmitz was sick since December and kept closed his store in the mornings, also earlier in the night. This was what improved our income, not you."

She then told Frank that the German had sold out and two Norwegians were opening up today.

Frank flushed. "I knew that Schmitz was sick and kept his store closed sometimes, but that isn't what made your business get better. What did that was how hard I worked building up the trade. And I bet I can keep this place in the shape it is, even with two Norwegians around the corner or three Greeks. What's more, I bet I can raise the take-in higher."

Though she was half-inclined to believe him, she couldn't.

"Wait, you'll see how smart you are."

"Then let me have a chance to show you. Don't pay me anything, the room and meals are enough."

"What," she asked in desperation, "do you want from us?"

"Just to help out. I have my debt to Morris."

"You have no debt. He has a debt to you that you saved him from the gas."

"Nick smelled it first. Anyway I feel I have a debt to him for all the things he has done for me. That's my nature, when I'm thankful, I'm thankful."

"Please don't bother Helen. She is not for you."

"I won't."

She let him stay. If you were so poor where was your choice?

Taast and Pederson opened up with a horseshoe of spring flowers in their window. Their pink handbills brought them steady business and Frank had plenty of time on his hands. During the day only a few of the regulars came into the grocery. At night, after the Norwegians had closed, the grocery had a spurt of activity, but when Frank pulled the strings of the window lights around eleven, he had only fifteen dollars in the register. He didn't worry too much. Monday was a slow day anyway, and besides, people were entitled to grab off a few specials while they could get them. He figured nobody could tell what difference the Norwegians would make to the business until a couple of weeks had gone by, when the neighborhood was used to them and things settled back to normal. Nobody was going to give specials away that cheap every day. A store wasn't a charity, and when they stopped giving something for nothing, he would match them in service and also prices and get his customers back.

Tuesday was slow, also as usual. Wednesday picked up a little, but Thursday was slow again. Friday was better. Saturday was the best day of the week, although not so good as Saturdays lately. At the end of the week the grocery was close to a hundred short of its recent weekly average. Expecting something like this, Frank had closed up for a half hour on Thursday and taken the trolley to the bank. He withdrew twenty-five dollars from his savings account and put the money into the register, five on Thursday, ten on Friday and ten on Saturday, so that when Ida wrote the figures down in her book each night she wouldn't feel too bad. Seventy-five less for the week wasn't as bad as a hundred.

Morris, better after ten days in the hospital, was brought home in a cab by Ida and Helen and laid to bed to convalesce. Frank, gripping his courage, thought of going up to see him and this time starting out right, right off. He thought of bringing him some fresh baked goods to eat, maybe a piece of cheese cake that he knew the grocer liked, or some apple strudel; but the clerk was afraid it was still too soon and Morris might ask him where he had got the money to buy the cake. He might yell, "You thief, you, the only reason you stay here still is because I am sick upstairs." Yet if Morris felt this way he would already have told Ida what Frank had done. The clerk now was sure he hadn't mentioned it, because she wouldn't have waited this long to pitch him out on his ear. He thought a lot about the way Morris kept things to himself. It was a way a person had if he figured he could be wrong about how he sized up a situation. It could be that he might take a different view of Frank in time. The clerk tried to invent reasons why it might be worth the grocer's while, after he got on his feet again, to keep him on in the grocery. Frank felt he would promise anything to stay there. "Don't worry that I ever will steal from you or anybody else any more, Morris. If I do, I hope I drop dead on the spot." He hoped that this promise, and the favor he was doing him by keeping the store open, would convince Morris of his sincerity. Yet he thought he would wait a while longer before going up to see him.

Helen hadn't said anything to anybody about him either and it wasn't hard to understand why. The wrong he had done her was never out of his mind. He hadn't intended wrong but he had done it; now he intended right. He would do anything she wanted, and if she wanted nothing he would do something, what he should do; and he would do it all on his own will, nobody pushing him but himself. He would do it with discipline and with love.

All this time he had snatched only glimpses of her, though his heart was heavy with all he hoped to say. He saw her through the plate glass window—she on the undersea side. Through the green glass she looked drowned, yet never, God help him, lovelier. He felt a tender pity for her, mixed with shame for having made her pitiable. Once, as she came home from work, her eyes happened to look into his and showed disgust. Now I am finished, he thought, she will come in here and tell me to go die some place; but when she looked away she was never there. He was agonized to be so completely apart from her, left apologizing to her shadow, to the floral fragrance she left in the air. To himself he confessed his deed, but not to her. That was the curse of it, to have it to make but who would listen? At times he felt like crying but it made him feel too much like a kid to cry. He didn't like to, did it badly.

Once he met her in the hall. She was gone before he could move his lips. He felt for her a rush of love. He felt, after she had left, that hopelessness was his punishment. He had expected that punishment to be drastic, swift; instead it came slowly—it never came, yet was there.

There was no approach to her. What had happened had put her in another world, no way in.

Early one morning, he stood in the hall till she came down the stairs.

"Helen," he said, snatching off the cloth cap he now wore in the store, "my heart is sorrowful. I want to apologize."

Her lips quivered. "Don't speak to me," she said, in a voice choked with contempt. "I don't want your apologies. I don't want to see you, and I don't want to know you. As soon as my father is better, please leave. You've helped him and mother and I thank you for that, but you're no help to me. You make me sick."

The door banged behind her.

That night he dreamed he was standing in the snow outside her window. His feet were bare yet not cold. He had waited a long time in the falling snow, and some of it lay on his head and had all but frozen his face; but he waited longer until, moved by pity, she opened the window and flung something out. It floated down; he thought it was a piece of paper with writing on it but saw that it was a white flower, surprising to see in wintertime. Frank caught it in his hand. As she had tossed the flower out through the partly opened window he had glimpsed her fingers only, yet he saw the light of her room and even felt the warmth of it. Then when he looked again the window was shut tight, sealed with ice. Even as he dreamed, he knew it had never been open. There was no such window. He gazed down at his hand for the flower and before he could see it wasn't there, felt himself wake.

The next day he waited for her at the foot of the stairs, bareheaded in the light that fell on his head from the lamp.

She came down, her frozen face averted.

"Helen, nothing can kill the love I feel for you."

"In your mouth it's a dirty word."

"If a guy did wrong, must he suffer forever?"

"I personally don't care what happens to you."

Whenever he waited at the stairs, she passed without a word, as if he didn't exist. He didn't.

If the store blows away some dark night I might as well be dead, Frank thought. He tried every way to hang on. Business was terrible. He wasn't sure how long the grocery could last or how long the grocer and his wife would let him try to keep it alive. If the store collapsed everything would be gone. But if he kept it going there was always the chance that something might change, and if it did, maybe something else might. If he kept the grocery on its feet till Morris came down, at least he would have a couple of weeks to change how things were. Weeks were nothing but it might as well be nothing because to do what he had to do he needed years.

Taast and Pederson had the specials going week after week. They thought of one come-on after another to keep the customers buying. Frank's customers were disappearing. Some of them now passed him in the street without saying hello. One or two crossed the trolley tracks and walked on the other side of the street, not to have to see his stricken face at the window. He withdrew all he had left in the bank and each week padded the income a little, but Ida saw how bad things were. She was despondent and talked of giving the place over to the auctioneer. This made him frantic. He felt he had to try harder.

He tried out all sorts of schemes. He got specials on credit and sold half the stuff, but then the Norwegian began to sell it cheaper, and the rest remained on his shelves. He stayed open all night for a couple of nights but did not take in enough to pay for the light. Having nothing much to do, he thought he would fix up the store. With all but the last five dollars from the bank account, he bought a few gallons of cheap paint. Then removing the goods from one section of the shelves, he scraped away the mildewed paper on the walls and painted them a nice light yellow. When one section was painted he went to work on the next. After he had finished the walls he borrowed a tall ladder, scraped the ceiling bit by bit and painted it white. He also replaced a few shelves and neatly finished them in dime store varnish. In the end he had to admit that all his work hadn't brought back a single customer.

Though it seemed impossible the store got worse.

"What are you telling Morris about the business?" Frank asked Ida.

"He don't ask me so I don't tell him," she said dully.

"How is he now?"

"Weak yet. The doctor says his lungs are like paper. He reads or he sleeps. Sometimes he listens to the radio."

"Let him rest. It's good for him."

She said again, "Why do you work so hard for nothing? What do you stay here for?"

For love, he wanted to say, but hadn't the nerve. "For Morris."

But he didn't fool her. She would even then have told him to pack and go, although he kept them for the moment off the street, had she not known for a fact that Helen no longer bothered with him. He had probably through some stupidity fallen out of her good graces. Possibly her father's illness had made her more considerate of them. She had been a fool to worry. Yet she now worried because Helen, at her age, showed so little interest in men. Nat had called but she wouldn't go near the phone.

Frank scraped down on expenses. With Ida's permission he had the telephone removed. He hated to do it because he thought Helen might sometime come down to answer it. He also reduced the gas bill by lighting only one of the two radiators downstairs. He kept the one in the front lit so the customers wouldn't feel the cold, but he no longer used the one in the kitchen. He wore a heavy sweater, a vest and a flannel shirt under his apron, and his cap on his head. But Ida, even with her coat on, when she could no longer stand the emptiness of the front, or the freezing back, escaped upstairs. One day she came into the kitchen, and seeing him salting a soup plate of boiled potatoes for lunch, began to cry.

He thought always of Helen. How could she know what was going on in him? If she ever looked at him again she would see the same guy on the outside. He could see out but nobody could see in.

When Betty Pearl got married Helen didn't go to the wedding. The day before she apologized embarrassedly, said she wasn't feeling too well—blamed her father's illness. Betty said she understood, thinking it had something to do with her brother. "Next time," she remarked with a little laugh, but Helen, seeing she was hurt, felt bad. She reconsidered facing the ceremony, rigmarole, relatives, Nat or no Nat—maybe she could still go; but couldn't bring herself to. She was no fixture for a wedding. They might say to her, "With such a face, go better to a funeral." Though she had many a night wept herself out, her memories kept a hard hold in her mind. Crazy woman, how could she have brought herself to love such a man? How could she have considered marrying someone not Jewish? A total, worthless stranger. Only God had saved her from a disastrous mistake. With such thoughts she lost all feeling for weddings.

Her sleep suffered. Every day she dreaded every night. From bedtime to dawn she eked out only a few wearisome unconscious hours. She dreamed she would soon awake and soon awoke. Awake, she felt sorry for herself, and sorrow, no soporific, induced sorrow. Her mind stamped out endless worries: her father's health, for instance; he showed little interest in recovery. The store, as ever. Ida wept in whispers in the kitchen. "Don't tell Papa." But they would sometime soon have to. She cursed all grocery stores. And worried at seeing nobody, planning no future. Each morning she crossed off the calendar the sleepless day to be. God forbid such days.

Though Helen turned over all but four dollars of her check to her mother and it went into the register, they were always hard up for cash to meet expenses. One day Frank got an idea about how he might lay hold of some dough. He thought he would collect an old bill from Carl, the Swedish painter. He knew the painter owed Morris over seventy bucks. He looked for the housepainter every day but Carl did not come in.

One morning Frank was standing at the window when he saw him leave Karp's with a wrapped bottle in his pocket.

Frank ran out and reminded Carl of his old bill. He asked him to pay something on the account.

"This is all fixed up with me and Morris," the painter answered. "Don't stick your dirty nose in."

"Morris is sick, he needs the dough," Frank said.

Carl shoved the clerk aside and went on his way.

Frank was sore. "I'll collect from that drunk bastard."

Ida was in the store, so Frank said he would be back soon. He hung up his apron, got his overcoat and followed Carl to his house. After getting the address, he returned to the grocery. He was still angered at the painter for the way he had acted when he had asked him to pay his bill.

That evening he returned to the shabby four-story tenement and climbed the creaking staircase to the top floor. A thin, dark-haired woman came wearily to the door. She was old until his eyes got used to her face, then he realized she was young but looked old.

"Are you Carl the painter's wife?"

"That's right."

"Could I talk to him?"

"On a job?" she said hopefully.

"No. Something different."

She looked old again. "He hasn't worked for months."

"I just want to talk to him."

She let him into a large room which was a kitchen and living room combined, the two halves separated by an undrawn curtain. In the middle of the living room part stood a kerosene heater that stank. This smell mixed with the sour smell of cabbage cooking. The four kids, a boy about twelve and three younger girls, were in the room, drawing on paper, cutting and pasting. They stared at Frank but silently went on with what they were doing. The clerk didn't feel comfortable. He stood at the window, looking down on the dreary lamplit street. He now figured he would cut the bill in half if the painter would pay up the rest.

The painter's wife covered the sizzling frying pan with a pot lid and went into the bedroom. She came back and said her husband was sleeping.

"I'll wait a while," said Frank.

She went back to her frying. The oldest girl set the table, and they all sat down to eat. He noticed they had left a place for their old man. He would soon have to crawl out of his hole. The mother didn't sit down. Paying no attention to Frank, she poured skim milk out of a container into the kids' glasses, then served each one a frankfurter fried in dough. She also gave everybody a forkful of hot sauerkraut.

The kids ate hungrily, not talking. The oldest girl glanced at Frank then stared at her plate when he looked at her.

When the plates were empty she said, "Is there any more, Mama?"

"Go to bed," said the painter's wife.

Frank had a bad headache from the stink of the heater.

"I'll see Carl some other time," he said. His spit tasted like brass.

"I'm sorry he didn't wake up."

He ran back to the store. Under the mattress of his bed he had his last three bucks hidden. He took the bills and ran back to Carl's house. But on the way he met Ward Minogue. His face was yellow and shrunken, as if he had escaped out of a morgue.

"I been looking for you," said Ward. He pulled Frank's revolver out of a paper bag. "How much is this worth to you?"

"Shit."

"I'm sick," sobbed Ward.

Frank gave the three bucks to him and later dropped the gun into a sewer.

He read a book about the Jews, a short history. He had many times seen this book on one of the library shelves and had never taken it down, but one day he checked it out to satisfy his curiosity. He read the first part with interest, but after the Crusades and the Inquisition, when the Jews were having it tough, he had to force himself to keep reading. He skimmed the bloody chapters but read slowly the ones about their civilization and accomplishments. He also read about the ghettos, where the half-starved, bearded prisoners spent their lives trying to figure it out why they were the Chosen People. He tried to figure out why but couldn't. He couldn't finish the book and brought it back to the library.

Some nights he spied on the Norwegians. He would go around the corner without his apron and stand on the step of Sam Pearl's hallway, looking across the street at the grocery and fancy delicatessen. The window was loaded with all kinds of shiny cans. Inside, the store was lit as bright as day. The shelves were tightly packed with appetizing goods that made him feel hungry. And there were always customers inside, although his place was generally empty. Sometimes after the partners locked up and went home, Frank crossed to their side of the street and peered through the window into the dark store, as if he might learn from what he saw in it the secret of all good fortune and so change his luck and his life.

One night after he had closed the store, he took a long walk and stepped into the Coffee Pot, an all-night joint he had been in once or twice.

Frank asked the owner if he needed a man for night work.

"I need a counterman for coffee, short orders, and to wash the few dishes," the owner answered.

"I am your boy," said Frank.

The work was from ten to six A.M. and paid thirty-five dollars. When he got home in the morning, Frank opened the grocery. At the end of a week's working, without ringing it up, he put the thirty-five into the cash register. This, and Helen's wages, kept them from going under.

The clerk slept on the couch in the back of the store during the day. He had rigged up a buzzer that waked him when somebody opened the front door. He did not suffer from lack of sleep.

He lived in his prison in a climate of regret that he had turned a good thing into a bad, and this thought, though ancient, renewed the pain in his heart. His dreams were bad, taking place in the park at night. The garbage smell stank in his nose. He groaned his life away, his mouth crammed with words he couldn't speak. Mornings, standing at the store window, he watched Helen go off to work. He was there when she came home. She walked, slightly bowlegged, toward the door, her eyes cast down, blind to his presence. A million things to say, some extraordinary, welled up in him, choked his throat; daily they died. He thought endlessly of escape, but that would be what he always did last—beat it. This time he would stay. They would carry him out in a box. When the walls caved in they could dig for him with shovels.

Once he found a two-by-four pine board in the cellar, sawed

off a hunk, and with his jackknife began to carve it into something. To his surprise it turned into a bird flying. It was shaped off balance but with a certain beauty. He thought of offering it to Helen but it seemed too rough a thing—the first he had ever made. So he tried his hand at something else. He set out to carve her a flower and it came out a rose starting to bloom. When it was done it was delicate in the way its petals were opening yet firm as a real flower. He thought about painting it red and giving it to her but decided to leave off the paint. He wrapped the wooden flower in store paper, printed Helen's name on the outside, and a few minutes before she came home from work, taped the package onto the outside of the mailbox in the vestibule. He saw her enter, then heard her go up the stairs. Looking into the vestibule, he saw she had taken the flower.

The wooden flower reminded Helen of her unhappiness. She lived in hatred of herself for having loved the clerk against her better judgment. She had fallen in love, she thought, to escape her predicament. More than ever she felt herself a victim of circumstance—in a bad dream symbolized by the nightmarish store below, and the relentless, scheming presence in it of the clerk, whom she should have shouted out of the house but had selfishly spared.

In the morning, as he aimed a pail of garbage into the can at the curb, Frank saw at the bottom of it his wooden flower.

On the day he had returned from the hospital Morris felt the urge to jump into his pants and run down to the store, but the doctor, after listening to his lungs, then tapping his hairy knuckles across the grocer's chest, said, "You're coming along fine, so what's your big hurry?" To Ida he privately said, "He has to rest, I don't mean maybe." Seeing her fright he explained, "Sixty isn't sixteen." Morris, after arguing a bit, lay back in bed and after that didn't care if he ever stepped into the store again. His recovery was slow.

With reservations, spring was on its way. There was at least more light in the day; it burst through the bedroom windows. But a cold wind roared in the streets, giving him goose pimples in bed; and sometimes, after half a day of pure sunshine, the sky darkened and some rags of snow fell. He was filled with melancholy and spent hours dreaming of his boyhood. He remembered the green fields. Where a boy runs he never forgets. His father, his mother, his only sister whom he hadn't seen in years, gottenyu. The wailing wind cried to him. . . .

The awning flapping below in the street awoke his dread of the grocery. He had not for a long time asked Ida what went on downstairs but he knew without thinking. He knew in his blood. When he consciously thought of it he remembered that the register rang rarely, so he knew again. He heard heavy silence below. What else can you hear from a graveyard whose noiseless tombstones hold down the sick earth? The smell of death seeped up through the cracks in the floor. He understood why Ida did not dare go downstairs but sought anything to do here. Who could stay in such a place but a goy whose heart was stone? The fate of his store floated like a black-feathered bird dimly in his mind; but as soon as he began to feel stronger, the thing grew lit eyes, worrying him no end. One morning as he sat up against a pillow, scanning yesterday's *Forward,* his thoughts grew so wretched that he broke into sweat and his heart beat erratically. Morris heaved aside his covers, strode crookedly out of bed and began hurriedly to dress.

Ida hastened into the bedroom. "What are you doing, Morris—a sick man?"

"I must go down."

"Who needs you? There is nothing there. Go rest some more."

He fought a greedy desire to get back into bed and live there but could not quiet his anxiety.

"I must go."

She begged him not to but he wouldn't listen.

"How much he takes in now?" Morris asked as he belted his trousers.

"Nothing. Maybe seventy-five."

"A week?"

"What else?"

It was terrible but he had feared worse. His head buzzed with schemes for saving the store. Once he was downstairs he felt he could make things better. His fear came from being here, not where he was needed.

"He keeps open all day?"

"From morning till night—why I don't know."

"Why he stays here?" he asked with sudden irritation.

"He stays," she shrugged.

"What do you pay him?"

"Nothing—he says he don't want."

"So what he wants—my bitter blood?"

"He says he wants to help you."

He muttered something to himself. "You watch him sometimes?"

"Why should I watch him?" she said, worried. "He took something from you?"

"I don't want him here no more. I don't want him near Helen."

"Helen don't talk to him."

He gazed at Ida. "What happened?"

"Go ask her. What happened with Nat? She's like you, she don't tell me anything."

"He's got to leave today. I don't want him here."

"Morris," she said hesitantly, "he gave you good help, believe me. Keep him one more week till you feel stronger."

"No." He buttoned his sweater and despite her pleading went shakily down the stairs.

Frank heard him coming and grew cold.

The clerk had for weeks feared the time the grocer would leave his bed, although in a curious way he had also looked forward to it. He had spent many fruitless hours trying to construct a story that would make Morris relent and keep him on. He had planned to say, "Didn't I starve rather than to spend the money from the holdup, so I could put it back in the register—which I did, though I admit I took a couple of rolls and some milk to keep myself alive?" But he had no confidence in that. He could also proclaim his long service to the grocer, his long patient labor in the store; but the fact that he had stolen from him during all this time spoiled his claim. He might mention that he had saved Morris after he had swallowed a bellyful of gas, but it was Nick who had saved him as much as he. The clerk felt he was without any good appeal to the grocer—that he had used up all his credit with him, but then he was struck by a strange and exciting idea, a possible if impossible ace in the hole. He figured that if he finally sincerely revealed his part in the holdup, he might in the telling of it arouse in Morris a true understanding of his nature, and a sympathy for his great struggle to overcome his past. Understanding his clerk's plight—the meaning of his long service to him—might make the grocer keep him on, so he would again have the chance to square everything with all concerned. As he pondered this idea, Frank realized it was a wild chance that might doom rather than redeem him. Yet he felt he would try it if Morris insisted he had to leave. What could he lose after that? But when the clerk pictured himself saying what he had done and had been forgiven by the grocer, and he tried to imagine the relief he would feel, he couldn't, because his overdue confession wouldn't be complete or satisfying so long as he kept hidden what he had done to his daughter. About that he knew he could never open his mouth, so he felt that no matter what he did manage to say there would always be some disgusting thing left unsaid, some further sin to confess, and this he found utterly depressing.

Frank was standing behind the counter near the cash register, paring his fingernails with his knife blade when the grocer, his face pale, the skin of it loose, his neck swimming in his shirt collar, his dark eyes unfriendly, entered the store through the hall door.

The clerk tipped his cap and edged away from the cash register.

"Glad to see you back again, Morris," he said, regretting he hadn't once gone up to see him in all the days the grocer had been upstairs. Morris nodded coldly and went into the rear. Frank followed him in, fell on one knee, and lit the radiator.

"It's pretty cold here, so I better light this up. I've been keeping it shut off to save on the gas bill."

"Frank," Morris said firmly, "I thank you that you helped me when I took in my lungs so much gas, also that you kept the store open when I was sick, but now you got to go."

"Morris," answered Frank, heavy-hearted, "I swear I never stole another red cent after that last time, and I hope God will strike me dead right here if it isn't the truth."

"This ain't why I want you to go," Morris answered.

"Then why do you?" asked the clerk, flushing.

"You know," the grocer said, his eyes downcast.

"Morris," Frank said, at agonizing last, "I have something important I want to tell you. I tried to tell you before only I couldn't work my nerve up. Morris, don't blame me now for what I once did, because I am now a changed man, but I was one of the guys that held you up that night. I swear to God I didn't want to once I got in here, but I couldn't get out of it. I tried to tell you about it—that's why I came back here in the first place, and the first chance I got I put my share of the money back in the register—but I didn't have the guts to say it. I couldn't look you in the eye. Even now I feel sick about what I am saying, but I'm telling it to you so you will know how much I suffered on account of what I did, and that I am very sorry you were hurt on your head—even though not by me. The thing you got to understand is I am not the same person I once was. I might look so to you, but if you could see what's been going on in my heart you would know I have changed. You can trust me now, I swear it, and that's why I am asking you to let me stay and help you."

Having said this, the clerk experienced a moment of extraordinary relief—a treeful of birds broke into song; but the song was silenced when Morris, his eyes heavy, said, "This I already know, you don't tell me nothing new."

The clerk groaned. "How do you know it?"

"I figured out when I was laying upstairs in bed. I had once a bad dream that you hurt me, then I remembered—"

"But I didn't hurt you," the clerk broke in emotionally. "I was the one that gave you the water to drink. Remember?"

"I remember. I remember your hands. I remember your eyes. This day when the detective brought in here the holdupnik that he didn't hold me up I saw in your eyes that you did something wrong. Then when I stayed behind the hall door and you stole from me a dollar and put in in your pocket, I thought I saw you before in some place but I didn't know where. That day you saved me from the gas I almost recognized you; then when I was laying in bed I had nothing to think about, only my worries and how I threw away my life in this store, then I remembered when you first came here, when we sat at this table, you told me you always did the wrong thing in your life; this minute when I remembered this I said to myself, 'Frank is the one that made on me the holdup.' "

"Morris," Frank said hoarsely, "I am sorry."

Morris was too unhappy to speak. Though he pitied the clerk, he did not want a confessed criminal around. Even if he had reformed, what good would it do to keep him here—another mouth to feed, another pair of eyes to the death watch?

"Did you tell Helen what I did?" sighed Frank.

"Helen ain't interested in you."

"One last chance, Morris," the clerk pleaded.

"Who was the antisimeet that he hit me on the head?"

"Ward Minogue," Frank said after a minute. "He's sick now."

"Ah," sighed Morris, "the poor father."

"We meant to hold Karp up, not you. Please let me stay one more month. I'll pay for my own food and also my rent."

"With what will you pay if I don't pay you—with my debts?"

"I have a little job at night after the store closes. I make a few odd bucks."

"No," said the grocer.

"Morris, you need my help here. You don't know how bad everything is."

But the grocer had set his heart against his assistant and would not help him stay.

Frank hung up his apron and left the store. Later, he bought a suitcase and packed his few things. When he returned Nick's radio, he said good-bye to Tessie.

"Where are you going now, Frank?"

"I don't know."

"Are you ever coming back?"

"I don't know. Say good-bye to Nick."

Before leaving, Frank wrote a note to Helen, once more saying he was sorry for the wrong he had done her. He wrote she was the finest girl he had ever met. He had bitched up his life. Helen wept over the note but had no thought of answering.

Although Morris liked the improvements Frank had made in the store he saw at once that they had not the least effect on business. Business was terrible. And with Frank's going the income shrank impossibly lower, a loss of ten terrible dollars from the previous week. He thought he had seen the store at its worst but this brought him close to fainting.

"What will we do?" he desperately asked his wife and daughter, huddled in their overcoats one Sunday night in the unheated back of the store.

"What else?" Ida said, "give right away in auction."

"The best thing is to sell even if we have to give away,"

Morris argued. "If we sell the store we can also make something on the house. Then I can pay my debts and have maybe a couple thousand dollars. But if we give in auction how can I sell the house?"

"So if we sell who will buy?" Ida snapped.

"Can't we auction off the store without going into bankruptcy?" Helen asked.

"If we auction we will get nothing. Then when the store is empty and it stays for rent, nobody will buy the house. There are already two places for rent on this block. If the wholesalers hear I went in auction they will force me in bankruptcy and take away the house also. But if we sell the store, then we can get a better price for the house."

"Nobody will buy," Ida said. "I told you when to sell but you wouldn't listen."

"Suppose you did sell the house and store," Helen asked, "what would you do then?"

"Maybe I could find a small place, maybe a candy store. If I could find a partner we could open up a store in a nice neighborhood."

Ida groaned. "Penny candy I won't sell. Also a partner we had already, he should drop dead."

"Couldn't you look for a job?" Helen said.

"Who will give me at my age a job?" Morris asked.

"You're acquainted with some people in the business," she answered. "Maybe somebody could get you a cashier's job in a supermarket."

"You want your father to stand all day on his feet with his varicose veins?" Ida asked.

"It would be better than sitting in the freezing back of an empty store."

"So what will we do?" Morris asked, but nobody answered.

Upstairs, Ida told Helen that things would be better if she got married.

"Who should I marry, Mama?"

"Louis Karp," said Ida.

The next evening she visited Karp when he was alone in the liquor store and told him their troubles. The liquor dealer whistled through his teeth.

Ida said, "You remember last November you wanted to

send us a man by the name Podolsky, a refugee he was interested to go in the grocery business?"

"Yes. He said he would come here but he caught a cold in his chest."

"Did he buy some place a store?"

"Not yet," Karp said cautiously.

"He still wants to buy?"

"Maybe. But how could I recommend him a store like yours?"

"Don't recommend him the store, recommend him the price. Morris will sell now for two thousand cash. If he wants the house we will give him a good price. The refugee is young, he can fix up the business and give the goyim a good competition."

"Maybe I'll call him sometime," Karp remarked. He casually inquired about Helen. Surely she would be getting married soon?

Ida faced the way she hoped the wind was blowing. "Tell Loius not to be so bashful. Helen is lonely and wants to go out with somebody."

Karp coughed into his fist. "I don't see your clerk any more. How is that?" He spoke offhandedly, walking carefully, knowing the size of his big feet.

"Frank," Ida said solemnly, "don't work for us any more. Morris told him to leave, so he left last week."

Karp raised bushy brows. "Maybe," he said slowly, "I will call Podolsky and tell him to come tomorrow night. He works in the day."

"In the morning is the best time. Comes in then a few Morris' old customers."

"I will tell him to take off Wednesday morning," Karp said.

He later told Louis what Ida had said about Helen, but Louis, looking up from clipping his fingernails, said she wasn't his type.

"When you got gelt in your pocket any woman is your type," Karp said.

"Not her."

"We will see."

The next afternoon Karp came into Morris's and speaking as if they were the happiest of friends, advised the grocer; "Let Podolsky look around here but not too long. Also keep your mouth shut about the business. Don't try to sell him anything. When he finishes in here he will come to my house and I will explain him what's what."

Morris, hiding his feelings, nodded. He felt he had to get away from the store, from Karp, before he collapsed. Reluctantly he agreed to do as the liquor dealer suggested.

Early Wednesday morning Podolsky arrived, a shy young man in a thick greenish suit that looked as if it had been made out of a horse blanket. He wore a small foreign-looking hat and carried a loose umbrella. His face was innocent and his eyes glistened with good will.

Morris, uneasy at what he was engaged in, invited Podolsky into the back, where Ida nervously awaited him, but the refugee tipped his hat and said he would stay in the store. He slid into the corner near the door and nothing could drag him out. Luckily, a few customers dribbled in, and Podolsky watched with interest as Morris professionally handled them.

When the store was empty, the grocer tried to make casual talk from behind the counter, but Podolsky, though constantly clearing his throat, had little to say. Overwhelmed by pity for the poor refugee, at what he had in all probability lived through, a man who had sweated blood to save a few brutal dollars, Morris, unable to stand the planned dishonesty, came from behind the counter, and taking Podolsky by the coat lapels, told him earnestly that the store was rundown but that a boy with his health and strength, with modern methods and a little cash, could build it up in a reasonable time and make a decent living out of it.

Ida shrilly called from the kitchen she needed the grocer to help her peel potatoes, but Morris kept on talking till he was swimming in his sea of woes; then he recalled Karp's warning, and though he felt more than ever that the liquor dealer was thoroughly an ass, abruptly broke off the story he was telling. Yet before he could tear himself away from the refugee, he remarked, "I could sell for two thousand, but for fifteen-sixteen cash, anybody who wants it can take the store. The house we will talk about later. Is this reasonable?"

"Why not?" Podolsky murmured, then again clammed up.

Morris retreated into the kitchen. Ida looked at him as if he had committed murder but did not speak. Two or three more people appeared, then after ten-thirty the dry trickle of customers stopped. Ida grew fidgety and tried to think of ways to get Podolsky out of the place but he stayed on. She asked him to come into the back for a glass of tea; he courteously refused. She remarked that Karp must now be anxious to see him; Podolsky bobbed his head and stayed. He tightened the cloth around his umbrella stick. Not knowing what else to say she absently promised to leave him all her recipes for salads. He thanked her, to her surprise, profusely.

From half past ten to twelve nobody approached the store. Morris went down to the cellar and hid. Ida sat dully in the back. Podolsky waited in his corner. Nobody saw as he eased himself and his black umbrella out of the grocery and fled.

On Thursday morning Morris spat on his shoebrush and polished his shoes. He was wearing his suit. He rang the hall bell for Ida to come down, then put on his hat and coat, old but neat because he rarely used them. Dressed, he rang up "no sale" and hesitantly pocketed eight quarters.

He was on his way to Charlie Sobeloff, an old partner. Years ago, Charlie, a cross-eyed but clever conniver, had come to the grocer with a meager thousand dollars in his pocket, borrowed money, and offered to go into partnership with him—Morris to furnish four thousand—to buy a grocery Charlie had in mind. The grocer disliked Charlie's nervousness and pale cross-eyes, one avoiding what the other looked at; but he was persuaded by the man's nagging enthusiasm and they bought the store. It was a good business, Morris thought, and he was satisfied. But Charlie, who had taken accountancy in night school, said he would handle the books, and Morris, in spite of Ida's warnings, consented, because, the grocer argued, the books were always in front of his eyes for inspection. But Charlie's talented nose had sniffed the right sucker. Morris never looked at the books until, two years after they had bought the place, the business collapsed.

The grocer, stunned, heartbroken, could not at first understand what had happened, but Charlie had figures to prove that the calamity had been bound to occur. The overhead was too high—they had paid themselves too high wages—his fault, Charlie admitted; also profits were low, the price of goods increasing. Morris now knew that his partner had, behind his back, cheated, manipulated, stolen whatever lay loose. They sold the place for a miserable price, Morris going out dazed, cleaned out, whereas Charlie in a short time was able to raise the cash to repurchase and restock the store, which he gradually worked into a thriving self-service business. For years the two had not met, but within the last four or five years, the ex-partner, when he returned from his winters in Miami, for reasons unknown to Morris, sought out the grocer and sat with him in the back, his eyes roving, his ringed fingers drumming on the table as he talked on about old times when they were young. Morris, through the years, had lost his hatred of the man, though Ida still could not stand him, and it was to Charlie Sobeloff that the grocer, with a growing sense of panic, had decided to run for help, a job—anything.

When Ida came down and saw Morris, in his hat and coat, standingly moodily by the door, she said in surprise, "Morris, where you going?"

"I go to my grave," the grocer said.

Seeing he was overwrought, she cried out, clasping her hands to her bosom, "Where do you go, tell me?"

He had the door open. "I go for a job."

"Come back," she cried in anger. "Who will give you?"

But he knew what she would say and was already in the street.

As he went quickly past Karp's he noticed that Louis had five customers—drunkards all—lined up at the counter and was doing a thriving business in brown bottles. *He* had sold only two quarts of milk in four hours. Although it shamed him, Morris wished the liquor store would burn to the ground.

At the corner he paused, overwhelmed by the necessity of choosing a direction. He hadn't remembered that space provided so many ways to go. He chose without joy. The day, though breezy, was not bad—it promised better, but he had little love left for nature. It gave nothing to a Jew. The March wind hastened him along, prodding the shoulders. He felt weightless, unmanned, the victim in motion of whatever blew at his back; wind, worries, debts, Karp, holdupniks, ruin. He did not go, he was pushed. He had the will of a victim, no will to speak of.

"For what I worked so hard for? Where is my youth, where did it go?"

The years had passed without profit or pity. Who could he blame? What fate didn't do to him he had done to himself. The right thing was to make the right choice but he made the wrong. Even when it was right it was wrong. To understand why, you needed an education but he had none. All he knew was he wanted better but had not after all these years learned how to get it. Luck was a gift. Karp had it, a few of his old friends had it, well-to-do men with grandchildren already, while his poor daughter, made in his image, faced—if not actively sought—old-maidhood. Life was meager, the world changed for the worse. America had become too complicated. One man counted for nothing. There were too many stores, depressions, anxieties. What had he escaped to here?

The subway was crowded and he had to stand till a pregnant woman, getting off, signaled him to her seat. He was ashamed to take it but nobody else moved, so he sat down. After a while he began to feel at ease, thought he would be satisfied to ride on like this, provided he never got to where he was going. But he did. At Myrtle Avenue he groaned softly, and left the train.

Arriving at Sobeloff's Self-Service Market, Morris, although he had heard of the growth of the place from Al Marcus, was amazed at its size. Charlie had tripled the original space by buying the building next door and knocking out the wall between the stores, later running an extension three-quarters of the way into the back yards. The result was a huge market with a large number of stalls and shelved sections loaded with groceries. The supermarket was so crowded with people that to Morris, as he peered half-scared through the window, it looked like a department store. He felt a pang, thinking that part of this might now be his if he had taken care of what he had once owned. He would not envy Charlie Sobeloff his dishonest wealth, but when he thought of what he could do for Helen with a little money his regret deepened that he had nothing.

He spied Charlie standing near the fruit stalls, the balabos, surveying the busy scene with satisfaction. He wore a gray Homburg and blue serge suit, but under the unbuttoned suit jacket he had tied a folded apron around his silk-shirted paunch, and wandered around, thus attired, overseeing. The grocer, looking through the window, saw himself opening the door and walking the long half block to where Charlie was standing.

He tried to speak but was unable to, until after so much silence the boss said he was busy, so say it.

"You got for me, Charlie," muttered the grocer, "a job? Maybe a cashier or something? My business is bad, I am going in auction."

Charlie, still unable to look straight at him, smiled. "I got five steady cashiers but maybe I can use you part time. Hang up your coat in the locker downstairs and I'll give you directions what to do."

Morris saw himself putting on a white duck jacket with "Sobeloff's Self-Service" stitched in red over the region of the heart. He would stand several hours a day at the checking, adding, ringing up the cash into one of Charlie's massive chromium registers. At quitting time, the boss would come over to check his money.

"You're short a dollar, Morris," Charlie said with a little chuckle, "but we will let it go."

"No," the grocer heard himself say. "I am short a dollar, so I will pay a dollar."

He took several quarters out of his pants pocket, counted four, and dropped them into his ex-partner's palm. Then he announced he was through, hung up his starched jacket, slipped on his coat and walked with dignity to the door. He joined the one at the window and soon went away.

Morris clung to the edge of a silent knot of men who drifted along Sixth Avenue, stopping at the employment agency doors to read impassively the list of jobs chalked up on the blackboard signs. There were openings for cooks, bakers, waiters, porters, handymen. Once in a while one of the men would secretly detach himself from the others and go into the agency. Morris followed along with them to Forty-fourth Street, where he noted a job listed for countermen behind a steam counter in a cafeteria. He went one flight up a narrow staircase and into a room that smelled of tobacco smoke. The grocer stood there, uncomfortable, until the big-faced owner of the agency happened to look up over the roll-top desk he was sitting at.

"You looking for something, mister?"

"Counterman," Morris said.

"You got experience?"

"Thirty years."

The owner laughed. "You're the champ but they want a kid they can pay twenty a week."

"You got something for a man my experience?"

"Can you slice sandwich meat nice and thin?"

"The best."

"Come back next week, I might have something for you."

The grocer continued along with the crowd. At Forty-seventh Street he applied for a waiter's job in a kosher restaurant but the agency had filled the job and forgotten to erase it from their sign.

"So what else you got for me?" Morris asked the manager.

"What work do you do?"

"I had my own store, grocery and delicatessen."

"So why do you ask for waiter?"

"I didn't see for counterman anything."

"How old are you?"

"Fifty-five."

"I should live so long till you see fifty-five again," said the manager. As Morris turned to go the man offered him a cigarette but the grocer said his cough kept him from smoking.

At Fiftieth he went up a dark staircase and sat on a wooden bench at the far end of a long room.

The boss of the agency, a man with a broad back and a fat rear, holding a dead cigar butt between stubby fingers, had his heavy foot on a chair as he talked in a low voice to two gray-hatted Filipinos.

Seeing Morris on the bench he called out, "Whaddye want, pop?"

"Nothing. I sit on account I am tired."

"Go home," said the boss.

He went downstairs and had coffee at a dish laden table in the Automat.

America.

Morris rode the bus to East Thirteenth Street, where Breitbart lived. He hoped the peddler would be home but only his son Hymie was. The boy was sitting in the kitchen, eating cornflakes with milk and reading the comics.

"What time comes home papa?" Morris asked.

"About seven, maybe eight," Hymie mumbled.

Morris sat down to rest. Hymie ate, and read the comics. He had big restless eyes.

"How old are you?"

"Fourteen."

The grocer got up. He found two quarters in his pocket and left them on the table. "Be a good boy. Your father loves you."

He got into the subway at Union Square and rode to the Bronx, to the apartment house where Al Marcus lived. He felt sure Al would help him find something. He would be satisfied, he thought, with little, maybe a night watchman's job.

When he rang Al's bell, a well-dressed woman with sad eyes came to the door.

"Excuse me," said Morris. "My name is Mr. Bober. I am an old-time customer Al Marcus's. I came to see him."

"I am Mrs. Margolies, his sister-in-law."

"If he ain't home I will wait."

"You'll wait a long time," she said, "they took him to the hospital yesterday."

Though he knew why he couldn't help asking.

"Can you go on living if you're already dead?"

When the grocer got home in the cold twilight Ida took one look at him and began to cry.

"What did I tell you?"

That night Morris, alone in the store after Ida had gone up to soak her poor feet, felt an uncontrollable craving for some heavy sweet cream. He remembered the delicious taste of bread dipped in rich milk when he was a boy. He found a half-pint bottle of whipping cream in the refrigerator and took it, guiltily, with a loaf of stale white bread, into the back. Pouring some cream into a saucer, he soaked it up with bread, greedily wolfing the cream-laden bread.

A noise in the store startled him. He hid the cream and bread in the gas range.

At the counter stood a skinny man in an old hat and a dark overcoat down to his ankles. His nose was long, throat gaunt, and he wore a wisp of red beard on his bony chin.

"A gut shabos," said the scarecrow.

"A gut shabos," Morris answered, though shabos was a day away.

"It smells here," said the skinny stranger, his small eyes shrewd, "like a open grave."

"Business is bad."

The man wet his lips and whispered, "Insurinks you got—fire insurinks?"

Morris was frightened. "What is your business?"

"How much?"

"How much what?"

"A smart man hears one word but he understand two. How much you got insurinks?"

"Two thousand for the store."

"Feh."

"Five thousand for the house."

"A shame. Should be ten."

"Who needs ten for this house?"

"Nobody knows."

"What do you want here?" Morris asked, irritated.

The man rubbed his skinny, red-haired hands. "What does a macher want?"

"What kind of macher? What do you make?"

He shrugged slyly. "I make a living." The macher spoke soundlessly. "I make fires."

Morris drew back.

The macher waited with downcast eyes. "We are poor people," he murmured.

"What do you want from me?"

"We are poor people," the macher said, apologetically. "God loves the poor people but he helps the rich. The insurinks companies are rich. They take away your money and what they give you? Nothing. Don't feel sorry for the insurinks companies."

He proposed a fire. He would make it swiftly, safely, economically—guaranteed to collect.

From his coat pocket he produced a strip of celluloid. "You know what is this?"

Morris, staring at it, preferred not to say.

"Celluloy," hissed the macher. He struck a large yellow match and lit the celluloid. It flared instantly. He held it a second then let it fall to the counter, where it quickly burned itself out. With a *poof* he blew away nothing. Only the stench remained, floating in air.

"Magic," he hoarsely announced. "No ashes. This is why we use celluloy, not paper, not rags. You push a piece in a crack, and the fire burns in a minute. Then when comes the fire marshal and insurinks investigator, what they find?—nothing. For nothing they pay cash—two thousand for the store, five for the house." A smile crawled over his face.

Morris shivered. "You want me I should burn down my house and my store to collect the insurance?"

"I want," said the macher slyly, "tsu you want?"

The grocer fell silent.

"Take," said the macher persuasively, "your family and go for a ride to Cunyiland. When you come back is the job finished. Cost—five hundred." He lightly dusted his fingers.

"Upstairs lives two people," muttered the grocer.

"When they go out?"

"Sometimes to the movies, Friday night." He spoke dully, not sure why he was revealing secrets to a total stranger.

"So let be Friday night. I am not kosher."

"But who's got five hundred dollars?"

The macher's face fell. He sighed deeply. "I will make for two hundred. I will do a good job. You will get six—seven thousand. After, pay me another three hundred."

But Morris had decided. "Impossible."

"You don't like the price?"

"I don't like fires. I don't like monkey business."

The macher argued another half hour and departed reluctantly.

The next night a car pulled up in front of the door, and the grocer watched Nick and Tessie, dressed for a party, get in and drive off. Twenty minutes later Ida and Helen came down to go to a movie. Helen had asked her mother to go with her, and Ida said yes, seeing how restless her daughter was. When he realized that the house was deserted, Morris felt suddenly agitated.

After ten minutes, he went up the stairs, and searched in a camphor-smelling trunk in the small room for a celluloid collar he had once worn. Ida saved everything, but he couldn't locate it. He searched in Helen's bureau drawer and found an envelope full of picture negatives. Discarding several of her as a school girl, Morris took some of boys in bathing suits, nobody he recognized. Hurryng down, he found matches and went into the cellar. He thought that one of the bins would be a good place to start the fire but settled instead on the air shaft. The flames would shoot up in an instant, and through the open toilet window into the store. Gooseflesh crept over him. He figured he could start the fire and wait in the hall. Once the flames had got a good start, he would rush into the street and ring the alarm. He could later say he had fallen asleep on the couch and had been awakened by the smoke. By the time the fire engines came, the house would be badly damaged. The hoses and axes would do the rest.

Morris inserted the celluloid strips into a crack between two boards, on the inside of the dumb-waiter. His hand shook and he whispered to himself as he touched the match to the negatives. Then the flame shot up in a stupefying stench and at once crawled up the wall of the dumb-waiter. Morris watched, hypnotized, then let out a terrible cry. Slapping frantically at the burning negatives, he knocked them to the cellar floor. As he hunted for something with which to beat out the fire in the dumb-waiter, he discovered that the bottom of his apron was burning. He smacked the flames with both hands and then his sweater sleeves began to blaze. He sobbed for God's mercy, and was at once roughly seized from behind and flung to the ground.

Frank Alpine smothered the grocer's burning clothes with

his overcoat. He banged out the fire in the dumb-waiter with his shoe.

Morris moaned.

"For Christ sake," Frank pleaded, "take me back here."

But the grocer ordered him out of the house.

Saturday night, about one A.M., Karp's store began to burn.

In the early evening, Ward Minogue had knocked on Frank's door and learned from Tessie that the clerk had moved.

"Where to?"

"I don't now. Ask Mr. Bober," Tessie said, anxious to get rid of him.

Downstairs, Ward peered through the grocery window and seeing Morris, hurriedly withdrew. Though alcohol nauseated him lately, his thirst for a drink was killing him. He thought if he could get a couple of swigs past the nausea he would feel better. But all he had in his pocket was a dime, so he went into Karp's and begged Louis to trust him to a cheap fifth of anything.

"I wouldn't trust you for a fifth of sewer water," Louis said.

Ward grabbed a bottle of wine from the counter and flung it as Louis' head. He ducked but the wine smashed some bottles on the shelf. As Louis, yelling murder, rushed into the street, Ward snatched a bottle of whiskey and ran out of the store and up the block. He had gone past the butcher's when the bottle slipped from under his arm and broke on the sidewalk. Ward looked back with anguish but kept on running.

By the time the cops came Ward had disappeared. After supper that night, Detective Minogue, roaming the cold streets, saw his son in Earl's bar, standing over a beer. The detective went in by the side door but Ward saw him in the mirror and bolted out the front. Although short of breath, driven by great fear, he ran toward the coal yard. Hearing his father behind him, Ward leaped across the rusted chain stretched in front of the loading platform and sped over the cobblestones toward the back of the yard. He scrambled under one of the trucks in the shed.

The detective, calling him filthy names, hunted him in the dark for fifteen minutes. Then he took out his pistol and fired a shot into the shed. Ward, thinking he would be killed, crawled out from under the truck and ran into his father's arms.

Though he pleaded with the detective not to hurt him, crying he had diabetes and would surely get gangrene, his father beat him mercilessly with his billy until Ward collapsed.

Bending over him, the detective yelled, "I told you to stay the hell out of this neighborhood. This is my last warning to you. If I ever see you again, I'll murder you." He dusted his coat and left the coal yard.

Ward lay on the cobblestones. His nose had been gushing blood but it soon stopped. Getting up, he felt so dizzy he wept. He staggered into the shed and climbed into the cab of one of the coal trucks, thinking he would sleep there. But when he lit a cigarette he was overcome with nausea. Ward threw the butt out and waited for the nausea to leave him. When it did he was thirsty again. If he could climb the coal yard fence, then some of the smaller ones beyond it, he would land up in Karp's back yard. He knew from having cased the place once that the liquor store had a barred window in the back, but that the rusty iron bars were old and loose. He thought that if he got his strength back he could force them apart.

He dragged himself over the coal yard fence, then more slowly over the others until he stood at last in Karp's weedy back yard. The liquor store had been closed since midnight and there were no lights burning in the house. Above the dark grocery one of Bober's windows was lit, so he had to be careful or the Jew might hear him.

Twice, at intervals of ten minutes, he tried to bend the bars but failed. The third time, straining till he shook, he slowly forced the inside two apart. The window was unlocked. Ward got his fingertips under it and lifted it with care because it squeaked. When it was open, he squeezed through the bent bars, squirming into the back of the liquor store. Once in there he laughed a little to himself and moved around freely, knowing Karp was too cheap to have a burglar alarm. From the stock in the rear Ward sampled and spat out three different brands of whiskey. Forcing himself, he gurgled down a third of a bottle of gin. In a couple of minutes he forgot his aches and pains and lost the sorrow he had been feeling for himself. He snickered when he imagined Louis' comic puss as he found the empty bottles all over the floor in the morning. Remembering the cash register, Ward staggered out front and rang it open. It was empty. He angrily smashed a whiskey bottle on it. A feeling of nausea gagged him and with a croak he threw up over Karp's counter. Feeling better, he began by the light of the street lamp to smash the whiskey bottles against the cash register.

Mike Papadopolous, whose bedroom was right above the front part of the liquor store, was awakened by the noise. After five minutes he figured something was wrong so he got up and dressed. Ward had, in the meantime, destroyed a whole shelf of bottles, when he felt a hunger to smoke. It took him two minutes to get a match struck and the light touching his butt. He tasted the smoke with pleasure as the flame briefly lit his face, then he shook the match and flipped it over his shoulder. It landed, still burning, in a puddle of alcohol. The fire flew up with a zoom. Ward, lit like a flaming tree, flailed at himself. Screaming, he ran through the back and tried to get out of the window but was caught between the bars and, exhausted, died.

Smelling smoke, Mike came down in a rush and seeing fire in the store, raced to the drugstore corner to turn in the alarm. As he was running back, the plate glass window of the liquor store exploded and a roaring flame boiled up in the place. After Mike had got his mother and the upstairs tenants out of the house, he ran into Bober's hall, shouting there was a fire next door. They were all up—Helen, who had been reading when the window crashed, had run up to call Nick and Tessie. They left the house, bundled in sweaters and overcoats, and stood across the street, huddled together with some passer-by, watching the fire destroy Karp's once prosperous business, then devour the house. Despite the heavy streams of water the firemen poured into the flames, the fire, fed by the blazing alcohol, rose to the roof, and when it was at last smothered, all that was left of Karp's property was a gutted, dripping shell.

As the firemen began with grappling hooks to tear out the burned fixtures and heave them onto the sidewalk, everybody fell silent. Ida moaned softly, with shut eyes thinking of Morris's burned sweater that she had found in the cellar, and the singed hair she had noticed on his hands. Sam Pearl, lost without his bifocals, mumbled to himself. Nat, hatless, an overcoat on over pajamas, edged close to Helen until he stood by her side. Morris was fighting a tormenting emotion.

A car drew up and parked beyond the drugstore. Karp got out with Louis and they crossed the hose-filled street to their store. Karp took one unbearable look at his former gesheft, and though it was for the most part insured, tottered forward and collapsed. Louis yelled at him to wake up. Two of the firemen carried the stricken liquor dealer to his car, and Louis frantically drove him home.

Afterward Morris couldn't sleep. He stood at his bedroom window in his long underwear, looking down at the pile of burned and broken fixtures on the sidewalk. With a frozen hand the grocer clawed at a live pain in his breast. He felt an overwhelming hatred of himself. He had wished it on Karp—just this. His anguish was terrible.

Sunday, the last of March, was overcast at eight A.M., and there were snow flurries in the air. Winter still spits in my face, thought the weary grocer. He watched the fat wet flakes melt as they touched the ground. It's too warm for snow, he thought, tomorrow will come April. Maybe. He had awakened with a wound, a gap in his side, a hole in the ground he might fall through if he stepped outside where the liquor store had been. But the earth held him up and the odd feeling wore off. It went as he reflected it was no use mourning Karp's loss; his pocketbook would protect him from too much pain. Pain was for poor people. For Karp's tenants the fire was a tragedy, and for Ward Minogue, dead young; maybe also for the detective, but not for Julius Karp. Morris could have used the fire, so Karp had got it for free. Everything to him who has.

As the grocer was thinking this, the liquor dealer, apparently the victim of a sleepless night, appeared in the falling snow and entered the grocery. He wore a narrow-brimmed hat with a foolish little feather in the band and a double-breasted overcoat, but despite his stylish appearance, his eyes, with dark bags under them, were filled with gloom, his complexion pasty, lips blue. Where his forehead had smacked the sidewalk last night he wore a plaster patch—an unhappy figure, the loss of his business the worst that could happen to him. He couldn't stand the vision of dollars he might be taking in, flying daily away. Karp seemed embarrassed, ill. The grocer, his shame awakened, invited him into the back for tea. Ida, also up early, made a fuss over him.

Karp took a hot sip or two of tea, but after setting the cup down, hadn't the strength to lift it from the saucer. After a fidgety silence he spoke. "Morris, I want to buy your house. Also the store." He drew a deep, trembly breath.

Ida let out a stifled cry. Morris was stupefied.

"What for? The business is terrible."

"Not so terrible," cried Ida.

"Don't interest me the grocery business," Karp gloomily replied. "Only the location. Next door," he said, but couldn't go on.

They understood.

He explained it would take months to rebuild his house and place of business. But if he took over Morris's store he could have it refixtured, painted, stocked in a couple of weeks, thus keeping to a minimum his loss of trade.

Morris couldn't believe his ears. He was filled with excitement and dread that somebody would tell him he had just dreamed a dream, or that Karp, fat fish, would turn into a fat bird and fly away, screeching, "Don't you believe me," or in some heartbreaking way change his mind.

So he put his foot on anticipation and kept his mouth shut, but when Karp asked him to name his price the grocer had one ready. "Nine thousand for the house—three down, my equity—and for the store twenty-five hundred cash. After all, bad as it was, the grocery was a going business, and for the refrigerator alone he had paid nine hundred dollars. With trepidation he figured a fair fifty-five hundred in cash in his hands, enough after he had paid his debts to look for a new business. Seeing Ida's astonished expression, he was surprised at his nerve and thought Karp would surely laugh him in the face and offer less—which he would grab anyway; but the liquor dealer listlessly nodded. "I will give you twenty-five hundred for the store, less the auction price of stock and fixtures."

"This is your business," Morris replied.

Karp could not bear to discuss the terms any further. "My lawyer will draw the contract."

When he left the grocery, the liquor dealer vanished in the swirling snow. Ida wept joyfully, while Morris, still stunned, reflected that his luck had changed. So had Karp's, for what Karp had lost he had in a sense gained, as if to make up for the misery the man had caused him in the past. Yesterday he wouldn't have believed how things would balance out today.

The spring snow moved Morris profoundly. He watched it falling, seeing in it scenes of his childhood, remembering things he thought he had forgotten. All morning he watched the shifting snow. He thought of himself, a boy running in it, whooping at blackbirds as they flew from the snowy trees; he felt an irresistible thirst to be out in the open.

"I think I will shovel the snow," he told Ida at lunchtime.

"Go better to sleep."

"It ain't nice for the customers."

"What customers—who needs them?"

"People can't walk in such high snow," he argued.

"Wait, tomorrow it will be melted."

"It's Sunday, it don't look so nice for the goyim that they go to church."

Her voice had an edge to it. "You want to catch pneumonia, Morris?"

"It's spring," he murmured.

"It's winter."

"I will wear my hat and coat."

"Your feet will get wet. You have no galoshes."

"Only five minutes."

"No," she said flatly.

Later, he thought.

All afternoon the snow came softly down and by evening it had reached a depth of six inches. When the snowing stopped, a wind rose and blew clouds of it through the streets. He watched at the front window.

Ida hung over him all day. He didn't get out till late. After closing he had sat relentlessly over a piece of store paper, writing a long list, until she grew impatient.

"Why do you stay so late?"

"I figure the stock for the auctioneer."

"This is Karp's business."

"I must help, he don't know the prices."

Talk of the store's sale relieved her. "Come up soon," she yawned.

He waited until he felt she was asleep, then went down to the cellar for the shovel. He put on his hat and a pair of old gloves and stepped out into the street. To his surprise the wind wrapped him in an icy jacket, his apron flapping noisily. He had expected, the last of March, a milder night. The surprise lingered in his mind but the shoveling warmed him. He kept his back to Karp's burned hole, though with the black turned white it wasn't too hard to look at.

Scooping up a shovelful of snow he heaved it into the street. It turned to dust in mid-air and whirled whitely away.

He recalled the hard winters when he had first come to America. After about fifteen years they turned mild but now they were hard again. It had been a hard life, but now with God's help he would have an easier time.

He flung another load of snow into the street. "A better life," he muttered.

Nick and Tessie came home from somewhere.

"At least put something warm on, Mr. Bober," advised Tessie.

"I'm almost finished," Morris grunted.

"It's your health," said Nick.

The first floor window shot up. Ida stood there in her flannel nightgown, her hair down.

"Are you crazy?" she shouted to the grocer.

"Finished," he answered.

"Without a coat—are you crazy?"

"Took me ten minutes."

Nick and Tessie went into the house.

"Come up now," Ida shouted.

"Finished," Morris cried. He heaved a last angry shovelful into the gutter. A little of the sidewalk remained to be cleaned but now that she was nagging he felt too tired to do it.

Morris dragged the wet shovel into the store. The warmth struck him across the head. He felt himself reeling and had a momentary fright but after a glass of hot tea with lemon felt rested.

As he was drinking the tea it began to snow again. He watched a thousand flakes push at the window, as if they wanted to snow through the glass and in the kitchen. He saw the snow as a moving curtain, and then, he saw it in lit single flakes, not touching each other.

Ida banged hard on the floor, so he finally closed and went upstairs.

She was sitting in her bathrobe with Helen in the living room, her eyes dark with anger. "Are you a baby you had to go out in the snow? What's the matter with such a man?"

"I had my hat on. What am I, tissue paper?"

"You had pneumonia," she shouted.

"Mama, lower your voice," Helen said, "they'll hear upstairs."

"Who asked him to shovel snow, for God's sakes?"

"For twenty-two years stinks in my nose this store. I want to smell in my lungs some fresh air."

"Not in the ice cold."

"Tomorrow is April."

"Anyway," Helen said, "don't tempt fate, Papa."

"What kind of winter can be in April?"

"Come to sleep." Ida marched off to bed.

He sat with Helen on the couch. Since hearing of Karp's visit that morning she had lost her moodiness, looked again like a happy girl. He thought with sadness how pretty she was. He wanted to give her something—only good.

"How do you feel that I am selling the house and store?" he asked her.

"You know how I feel."

"Tell me anyway."

"Refreshed."

"We will move to a better neighborhood like you like. I will find a better parnusseh. You will keep your wages."

She smiled at him.

"I remember when you were a little baby," Morris said.

She kissed his hand.

"I want the most you should be happy."

"I will be." Her eyes grew wet. "If you only knew all the good things I'd like to give you, Papa."

"You gave me."

"I'll give you better."

"Look how it snows," said Morris.

They watched the snow through the moving windows, then Morris said good night.

"Sleep well," Helen said.

But he lay in bed restless, almost dejected. There was so much to do, so many changes to make and get used to. Tomorrow was the day Karp would bring the deposit. Tuesday the auctioneer would come and they would go over the goods and fixtures. Wednesday they could hold the auction. Thursday, for the first time in almost a generation, he would be without a place of business. Such a long time. After so many years in one place he hated the thought of having to get used to another. He disliked leaving the neighborhood though he hadn't liked it. It made him uncomfortable to be in a strange place. He thought uneasily of having to locate, appraise, and buy a new store. He would prefer to live above the store, but Helen wanted them to take a small apartment, so let it be a small apartment. Once he had the store he would let them look for a place to live. But the store he would have to find himself. What he feared most was that he would make another mistake and again settle in a prison. The possibility of this worried him intensely. Why would the owner want to sell? Would he be an honest man or, underneath, a thief? And once he had bought the place, would business keep up or go down? Would times stay good? Would he make a living? His thoughts exhausted him. He could feel his poor heart running a race against the merciless future.

He fell heavily asleep but awoke in a couple of hours,

drenched in hot sweat. Yet his feet were freezing and he knew that if he kept his thoughts on them he would break into shivering. Then his right shoulder began to hurt, and when he forced himself to take a deep breath, his left side pained him. He knew he was sick and was miserably disappointed. He lay in the dark, trying not to think how stupid it had been to shovel the snow. He must have caught a chill. He thought he would not. He thought he was entitled, after twenty-two years, to a few minutes of freedom. Now his plans would have to wait, although Ida could finish the business with Karp and make arrangements with the auctioneer. Gradually he accepted the thought that he had a cold—maybe flu. He considered waking her to call a doctor but who could they call without a telephone? And if Helen got dressed and used Sam Pearl's phone, what an embarrassment that would be, waking up a whole family when she rang their bell; also arousing a doctor out of his precious sleep, who would say after examining him, "Mister, what's all the excitement? You got the flu, so stay in bed." For such advice he didn't need to call a doctor in his nightshirt. He could wait a few hours till morning. Morris dozed but felt fever shake him in his sleep. He awoke with his hair stiff. Maybe he had pneumonia? After a while he grew calmer. He was sick but sickness was nothing new to him. Probably if he hadn't shoveled snow he would have got sick anyway. In the last few days he hadn't felt so well—headachy, weak in the knees. Yet though he tried to resign himself to what had happened, he felt enormously bitter that he had become ill. So he had shoveled snow in the street, but did it have to snow in April? And if it did, did he have to get sick the minute he stepped out into the open air? It frustrated him hopelessly that every move he made seemed to turn into an inevitable thing.

He dreamed of Ephraim. He had recognized him when the dream began by his brown eyes, clearly his father's. Ephraim wore a beanie cut from the crown of an old hat of Morris's, covered with buttons and shiny pins, but the rest of him was in rags. Though he did not for some reason expect otherwise, this and that the boy looked hungry shocked the grocer.

"I gave you to eat three times a day, Ephraim," he explained, "so why did you leave so soon your father?"

Ephraim was too shy to answer, but Morris, in a rush of love for him—a child was so small at that age—promised him a good start in life.

"Don't worry, I'll give you a fine college education."

Ephraim—a gentleman—averted his face as he snickered.

"I give you my word . . ."

The boy disappeared in the wake of laughter.

"Stay alive," his father cried after him.

When the grocer felt himself awaking, he tried to get back into the dream but it easily evaded him. His eyes were wet. He thought of his life with sadness. For his family he had not provided, the poor man's disgrace. Ida was asleep at his side. He wanted to awaken her and apologize. He thought of Helen. It would be terrible if she became an old maid. He moaned a little, thinking of Frank. His mood was of regret. I gave away my life for nothing. It was the thunderous truth.

Was the snow still falling?

Morris died in the hospital, three days later, and was buried the day after in an enormous cemetery—it went on for miles—in Queens. He had been a member of a burial society since coming to America and the services took place in the Society's funeral parlor on the Lower East Side, where the grocer had lived as a young man. At noon in the chapel's antechamber, Ida, gray-faced and in mourning, every minute on the edge of fainting, sat in a high-backed tapestried chair, rocking her head. At her side, wasted, red-eyed from weeping, sat Helen. Landsleit, old friends, drawn by funeral notices in the Jewish morning papers, lamented aloud as they bent to kiss her, dropping pulpy tears on her hands. They sat on folding chairs facing the bereaved and talked in whispers. Frank Alpine stood for a moment, his hat uncomfortably on, in a corner of the room. When the place grew crowded he left and seated himself among the handful of mourners already assembled in the long narrow chapel, dimly lit by thick, yellow wall lamps. The rows of benches were dark and heavy. In the front of the chapel, on a metal stand, lay the grocer's plain wooden coffin.

At one P.M., the gray-haired undertaker, breathing heavily, escorted the widow and her daughter to the front row on the left, not far from the coffin. A wailing began among the mourners. The chapel was a little more than half-full of old friends of the grocer, a few distant relatives, burial society acquaintances, and one or two customers. Breitbart, the bulb peddler, sat, stricken, against the right wall. Charlie Sobeloff, grown heavy-faced and stout, appeared, with Florida tan and sad crossed eye, together with his stylish wife, who sat staring at Ida. The entire Pearl family was present, Betty with her new husband, and Nat, sober, concerned for Helen, wearing a black skull cap. A few rows behind them was Louis Karp, alone and ill at ease among strangers. Also Witzig, the baker, who had served Morris bread and rolls for twenty years. And Mr. Giannola, the barber, and Nick and Tessie Fuso, behind whom Frank Alpine sat. When the bearded rabbi entered the chapel through a side door, Frank took off his hat but quickly put it on again.

The secretary of the Society appeared, a soft-voiced man with little hair, his glasses lit with reflections of the wall lamps, and read from a handwritten paper praise for Morris Bober and lamentation for his loss. When he announced the body could be seen, the undertaker and his assistant, a man in a chauffeur's cap, lifted the coffin lid and a few people came forward. Helen wept profusely at her father's waxen, berouged image, the head wrapped in a prayer shawl, the thin mouth slightly twisted.

Ida flung up both arms, crying in Yiddish at the corpse, "Morris, why didn't you listen to me? You went away and left me with a child, alone in the world. Why did you do it?" She broke into racking sobs and was gently escorted by Helen and the breathless undertaker to her seat, where she pressed her wet face against her daughter's shoulder. Frank went up last. He could see, where the prayer shawl fell back a little, the scar on the grocer's head, but outside of that it wasn't Morris. He felt a loss but it was an old one.

The rabbi then prayed, a stocky man with a pointed black beard. He stood on the podium near the coffin, wearing an old Homburg, a faded black frock coat over brown trousers, and bulbous shoes. After his prayer in Hebrew, when the mourners were seated, in a voice laden with sorrow he spoke of the dead man.

"My dear friends, I never had the pleasure to meet this good grocery man that he now lays in his coffin. He lived in a neighborhood where I didn't come in. Still and all I talked this morning to people that knew him and I am now sorry I didn't know him also. I would enjoy to speak to such a man. I talked to the bereaved widow, who lost her dear husband. I talked to his poor beloved daughter Helen, who is now without a father to guide her. To them I talked, also to landsleit and old friends, and each and all told me the same, that Morris Bober, who passed away so untimely—he caught double pneumonia from shoveling snow in front of his place of business so people could pass by on the sidewalk—was a man who couldn't be more honest. Such a person I am sorry I didn't meet sometime in my life. If I met him somewhere, maybe when he went to visit in a Jewish neighborhood—maybe at Rosh Hashana or Pesach—I would say to him, 'God bless you, Morris Bober.' Helen, his dear daughter, remembers from when she was a small girl that her father ran two blocks in the snow to give back to a poor Italian lady a nickel that she forgot on the counter. Who runs in wintertime without hat or coat, without rubbers to protect his feet, two blocks in the snow to give back five cents that a customer forgot? Couldn't he wait till she comes in tomorrow? Not Morris Bober, let him rest in peace. He didn't want the poor woman to worry, so he ran after her in the snow. This is why the grocer had so many friends who admi-red him."

The rabbi paused and gazed over the heads of the mourners.

"He was also a very hard worker, a man that never stopped working. How many mornings he got up in the dark and dressed himelf in the cold, I can't count. After, he went downstairs to stay all day in the grocery. He worked long long hours. Six o'clock every morning he opened and he closed after ten every night, sometimes later. Fifteen, sixteen hours a day he was in the store, seven days a week, to make a living for his family. His dear wife Ida told me she will never forget his steps going down the stairs each morning, and also in the night when he came up so tired for his few hours' sleep before he will open again the next day the store. This went on for twenty-two years in this store alone, day after day, except the few days when he was too sick. And for this reason that he worked so hard and bitter, in his house, on his table, was always something to eat. So besides honest he was a good provider."

The rabbi gazed down at his prayer book, then looked up.

"When a Jew dies, who asks if he is a Jew? He is a Jew, we don't ask. There are many ways to be a Jew. So if somebody comes to me and says, 'Rabbi, shall we call such a man Jewish who lived and worked among the gentiles and sold them pig meat, trayfe, that we don't eat it, and not once in twenty years comes inside a synagogue, is such a man a Jew, rabbi?' To him I will say, 'Yes, Morris Bober was to me a true jew because he lived in the Jewish experience, which he remembered, and with the Jewish heart.' Maybe not to our formal tradition—for this I don't excuse him—but he was true to the spirit of our life—to want for others that which he wants also for himself. He followed the Law which God gave to Moses on Sinai and told him to bring to the people. He suffered, he endu-red, but with hope. Who told me this? I know. He asked for himself little—nothing, but he wanted for his beloved child a better existence than he had. For such reasons he was a Jew. What more does our sweet God ask his poor people? So let Him now take care of the widow, to comfort and protect her, and give to the fatherless child what her father wanted her to have. 'Yaskadal v'yiskadash shmey, rabo. B'olmo divro . . .' "

The mourners rose and prayed with the rabbi.

Helen, in her grief, grew restless. He's overdone it, she thought. I said Papa was honest but what was the good of such honesty if he couldn't exist in this world? Yes, he ran after this poor woman to give her back a nickel but he also trusted cheaters who took away what belonged to him. Poor Papa; being naturally honest, he didn't believe that others come by their dishonesty naturally. And he couldn't hold onto those things he had worked so hard to get. He gave away, in a sense, more than he owned. He was no saint; he was in a way weak, his only true strength in his sweet nature and his understanding. He knew, at least, what was good. And I didn't say he had many friends who admired him. That's the rabbi's invention. People liked him, but who can admire a man passing his life in such a store? He buried himself in it; he didn't have the imagination to know what he was missing. He made himself a victim. He could, with a little more courage, have been more than he was.

Helen prayed for peace on the soul of her dead father.

Ida, holding a wet handkerchief to her eyes, thought, So what if we had to eat? When you eat you don't want to worry whose money you are eating—yours or the wholesalers'. If he had money he had bills; and when he had more money he had more bills. A person doesn't always want to worry if she will be in the street tomorrow. She wants sometimes a minute's peace. But maybe it's my fault, because I didn't let him be a druggist.

She wept because her judgment of the grocer was harsh although she loved him. Helen, she thought, must marry a professional.

When the prayer was done the rabbi left the chapel through the side door, and the coffin was lifted by some of the Society members and the undertaker's assistant, carried on their shoulders outside, and placed in the hearse. The people in the chapel filed out and went home, except Frank Alpine, who sat alone in the funeral parlor.

Suffering, he thought, is like a piece of goods. I bet the Jews could make a suit of clothes out of it. The other funny thing is that there are more of them around than anybody knows about.

In the cemetery it was spring. The snow had melted on all but a few graves, the air was warm, fragrant. The small group of mourners following the grocer's coffin were hot in their overcoats. At the Society's plot, crowded with tombstones, two gravediggers had dug a fresh pit in the earth and were standing back, holding their shovels. As the rabbi prayed over the empty grave—from up close his beard was thick with gray—Helen rested her head against the coffin held by the pallbearers.

"Good-by, Papa."

Then the rabbi prayed aloud over the coffin as the gravediggers lowered it to the bottom of the grave.

"Gently . . . gently."

Ida, supported by Sam Pearl and the secretary of the Society, sobbed uncontrollably. She bent forward, shouting into the grave, "Morris, take care of Helen, you hear me, Morris?"

The rabbi, blessing it, tossed in the first shovelful of earth.

"Gently."

Then the diggers began to push in the loose earth around the grave and as it fell on the coffin the mourners wept aloud.

Helen tossed in a rose.

Frank, standing close to the edge of the grave, leaned forward to see where the flower fell. He lost his balance, and though flailing his arms, landed feet first on the coffin.

Helen turned her head away.

Ida wailed.

"Get the hell out of there," Nat Pearl said.

Frank scrambled out of the grave, helped by the diggers. I spoiled the funeral, he thought. He felt pity on the world for harboring him.

At last the coffin was covered, the grave full, running over. The rabbi said a last short Kaddish. Nat took Helen by the arm and led her away.

She gazed back once, with grief, then went with him.

Louis Karp was waiting for them in the dark hallway when Ida and Helen returned from the cemetery.

"Excuse me for bothering you on this sad occasion," he said, holding his hat in his hand, "but I wanna tell you why my father couldn't get to the funeral. He's sick and has to lay flat on his back for the next six weeks or so. The other night when he passed out at the fire, we found out later he had a heart attack. He's lucky he's still alive."

"Vey is mir," muttered Ida.

"The doctor says he's gonna have to retire from here on in," Louis said, with a shrug, "so I don't think he'll wanna buy your house any more. Myself," he added, "I got a job of salesman for a liquor concern."

He said good-by and left them.

"Your father is better off dead," said Ida.

As they toiled up the stairs they heard the dull cling of the register in the store and knew the grocer was the one who had danced on the grocer's coffin.

Frank lived in the back, his clothes hung in a bought closet, sleeping under his overcoat on the couch. He had used their week of mourning, when mother and daughter were confined upstairs, to get the store going. Staying open kept it breathing, but beyond that things were rocky. If not for his thirty-five dollars in the register he would have had to close up. Seeing he paid his little bills, the wholesalers extended credit. People stopped in to say they were sorry Morris was dead. One man said the grocer was the only storekeeper that had ever trusted him for anything. He paid Frank back eleven dollars that he owed Morris. Frank told anybody who asked that he was keeping the business going for the widow. They approved of that.

He gave Ida twelve dollars a week rent and promised her more when times got better. He said when they did, he might buy the store from her, but it would have to be on small installments because he had no money for a down payment. She didn't answer him. She was worried about the future and feared she might starve. She lived on the rent he paid her, plus Nick's rent, and Helen's salary. Ida now had a little job sewing epaulettes for military uniforms, a bag of which Abe Rubin, a landsman of Morris's, delivered in his car every Monday morning. That brought in another twenty-eight to thirty a month. She rarely went down to the store. To speak to her, Frank had to go upstairs and knock on her door. Once, through Rubin, someone came to look at the grocery and Frank was worried, but the man soon left.

He lived in the future, to be forgiven. On the stairs one

morning he said to Helen. "Things are changed. I am not the same guy I was."

"Always," she answered, "you remind me of everything I want to forget."

"Those books you once gave me to read," he said, "did you understand them yourself?"

Helen waked from a bad dream. In the dream she had got up to leave the house in the middle of the night to escape Frank waiting on the stairs; but there he stood under the yellow lamp, fondling his lascivious cap. As she approached, his lips formed, "I love you."

"I'll scream if you say it."

She screamed and woke.

At a quarter to seven she forced herself out of bed, shut off the alarm before it rang and drew off her nightgown. The sight of her body mortified her. What a waste, she thought. She wanted to be a virgin again and at the same time a mother.

Ida was still asleep in the half-empty bed that had for a lifetime served two. Helen brushed her hair, washed, and put on coffee. Standing at the kitchen window, she gazed out at the back yards in flower, feeling sorrow for her father lying in his immovable grave. What had she ever given him, ever done to make his poor life better? She wept for Morris, thinking of his compromises and surrenders. She felt she must do something for herself, accomplish some worthwhile thing or suffer his fate. Only by growing in value as a person could she make Morris's life meaningful, in the sense that she was of him. She must, she thought, in some way eventually earn her degree. It would take years—but was the only way.

Frank stopped waiting for her in the hall. She had cried out one morning, "Why do you force yourself on me?" and it had struck him that his penitence was a hammer, so he withdrew. But he watched her when he could, through an opening in the tissue paper backing of the store window. He watched as if he were seeing for the first time her slender figure, high small breasts, the slim roundness of her hips and the exciting quality of her slightly bowed legs. She always looked lonely. He tried to think what he could ever do for her and all he could think of was to give her something she had no use for, that would end up in the garbage.

The idea of doing something for her seemed as futile as his other thoughts till one day, the tissue paper held a little aside as he watched her impassively entering the house, he had a thought so extraordinary it made the hair on the back of his neck stiffen. He figured the best thing he could do was help her get the college education she had always wanted. There was nothing she wanted more. But where, if she agreed to let him—he doubted it every minute it was in his mind—could he get the money unless he stole it? The more he pondered this plan, the more it excited him until he couldn't stand the possibility it might be impossible.

He carried in his wallet the note Helen had once written him, that she would come up to his room if Nick and Tessie went to the movies, and he read it often.

One day he got another idea. He pasted a sign in the window: "Hot Sandwiches And Hot Soups To Go." He figured he could use his short-order cooking experience to advantage in the grocery. He had some handbills printed, advertising these new things and paid a kid half a buck to deliver them to places where there were working men. He followed the boy for a couple of blocks to see that he didn't dump the papers into a sewer. Before the end of the week a few new people were coming in at lunch and suppertime. They said this was the first time you could get any hot food to take out in the neighborhood. Frank also tried his hand at ravioli and lasagna once a week, making them from recipes he got out of a cookbook in the library. He experimented with baking small pizzas in the gas stove, which he sold for two bits apiece. The pasta and pizzas sold better than the hot sandwiches. People came in for them. He considered putting a table or two in the grocery but there was no room, so all the food had to go.

He got another little break. The milkman told him the two Norwegians had taken to yelling at each other in front of their customers. He said they were making less than they had expected. The store was fine for one man but not for two, so they each wanted to buy the other out. Pederson's nerves couldn't stand the fighting, and Taast bought him out at the end of May and had the place all to himself. But he found that the long hours alone were killing his feet. His wife came in to help out around suppertime; however Taast couldn't stand being away from his family every night, when everyone else was free and at home, so he decided to close at seven-thirty and stop fighting Frank until almost ten. These couple of hours all to himself at night helped Frank. He got back some of the customers who came home from work late, and also the housewives who at the last minute needed something for breakfast. And Frank noticed from peering into Taast's window after he was closed, that he was no longer so generous with the specials.

The weather turned hot in July. People cooked less, lived more on delicatessen, canned goods, bottled drinks. He sold a lot of beer. His pastas and pizzas went very well. He heard that Taast had tried making pizzas but they were too doughy. Also, instead of using canned soups, Frank made a minestrone of his own that everybody praised; it took time to cook up, but the profit was better. And the new things he was selling pushed other goods along. He now paid Ida ninety a month for rent and the use of her store. She was earning more money on her epaulettes, and did not think so often that she would starve.

"Why do you give me so much?" she asked him when he raised the money to ninety.

"Maybe Helen could keep some of her wages?" he suggested.

"Helen isn't interested any more in you," she said sternly.

He didn't answer her.

But that night after supper—he had treated himself to ham and eggs and now smoked a cigar—Frank cleared the table and sat down to figure out how much it would cost to support Helen in college if she would quit her job and give all her time to education. When he had figured out the tuition from the college catalogues he had collected, he saw he couldn't do it. His heart was heavy. Later he thought maybe he could work it if she went to a free college. He could give her enough for her daily expenses and also to make up whatever money she now gave her mother. He figured that to do it would be a rocky load on his head, but he *had* to do it, it was his only hope; he could think of no other. All he asked for himself was the privilege of giving her something she couldn't give back.

The big thing, exciting yet frightening, was to talk to her, say what he hoped to do. He always had it in mind to say but found it very hard. To speak to her, after all that had happened to them, seemed impossible—opening on peril, disgrace, physical pain. What was the magic word to begin with? He despaired he could ever convince her. She was remote, sinned against, unfeeling, or if she felt, it was disgust of him. He cursed himself for having conceived this mess he couldn't now bring himself to speak of.

One August night after he had seen her come home from work in the company of Nat Pearl, sick of the misery of unmotion, Frank made himself move. He was standing behind the counter piling bottles of beer into a woman's market bag when he caught sight of Helen going by with some books on her arm. She was wearing a new summer dress, red trimmed with black, and the sight of her struck him with renewed hunger. All summer she had wandered at night alone in the neighborhood, trying to outwalk her loneliness. He had been tempted to close up and follow her, but until he had his new idea he could not think what he dared say that she wouldn't run from. Hurrying the customer out of the store, Frank washed, slicked back his hair and quickly changed into a fresh sport shirt. He locked the store and hurried in the direction Helen had gone. The day had been hot but was cooling now and still. The sky was golden green, though below the light was dark. After running a block he remembered something and trudged back to the store. He sat in the back listening to his heart hammering in his ears. In ten minutes he lit a lamp in the store window. The globe drew a ragged moth. Knowing how long she lingered among books, he shaved. Then locking the front door again, he went toward the library. He figured he would wait across the street till she came out. He could cross over and catch up with her on her way home. Before she could even see him, he would speak his piece and be done with it. Yes or no, she could say, and if no, he would shut the joint tomorrow and skiddoo.

He was nearing the library when he glanced up and saw her. She was about half a block away and walking toward him. He stood there not knowing which way to go, dreading to be met by her as lovely as she looked, standing like a crippled dog as she passed him. He thought of running back the way he had come, but she saw him, turned and went in haste the other way; so, reviving an old habit, he was after her, and before she could deny him, had touched her arm. They shivered. Giving her no time to focus her contempt, he blurted out what he had so long saved to say but could not now stand to hear himself speak.

When Helen realized what he was offering her, her heart moved violently. She had known he would follow and speak, but she could never in a thousand years have guessed he would say *this*. Considering the conditions of his existence, she was startled by his continuing ability to surprise her, make God-knows-what-next-move. His staying power mystified and frightened her, because she felt in herself, since the death of Ward Minogue, a waning of outrage. Although she detested the memory of her experience in the park, lately it had come back to her how she had desired that night to give herself to Frank, and might have if Ward hadn't touched her. She had wanted him. If there had been no Ward Minogue, there would have been no assault. If he had made his starved leap in bed she would have returned passion. She had hated him, she thought, to divert hatred from herself.

But her response to his offer was an instantaneous no. She said it almost savagely, to escape any possibility of being directly obligated to him, of another entrapment, nausea.

"I couldn't think of it."

He was astonished to have got this far, to be walking at her side—only it was a night in a different season, and her summer face was gentler than her winter one, her body more womanly; yet it all added up to loss, the more he wanted her the more he had lost.

"In your father's name," he said. "If not for you, then for him."

"What has my father got to do with it?"

"It's his store. Let it support you to go to college like he wanted you to."

"It can't without you. I don't want your help."

"Morris did me a big favor. I can't return it to him but I might to you. Also because I lost myself that night—"

"For God's sake, don't say it."

He didn't, was dumb. They walked dumbly on. To her horror they were coming to the park. Abruptly she went the other way.

He caught up with her. "You could graduate in three years. You wouldn't have any worry about expenses. You could study all you want."

"What would you expect to get from this—virtue?"

"I already said why—I owe something to Morris."

"For what? Taking you into his stinking store and making a prisoner out of you?"

What more could he say? To his misery, what he had done to her father rose in his mind. He had often imagined he would someday tell her, but not now. Yet the wish to say it overwhelmed him. He tried wildly to escape it. His throat hurt, his stomach heaved. He clamped his teeth tight but the words came up in blobs, in a repulsive stream.

He spoke with pain. "I was the one that held him up that time. Minogue and me. Ward picked on him after Karp ran away, but it was my fault too on account of I went in with him."

She screamed and might have gone on screaming but strangers were staring.

"Helen, I swear—"

"You criminal. How could you hit such a gentle person? What harm did he ever do you?"

"I didn't hit him, Ward did. I gave him a drink of water. He saw I didn't want to hurt him. After, I came to work for him to square up what I did wrong. For Christ's sake, Helen, try to understand me."

With contorted face she ran from him.

"I confessed it to him," he shouted after her.

He had managed well in the summer and fall, but after Christmas business dragged, and though his night salary had been raised five bucks, he found it impossible to meet all his expenses. Every penny looked as big as the moon. Once he spent an hour searching for a two-bit piece he had dropped behind the counter. He tore up a loose floor board and was elated to recover more than three dollars in green and grimy coins that Morris had lost during the years.

For himself he spent only for the barest necessities, though his clothes were falling apart. When he could no longer sew up the holes in his undershirts he threw them away and wore none. He soaked his laundry in the sink and hung it to dry in the kitchen. He was, as a rule, prompt in his payment of jobbers and wholesalers, but during the winter he kept them waiting. One man he held off his neck by threatening to go bankrupt. Another he promised tomorrow. He slipped a couple of bucks to his most important salesman, to calm them at the office. Thus he kept going. But he never missed a payment of rent to Ida. He valued his payments to her because Helen had returned to night college in the fall, and if he didn't give the ninety to Ida, Helen wouldn't have enough for her own needs.

He was always tired. His spine ached as if it had been twisted like a cat's tail. On his night off from the Coffee Pot he slept without moving, dreaming of sleep. In the dead hours at the Coffee Pot, he sat with his head on his arms at the counter, and during the day in the grocery he took catnaps whenever he could, trusting the buzzer to rouse him, although other noises did not. When he awoke, his eyes were hot and watery, his head like porous lead. He grew thin, his neck scrawny, face bones prominent, his broken nose sharp. He saw life from a continual wet-eyed yawn. He drank black coffee till his stomach turned sour. In the evening he did nothing—read a little. Or he sat in the back with the lights out, smoking, listening to the blues on the radio.

He had other worries, had noticed Nat was hanging around Helen more. A couple of times a week the law student drove her home from work. Now and then, over the week end, they went for a ride at night. Nat would toot his horn in front of the door and she came out dressed up and smiling, neither of them noticing Frank, in open sight. And she had had a new telephone put in upstairs, and once or twice a week he heard it ring. The phone made him jumpy, jealous of Nat. Once on his night off from the Coffee Pot, Frank woke abruptly when

Helen and somebody came into the hall. Sneaking into the store and listening at the side door, he could hear them whispering; then they were quiet and he imagined them necking. For hours after, he couldn't get back to sleep, desiring her so. The next week, listening at the door, he discovered the guy she was kissing was Nat. His jealousy ate him good.

She never entered the store. To see her he had to stand at the front window.

"Jesus," he said, "why am I killing myself so?" He gave himself many unhappy answers, the best being that while he was doing this he was doing nothing worse.

But then he took to doing things he had promised himself he never would again. He did them with dread of what he would do next. He climbed up the air shaft to spy on Helen in the bathroom. Twice he saw her disrobe. He ached for her, for the flesh he had lived in a moment. Yet he hated her for having loved him, for to desire what he had once had, and hadn't now, was torture. He swore to himself that he would never spy on her again, but he did. And in the store he took to cheating customers. When they weren't watching the scale he short-weighted them. A couple of times he shortchanged an old dame who never knew how much she had in her purse.

Then one day, for no reason he could give, though the reason felt familiar, he stopped climbing up the air shaft to peek at Helen, and he was honest in the store.

One night in January Helen was waiting at the curb for a trolley. She had been studying with a girl in her class and afterward had listened to some records, so she had left later than she had planned. The trolley was late in coming, and though she was cold, she was considering walking home, when she began to feel she was being watched. Looking into the store before which she was standing, she saw nobody there but the counterman resting his head on his arms. As she observed him, trying to figure out why she felt so strange, he raised his sleepy head and she saw in surprise that it was Frank Alpine. He gazed with burning eyes in a bony face, with sad regret, at his reflection in the window, then went drunkenly back to sleep. It took her a minute to realize he hadn't seen her. She felt the momentary return of an old misery, yet the winter night seemed clear and beautiful.

When the trolley came, she took a seat in the rear. Her thoughts were heavy. She remembered Ida saying Frank worked some place at night but the news had meant nothing to her. Now that she had seen him there, groggy from overwork, thin, unhappy, a burden lay on her, because it was no mystery who he was working for. He had kept them alive. Because of him she had enough to go to school at night.

In bed, half-asleep, she watched the watcher. It came to her that he had changed. It's true, he's not the same man, she said to herself. I should have known by now. She had despised him for the evil he had done, without understanding the why or aftermath, or admitting there could be an end to the bad and a beginning of good.

It was a strange thing about people—they could look the same but be different. He had been one thing, low, dirty, but because of something in himself—something she couldn't define, a memory perhaps, an ideal he might have forgotten and then remembered—he had changed into somebody else, no longer what he had been. She should have recognized it before. What he did to me he did wrong, she thought, but since he has changed in his heart he owes me nothing.

On her way to work one morning a week later, Helen, carrying her brief case, entered the grocery and found Frank hidden behind the tissue paper of the window, watching her. He was embarrassed, and she was curiously moved by the sight of his face.

"I came in to thank you for the help you're giving us," she explained.

"Don't thank me," he said.

"You owe us nothing."

"It's just my way."

They were silent, then he mentioned his idea of her going to day college. It would be more satisfying to her than at night.

"No, thank you," Helen said, blushing. "I couldn't think of it, especially not with you working so hard."

"It's no extra trouble."

"No, please."

"Maybe the store might get better, then I could do it on what we take in here?"

"I'd rather not."

"Think about it," Frank said.

She hesitated, then answered she would.

He wanted to ask her if he still had any chance with her but decided to let that wait till a later time.

Before she left, Helen, balancing the brief case on her knee, unsnapped it and took out a leather-bound book. "I wanted you to know I'm still using your Shakespeare."

He watched her walk to the corner, a good-looking girl, carrying his book in her brief case. She was wearing flat-heeled shoes, making her legs slightly more bowed, which for some reason he found satisfying.

The next night, listening at the side door, he heard a scuffle in the hall and wanted to break in and assist her but held himself back. He heard Nat say something harsh, then Helen slapped him and he heard her run upstairs.

"You bitch," Nat called after her.

One morning in the middle of March the grocer was sleeping heavily after a night off from the Coffee Pot, when he was awakened by a pounding on the front door. It was the Polish nut wanting her three-cent roll. She came later these days but still too early. The hell with all that, he thought, I need my sleep. But after a few minutes he grew restless and began to dress. Business still wasn't so hot. Frank washed his face before the cracked mirror. His thick hair needed cutting but it could wait one more week. He thought of growing himself a beard but was afraid it would scare some of the customers away, so he settled for a mustache. He had been letting one grow for two weeks and was surprised at the amount of red in it. He sometimes wondered if his old lady had been a redhead.

Unlocking the door, he let her in. The Polish dame complained he had kept her waiting too long in the cold. He sliced a roll for her, wrapped it, and rang up three cents.

At seven, standing by the window, he saw Nick, a new father, come out of the hall and run around the corner. Frank hid behind the paper and soon saw him return, carrying a bag of groceries he had bought in Taast's store. Nick ducked into the hallway and Frank felt bad.

"I think I will make this joint into a restaurant."

After he had mopped the kitchen floor and swept the store, Breitbart appeared, dragging his heavy boxes. Lowering the cartons of bulbs to the floor, the peddler took off his derby and wiped his brow with a yellowed handkerchief.

"How's it going?" Frank asked.

"Schwer."

Breitbart drank the tea and lemon that Frank cooked up for him, meanwhile reading his *Forward.* After about ten minutes he folded the newspaper into a small, thick square and pushed it into his coat pocket. He lifted the bulbs onto his itchy shoulders and left.

Frank had only six customers all morning. To keep from getting nervous he took out a book he was reading. It was the Bible and he somctimes thought there were parts of it he could have written himself.

As he was reading he had this pleasant thought. He saw St. Francis come dancing out of the woods in his brown rags, a couple of scrawny birds flying around over his head. St. F. stopped in front of the grocery, and reaching into the garbage can, plucked the wooden rose out of it. He tossed it into the air and it turned into a real flower that he caught in his hand. With a bow he gave it to Helen, who had just come out of the house. "Little sister, here is your little sister the rose." From him she took it, although it was with the love and best wishes of Frank Alpine.

One day in April Frank went to the hospital and had himself circumcised. For a couple of days he dragged himself around with a pain between his legs. The pain enraged and inspired him. After Passover he became a Jew.